# AMERICAN WOMEN OF MYSTERY

Three Classic Mystery Novels by American
Women Authors of the 1930's

## Edited by Greg Fowlkes

# AMERICAN WOMEN OF MYSTERY

## Published by Resurrected Press

This classic book was handcrafted by Resurrected Press. Resurrected Press is dedicated to bringing high quality classic books back to the readers who enjoy them. These are not scanned versions of the originals, but, rather, quality checked and edited books meant to be enjoyed!

Please visit ResurrectedPress.com to view our entire catalogue!

**Like us on Facebook to stay up-to-date on all of our latest releases: http://www.facebook.com/ResurrectedPress**

ISBN 13: 978-1-943403-34-9

Printed in the United States of America

# FOREWORD

The three novels presented in this collection were all written by American women and published in the 1930's. While the 1920's and 1930's have been called "The Golden Age of British Detective Fiction," it was also an important period in the evolution of the genre in America. It saw the development of the hard-boiled detective in the hands of authors such as Dashiell Hammett, as well as more genteel efforts by S. S. Van Dine and Ellery Queen.

American women authors were an important part of this era. Indeed, American women had been pioneers of the genre with authors such as Anna Katherine Green, Carolyn Wells, and Mary Roberts Rinehart writing mysteries long before their British counterparts were being published, and had as much of an impact on the form mystery fiction took in America as their male colleagues.

There are a number of similarities to the three authors represented in this book, Anne Austin, Dorothy Bennett, and Harriette Ashbrook. All were in their early to mid-thirties (Bennett was twenty-nine when *Murder Unleashed* was published), all featured male characters as their main protagonists, and all placed their novels in an urban setting (New York in the case of Ashbrook, San Francisco for Bennett, and the small fictional Midwestern city of Hamilton by Austin.) While none of these three novels is particularly bloody in comparison to the hard-boiled fiction of the time, there is an edginess to them that separates them from the "cozy mysteries" that were so common in Britain in the period. Despite the similarities, though, each of these three authors takes a distinctive approach to their writing.

Anne Austin began her career writing romance novels, but switched over to mysteries to meet the demands and taste of her audience. She wrote six mysteries in all, the last five featuring James Dundee, a special investigator in the District Attorney's office. While in the first of the Dundee books she shows some of her roots as a romance writer, the last two books in the series take on a much darker and mature tone. Dundee is a handsome, likable young man, just the sort that would appeal to her readers, many of who read the books in the form of newspaper serials. But *One Drop of Blood*. which takes place in a sanatarium where the lead psychiatrist has been found murdered places the investigator in a more precarious situation than in the earlier books when he goes undercover in the institution.

Ashbrook's book is quite different than Austin's. Her detective, Phillip (Spike) Tracy, is a clever amateur whose approach to detection and, for that matter, life resembles Nick Charles in Hammett's *The Thin Man*, in that it involves a great deal of drinking and light hearted banter. He delights in being a thorn in the side of his staid brother the prosecuting attorney for New York city. Ashbrook's approach to crime is both serious and amusing at the same time, and while this is a difficult tightrope to balance on, she does a masterful job of it in *The Murder of Cicely Thane* and the subsequent books in the series.

Bennett's book, *Murder Unleashed,* comes the closest of the three to crime noir. The central character is a man with a secret in his past, one that entangles him in a murder case where he is the prime suspect. The San Francisco of the novel is one that would be was familiar to a reader of *The Maltese Falcon* and there is very much a sense that the characters in it are "playing for keeps." Despite the fact that Bennett was the youngest of the authors when her novel is published it's treatment is darker and more adult. It is unfortunate that Bennett had only one more mystery published.

While their authors may not be well known today, these three novels present an interesting cross section of the detective fiction that was being produced by American women in the 1930's. While they may diverge in approach, they were all written with a distinctly American viewpoint. It is my hope that they will both entertain and enlighten their readers.


Greg Fowlkes
Editor-In-Chief
Resurrected Press
www.ResurrectedPress.com

# RESURRECTED PRESS CLASSIC
## MYSTERY CATALOGUE

**E. C. Bentley**
*Trent's Last Case: The Woman in Black*

**Ernest Bramah**
*Max Carrados Resurrected:*
*The Detective Stories of Max Carrados*

**Agatha Christie**
*The Secret Adversary*
*The Mysterious Affair at Styles*

**Octavus Roy Cohen**
*Midnight*

**Freeman Wills Croft**
*The Ponson Case*
*The Pit Prop Syndicate*

**J. S. Fletcher**
*The Herapath Property*
*The Rayner-Slade Amalgamation*
*The Chestermarke Instinct*
*The Paradise Mystery*
*Dead Men's Money*
*The Middle of Things*
*Ravensdene Court*
*Scarhaven Keep*
*The Orange-Yellow Diamond*
*The Middle Temple Murder*
*The Tallyrand Maxim*
*The Borough Treasurer*
*In the Mayor's Parlour*
*The Saftey Pin*

## R. Austin Freeman

*The Mystery of 31 New Inn from the Dr. Thorndyke Series*
*John Thorndyke's Cases from the Dr. Thorndyke Series*
*The Red Thumb Mark from The Dr. Thorndyke Series*
*The Eye of Osiris from The Dr. Thorndyke Series*
*A Silent Witness from the Dr. John Thorndyke Series*
*The Cat's Eye from the Dr. John Thorndyke Series*
*Helen Vardon's Confession: A Dr. John Thorndyke Story*
*As a Thief in the Night: A Dr. John Thorndyke Story*
*Mr. Pottermack's Oversight: A Dr. John Thorndyke Story*
*Dr. Thorndyke Intervenes: A Dr. John Thorndyke Story*
*The Singing Bone: The Adventures of Dr. Thorndyke*
*The Stoneware Monkey: A Dr. John Thorndyke Story*
*The Great Portrait Mystery, and Other Stories: A Collection of Dr.
John Thorndyke and Other Stories*
*The Penrose Mystery: A Dr. John Thorndyke Story*
*The Uttermost Farthing: A Savant's Vendetta*

## Arthur Griffiths

*The Passenger From Calais*
*The Rome Express*

## Fergus Hume

*The Mystery of a Hansom Cab*
*The Green Mummy*
*The Silent House*
*The Secret Passage*

## Edgar Jepson

*The Loudwater Mystery*

## A. E. W. Mason

*At the Villa Rose*

## A. A. Milne

*The Red House Mystery*

## Baroness Emma Orczy

*The Old Man in the Corner*

## Edgar Allan Poe

*The Detective Stories of Edgar Allan Poe*

## Arthur J. Rees
*The Hampstead Mystery*
*The Shrieking Pit*
*The Hand In The Dark*
*The Moon Rock*
*The Mystery of the Downs*

## Mary Roberts Rinehart
*Sight Unseen and The Confession*

## Dorothy L. Sayers
*Whose Body?*

## Sir William Magnay
*The Hunt Ball Mystery*

## Mabel and Paul Thorne
*The Sheridan Road Mystery*

## Louis Tracy
*The Strange Case of Mortimer Fenley*
*The Albert Gate Mystery*
*The Bartlett Mystery*
*The Postmaster's Daughter*
*The House of Peril*
*The Sandling Case: What Would You Have Done?*

## Charles Edmonds Walk
*The Paternoster Ruby*

## John R. Watson
*The Mystery of the Downs*
*The Hampstead Mystery*

## Edgar Wallace
*The Daffodil Mystery*
*The Crimson Circle*

## Carolyn Wells

*And much more!*
*Visit ResurrectedPress.com for our complete*
*catalogue*

Like us on Facebook to stay up-to-date on all of our latest
releases: http://www.facebook.com/ResurrectedPress

# TABLE OF CONTENTS

# ONE DROP OF BLOOD
## BY ANNE AUSTIN

One Drop of Blood
*by* Anne Austin

R. P.

A Resurrected Press Mystery

## ORIGINALLY PUBLISHED 1932

## EDITOR'S NOTES:
# ONE DROP OF BLOOD
### BY ANNE AUSTIN

Anne Austin started out her literary career writing romance novels about young women overcoming adversity and finding true love, but within a few years turned to the mystery genre as more rewarding or at least more marketable. Her first mystery was *The Black Pigeon*. She then began writing a series of novels featuring James "Bonnie" Dundee that spanned the decade of the 30's. Dundee was a Special Investigator for the Office of the District Attorney in the town of Hamilton.

The series began with *The Avenging Parrot* in 1930, continued on with *Murder Backstairs, Murder at Bridge, One Drop of Blood* before ending with *Murdered But Not Dead* in 1939. Several of the early novels also appeared in serial format in various newspapers.

The events in *One Drop of Blood* take place at the Mayfield Sanitarium, a psychiatric hospital that caters to a mostly wealthy and middle class clientel. Rather than an asylum for the criminally insane, Mayfield deals with patients with nerosies, substance abuse problems, or who just feel the need for a "rest cure," a time out from the rigors of modern life.

A sanitarium can provide a fertile ground for a mystery writer. The action is confined to a small locale with a limited number of characters in much the same way that the small English village has served as a setting for so many British mysteries. Also, as many of the residents are by definition, not completely sane, one can deal with imaginary motives as well as real ones. Because of these facts, psuchiatric facilities have featured in a number of mysteries over the years, often with the detective going undercover as one of the patients. The earliest example that I know of is 1912 novel *The Ivory Snuff Box* by Arnold Fredericks (Frederic Arnold Kummer).

The public's fascination with such psychiatry was particularly high in the period when this book was written. Those with mental problems were no longer just being locked away and forgotten in asylums. Advances in medicine and the work of people such as Freud and Jung gave hope of real treatments for various forms of insanity. Mental problems were being seen as a disease, and not just a sign of a weak character or a bad blood line. With the promise of treatment, psychiatric problems were no longer something that had to be hushed up, but could now be discussed openly over dinner of cocktails.

However, along with the advances came the quacks and charlatans promising miracle cures. Some of these practicioners were merely following pet theories with little basis in science, but there were also those who were willing to abuse their patient's trust for profit or fame. There were certainly some questionable practices such as lobotomies that came out of this period.

This is the popular image of an upscale sanitarium which serves as a backdrop for *One Drop of Blood*. When the head doctor at the facility is murdered, the list of suspects includes not only the patients, but some of the staff as well. But Austin forgoes some of the more lurid staples of such environments, and when Dundee goes undercover he is not subject to drugs or other treatments for Mayfield is really quite a pleasant place, except for the murder, of course.

Anne Austin is not well known today, a product of a decade eighty years in the past. Yet her mysteries are not without their charm and interest. It is therefore with pleasure that Resurrected Press brings you this new edition of *One Drop of Blood*.

**About the Author**

Born in 1895, Anne Austin began by writing romance novels about young women in the mid 1920's but soon turned her talents to producing a string of mysteries through the 1930's, some of which appeared as serials in newspapers.. Many of these mysteries feature as the detective "Bonnie" Dundee, Special Investigator for the District Attorney, including *Murder Backstairs*, *The Avenging Parrot*, *Murder at Bridge*, and *One Drop of Blood*. Several of her mysteries were translated into French, including *Le Pigeon Noir* and *Le Crime Parfume*. Despite her success as a novelist, Anne Austin disappears from the public record after the 1930's.

# ONE DROP OF BLOOD

## CHAPTER I

"SURE you wouldn't be better off in a hospital, Chief?" James F. Dundee rose, to end his call upon the district attorney, who had been laid very flat by an attack of pleurisy.

Sanderson started to chuckle, then clapped a hand to his right side, as a grimace of pain contracted his pleasantly homely, freckled face. "Whoever first described this pain as like the thrust of a knife hit on the only apt simile for it in the English language," he groaned, but his gray eyes twinkled affectionately at his "special investigator." "No, Bonnie me lad, as Captain Strawn calls you, I haven't the heart to cheat my sister of the thrill of playing nurse. She has a passion for thermometers, hot water bottles and in valid trays, that amounts to an obsession. Our mother used to say that Nell would resort to feeding the family small doses of poison, if she couldn't get hold of an invalid in any other way."

"Well, don't let her kill you with kindness," Dundee grinned. "Things are dismally quiet now, but we're just about due for another crime wave."

"Can't kill a husky like me," District Attorney Sander son boasted. "I'll be thirty six in July, but damned if I don't feel more like a colt than I did at twenty one. . . . By the way, what do you hear from—from Penny?"

Dundee stopped halfway to the door of the sickroom. "From Penelope Crain?" he asked, as if it had required a prodigious feat of memory to dig up the full name of his chief's former secretary. "Haven't had a letter for months. . . . How is she liking law school by this time? A grand little female spellbinder Penny ought to make, that is, if she can keep from bawling out the judge when he makes a decision she doesn't like."

"She *is* a peppery little piece," Sanderson agreed, grinning broadly, but to Dundee's amazement his chief's freckled face was turning a fiery red.

"Are—congratulations in order, Chief?" he managed to ask, with great cheeriness, but his heart contracted sharply with a return of the old pain of which he had thought it cured. Darling little Penny! Clever, quick, thorny little Penny, who had helped him so marvelously, so chummily in the solving of the famous Bridge Murder Mystery.

"I—I thought maybe she'd written you," Sanderson stammered. "You two were great friends, weren't you? I confess I was afraid you'd beaten me to the prize, Bonnie."

"Oh, no! No!" Dundee reassured him, with unnecessary vehemence. "Nothing like that, Chief! I'll have to be making a lot more money and have a more dignified job than that of a common 'dick' before I can ask a girl like Penny Crain to marry me."

"I'm afraid there isn't another girl like Penny Crain," Sanderson smiled almost fatuously. "But you're not a 'common dick,' and you know it. You're an expert criminologist, and I'm damned proud to have you attached to my office. . . . You're not quoting Penny, by any chance?"

"I never gave her a chance to turn me down," Dundee answered, his blue eyes frank and friendly again. "But I don't mind telling you that you're the luckiest man in the world, Mr. Sanderson. . . . When is it to be?"

"Oh, not for another year yet," the district attorney answered, with sudden glumness. "Penny insists on graduating from law school—Now, who the devil can be ringing me at this time of the night?" He stilled the clamor of the telephone bell by lifting the receiver. "Hello! . . . Yes, this is the district attorney speaking . . . Dr. who? . . . Oh, yes, Dr. Cantrell . . . What's that? . . . *Dr. Koenig!?* My God! ... Yes ... Yes ... How long—? . . . Yes, I see . . . Any idea who—? ... I see ... You have my heartfelt sympathy, Dr. Cantrell. It's a national tragedy. . . . No, Doctor, I'm sorry to say I can't come in person. A nasty attack of pleurisy. But I'll send young Dundee, special investigator attached to my office. I consider him the ablest detective I have ever met. . . . Thanks. By the way, have you notified the police? . . . Then I'll call them for you . . . No, no. I'm quite equal to it. Glad to relieve you of the job. You'll see that nothing is disturbed, of course. . . . Terribly sorry, Doctor. Good bye."

Dundee waited tensely, like a hunter poised to take a fence. Very slowly the district attorney replaced the telephone receiver.

"Dr. Carl Koenig," he began heavily, "was murdered tonight in his office at the Mayfield Sanitarium. Exit a fine man and a great psychiatrist. . . . The back of his head cracked open—God!"

"Who did it?—a loony patient?" Dundee asked.

"That will be the conclusion both police and newspapers will jump at, of course, since it seems to be one of those motiveless, clueless mysteries," Sanderson answered. "That was Dr. Cantrell on the phone—medical head of the sanitarium, and sort of a partner, I believe. . . . Well, hop to it, boy, and keep in touch with me. Why, damn it! Koenig was a *friend* of mine, as well as the finest alienist I ever had on the witness stand."

But Dundee did not "hop" instantly. "Can you give me a line on the sanitarium, Chief? Are most of the patients crazy?"

"Not by any means," Sanderson assured him. "Only a small minority of the patients have been 'committed'— that is, adjudged insane in court. Those are in a locked ward, of course. Then there's quite a large group of more or less mild psychopathic cases, voluntary patients—cases of senility, incipient paresis, epilepsy, manic depression, chronic alcoholism, amnesia, aphasia, and victims of all sorts of complexes, psychoses and neuroses, harmful, usually, to no one but themselves. In addition, the place has become the most fashionable 'rest cure' and convalescent home in the state. Society women go there to indulge in 'nervous prostration' or the luxury of being psychoanalyzed, and rich men to be 'boiled out' after a prolonged spree. A good example of the latter is that handsome scapegrace, young Webster. He's in and out of the place half a dozen times a year—seems to enjoy it."

"Expensive?" Dundee interrupted.

"A big price range, but they've rather gone in for luxury for those that can afford it," Sanderson answered. "Suites of sitting room, bedroom and bath, at a hundred and fifty a week, I believe, and even separate cottages that are pretty darned ultra. Dr. Koenig's reputation as a psychiatrist, neurologist and psychoanalyst is so great that he's been the making of the place from a financial standpoint. It's now considered smart to go to Mayfield for treatment, whereas it used to be considered a disgrace to have to go into a 'mental hospital.' "

"Know anyone else there, sir?"

"I think not. No, wait! Bruce Cantrell found himself a peach of a wife among the patients, one of our society girls who went there to be psychoanalyzed a year or so ago. Claire Hobson, she was; pretty and rich as butter. . . . But you'd better get going, my lad."

"Right, sir! But give me a ten or fifteen minutes start before you notify Captain Strawn, won't you? I'd like to have a few uninterrupted moments on the scene of the crime. By the way, where is the sanitarium?"

Within two minutes Dundee had his roadster headed south, his foot pressing hard upon the accelerator, for there was little traffic in the streets of Hamilton at that hour of the night—a quarter to eleven. The cool June breeze lifted the crisp waves of his Irish black hair, hat-free, and fanned into flame the recently quenched fires of hope and ambition. Life was good, when it could so easily fling one into a big new job, the kind of adventure he liked best in the world. A new job, a new—Good Lord! He caught himself up sharply, half amused and half ashamed. He'd almost said, "A new job, a new girl!" Of course he was miserable. Hadn't he lost precious, funny, peppery little Penny? Ye e es. But Well, he told himself defiantly, every one of his three big jobs heretofore in Hamilton had brought him a new girl. Why not admit it? Hadn't he felt almost as badly over Norma Paige's being disgustingly satisfied with Walter Styles; over Gigi Berkeley's being just a little too young to be taken seriously? And now Penny Crain had broken his heart. . . . But was it really broken? Wasn't it true that, a mystery triumphantly solved, a murderer unmasked, the romantic adventure which had gone hand in hand with the adventure of crime detection always displayed an alarming tendency to write Finis for itself too? Perhaps—and he grinned at the drought—if he ran into an unsolvable crime and a lovable girl at the same time, he'd be permanently intrigued by both. . . .

*A new job, a new girl,* his blood persisted in singing to the hum of his speeding motor. . . . But that was absurd, his common sense objected. What more unlikely place for romance than a sanitarium for "mental" cases?

Suddenly his handsome young face became grim and purposeful, as, throwing off nonsense, he recalled the first and last time he had seen the famous psychiatrist. Dr. Carl Koenig had been called by District Attorney Sander son as an expert witness, to testify as to the legal sanity of a confessed murderer on trial for his life, and whom brilliant defense attorneys were trying to save on a plea of insanity.

As if he were before him then, in a phantom witness box, Dundee saw the thin, dark, rather small man, with his lean, clever face uplifted in an attitude of patient listening, as a defense attorney read a long hypothetical question requiring the alienist's uncompromising "Yes" or "No." He saw those smoky dark eyes, sad eyes they were, light up for an instant with a gleam of humor, as he uttered an answer which confounded his heckler. The face of a scholar and of an ascetic, a Christlike face, the lips thin but mobile, the swart skin drawn tight over high cheek bones, the nose high bridged and wide nostrilled. Not a man to be greeted as "Doc" and clapped on the back. Not a man for a patient to get chummy with, but a man of such sincere humanitarianism, Dundee believed, that any patient could trust him with any secret, however vile and shameful, and find in his tortured mind a great peace after the telling. . . .

And now the famous healer of sick minds was dead. Murdered. As unjustly dead as was justly dead the murderer against whom he had given expert testimony. Would there be another courtroom battle between alienists, with perhaps the ghost of the great Koenig whispering in a colleague's ear: "Forgive him. He knew not what he did."

His speedometer told Dundee that he had been traveling for nearly five miles along Mirror Lake Road. He slowed down, and began to search for the highway sign that would tell him when he had reached Willow Creek Drive, the turning which would take him, after a hundred yards' or so, to Mayfield Sanitarium.

If he had known the road and had been driving fast he would probably not have noticed, in the darkness which was doubly black in contrast with the light from his head lamps, that which caused him to step so hard and so suddenly upon his footbrake that he was almost catapulted over his own windshield.

And if her dress had not been white— But he did see and he did stop, after swerving his car so that the head lights threw their bright glare across the huddled body of a girl.

For a moment he thought she was dead, her fragile body crushed and flung into the roadside weeds by a hit and run driver. But as he knelt to lift her she moaned faintly, and the largest pair of dark blue eyes he had ever seen fluttered open and gazed upward at him with curious trustfulness, as if she were looking at a very old friend.

"Hello!" he greeted her happily, out of the profound ness of his relief.

"How do you do?" she returned with quaint politeness, lifting a hand feebly to push back the tumbled golden chestnut curls from her childlike forehead. But with the gesture she seemed to remember many things. Fear distorted her delicate, very white face.

"Are you a—a policeman?" she amazed him by asking, as she cowered away from the hands which were extended to help her rise.

"No," Dundee answered, truthfully enough. "Why?"

But she was not satisfied. One fragile, beautifully kept hand fluttered to his coat and turned back the left lapel. Reassured, she sighed and sank back upon her pillow of dusty weeds.

"I think," she said faintly, without answering his question, "I've sprained my ankle. Probably it's broken. It hurts dreadfully. ... I was running away," she explained simply. "Will you help me to run away?"

"We'll discuss that later," Dundee retorted cheerfully. "First, I'm going to take you to Mayfield Sanitarium— "

"No, no! Not there!" she panted, her whole body shrinking away from him. "Any place else—a hospital in Hamilton—anywhere "

"But I'm on my way there myself, and it's the nearest," Dundee reasoned with her gently.

"*You*—going to Mayfield?" she cried in horror.

"You poor kid!" Dundee ejaculated, but he was smiling. "You've got an idea that all the patients there are crazy. Isn't that it?"

"No." She shook her head and closed her eyes with great weariness. "It's—Mayfield I'm running away from."

"And you thought I was a policeman sent to bring you in—dead or alive?" Dundee asked, smiling more broadly. Then a cold chill raced down his spine. Only *insane* patients could fear such an aftermath to running away —those who had been committed. . . . Was this lovely, frail girl—*crazy?*

"Yes, yes!" she answered quickly. "I was afraid they'd —missed me and sent the police after me. I was afraid they'd put me in the locked ward for running away."

"Then you're not a locked ward patient?" he asked tactlessly.

"I—a *locked ward* patient?" she echoed indignantly. "Certainly not! I'm there for—for nerves."

"I see," Dundee said gently, not believing her for an instant. What a terrible pity that one so young, so lovely should be demented. . . . "But I'll really have to take you back, you know, since I have to go there myself "

"It's long past visiting hours," the girl protested. "And you can't be going as a patient. I'm sure you're not nervous, or—or anything queer, and you look awfully healthy "

Dundee made a sudden resolve. "I'm sorry to say I *am* going as a patient. I've been working too hard," he went on, lying gracelessly but convincingly. "My doctor orders rest and regular hours—that sort of thing. You see," and he grinned, making use of his earlier reflections on his susceptibility, "I'm subject to heart attacks. No organic disease; purely—er, functional, but quite distressing at the time."

"Oh!" the girl breathed softly, and stroked his hand with a rose tipped, slim forefinger. "I'm so sorry."

"And I'm afraid," Dundee took advantage of her shamelessly but truthfully, "that I feel an attack coming on now."

"Then—then good bye," she quavered, and lay back on her bed of weeds. "Please don't tell anyone you saw me."

"Silly! Do you think I'm going to leave you here?" And over her hysterical protests Dundee lifted her feather weight but rather long body in his arms and carried her to his roadster.

After the car was bowling along the highway again the girl suddenly ceased to struggle and protest. Dundee had removed the little white sandal from her badly swollen left foot, which she now nursed against her right knee, whimpering softly with pain.

"What's your name?" Dundee asked, partly to divert her. "Mine is Dundee," he added, for he had determined not to resort to the use of an alias. Outside of newspaper and police circles he was known scarcely at all. There was scant probability that any patient at Mayfield Sanitarium woula recognize his name or suspect his connection with the district attorney's office.

"E Enid Rambler," she told him, and Dundee wondered if her "nerves" caused her to stammer.

"That's a pretty name," Dundee commented idly. "I don't think I've ever known any Ramblers except the ancient automobiles of that name."

Oddly enough, the girl shrank from him at that. . . . A queer little thing she was. . . .

Isn't this where we turn?" He slowed the car to scan a highway sign. "Yes. Willow Creek Drive. You were going to let me miss my turn, weren't you?"

Sulking, Dundee decided, as she did not answer. But after he had made the right hand turn, a swift glance told him that she was not sulking. The expression on her rigid face and in her unwinking, staring eyes was that of hope less despair.

"Why were you running away?" he asked, very gently.

She appeared not to have heard.

Suddenly the detective instinct in him asserted itself over the knight to ladies in distress. "*When* did you run away?"

She answered that, dully: "I don't know what time it was. I was nervous. I get that way—hysterical. I can't sit still or lie still. I wandered around, looking for the head nurse, Miss Lacey, or for one of the doctors to give me a bromide. But I couldn't find anyone, so I—I walked about the grounds for a—a long time. Then I ran away. The gates are never locked."

Even if the gates she had referred to had not loomed ahead of him then he would not have dared question her further, for fear of exciting her suspicions as to his business at Mayfield. He swung his roadster between the high stone pillars and drove slowly along the winding, box hedged driveway. On either side lay acres of beautifully kept lawn, studded with formal flower beds and majestic trees, the whole faintly lighted by powerful electric lamps set at intervals along the base of the high wrought iron fence.

"Don't take me to the offices," the girl begged, her hands gripping his right arm with sudden vehemence. "Take me nearly to the door of the cottage I live in, and let me out. Then drive away and I'll call for help. A nurse will be sure to hear me. Please, please! If they know I've run away "

Because of the mounting hysteria in her voice Dundee agreed, silently regretful that he would have to betray her to Captain Strawn, turn her over to him for questioning. For even if she did not know that Dr. Koenig had been murdered, by her own confession she had been "wandering around" either shortly before or shortly after the murder. Probably the girl herself did not have the least idea how long she had lain unconscious after spraining her ankle, but Strawn would certainly pounce upon her. . . .

"Stop here!" the girl commanded. "That's my cottage over there. I'll crawl along on my hands and knees till I get to the steps, and I'll tell Miss Hunter—she's the night attendant—that I sprained my ankle while walking on the grounds "

"Do you have a cottage to yourself?" Dundee asked, as he stopped the car.

"Oh, no. Just a suite. There are six suites in Sunflower Court. They're built around a patio, where we can sit when we don't want to be on the main lawn with the other patients," Enid Rambler explained hurriedly. "There's a vacancy. Maybe they'll assign you to it," she added shyly, but hopefully.

"That would be nice," Dundee agreed, his mind instantly made up to subject the county to that expense, however large it might be. "Sure you'll be all right?—not faint again?"

"Sure," she whispered. "And thank you with all my heart, Mr. Dundee. Only—I wish you hadn't made me come back," she added, terror again stamping her delicate, mobile face. "The main building is straight ahead. It's the biggest building. You can't miss it."

Ruefully aware that the accident of his discovering the crippled runaway had cost him several of the precious minutes by which he had planned to beat Captain Strawn to the scene of the crime, Dundee drove rapidly up the driveway and stopped in a vacant space in a row of several cars parked diagonally in front of the main building. To his vast relief, Captain Strawn's car was not among them, nor was any policeman on guard.

He was walking toward the steps leading to the broad porch of the cream colored brick building when a man stepped from behind one of the white Doric columns, a flashlight and a metal box in his hands.

"I'm the night watchman, sir. Who you want to see?"

"Dr. Cantrell. He's expecting me."

"You're from the district attorney's office, sir?"

"Yes."

"I'll take you in, sir. I was just going to register the hour on my rounds. Eleven o'clock, but—" and the grizzled, heavy bodied man sighed, as he pointed to the dial of the boxed clock he was carrying, "all is not well. . . . It's a sad night for Mayfield, sir, a mighty sad night."

"You check in here every hour?" Dundee asked.

"Yes, sir. And patrol the grounds and buildings all night long."

"Did you see or hear anything at all unusual tonight?"

"No, sir. That is, not until Miss Hunter, who's night attendant over at Sunflower Court told me to look about the grounds for one of her patients—a young lady by the name of Rambler. Rambler by name, and now rambler in fact, it looks like, sir "

"I found her unconscious on the highway. A sprained ankle. I've just set her down at Sunflower Court," Dundee explained impatiently. "And please tell Miss Hunter for me to keep the girl under constant supervision for the rest of the night. . . . Now, outside of Miss Rambler's disappearance ?"

"Nothing, sir, until Dr. Cantrell blew his whistle for me half an hour ago. I was over at Ten'—that's what we call the locked ward, sir— and when I got here Dr. Cantrell told me Dr. Koenig had been killed, and asked me if I'd seen any suspicious characters about, but I told him, with all the comings and goings tonight "

"What's that?" Dundee cut in sharply.

"We have a picture show every Wednesday night, sir, in the O. T. Shop, and nearly all the patients are allowed to invite guests to see the show, so there's always a lot of strangers about of a Wednesday night."

"Where and what is the O. T. Shop?" Dundee asked.

"O. T. stands for Occupational Therapy, sir," the night watchman answered, with a trace of condescension. "Where the patients make baskets and shawls and hooked rugs and pottery. It's good for their nerves, sir. The O. T. Shop is in this building, sir, a big room at the center back. Talking pitchures we have, sir. We spare no expense "

Dundee grinned at the proud use of the personal pronoun, but he made haste to interrupt. "And at what time was the show over tonight?"

"It was an extry long pitchure, a fine new talkie called 'Manslaughter,' all about a girl that gets sent to prison for killing a traffic cop with her automobile "

"Yes, yes, I know! But when was it over?"

"There was a comedy first," the night watchman went on, a little offended, "and then the feature pitchure, and futhermore the operator was nearly an hour late getting here, so it was just turned ten, because it was almost time for me to clock in—"

"And you'd been watching the show, of course?" Dundee pounced.

"Off and on, sir, everything being quiet like," the man admitted.

"So that Dr. Koenig could have been murdered while you were enjoying 'Manslaughter,' " Dundee drove in his point relentlessly. Then: "Are any patients quartered in this building?"

"No," Whalen answered flatly, omitting the "sir." "Some of the staff have apartments on the second floor, and downstairs we have the doctors' offices, and the chartroom where Miss Lacey—she's the head nurse—has her desk, and then there's a big living room with a fireplace for the use of the patients, besides the O. T. Shop. And in the left wing there's the main kitchen, the staffs dining room, and another dining room for the men patients who don't want trays in their rooms."

"We'll go in now," Dundee cut into the watchman's volubility. "Is this door usually closed?"

"No, sir, except in cold weather, and then it's not locked. There's likely to be comings and goings all night, and the night head nurse is on duty in the chartroom. But the other outside doors to the doctors' offices are locked at night, after the secretary, Miss Home, is gone, unless one of the doctors is working late."

"Other outside doors?" Dundee repeated. "How many are there?"

"There's an outside front entrance, sir, just to the right of this porch, leading into the reception room where Miss Home and Dr. Harlow—that's Dr. Koenig's young lady doctor—do their work, and where patients and visitors are received," the night watchman explained, with a returning relish of his importance as guide. "Dr. Koenig's office is right behind the little reception room, and to the right of his office with a door between is Dr. Cantrell's office. And there's a back outside door to Dr. Cantrell's office. He uses it to go home, sir. His house is about two hundred feet back of the office."

Without comment, Dundee followed the watchman into a large central hall, pleasantly furnished with lamps, chairs and settees.

"This first door on your right opens into the reception room, and that next one into Dr. Koenig's office," Whalen continued, then, shaking his grizzled head lugubriously: "And this is the first time I ever knowed the Big Doctor's door to be shut when he was in his office. Always open it was, sir, no matter how busy he might be "

"Why?" Dundee asked, surprised.

"Because, sir, a lot of our patients are not exactly what you'd call theirselves, in a manner of speaking, and they get so nervous and upset that nothing will do them any good but to speak to Dr. Koenig himself. So they ain't no red tape here, Mister. A patient can—I mean could walk right in on the Big Doctor and have a chin with him any time of the day or night, if he was in his office. I don't know what we'll do without him. Looks to me like the place will go to the dogs "

"I hope not. . . . This is the living room for the patients' use, I suppose?" and Dundee nodded toward the wide, arched doorway on his left, beyond which he could see a piano, a huge sofa, a set up bridge table, smoking stands, overstuffed armchairs, and floor lamps.

"Yes, sir. It's used mostly by the bridge players in the evening after it gets too dark to play on the lawn."

"Was there a game this evening?" Dundee asked hope fully, since players would have a clear view of the doctor's office directly across the hall.

"No, sir, more's the pity," the watchman answered gloomily. "You see, sir, nearly all the patients was attending the pitchure show this evening. Like as not, if the bridge game had been going on as usual the murderer— may he burn in hell!—wouldn't have had a chance to kill the poor doctor and wreck his office without somebody hearing the fuss he made."

"You're probably right," Dundee assured him, then wheeled to face a small, gray haired, pale faced nurse who had entered from the porch. "Good evening. I've come to see Dr. Cantrell. He's expecting me."

"Oh, yes, sir," the nurse gasped. "I'm sorry I wasn't here when you arrived. I was busy giving a hypodermic to a patient in 'Ten.' I'll tell Dr. Cantrell you're here, Mr.—?"

"Dundee, from the district attorney's office. . . . Just a minute, Mr. Whalen," the detective halted the watchman, who was moving on. "I may find it necessary to stay on here for a day or two, and if I do it will be as a patient. You understand? None of the patients is to know what I am here for."

"Yes, sir, yes, sir!" Whalen answered eagerly, gloom giving way to keen relish.

And the nurse smiled at Dundee from tear reddened eyes before scurrying across the hall to knock at the reception room door.

Dundee was not kept waiting. Two men and two women rose to receive him as the night nurse slipped away, closing the door after her. A rather stout man, of perhaps forty, advanced with outstretched hand.

"Mr. Dundee? I'm Dr. Cantrell, medical head of Mayfield Sanitarium."

Burning, deep sunken black eyes under an incongruous thatch of rust colored hair held Dundee's eyes briefly before the doctor continued:

"And this is Dr. Harlow—Dr. Justine Harlow, Dr. Koenig's assistant psychiatrist."

He paused impatiently for the small and very girlish, pretty young doctor to shake hands with the detective; then:

"And this is Mr. Baldwin, our business manager, and a partner with Dr. Koenig and myself. . . . And this is Miss Lacey, our head nurse."

Dundee shook hands first with the nurse, whose Irish youthfulness of face was belied by the threads of white in her curling black hair, then gave his attention to the business manager. And he felt a swift, unreasoning dislike of Mr. Baldwin. In the first place, the man was physically most unattractive, with his insignificant, round shouldered body, his glistening, egg shaped head whose bald area was fringed with thin, white hair, his curiously dead looking brown eyes, and his hooked nose pointing to a tightly pursed mouth. But it was something more subtle than physical appearance which repelled Dundee. He fumbled for an explanation and found it before Baldwin's limp hand had quickly released his own firm clasp. There was a complete absence of decent grief in the man. His partner had been brutally murdered, and this man was not grieving. He was angry, disturbed, indignant. But he was not grief stricken. The obvious desolation of the two women and the burning sorrow in the medical doctor's eyes put him to shame. And they were all aware, too, of Baldwin's callousness to the tragedy, for Dundee was positive that they shrank from him, huddled together spiritually for consolation.

As the detective was about to voice his personal grief for the man he had seen only once, but had respected and admired deeply, the business manager cut in sharply:

"Yes, yes. But there is something I must request immediately, sir, immediately! Since you are representing the district attorney, and will therefore have prestige with the reporters who are certain to flock around like vultures, I must insist—" He may have realized that he was going too far, for the pursed lips sucked in a whistling breath before shaping more tactful words. "I must beg of you, Mr. Dundee, to do everything in your power to keep the press from jumping to the conclusion that one of our patients murdered Dr. Koenig!"

"But—if the evidence points to that conclusion?" Dundee asked mildly.

"If it does, I assure you that the murderer faked it very cleverly," Baldwin assured him vehemently. "Wouldn't that be the natural thing for the fiend to do? Not only to throw suspicion from himself, but to bring ruin upon the institution which Dr. Koenig's great skill and outstanding reputation have built up. And I must ask you to help defeat that base intention, Mr. Dundee. Prospective patients will shun us like the plague if they are led to believe that not even the doctors themselves are safe from the violence of demented patients. I tell you, sir, every precaution is taken here—"

"May I see the body, please?" Dundee interrupted curtly. The old fool! Did he think he was making a speech before a jury? And was he so concerned with balance sheets that he would be more than willing to have his partner's death unavenged, if the murderer should indeed be one of his precious and profitable patients? Every precaution indeed! When he—Dundee himself—had found a patient unconscious by the roadside a mile from the sanitarium; when he had been in the hall of the main building for minutes before even a nurse had appeared; when Dr. Koenig's office had been accessible that night from at least three unlocked doors, while visitors and patients had swarmed in and out of the building!

It was Dr. Cantrell who, after a glance of bitter contempt at his partner, was about to lead the way into the small office where the murder had been committed, when the outside door was opened unceremoniously and a very plump, cherubic man bounded into the room.

"Hello, folks! 'Happy' Day is here again!" the man yodeled, his round face one vast smile, which abated some what with embarrassment as his beaming brown eyes encountered Dundee. "Scuse! Didn't know you were busy!"

"It's all right, 'Happy'," Dr. Harlow quavered, as if his joyousness hurt every nerve in her body. "I'm glad you got my message. It's your friend, Archie, this time. He's over in 'Ten.' "

"Thanks, doc! That's swell. Archie's a great kid. Believe me, I'm glad to get another case so soon. I feel like a fish out of Water when I'm not at Mayfield."

Dundee permitted the man to bounce blithely away, before he asked Dr. Harlow: "And who is the happy young man?"

The girl doctor smiled tremulously. "His nickname does suit him, doesn't it? His name is Howard Day, but everyone calls him 'Happy' Day. He is one of our most popular attendants. The case he had been on for a long time was transferred Monday to the State Hospital for Mental Diseases, and he has been 'on call' since."

Because time was pressing, and Strawn was overdue, Dundee forebore to inquire into the popular attendant's new case. His chief interest now lay in the murdered doctor's office. And one sweeping glance sufficed to show Dundee that Business Manager Baldwin had good cause to fear that suspicion would fall upon one of Mayfield's demented patients.

# CHAPTER 2

A CLEANING woman, after one indignant look at Dr. Carl Koenig's office, would have muttered: "Looks like a cyclone had struck it!" And Special Investigator Dundee could think of no better simile. But apparently it had been a cyclone of fury, of unreasoning, destructive rage that had swept through the private sanctum of the great psychiatrist, striking with deadly aim at the doctor himself, then spending itself upon the victim's possessions.

Over a thick, taupe colored rug cluttered with letters and books, finely torn scraps of paper, and an overturned floor lamp and smoking stand, Dundee picked a cautious path to the dead man's desk.

The body, seated in a swivel chair, was so bowed that the forehead of the dead man's face, which was sharply turned to the left, rested upon the big blotter that protected nearly half the surface of the flat topped desk. The left arm was stretched across the desk, but the other arm dangled against the chair, the palm of the hand turned outward with the fingers curled almost to the tip of the thumb.

The cause of death was apparent at a glance. Blows from some ax like instrument upon the back of the head, slightly to the left, had shattered the skull. Dundee quickly averted his eyes from the nauseating spectacle, and sought the weapon.

He did not have far to search. On the rug, almost touching one of the curved legs of the swivel chair, lay a small bronze replica of the famous sculpture, "The Discus Thrower." And it had been the sharp edge of the discus itself which had crashed through the skull of the doctor, for it bore traces of its gruesome use—a few short black hairs matted to the bronze with dried blood.

Inserting the toe of his boot beneath the body of the bronze athlete, Dundee raised the statue an inch or so from the rug, stared thoughtfully for a moment, then let it sink slowly into its former place.

"At what time was the murder discovered?" Dundee asked, as his eyes took in the disorder of the desk: pulled out drawers, a flower vase and an inkwell both over turned upon the blotter, ashes and stubs scattered from a metal cigarette tray and wet from the same fluids which had stained the bowed face of the dead man. The three lovely roses, which almost touched the nose that could no longer inhale their fragrance, had also been stained with ink. Unusual roses they were, too: their gold tipped petals shading into a deep, rosy saffron. Still crisply fresh and only half opened. . . .

"At about ten twenty five," Dr. Cantrell answered. "Miss Lacey—"

"Just a minute. I'll get her story later. When did you view the body?"

"Not more than three minutes after Miss Lacey discovered what had happened. I was at home. She called me on the telephone. My house is only two or three hundred feet back of this suite of offices. I answered the telephone myself and came immediately."

"Did you make any tests to determine how long the doctor had been dead?"

"Yes. I took the body temperature, and tested for rigor mortis, which had not set in to any appreciable extent," Dr. Cantrell replied. "To the best of my ability to calculate, Dr. Koenig had then been dead about forty five minutes."

"Which, you would say, places the murder at approximately nine forty five?"

"Yes. Of course there could well be a leeway of five or ten minutes."

"In your opinion—and of course you understand that all your findings will be checked by the coroner, Dr. Price, when he arrives— was death instantaneous?"

"Not a doubt of that," Dr. Cantrell answered.

"Another thing, doctor," Dundee continued, his eyes again flicking a reluctant glance at the broken head. "Would you say that a person of extraordinary strength struck that blow?"

Dr. Cantrell seemed to weigh his words very carefully before uttering them. Then: "Not necessarily, Mr. Dundee. My examination of the wound shows that Dr. Koenig's skull was rather thinner than the average. The weapon, you will notice, weighs at least fifteen pounds, I should judge "

"Have you touched it?" Dundee interrupted sharply.

"Certainly not. But the statuette is of solid bronze and is more than eighteen inches tall. The pedestal alone—"

"Could a woman have struck that blow?" Dundee interrupted again.

Again the doctor hesitated. "Ye—es, especially if the woman were under terrific mental stress—"

"Yes, I understand that insanity—whether temporary or chronic— lends abnormal strength to a person in a homicidal rage," Dundee cut in.

The medical head of Mayfield Sanitarium was silent, his face rigid, his burning black eyes fixed upon some terrible picture which only he could see.

"Then you, too, are afraid that one of your patients did this thing?" Dundee asked.

He had not heard the door open and he wheeled in surprise as a woman's faltering but very musical voice called from the doorway:

"Please, Mr. Dundee! There's something I *must* say."

"Certainly, Dr. Harlow. . . . Will you come in?"

The small, girlish doctor advanced gingerly, her little low heeled patent leather pumps as careful not to tread upon the litter as the detective's had been. Very pretty, indeed, she was, Dundee observed appreciatively, although amber rimmed spectacles detracted from the beauty of her large, gray green eyes, and her magnificent red hair, which she wore in great coils over her ears, had become sadly disordered in the storm of grief through which she had undoubtedly passed. She was still in uniform—stiffly starched white linen, with only a severe little black crepe de chine jacket and the absence of a cap to distinguish her from the institution's nurses.

"I overheard what you asked Dr. Cantrell," she began as she stood before him, her lovely voice becoming quite steady with the professional authority that sat quaintly upon her smallness and girlishness. "Please remember that I am speaking as a doctor, as a psychiatrist, when I beg you not to voice any such theory to reporters."

"May I ask why?"

"I can't expect you to be in sympathy with our problems here," the little doctor began, a note of despair in her voice. "But if the morning papers print a theory that a patient here is the—the murderer " She flinched at the word, then brought it out bravely—"it will do untold damage here, not only among those who are mentally ill, but throughout the institution. It would simply create a panic. We could not possibly hire enough attendants and special nurses to handle the situation of a sanitarium full of terror stricken patients, each one fearing he or she might be the next victim. And even if we doubled our staff, the patients, believing *we* feared for their safety " The beautiful voice broke, and the girl doctor's small but very firm hands stretched toward the detective appealingly.

"I understand," Dundee assured her gently.

"Oh, I hope you do!" she breathed, almost prayerfully. "But there's still—another angle. I can illustrate by telling you that when one patient commits suicide—and in spite of our vigilance that does happen sometimes—we can count on five attempted suicides when the news gets about. Do you—see what I mean?" she persisted, her gray green eyes wide with a very real terror.

"I think I do," Dundee answered slowly. "You mean—the power of suggestion might bring about other murders, or attempted murders?"

"Yes," the little doctor nodded. "And undoubtedly a flurry of confessions, which would only hinder you in your work."

"I am sure you are right," Dundee assured her, with entirely respectful admiration. "And I'll gladly do all I can, not only because I want to help, but—*because I do not believe Dr. Koenig was murdered by a person in a homicidal rage!"*

Dundee watched her face keenly as he spoke the slow, emphasized words. He saw relief give place to blankness, then—and he was very sure of that—startled fear flickered in those candid eyes and twitched her pretty, rougeless lips.

It was with obvious effort that she spoke again, after a shuddering intake of breath: "Then—you don't think a patient did it?"

"I didn't say that," Dundee reminded her, and he was sure she was again relieved. "Of course I have no power to dictate what Captain Strawn of the Homicide Squad shall say to the press, but, for my part, if I cannot escape the reporters entirely, I shall voice no theories and make no statements as to the murderer unless our investigation tonight succeeds far beyond my expectations. . . . And by the way, I wonder what is detaining the captain so long. The District Attorney was to telephone him—"

"Oh!" Dr. Harlow gasped, flushing. "He's in the reception room now. That's what I came to tell you, but I wanted to enlist your help first. Shall I show him in here? He has been questioning Mr. Whalen, our night watchman."

"Good! I've already talked to Whalen," Dundee said. "Show the Captain in when he's ready."

A moment after the girl doctor had left, Captain John Strawn, Chief of the Homicide Squad, bulked large in the doorway, a reluctant grin pulling downward one corner of his typical policeman's mouth.

"Well, Bonnie me lad, I see you've taken the first trick," the gray haired detective greeted the former member of his squad. "You've beat me to the game by a good half hour, I take it. Sanderson vows he tried that long to reach me. Matter of fact, I took my wife for a drive after a movie."

"Sure it was your wife, Chief?" Dundee gibed affectionately, as he shook hands. "Dr. Cantrell, Captain Strawn."

"Glad to meetcha, Doc, though I wish it was a happier time and place," the old detective boomed, shaking hands with the proper touch of solemnity. "Well, Bonnie! Got your murderer all picked out?"

"I wish it were that easy, Captain."

"What!" Strawn ejaculated, his keen gray eyes again sweeping the disorder of the room and the corpse at the desk. "Here we have a nut hospital, the brain doctor's head bashed in with the handiest weapon, and his office left in one hell of a mess. Plain sailing, Bonnie. Some loony patient comes in to talk with the doc, gets sore, runs amok and kills him. . . . Don't it look that way to you, Dr. Cantrell?"

The medical head of the sanitarium glanced at Dundee, then shrugged helplessly, without answering in words.

"Now, what does he mean by that?" Dundee reflected silently. "Does he agree, along with Dr. Harlow and Baldwin, or—does he just want me to think he agrees?"

"Sure I'm right," Strawn went on emphatically, as if Dr. Cantrell had confirmed his suspicion. "Got a lot of nuts here who could a done it, eh, Doc?"

"I do not feel qualified to answer that question, sir," Dr. Cantrell answered stiffly. "My work is purely medical. I am not a psychiatrist. But I may say that all patients who have shown any tendency to harm themselves or others are kept in a locked ward—Ward Ten, we call it, and are under constant observation when not locked in their rooms. But I suggest you question Dr. Harlow, the assistant psychiatrist, along these lines."

"I'll do that! Don't worry," Strawn retorted, stung by the doctor's attitude. "But I've already had a talk with your night watchman, Whalen, and he tells me there was a picture show in what he calls the O. T. Shop this evening. Moreover, he says that five of the crazy patients out of Ten' attended the show. Saw 'em himself," Strawn added triumphantly.

"If he saw them, then he also saw their attendants," Cantrell retorted coldly.

"It was pretty dark in the O. T. Shop while the pictures was being run, wasn't it? ... Well, then! . . . And by the way, Doctor, it struck me as being kinda funny that a picture called 'Manslaughter' would be picked out to amuse a bunch of nuts and nervous patients."

"I thought of that, too, Captain," Dundee commented approvingly. "I admit I don't know the story, but I have been wondering about—the power of suggestion."

"I saw the picture Monday evening in Hamilton," Dr. Cantrell said, plainly on the defensive. "Certainly it would have no power to suggest the crime that was committed here tonight, since 'Manslaughter' is the story of a girl who kills a traffic policeman who has been chasing her for speeding. Accidental homicide, in other words, though the girl in the case was extremely culpable and deserved the prison sentence she received. I feel sure that there was nothing unduly exciting, even to the very nervous, and that, on the contrary, the punishment of the girl would have a salutary effect on any patient with tendencies to violence. In fact, I feel safe in assuming that our business manager, Mr. Baldwin, had just such an effect in mind when he chose the picture for tonight's run. His choice of pictures is limited, also, since Dr. Koenig had banned the showing of gangster pictures and movies which were decidedly 'sexy.' "

"Why?" Strawn demanded.

"Gangster pictures are full of violence, shooting and sudden death," Cantrell explained impatiently, "and the so called 'sexy' pictures, in Dr. Koenig's opinion, would cause decidedly erotic reactions among the psychopathic patients, as well as create a restlessness among our other patients who are temporarily deprived of the society of their mates or sweethearts."

"You mean the loony patients are apt to be nuts on sex, eh?" Strawn decoded the doctor's academic explanation.

"To put it crudely—yes!"

"Must cost you a lot to rent a popular movie like that," Strawn ruminated.

"Not an excessive amount," Cantrell answered coldly. "One of Dr. Koenig's grateful patients donated the rather expensive machines for the showing of talking pictures, and Mr. Baldwin has made an arrangement with the Hamilton theaters whereby, at a nominal sum in addition to the payment for the operator's services, he secures first class pictures. We usually show a comedy, which is secured from one theater, and a feature picture from another. As you know, the downtown theaters have two hour programs. We arrange for the transportation of the films, picking them up as soon as the theater operators have finished running them, and returning them before they are needed for the next show."

"I see," Strawn admitted. "Now, Doc, you were called in to view the body right after it was discovered, weren't you?"

Dundee, already familiar with the forthcoming questions and answers, began to wander about the room, minutely investigating its disorder. He paused first at the desk, considered it thoughtfully, then concentrated upon the low typewriter table placed near the end of the desk, farthest from the door into the hall, and at right angles to the desk. The table was large enough to hold a telephone of the French type, a stack of typewriter paper, and a portable machine. Nothing here was disarranged, except that the ribbon had been yanked from the typewriter's spools and lay in purple coils upon the keys. But there was something else, Dundee discovered. He had almost missed it, for the torn scrap of paper was nearly hidden under the rubber platen or the typewriter. Someone, whether Dr. Koenig, dissatisfied with what he had written, or his murderer, had snatched from the machine the last sheet of paper upon which the doctor would ever type. And, remembering the quietness and calmness of the alienist upon the witness stand, Dundee could not believe that it was Koenig's hand which had done the violent snatching.

With increasing excitement, the young detective continued his wandering. Kneeling, he examined the over turned floor lamp, carefully scrutinizing the socket, the globe and the decorated parchment shade. Next he paused before the large bookcase, principally devoted to textbooks on mental diseases. The gaps in the rows were accounted for by the books scattered over the floor. Kneeling before the book nearest the case, he lifted it very carefully, then examined the thick pile of the rug in a circle of at least three feet in diameter. He repeated the strange procedure with all the scattered books, then, more than satisfied, turned his attention to the five drawer steel filing cabinet set against the wall between the bookcase and the door leading into the reception room. All the drawers had been pulled approximately halfway out, and a glance was enough to show Dundee that the cabinet contained a well indexed file of patients' case histories, everyone in its own manila folder, labeled with the patient's name. A number of the folders had been partially withdrawn and left sticking out of the file drawers at untidy angles.

With a sharp exclamation below his breath, Dundee grasped a corner of one of the folders, tested it for smoothness and weight, then again dropped to his knees and searched among the finely torn scraps of paper that littered the rug. He found what he was looking for, then hurried back to the filing cabinet, where he further satisfied himself by comparing the fragment with the manila folder he had been fingering.

Slowly he strolled to the room's one window, set almost in the corner of the back wall of the office. The shade was drawn exactly flush with the sill, but the silk pongee curtains were pushed to either end of their rod. By means of its cord, Dundee raised the shade, and. peered out upon a faintly lighted bit of garden, through which a cement path led to the Cantrell home. The window was closed but not locked. . .

After a few moments of deep thought, he wheeled abruptly from the window and pushed wide the partly open door between Dr. Koenig's office and the room beyond. Dr. Cantrell's office was somewhat larger than the psychiatrist's. In addition to the locked door in the back wall, there were three screened windows, all locked and with drawn shades.

It was a typical medical doctor's private office: scales for weighing patients and measuring their height; a long, high, narrow table covered with brown leather, and used in making physical examinations; a white enameled instrument cabinet, which Dundee found to be locked; an instrument sterilizer; a hand basin with running water; two lidded metal hampers; a file cabinet, a large, flat topped desk, a swivel chair, two straight chairs, and a well stocked bookcase, which was topped with a leather framed photograph of a beautiful girl, whose silver blonde hair was in enchanting contrast to large, liquid black eyes. Cantrell's wife, of course. . . . .

Here was perfect order, apparently. But Dundee left nothing to chance. He made a thorough tour of the room, looking for any faintest trace of the murderer's visit. And at last he was triumphantly justified.

He had pressed his foot upon the pedal which raised the lid of the smaller of the two white enameled hampers, and had gasped at his discovery.

"Bloodstained swabs!" he gloated. "And rubber gloves. ... Of course he would wear rubber gloves. And what more certain than that he would find a pair in Dr. Cantrell's office!"

Stooping, he fished out the two red rubber gloves, one badly torn at the wrist. But strangely enough Dundee was disappointed with his first examination of the find. Then he swiftly turned the gloves inside out and let his eyes run eagerly over the tips of the thumbs and fingers. And he found what he was looking for.

"Hey, Bonnie! Stealing another march on me?" Captain Strawn boomed from the doorway, his bulk almost hiding the doctor, who stood behind him.

"I'm afraid I am," Dundee assented gravely. "Will you come here a moment, Dr. Cantrell?"

When the doctor had joined him Dundee pointed rather melodramatically to the blood soaked gauze swabs in the hamper. "A tidy murderer, after all, in spite of the mess he made in that other office!"

Dr. Cantrell laughed, a sharp, mirthless bark. "I'm afraid I'm the tidy one, but—not the murderer. I dropped those swabs into that hamper myself. One of the male patients, who has the reputation of being rather an exhibitionist, and given to half hearted attempts at suicide, which he takes good care will not be fatal, slashed his arm from the wrist almost to the elbow this evening, and I dressed it. Miss Caplan, the night nurse, helped me."

Dundee did not seem so dashed as Strawn, broadly grinning, evidently expected him to be.

"And these rubber gloves, doctor?"

"Miss Caplan wore them. There was not time for her to 'scrub up.' She put the gloves on and applied a tourniquet, while I washed my hands with an antiseptic before sewing up the wound," Dr. Cantrell explained.

"Did you notice whether she tore them when she removed the gloves?" Dundee asked. "And whether she discarded them?"

"I didn't notice," Cantrell answered, then caught him self up short. "Yes. I do remember seeing her take them off. But—*she didn't drop them into that hamper!* It's used for waste stuff only, such as the swabs we used in staunching the blood and cleansing the wound. I distinctly remember seeing her drop them into the instrument tray she had got ready for me. Here's the tray on top of the cabinet," he added, frowning slightly. "I see that Miss Caplan did not sterilize the instruments and return them to the cabinet. Called away, I presume."

"Then the gloves she had used were in plain sight and accessible to anyone who wanted to use them?" Dundee persisted.

"Apparently so," Dr. Cantrell admitted. "But I can't see—"

"Where did Miss Caplan get the rubber gloves?"

"Out of the cabinet, of course. It is kept locked, so that no patient with suicidal tendencies can possibly get at a sharp instrument. As an added precaution, the windows and doors of this office are always kept locked when I am not using it."

"Then you locked the door between your office and Dr. Koenig's when you finished in here this evening?" Dundee asked.

"No. Dr. Koenig was in his office, and I left this door ajar in case he might have occasion to use my office," Dr. Cantrell replied. "Naturally he had a key, and I left the door ajar as a courtesy."

"What's all the Sherlocking for, Bonnie?" Strawn interrupted disgustedly. "The case will be as good as closed as soon as Carraway photographs the fingerprints. The nut murderer must have left hundreds of 'em—"

"Not so nutty, I'm afraid," Dundee cut in. "At any rate he had his wits sufficiently about him to don rubber gloves before stepping into the role of 'homicidal maniac.' "

"How do you know he wore the gloves?" Strawn demanded belligerently. "Just because you find a torn pair in a waste hamper "

"Whoa, Captain!" Dundee grinned. "Am I the lad for jumping at conclusions? . . . Dr. Cantrell, is it likely or even possible, in your opinion, that anyone connected with the sanitarium—yourself, Dr. Koenig, or the nurse—used these gloves tonight to keep his or her hands clean while changing or untangling the ribbon on a typewriter?"

"Certainly not! Those gloves were soiled—stained with blood," Dr. Cantrell assured him coldly. "If Dr. Koenig —and he was the only one using a typewriter this evening, to my knowledge—had wanted to wear rubber gloves while changing a ribbon, he would have got a clean pair out of the cabinet. He had a key, of course."

"Just as I thought," Dundee nodded. "The *inside* of the gloves was stained with blood when the murderer put them on "

"The inside?" Strawn repeated, frowning.

"I am assuming that the nurse removed them in the natural way—shucked them off so that they were turned inside out," Dundee explained. "When the murderer pulled them on, he did not see the bloodstains. But when he took them off it was not to clean them tidily of blood spots, but to wash away any possible trace of his finger prints from the inside of the gloves—which was then the *outside*, of course, since he had shucked them off his hands, turning them by doing so. And, unidentifiable, it is true, the towel he spread across his hands while manipulating the washing and drying of the gloves is now in the other hamper. Just my opinion, of course, but it is the obvious thing for him to have done. You see, he was canny enough to take no chances. *Or so he thought!* He forgot to cleanse again what had become the *inside* of the gloves when he shucked them off. Look, Doctor! Don't you agree with me that the forefinger and thumb of this glove, which I turned after I found the pair, are stained with purple typewriter ribbon ink?"

"It looks like it," Dr. Cantrell agreed, furrowing his brows as he studied the glove extended for his inspection. "But how—?"

"Just a little souvenir of the murderer's 'mad rage,' which by the way, was probably the most noiseless, methodical 'mad rage' on record!"

# CHAPTER 3

"Noiseless" ejaculated Captain Strawn, as he stepped back into the dead doctor's office. With this room in the mess it is? Books thrown around, this big lamp and the smoking stand turned over–"

"All of which is exactly what the murderer counted on your saying" Dundee assured his former chief. "But I'll wager only two sounds could have been heard, even faintly outside one cf these closed doors tonight. The first, made before the murderer had put on the rubber gloves, of course was the sound of the blow, or blows, which did the deed. And the second was the much fainter and not at all suspicious sound of paper being torn."

"You're cuckoo, Bonnie!" Strawn was becoming angry. "Why when he flung down the statue—"

"Yes. If he had flung it down. But it just happens that there is proof that he laid it down beside the doctor's chair — very carefully, without any noise whatever, after wiping it clean of his fingerprints."

"You can't know that!" Strawn protested hotly.

"Look. Chief." Dundee urged, as he again inserted the toe of his boot beneath the prone statue of "The Discus Thrower," raising it slightly from its resting place on the rug. "The pile of the rug is mashed down only very slightly. If the statue had been hurled or even dropped from a height of a few feet — say from the hand of the murderer — there would be deep indentations in the pile of the rug, where the sharp edges of the statue struck. After Carraway quite unsuccessfully tests it for finger prints, I can demonstrate my point to you, if you wish. But I can convince you otherwise, I believe. . . . Look at this lamp'"

"Well, what about it? Toppled over, ain't it?" Strawn growled.

"But oh, so gently!" Dundee smiled. "The globe is not broken, you notice, though the lamp standard is a heavy metal one. The socket is not bent even slightly, as invariably happens when I tip over a floor lamp by catching my foot in the cord. And, lastly, the light wire frame of the shade is not bent, either. . . . Now for the books. . . . Dr. Cantrell, will you be good enough to take a book from that bookcase and hurl it across the room?"

Frowning, as if he resented this attack upon his dignity, Dr. Cantrell obeyed, throwing the volume with consider able force. Dundee, with Strawn at his heels, strolled over to where the book lay open, face downward, some of the leaves ruffled and bent, and one of the stiff corners of the binding sadly broken.

"That's the way a thrown book usually looks," Dundee pointed out. "But look at the books our murderer deposited over the room. Two are open, face downward, but quite tidily so, with no leaves crumpled, no corners broken. The other five books are very decorous indeed, showing no signs whatever of having been hurled—not even a strain on the ribs. . . . No, Captain. These books were never thrown. They were very carefully and noiselessly deposited on the floor. . . . But that's not all!"

And Dundee led the way to the psychiatrist's desk. "Here we have an overturned, very fragile crystal vase. It is not broken, you see. Moreover, it was carefully laid on its side *on the blotter,* although, judging by this dust free circle near the back of the desk which fits the size of the base of the vase, the murderer had to move it nearly two feet, before his 'rage' overcame him. ... I wonder," he said softly, "if this was a sardonic touch: the overturning of the vase so that the roses would exude their fragrance directly against a nose which would never smell roses again?"

"Don't go fancy on us, Dundee," Strawn snorted with disgust.

"Sorry!" Dundee apologized, his blue eyes twinkling. "Now for the inkwell. You'll observe that it lies half on, half off the blotter. But there is not even a faint scar on the mahogany, as would have been inevitable if the murderer had picked up the heavy inkwell and dashed it down. Right?"

"Maybe," Strawn conceded grudgingly.

"And here is where the murderer over reached himself," Dundee went on, pointing to the coils of purple ribbon lying across the typewriter keys. "A nice little touch, that. But in adding it, the murderer stained his rubber gloves, and then left faint smudges on the case history he tore into exceedingly fine fragments, as well as on case histories whose folders he touched while searching for the one he wanted to destroy."

"Case histories!" Dr. Cantrell exclaimed. "Good Lord, Dundee! Are you sure? Why, that's a calamity!"

"Calamity?" Strawn boomed. "It's a lucky break for us, you mean. Find the guy whose case history is missing "

"Just what did you mean, Dr. Cantrell?" Dundee asked curiously.

The doctor wiped his forehead with a newly unfolded handkerchief. "Only that case histories are sacred, and guarded above anything else in the institution. If anyone has wantonly destroyed some of them it will be a very serious loss."

"I take it, then, that this filing cabinet is usually kept locked?" Dundee asked.

"Always," the doctor answered emphatically. "And there are only four keys in existence. Dr. Koenig had one, Dr. Harlow has another, Miss Home, the secretary, has the third, and I have the fourth myself. Since the cabinet is open, Dr. Koenig must have been making some additions to a case history this evening."

"Was Dr. Koenig in the habit of typing such things himself?"

"Oh, yes. He was an expert on the typewriter, and he never bothered to wait to dictate, if the secretary wasn't available."

"Then we can assume that Dr. Koenig was typing an addition to a case history on the sheet of paper that the murderer tore from the machine?" Dundee persisted.

"If a sheet of paper *was* torn from the machine—yes!" Dr. Cantrell answered. "Dr. Koenig almost never wrote letters in the evening, but frequently worked on the histories."

"Listen, Doc!" Strawn interrupted excitedly. "Do the nutty patients know their what d' you call it?—their diagnosis? I mean, does the brain doctor tell 'em the technical names for their troubles?"

"Certainly not, as a rule," Dr. Cantrell answered, with great dignity. "Naturally some of the patients are educated enough to know the technical terms without being told, and have enough self knowledge to know their own diagnoses. Epileptics, for instance, and most manic depressives "

"But now looky here!" Strawn interrupted impatiently. "Suppose a guy come in here tonight to have a chin with the brain doctor. The doctor looks up, says wait a minute, and goes on with his typing. But the patient comes close, bends over, sees what the doc is writing, and— *it's all about this patient*, see? With terrible sounding words that the patient don't understand but which sound like an insult to him. . . . See? . . . Well, the patient backs off, the doc keeps on typing, the patient sneaks the statue off that bookcase where you said it was kept, and bangs the doctor over the head. Then he jerks the sheet of paper out of the typewriter, tears it up; finds the rest of the case history open on the doc's desk, tears it up, too—"

"First calming down enough to hunt for and find a pair of rubber gloves, so as to make sure of leaving no finger prints," Dundee interrupted. "Wait, Chief! I'm not saying you aren't right. In fact, there are strong indications that you are "

"Spoken like the sport you are, lad!" Strawn beamed. "Sure I'm right! This bird gets cagey. He says to himself, 'If I tear up only my own case history, they'll pin it on me sure, when they check up on the case history file. So I'll destroy one or two more, just to put 'em off the track!' . . . Which he does."

"Thereby proving himself a very level headed, calculating 'nut' as you call him, Chief," Dundee smiled.

"A great many psychopathic patients are not 'insane' at all, in the sense that the layman understands the term," Dr. Cantrell volunteered. "They are quite capable of sane, sound reasoning. And, at the risk of poaching upon Dr. Harlow's preserves, I may add that we are quite familiar here with the extreme cunning of some of the definitely insane."

"The *legally* insane?" Dundee asked.

"Yes."

"But would not a legally insane patient—and he must know his legal status if he has been committed after having been adjudged insane—*know that he could not be held accountable for his crime*, and therefore not take the trouble to set the stage as this murderer did?"

"That is true," Cantrell admitted. "But it is also true no patient, however insane, would relish the idea of being transferred to an asylum for the criminally insane. I assure you that even our locked ward here is heaven compared to such a place."

"And you have already assured me that your definitely insane patients are kept under constant observation in the locked ward," Dundee reminded him.

"That is true," Cantrell assented shortly. "Every patient who has been committed after being adjudged insane is kept in the locked ward. But we have a few patients who have not been committed, who are here voluntarily or because their relatives have placed them here, and who, because they have shown no disposition toward running away or toward violence, are permitted to live in the cottages, although they *could* be legally committed, if a charge were made."

"Why, looky, my lad!" Strawn became excited again. "That's the ticket, right there! Our friend the murderer is one of these patients who don't even know he's loony, because the family has been protecting him, see? And he sees the doc writing it all out—how crazy he is, and that he ought to be locked up, maybe. . . . Look at it this way, Bonnie! Supposing you're here, with the folks kidding you that you're here for 'nerves.' You're restless, don't like it here much, have come in to ask the doc to let you go home. Well, you take a peep at what the doc's writing, and you find out that he thinks you're bugs; not only that, but a dangerous lunatic. *And you know that what this doc says will be gospel to the lunacy commission!* Not only that, but, being loony, you jump to the conclusion that they're trying to frame you, put you away to get hold of your fortune, or something like that," the Chief of the Homicide Squad ended lamely, aware of the movie melodrama tinge to his last few words.

"Pretty clever, Captain," Dundee applauded. "And of course if his case history is destroyed and the doctor whose word is gospel with the lunacy commission is dead, your theoretical murderer would feel doubly safe."

"Exactly!" Strawn agreed with great satisfaction. "Come in!" he bawled, as he was interrupted by a knock on the door. "What is it, little lady?"

Dr. Harlow, her dignity affronted, tried her best to look three inches taller and ten years older, as she announced: "Dr. Price, the coroner, is here with the morgue ambulance." But her voice broke childishly on the dreadful word.

"Come on in, Price!" Strawn bawled, through the partly opened door, and the coroner obeyed, his thin legs very spry, but a look of real regret on his nice old face.

"Too bad, Captain, too bad! . . . How're ye, Bonnie? . . . Had the pleasure of knowing Dr. Koenig. Fine man! Fine man! . . . Hmm! Death must have been instantaneous. A very nasty blow. Hmm."

"Carraway!" Strawn called. "Bring in your camera, and get busy!"

The fingerprint expert, who was also the police department's official photographer, sauntered into the office, carrying camera and tripod, as well as the box containing his fingerprinting paraphernalia.

"Pictures of the corpse after Doc Price has finished with it," Strawn directed. "Also of the room from all angles. Then pick up any fingerprints you can find on the desk, the flower vase, the inkwell, that statue laying there, the smoking stand, the lamp, the books and the doorknobs. Also, gather up all them scraps of paper on the floor and go over every one of them with your powder. ... By the way, little lady," and he turned to Dr. Harlow, "whose fingerprints would normally be on the case histories?"

"Case histories!" she repeated, the same acute dismay in her voice as had characterized Dr. Cantrell's at the mention of those important documents.

"Sure! The murderer tore up some of 'em, including his own, to my way of thinking!" Strawn told her. "Now, who's been handling them in the ordinary course of duty?"

"Why—" she began, her voice still flat with dismay. Then, more firmly: "Only Dr. Koenig, myself, and the secretary, Miss Home. . . . That is," she amended conscientiously, "we are the only three who have handled the case histories during the last five years, with the exception of temporary stenographers, who have relieved Miss Home when she was on vacation."

"Five years?" Strawn pounced. "Mean to say a kid like you has been a doctor for five years?"

"I'm twenty nine years old," Dr. Harlow informed him, with great dignity. "Dr. Koenig took me on as his assistant when he became head psychiatrist here, five years ago."

"And who was here ahead of him?" Strawn asked.

"Dr. Cyrus Mayfield," the girl doctor answered in a low voice, as she shot a strange glance at Dr. Cantrell. pushing a loose strand of curling red hair off her forehead.

"And where is this Dr. Mayfield now, Dr. Harlow?" Dundee interrupted, since he was sure that that was the one question the diminutive doctor most wished not to hear.

"Why, he—he's " The girl drew a deep breath,

"Dead?" Dundee helped her gently.

"His—*body* is alive," the girl answered, her voice quivering.

# CHAPTER 4

"JUST what do you mean, Dr. Harlow?" Dundee persisted. "You put it very strangely—'his *body* is alive.' "

Before the girl doctor could answer, Baldwin, the business manager, stepped into the office from the reception room.

"Let me explain, Justine," he commanded curtly. "She means exactly what she says, Dundee. Dr. Mayfield's body is alive, but his mind is practically dead. He is and has been for about six years the victim of senility—or, in medical terms, senile dementia."

"And where is Dr. Mayfield now?" Dundee asked.

"In his apartment upstairs," Baldwin astounded him by announcing calmly. "I may explain that when Dr. Mayfield's condition became painfully apparent, some six years ago, his daughter, Harriet, who is now Madame Arnaud and a resident of Paris, took her father abroad for rest and treatment. He became worse steadily, and when I met them on a ship returning to America, Miss Mayfield told me that it would be necessary to have her father adjudged incompetent, in order to protect his estate and to permit the sanitarium to pass into other hands. Dr. Cantrell was with the party, as Dr. Mayfield's physician, and it was at his suggestion that the two of us conferred on the possibility of a three way partnership—neither of us having money enough to purchase the sanitarium outright."

"That is correct," Dr. Cantrell corroborated him. "But let me add that the original suggestion of such a partnership came from Miss Mayfield, who also suggested that we approach Dr. Koenig, whom she and Dr. Mayfield knew personally, and in whom she had the highest confidence. After the legal steps had been taken here in Hamilton, the partnership was formed, one of the conditions of sale being that Dr. Mayfield be taken care of here for the rest of his life, retaining his former apartment upstairs, and—" He hesitated and glanced uneasily at Dr. Harlow.

"Yes?" Dundee prompted.

Dr. Harlow obeyed the unspoken appeal in her colleague's eyes. "Miss Mayfield also stipulated that her father never be told that he was no longer head of the sanitarium. . . . It is a characteristic of senility, you know, that the patient believes he is still in his mental prime, and quite capable of managing his own affairs."

"I see," Dundee said slowly, as he pondered frowningly upon what he had heard.

"I say, Bonnie!" Strawn ejaculated. "We're onto some thing, sure as you live! . . . Listen, little doctor!" and he turned to Dr. Harlow. "Dr.

Koenig kept a case history on the old doc, same as on any other patient, I take it?"

"Yes," the girl admitted, startled.

"Is this loony old doctor bedridden, by any chance?" Strawn went on, with mounting excitement.

"No. He is quite feeble, and in bed a good many hours of the day, but— "

"He can walk all right, can't he? Get up and downstairs without help?" Strawn persisted.

"Yes. He spends a part of each day, when the weather permits, in a little private garden."

"And where is that?"

"Behind these offices, between here and Dr. Cantrell's house," the girl answered faintly.

"All right!" Strawn struck his hands together triumphantly. "The old doctor thinks he's still the big cheese here and thinks Dr. Koenig is just his hired assistant. . . . That so?"

"Yes," the girl answered, rather defiantly.

"Look, then! Dr. Mayfield wanders downstairs, sees Dr. Koenig in his office, drops in to give him some 'orders', finds him actually writing some additional notes for *his own case history*, tumbles to the deception that's been played on him, and—kills him!"

Dr. Harlow flung back her head. Her cheeks were white and her gray green eyes blazing behind their horn rimmed spectacles. "That's absurd! Dr. Mayfield hasn't the physical strength to strike a blow like that!"

"Do you agree, Dr. Cantrell?" Dundee asked quietly.

"I—don't know," the medical head answered haltingly. "When he's crossed, he shows—surprising strength "

"For instance?" Dundee cut in.

"Well, he refuses to let an attendant stay near him," Dr. Cantrell answered, still very slowly. "Naturally I have convinced him that he is not a well man, physically, and that he mustn't tax his strength by attending to too many 'duties,' and the presence of a nurse is explained in that way. But he drives his male attendant out of the room, whenever he has a lucid interval. Those are becoming increasingly rare, I may add."

"Can either of you tell me when Dr. Koenig last saw Dr. Mayfield professionally?"

Both doctors hesitated, and then it was Dr. Harlow who answered defiantly: "This afternoon. Dr. Koenig was with Dr. Mayfield for only a few minutes, and when he returned to his office he called me in and told me he was thinking of cabling to Madame Arnaud, since, in his opinion, the old doctor had no more than a few months to live. . . .

*Senile dementia*," she added in her professional voice, "usually terminates fatally in about five years."

"May I see Dr. Mayfield's case history, Dr. Harlow?" Dundee asked suddenly.

The little doctor again tried to look three inches taller than her five feet one. "The case histories of our patients are sacred, Mr. Dundee," she told him severely. "Only when you can show me a court order—"

"Then," and Dundee smiled at her very winningly, for her dignity and her loyalty aroused both his admiration and his amusement, "will you—just to clear things up a bit—look in the files and see if Dr. May field's history is there?"

"Won't find it," Strawn whispered to Dundee, as the girl obeyed. "Sure as you're alive, the old boy destroyed it."

"Here it is," Dr. Harlow called, her voice very cold.

"Just a minute, doctor!" Dundee sprang across the room. "Was it by any chance in one of the folders that was sticking almost half out of the files?"

"No. It was in its place," she answered triumphantly.

"Then—" and Dundee glanced at Strawn, his eye brows cocked, "will you just glance at it and see if Dr. Koenig made any additions to day?"

The girl turned the loose pages until she came to the last. "Yes," she said. "He has recorded a very brief and very mild attack of *senile delirium*, which was the cause of his visit to Dr. Mayfield this afternoon. The next attack," she explained, "will probably end in death. . . . Dr. Koenig prescribed a sedative, and I feel sure Dr. Mayfield has been sleeping ever since the attack."

"He has an attendant at night, of course?"

"Yes. But the attendant keeps out of sight, sitting just outside the bedroom door, in the sitting room of the suite."

"Let me have a crack at that attendant!" Captain Strawn commanded belligerently. Not easily would he relinquish his pet theory! "Cain!" he bawled, and one of his plain clothes squad appeared almost instantly in the doorway. "Show this man the way, Doctor."

With head high and cheeks scarlet, Dr. Harlow left the room in advance of Detective Cain.

"All finished, Dr. Price?" Dundee asked.

"Some minutes ago, and Carraway has made his pictures of the body," the little old coroner answered testily. "Any questions? . . . Make 'em snappy! I'm getting old and I've got the post mortem ahead of me yet tonight."

"Did you find the skull to be of the usual thickness?" Dundee asked, remembering Dr. Cantrell's opinion.

"No. On the contrary. Very thin skull."

"At approximately what hour do you calculate that death occurred?" Strawn took a hand.

"Somewhere between half past nine and ten o'clock this evening," the coroner answered. "By the way, Doctor," and he turned to Cantrell, "what time did Dr. Koenig dine? That will help me fix the time of death more accu rately, after I've examined the stomach contents."

"At six o'clock promptly, in the staff dining room," Dr. Cantrell replied. "The patients have their dinner between eleven thirty and twelve, and their supper between five and five thirty, but the members of the staff have dinner together at six o'clock."

"Any other wounds or abrasions of any kind, besides the head wound?" Dundee asked, as a matter of form.

"A bruise on the chin, slightly to the right of the mouth," Dr. Price answered laconically.

"What!" Dundee exclaimed. "I don't see how that happened. The head was bowed in such a position that only the forehead struck the desk at all."

"Well, then, you've got something to play sleuth with," Price twinkled. "For the forehead is not bruised, and the chin is. In my opinion—to be verified by the post mortem, of course—the bruise was made *after death*. . . . Would you care to look, Doctor?"

The two medical men returned to the body, consulted together in low tones, then retraced their steps to where Dundee was standing, deep in thought.

"I am inclined to agree with Dr. Price," Cantrell announced tiredly.

"I confess that's a poser," the detective said, frowning, but his reflections were interrupted by the return of Cain and Dr. Harlow, followed by a young man in the white uniform of an attendant.

"Found this bird asleep at the switch, Chief," Cain blurted out. "His patient, a white haired old gent, was reading in bed."

"*Reading*, was he?" Strawn boomed. "Thought you said the old doc was clear gone in the upper story, little lady!"

"He has lucid intervals, and such an interval is likely to follow an attack of senile delirium," Dr. Harlow answered with dignity. "Though I confess I expected the sedative to keep Dr. Mayfield asleep longer than it did."

"So you were snoozing on the job, eh?" Strawn lashed out at the cringing attendant. "What's your name?"

"Peters, sir. I'm afraid I did doze off "

"Doze!" Cain repeated contemptuously. "This baby had to be shook before he opens his peepers "

"You see, sir," the attendant stammered, "my wife is pretty sick, and I didn't get any sleep at all today. But I give you my word I hadn't been dozing more than a few minutes. Dr. Mayfield was sleeping "

"So you thought you'd keep him company in slumberland!" Strawn snarled.

"I'm sorry if any harm's been done " the poor young man began timidly, well aware that he had lost his job.

"Harm?" Strawn snorted. "Just a little matter of murder, that's all. . . . All right, Price. You can take the body away."

While the morgue ambulance crew were busy with the stretcher, Peters cowered, trembling and white faced, against the door leading into the hall.

"Now, young fellow," Strawn began again, when the body had been removed. "Just what were you doing between nine and ten o'clock tonight?"

"Sitting outside Dr. Mayfield's door," the attendant quavered. "I was reading a detective story, but it was hard to keep my mind on the story, because I could hear the voices from the talking picture right under Dr. Mayfleld's apartment."

"So you went down to have a look at the pictures your self?" Strawn pounced.

"No, sir!" the attendant denied emphatically.

"Cain! How close to the bedroom door was this man's chair?"

"About two feet away from it, sir."

"Room for the old man to pass without waking up this bird?"

"Yes, sir."

"Listen, you! Does your patient ever get up and wander around at night?"

"Some—sometimes," Peters stammered. "But I always persuade him to get back to bed."

"Did he get out of bed tonight?"

"No, sir!"

"You mean, if he did, he didn't wake you up!" Strawn corrected contemptuously. "Cain, you go with this baby and keep him company for the rest of the night. And listen hard for anything the old gentleman may say."

"You know, Chief," Dundee began mildly, when the two men had left the room, "I don't really believe that feeble old doctor murdered Koenig. Remember, his case history, with today's addition to it, was left in the files. That fact alone destroys your theory. But there is another point. *Case histories are sacred to a physician!* You have heard both Dr. Harlow and Dr. Cantrell say so, and have seen their dismay at the idea of case histories being destroyed. Dr. Mayfield was, first and last, a doctor, a psychiatrist. To him, too, case histories would be sacred. Granted that he would destroy his own, in a fit of rage, I believe it is psychologically impossible for him to destroy others."

"Tommyrot!" Strawn snorted.

"Am I right, Dr. Harlow?"

"Absolutely!" the girl doctor assured him eagerly. "Even in his present condition, Dr. Mayfield's every lucid and—delusional thought is connected with his work. He was and still is devoted to it. In fact, his devotion is so strong that we have to humor him when he desires to interview patients."

"He actually treats patients?" Dundee asked, in astonishment.

"Oh, yes, or he thinks he does. He questions them quite in his old manner. ... Of course," she added, "we send him only those patients who were here when he was still in charge, and whom he remembers. Sometimes he sends for a patient who is dead or who has left, and we persuade him to talk to another of the old stand bys. They are very kind to him. They understand, and enjoy their visits."

"Very interesting," Dundee commented absently. Then: "Dr. Harlow, have you a list of all the patients who are here at present?"

"Yes, of course. In the chartroom, with the room or suite number opposite the name of each patient, for the convenience of the head nurse."

"Then will you please check the file, and tell us which case histories are missing?"

As Dr. Harlow left the office, Carraway sauntered up to his chief.

"What luck?" Strawn asked the fingerprint expert.

"A world of prints, most of 'em not so new," Carraway answered. "But none at all on the statue. Been wiped clean."

"What about those fine torn scraps of paper?" Dundee asked.

"Four sets of prints, taking the whole heap of scraps," Carraway answered. "A man's fingerprints—I've compared them with the corpse's and they match—and three sets that look like they belong to women. Smaller, with the ridges more delicate and less pronounced, you know."

"Confirming my suspicion that the murderer wore gloves," Dundee commented. "Undoubtedly the women's prints will be found to belong to Dr. Harlow and a couple of stenographers—easy enough to check the correspondence files for similar prints. . . . Anything else, Carraway?"

"A flock of prints that I got from doorknobs and doors and door frames. . . . Say, I supposed you noticed that smear on the desk?"

"What smear?" Dundee was plainly chagrined.

"Looks like where somebody wiped off blood," Carraway answered nonchalantly. "You and the Captain were both busy, and I took the liberty of wiping the spot some more with the damp end of a towel. Dr. Price said it was blood, all right, but he's going to make a report later. . . . Look! You can see where I wiped the desk. I didn't make the smear any bigger."

Both Strawn and Dundee bent over the spot which was easily discernible near the right hand corner of the desk. The dampness of the towel and the original stain had dulled the bright polish of the mahogany.

"That's damned odd," Dundee said slowly. "Look, Chief! Here's something that looks like blood on the blotter, too, which we couldn't have seen without lifting up the head."

"I believe I can explain that stain," Dr. Cantrell interrupted. Uninvited, he had come close. "A blow such as killed Dr. Koenig causes a slow oozing of blood from the ears. As the head was resting, the right ear would have been directly over that spot on the blotter."

"Is that so?" Dundee commented, still frowning. "But —*why the blood on the corner of the desk?* How did it get 'way over there, why should the murderer wipe it up, and what did he wipe it *with?* ... By Jove! Those blood stained swabs in the hamper!"

"I have explained them," Dr. Cantrell reminded him.

"Yes, *but there they were*, some of them not so badly soiled!" Dundee pointed out. "When the murderer discarded the rubber gloves, he must have seen them. All nicely made to order for his purpose! A little more blood on one of those swabs would never be noticed—and blood on the corner of the desk doesn't fit into the picture our murderer is painting. . . . Well, we have a couple of posers, Chief. A bruise that has no business to be on the doctor's chin; blood that couldn't logically be on this corner of the desk—"

"Why should the murderer bother about the blood and whether it could be explained?" Strawn objected.

"That's exactly what I should like to know," Dundee admitted, very thoughtfully. "There's the key to the puzzle—or I'm much mistaken!"

With his hands in his pockets he bent a brooding gaze upon the dead doctor's desk. Nothing there to explain the bruise made *after death*. True, there were the ash tray, the overturned vase, the inkwell, a couple of pencils, and a penholder. But all these objects had been well away from the doctor's bowed face. Granted, for the sake of argument, that the chin had struck one of these objects: why had the murderer removed it?

His puzzled, roving eyes came to rest upon a small, loose leaf desk calendar, which, curiously enough, had not been disturbed by the murderer. The used leaves had been turned back over the metal rings, and the exposed leaf bore the date of the following day, Thursday, June 4th. The doctor had obviously used the calendar as a memory tickler, for, in pencil, were the notations:

*Call Morse*
*Inner spring mattresses*
*Dr. Sandlin*

The last two words were heavily underlined.

"Dr. Harlow!" Dundee called suddenly to the girl who was busy at the case history file. "Who is Dr. Sandlin?"

The little doctor stared blankly then shook her head. It was the business manager, Baldwin, who threw a bomb shell into the quiet room with his answer.

# CHAPTER 5

"DR. SANDLIN," the business manager announced calmly, "is the psychiatrist whom Dr. Koenig hoped to be able to hire to take Dr. Harlow's place here."

Dr. Cantrell's reaction to the news was apparently blank surprise, but it was to Justine Harlow's vivid little face that Dundee shifted his eyes. She looked as if she had been knocked almost senseless by a blow in the solar plexus. Her small body seemed bent and shrunken in the suddenly too large white uniform. Every scrap of color had left her cheeks, leaving them waxen and drawn. Even her eyes were changed in color, the green being scarcely noticeable now.

"No, no! I—don't believe it," her white lips quivered, the voice so low that Dundee could scarcely distinguish the words.

"This is the first intimation you have had that you were not— giving entire satisfaction?" Dundee asked, and was instantly ashamed of the wording. As if she were a servant girl!

The girl doctor did not answer, except to straighten her small body as if to brace it for the new blow he had dealt her.

"Dr. Koenig was extremely fond of Justine—of Dr. Harlow, I mean," Dr. Cantrell put in, emphatically. "I am afraid Mr. Baldwin misunderstood something our colleague said—"

"Not a chance!" Baldwin denied brusquely. "The doctor and I had a business conference this afternoon—informal, of course, or you would have been included, Bruce. You see, Dundee, Dr. Koenig had returned late Monday, from a three weeks' trip, and there were a number of matters I had to take up with him."

"What was the nature of the trip?" Dundee asked.

"Partly business, partly a lecture tour," Baldwin answered. "Business took him to New York, where he completed negotiations with the principal creditors of a sanitarium at Meridian, about a hundred miles from here, to take over their patients and some of their equipment. A good stroke of business for Mayfield, since we eliminate our only local competition, and increase our prestige enormously. We already have plans under way for the building of one large new cottage."

"And we were agreed that it meant the hiring of another assistant to Dr. Koenig," Dr. Cantrell added curtly. "A male assistant. But I feel absolutely sure that Dr. Koenig had no intention of dispensing with Dr. Harlow's services."

"What makes you feel so certain, Doctor?" Dundee asked, his pitying eyes still fixed on Dr. Harlow's white face.

"Because I know how much Dr. Koenig valued her, both as a friend and as an assistant," the medical man retorted stoutly. "I hope I am not betraying his confidence when I say that his appreciation of Dr. Harlow is amply proved by the terms of Dr. Koenig's will."

"Ah!" Dundee breathed. "And—you know the terms of that will, Doctor?"

"I do, because I was one of the witnesses when it was signed. My wife was another. By the terms of that will, drawn by Clifford Forrest, Dr. Koenig's attorney, Justine Harlow and Norah Lacey, our head nurse, share equally in the estate, which of course includes Dr. Koenig's third interest in Mayfield Sanitarium."

"You mean to say that those two girls are to have an equal say so with you and me?" Baldwin demanded, his lips twisted with anger.

"I'm satisfied!" Cantrell retorted curtly.

Dundee saw the girl draw a deep, quivering breath, which seemed to bring color to her cheeks and a sparkle to her eyes, as well as tears.

"I knew it!" she cried. "I knew he was too big a man to let one little disagreement turn him against me!"

"So you had a quarrel with the Big Doctor, eh?" Strawn pounced, as if to say, "Now we're getting somewhere!"

"Certainly not!" Justine Harlow flared indignantly. "It was only the slightest disagreement—purely professional!"

"So the doctor thought you were getting too big for your britches, eh?" Strawn suggested vulgarly. "When did this quarrel take place?"

The girl's cheeks were scarlet. "I refuse to discuss the matter if you insist upon calling it a quarrel!"

"Easy, Chief!" Dundee warned, in a low voice. "Dr. Harlow," he began, in a friendly, casual voice: "It is natural enough for two physicians to disagree about a diagnosis or the treatment of a case. I take it that you and Dr. Koenig did disagree in regard to some patient?"

"Yes," the girl answered, turning to the young detective and ignoring the older. "It was really too trivial for me even to remember, until—until it appeared that Dr. Koenig wished to replace me. Professional ethics forbid me to go into details, but the disagreement was over a young girl patient who has been almost entirely under my care. I thought her condition much more serious—increasingly serious—than Dr. Koenig, who had been away a good deal since the girl came here, was inclined to regard it."

"Are you, by any chance, referring to a girl named Enid Rambler?" Dundee asked.

The girl's eyes widened. "I am, as a matter of fact, but—"

"Then let me assure you that I believe you were right, and Dr. Koenig wrong for once," Dundee said quietly. "The young lady was in so serious a state tonight that she became hysterical and tried to run away from the sanitarium."

"And got herself arrested for disturbing the peace?" Baldwin cut in.

"No. She was very quiet when I found her—unconscious, in fact. In a ditch by the roadside, with a sprained ankle. I brought her back."

"*Enid Rambler?*" Dr. Harlow asked, incredulity written all over her expressive face. "I can't imagine Enid's *running away*—"

"Why not?" Dundee forestalled Strawn, who was chewing his gray mustache in a way that portended a new theory.

"Because Enid Rambler has consistently refused to leave the grounds, even with other patients or for a drive with me," Dr. Harlow answered, her brows still knit with perplexity, and professional ethics apparently forgotten. "Why, Enid would run like a deer to keep from meeting a stranger! If a patient begged her to meet his visitors, she refused, and hid in her room until the visitors were gone. And the very suggestion that she must try to get well so that she could leave was enough to send her into hysterics."

"Then it's about time I had a go at that young lady!" Strawn interrupted grimly. "If Dundee found her on the roadside, after she'd run away from the sanitarium, and if what Dr. Harlow tells us is true, it's a cinch she had one swell reason for running away this particular night. And say! The Big Doctor was anxious to get rid of her, wasn't he? Wanted to send her away and you said she wasn't able to go—eh, little lady?"

Justine Harlow's cheeks again burned scarlet in resentment of the insinuation behind the old detective's words. "That's not true!" she flashed. "I suggested to Dr. Koenig that the girl should be thoroughly psychoanalyzed, to rid her of two complexes: one a fear of crowds, strangers; the other a very definite claustrophobia."

"Says which?" Strawn frowned at the unfamiliar word.

"Claustrophobia consists of an inability on the part of the patient to remain in a closed space," Dr. Harlow enlightened him crisply. "It also frequently exhibits itself in a desire for unusually large rooms."

"So she hates locked doors and *little rooms*, does she?" Strawn commented grimly. "Wouldn't like prison cells *a tall!* . . . Looky, Bonnie! This girl comes here for the express purpose of *getting Koenig!* He don't know her, or she wouldn't take the chance. But let's say she wants to avenge some wrong done to a member of her family. I'll grant it may have been one of them fancied wrongs you read about in books. But Koenig gets suspicious. He won't treat her himself, but gives the job to Dr. Harlow, and he wants the little doctor here to *hustle her out.* . . . Get me? . . . Well, she gets wind of his intentions some how, and she don't lose any more time. Picks a night when a lot of strangers are coming and going, does the job, plans it to look like the work of one of the nuts, and beats it. What's more, I don't doubt she got this here glostrophobia or whatever you call it. A girl all steamed up to murder a man in cold blood is apt to think a mighty lot about prison cells. And to take every precaution to see that she don't get stuck into one!"

Dundee shook his head. "Somehow—and mind you, I've had quite a talk with the girl, Chief—I can't picture Enid Rambler as the cold blooded murderer who could strike down a man, don rubber gloves, disrupt the room to look as if a homicidal maniac had done the deed, and then —run away. You see, Captain the two sets of characteristics don't jibe. If the murderer lives here, he—or she— didn't lose his or her head and run away! Too cool a head for that! But I grant you that *something* happened to panic the girl, and that that something may very well be connected with the murder."

"I'll say it's connected!" Strawn snorted. "Did you finish checking that file, little lady?"

"Yes. I was just finishing when Mr. Dundee called me."

"Then I'll wager my shield you found this Rambler baby's case history among the missing!" Strawn challenged her triumphantly.

"Then you lose your shield," the young doctor told him coolly. "There are two case histories missing, the patients being Samuel Rowan and Archibald Webster."

The last name rang a bell in Dundee's memory. What was it Sanderson had said?—"rich, handsome scapegrace, young Webster. ... In and out of the place half a dozen times a year—"

But Strawn was crawfishing with ease: "That don't mean nothing, but that the dame is smarter than I give her credit for. Fixed it so's the blame would fall on two other guys—take your choice, or, better still, take the guy who can't give an ironclad alibi."

Dundee smiled. "I'm afraid I'm more interested, at the moment, in the 'two other guys,' Captain, than I am in Miss Rambler. Can any of you tell us whether either or both of these patients attended the movie?"

Baldwin, Cantrell and Dr. Harlow shook their heads. Then the girl doctor suggested: "I feel sure Miss Caplan, the night head nurse, could answer that question. I'll call her." She went to the door leading into the main hall, opened it, and called: "Rose! Rose! . . . Will you come here, please?"

The thin, gray haired, pale faced nurse who had received Dundee came hurrying across the hall, frightened deference in her voice as she answered: "Yes, Dr. Harlow?"

"These gentlemen wish to question you, Rose. Don't be afraid to tell anything you know, or to answer any question whatever."

Strawn waved her to Dundee, as if granting the younger detective's greater ability where the questioning of women was concerned.

"At what time did you come on duty, Miss Caplan?" Dundee asked, accepting the task gladly.

"At seven o'clock," the nurse quavered.

"And at what time did the patients begin to gather for the picture show?"

"About fifteen minutes after I came on duty. Our movies usually start about 7:20, but, due to a misunderstanding on the operator's part, because the downtown theaters had changed their schedules, the first picture did not start until eight o'clock this evening," the nurse answered painstakingly, little gasps punctuating her sentences.

"And did the patients wait in the O. T. Shop all that time?" Dundee continued.

"Some did, laughing and talking together in groups. Some strolled about the grounds until they saw the car arrive with the films."

"Were you in a position to note all arrivals and departures, and returns?"

"Yes, sir, except when the phone rang. And even when I had to talk over the phone I kept an eye on the hall. You see, the door to the chartroom is very close to the door into the O. T. Shop, and I kept a watch because I was afraid something might happen—with the patients getting restless and excitable—"

"I understand," Dundee assured her, as her voice trembled to an uncertain pause. "Now, Miss Caplan, can you tell us whether Mr. Rowan and Mr. Webster attended the show?"

"Mr. Rowan did," the nurse answered more confidently. "I noticed him particularly, because"—and she turned shining, glad eyes upon Dr. Harlow, as if to share her pleasure—"*he talked and laughed* with two of the patients while they were waiting for the films to come!"

"And is that extraordinary^' Dundee asked quickly.

"Very extraordinary," Dr. Harlow replied. "Poor Mr. Rowan has been almost completely silent for two years. No one could reach him, no one could make him talk. But this afternoon he walked into Dr. Koenig's office and voluntarily began to talk. He talked for three hours— until Dr. Koenig had to make him stop. The doctor was jubilant, told me he was sure Rowan could be cured now—"

"What did Rowan talk about?" Dundee asked.

The little doctor stiffened. "I don't know," she answered coldly, "and if I did, professional ethics—"

"Ethics be damned, Doctor—begging your pardon," Strawn interrupted. "Get wise, little lady! This is *murder!*"

"I have told you I don't know. Dr. Koenig did not have an opportunity to go into Rowan's case with me then."

"But in all probability he made some additions to Rowan's case history this evening?" Dundee suggested.

"It is quite likely. He worked steadily all evening."

"Did he tell you—or you " and Dundee turned first to Cantrell and then to Baldwin, "what Rowan talked about? It must have been a rather important unburdening, if it unlocked a silence of two years' duration."

"No," Dr. Cantrell answered flatly.

"No," Baldwin said, too, then: "But he did remark to me that if a psychiatrist chose to, he could give the police plenty to keep them busy!"

"Did he make that remark apropos of Rowan?"

"No. But Rowan had just left. I passed him in the hall, on my way into Dr. Koenig's office. It was just a few minutes before five—supper time for the patients. Dr. Koenig was pretty 'high,' and I took the remark to refer to the last patient he'd been seeing. A success like that always stirred him up, made another man out of him."

"And it was during this same visit that Dr. Koenig mentioned Dr. Sandlin?" Dundee remembered to ask.

"Yes."

"What time does Miss Home, the secretary, leave?"

"At five," Baldwin answered. "She came in to say good night while I was still with the doctor."

"Thanks. . . . Now, Miss Caplan, will you tell us whether Mr. Rowan stayed for the entire showing of the pictures?"

"So far as I know, he did. I saw him come out with the others when the program was over."

"Is there more than one door to the O. T. Shop?" Dundee asked.

"Yes. There are two other doors. One opens out onto the back lawn, and another leads into the storeroom, back of Mr. Baldwin's office."

"Were these doors locked?"

"The door into the storeroom was," the nurse answered. "Mr. Baldwin has one key, and the other is kept in a desk drawer in the chartroom. The storeroom door is always locked. But the other door was open for the sake of coolness—it was a hot night."

"Then it was possible, while the shop was dark for the showing of pictures, for a patient or a patient's visitor to slip out of that back door without being noticed?"

"Possible, of course," the nurse answered hesitantly.

"Very possible to leave—and return unnoticed?"

"I suppose so. But of course some of the other patients would have noticed"

"Engrossed in so thrilling a picture as 'Manslaughter'?" Dundee was skeptical.

"I—"

"Did *you* notice anyone leave in that way?" Strawn pounced.

"No!" the nurse cried, too emphatically, her face turning too pale.

To Strawn's disgust, Dundee seemed to take sides with the nurse, for he assured her soothingly: "I understand, Miss Caplan. You mean to say, don't you, that you were not in a position to observe arrivals and departures *after* the show had started, since you were at your post in the chartroom?"

"Yes!" the girl fell into the trap. "Of course! I was in the chartroom—"

"But," Dundee interrupted»her regretfully, his brows knit as if in great perplexity, "I've just remembered that Miss Rambler said she couldn't find you in the chartroom after she left the O. T. Shop in the middle of the feature picture. She said she was looking for a nurse to give her a sedative. . . . But perhaps," he continued guilefully as the nurse's pale face became ashen, "you were called away on some duty?"

The woman turned hunted eyes from face to face, but in that circle of stern judges there was only one friendly, pitying pair of eyes.

"Don't be frightened, Rose. We all know how conscientious you are. Simply tell the exact truth," Dr. Harlow urged.

"I—I was looking at 'Manslaughter,' too," Miss Caplan gasped. "I—I knew I could hear my phone ring. I was just inside the door to the shop—"

"But, of course," Dundee suggested casually, "the door was closed because the light from the hall would have interfered with the showing of the pictures."

"Yes, sir," the badgered woman admitted in a low voice.

"Another thing is puzzling me," Dundee went on. "Dr. Harlow has told us that Miss Rambler had a complex against encountering strangers, and yet there were a number of visitors who came with patients to see the show this evening."

"Enid—I mean, Miss Rambler, came in when the shop was dark for the showing of the pictures, and she left before 'Manslaughter' ended," Miss Caplan explained in a rush, then clapped her hand to her mouth as she realized, too late, that she had revealed what she had been trying to conceal.

Dundee showed no triumph, as he asked: "Can you tell us approximately the time Miss Rambler arrived for the pictures, and the time she left?"

"The comedy had been on about ten minutes, so it must have been about ten minutes after eight when Enid—Miss Rambler—slipped in," the nurse answered hopelessly. "It was pretty dark, but I suppose she recognized me standing there by the door when she opened it and let a bit of light in. Anyway, I recognized her, and put out my hand. She—

she took it and squeezed it and said, 'Aren't I brave?' Then she edged along the wall till she got to the back of the room, and I saw her hesitate, then creep along in the dark until she found a seat near the back door. I knew she would want to escape before the lights went up, and I didn't think anything about it when I saw her slip out when 'Manslaughter,' the second picture, was about half finished."

"Listen, Doc!" Strawn cut in, turning to Dr. Cantrell. "You said, when you was telling us about that picture, that it was about a girl that got sent to prison, didn't you? . . . Well, then, whereabouts in the fillum do they show her in a cell? *About halfway through it,* eh?"

"There you are, Bonnie!" Strawn spread his hands in a gesture of triumph.

"I—believe so," Cantrell answered coldly.

"But exactly *where* am I?" Dundee grinned. "It seems to me that the sight of another girl in prison would act as a deterrent to a girl who already has claustrophobia—not as an incentive for her to go out and kill a man! . . . What do you think, Dr. Harlow?"

"I think Enid's leaving the picture and subsequently running away was caused by an acute attack of claustrophobia," the little doctor answered emphatically. "It is a well known fact that a girl, viewing a motion picture, puts herself in the place of the heroine, consciously or unconsciously. Temporarily, Enid Rambler was the girl in the picture, and she could not bear the close quarters or the locked door. Her other complex—fear of strangers from the outside world—made her control herself until she was safely out of the shop. Then, I don't doubt, she became hysterical. It is likely, too, that for the first time she visualized the sanitarium as a sort of prison, and the impulse to escape became stronger than her fear of the world."

"I think that is quite clear," Dundee commented respectfully.

"Just a heap of words, if you ask me!" Strawn brushed it aside violently. "A pretty woman could always make you believe black is white, Bonnie me boy! Just let me have a whack at this Rambler dame!"

It was the timid nurse who flared the answer: "She didn't have a thing to do with that awful murder! Enid Rambler is the sweetest, kindest, most lovable—" She stopped suddenly, her voice choked with tears.

"Pretty fond of her, ain't you, sister?" Strawn asked sarcastically.

"I certainly am! But so is nearly everybody else! But why pick on her? She wasn't the only one who left the shop while the pictures were on!"

"Ah!" Dundee said softly, about to reap the harvest of patience and tact. "You saw someone else leave, Miss Caplan?"

"Two others!" she affirmed emphatically. "Archie Webster and a man who was visiting him this evening!"

# CHAPTER 6

"WELL, sister, your eyesight and memory are sure improving fast!" Captain Strawn commended the nurse sarcastically. "Take a good long think and see if you can't conveniently remember a few more patients who strolled out of the *dark* shop tonight."

"Others may have left, but I saw only those three," Miss Caplan retorted angrily. "The phone rang twice and once Mrs. Appleby came over to ask for a sedative for her patient, so I was out of the shop three times while the pictures were being shown."

"But you're sure about Mr. Webster and his visitor, Miss Caplan, in spite of the shop's being dark?" Dundee asked, his voice very gentle.

"I am," she answered earnestly. "You know how your eyes get accustomed to the dark. And the shop is narrow, although it's quite long."

"How did you identify these two men in the gloom?" Dundee persisted.

"Well, Mr. Webster is a very unusual type," the nurse replied confidently. "He's the tallest patient we have here, and very broad shouldered. This evening he was wearing a red and white striped blazer, which showed up clearly. And I noticed his friend very particularly, because he was so awfully fat and short—like a balloon that's been blown up till it's ready to burst. ... I don't know his name."

"They left together, of course?"

"No. The fat man left first, and about five minutes later I saw Mr. Webster leave. They both had seats near the door, in the same row where Enid sat."

"Did Webster speak to the girl before he left?"

"Oh, she'd already left, just a minute or so before the fat man did."

"But Webster knows Miss Rambler, of course?"

"Ye—es," the nurse admitted. "He seems to be terribly in love with Enid, but I don't think she cares especially for him."

"There was no reason why you should have had Mr. Webster followed?"

The nurse flushed and looked toward Dr. Harlow entreatingly. "I— well, it *would* have been safer—"

"What do you mean?" Dundee asked sharply.

"Well, you see," the nurse stammered, "Archie—Mr. Webster—got drunk. We had to—to put him in the locked ward, because he became violently quarrelsome."

"Hmm. . . . So he'd slipped out to do a little intensive drinking with his friend, I suppose?"

"He couldn't have got the whisky any other way," Miss Caplan assured him defiantly. "1 think that fat man was just a bootlegger—"

"When, exactly, was Webster's condition discovered?" Dundee interrupted.

"When the movies were over and the patients and their visitors were leaving the shop," Miss Caplan told him.

"Archie came lurching into the hall from the front porch, and tried to pick a quarrel with Mr. Rowan. Archie is usually the sweetest tempered person in the world, but when he's drinking. . . . Well, he said Mr. Rowan had insulted him yesterday by not speaking to him, and that he could whip ten Rowans with his hands tied behind him. I thought," she added, "that it was too bad he had to pick on Mr. Rowan, because it was the first time the poor man had ever attended one of our movie shows, and I did want him to keep on being happy—"

"What happened?"

"Mr. Rowan simply knocked Archie down with one blow and walked out," the nurse said, with a trace of pride. "Mr. Whalen had just come to 'clock in,' since it was ten o'clock, and he helped two of the attendants to carry Archie off to 'Ten.' Dr. Harlow heard the racket and came down from her apartment upstairs, and she and I went over to 'Ten' with Archie."

"And the fat man?"

"I didn't see him, and Mr. Whalen couldn't find him anywhere on the grounds."

"You observed the patient closely, of course, Dr. Harlow?" Dundee turned deferentially to the little doctor.

"Naturally, but his condition was obvious. He was quite drunk. I administered a sedative, which took effect very rapidly."

"Then he's asleep now, I suppose," Dundee commented regretfully. "No chance to question him before morning?"

"It would be very unwise, and, in my opinion, quite useless to arouse him," Dr. Harlow answered emphatically. "Archie will keep. Besides being in the locked ward, he will be watched every minute by 'Happy' Day, the attendant you saw arrive this evening."

"What is Webster's trouble?"

"Periodic drunkenness. But he is not, medically speaking, a true alcoholic," Dr. Harlow told him. "He's a very rich and idle young man, given to excesses of many sorts, I am afraid. His father persuades him to enter Mayfield voluntarily for hydrotherapy and enforced abstinence. That is all the treatment he needs."

"Too bad the abstinence wasn't enforced this time," Strawn commented sourly.

"It is," the little doctor agreed sturdily. "But it is not entirely our fault. We have told his father that it is unwise for Archie to have visitors, but his father argues that only by dealing very tactfully with the boy and permitting him a degree of liberty here, can he induce him to come for treatment. But I made Mr. Webster agree to his having an attendant if Archie again succeeded in getting liquor while in our charge. He likes Happy—everyone does; so I don't anticipate any trouble on that score."

"Let's return to Miss Rambler for a moment," Dundee suggested. "You may go back to your work, Miss Caplan, and thank you very much. . . . Now, Dr. Harlow, will you tell me frankly what Dr. Koenig thought of Miss Rambler's case?"

The doctor hesitated, then apparently decided to waive professional ethics. "Dr. Koenig was of the opinion that, for some unknown reason, Enid was malingering—that is, faking symptoms and exaggerating her probably natural tendency to hysteria."

"Did he say why he thought so?"

"He—thought she was having so good a time here that she didn't want to leave. I granted that she was extremely popular with our men patients, but I pointed out that so pretty and charming a girl and one who was apparently a rich orphan would be popular anywhere, if it were not for her fear of strangers."

"Then her fear of strangers does not extend to new patients?"

"We—ell, yes," the girl hesitated. "When she first came we could not induce her to leave her suite—the largest in the sanitarium, by the way. But she still avoids new patients, does not make friends until they have taken her unawares and—shown themselves friendly. As I said, she is extremely popular, especially with the men. I am afraid most of our women patients are a little jealous of her beauty and her very smart clothes, but all the nurses and attendants are devoted to her."

"But Dr. Koenig considered her a disturbing influence?" Dundee guessed.

"Yes, for both reasons. I may as well be frank. There have been two or three fights—nothing really serious, of course—among the men who are infatuated with her. And one of the women patients—a former trained nurse who has been a sort of pensioner of Dr. Koenig's since she be came paretic about a year ago—had to be put temporarily in 'Ten' for tearing to pieces three or four of Enid's prettiest dresses."

"But you are still of the opinion that Miss Rambler is definitely ill?" Dundee asked.

"Yes, I am, and I feel sure Dr. Koenig would have agreed with me if he had had more opportunity to observe her," the young doctor answered stoutly. "When I failed to get at the source of her complexes, I suggested to Dr. Koenig that he try to get her consent to psychoanalysis."

"And did he talk with Miss Rambler after you made that suggestion?"

"Not to my knowledge."

"Did Miss Rambler appeal to either of you two doctors for a sedative this evening?"

It was Dr. Cantrell who answered first. "Not to me. I was at home all evening, but was not called and received no visitors."

"I was out from immediately after eight until five minutes to ten," Dr. Harlow told him.

"Alone?" Strawn shot at her.

"Yes!" the girl answered, the gray green eyes flashing angrily. "I was out in my car, taking a long drive for relaxation and fresh air."

"*Worried* about something, and wanted to get off to yourself?" Strawn insinuated.

"Not at all!" the girl flashed. "I am in the habit of taking a drive whenever I have the opportunity, that is, when Dr. Koenig is—was—on hand to take care of any emergency that might arise. It is a confining life."

"Perhaps that is another reason why he planned to take on an additional assistant," Dundee suggested tactfully.

"I tell you Koenig said he was going to *replace* the girl," Baldwin, who had been silent for a long time, burst out.

"Did he give you any reason for his decision to dismiss Dr. Harlow?"

"Yes. He said Justine was too credulous, an impractical idealist, and inclined to let her heart run away with her head," the business manager answered without hesitation. "Then of course there was the question of expense. We didn't feel that we could afford two assistant psychiatrists just yet, and Koenig said a man would be required to handle the batch of new patients we'll be getting. The Meridian Sanitarium has been catering largely to alcoholics and drug addicts, and a doctor who has specialized in those fields as well as in general psychiatry will be badly needed. And I agreed that, what with the expense of new building and furnishing, we would not be in a position to afford two assistants for him, since Dr. Cantrell will also require an assistant in the medical department."

"It's you who are always harping on economy and cutting down expenses!" the girl cried indignantly. "Dr. Koenig never considered expense for a minute when the good of the patients was jeopardized. He had to fight you every inch of the way to put improvements through. . . . Look!" and she pointed a trembling forefinger at the dead doctor's desk calendar. "There's a notation—'inner spring mattresses.' He told me this very morning that, in spite of your opposition, he was going to replace every mattress in the sanitarium with the finest inner spring box mattresses."

"He said the same to me," Dr. Cantrell upheld her. "Baldwin was holding out for having the old mattresses renovated at a nominal cost."

Captain Strawn thrust both hands into his pockets and looked the business manager up and down with narrowed gray eyes.

"So you and Koenig had your *spats*, too, eh?"

"We had differences of opinion—yes!" Baldwin replied defiantly. "The business manager of any institution has a constant fight on his hands to keep down expenses. That's what business managers are for."

"Then I take it there wasn't much love lost between you and the doctor?" Strawn went on, rocking back and forth on his heels.

"That's a nasty crack, but I'll answer it frankly," Baldwin retorted, a glow of anger lighting up his usually cold, emotionless eyes. "I'm not a sentimentalist, like these two!" and he indicated Dr. Harlow and Dr. Cantrell with a contemptuous wave of his claw thin hand. "But I had the highest respect for Dr. Koenig—as a psychiatrist. He made this sanitarium! As its business manager I can tell you that in Dr. Koenig's death Mayfield has suffered the greatest calamity that could happen to it. And as Mayfield's *business manager*, I mourn Dr. Koenig's death with all my heart. But I couldn't be truthful and say that I have lost a bosom friend. We shared a cottage on the grounds and a manservant; we ate most of our meals together when the doctor wasn't away on a lecture trip— every trip being good business, I assure you!—and spent a good many hours in each other's company, in the way of business. But we were not congenial. Now—take that and make the most of it!"

In spite of his instinctive dislike of the man, of his cold bloodedness and obvious mercenariness, Dundee could not help admiring the business manager's fearless frankness. Certainly this man, together with Dr. Cantrell, had every thing to lose and apparently nothing to gain by Dr. Carl Koenig's death.

"And have you any plans for replacing the man who 'made Mayfield'?" Strawn asked, his voice still edged with sarcasm. "Somebody who'll be a little easier for the business office to handle?"

"That question is in pretty bad taste, Captain Strawn," Dr. Cantrell interjected quietly. "For two reasons. First: Dr. Koenig is so recently dead and so tragically dead that none of us has given any thought to his possible successor. Second: the implied insinuation against Mr. Baldwin is unwarranted. It is my experience that an institution's business manager is usually not very popular with the doctors, who are nearly always impractical outside their own particular field. Mr. Baldwin is no exception, but both Dr. Harlow and I can tell you that, in the last analysis, he has the good of Mayfield at heart as much as any of us. ... Isn't that correct, Justine?"

Dundee was sure the "Yes" cost the girl doctor a real effort.

"Thanks!" Baldwin said gruffly, then cleared his throat before going on: "As for a successor to Dr. Koenig, that's entirely out of my line. My only concern is that we get a man of whom Koenig himself would have approved."

"Meaning this Dr. Sandlin, eh?" Strawn caught him up. "Friend of yours, eh?"

"I've never met the man in my life," Baldwin denied scornfully. "Everything in the world that I know of him is what Dr. Koenig told me—and that was precious little. I gathered that Dr. Koenig had a talk with him while he was on this last trip, though I don't even know where Sandlin is located."

"I do," Dr. Harlow said very quietly, but with an almost fanatic light in her eyes. "He's on the staff of a private sanitarium near Chicago. And Dr. Koenig lectured on mental hygiene at the Medical College of Northwestern University while he was on this trip. Doubtless he interviewed Dr. Sandlin when he was in Chicago, and I, for one—if I really have any right to do so—will cast my vote for him. Dr. Koenig's wishes have been and always will be sacred to me!"

"Same here!" Dr. Cantrell said emphatically if inelegantly.

"No use being hasty," Baldwin reminded his two associates. "Dr. Koenig undoubtedly thought this Sandlin would fill the bill of assistant, but as far as being head psychiatrist here is concerned "

"At least, he shall be on the staff," Justine Harlow interrupted stubbornly. "He can—have—my place," she added haltingly, her voice choking. "For if Dr. Koenig really didn't want me to stay, that wish of his is sacred to me, too."

Dr. Cantrell shot a venomous look at Baldwin, as he reached for the girl's small, firm hand and gripped it hard. "I don't believe Carl had the least idea of dismissing you, Justine. Any such idea, I am sure, originated with Mr. Baldwin, as an economy move "

"Are you intimating that I lied, Bruce?" Baldwin interrupted furiously.

"Not at all," Dr. Cantrell assured him coldly. "I merely mink it quite possible that you misunderstood Dr. Koenig."

"It occurs to me," Dundee interrupted what promised to be a quarrel, "that if Dr. Koenig seriously considered dismissing Dr. Harlow, he would first take steps to change his will. Does anyone know Attorney Forrest's telephone number?"

"He is my attorney also," Cantrell told him. "The office number is Main 0300, the residence number Mirror 3421. But it is after midnight now "

"Sorry!" Dundee smiled, and reached for the telephone on the dead man's typewriter table. As he dialed the second number, he kept his eyes on the three most concerned, but observed no expression more incriminating than tense expectancy.

"Hello! I'm sorry to be calling so late, but it is quite important. May I speak with Mr. Forrest, please?" He listened for a moment, disappointment clouding his blue eyes. Then: "I wonder if you could tell me, Mrs. Forrest, whether Dr. Carl Koenig tried to reach his attorney this evening? . . . He *did?* Then did he tell you the nature of the business on which he wished to consult your husband? This is Dundee, of the District Attorney's office. . . . No? ... Oh! I see! . . . Thank you very much, Mrs. Forrest."

He replaced the hand telephone slowly. "I didn't want to spoil her sleep by telling her the news. . . . Mrs. Forrest told me, Captain, that Dr. Koenig telephoned about half past nine this evening, asking for Forrest, who is out of town. Mrs. Forrest told him the lawyer would be back in the morning, and hoped there was nothing urgent that could not wait until then."

"Well?" Strawn prodded, as the young detective paused, frowning.

"Dr. Koenig replied that the matter *was* urgent, and that *he would attend to it himself tonight.'"

"Well! Well! Well!" and Strawn rocked back and forth on his heels. "Three guesses, my lad, as to what the doctor was writing on that sheet that was torn out of his typewriter! Wants a lawyer quick. Can't wait till morning——"

"I'm afraid you're jumping pretty high to reach that conclusion, Captain," Dundee warned, averting his eyes from the girl doctor's blanching cheeks.

"High, nothing! The Big Doctor tells Baldwin here that he's going to replace the lady doctor. She's down in his will for one half his estate. Believe me, boy, whatever it was that made Koenig determine to get rid of the girl— and I'm sorry to be as blunt as this, little lady!—was serious enough to make him determined to draw up a new will without even waiting until morning! . . . And even then he wasn't quick enough!"

"I—Oh, Bruce!" It was not a dignified doctor, but a desolate girl who clung, shuddering, to the only friend she had in the room.

Cantrell hugged the girl close for a moment, then strode swiftly toward Strawn, his black eyes blazing, his right hand knotted into a powerful fist.

"Just a minute, Doctor!" Dundee commanded, stepping between the two. "I agree with you that Captain Strawn is a bit hasty. It is pure supposition that Koenig wanted to see his lawyer about changing his will, and even if that was his intention, we must not overlook the f act that the will names *two* beneficiaries."

"Norah Lacey is just as much above suspicion as Dr. Harlow is!" Cantrell assured him savagely. "Oh, I can see what you're getting at, all right! Anyone unlucky enough to be named in a murdered man's will is bound to have the police yelling 'Motive!' at him—or her. But it's a damned outrage that the two finest women I've ever known—barring my wife, of course," he amended tardily, "should have to submit to being suspected of killing the greatest man that ever lived!"

To Dundee's amazement, the business manager joined his partner in defending the weeping little doctor.

"I'm no sentimentalist—far from it!" Baldwin began grimly, "but I'm a just man. And I'll frankly confess that, if I'd known the line you were going to take, Captain Strawn, I'd have bitten out my tongue before I should have said what I did of Koenig's intention to replace Dr. Harlow. And don't forget that I'm as anxious as you are— far more so!—to have this nasty business cleaned up. But I repeat I'm just a man. And I can't stand by without a word and hear you try to pin the job on this girl. Carl Koenig was God to her. A blind man or a fool could have seen that she worshiped the ground he walked on. . . . *Kill* him? Not if he'd been a billionaire and had left her every dime of his fortune! *Kill* him because they'd had a disagreement? Bosh! The girl would have let him shave her head, clip her ears and cut off her nose, if he'd wanted to! *Kill* him because he intended to replace her? Bosh, again! If he had told her it was to his best interest to have a man assistant, she'd have kissed his feet when she told him good bye! . . . And what's more, literally the same applies to Norah Lacey! Sentimental fools, but —there you are!"

"You're pretty eloquent, Mr. Baldwin," Dundee commented drily.

"I'm merely being just. And not wholly disinterested either," the business manager retorted savagely. "I have Mayfield's welfare at heart. It's my job to safeguard that welfare. And God knows we're in for enough scandal through the very fact that a murder has been committed here, without it's being broadcast that one of the staff is under suspicion of having killed the Big Doctor."

"Spoken from the heart," Dundee murmured. "At least, Baldwin, you make no bones about being mercenary. It's quite refreshing to find a man so free from hypocrisy."

"Your opinion of me does not interest me in the slight est," Baldwin told him sourly. "Just stick to your job. Find the murderer with the least possible delay, keep your 'theories' out of the papers, and above all, don't waste time barking up the wrong tree."

"Now that we've got our orders, Captain Strawn," Dundee said wryly, "don't you think we'd better see Miss Lacey?"

"Collins!" Strawn bawled, and a plainclothesman almost instantly opened the door between the office and the reception room. "Come on in and shut the door. . . . Now, anything to report?"

"Yes, sir. Pretty soon after you come in here, a nurse by the name of Hunter come and told Miss Lacey that a patient named Rambler was in a pretty bad state, and Miss Lacey beat it with her over to a cottage they call Sunflower Court. I trailed along and waited outside the patient's door. She was taking on something terrible, but this Lacey dame quieted her down. Come out and fixed a shot in the arm for her, and then set with her till she was asleep. Then we come back over here, and that's all."

"All right! Send Miss Lacey in, Collins," Strawn ordered.

The tip of the nurse's little Irish nose was scarlet, and dark circles emphasized the grief in her tear reddened eyes. Her white cap with its black ribbon band sat askew on her gray threaded black curls, a fact of which she was as desolately unconscious as she was of the streaks which tears had left on her freckled cheeks.

She must have been thirty five years old, but she looked curiously like an inconsolable child as she hesitated just inside the door, little hiccoughy sobs breaking up her words:

"You—wanted—to see me?"

Because she had looked straight into his eyes, Dundee took upon himself the duty of questioning her.

"I believe it was you who discovered what had happened here this evening, Miss Lacey," he began very gently. "Will you tell us about it?"

"At ten twenty I went up to my apartment on the second floor to change into my uniform. I always relieve Miss Caplan while she's at supper, if I'm in. She has supper between half past ten and eleven "

"Hold on a minute, sister!" Strawn interrupted rudely. "You say you went upstairs at twenty past ten. Where were you before that time?"

"I was—out," the nurse answered defiantly.

"Out where?" Strawn demanded. "And who were you with?"

"I was alone. I—I went to a movie."

"Yeah? What movie did you see, sister?"

The nurse's eyes widened as she stared at him, then the tear reddened lids hid them for a moment before she answered:

"I went to the Symphony. I saw 'His Wife's Lover.' "

"Just a minute, Captain," Dundee interrupted Strawn's next question.

And very slowly, his eyes on the nurse's paling face, he drew a folded theater program from his inside breast pocket.

# CHAPTER 7

"I THINK, Captain Strawn," Dundee said quietly, "that Miss Lacey would like to revise her story as to where she spent the evening. Am I not right, Miss Lacey?"

"No!" the nurse answered dully. "I went to the Symphony. I saw 'His Wife's Lover.' I can tell you everyone that's in it and the story, too, if you don't believe me."

"I'm quite sure you saw the picture, Miss Lacey, but that you did not see it this evening," Dundee contradicted more sternly. "You see, it happens that the Symphony changed its schedule only last Saturday. That is, the programs are changed now on Saturday and Wednesday, instead of Sunday and Thursday. I, too, saw 'His Wife's Lover'—a very poor picture, by the way, one whose story I really couldn't bear to hear again. But because the feature which began its run *today* is one that I'd hate to miss I kept the program with its announcement of future attractions. Would you like to see it, Miss Lacey?"

"No!" The woman repudiated the proffered sheet with a violent gesture.

"But I'm afraid it will be necessary for you to answer Captain Strawn's question as to where you did spend the evening, Miss Lacey. Naturally, if such an answer would tend to—incriminate—"

"Incriminate? *Me?*" The nurse's voice shrilled. "Dr. Koenig was the best friend I ever had, the finest man that ever lived! I'd have *died* for him, and then—you *dare* insinuate that I— "

"Please, Miss Lacey! It's your own refusal to tell the truth that is involving you," Dundee assured her curtly.

"All right! I'll tell," the nurse capitulated wearily. "I was lying. I saw that picture Sunday night. I spent this evening with friends. I didn't want to drag them into this—"

"Your friends' names?" Dundee prodded.

Norah Lacey cast a despairing glance at Justine Harlow, then flung up her head defiantly. "I spent the evening, from eight o'clock until ten, with Mrs. Satterlee and her daughter, Mabel."

"Surely that's an innocent diversion," Dundee commented drily. "Their address and—telephone number?"

"They live on Vine Street in Hamilton—5540 Vine Street," the nurse told him reluctantly.

"And the telephone number?" Dundee insisted.

"Can't you take my word for it that I was there?" Norah Lacey protested, almost wailing. "The number is Lakewood 0341, but—" and she sprang forward as if to prevent Dundee by force from using the telephone which he had picked up. "*Please* don't call them now. It's so late. You might wake up the " She gasped, then completed her sentence: "—the old lady."

With his eyes steadily upon her, the young detective called the number. To his surprise the call was completed almost immediately. A girl's voice, which, as the conversation continued, betrayed its owner's Southern origin, drawled "Hel—lo—o—o!"

"I'm speaking from Mayfield Sanitarium, Miss Satterlee. Will you please tell me whether Miss Norah Lacey was there this evening?"

"Oooh!" the soft voice cooed consternation. "Hasn't she got home yet? She left here simply ages ago."

"Can you tell me just when she did leave?" Dundee asked.

"Why, yes, sir." The drawl was becoming anxious. "It was exactly ten o'clock. Miss Lacey said she'd have to be back at the sanitarium in time to change into her uniform before half past ten. She always leaves exactly at ten. I simply can't imagine "

"Don't be alarmed, Miss Satterlee," Dundee interrupted soothingly.

"But I'm simply scared to death," the soft voice mourned. "Won't you please tell her to call up Mabel the very minute she gets back?"

Having given the promise, Dundee said good night, with apologies, and rather thoughtfully relayed the conversation to Strawn.

The Chief of the Homicide Squad was at heart a kindly man. "Looks all right for you, sister," he told the nurse grudgingly, "but I can't see what you made such a to do about. Better call up your friend in a minute or two. . . . Now get along with your story."

Relief made the woman's face almost radiant. "I'm sorry, but I didn't want my friends to be bothered. . . . Well, I changed into my uniform and came downstairs. It lacked about five minutes of half past ten, and I thought I'd get a book out of Dr. Koenig's office. Doctor had shown me a new textbook on psychiatry which the author had autographed and sent to him, and I thought I'd read while I was relieving Miss Caplan, though it wasn't likely that I'd not be interrupted. The patients are apt to be restless after the movies, and I'd been told the pictures lasted late—till ten o'clock—and nine is bedtime here. . . . Well, anyway " and she raised one of her clenched fists to press the knuckles against her trembling lips, "I tried the door that opens into the main hall, and I found it locked, of course, but I didn't know what to think when my key wouldn't work."

"Then you have a key to Dr. Koenig's office?" Strawn cut in.

"Certainly," the nurse answered with a flash of resentment. "So has Miss Caplan, and Miss Home, Doctor's secretary, has one, too, of course. Well, I thought maybe Doctor had turned the bolt on the door— it has a Yale lock—and had forgot about it, so I went through the door that leads from the main hall into the reception room—"

"That door was not locked?" Dundee interrupted.

"No, because patients are brought in at all hours, and that room is kept ready to receive them. I tried the door into this office, and it was locked, as I expected, but my key worked, and I entered. There's a light switch just inside the door "

"Then there was no light on in here when you entered?"

"No, of course not. If there had been, I should have seen it from the transom outside in the hall, and I'd have knocked, supposing Dr. Koenig was still working. I pushed the switch button, and—and I saw him—sitting there " Norah Lacey covered her face with her shaking hands.

"I know it's hard, Miss Lacey," Dundee sympathized. "Did you touch the—touch him?"

"I—no, I could see he—was His head— "

"Just what did you do?"

"I—ran," the nurse confessed miserably. "I ran and unbolted the door and ran on into the chartroom. Miss Caplan, knowing I was ready to relieve her, had gone on to her supper, and I Well, finally I managed to call Dr. Cantrell on the telephone. Then I ran upstairs and told Dr. Harlow. She was just getting into bed, and while she was dressing I ran back downstairs and waited for Dr. Cantrell in the reception room. When I heard him come into Dr. Koenig's office—"

"You came in through your own office, I suppose, Doctor?" Dundee turned to Cantrell.

"Of course! It's the shortest route, and the one I always use. I unlocked the outside door of my office, and found the door between the two offices ajar, just as I had left it shortly after seven o'clock."

"Thank you. . . . Now, Miss Lacey, was this office left exactly as you found it?"

"It was. Except that I unbolted the door into the hall, just as I told you."

"Dr. Cantrell?"

"I disturbed nothing. I even took care not to shift the body in the slightest when I took the temperature, in an effort to decide how long Dr. Koenig had been dead."

"But you used the telephone later to call the district attorney?"

"No. Not the instrument in this office. I used the phone in the chartroom."

"By the way, are your telephones on a switchboard?" Dundee asked.

"No," Cantrell answered. "We have three outside lines. This telephone is on one of them. This instrument and the one on my desk are extensions from the telephone in the reception room. During the day, Miss Home, the secretary, answers the telephone, and notifies either myself or Dr. Koenig of a call by pushing the correct button on her desk. Mr. Baldwin has another of the outside lines, with an extension on his secretary bookkeeper's desk. The third line, which is listed as 'Mayfield Sanitarium (Information),' is in the chartroom. In addition we have an intercommunicating telephone system between all of the cottages, the chartroom, my home, the head nurses' apartment on the second floor, and Dr. Harlow's apartment on the same floor."

"I see," Dundee commented, cocking an amused eye brow at Strawn's impatience. "Where were you when the crime was discovered, Mr. Baldwin?"

"In the cottage I share—did share, rather," the business manager amended without emotion, "with Dr. Koenig. Bruce—Dr. Cantrell— called me on the intercommunicating telephone at ten thirty five. I had not gone to bed, so I came right over. We talked things over a bit, had Whalen in to see if he could tell us anything, then I suggested that we call the district attorney, rather than the police. Dr. Cantrell agreed, and called Sanderson himself."

"And how did you spend the evening, Mr. Baldwin?" Dundee asked.

"Working," Baldwin told him curtly. "Went back to my office directly after dinner. Carl—Dr. Koenig—and I left the dining room together, and parted just outside his door in the main hall. I had some estimates on the new two story building which will be required to house the new patients, and I wanted to go over them in detail. Also, since it's just after the first of the month, I had a flock of sanitarium bills that required my O. K. before the bookkeeper could pay them."

"How late did you work?" Dundee persisted.

"I can't say to the minute," the business manager answered, frowning, "but it must have been about half past nine. My office opens into the main hall just to the left of the staircase, and I pass this door on my way out. It was ajar."

"Did you see Dr. Koenig?" Dundee asked.

"I did. But he did not see me. He was typing, so his back was turned to the door. There was no reason why I should interrupt him, so I passed on through the hall and went straight to our cottage."

"Did you see anyone at all, except Dr. Koenig, in this building?"

"No one at all," Baldwin answered emphatically. "I remember glancing into the patients' living room across the hall, as I passed, but it appeared to be deserted. Naturally I did not give it more than a passing glance."

"And on your way to your cottage?"

"No one at all," came the unequivocal answer. "I still had my mind on the plans for the new building, and I don't remember looking about at all as I walked."

Dundee lapsed into a thoughtful silence, and it was Strawn who took up the burden of the investigation.

"We can take it for granted that the doctor was alive at half past nine or thereabout. Now, speak up! Anybody see him alive after that time?"

There was a throbbing silence.

"How about you, little doctor?" the Chief of the Homicide Squad demanded, pointing a finger at Justine Harlow. "You got home at five minutes to ten, you say, and you must have passed through the main hall. Was the doctor's door open then?"

"No. And there was no light showing through the transom. I was a little surprised, since Dr. Koenig had said he would work until I returned," Dr. Harlow answered.

"But you made no inquiries as to when the doctor had left?" Strawn demanded, accusingly.

The girl flushed, but she answered steadily: "No. I knew he was tired, and I concluded that he had gone to bed. Since he lived on the grounds, he would have been accessible in case of emergency. Shortly after I got in, Miss Caplan called me to help her handle Archie Webster, but there was no reason at all to call Dr. Koenig."

"What about you, Cantrell?" Strawn leveled his forefinger at the medical man.

"I did not see or communicate with Dr. Koenig after about seven fifteen, when I finished sewing up Chester's slashed arm," Cantrell answered positively. "Carl—Dr. Koenig—looked on as I worked, and gave young Chester a good tongue lashing for the trouble he had caused. When I had finished with the boy—"

"Bawled him out, did he?" Strawn pounced. "Kinda funny way for a brain doctor to treat a patient, ain't it?"

"Not at all!" Justine Harlow took up the cudgels spiritedly. "It's exactly the right way to treat a patient like Luke Chester. He hasn't the slightest intention of committing suicide, but because his father has forbidden his marriage with a middle aged adventuress, he has been punishing his family and indulging his own love of excitement and the limelight by very half hearted suicide attempts. His father got tired of the excitement and put him in here. There's nothing actually wrong with the boy mentally, except a perverted desire for sympathy and excitement."

"Not at all!" Dr. Harlow retorted. "He was devoted to Dr. Koenig, as are all our patients. In fact, he was pleased that Dr. Koenig should take time to give him a good, stiff lecture. He voluntarily promised to ask to be put into 'Ten,' the locked ward, the next time the urge came on him to 'commit suicide.' And of course," she smiled, for the first time that evening, "he'll enjoy himself immensely when he does go into 'Ten.' A new and different way of getting into the limelight."

"But the boy got good and sore at the doctor, eh?" Strawn guessed.

"Each to his own fancy!" Strawn growled. "Now, Cantrell! You say you didn't see or communicate with Dr. Koenig after seven fifteen. Where were you from that time on?"

"At home, subject to call. No call came."

"Anyone to back up that alibi?" Strawn demanded crudely.

"Alibi?" Cantrell repeated angrily. "Don't you think, sir, that the use of that word is a little premature?"

"I take it, then, that you are going to say you were alone," Strawn caught him up shrewdly.

"As a matter of fact, I *was* alone after eight o'clock," Cantrell answered, with an obvious effort to control his anger. "That is, I was alone in the living room of my house, my wife having gone to bed very shortly after dinner, with one of her severe neuralgic headaches. Naturally she can not support my 'alibi,' as you call it, since our bedroom is so far separated from the living room that I could have left the house and returned half a dozen times without her hearing me."

"Have you told her the news of the murder?"

"I looked in on her when I left, and found she was asleep. I did not wake her."

"'Then we'd better get hold of her right now, don't you think, Bonnie?" and Strawn turned to the younger detective.

Dundee glanced at the medical man's flushed cheeks and blazing eyes. "Hardly necessary, is it, Chief?" he answered lazily. "The doctor has already admitted that his wife cannot corroborate his story of not having left the house, and if Mrs. Cantrell is ill, it seems rather a shame to disturb her. . . . Your wife was formerly a patient of Dr. Koenig's, I believe?"

"She was," Cantrell answered, more pleasantly. "Not a 'mental' case in the usual sense of the word, Claire was a neurasthenic. Dr. Koenig psychoanalyzed her and she has been a very normal and happy girl ever since."

"You don't say!" Strawn commented. "By the way, Doc, how old are you?"

Again the doctor's eyes blazed wrath, but he answered with savage brevity: "Forty nine!"

"And how old is that pretty little wife of yours?" Strawn grinned.

"Look here!" The doctor almost choked with anger. "I don't know why you're wasting time on damn fool questions My wife is twenty four years old, if that fact concerns you in the least!"

Strawn's advice to the medical man that he keep a civil tongue in his head was interrupted by the appearance of Detective Harmon from the reception room, his heavy face red and damp with perspiration.

"I can't hold off them newspaper boys much longer, Chief!" he protested apologetically. "They're threatenin' to bust down this door if you don't give 'em a story within five minutes, so's they can catch their home edition deadlines."

"Tell 'em to go to hell!" Strawn growled. "I ain't running the Homicide Bureau on newspaper deadlines... . You want to see 'em, Bonnie?"

"No, Captain," Dundee smiled, for he well knew his old chief's love of publicity. "I'm not in the picture officially—at least not yet. Keep my name out of it, will you?"

"Blamed if I know what to tell the boys," Strawn worried, scratching his thick gray hair.

"Personally, I don't think it would be wise to let them see this room," Dundee suggested tactfully. "I think we are agreed that this is merely a well set stage—just a little too well set; but I believe the less said about it in the papers, the better. No use tipping off the murderer that he overplayed his hand."

"How's this, lad?" Strawn was still thoughtfully scratching his scalp. "Owing to the fact that they was a lot of visitors here tonight, on account of the movies, the police have a theory that the murderer sneaked in unnoticed, and killed the doctor to even up some old score. I can hint that we're on the track of the relative of some killer that the doctor, as an alienist in court, helped to hang by testifying he wasn't insane. It's a cinch Koenig made a slew of enemies that way, first and last."

"A good idea!" Dundee applauded sincerely, and Dr. Harlow gave a quick, tremulous sigh of relief.

As Detective Harmon returned to the impatient reporters, Strawn rocked back and forth on his heels, his chest expanded with satisfaction in his own cleverness and Dundee's appreciation of it. "Now, folks," he began pompously, "what I've just said brings up a mighty important question, and I want all of you to think seriously and answer truthfully: did Dr. Koenig have any enemies that any of you know about?"

After a suitably long and solemn pause Dr. Harlow spoke up, her lovely voice very earnest and reasonable: "You yourself, Captain Strawn, have hit upon one class of enemies that any alienist is sure to have. Dr. Koenig was famous as an expert witness on legal insanity, and he has taken the stand in almost every state in the Union. Whether he testified for the prosecution or for the defense, almost every important trial brought its aftermath of death threats for the doctor. Sometimes the relatives of a murderer's victim threatened his life, because he helped to send the murderer to an insane asylum instead of to the death house. More often, of course, the relatives of criminals who received long term sentences or the death penalty swore to be avenged."

"Did the doctor keep those letters?" Dundee asked.

"Not one of them. Nor did he bother to turn them over to the police. He did not have an atom of fear in his make up," the little doctor answered emphatically.

"Any other enemies?" Strawn prodded.

"As an alienist in court and as a member of the lunacy commission," Dr. Harlow answered, "Dr. Koenig some times balked a well planned conspiracy on the part of scheming relatives to have a rich member of the family 'put away,' in order to get control of his or her property. And I should also explain that every patient, at a certain stage in the treatment, hates his psychiatrist, because the doctor forces him to face some bitter truth about himself. But once that truth is faced and understood, and mental healing has begun, it is just as natural to love the psychiatrist with a deep devotion."

"So you admit that a patient could have been at the hating stage in the treatment, and hated the doctor enough to kill him?" Strawn bore down on her.

"I admit the possibility—yes!" the young doctor said quietly. "But I cannot reconcile the scheming and planning *after* the murder with the impulsive act of an enraged patient."

"How about this chap Rowan?" Strawn suggested. "By all accounts, he was the last patient to have an interview with the doctor, and according to Miss Caplan he has a violent temper—took a sock at Webster and knocked him flat."

"Samuel Rowan did have a three hour interview with Dr. Koenig this afternoon," Dr. Harlow admitted. "But when he left this office he was a changed man—relieved, buoyant, sociable, in contrast to two years of almost total silence. Dr. Koenig was jubilant, as Mr. Baldwin has told you. And Rowan was so much a new man that he attended the picture show for the first time since he's been here, and chatted and laughed with the other patients almost as normally as if he'd never been ill. Of course he was, and will be for a time, in a state technically called 'elation'— the pendulum having swung from extreme depression to extreme well being, based on relief. When he is really completely normal again he will be neither depressed nor elated. But I can assure you, from all my past experience, that Samuel Rowan was worshiping Dr. Koenig as his savior this evening."

"Just the same, I'd like to have a little powwow with Mr. Samuel Rowan!" Strawn interrupted her eloquence belligerently. "This is the way I look at it, Bonnie! Here's a bird that's had something pretty fierce on his chest for two years. He spills it to the Big Doctor. Sure he's relieved! Every crook is, when he confesses! Haven't I seen a Bluebeard dance a jig and sing a jazz song, after I'd third degreed him into telling where he'd buried the bodies of his four missing wives? . . . Well, this

Rowan, chap feels swell until he sees that movie, 'Manslaughter,' where the girl gets sent to the 'pen.' And he don't feel so good. He gets to worrying, see? That damned doctor knows too much! And Rowan wonders how the hell he happened to go so cuckoo as to spill the beans. Why, the doc can notify the police and it'll be the 'pen' for Sammy Rowan! What does he do? He slips out of the dark shop, and into the doc's office. And the first thing he sees is his case history lying on the doc's desk, and the doc typing it all out—what he'd told him, and what's enough to send him up maybe for the rest of his life. Get it? He don't stop to reason that the doc can't squeal on him, on account of professional ethics. He ain't taking no chances! He kills the doctor, and tears up his case history. But this bird ain't crazy, and he knows he can't get away with it on no insanity plea. So he fixes things up to look like one of the nuts did it, and then strolls away and into the shop again by the back door. . . . Get it, boy?"

Dundee nodded slowly. It really was amazingly convincing. And he had no better theory of his own to offer. None half so good, if he would admit the truth. But still

"Why, boy, it's air tight!" Strawn jubilated. "Mr. Baldwin here has already told us what the doc said to him *after Rowan bad had his powwow!* Just what was the words the doc used, sir?"

Baldwin, answered reluctantly: "Dr. Koenig remarked that, if a psychiatrist chose to, he could give the police plenty to keep them busy. But he did not mention Rowan by name. I admit that your theory sounds very plausible, Captain, but I feel absolutely sure that you are making a mistake—"

"So do I, Roger!" Justine Harlow cut in, her lovely voice warm and rich with gratitude.

The business manager flushed with pleasure at the girl's first use that evening—and Dundee suspected it was the very first—of his Christian name.

"I'm beginning to think," Strawn began savagely, "that nobody around here wants the doctor's murder cleared up! But the police do! And I'll thank you to send for this Rowan bird without any more shillyshallying!"

Dr. Harlow's small face flamed with anger, but her voice was steady with professional dignity and authority:

"I am sorry to have to refuse that request, Captain Strawn! Unless you show me a warrant for Samuel Rowan's arrest you cannot see him tonight!"

# CHAPTER 8

DUNDEE grinned his delight in the little doctor's spunk, but Captain Strawn glared at her as if he would love to spank her.

Dr. Harlow continued implacably: "Mr. Rowan has gone through the most exciting day of his life, and to haul him out of his sleep now to question him ruthlessly about a murder would work an injury to his precarious mental condition which I, as his doctor, cannot permit."

"I agree with Dr. Harlow, and stand back of her in that decision!" Bruce Cantrell stated uncompromisingly.

Before the outraged Chief of the Homicide Squad could spit out the words which were almost choking him, Dundee interposed: "Rowan will keep until morning, Chief. I am sure the doctors will see the advisability, however, of having a detective stationed outside his door—"

"Certainly!" Dr. Harlow agreed crisply.

"God! What a case!" Strawn exploded, and stamped out of the office into the reception room, where the reporters were almost ready to tear him limb from limb.

"We are all very tired, Mr. Dundee," Dr. Harlow reminded the detective who remained.

He regarded the little fighter with genuine compassion. She looked wizened and blanched with fatigue. And nervous reaction to the shock of the murder was showing itself now in half a dozen twitching muscles in face and hands. Tardily he remembered the other woman whom Dr. Koenig had left the richer in worldly goods by his tragic death.

Norah Lacey had long since sunk almost out of sight in a huge leather chair in the farthest corner of the room. A crooked arm shielded her face, but Dundee could see slow tears trickling down her wan, freckled cheeks, and dropping with tiny splashes upon the stiffness of her uniform. . . .

"I'm terribly sorry," he said gently, turning back to the girl doctor. "I am sure we shall all be the better for a few hours' rest. I don't believe there is much more that either Captain Strawn or I can do tonight. By the way, I understand that there is a vacant suite in Sunflower Court. If you will permit me "

"We shall be glad to have you as our guest," she assured him with something more than perfunctory polite ness, "for as long"—and she drew a sharp breath—"as it may seem necessary for you to remain on the ground. I'll telephone to Miss Hunter to make you comfortable. . . . Oh, Mr. Dundee! Please believe that we all want to help! You seem so—

so understanding, so—kind! You must realize that we who are left must safeguard our patients as *he* would have wished us to—"

"I do understand," Dundee assured her humbly, for he could have knelt before her loyalty and courage. "I'll help you to the very best of my ability. . . . Now, if you will trust me here alone—" he suggested tactfully.

But before the two doctors, the nurse and the business manager had obeyed his suggestion, the girl psychiatrist had locked the precious case history file and had asked for and received from the detective the key to it which lay among the few possessions taken from the murdered man's pockets. Strawn might have considered his yielding a weakness, but Dundee had a profound respect for Justine Harlow's attitude toward the secrets that filing cabinet held. And he felt fairly sure that none of those secrets had any place in the mystery he was investigating.

"You will not try to piece together those tiny scraps of the destroyed case histories?" she had asked him anxiously. "I know they are "evidence," but—"

"I'm afraid that would take many days and a Job's patience," he reassured her, and a singularly sweet smile rewarded him.

When he was alone, awaiting Strawn, who was still busy with the newspaper men, Dundee poked tentatively at the great mound or scraps which Carraway, the fingerprint expert had examined and then left in a glass letter tray upon the dead man's desk.

A superhuman task, indeed, to paste these fragments into two complete case histories! But what a reward for patience it might be! What dark secret had clouded Samuel Rowan's mind and sealed his lips for two long years? If Rowan himself did not choose to tell—and why should he?—was that secret to be locked forever in the dead doctor's brain? And that other case history which the murderer had destroyed. Why had he chosen Archie Webster's record of drinking debauches and probably mild attacks of delirium tremens? Had he chosen hit or miss, as part of his scheme for making this murder look like the work of a demented patient, or had he, as Strawn believed, destroyed his own record, and that of another patient merely as camouflage?

Samuel Rowan. . . . Archibald Webster. . . . Both *current* patients, while the files were crowded with case histories of the dead or departed. And had chance or a diabolical schemer hit upon two patients who could not possibly furnish the police with an unassailable alibi? Had the murderer possibly seen Webster leave the O. T. Shop, just as Miss Caplan had seen him? *And who was Webster's visitor?* If Strawn was right in his theory, Rowan could have seen Webster and his friend leave; could have made use of that knowledge with the cold blooded intention of "framing" the young scapegrace for his crime. Certainly there had been bad blood between the two men. . . . But—and Dundee caught himself up short—if Rowan had actually sneaked out of the shop, committed murder, framed Webster, and crept back into the O. T. Shop while the movie was still on, would he have been so foolhardy as to make himself conspicuous and label him self violent, by knocking young Webster down? But might not a super clever man have done just that? How better to prove that he had stayed in the shop all evening and had left with the crowd, than to make a scene out of what might have passed unnoticed?

Dundee propped his elbows on the dead doctor's desk and rested his head upon his cupped hands, for he too was very tired. He had had a hard day. . . .

"Damn that blood smear!" he groaned, as his heavy eyes rested on the whitish spot on the comer of the desk.

How big had the smear been before Carraway had officiously dabbed at it with a wet towel end, to make sure that it *was* blood? And what the devil was blood doing there, anyway?

It simply did not fit into the picture. He closed his eyes and again visualized the murder drama. The doctor tapping away at the typewriter keys, not hearing the soft, stealthy footsteps, which came from the reception room, on through the open door and across the thick rug to the doctor's very chair.

But wait! If the doctor had been typing, he would have been sitting in such a position that, out of the corner of his eye at least, he would have caught sight of that stealthy, approaching figure. For the typewriter table was at right angles to the desk, which was set against the wall almost directly opposite the door into the reception room.

Dundee frowned. There were two alternatives, of course. Either the doctor was bent over work at his desk, with his back squarely to the door, and the entry had been so noiseless that he had not heard a sound, or he had been typing, and the sight of his visitor had not surprised or alarmed him. Someone he knew! Someone he was accustomed to seeing. Someone who was privileged to walk into that office unannounced! But any member of the staff or any patient in Mayfield could do that!

Dundee again concentrated on visualizing the murderer's movements. The doctor had not been alarmed; had continued with his typing, with perhaps a word to his caller. The murderer had strolled to the doctor's chair, and had glanced over those bowed shoulders at the sheet of paper in the machine. What had he read there? Somewhere in that mound of fine torn scraps was the answer— if Dundee was not guessing wildly. But if he was right, whatever the murderer had read had been so great a shock to his mind or so horrible a menace to his liberty that only by destruction of the writer as well as of the written words could the doctor's caller ever feel safe again. The doctor—Dundee let the imaginary film unwind rapidly—had gone on with his typing, unaware that his visitor had peeked. The murderer had withdrawn a few steps, involuntarily; had backed slowly away in horror, a terrible resolution already forming in his shocked brain. He had backed to the open door leading into the hall, had silently drawn it shut. And if the doctor had heard the click of the lock, he had undoubtedly surmised that his visitor desired privacy for his interview. Then the murderer's eyes had fallen on the heavy bronze statue atop the bookcase so near at hand, in the corner between the two doors. Without pausing for reflection, he had seized the statue, stepped swiftly and silently back to the doctor's chair, and had brought the thing crashing down on that bowed, intent head.

For only by that hypothesis could Dundee account for the bruise upon the murdered psychiatrist's chin. Certainly the blow struck in that way would force the head down so violently that the chin could be bruised upon the frame of the typewriter. And naturally it had been necessary to swing the swivel chair so that the head was no longer jammed against the typewriter, since the incriminating sheet of paper must be removed from the machine and destroyed. But Dundee could picture the Unknown recoiling from the machine, even as his fingers were reaching for the all important paper. Fingerprints! The statue, which he had carefully and silently laid on the rug beside the swivel chair, could be wiped clean of betraying prints, but he must touch nothing else with uncovered fingers. Gloves! But it was summertime, and he had no gloves with him. But through the half open door into Dr. Cantrell's office he could see the white enamel instrument cabinet. Of course! Doctors always used rubber gloves in making examinations. And silently he had tiptoed into the medical man's office. There, as if Fate were on his side, he had found the soiled rubber gloves which the night nurse had left lying on top of the cabinet in the instrument tray.

No use picturing all that had followed. It was quite obvious how the murderer's mind had worked. This was primarily a sanitarium for the treatment of mental diseases. There, too, Fate had been working for him. What easier than to "wreck" the room, so that police and hospital authorities would jump to the conclusion that one of the psychopathic patients had gone berserk and had murdered in a homicidal rage?

But—how had blood come to be upon the corner of the doctor's desk? The head wound had bled but little, most of the blood matting in the hair and the rest trickling down the neck to disappear beneath the collar. And the blood that had slowly oozed from the right ear had soaked into the blotter. Dundee swung himself in the swivel chair until he faced the typewriter, bent his head until it touched the machine, then raising his head only slightly, he swung the chair until his forehead came to a rest upon the desk. No! The blood *could not* have been flung to the corner of the desk in that way! But how—*how?*

Temporarily abandoning that poser, the detective asked himself *who* the murderer could be. If his reconstruction of the crime was even approximately the truth, Dundee knew certain things about him.

First: the murderer was someone who was privileged to enter that office unceremoniously.

Second: the murderer was probably someone who was occupying the doctor's attention at the very moment he had entered the office. Now, what had the doctor been typing? One of three things, obviously: an addition to a case history; a change in his will; or a letter.

Third: the murderer was quick witted and cold blooded.

Fourth: he was apparently familiar with the names of the current patients. Or had his choice of case histories to be destroyed been hit or miss?

As he made his points, Dundee wrote them on a fresh sheet of paper which he had rolled into the typewriter. Now he paused and stared at the second paragraph, frowning intently. "An addition to a case history." . . . Only patients figured in case histories No, wait! Doctors and nurses must be mentioned in them, too! And the head psychiatrist had been away for three weeks. The mental welfare and the very lives of his patients had been in the hands of Dr. Cantrell, Dr. Harlow, Norah Lacey, Rose Caplan, and a small army of attendants.

After so long an absence Dr. Koenig had undoubtedly been besieged by patients. Was it possible—and Dundee sat up, startled, at the new train of thought—that a patient had complained to the Big Doctor of brutal treatment suffered during his absence? Or of criminal neglect on the part of some member of the staff or of an attendant? And if so, would not Dr. Koenig have recorded the accusation in the patient's case history, labeling it, possibly, as evidence of a "persecution complex" or a delusion? But suppose the accused—attendant, doctor, or trained nurse— had seen the accusation being typed out by the doctor, *and had known it to be true?* Had known that investigation would bring about dismissal or disgrace? And was it not possible, too, that Dr. Koenig had summoned the accused, to confront him or her with the patient's serious charge? Such speculation had endless possibilities. An attendant or a doctor who had criminally assaulted a girl patient. Such a girl as Enid Rambler, for instance. A subtle drug administered to produce the symptoms of insanity. Criminal malpractice, resulting in the death of a patient during the head doctor's absence. Bribery of a doctor or an attendant or a nurse by the relative of a patient, so that the patient would be kept wrongfully incarcerated. Such things had been done, Dundee knew. Wives of rich old men had been known to put their undesirable husbands away in just such institutions as this, so that they might enjoy the poor devil's money unhampered. With the collusion of a doctor, tempted by a heavy bribe—

Dundee's head swam. He closed his eyes and pressed his fingers into his temples. But he could not drive away the hideous possibility that lurked behind all these speculations. Finally he faced it squarely.

Roger Baldwin, Koenig's partner and certainly in his confidence where business matters were concerned, was authority for the statement that Dr. Koenig had planned to dismiss Justine Harlow and secure another assistant psychiatrist in her place. A sudden decision, undoubtedly, since neither the girl doctor nor the medical head of Mayfield had known of it. But the girl was co legatee with Norah Lacey in his will. That, certainly, was a fact, since Dr. Cantrell and his wife had witnessed the will. And it was as indisputably a fact that Dr. Koenig had been in pressing need of the services of a lawyer, that he had called his attorney that night, and, finding that he was out of town, had told Mrs. Forrest that he would attend to the matter himself, since it could not wait until morning.

And Justine Harlow herself had admitted that she had had a "disagreement" with the Big Doctor on the subject of Enid Rambler. And Enid Rambler was certainly a girl of wealth. Was it possible that the girlish, loyal seeming little doctor had succumbed to the temptation of a huge bribe to aggravate the girl's mental condition until she should finally be a fit subject to be "committed" by a lunacy commission?

No! Dundee surprised himself by crashing his fist upon the dead doctor's desk. It was unthinkable! That girl was all she seemed to be, or he was crazier than any inmate of Mayfield Sanitarium. But—*the doctor had determined to dismiss her*. The doctor had telephoned his lawyer. . . . And the vicious circle began to spin again in the detective's head. Justine Harlow was a graduate of medical school as well as of psychiatry. *She knew drugs*. And some secret anxiety had gnawed at her nerves all evening. . . .

Dundee was so sunk in miserable speculation that he did not hear the door open.

"Well, boy! I've got rid of them damned reporters at last!" Strawn boomed. "And say, one of the boys spun a theory that ain't so dusty."

"Yeah?" Dundee asked wearily, without turning to face his old chief.

"Yeah! Says me!" Strawn retorted. "Creston, of *The News*. His idea is that Doc Koenig was in collusion with some rich woman to keep her hubby shut up here, then go before the lunacy commission and swear he's a nut, so that the wife could get herself appointed the guardian of his person and of his property—"

"I thought of that," Dundee interrupted wearily. "But Koenig was too big a man for that."

"Every man's got his price," Strawn quoted cynically. "And I got a hunch of my own. The Big Doc was away for three weeks. Just got back. This girl doctor probably don't get a whale of a salary, and if a rich dame come along and offered her—"

"Great minds run in the same channel, Chief—to quote another old saw," Dundee interrupted, grinning wryly. "I'd just been going over that very possibility, and—I can't believe it! Not of that girl!"

"Because she's got red hair and green eyes, and a cute way of wrinkling her nose when she grins?" Strawn cut in slyly. "Well, you needn't tear your shirt, lad! I'm thinking it's that Rowan bird, and I'll be after him bright and early in the morning. I'm leaving Harmon and Clinton on guard outside these doors, and shoving off myself. What about you?"

"I now become an inmate of Mayfield Sanitarium," Dundee grinned. "My temporary address is Sunflower Court."

"Next door to the Rambler baby, eh? Gonna sit up with her and hold her little white hand? . . . Well, I'd rather pound my ear. "Night!"

"Just a minute, Captain. I'm taking charge of this trayful of scraps, if you don't mind."

"Sure! Paste 'em up, if you like. I never was any good at jigsaw puzzles, and there ain't a man on the squad I feel like giving a week off to do the job. But don't take any chances with that trash, Bonnie. I'm betting the district attorney can make a rope out of it to hang Rowan with."

"If," Dundee replied slowly, "it's the stuff that hangman's rope is made of, why do you suppose the murderer left it lying about? Why didn't he burn it?

# CHAPTER 9

UNESCORTED, Special Investigator Dundee crossed the driveway before the main building and struck off across the dew wet, thick grassed lawn toward Sunflower Court. Except for a small cottage in the far corner of the grounds, the building in which he was to be housed was the only structure to the left of the long, U shaped driveway. In the faint light diffused by the powerful lamps set at intervals along the high iron fence Dundee saw, in this segment of the vast grounds, a croquet field, a miniature golf course, a large flower bed encircling a fountain, two huge, colorful umbrellas with their scalloped edges fluttering in the flower scented night air, three iron tables topped with gay oilcloth, and numerous striped canvas chairs, with canopies to protect the patient's eyes from the glare of the summer sun. Truly, these looked like the grounds of a fashionable resort hotel.

And when he had inspected his suite in Sunflower Court he knew that for such luxury and comfort a hotel visitor would pay even more than Mayfield Sanitarium exacted of its wealthy patients.

Miss Hunter, the nurse in charge of Sunflower Court, and whose name had bobbed up frequently during the long hours of the investigation into the murder of Dr. Carl Koenig, greeted the detective as he was crossing the cement floored porch of the stucco building. And she chuckled richly as he was momentarily dumb with astonishment.

"I know I'm big," she laughed, as she extended the largest arm Dundee had ever seen on a woman, "but I wouldn't hurt a fly. You'll get used to me. . . . Come along in, sir, and make yourself at home."

Dundee grinned apologetically and stepped into a pleasant, charmingly furnished room, which jutted out upon the porch. A chart table and a signal board above it were the only features to distinguish the room as in anyway connected with a hospital.

"Everything quiet now, nurse?" he asked in a low voice.

"Yes, thank heaven!" the huge nurse sighed, but she could not make her great, red, freckled face look lugubrious to save her life. "And what a night it's been! Honest, my feet are killing me. . . . Have you found out who did that awful thing, sir? Let me tell you, Mr. Dundee, a finer man and a greater doctor than Dr. Koenig never drew breath of life."

"I'm afraid I don't know any better than you who did the deed, Miss Hunter," Dundee told her regretfully. "How is Miss Rambler? It was I who found her and brought her back, you know."

"Poor lamb! She'd have had a conniption fit if she'd known you were a detective. . . . She's asleep now, bless her heart, but she wouldn't shut an eye till Miss Lacey gave her a hypo and promised to sit with her until it took effect."

"Has she an attendant?" Dundee asked.

"Sure! Crippled like she is with that sprained ankle, poor kid! But she hasn't needed an attendant before this. . . . Would you like to go to your rooms now, sir?"

Dundee followed her into a narrow hall, which, midway its length, gave upon an immaculate kitchen.

"Most of the food is cooked in the main kitchen, and brought over," Miss Hunter explained, "but the trays and extra delicacies are prepared here, as well as the nine o'clock nourishments. . . . This way out, sir."

Dundee found himself facing a long open court, carpeted with grass, bordered and gemmed with flower beds. A narrow, roofed porch hugged the building on all sides, except the far end, which was guarded by a spiked iron fence.

"Nice little private garden, isn't it?" boasted the nurse in charge of Sunflower Court. "The gate at the end is always kept locked, and there's no other way out except through my office, so you see the patients are pretty safe here."

The mountainous, jolly nurse leading the way, they walked softly for a few feet along the left side of the court, before Miss Hunter paused at a door marked with a gleaming brass "B."

There was a tiny hall, and to the right of it a large, luxuriously furnished sitting room, complete with easy chairs, radio cabinet, bookcase, down stuffed couch, coffee table, end tables, and rather good bric a brac and pictures. Gold silk curtains and a golden brown velvet rug gave the room a rich glow of comfort.

"And here's your bedroom," Miss Hunter told him proudly, as she ushered him into a large, exquisitely appointed chamber. The color scheme was daffodil and green, carried out in the painted furniture, the window drapes, bedspread and rug.

"We usually put a woman here," Miss Hunter admitted, as Dundee grinned at the thought of his occupying so feminine a bower. "This is the bathroom. It has a door into the sitting room, too, to make it convenient for the attendant, which you'll not be needing, of course."

The green and yellow bathroom was as luxurious as the rest of the suite.

"There are six apartments in the court, I believe?" Dundee asked, when he had sufficiently praised his quarters.

"That's right. Miss Rambler has Suite C, next to you toward the end of the court. It and Suite F are even larger than this."

"Who are the other patients in the court?"

"Well, a real old lady, by the name of Horton, has A," Miss Hunter began. "That's on the other side of yours. And across the court in D we have a Mrs. Morse— "

"*Morse?*" Dundee repeated. He saw again the two words "Call Morse," which headed the three notations on the dead doctor's calendar.

"Yes. Do you know her? Poor thing! She's been awfully 'queer' for months, but she's much better now. Or, rather, she was until tonight, when she got all upset again."

"What happened to upset her tonight?" Dundee asked sharply. "Did she go to the movie?"

"No. Her husband visited with her from about half past seven until nearly nine, and when he came through my office on his way out he said he had never seen his wife in better spirits," Miss Hunter explained. "He acted just tickled to death, poor man. But it wasn't more'n fifteen minutes before she was taking on something terrible. Her nurse—she has three attendants, on eight hour shifts—had gone to our kitchen to fix her nine o'clock nourishment, and when Miss Macy took her her hot chocolate and toast she found Mrs. Morse moaning and shuddering, her head all covered up with a sheet. She rang for me and I had to get Miss Caplan to come over and give her a strong sedative."

"Did Mrs. Morse say what had upset her?" Dundee asked.

"No. She wouldn't say anything except that she was going to kill herself. . . . And here we'd been singing Hallelujah because she was cured," the fat nurse sighed.

"Cured? You mean a sudden cure?" Dundee asked, startled.

"It was like a miracle!" Miss Hunter assured him solemnly. "You know Dr. Koenig had been gone for three weeks. Well, it seems that he did a lot of studying about Mrs. Morse's case while he was gone, because as soon as he got back—"

"What was wrong with Mrs. Morse?" Dundee interrupted.

"Some kind o' delusion, I guess you'd call it," Miss Hunter answered. "You see, Mr. Dundee, I'm not a trained nurse—just head attendant here; so I don't know all the doctor book names for things. . . . Well, anyway, Mrs. Morse never would say 'I' or 'me' "

"What's that?" Dundee puzzled.

"It was like this, sir," the nurse explained patiently. "If anybody spoke to her, said 'How are you, Mrs. Morse?,' for instance, she'd say, '*She* is very well, thank you,' or, '*She* says she doesn't feel well to day.' It was the same every time she referred to herself. Never did say 'I' until Tuesday, after she'd had a long talk with Dr. Koenig. You could have knocked me down with a feather, big as I am, when I come on duty Tuesday night and she answered me just like anybody else. She spoke right up: Tm feeling fine, Miss Hunter!' she said, and I ain't ashamed to tell you I broke right down and cried, I was so happy to see the poor darling was cured."

"You say she talked with Koenig on Tuesday?" Dundee asked, frowning.

"Yes, sir. You see, Doctor had been psychoanalyzing her for weeks, and the word went round that he'd finally hit on whatever it was that had got her poor mind all kinked up. A complex, they call it. Or maybe it's a psychosis."

"Do you know whether Mr. Morse saw Dr. Koenig this evening, before or after he visited his wife?" Dundee persisted.

"I guess he did," the nurse admitted, her hazel eyes widening. "He said he was going to drop in and speak to the doctor, to ask him when he could take his wife home."

Dundee stared silently into the nurse's apprehensive eyes, his mind buzzing with questions and conjectures.

"Is Mrs. Morse's attendant thoroughly reliable?" he asked at last. "She must not be left alone an instant."

"You—don't think ?" the nurse gasped.

"I don't think anything!" Dundee retorted curtly. "But Mrs. Morse must be guarded every second of the day and night! . . . Now, who are the other patients in the court?"

The nurse looked like a huge child whose feelings had been wounded. "Mr. Salter has E, the suite next to Mrs. Morse, and Archie Webster is in F. That is, he was until they put him in 'Ten' tonight. I expect he'll be back here in the morning. He's an awfully sweet boy, except when he's drinking– "

"So I've heard," Dundee interrupted drily, for he was a little tired of hearing Archie Webster's praises sung by infatuated nurses. "Who is Mr. Salter? The name sounds familiar."

"Howard Salter, the writer," the nurse explained. "He writes Western novels—the most exciting things! But you don't dare mention them to him. They say he hates his books like poison, but they've made him rich enough to afford Suite F, which is two hundred dollars a week—the same price as Enid's. The rest of these apartments are only a hundred and fifty."

"Did Mr. Salter go to the movies tonight?" Dundee asked.

"No. He hates the movies, too, though I've heard that five or six of his novels have been made into pictures."

"Perhaps that is why Mr. Salter doesn't like the movies," Dundee smiled. "Just what did Mr. Salter do with his evening?"

"Sally Porter, the girl he's going to marry if he ever gets well– "

"And what's wrong with him?" Dundee interrupted.

"He's what they call a manic depressive," Miss Hunter elucidated, obviously proud of her knowledge. "Manic depressives ain't really crazy, you know—just 'mentally sick.' They're in a sort of black despair. They can't bear themselves and they think the whole world's a sink of sin and sorrow, I guess. But they always come out of it, just like Mr. Salter's doing. He's been just fine for four or five days, and his girl friend was mighty happy tonight. I guess they'll be getting married soon."

"How long did Miss Porter stay with Mr. Salter?"

"I don't know exactly," the nurse confessed. "She come about eight and him and her took a little drive in her car, then they sat out on the lawn. Mr. Salter come in alone about five minutes to nine and I gave him his bromide, which he takes at nine every night. All the manic depressives are given bromides at night so they won't lie awake and brood."

"Has Mr. Salter an attendant?"

"Oh, no! Not since he's been getting better. He had an attendant at night as long as there was any danger of him committing suicide, like he threatened to do when he first came here. But I make the rounds every half hour. The patients ain't allowed to lock their bedroom doors, and I peep in to see if them that haven't attendants are all right. Just now Mr. Salter is the only patient I have to keep an eye on, so if you'll excuse me– There's pajamas and a dressing gown on your bed, and a new toothbrush and a shaving kit in your bathroom. Mr. Baldwin brought them over before you got here."

"Decent of him," Dundee said with an effort, for he hated the idea of being under any obligation to the only person he had met that evening whom he did not like. "I'm sure I'll be very comfortable, Miss Hunter. And thanks for everything."

"I'm afraid I've talked too much," the big nurse apologized, but her face was one vast smile of hospitality and genuine friendliness. "Good night, sir. Just ring if you want anything. You'll find the bell cord hanging from the head of your bed."

Tired though he was Dundee found that he could not lay himself down to sleep. He had counted on the warm shower to relax his nerves, but they remained annoyingly taut. At last, clad in the delft blue silk pajamas, black satin dressing gown and dark blue leather slippers which Roger Baldwin had thoughtfully provided for him, the young detective stepped out of his miniature hall into the silent, flower fragrant patio. Perhaps a walk in the balmy June air would help. . . .

He strolled noiselessly, hands deep in the big pockets, his brows knit with perplexed thought. If he only had something to read. . . . The bookcase in his room was empty, awaiting the patient's choice of literature—

"What luck!" he ejaculated to himself, as he saw a book lying open and face down upon one of the iron tables set at intervals along the roofed porch of the patio. There was not light enough from the small electric lanterns which swung from every door along the court, but he thrust the volume into his dressing gown pocket, and continued his stroll to the spiked fence at the rear.

Grinning at the thought that he was as well locked up as any psychopathic resident of the court, Dundee idly shook the heavy iron gate set in the center of the fence. But the grin was wiped off instantly. *The gate was not locked.*

Miss Hunter raised startled eyes from the hooked rug she was working on, as the newcomer she thought asleep confronted her.

"You said that gate at the rear was always kept locked!" he reminded her grimly. "Well, it's not locked now!"

"Not locked?" the nurse repeated blankly. "Oh! Then Frank, the kitchen man, must have forgot to lock it after he brought the supper wagon through. But surely there's no harm done– "

"More harm may have been done than you suspect," Dundee interrupted darkly. "Dr. Koenig was murdered tonight, and Mrs. Morse was mysteriously thrown into a panic. . . . Have you a key to that gate?"

"Yes, sir!" the nurse quavered. "I'll go lock it now. Such a thing has never happened before "

"Who else has a key?"

"There's one in the chartroom in the main building, and Frank has one."

"See that Mrs. Morse's nurse doesn't go to sleep on the job tonight!" the detective warned her, and then left the room as unceremoniously as he had come.

He was strangely disturbed. And his scalp was prickling with the same premonitory unease which had served to warn him of danger so many times in the past. Morse. ... Morse. . . . "Call Morse." . . . The name writhed through his brain. . . . Mrs. Morse had been almost miraculously cured by Dr. Koenig only the day before. Her husband had come to rejoice over her cure, to plan to take her home. But had he really rejoiced? Had the unexpected cure of his wife upset some vile, deep laid scheme? Had Morse stopped in to see the doctor who had wrought the miracle? If so, why had Dr. Koenig not crossed out the notation on his calendar "Call Morse." Had death itself interfered with his meticulous efficiency?

With sudden resolution, Dundee knocked upon the door of Suite D. An elderly woman in nurse's uniform answered his knock, then drew back in startled amazement at sight of her informally dressed caller.

"You are Mrs. Morse's nurse?" Dundee asked curtly, in a low voice.

"Yes, sir. Mrs. Appleby is my name."

"I'm Dundee, of the district attorney's office. I am occupying Suite B, *as a patient*, until the mystery of Dr. Koenig's death is cleared up. You'll remember that, I hope? . . . Very well. Is your patient asleep?"

"Yes, sir," the woman breathed.

"I understand that Mrs. Morse was unaccountably upset this evening after her husband's visit," Dundee went on, keeping his voice very low. "I want you to tell me about it. You were with her while Mr. Morse was here?"

"Not in the sitting room with them—no, sir. I never like to intrude. Part of the time I was in the bedroom, but most of the time I was out in the patio, dose enough to hear if I was called."

"Tell me! When did you first notice that Mrs. Morse was upset?"

"I came in when I saw Mr. Morse leave," the nurse answered, her voice frightened. "I couldn't find Mrs. Morse at first, but then I heard the water running in the bathtub. I called to her and she said she was going to take a hot bath. I thought her voice sounded a little queer, but she never likes to have me help her with her bath, so I turned down the bed, and then went to fix her nine o'clock nourishment. When I got back with it—I was gone about fifteen minutes, making toast and hot chocolate, and having to whip the cream and everything– "

"And gossip with the other nurses, I suppose!" Dundee cut in grimly.

"I had no reason to think Mrs. Morse wasn't quite all right!" the elderly woman flared. "She was in high spirits before Mr. Morse came, seemed to be as well as anybody."

"And what state did you find her in?" Dundee asked more gently.

"She was in bed, with the sheet over her head. And she was crying and moaning– "

"Any words you could distinguish?" Dundee interrupted.

"All she said was 'Too late! Too late!—over and over! But I couldn't make her tell me what she meant. And she was in such a state that I didn't worry her much with questions. I rang for Miss Hunter, and she got Miss Caplan to give Mrs. Morse a strong sedative."

"Is it your opinion that something Mr. Morse said or did to his wife caused this upset, or that it was something that happened while you were in the kitchen?"

"I don't know, sir, since I didn't see her at all until I got back with the nourishment."

Dundee gave it up for then, and, with a word of apology and thanks, departed for his own suite.

Determined to "Call Morse" himself the next morning, and equally as determined to dismiss the matter from his mind for the night, the weary young detective stretched out between the smooth, fresh sheets of his bed. The book he had found in the patio proved to be a mystery story, and, grinning in anticipation of the technical flaws he was very apt to spot in it, he adjusted the bedside lamp for reading.

"Murder Without Motive." . . . Not a bad title, that. And it must be a popular book among the patients, Dundee concluded, after a glance at its dog eared condition. An envelope pasted upon the fly leaf bore the printed words: "Ex libris Mayfield Sanitarium. . . . Guests are kindly requested to return books to the library as soon as they have read them."

He settled himself to read, slightly annoyed by the fact that some previous reader had underlined significant sentences and phrases on almost every page. The story concerned the apparently motiveless, brutal slaying of a housewife at work in her own kitchen. After a crisply sensational first chapter, the story meandered rather dully, Dundee thought, but perhaps that was because a far more baffling mystery in real life persisted in distracting his attention from the printed pages.

Suddenly, however, he uttered a sharp exclamation. No need for the penciled underlining to attract his attention to these words, uttered by the amateur detective whose "brilliant work was putting the police force to shame," as the author assured the reader:

*"No, Sergeant. I am afraid you are wrong. Don't waste time looking for a foppishly dressed man, the kind, as you say, who wears gloves in July. Poor Mrs. Stone furnished her murderer with gloves. Look!" And Hartley Jarnegan pointed dramatically at a pair of innocent looking rubber gloves lying atop a bar of yellow soap in the soap dish above the kitchen sink.*

Dundee whistled. *Rubber gloves!* Had he stumbled upon an odd coincidence, or had the prospective murderer, reading this very book, stored away in his subconscious mind a fact that had proved to have a sinister usefulness?

Was it his hand—or *her* hand—which had underlined these pages so liberally? The story forgotten, Dundee turned rapidly through the book, searching every page for a scribbled word, a marginal comment or query. But there was nothing upon which a handwriting expert could exercise his craft. Who had read this book? Dozens, apparently, but Dundee determined to have a look at the withdrawal card which undoubtedly reposed this minute in the sanitarium's library card file.

Another chore for the morning, which promised to be a very busy one. He ticked off his tasks upon his fingers:

Check up Norah Lacey's alibi. That would necessitate a trip to the Satterlee home in Hamilton.

Call Morse, to find out what had taken place during his visit with his wife, and whether he had called upon Dr. Koenig.

Interview Mrs. Cantrell.

Check the doctor's visitors, including patients, since his return on Monday, with the secretary, Miss Home.

Visit Enid Rambler, in the guise of fellow patient.

Listen in on Strawn's questioning of Rowan and Webster.

Circulate among patients on the lawn, to hear comment on the doctor's murder.

Call on the district attorney, to report progress—or lack of it!

Dundee sighed as wearily as if he had already performed these labors. Then sleep descended upon him so suddenly that he could scarcely arouse himself to turn off his bedside lamp.

A knock startled him into instant wakefulness. He was sure he had just that minute dozed off, but the sun was shining brilliantly through the flowered silk curtains at his bedroom windows.

Miss Hunter's vast bulk filled the door, but over her shoulder Dundee saw the hennaed and marcelled head of a stranger.

"Good morning, Mr. Dundee!" the big nurse greeted him heartily. "I brought Miss Doty—Lurline Doty—in to meet you. She's in charge here during the day.

"My, Mr. Dundee! I won't know how to act with a detective watching me!" the newcomer babbled, a hint of hysteria in her voice and in her rounded blue eyes. "I'm still all of a tremble. I didn't know a blessed thing until I come on duty ten minutes ago—"

"Yes. It's pretty bad," Dundee agreed curtly. "Every thing quiet, Miss Hunter?"

To his astonishment the night nurse flushed darkly behind her freckles and her hazel eyes avoided his. "Everything's quiet—*now*. I wanted to wake you up last night to tell you, seeing as how you're the detective, but Dr. Harlow wouldn't let me—"

Dundee sat bolt upright in bed. "For God's sake, what happened? Is Mrs. Morse— ?"

"No, sir. It was Mr. Salter!"

# CHAPTER 10

"DR. HARLOW, why wasn't I told last night that Howard Salter had tried to commit suicide?"

The little doctor, her coiled red braids gleaming, her uniform crisply immaculate, opened wider the door to her apartment on the second floor of the main building, with a gesture which invited the outraged young detective to enter.

"Why should I have told you?" she countered. Then, with a hint of laughter in her lovely voice: "But how stupid of me! I remember now that it is a crime to commit suicide. Naturally you wanted to arrest him! But isn't it rather early in the morning for you to bully me, Mr. Dundee? I haven't even been fortified by breakfast. . . . By the way, have you?"

"No. I came here as soon as Miss Hunter told me what had happened."

"Charlotte Hunter always did talk too much," the girl reflected with mock sadness. "Pardon me!" and she stepped to a table which held two telephones and a black metal box with perhaps a dozen pairs of push buttons. After a moment of manipulation she spoke into a receiver:

"The kitchen? . . . Joe? . . . Dr. Harlow speaking. Send up two breakfast trays as soon as possible."

"That's kind of you," Dundee admitted, a little less stiffly. "But you must realize, Doctor–"

He was interrupted by the ringing of a telephone bell. Justine Harlow, who still stood by the table, picked up the instrument she had used in her house call.

"Dr. Harlow speaking. . . . Yes, Miss Lacey. . . . Very well." She replaced the receiver and reached for the other instrument, her eyes on Dundee. "Good morning, Captain Strawn. . . . No, not very well, thank you. . . . Yes, I had thought of that, and I've given orders that all morning papers are to be withheld from the patients. . . . I beg your pardon? . . . Why, ye es, I suppose so. ... What time? . . . Very well. Good bye!"

She slowly hung up the receiver and faced Dundee. "Captain Strawn will be here about eight o'clock with the police stenographer, to question every patient in his room. He has asked that no patient be informed of the doctor's death, or permitted to see a newspaper. He will begin the rounds at nine, he says, and until then patients are to be allowed to follow their regular routine. ... I suppose," she concluded dejectedly, "that some sort of examination of the patients is necessary, but—there's a hard day ahead for doctors and nurses. . . . Will you accompany Captain Strawn on his rounds?"

"Remember I'm here as a patient," Dundee reminded her. "But about Salter—"

"Come in! . . . Good morning, Joe. . . . Put the trays on the table between the windows. . . . That's fine. Thanks!"

A minute later Dundee was facing the little doctor across the improvised breakfast table, and was accepting a cup of coffee.

"Now, if you'll let me have just two swallows of coffee," she begged, and raised her own cup to her pretty, unrouged mouth. "Now! I'm beginning to feel human. ... In the first place, I didn't call you last night, or rather at two o'clock this morning, because I was too busy to think of anything or anybody but Howard Salter. In the second place, the poor man was too near dead to be questioned, and you would have been terribly in the way."

"Just what happened?" Dundee asked. "Miss Hunter was called away before she could give me more than the bare fact that he had tried to kill himself."

"He slashed his wrist with a safety razor blade. Fortunately, he neglected to turn off the bathroom light and shut the door, and Miss Hunter, on her two o'clock visit to see if he was resting—she makes the rounds every half hour—saw the light and investigated. She found Mr. Salter unconscious and soaked with blood. But for a lucky chance I am afraid he would have been dead by now—"

"You mean the bathroom light?" Dundee interrupted.

"No. The lucky chance was that we were able to give a blood transfusion immediately. We make a blood test of every patient who comes in, and also classify his blood according to type. Howard Salter's blood happens to be the rarest type. Of course we have a file of blood donors, classified according to type, but there was no time to send into Hamilton for a registered donor. Mr. Baldwin, whom Miss Lacey had aroused to send on errand into Hamilton, regardless of the apparent hopelessness of the case, volunteered the information that he is what we call a 'universal donor'—that is, his blood can fuse with any other type— and offered his own blood to save Salter's life. Dr. Cantrell and I performed the transfusion operation, and Howard Salter will live."

"Baldwin doesn't look as if he has much blood to spare," Dundee commented with a trace of malice, then, ashamed of himself, he added: "It was decent of him."

"Oh, Roger wouldn't thank you for the compliment!" Justine Harlow laughed. "He'd shut you up by saying it was good business to save a patient who can afford a suite in Sunflower Court. But it was decent of him. Perhaps Roger Baldwin is a much better man than he gives himself credit for being."

"Did Salter talk at all? Give any reason for his act?"

"He cursed us feebly for saving his life," the little doctor twinkled. "And insisted that it was better to be dead than insane. I tried to convince him that he was in no danger of losing his mind, but there's no reasoning with a manic depressive in a suicidal mood."

"And yet Miss Hunter told me last night that Howard Salter was greatly improved—that he'd be able to leave soon and get married," Dundee told her, frowning thoughtfully.

"Yes. I confess I was surprised. Dr. Koenig and I both thought he was almost cured."

"What is the cause of his trouble?" Dundee wanted to know.

"A conviction of personal failure," Dr. Harlow answered succinctly. "He is a writer—very well known for his Western stories. But it seems that for two or three years he has hated the sort of book he writes, and wanted to do 'bigger and better' things—serious novels, as he calls them. I understand from Sally Porter, the girl he is engaged to, that his present breakdown was caused by two things. Every house in the publishing business rejected a 'serious' novel Salter had worked on intermittently for two years, and he could not write even the first chapter of a Western story he had contracted to deliver by May first. He was in speechless, black despair when he came here about the middle of April, but oddly enough this is the first time he had tried to carry out his threats to commit suicide."

"Salter has the rooms next to Mrs. Morse, hasn't he?" Dundee asked thoughtfully.

"Why, yes!"

"Rather odd, isn't it? Yesterday Mrs. Morse was considered cured. And yesterday Howard Salter seemed to be almost normal. A rather strange coincidence, isn't it, that both of them should have a serious relapse last night?"

"I don't know what you're talking about!" the girl cried sharply. "I haven't heard a word about Mrs. Morse's relapse. . . . Wait a minute!" and she sprang up from the breakfast table and ran to the telephone table. In a moment she was giving a curt order: "Miss Lacey, send me up the night reports from Sunflower Court immediately!"

While she was waiting, her small body tense with impatience, Dundee asked: "Did Salter have an interview with Dr. Koenig after the doctor's return from his trip?"

To his surprise the little doctor flushed. "I—don't think so. In fact, I'm fairly sure he did not. You see, our patients are a queer lot. They become unreasoningly attached to the psychiatrist who first gains their confidence, and they resent any interference whatever. It happens that Dr. Koenig was out of town when Howard Salter first came, and that he became so devoted to me that he never sought out Dr. Koenig at all."

In fact, he refused to talk at all the one time Dr. Koenig summoned him to his office."

"Have you read Salter's 'serious' novel?" Dundee asked, idly enough.

"No. But Dr. Koenig read it. Sally Porter took charge of the manuscript when Howard came, and just a day or so before Dr. Koenig left on this last trip she brought it in to him and asked his opinion. She hoped it would give the doctor a clew to Howard's mental condition. Doctor read it on the train."

"And his opinion of it?" Dundee asked, strangely eager.

"He said it was terrible," Dr. Harlow answered simply. "Fumbling in style, almost amateurish, erotic and futile."

"I wonder," Dundee said slowly, "if last night, while Sally Porter and Howard Salter were walking on the lawn, they dropped in to ask the doctor his opinion and—he told them what you've told me!"

The girl's eyes widened and she paled, but her voice was quite steady: "If they asked him, he told them the truth. Carl—Dr. Koenig— was almost ruthlessly honest. He found honesty the best medicine in treating manic depressives."

"Strong medicine—in this case!" Dundee commented grimly.

"You don't think—? . . . Come in! ... Thank you, Mary. Yes, that's all."

The gingham frocked girl, who, Dundee guessed, was a maid, handed a sheaf of chart sheets to the little doctor, and scurried out of the room as if terrified.

Dr. Harlow shuffled the sheets until she found the night report on Mrs. Morse. He watched her read, saw her cheeks pale and her lips tighten.

"But—there's something wrong here!" she gasped. "*Mrs. Morse doesn't hear voices!* She never has! It doesn't fit—"

"*Voices?*" Dundee echoed incredulously. "Miss Hunter did not tell me last night that Mrs. Morse claims to have heard voices—"

"Only because Miss Hunter did not know it when she talked with you," the doctor assured him, with a little click of her teeth. "She seems to have told you everything else she ever knew. . . . Mrs. Appleby, Mrs. Morse's night attendant, records that at five o'clock this morning Mrs. Morse awoke, began to cry hysterically, and then confessed that 'the voice of God' had spoken to her; that she had heard His voice quite plainly while Mrs. Appleby was preparing her nine o'clock nourishment. . . . But it's absurd. Mrs. Morse is not subject to auditory hallucinations. Her case was a remarkable one—that of a pseudo split psyche due to a submerged conviction of unpardonable sin. But Dr.

Koenig cured her! I tell you, she was absolutely and definitely cured!"
she insisted, a note of hysteria in her own voice.

"Will you tell me what, exactly, caused Mrs. Morse's illness?"
Dundee asked earnestly. "Believe me, I consider it important that I
know."

"A patient's case history is sacred," the girl reminded him in her
most professional manner.

"Dr. Harlow, do you want Howard Salter to be cured of his fear that
he has suddenly become insane, and Mrs. Morse to be saved from
probable insanity?" Dundee demanded very solemnly.

"Of course! But–"

"I'm afraid there is someone who doesn't want one of those patients
ever to be able to leave!" Dundee interrupted grimly. "I'm a detective,
not a psychiatrist, so it is becoming quite plain to me that Mrs. Morse
*did* hear a voice last night. But it was not the 'voice of God'!"

"I don't understand!"

"And I only have a glimmer," Dundee assured her. "Which is why I
want you to tell me what brought about Mrs. Morse's 'split psyche.' "

"Very well!" she conceded crisply. "Mrs. Morse was born and reared
a Catholic. During adolescence she drifted away from the Church, and
fancied herself almost an agnostic. While still in that state of rebellion
against religion, she married—by civil ceremony only—a non Catholic,
a man who is really an agnostic. They had four children in ten years.
The youngest was two years old when Mrs. Morse began to show
symptoms of mental derangement. Finally, she repudiated her ego
entirely— refused to be herself any longer. She–"

"– referred to herself always in the third person," Dundee
completed the sentence for the doctor.

"Oh, that Hunter!" Dr. Harlow smiled, wrinkling her nose in the
quaint gesture Dundee was beginning to watch for. "Yes.
Subconsciously, you see, she had denied her own identity, *in order to
escape the consequences of what she believed to be an unpardonable sin.*
That sin, of course, was her marriage, which, to the true Catholic she
was at heart, was no marriage, but adultery. Her children born in sin
and not baptized–"

"And all this was entirely in the unconscious?" Dundee asked,
wonderingly.

"Oh, yes! Dr. Koenig dug deep, in psychoanalysis, before he found
the root of the mental evil," Dr. Harlow answered, pride in her dead
hero enriching her beautiful voice. "He had a long talk with Mrs. Morse
on Tuesday, then sent for Mr. Morse. You see, her cure was in her
husband's power. Dr. Koenig asked him if, to save his wife, he would be
willing to remarry her, with a priest officiating and blessing the union,
and then have his children baptized."

"And what did Morse say?" Dundee demanded tensely.

"He said he would get the Pope himself to marry them, if it would save his wife's mind."

"Then why did Mrs. Morse hear 'the voice of God' crying to her that it was 'Too late! Too late!'?" Dundee leaned close to inquire, his blue eyes gleaming with excitement. "For I'm sure Mrs. Morse will tell you that those are the words she heard. Mrs. Appleby told me last night— even then I was oddly disturbed by Mrs. Morse's strange relapse—that the woman would tell her nothing, would only moan, 'Too late! Too late!' . . . Remember! *Her husband had left her only a few minutes before!*"

"Yes—so the report says," Dr. Harlow agreed, her voice dragging. "But Mr. Morse is a good man—" she protested despairingly.

"I'm afraid Dr. Koenig was right. You're a credulous child, who lets her heart run away with her head," Dundee smiled. "By the way, do you have any idea why Dr. Koenig made the notation, 'Call Morse,' on his desk calendar?"

"Yes. He made the notation yesterday morning when he was talking to me about Mrs. Morse," Dr. Harlow told him, and Dundee saw her cheeks grow paler and the gray green eyes widen behind their spectacles. "You see, the Morse baby has died since Mrs. Morse came here, and she has never been told, because Dr. Koenig feared the effect it might have on her mind. He suddenly remembered about the baby yesterday, and tried to call Mr. Morse then. But his secretary reported that he was out of town on business, and would not return until today. So Dr. Koenig wrote that notation to remind himself to call Mr. Morse today, in order to warn him against telling his wife until she is stronger."

"And Morse visited his wife last night!" Dundee reminded her grimly.

"But what you're thinking is fantastic!" Dr. Harlow protested vehemently. "I tell you, he is a good man, and a devoted husband! It's absolutely criminal of you to accuse him of telling her of the unbaptized baby's death, then of sneaking under her window to wail 'Too late! Too late!,' in order to drive her crazy again! Call me a credulous fool if you like!" and she stamped her foot, "but I know–"

"Do you happen to know *this?*" Dundee interrupted gently but firmly. "Did Mrs. Morse, rich in her own *right*, marry a poor man as well as an agnostic?"

"I do not!" she flared.

"It should be rather easy to find out," Dundee reflected aloud, as he rose to leave.

"But what has all this to do with Howard Salter?" she detained him.

"That, with your permission," Dundee assured her gravely, "is what I am going to find out. As I said before, I am a detective, not a psychiatrist, but I have a hunch that I am going to be the Miracle Man in person this morning."

"Exactly what do you mean?" the girl demanded.

"Only that, as one poor devil of a patient calling on another, I'm going to have a pleasant little visit with Howard Salter. After that visit, you will either find your manic depressive quite cured of his fear of insanity, or—he may be fervently wishing he had succeeded last night!"

"I forbid—" the little doctor began, imperiously.

"I really don't think you'd better," Dundee interrupted gently, and, as she stood staring dumbly after him, he strode from the room.

It was still too early—not yet eight o'clock—for patients to be out and on the grounds. The only persons Dundee encountered, as he left the main building and set off across the lawn to Sunflower Court, were the two plainclothesmen Captain Strawn had left to guard the suite of offices in which the murder had been committed. He had already spoken to both of them, and had learned that the only disturbance during the night had occurred when Dr. Cantrell and Miss Lacey had asked permission to enter the former's office shortly after two o'clock in the morning, for the purpose of getting instruments needed in dealing with the attempted suicide.

His parley with Miss Doty, the day nurse in charge of Sunflower Court, was brief but effective. Very meekly, the henna haired, blue eyed girl led the way to Suite E, the door of which was opened by a male attendant.

"This is Mr. Dundee, Roy," she whispered. "He wants to have a private talk with your patient."

"I'm afraid you'll have to do most of the talking, sir," the attendant deprecated respectfully, aware obviously of Dundee's status. "He ain't said 'Yea,' 'Nay' or 'Go to hell!' since I come on duty."

"How is he physically?"

"Oh, fine! Old Baldwin's pint of blood has put roses in his cheeks. Pulse fine, temperature normal."

And indeed Howard Salter did not look like a man who had been snatched from the jaws of death only a few hours before. His long body was not thin, and there was a faint, natural color in his swarthy, handsome young face. Only his gray eyes, which gazed dully and without surprise, at the detective, gave a hint of the strain through which he had passed.

"Good morning, Mr. Salter," Dundee began, with the winning diffidence he knew so well how to assume. "I'm a new patient here, and sort of restless, so I thought I'd drop in—"

The man in the bed closed his eyes and his nostrils flared, but to Dundee's relief he did not order him out of the room.

"I wouldn't butt in on a sick man like this," Dundee went on, awkwardly and apologetically, "but there's something on my mind, and I hoped you might be able to tell me whether I'm going cuckoo or–"

"What's that?" the sick novelist interrupted sharply, his eyes blazing open.

"Miss Hunter kidded me and said she guessed it was high time I came here," Dundee went on guilelessly. "She said I'd had an 'auditory hallucination' or some rot like that, and got me scared stiff–"

"What the devil are you talking about?" the sick man almost shouted, raising himself upon an elbow. "Are you trying to say you heard something queer last night?"

"Either I actually heard a voice, or I belong in 'Ten,' " Dundee laughed awkwardly. "I thought maybe if I could find somebody else that had heard the same thing–"

"Was it a voice, like a Banshee wail, moaning 'Too late! Too late!'?" the sick man demanded feverishly. "For God's sake, man–"

"By George! You heard it, too, and I'm not crazy!" Dundee pretended to exult, slapping his knee joyously.

The novelist fell back upon his pillows. A brighter color glowed in his cheeks and his eyes lost their dullness, sparkled with new life and hope. "And I'm not crazy, either, it seems!" he gasped. "Man! You're a lifesaver, whoever you are! I heard that damned voice. I'd just gone to sleep. Had a bromide, you know," the writer went on, almost babbling in the blessedness of relief. "It was a long drawn out moan–"

"Would you say it was a man's voice or a woman's?" Dundee interrupted.

"God knows. It sounded like nothing human," the novelist assured him. "Just those two words, over and over, 'Too late! Too late!' I'd hate to tell you what I thought it was–"

" 'The voice of God,' perhaps?" Dundee dared interrupt again.

"Something like that," the other grinned. "I thought it was a message meant for no other ears but mine. 'Too late,' it said to me, "for you to write a great book, Howard Salter. 'Too late,' even, for me to write the popular trash I've been grinding out for years. 'Too late'— because my mind was tottering, was going even as I listened. ... I tried to kill myself. Didn't fancy being a raving lunatic locked up in "Ten,' " he added simply.

"You and me both!" Dundee agreed, still in the role of awkward new patient. "Not even to make an interesting case for the Big Doctor, as they call him. ... What sort of a chap is Koenig anyway, old man?"

He watched the novelist narrowly, as he put the apparently innocent question, but the now happy gray eyes did not change expression.

"One of the best," Salter assured him heartily. "But I'm Doctor Harlow's patient. She's a peach, and got a head on her like old Socrates himself. I do want to see Koenig today, however, if they'll let me up, and I feel like a million dollars now. Miss Porter, the girl I'm engaged to—you'll be meeting Sally—told me last night that she'd given the Big Doctor my novel to read, and I want to chin with him about it. If he says it's rot, I'll take it standing, and begin over again! . . . Come in often, Dundee. Glad to see you any time."

Dundee shook hands. The man in the bed had answered the one question he had not dared to ask him. Howard Salter had not talked with Dr. Koenig last night. Moreover, Salter did not know that the great psychiatrist was dead. So sure was he of these two things that Dundee unhesitatingly shook hands with the man he had "healed."

# CHAPTER 11

As Dundee stepped into the patio out of the tiny hall of Suite E, he almost bumped into Salter's attendant, carrying a tray which held nothing but a pint bottle of milk and a glass.

"If this is Mr. Salter's breakfast, you'd better add a couple of eggs, some bacon and a stack of toast," the detective advised blithely. "Your patient says he feels like a million dollars now, and he had a hungry gleam in his eye when I left."

"Thought you was a detective, not a doctor," the attend ant chuckled. "Say, mister, Dr. Harlow just phoned over that she wants to see you right away. She's in her private office on the second floor of the main building."

Grinning at this evidence that the little doctor had her share of the feminine vice, curiosity, Dundee set out to obey the summons. But as he crossed the front porch of Sunflower Court he determined to let her wait a bit while he studied the scene of last night's minor mystery— "the voice of God."

Whoever, with fiendish cruelty, had wailed those sinister words in a sepulchral, well disguised voice, must have stood or crouched beneath the windows of the adjoining bedrooms of Suites D and E, the first occupied by Mrs. Morse, the second by Howard Salter. Sunflower Court, he discovered, was enclosed on all sides but the front with a high box hedge. Inside the hedge there was a narrow cement walk, bordered on both sides by grass and flowers. The hedge ended opposite the front corner of Mrs. Morse's bedroom. The nocturnal wailer must have bided his time and slipped inside the hedge; must have crouched beneath the window of the patient chosen to be the victim of his cruel plot. Who was that chosen victim? For surely the plotter had intended that only one person should hear and be terrified into hysteria or into a relapse into insanity. An audience of *two* patients would defeat his purpose— had, in fact, defeated it. For, just as Howard Salter had been "cured" by the assurance that other ears had heard that voice, so would Mrs. Morse, Dundee hoped and believed, be restored to sanity, if not to happiness. Yes, it was quite clear that the plotter had felt sure, before he sent that sepulchral wail floating through open windows, that only *one* patient would hear it. And, logically, that patient was Mrs. Morse. Her light was on. The watcher could see that she was alone; knew, possibly, that her nurse was in the kitchen. On the other hand, Salter's light was out. By his own account, he was asleep when the wailing voice had startled him into wakefulness and the conviction that his mind was tottering. Had that sinister plotter beneath the window seen

Salter strolling on the lawn with his fiancee? Had he counted on the fact that Salter was still out? Or had he known merely that a movie was being shown that evening, an attraction that could be counted upon to lure all of Mayfield's guests into the O. T. Shop? All, that is, who were able to attend— *except Mrs. Morse.* How had he known of that exception? And the logical answer to that was: *because he had just left her in her room.*

"I'm getting as acrobatic at jumping to conclusions as Captain Strawn himself," Dundee gibed mentally, but he could find no reason to climb down from the height his speculations had carried him to.

Very softly, professional curiosity being stronger than his reluctance to play eavesdropper, the detective crept along the inside of the hedge until he stood squarely opposite the first of Mrs. Morse's bedroom windows. The shade was up and the silk curtains pushed aside to admit the brilliant morning sun.

His view unobstructed, Dundee gazed eagerly into the luxurious room. The bed was placed along the wall near the window, so that the patient, propped on pillows, presented her profile to the eavesdropper. Dundee caught his breath with admiration and pity, then held it lest he make the slightest sound. It was like looking upon a life size picture representing "The Grieving Madonna." Long, rippling black hair framed a face of extraordinary purity and pallor. The thin, white fingers of the woman's beautiful hands were laced to support her chin, and to receive, like a chalice, the tears that strained slowly through the thick, long, black lashes of her closed eyes. Her eyes would be black, too, Dundee told himself; large, and heavy with sorrow. She seemed neither old nor young— an ageless, heartbreakingly beautiful incarnation of Motherhood and Despair.

When he had escaped without betraying himself, Dundee struck off hurriedly across the lawn. Thank God, part of her burden could be lifted. One of her unbaptized children was dead, but soon Dr. Harlow could convince her that God had not spoken out of the night to condemn her.

Three or four of the patients, ignorant of the tragedy, had come out for early morning air and sunshine. An extremely thin, gray haired woman was idly slashing at croquet balls with a mallet. A young man, who seemed to be partially paralyzed, was staggering along on tiptoe, eyes bulging out of a drawn, distorted face. A very large, hideously ugly woman, with thin, greasy blonde hair, crimson cheeks and thick, wet lips, was squatting before a flower bed, wantonly tearing the blooms from their stalks. As Dundee passed near, she looked up and laughed— a horrible peal of shrill notes that made the detective's scalp tingle.

"She ain't laughing at you, Buddy! She's laughing at life. . . . Ain't you, Rosie?"

It was a blithe voice, and a vaguely familiar one. Dundee turned toward the driveway, and saw two men crossing it. He paused until they had almost reached him, then took a step or two to meet them.

"Mr. Day, isn't it? I believe I saw you last night."

"Sure. 'Happy' Day in person. I've even got a theme song all my own. . . . Say, Buddy, I didn't catch your name. . . . Dundee? Scotch Irish, ain't you? . . . Meet my pal, Archie Webster."

Turning from the plump, jolly attendant, Dundee shook hands with the man he had heard so much about the night before, and who, apparently, had lost no time in getting out of Ten,' the locked ward. Yes, young Webster was amazingly good looking, he decided. Tall, broad shouldered, with an athlete's waist, as yet unspoiled by the liquor he liked too well. Light brown hair, thick and curling back from a handsome brow. Merry eyes of a clear leaf brown, the whites only slightly bloodshot from last night's spree. Firm fleshed, ruddy cheeks, lightly tanned. A wide mouth, smiling to show splendid teeth.

"Happy is being tactful, Dundee," Archie Webster laughed. "The horrid truth is that I'm a patient just out of Ten,' and it's Happy's job to see that I don't get caught by the Demon Rum. . . . Haven't got a flask on your hip, have you? I could do with a tastier pick me up than the Eno's salts highball they gave me over in Ten' this morning."

"Afraid I haven't," Dundee answered, "but maybe your bootlegger will be around again today."

"My bootlegger?—*again today?*" young Webster repeated, in a puzzled voice. Then he laughed, a frank roar of mirth. "You don't mean to tell me Fatty was a bootlegger, and I—*I!*—didn't tumble! Well, Happy, that's one on me! That pint he slipped me was just a sample, and I didn't realize it—"

"Perhaps I'm the one that was mistaken," Dundee interrupted ruefully. "If so, my apologies to your friend—"

"No friend of mine!" Webster cut in, still laughing. "Never saw him before last night. Don't even know his name. But I don't look a gift horse in the mouth, so when he slipped me what was left of the pint after we'd both had a pull at it, I invited him to see the movies with me, no questions asked. Matter of fact, he was asking enough questions for both of us."

"Curious about the nuts, I guess," Happy Day chuckled. "All visitors are. But who did this chap come to see, if it wasn't you, Archie?"

"Damned if I know," Webster answered, serious for the moment. "I was strolling on the lawn with Enid—that's Miss Rambler, Dundee; the belle of Mayfield—when up walks this fat bird, and Enid runs like a rabbit. Afraid of strangers, the funny kid! Well, he asked me if I'd like a nip, and I said, 'Do I look crazy?' So we had a drink and then he began to ask all sorts of questions about Enid, because she'd run away, I suppose. I wasn't putting out much, but he hung around, and finally we went into the O. T. Shop to see the movies. I guess he'd seen 'Manslaughter' before; anyway, he ducked out before the picture was finished "

"Probably to get better acquainted with Miss Rambler," Dundee suggested.

"Say! That's a thought! Come to think of it, she had left just before that fat bozo ducked! Well, the fat old chaser!" Webster exclaimed in deep disgust. "I'd have hunted him up and socked him one, if I had suspected that was his game."

"As it was, I suppose you just sat tight and enjoyed the show," Dundee suggested craftily.

"Well, no, I ducked, too," Webster confessed, with a rueful grin. "That pint of the best was burning a hole in my hip pocket. Unfortunately, I couldn't find anybody to share it with me, so it landed me in Ten."

"How was that?" Dundee asked sympathetically.

Webster grinned. "When I get likkered up, I get notions in my head. And last night it struck me all of a sudden that Sam Rowan hadn't been behaving exactly like a buddy of mine—not speaking, and all that sort of thing. So I called him for it, and he swung a mean one at my jaw. If I hadn't been staggering already, that old bag o' bones couldn't have even jarred me. As it was, he knocked me flat. And it was me they put in Ten," he added in an injured voice, but with a gleam of mirth in his eyes. "Rowan's all right. My fault. . . . Well, cheerio, old sport! Glad to have you here. Not a bad hole. The Big Doctor's a great guy. . . . And the *little doctor*—Oh, baby!"

"Come along and get your hydro now, Archie," the attendant urged. "See you later, Dundee. . . . Play bridge? Poker?"

"Both," Dundee assured him.

"Then we'll be seeing you," 'Happy' Day promised blithely, linking a chummy arm in that of his patient.

Hardly the type to commit murder, Dundee reflected, as he watched Archie Webster swing jauntily along the driveway. A likeable youngster in spite of, or perhaps because of, his frank weaknesses. But as the detective continued on his way to the second floor of the main building his mind was more engrossed with the problem of the fat unknown, his unexplained visit, his persistent interest in Enid Rambler, and his disappearance. Well, Strawn had an excellent machinery for searching for mysterious strangers. And he could undoubtedly get an accurate description from Webster, when he questioned that unregenerate young man. . . .

"I thought you were never coming!" Justine Harlow scolded from the top landing of the stairway.

"The time seemed long because you're eaten up with curiosity," Dundee scolded in turn. "How about giving me a job here as your assistant? I've already cured one of your patients of a neurosis, and can guarantee to do the same for another."

"You mean Salter—?" she demanded, her gray green eyes widening.

"I mean that Salter heard 'the voice of God,' too," he elucidated. "I mean further that he now knows he was not the only one who heard it, and that it was not the voice of God, but of a devil in human form. . . . Pardon the melodrama, Doctor, but I'm feeling rather strongly on the subject, and I'll be happier when I know that you've taken the same good news to poor Mrs. Morse. ... Of course, in a sense, it is 'too late' for her, since her baby died unbaptized—"

"But he didn't!" she cried, and her voice shook with emotion. "That's why I sent for you. Mr. Morse is here now with his mother in law, Mrs. Prade. Mrs. Prade is a devout Catholic, of course, and it seems that she smuggled a priest into the Morse home and had the little fellow baptized before he died. Mr. Morse didn't know about it. Mrs. Prade thought he'd object, you see—"

"And they're here now?" Dundee interrupted eagerly. "I want a look at Morse. Why are they here so early?"

"I'll let you talk to him," Dr. Harlow offered, and led the way into a small but comfortably furnished office opposite her apartment.

"Mrs. Prade, Mr. Morse, this is Mr. Dundee, of the district attorney's office," the doctor announced, and the detective found himself shaking hands, first with a stout, elderly woman, then with a heavy, middle aged man. Morse, Dundee thought, might have posed for an artist as the typical American business man. Neither handsome nor homely; strong, rather heavy features; shrewd but kindly brown eyes; thick, smoothly brushed gray hair, quietly expensive suit of brown homespun.

"Glad to meet you, Mr. Dundee," Morse said, clipping his words like a busy executive. "The doctor here tells me you've stumbled upon something that closely concerns my wife."

"I'm afraid I have," Dundee admitted seriously. "But first, will you tell me how you happen to be calling so early this morning?"

"For two reasons, sir," Morse answered curtly. "Last night when I visited my wife—the first visit I have had with her since she has become—well, herself again, she began to ask all sorts of questions about the children. On my previous visits she never mentioned them. That was part of her—trouble. She acted as if they did not belong to her, as if she had no responsibility for them."

"I understand," Dundee assured him. "I have heard Dr. Koenig's diagnosis of her trouble."

The big man touched his forehead with a fine linen handkerchief. "It has been pretty bad, sir, but thank God the doctor got at the root of the trouble."

"I always did say—" the mother in law began importantly.

"Yes, Mother, you did," Morse agreed. "Well, last night when she asked about the children I knew she was really cured. But when she wanted to know all about the baby " his voice broke, and his mother in law crossed herself, facile tears springing into her eyes.

"You told her he was dead?" Dundee asked.

"No. I put her off as best I could, but she *sensed* some thing was wrong—mighty wrong," Morse told him, again touching his forehead with the linen square. "She asked me pointblank if he was dead, but I put her off again, told her he was 'asleep that minute.' But I was sure she wasn't fooled. It's hard to fool a mother, sir," he added sententiously. "But for my sake she played the game. Didn't get hysterical or anything like that. But I made up my mind to speak to Koenig and get him to tell her the truth. I thought it best for her to stay here until she'd got over the shock."

"So you called on the doctor last night?" Dundee asked, tense with excitement.

"No. The doctor was in, but I could tell he was busy, and I didn't feel much like waiting," Morse answered. "Besides, I couldn't help hearing and it embarrassed me—"

"Tell me exactly what you heard or saw!" Dundee demanded sternly.

"We—ell, it wasn't anything much," the big man deprecated, flushing, "but that's the second reason I dropped in so early this morning. I thought it just might have something to do with what happened here last night—"

"Go on!" Dundee almost shouted.

"Well, Miss Hunter had told me the doctor was in his office, so I went to the reception room," Morse began reluctantly. "It was then close on to nine o'clock. I was just about to knock when I heard a woman's voice. I thought it was a patient, of course, and I suppose it was. Anyway, she was crying and talking at the same time—"

"Could you distinguish what they said?" Dundee urged, as the narrator paused.

"Not a great deal of it. It seemed like he was trying to get rid of the woman, and she didn't want to go," Morse answered slowly. "I heard her say something like: 'I won't leave you! You can't make me!' And the doctor tried to pacify her. I heard him say, 'But my darling girl!' and then the woman began to carry on pretty bad–" Again Morse's voice dragged to an embarrassed halt.

"Did you hear anything else they said?" Dundee prodded.

"Well, the girl said something about he'd made her love him, and now he hated her, and she could kill him when he looked at her like that," the man continued uncomfortably. "Just the sort of thing a woman will say when she's all worked up, and not mean a thing by it."

Dundee glanced at Justine Harlow. If she had died while the man was talking, her face could not have been more rigid, more ghastly in its pallor.

"And the doctor?" the detective asked dutifully, but his voice was flat and colorless. He was not enjoying his job at that moment. "Did you hear his reply? And did he call the woman by name?"

"No. Or if he did, I did not hear the name," Morse assured him earnestly. "Once he said, "Child! Child!,' as if he was sorry for her and sort of hopeless. And fond of her, too. Then when she began to pound him on the chest with her fists—or that's what it sounded like—I tiptoed out. I was feeling pretty uncomfortable."

"Would you recognize that voice—the woman's voice, I mean—if you heard it again?" Dundee asked, his eyes again resting upon the blighted face of the young doctor.

The man shook his head. He seemed relieved to be able to answer: "I'm afraid I wouldn't, sir. You see, she was crying all the time she was talking, and I'm sure her voice was a lot shriller than it would normally be."

Justine Harlow was not simply relieved. She looked as if she had signed a new lease on life.

"I see," Dundee commented grimly, and relapsed into a thoughtful silence, his blue eyes narrowed to slits.

The mother in law shifted in her chair, which creaked under her weight. "So my son in law dropped in at my house last night, to give me the news of Lora–"

"What time did Mr. Morse arrive at your house?" Dundee roused himself from his reverie to interrupt.

"Why, let me see," the woman ruminated. Then, eagerly: "I know! The Melody Boys were just finishing their program on the radio, and they go on at ten o'clock every night—I wouldn't miss 'em for a farm—so it must have been about twenty minutes after ten when Roland walked in."

"You live in Hamilton?" Dundee asked.

"Oh, yes, sir. On Maple Drive," she confirmed proudly, naming one of the most fashionable streets in the suburbs of the city.

"I drove around for an hour before I called on my mother in law," Roland Morse volunteered, but with no trace of belligerence. "I was pretty badly upset by my visit with Lora—my wife. Afraid the news of the baby's death might unhinge her poor brain again, and yet I realized it couldn't be kept from her any longer–"

"So the poor boy came to talk it over with me," the mother in law cut in. "Of course I was kind of surprised to see him–"

"Then Mr. Morse is not a frequent visitor?" Dundee interrupted swiftly.

The woman flushed and bridled. Morse's heavy cheeks turned a dull red.

"Well, no, sir, things being like they were," Mrs. Prade admitted. "I never have held with mixed marriages, even when a priest performs the ceremony. To my notion Lora and Roland aren't married at all–"

"Then you did not give your consent to the union?" Dundee broke in.

"Certainly not! But there wasn't any stopping Lora, her with her own money and all," the woman answered. "I always did say her grandfather made a terrible mistake, leaving her all that money with no strings tied to it–"

"Then Mrs. Morse is a very rich woman in her own right?" Dundee asked softly.

"Too rich!" Mrs. Morse's mother snapped. "It turned her head–"

"Now, Mother!" Roland Morse pleaded, the flush mounting to his iron gray hair.

"I'm only answering the gentleman's questions," his mother in law retorted acidly. "I said last night I'd for give you, when you and Lora are married in the Church, and I'll stick to it. But I'm no hypocrite. You're too old for Lora, and living in sin with you drove my poor girl crazy–"

Morse shrugged helplessly, and his eyes appealed to Dundee.

"I understand, Mrs. Prade," the detective began, coming briskly to the rescue, "that Mr. Morse called on you last night to tell you that your daughter had been almost miraculously restored to her right mind by Dr. Koenig, but that he feared the effect of the news of the baby's death. Is that right?"

"He wanted me to help him out," the mother in law answered. "And when he said he was more than willing to marry Lora in the Church, I told him that I'd put one over on him by having poor little Rollie baptized by Father Ryan. For a minute he looked pretty mad—yes, you did, Roland Morse!—but it didn't take him a minute to realize that I'd saved Lora from losing her mind all over again, and he was man enough to thank me. I told him I was coming here the first thing this morning and tell my poor girl the truth. A mother's love to comfort her and help her bear—"

"Just say to her," Dundee interrupted, with strange emphasis, his eyes upon Roland Morse, "that it is not *'too late! Too late!'*"

# CHAPTER 12

"I FEEL," Dundee told himself, with a rueful grin, as he strolled out of the main building of Mayfield Sanitarium, "like a Boy Scout with a holiday coming to him. Only eight o'clock, and I've already done two good deeds today."

But he paused on the lowest step of the three leading from the porch to the driveway, a frown banishing the grin. Was he giving too much time to the Morse mystery, and thereby neglecting the major mystery of the psychiatrist's murder? But "the voice of God" intrigued and tormented him. Roland Morse had had ample time to wail sepulchrally and disastrously under his wife's windows—and incidentally beneath Howard Salter's windows; pay that first actual or fictitious visit to the reception room; then bide his time until the mysterious and importunate woman visitor had left Koenig's office; then return and—

"But why the devil should he murder the doctor?" Dundee puzzled. "That fiendish wailing was amply sufficient to accomplish his purpose—or would have been, if Salter had not heard the fatal words, too. . . . Motive enough, God knows, if Morse *is* the schemer I'm making him out. A wife rich in her own right, who conveniently goes crazy enough for the courts to adjudge her incompetent and appoint her husband guardian of her person and her property. . . . The old lady let *that* cat out of the bag! . . . But why murder the doctor? Unless, of course, Morse's whole yarn about the sobbing female in Koenig's office is an out and out lie, the truth being that Koenig, on his way to pay a professional call on Mrs. Morse, caught Morse in his wailing act, and—"

But the detective's frown deepened. "That won't wash," he told himself disgustedly. "Leaves too many things unexplained. If Koenig caught Morse in the wailing act, why didn't he immediately reassure Mrs. Morse? And what did Morse do between nine o'clock and nine forty five, when Koenig was killed? Furthermore, would Koenig go on calmly working at his typewriter and let a dangerous man like Morse wander about the office until he maneuvered himself into a position to kill him? . . . No, Bonnie, my lad, *that* won't wash! But I'd wager a fortune, if I had it, that 'the voice of God' is mixed up in this murder—somehow!"

He was about to cross the driveway when he caught sight of a boy in overalls industriously polishing the hood of one of the parked cars—a trim little coupe next to his own roadster, which was sadly in need of the youth's ministrations.

"Neat little car," Dundee remarked idly, as he readied into his pocket for a dollar bill. "How about shining up my boat, young man?"

"Sure thing!" the boy beamed, his eyes on the bill. "Soon as I finish with Dr. Harlow's. ... I like to keep it looking like new—"

"It *is* new, isn't it?" Dundee asked, stepping upon the running board and peering in at the speedometer, which showed a mileage of 9,066.

"Had it nearly a year, she has," the boy informed him proudly. "I take care of it for her—gasoline, oil, tires, and everything. Had to have the crankcase drained yesterday. *She'd* never remember to, not even with that sticker on the dashboard—"

Suddenly Dundee leaned farther into the car, his eyes fixed incredulously upon the oil change sticker the boy was referring to. He read: "Drain oil at 10,055 miles," and, beneath, the name of the garage which had applied the sticker.

From experience, Dundee knew that a car owner was adjured, by all that was holy in motordom, to drain his crankcase every thousand miles.

"Well, young man, you won't have to worry about that crankcase for another thousand miles," the detective said casually, as he withdrew his head.

The boy peered in his turn, then, grinning at his own conscientiousness, he corrected his new client: "Gotta change again after 989 miles. She's drove eleven miles since yesterday."

"Right you are!" Dundee agreed heartily, but there was no satisfaction or triumph behind the words. "Give my bus a good rub, won't you? I'm afraid you'll have to use a little elbow grease on it."

So the little doctor had been lying when she said she had taken a long drive the night before! That innocent-looking sticker on the dashboard had betrayed her. Eleven miles in two hours!

Dundee's almost stunned brain had hardly begun to wrestle with all the implications of Justine Harlow's lie when he crossed the threshold of Sunflower Court. Lurline Doty looked up from her desk and cocked her hennaed head coquettishly.

"Aren't we the dreat big sheik, though?" she accused him playfully. "A certain boyful young lady is just dying to see you. . . . 'Course I haven't breathed a word about who you really are "

"Then don't begin now," Dundee interrupted rather curtly, for his stomach never reacted kindly toward baby talk. "You mean Miss Rambler, I suppose? . . . May I see her now?"

"You may!" The nurse bit off the words and buttoned her mouth into a thin streak of rouge.

"Ni—ize nursie!" Dundee forced himself to say in a coaxing voice as he passed her, and was rewarded by fluttering eyelids and smile curved lips. Silly, he told himself, to antagonize anyone who might be of help. . . .

A jolly looking, black haired little nurse answered his knock upon the patio door of Suite C.

"You're Mr. Dundee, aren't you?" she asked in a low voice, which sank into a whisper after he had admitted his identity. "She doesn't know a thing yet about Dr. Koenig. The poor child's been begging me for an hour to send for him. . . . Yes, Miss Rambler! It's Mr. Dundee. . . ,.. She's been asking for you, too, sir. . . . This way."

The detective led the way into the sitting room—a larger and even more luxurious one than his own, and discreetly disappeared into the bedroom beyond, closing the door softly.

"Do I make a satisfactory picture of an invalid?" the girl stretched upon the big couch demanded.

Dundee cocked his head and an eyebrow as he pretended to give serious consideration to the question, to which there could be but one answer. The girl, laughing, touched fingertips to her gleaming chestnut hair which was parted in the middle and arranged in loose curls that hung to her shoulders and mingled with the white ostrich feather trimming on her peacock blue silk robe—a blue that could not match that of her eyes for brilliance and beauty. The bandaged ankle was hidden beneath a flowered Spanish shawl.

"You'll do," he told her, as if grudgingly. Then: "What are those doing here so soon?" and he pointed to a pair of crutches propped against the foot of the couch.

"Resting quietly, thank you," she smiled at him. "And giving me a warm sense of security. They tell me that I can hobble away, even if I can't run. Sweet old crutches! I wouldn't go to sleep until Miss Lacey dug up a pair for me last night."

"Still feeling fugitive?" Dundee grinned.

"Off and on," she shrugged. Then words came tumbling out, as she raised herself upon an elbow and fixed him with her luminous blue eyes: "Listen, Mr. Dundee! I don't *want* to go! I want to stay right here *forever*, but I may have to go, and I want you to promise to help me—"

"To run away?" Dundee asked gently, ashamed of the role he was forced to play. "Hadn't you better tell me all about it?"

The girl stopped smiling and a wary look came into the deep blue eyes. "Oh!" she shrugged. "Just call it a— complex. A very popular word around here. . . . Tell me! Did you have an interview with Dr. Koenig last night?"

"I saw him," Dundee evaded, watching her intently. "But it was Dr. Harlow who admitted me."

"Isn't she a darling?" Enid Rambler exclaimed enthusiastically. "*She* is my friend. . . . But what did you think of Koenig?"

"A great man, I've been told," Dundee replied care fully. "Do you like him?"

The girl dropped her eyes, her fingers nervously plucking at the ostrich feathers about her throat. "I hardly know him," she said in a low voice, "but he looks—fascinating. And I *thought* he looked kind, but–" Her voice broke, and she was silent for a long minute. Then, lifting her head, the blue eyes met Dundee's bravely through a film of tears. "He isn't kind. He's cruel. He's going to—to have me taken away–"

"But, if you want to leave anyway," Dundee began, when her voice had choked so that she could not go on.

"At least I'd be *free* if I ran away!" the girl interrupted passionately. "I *won't* be locked up—Oh, my God! Who's that?"

Her terror was a sickening thing to see, but before Dundee could find words she was sitting up and clutching at his coat sleeve. "If it's Dr. Koenig, would you mind leaving us alone? I'm going to get down on my knees to him–"

There was the sound of a door opening, footsteps in the little hall. Then into the living room strode Captain Strawn of the Homicide Squad. At sight of his uniform the girl uttered a strangled cry, then collapsed against the pillows, her face as rigid and white as it would be in death.

Dundee turned his back upon the pitiful spectacle, and, winking at his one time chief, demanded indignantly: "What's wrong, Officer? What do you want here?"

Strawn took his cue. "Who are you, sir? . . . One of the patients? . . . Well, then," he commanded sternly, "stay where you are, and answer when you're spoken to. ... Now, young lady! Get a hold of yourself, and speak lively. Your name is Rambler, ain't it?"

The girl's eyes flew open and stared incredulously at the police officer. After a moment she answered, and her voice was stronger than Dundee had expected it to be.

"Yes! Enid Rambler. . . . And who are you?"

"I'm Captain John Strawn, Chief of the Homicide Squad of the Hamilton Police Department," Strawn in formed her grimly.

"Homicide?" she breathed, and fell back upon her pillows, her eyelids closing.

"Don't like the sound of that word, eh?" Strawn gibed. "Well, maybe you like the sound of *murder* a little better!"

"I say, Captain!" Dundee protested sincerely, and he did not wink this time. "Miss Rambler is not well, and I beg you "

"All right, all right! Keep your shirt on!" Strawn growled. "Now, young woman, I haven't any time to lose. Dr. Carl Koenig was murdered in his office last night–"

"*Dr. Koenig!*" The words brought the girl upright. Her blue eyes seemed to be starting from her head, but, to Dundee's amazed bewilderment, the expression that slowly dawned in them was relief. "But what—why—I don't see what *I* have to do with it "

"That's what I'm here to find out!" Strawn cut in sternly. "*After* he was murdered last night, *you* ran away from the sanitarium—"

The girl's laugh was hard for Dundee to bear. "And you're here because you think *I—I* killed him?" she cried hysterically. "Why, that's funny! Oh!" And her jangling laughter filled the room.

"Funny as hell!" Strawn agreed grimly. "Come on in, Brede!"

The anemic looking young man who held the job of police stenographer sidled into the room from the little hall, notebook in hand.

"I want a statement from you, young woman," Strawn told the girl, "and I'll warn you that we're already in possession of a good many facts about your movements last night, so you'd better talk fast and talk straight."

"What do you want to know?" Enid Rambler asked, almost coolly.

"Your movements from nine o'clock last night until you were brought back here, *after trying to escape.*"

Only then did the girl seem to realize the seriousness of the situation. The flush which had risen with her laughter died out of her cheeks. "From nine o'clock?" she repeated, as if sparring for time. "Why, at nine o'clock I was in the O. T. Shop, attending a motion picture show for the patients. I left when the feature picture was about half finished—"

"Why?" Strawn shot at her.

The girl drew a quick breath. "Because I was—nervous. And I didn't like the picture—"

"Because it was named 'Manslaughter'?" Strawn suggested.

"I didn't like it; that's all!" Enid Rambler retorted crisply. "I'm here for nerves, and I became too nervous to sit still any longer. I left the shop about half past nine, and tried to find someone who had authority to give me a dose of bromide. I got it every night until about a week ago, but Dr. Harlow wants me to try to sleep without it. Miss Caplan wasn't in the chartroom, and I didn't remember until later that she was watching the pictures. I wandered around the hall and living room of the main building for ten or fifteen minutes, then I went upstairs to see if Dr. Harlow was in. She wasn't, so I—"

"Why didn't you ask Koenig?" Strawn suggested sarcastically, as the girl's voice dragged to a pause.

"I—I thought of doing so," Enid told him slowly, reluctantly. "But— I knew he was busy—"

"How did you know that? You saw him, eh?" Strawn pounced.

"I told you I wandered around the hall," the girl answered defiantly. "When I first came into the hall from outside—I left the shop by the back door and walked around the main building—I saw him sitting at his desk. But his back was to the door and he was typing. I thought I could find someone else. Later, after I'd failed to find Dr. Harlow and had tried to walk off my nervousness–"

"Where did you walk?" Strawn cut in.

"Down to the big gates on Willow Creek Drive, and back. I walked slowly till I got to the gates, then I made up my mind to interrupt Dr. Koenig, so I hurried back. , But as soon as I entered the main hall I saw that his door was closed, although the light still showed through the transom."

"That was about what time?" Strawn demanded.

"I don't know," the girl answered, frowning. "Let me think. ... I looked at the clock in hall right after I'd left the picture show, and it was a minute or two after half past nine. I didn't notice the time when I returned to ask Dr. Koenig for the bromide, but it must have been about ten minutes to ten."

"Did you knock on his door?" Strawn asked, skepticism writ large on his face.

"No. I supposed he was interviewing a new patient, or an old one, and I did not dream of disturbing him by knocking."

"Did you *hear* anything to make you think he was busy with a patient?" Strawn asked craftily.

"Why, no—" the girl faltered. "I just saw the door was shut–"

"Come clean, Miss Rambler!" Strawn interrupted with sudden viciousness. "You know damn well the doctor was *dead* at ten minutes to ten–"

"*Dead—then?*" the girl scarcely breathed the words, and Dundee was afraid she had fainted when she fell back upon the couch, her right arm dangling till the lax fingers almost touched the floor.

"Just a minute, Captain!" he pleaded, as he sprang to a table, snatched a sheaf of roses from a vase, and hurried to the couch with the water.

"She's just stalling for time," Strawn muttered, but he waited until Dundee had dabbed at the girl's bluish lips and drawn cheeks with a water soaked handkerchief.

When she spoke at last, without opening her eyes, her voice was a thin thread of sound: "I'm sorry. . . . The shock. ... I didn't know—he was—dead–"

"Then, Miss Rambler!" Strawn almost thundered. "*Why did you run away?*"

The ghost of a laugh came from her pale lips. "There wasn't any reason why I should run away," she said strangely.

"But you did try to escape—and might have got away with it, too, if you hadn't sprained your ankle," Strawn reminded her relentlessly.

"I—can't explain," she answered colorlessly. "I'm a patient here. As Luke Chester says, none of us is here for flat feet. We're all ill, in one way or another. Dr. Harlow will tell you that I'm not—responsible for the way my nerves behave. Last night—" she went on, more strongly, and with a wary, calculating look in her dark blue eyes, "I acted on an uncontrollable impulse—"

"So you're going to frame up the good old 'insanity plea are you?" Strawn cut in brutally. "Well, let me tell you it won't work. Dr. Koenig knew you were stalling— that you didn't have any business to be here—"

"How do you know that?" the girl cried sharply.

"Because Dr. Harlow told me so," Strawn obliged. "Just yesterday she and Koenig had a run in over your case. She contended you were sick, and Koenig said there was nothing the matter with you; that you'd simply pulled the wool over the little lady doctor's eyes, in order to stay on here."

"Did he trouble to tell her why anyone would insist on staying in a place like this, if she was well?" Enid Rambler asked, her voice strangely cold and measured.

"I reckon you know the answer to that question better than Koenig did," Strawn accused. "I can make a pretty good guess myself, young woman. You stayed on here, *biding your time!* Koenig was nobody's fool. He sensed that you had some evil purpose, caught a look of hate in your eyes–"

"What *are* you talking about?" the girl interrupted scornfully. "I scarcely knew Dr. Koenig. I respected him highly, and knew that he did a great work here. Why on earth should *I* kill him?"

"I admit that we've got to find the motive," Strawn told her magnanimously. "Where's your home?"

The girl wilted visibly. "I—have no home. I am—an orphan–"

"Oh, yeah?" Strawn sneered. "Then where were you living before you came here?"

"At the—Randolph Hotel," she answered, but the pause was long enough to convince Dundee as well as Strawn that she was lying.

"And before that?"

The girl's eyelids flickered. "I lived in New York. With friends. The—Hendersons. They are touring in Europe now."

"Yeah?" Strawn was heavily sarcastic. "Got plenty of money, haven't you?" and his eyes swept the luxurious sitting room of Mayfield's most expensive suite.

"Enough," she answered curtly.

"What were you doing in Hamilton?"

"Oh, just breaking my trip to San Francisco," she answered nonchalantly. "I wasn't well, and was going to the Coast by easy stages."

"Yeah?" Strawn's vocabulary of sarcasm was strictly limited. "Now, young fellow!" and he turned abruptly to Dundee. "I hear it was you that found this girl on the roadside. . . . What time was that?"

"About eleven o'clock," Dundee answered easily, keep ing a straight face. "She was unconscious. I revived her and brought her here, since I was on my way to Mayfield anyway."

"How long had you been on the roadside?" Strawn turned again to the girl.

"I can't say exactly how long I was unconscious, if that is what you mean. I decided to run away just after"— she caught her breath sharply and paled—"very soon after I found Dr. Koenig's door closed and thought he was busy. I—just suddenly went to pieces when I couldn't get anyone to give me anything for my nerves. So—I ran away."

"Uh huh. . . . What are *you* here for? . . . Dundee's the name, ain't it?"

"Right!" and the young detctive grinned. "For a rest cure. Been working too hard. I also have occasional trouble with my heart."

"Yeah?" Strawn grinned wryly. "Well, I'm afraid you'll have another attack, if you hang around here," and he cast a meaning glance toward the beautiful girl on the couch. "Come along, Brede. . . . You understand, Miss Rambler, that I'm not through with you yet. And if you try to make another getaway you land in jail! . . . Say, wait a minute, Brede. . . . Miss Rambler, you say you roamed around the place, inside and out, for about twenty minutes, between half past nine and ten minutes to ten, and then lit out for town. . . . See anybody during any of them strolls of yours?"

Color flamed in the girl's cheeks. "You haven't believed a thing I've told you yet, so I don't expect you to believe this: *I saw no one.* No one at all, at any time, except Dr. Koenig sitting in his office at shortly after half past nine." Strawn, who had come close to the couch, was about to wheel toward the door, when he caught sight of the pair of crutches.

"Haven't lost any time, have you?" he grinned at the girl maliciously. "Now, you listen to me, young lady! Either you give me your word of honor that you'll stay right where you are, or I'll station one of my men outside that door to see that you do! Which will it be?"

"I'll make no promise!" Enid Rambler cried, and to Dundee's profound amazement there was a ring of exultation, rather than of defiant anger, in her clear voice. And now there was no fear in her beautiful eyes. . .

# CHAPTER 13

"WHEW!" Strawn whistled and mopped his brow, as Dundee joined him on the lawn in front of Sunflower Court. "What a girl! . . . But I didn't think she'd let you go so quick."

"In effect, Miss Rambler told me to run along and roll my hoop," Dundee laughed. "But not until she made sure that you had actually stationed a man outside her door."

"I swear I don't know what to make of that dame," Strawn worried. "First time I ever got mixed up with a bunch of nuts, and they're getting my goat. . . . But I called her bluff. Barney won't even let a mouse get past him."

"Which is exactly what the girl is counting on," Dundee retorted.

"What do you mean?" Strawn scowled.

"Isn't that rather obvious?" Dundee shrugged. "That girl was in a perfect lather of fear that she'd follow Dr. Koenig to the grave—until you kindly offered her the protection of a six foot plainclothes man. She knows some thing she doesn't dare tell, and yet"—he hesitated, his black brows drawn together in perplexity—"and yet, Chief, I'm absolutely convinced Enid Rambler did not know, until you told her, that Carl Koenig had been murdered."

"Then why the hell did she run away?" Strawn demanded angrily.

"Ask Enid Rambler. And she won't tell. ... By the way, I'll feel safer about that girl if you keep a man there day and night until this business is cleared up."

"Wasting a couple of good men, probably," Strawn grumbled.

"Then you don't think Miss Rambler is the murderess?" Dundee smiled.

"Don't ask me what I think!" Strawn growled. "I'm already fit to be tied. Before the day is over I'll have the police commissioner and the mayor and the chief of police, to say nothing of the newspapers, ganged up on me yelping for an arrest. . . . Coming along?"

"What's the program?"

"I'm gonna use a little of this here psychology you high brows are always spieling about," Strawn grinned. "Gonna quiz Rowan and Webster right on the scene of the crime, and see which cracks first. My own money's on Rowan. ... By the way, we checked that Lacey dame's alibi and it's watertight. But I'd still like to know why she's down in the doctor's will for half his estate."

"Then I wonder," Dundee mused, "why she gave a fake alibi the first time."

"Search me!" Strawn shrugged. "But old lady Satterlee and her daughter, Mabel, both swear she got to their house about eight o'clock and did not leave until exactly ten. So that's that. But if you want to hear me go for Rowan and Webster, sneak into Cantrell's office by the back door, and leave the connecting door ajar so's you can hear and not be seen, provided you still want to swank around here as a patient rich enough to afford a suite in Sunflower Court. . . . Here's a morning paper if you haven't seen it."

Automatically Dundee accepted both the invitation and the newspaper, but remained stockstill as Captain Strawn struck off across the lawn, trailed by a couple of his squad and by Brede, the stenographer.

When he did follow, skirting the main building to reach the back door of Cantrell's office, the heaviness of his heart made his feet drag. However much he wanted to, he could no longer dodge coupling the sickening discovery that Justine Harlow had lied with Morse's story of an hysterical woman pleading with Dr. Koenig just before nine o'clock. If that woman had not been Justine Harlow, then who could she have been? For Enid Rambler, as well as Norah Lacey, had an alibi—as yet uncorroborated except by Nurse Caplan—for the hour and a half between eight and nine thirty. But apparently Norah Lacey, as well as Justine Harlow, had been lying. . . .

"Come in, boy!" It was Strawn, holding the door open for him. "The show hasn't started yet, and I'm fixing you up a reserved seat. . . . See? I've hung this mirror so you can sit behind the connecting door and see what's going on in the other office. Cantrell and the little doctor both insist on listening in, too, to see that the mean old police man don't third degree their precious patients, so you'll have company in here."

The two doctors, who were seated opposite each other at Cantrell's desk, did not smile at or answer the captain's sally. The medical man was wearing a crisp, spotless suit of white linen, and a still bleeding cut on his cheek testified to a recent shave. But that was the extent of his morning freshness. He looked like a man who had not slept for a week, and who feverishly doubted his ability ever to sleep again. Justine Harlow sat grave and still, but to Dundee's quick eyes she seemed less worried than at any time since Dr. Koenig's murder had been discovered.

" 'Bout time for that secretary to show up, ain't it?" Strawn asked.

"Miss Home telephoned about half an hour ago, just after she'd read the morning paper," Dr. Harlow answered. "I told her to report for duty as usual, at nine o'clock."

"Pretty near nine now," Strawn grumbled, as he passed into the dead doctor's office, leaving the door half open.

Dundee took his seat behind it, and unfolded the paper Strawn had given him. "FAMOUS ALIENIST SLAIN" stretched in big, black type across the front page. As he read the story below Dundee mentally blessed Strawn for his discretion. Not even the exact hour of the doctor's murder, as arrived at by the coroner and Dr. Cantrell, had been given to the reporters. "Some time between eight and ten o'clock last night," the reporter on *The News* had written, "when all his patients who were not bedridden or confined to the locked ward were thrilling to a motion picture melodrama, fittingly entitled 'Manslaughter,' Dr. Carl Koenig, one of the five most famous psychiatrists in the United States, was brutally murdered in his private office in the main building of Mayfield Sanitarium."

And if the murderer had read that account in his morning paper, he must have been dismayed by the fact that his careful, "mad rage" wrecking of the office was not so much as mentioned. But that disappointment had probably been counteracted by the fact that there was also no mention of rubber gloves, and the absence of fingerprints upon the murder weapon.

"Captain John F. Strawn, Chief of the Homicide Squad, is working on a theory that one of the many enemies whom the great alienist made as an expert witness for and against criminals who rely upon the 'insanity plea' "

Dundee lowered his paper and fixed his eyes upon the mirror, for he had heard the door from the reception room open and, simultaneously, a genial, hearty voice calling out:

"Morning, Doctor!"

He saw Strawn swing himself around in the dead doctor's swivel chair, and could imagine the change of expression on the face of the man in the doorway.

"Your name Rowan?"

Dundee could not see the speaker but heard the answer, in a puzzled but still cheerful voice: "Yes, sir. I was told Dr. Koenig wanted to see me—"

"You were told," Strawn corrected grimly, "that you were wanted in Dr. Koenig's office—and you are! . . . Come on in! Sit down!"

The mirror showed a man advancing on slow feet to the chair Strawn was pointing at. Samuel Rowan was thin almost to emaciation, and stooping shoulders minimized his height to a bare average. Thick, slightly curling gray hair was matched in a short, stubby mustache, and contrasted sharply with the sunburned swarthiness of his lean face. Brown eyes, one of them clouded over with a cataract, were shielded by old fashioned, steel rimmed spectacles. His clothes—an old sweater and a pair of gray, baggy trousers, were marked with the unkempt shabbiness of a man who takes no interest in his personal appearance.

Either the man was a consummate actor and had had ample time to prepare himself for the ordeal he was about to endure, or he was genuinely puzzled but not frightened at finding himself face to face with a police captain, Dundee concluded, his eyes riveted upon the mirrored face of Samuel Rowan.

"Well, Rowan!" Strawn snapped. "You know why you're here, don't you?"

"I suppose I do," Rowan answered, surprisingly, "and I guess the sooner we get it over, the better. ... I have to appear in court in person, don't I?"

"You're damned right you do! . . . Pretty cool, ain't you, Rowan? Well, don't kid yourself you're going to sneak out of this on an insanity plea—"

Rowan half rose from his chair, his cheeks flushing darkly. "What the devil are you talking about? I'm as sane as you are—"

"That's swell!" Strawn cut in. "Now, come clean, Rowan! What did you do it for?"

The man sank back into his chair, staring blankly at his questioner. Then suddenly he began to laugh, a harsh, bitter sound that made Dundee's nerves tingle. "I see! Koenig was just stringing me, was he? Didn't believe a word I said. . . . Well! That's a good one on me!" And again that harsh, discordant laughter filled the room. "I keep my mouth shut for two years, and as soon as I open it—to a doctor, mind you!—the police are after me! That's good! That's rich!"

Before Dundee could realize her intention Justine Harlow was out of her chair and half across Cantrell's office. He made no effort to stop her and in a flash she was at Rowan's side, her small white hand closing firmly on his shoulder.

"Dr. Koenig did *not* betray your confidence, Mr. Rowan!" she cried, her eyes blazing upon Strawn. "What ever you said to Dr. Koenig is as safe as if it were still locked in your own brain! Remember that, Mr. Rowan!"

Strawn was on his feet, in a choking rage. "Do you want me to run you in for obstructing justice, young woman?"

"I don't care what you do to me," she blazed, "but have the decency to tell this patient why you are questioning him."

"He knows why! He's as good as confessed," Strawn answered savagely.

"Oh, no, he hasn't! If you have any sense at all, you'd know what he thought you were here for! Tell him, Mr. Rowan."

The man reached up a thin, trembling, brown hand to close over the little doctor's. "I thought—You see, sir, I was adjudged a mental incompetent by the court about eighteen months ago, and was made a ward of the county. Dr. Koenig was in court when my case came up and offered to take care of me here, free of charge. Yesterday I had a long talk with the doctor and when it was over I told him I was cured, and wanted to get out and get to work. He seemed to think I'd better stay on here for a while, to make an adjustment, as he put it, before I tried to take my place in the outside world. But when I saw you here instead of Dr. Koenig I thought he had concluded to let me go, and that you were to take me before the court, in order to have my status as a mentally competent person restored."

"So that's what you thought, eh?" Strawn sneered. "Had a powerful weight on your mind for two years, didn't you, Rowan?"

"I did," the man answered simply.

"Your *conscience* hurt you so bad that people thought you were crazy, didn't it?"

"Yes. I was put in the psychopathic ward of the county hospital for observation because I tried three times to commit suicide."

"And it felt pretty good to spill the beans to Koenig, didn't it?"

"Yes. But it was the fact that Dr. Koenig convinced me that I had nothing to blame myself for that cured me."

"Then why"—and Strawn leaned forward and shook an accusing forefinger in the man's face—"did you have to *kill* Koenig to make sure he'd keep his mouth shut?"

"Kill—Koenig?" the man echoed blankly, and his hand slowly released its clutch of Justine Harlow's fingers.

"You don't mean—?"

"Yeah! Murdered! In this office last night!" Strawn flung the words at the charity patient. "And the man that did it tore up your case history! You weren't taking any chances, were you, Rowan?"

"You mean—you're accusing *me*–?"

"You got me, Rowan! . . . And I've got you!" Strawn assured him grimly.

"But you—you can't " the man stammered, his tanned face turning yellow. "My God! I can't realize these things you're saying—When was the doctor killed?"

"You know damned well when he was killed," Strawn retorted. "And I have to hand it to you, Rowan, for choosing your time well. With everybody, including the night head nurse, shut up in the O. T. Shop watching the movies–"

"But I was there, too," Rowan cut in.

"Oh, sure! You took good care that everybody'd see you and hear you in the shop *before* the lights went off, and that you'd be seen coming out with the rest of the patients when the show was over," Strawn agreed, his voice heavy with sarcasm. "But who can you find to swear you didn't sneak out about half past nine and in again just before ten? Answer me that, Rowan!"

The man's pallor deepened. He seemed incapable of answering.

"Think, Mr. Rowan!" Dr. Harlow urged. "Whom did you sit beside?"

The man turned his head and stared up at her dumbly for a moment. Then he shook his head, and passed his hand across his spectacled eyes.

"Nobody," he admitted lifelessly. "I stood. The shop was crowded. I was talking to some of the patients until the lights went out, and then I couldn't find a seat easily, so I just stood, leaning against the wall."

"Which wall?" Strawn demanded.

"The back wall, near the door," Rowan confessed. "But I swear I did not leave the room between eight o'clock and ten, when the show was over."

"Near the door," Strawn repeated, with satisfaction. "Near the back door that was open all the time. . . . Now, Rowan, I want to know what you told Koenig yesterday."

"I won't tell you!" the patient retorted flatly.

And for ten minutes Dundee had to sit silently in his chair behind the door and listen to Captain Strawn batter at the man's amazing will power. He saw Samuel Rowan reduced to a pitiful, shivering wreck, but he also witnessed the complete defeat of Captain Strawn. Not one syllable regarding his past life would Rowan utter, and there was a flicker of triumph in his exhausted voice as he informed Strawn that he had drifted, an aimless, friendless wanderer, into Hamilton only a few weeks before he had been, made a ward of the county. But as to who he had been before those dark two years, and where he had come from— not one word.

And at last Strawn had been compelled to let him go, followed by a plainclothesman, who was charged with seeing that the suspect did not escape.

"I'll find out what crime he's hiding if I have to send his fingerprints and description to every chief of police in the country," Strawn vowed savagely, as Dundee joined him in the murdered man's office. "He had motive and I'll prove it. Motive and opportunity. That's enough!"

The word "motive" rang a bell in Dundee's mind. He turned to Dr. Harlow: "Do the patients sign for the books they take out of your library?"

"Why, yes."

"Then may I see the library card for *Murder Without Motive*?"

"Miss Home has charge of the library," Dr. Harlow told him. "I'll ask her to bring in the card. I'm sure she's in the reception room now."

"Ring for her!" Strawn commanded. "I want to see that young lady anyway. Chances are she's familiar with Rowan's case history as it was before Koenig made a report on yesterday's session, and can tell us where he came from."

Dundee rose, but Strawn remained sitting when the door opened and a girl hesitated upon the threshold, note book in a hand that was visibly trembling.

She was a pretty thing, Dundee noted with swift appreciation. Plump and dimpled and pink and white as a baby. A chemical blonde, perhaps, but the short, brassy ringlets that rioted all over her round head were in complete harmony with those round, baby blue eyes and that funny little button of a nose. Her soft, too small mouth was quivering like a grief stricken child's.

"What's your full name?" Strawn began with cruel abruptness.

"Maizie Home. ... I mean, it used to be Mary, but I changed it to Maizie "

"All right; Maizie it is," Strawn cut in, grinning slightly. "You know what happened here last night?"

"Yes, sir," she quavered, the blue eyes filling instantly with tears.

"What do you know about it?"

"Nothing! I don't know anything at all about it!" she denied frenziedly, the big eyes rolling an appeal to Dr. Harlow.

"How long have you worked for Dr. Koenig?"

"Nearly five years."

"How old are you?"

"Twenty two—I mean," the girl corrected her automatic lie, flushing scarlet, "I'm twenty four."

"You were here all day yesterday?" Strawn continued.

"From nine o'clock until five," she answered eagerly. "I don't even go out to lunch, except on special occasions. I eat in the staff dining room."

"Did anything unusual happen yesterday? Any mysterious visitors or telephone calls or telegrams, or anything of that sort for the doctor?"

"No, sir."

"Did Dr. Koenig seem to have anything on his mind— anything that worried or upset him?"

"Oh, no, sir! He was awfully busy, but then he always is– was– "

"Has anything at all unusual, anything you did not understand, for instance, happened here since Dr. Koenig returned from his trip Monday?"

"No, sir."

"Now, Miss Home, I want you to give me the name of everyone that came into this office yesterday to see Dr. Koenig."

"Let me think—Do you mean everybody, including the staff?"

"Everybody."

"Well, of course I was in and out all day," the girl began slowly. "And Dr. Harlow and Miss Lacey were in and out, too, and so was Dr. Cantrell. . . . Oh, yes! And Mrs. Cantrell. She came in during the morning to welcome the doctor home from his trip, and to ask him to dinner at her house on Thursday night—why, that would be tonight!" she discovered in awe, and the babyish mouth puckered.

"All right! Who else?" Strawn prodded impatiently.

"Let's see. . . . Oh, yes! Just after we'd finished lunch—that was about half past twelve—old Mr. Powell came to get Clyde's suitcase "

"Powell? Clyde?" Strawn repeated. "Who are they?"

It was Dr. Harlow who answered. "Clyde Powell was a patient here for years. A hopeless case—advanced stages of dementia praecox, with epileptiform seizures. Lately he had required day and night attendants, and his family was unable to pay for them, so they had him transferred Monday to the State Hospital for the Insane. I telephoned his father yesterday to ask him to call for a suitcase full of old clothes and worthless possessions that was not sent on with Clyde."

"And Powell saw Koenig, eh?" Strawn turned back to the secretary. "What was his attitude? Friendly?"

"Why, yes," the girl answered. "Of course he was all cut up over Clyde's having to go to the State Hospital, but he wanted to thank Dr. Koenig for having kept Clyde so long at a reduced rate. They only talked for a few minutes."

"All right. Who else?"

"Well, about one o'clock Dr. Koenig sent for Mrs. Morse, one of the patients," the secretary continued conscientiously. "She stayed about half an hour, and then Archie Webster's father came. Archie is another of the patients, and his father came to see him, and to ask Dr. Koenig how he was getting along–"

"Friendly, was he?" Strawn interrupted.

"Of course!" the girl retorted with some indignation. "Everybody thought the world of Dr. Koenig "

"*One* somebody didn't!" Strawn reminded her grimly. "But go on! How long was Mr. Webster with the doctor?"

"About fifteen minutes. When Mr. Webster left, Dr. Koenig went with him through the reception room where I was working, to the outside door, and I heard Dr. Koenig say, 'Don't worry, old man. She won't be here much longer ' "

" 'She'?" Dundee repeated. "Are you sure Dr. Koenig said 'she,' not 'he,' referring to Archie Webster?"

"I'm positive he said 'she,' because I said to myself, 'If they could see how Enid treats Archie, they wouldn't have any cause to worry about his marrying her.' "

"So you felt sure 'she' was Enid Rambler?" Dundee went on thoughtfully.

"Isn't it quite possible," Dr. Harlow suggested quietly, "that Dr. Koenig was referring to *me?*"

Now why the devil had she brought that up, Dundee wondered. Did she enjoy rubbing salt into the wound caused by the revelation that Dr. Koenig had planned to replace her?

"To *you,* Dr. Harlow?" Maizie Home cried incredulously. "Why, Dr. Koenig thought the sun rose and set in you, and you know it!"

"Then Dr. Koenig said nothing to you yesterday or before then about replacing Dr. Harlow with a male psychiatrist?"

"Of course not! I've heard him say a dozen times he couldn't do without Dr. Harlow!"

Dundee studied the girl through half closed eyes. Apparently she was telling the truth. And what she said merely corroborated the mute but powerful testimony of the doctor's will. But had Justine Harlow introduced the subject cunningly, for the purpose of eliciting this whole hearted corroboration? And what had happened to change Dr. Koenig's heart and mind so suddenly and so completely? For that change of heart had corroboration, too— in the scribbled notation "Sandlin" on the doctor's desk calendar, and in his direct statement to Roger Baldwin. . . . Eleven miles in two hours! . . . The voice of a woman pleading with Carl Koenig not to send her away...

There was something else, a question that had been demanding an answer.

"Miss Home," he asked, "who gave those roses"—and he pointed to the now sadly faded flowers on the dead man's desk—"to Dr. Koenig?"

"Roses?" the secretary repeated blankly. "*I* don't know! They weren't there when I left yesterday afternoon!"

# CHAPTER 14

AN hour later—a crowded but strangely fruitless hour—Dundee and Captain Strawn parted company temporarily, the chief of the Homicide Squad setting out with his stenographer and Dr. Harlow to make the rounds of those patients who had not yet been questioned, and the younger detective to report in person to the bed ridden district attorney.

But Dr. Cantrell detained Dundee. "My wife wishes very much to speak with you. I'd appreciate it if you would pay her a brief visit. You'll find her in the sun parlor."

"You've discussed the case fully with her, of course?" Dundee asked casually.

"Naturally," the doctor replied curtly. "As I told you, she was asleep when I was summoned here last night, and still asleep when I got home after one o'clock. I did not disturb her, but waited until after she had had her break fast this morning to tell her the bad news. She's very much upset, of course. My wife and I were Dr. Koenig's closest friends—except Dr. Harlow, of course."

There was so much tenseness and constraint in the doctor's jerky, almost defiant words that Dundee was very thoughtful as he took the path that connected the Cantrell home with the main building of the sanitarium.

A middle aged maid, whose eyes were puffed and red with weeping, conducted Dundee into the sun parlor. He found Claire Cantrell seated at a little wicker desk, her great brown eyes staring steadily at a large, leather framed photograph. A beam of sunlight lay in a broad band across her ash blonde hair, making it gleam like pale gold. She was extraordinarily beautiful.

Her voice was slow and deep and rich as she said, with out rising, her eyes still on the photograph of Dr. Carl Koenig: "A great man— pure and above reproach. As wise as Socrates and as gentle as Christ."

And somehow the words did not sound cheaply theatrical to Dundee.

"You were very fond of the doctor, Mrs. Cantrell?" he asked gently.

The sad brown eyes turned their beauty full upon him, but he was quick to note that no color rose to stain the clear creaminess of her cheeks. "I am afraid I almost worshiped Carl," she answered without hesitation. "Not only was he my closest friend, but he, as a doctor, made it possible for me to live fully."

And not even his death, Dundee reflected, had been able to destroy the poise and serenity that the doctor had helped her achieve. He had a sudden, amazing impulse to kiss one of her lovely, quiet hands, as tribute to her grave dignity and beauty.

But he said, almost brusquely professional: "You wished to see me, Mrs. Cantrell? You know something that may help us?"

"What I have to tell you," the slow, rich voice answered, "may have no bearing at all on Carl's death. But it puzzled me at the time, and since Bruce told me what happened so soon afterwards I can't get it out of my mind. ... As my husband told you, I retired at eight o'clock last night, with a severe neuralgic headache. Bruce gave me a dose of aspirin and luminol, and I was dozing before nine. Between our twin beds there is a telephone, or rather two telephones, one an instrument of the inter communicating system of the sanitarium, and the other a straight line out. Both have extensions in the front hall. At nine twenty—I looked at my watch as I picked up the receiver—there came three short buzzes, our call on the sanitarium telephone. It was Carl—"

Dundee was startled into rigid attention. "Why didn't Dr. Cantrell answer the call, since he knew you were asleep?"

"My husband did go to the front hall to answer, but hung up after a moment when it was evident that Carl wished to talk with me, not with him," she answered.

"But Dr. Cantrell made no mention of this call!" Dundee told her sharply.

"I know. He was very wrong, but his sole thought was to protect me from being questioned last night, when I was ill. Bruce—" and there was a throbbing note of tenderness in the rich voice, "is a very devoted and considerate husband, and he did not hear enough of the conversation to attach any significance to it."

"Just what did Dr. Koenig say?" Dundee tried gently to hurry her.

"The first thing he said was, 'Feeling better now, child?' Bruce had told him I had one of my headaches. I answered that I was, and he then asked if Justine was here with me. I told him she was not—"

"Did he say he wanted to see Dr. Harlow in his office?"

"No, but I inferred as much, of course," Mrs. Cantrell answered, with a trace of surprise at the question. "We talked on for a minute or so, idly, as friends do, but his voice seemed strained and tired and worried. I asked him what he was doing, and he said, 'Working on case histories, but not making much headway. The truth is, Claire, something happened this evening to shake my faith in human nature, but just hearing your voice has done a lot to restore it.' . . . I'm proud to say," the girl added, but without a trace of defiance, "that Carl was almost as fond of me as I was of him."

"I can believe that," Dundee assured her gravely. "But did he explain, give you any clew as to what had happened?"

"None at all, and I did not ask any questions. I supposed, naturally, that a patient had made some revelation that had shocked even Carl's understanding and tolerance."

Well, it looked as if Strawn might be right after all, and Rowan the one whose guilty secret must be protected at all costs, Dundee told himself ruefully. But—it was *Justine Harlow* the doctor had wanted to see. . . .

"All this is extremely important, I am sure, Mrs. Cantrell, and I thank you for telling it so freely and clearly—"

"But that is not all, Mr. Dundee," the girl surprised him by interrupting. "We talked on for a minute or so more—he advised me to stay in bed today and cautioned me to take care of myself—when suddenly he interrupted something unimportant I was saying. He cried out, 'Good Lord!,' in a voice I can only describe as horror stricken, and added immediately: 'So that's where I've seen those eyes before!' "

"Yes?" Dundee urged, as the girl paused. "What else? Surely he explained so strange a remark?"

"I asked him what he meant, but he answered evasively," the girl told him. "As nearly as I can remember, he said, 'I've just happened to stumble upon the missing link in a memory chain. . . . But I'll say good night now, my darling girl. I've got a nasty job to do, without wasting a minute's delay.' And he hung up the receiver. I was puzzled and troubled. I started to call Bruce and tell him about it, but my head had begun to throb violently again, and I knew that if I excited myself by talking any more, it would get worse."

"Your husband did not come to inquire what Dr. Koenig wanted?"

"No. Why should he?" Mrs. Cantrell asked. "It was the most natural thing in the world for Carl to call me, to ask how I was feeling."

"Can you recall, Mrs. Cantrell, at just what point in the conversation your husband replaced the receiver of the extension?"

"Not exactly, but very early—as soon as it was obvious that the call was for me only."

"May I ask, Mrs. Cantrell, if you and Dr. Harlow are good friends?"

"The best of friends," she answered emphatically. "I have known and loved Justine ever since I first came to Mayfield for psychoanalysis. She is an utter darling of a girl, and a splendid psychiatrist."

"Then it would be natural for Dr. Koenig to assume that Dr. Harlow would come straight to you, if she were in serious trouble?"

"Quite natural."

"Will you tell me this, Mrs. Cantrell: was Dr. Harlow in love with Dr. Koenig—or he with her?"

"You have no right to ask me that question," she replied with dignity, "but I will answer it. The answer is no. Dr. Harlow worshiped Dr. Koenig, but I am absolutely sure she did not love him, in the usual sense of the word. And Carl loved Justine only as a colleague and as a friend. ... I don't believe Carl was ever in love. He was an almost Christlike ascetic."

"Do you know personally of any woman who was in love with him?"

"I cannot answer that," she said, with dignity. "But I can tell you clumsily what Justine could express much more scientifically. Women patients are prone to fall in love with their analysts, at a certain stage of psychoanalysis. They make what is called a 'transference' of an unhealthy love from its previous object to the doctor. He encourages such a transference, but does not take advantage of it, if he is a reputable analyst. When the cure is completed, the patient is no longer in love with the doctor, but is ready for a normal life. I can assure you that Dr. Koenig was the soul of honor where his women patients were concerned. . . . And in every other respect. For instance, a practicing physician who is financially interested in a sanitarium is exposed to countless temptations—"

"Such as?" Dundee prompted, when the girl paused, as if she feared she was talking too much.

"It would be very easy for a doctor in Carl's position at Mayfield to retard rather than hasten the recovery of rich patients, or even of those who pay for moderately priced accommodations," Mrs. Cantrell explained quietly. "Carl almost leaned backward to escape any such accusation. Many women, and some men, too, find a place like Mayfield a heavenly refuge from life and all its demands and perplexities. After they are really well enough to be out, they want to stay on and on. Carl literally pushed them out, back into the world again. Naturally my husband, financially interested also, as you know, was in complete accord with Carl's principles—"

"But Business Manager Baldwin was not always so cheerful about seeing a well paying patient leave?" Dundee prompted, as she hesitated again.

"Roger Baldwin is not a doctor; he is a business man, and a very good one," Claire Cantrell reminded him. "But I admit that the difference of viewpoint did cause some friction—nothing serious, of course. For instance, Carl was quite upset when I saw him yesterday morning over the fact that poor Clyde Powell, who had been a paying patient for seven years, had been transferred to the State Hospital on Monday, all arrangements having been made before Carl returned. In fact, I am sure that if Carl had got here before Clyde's train left he would have got him back and kept him here as a charity patient."

"I see," Dundee nodded, then asked abruptly: "Did Dr. Koenig say anything at all to you or to your husband about his intention of replacing Dr. Harlow with a male assistant?"

"Not a word!" the girl flashed. "Bruce has told me what Roger Baldwin said, but I am sure Roger misunderstood something Carl said about taking on a second assistant. I am positive Carl had not the remotest intention of dismissing Justine."

"Not even if he discovered yesterday some serious error on her part, in the treatment of a patient?" Dundee persisted.

"He would have condemned the error itself, but not Justine's intentions," the girl assured him warmly. "He knew that Justine's principles were as high as his own."

"Candidly speaking, you believe Roger Baldwin lied?"

"I believe he is mistaken as to just what Carl said," she answered firmly.

"Your friends should prize your loyalty very highly, Mrs. Cantrell," Dundee said, sincerely, as he took her hand.

Her revelation of the telephone conversation had given the young detective so much food for thought that he was scarcely aware of the path he took as he left the Cantrell house. But when he almost stumbled against the footrest of a canopied lawn chair he discovered that he was cutting across a small rose garden which lay between the sanitarium driveway and the Cantrell home.

He was about to apologize for his clumsiness when he saw that the frail old man in the chair was fast asleep, his repose guarded by a white clad male attendant.

"It's Dr. Mayfield, sir," the attendant whispered.

Dundee halted and stared down at the sleeper with intense interest. Every line and contour of the face and head spelled nobility, high intelligence, thoroughbred ancestry and gentleness. But as the detective gazed down upon the old doctor, something like nausea clutched at the pit of his stomach. The unfairness of the tricks that life could play seemed suddenly more than he could bear. Why live decently, finely, cleanly—he asked himself—if at the end life could rob a man of the thing he held most dear, that which distinguished him from the beasts of the field?

"How is he today?" he asked the attendant, whom he beckoned to a safe distance from the sleeper.

"Seems to be in his right mind, when he's awake," the attendant answered. "But something's bothering him. He keeps demanding to see Dr. Koenig, and to humor him, I've told him Doctor's away on a trip."

Dundee nodded and walked on, but his lips silently formed the bitter words, "To humor him." Better a gangster's bullet in *his* spine, he decided, than that he should live on and on, until ultimately a paid caretaker of his body should murmur those words about him. . . .

But the zest for life was again strong within him when he reached the bedside of the pleurisy stricken district attorney.

"Time you were remembering you've got a boss, young fellow," Sanderson chided good naturedly. "What luck so far?"

"Swell luck!" Dundee grinned. "Within twelve hours I've met three of the prettiest women I've ever seen in my life. . . . Unfortunately one of them—and I'm not sure she isn't my favorite—insists on wearing horn rimmed spectacles to add to her dignity–"

"What the devil are you talking about?" Sanderson interrupted.

"Dr. Harlow, naturally—Justine Harlow," Dundee obliged. "A charming name, don't you think? Really, she's the cunningest little trick, especially when she's being the learned doctor–"

"If it won't bore you too much," Sanderson again interrupted acidly, "I'd like to hear a few details about a certain murder you're supposed to be investigating."

"Oh, *that!*" Dundee laughed and shrugged. "The truth is, I know so much about it that I'm afraid I don't know anything at all. . . . Does your doctor hold with having his patients told long, involved mystery stories?"

## CHAPTER 15

"WAIT a minute, Bonnie. My head's spinning," the district attorney pleaded, three quarters of an hour after Dundee had begun his recital.

"So is mine," Dundee admitted, and stretched prodigiously, his blue eyes twinkling as they rested on his chief's disturbed face.

"If it hadn't been for that damned movie in the what d'ye call it shop–"

"O. T. Shop," Dundee contributed helpfully. "But if it hadn't been for that damned movie, as you call it, think of the fun we'd miss playing 'Button, button, who's got the button?' with a whole squad of suspects. All of the patients would have been peacefully abed, since bedtime at Mayfield is nine o'clock."

"I'm not the glutton for suspects that you are," Sanderson reminded him testily. "Well, get along with it. You'd finished with Rowan, and I'm inclined to agree with Strawn that that bird'll bear checking up on."

"No doubt of that," Dundee agreed cheerfully. "I'm sure his story is an interesting human document, and one that quite possibly would complete a *dossier* in some police department, but–"

"All right, all right! What did Archie Webster have to say for himself when Strawn got hold of him this morning?"

"Oh, he's playing the same sort of game the Rambler girl is up to," Dundee told him. "Knows something he's not telling. But his story is straight enough, believe the story or not. He says he was sitting in the same row of seats at the movie as Enid Rambler, and that he noticed she was getting more and more nervous. Says he passed the word along to her that he had some first class whisky, which was exactly what she needed to brace her up. He says he also sent along the word that he'd be in a sort of little summerhouse in the northwest corner of the grounds, beyond the locked ward cottage. He left, went to the summerhouse, and waited for her to join him. He says she didn't come and he drank the whole pint himself, going back to the main building only in time to see the patients leaving the shop. He says his intention was to ask her to take a turn about the grounds with him before she went to bed, but that, tipsy as he was, he got into the mix up with Rowan, and did not even know she had ever left the movie."

"And I suppose the summerhouse is too far away from the main building for Archie to have seen anything?"

"It is."

"Then what the devil does he know that he's not telling?"

"*I* don't know," Dundee assured him plaintively. "I don't know a lot more than that, if you ask me—"

"And what about that mystery yarn—*Murder Without Motive*, that had the rubber gloves tip in it?" Sanderson asked irritably.

"Another washout. Miss Home, the secretary, says Koenig, who read nearly every mystery he could get his hands on, presented that book to the sanitarium library," Dundee told him. "And the library card shows that practically everyone whose name has been mentioned in the case so far has read the book. And I thought I was lucky to find that hot clew!" he gibed at himself.

"That fat man!" Sanderson ejaculated. "He'd stand a lot of explaining!"

"Strawn's got the 'dragnet,' as the papers call it, out for our fat friend," Dundee assured him. "Description: age, about forty; height approximately five feet five; weight no less than two hundred pounds, mostly under his belt; hair, scant, pepper and salt; eyes blue or gray. But unless he was kidding Archie Webster, the fat man's chief interest was in Enid Rambler, *to whom he did not speak—*"

"Met her outside," Sanderson supplied. "You say your self the girl knows who did it, or has strong suspicions, so strong she's afraid she'll get hers next, and that she won't tell because the murderer has something on her."

"Guess I'm stubborn," Dundee admitted ruefully, "but I can't approve of this mystery story unless the 'voice of God' is tied up nice and tight with the solution of Koenig's murder."

"Oh, don't bother about that voice," Sanderson advised. "Some nut with a religious complex, baying at the moon. Remember the place is full of nuts."

"Ye—es."

"If you want *my* theory, here it is," Sanderson went on, with increasing zest. "Claire Cantrell says—and I think we can bank on what she told you—that the doctor suddenly remembered where he'd seen somebody before, and that he was horrified. Now consider. Get the picture. The doctor's talking over the phone, sitting at his desk. His eyes rove, and light on something. All right! What was that something likely to be?"

"A case history, I suppose," Dundee admitted. "He told her he was working on case histories."

"Sure!" Sanderson was becoming jubilant. "The doctor sees a name—name of a person or a place—that makes his memory click. Now what is his memory most concerned with?"

"His work," Dundee answered dutifully. "And with out your prompting I can deduce that the phase of his work that horrified him most was murder trials, where he testified as to the defendants' sanity.

And I agree that if he suddenly realized that one of his patients was an escaped murderer—possibly a homicidal maniac—he'd get busy."

"Correct!" Sanderson snapped. "But remember it's *my* theory! Now what would a doctor do?"

"Send for the patient, verify his suspicion, then put him in the locked ward until he could be returned to the asylum for the criminally insane," Dundee answered promptly, with a grin. "Sorry, Chief, but I'd thought of all that, too, and the fact is that Koenig, so far as we can find out, sent for no patient in the sanitarium last night."

"But what if that patient had already seen him earlier in the day?" Sanderson suggested. "Suppose the patient had had a long powwow with the doctor, but had not told him the real truth. Suppose Koenig said something like this, 'Rowan, I've seen you somewhere before, but I can't place you!' What would you do if you were Rowan? Wouldn't you be tempted to have another chat with the doctor, to tell him some more lies to throw him more off the scent? . . . Well, that's exactly what Rowan does. He slips out of the shop, and into Koenig's office. And he sees Koenig has recognized him at last, and—the jig is up!"

"Sounds good, Chief," Dundee admitted. "But if Rowan *is* a homicidal maniac, why should he have to go to such pains to make the crime look like a maniac's work?"

Sanderson looked nonplussed for a moment, then brightened. "I got it! Rowan *isn't* a homicidal maniac, but a cold blooded murderer whom Koenig recognizes from having seen him before he committed his crime—for which he's a fugitive from justice. He knows Koenig ought to do his duty—turn him over to the authorities. So he kills him, but fixes up his defense *ahead of time.* In case he's caught, there's the evidence of the wrecked room and the fact that he's a patient to prove he had been a homicidal maniac all the time! . . . How's that?"

"Swell!" Dundee applauded feebly. "But—how does Enid Rambler fit into the picture?"

"That's easy!" Sanderson exulted. "She's got onto Rowan's trail. A relative of his first victim, probably. Unknown to Rowan, of course. So she leaves the movie to spill the beans to Koenig. She waits around, thinks he's busy. Then she hears or sees something that scares the wits out of her. Probably Rowan comes out of the doctor's office and she gives herself away to him. He threatens to kill her, and she runs away. Today she learns that Koenig was dead when Rowan came out of Koenig's office, and she knows he meant it when he said he'd kill her."

Dundee shook his head. "I don't believe she'd track down a murderer and then let him scare her off—not even after she found he'd killed Koenig," he said. "But it's the best theory so far, Chief, and I'll work on it."

"Yes, sir! You can't get away from the fact that Rowan's case history was torn up; that he'd had a long talk with Koenig; that no one can swear he didn't sneak out of the O. T. Shop; that he was still wrought up enough at ten o'clock to knock Webster down; and that he won't tell the police a thing concerning his past—doesn't dare tell! . . . And you can't get away from the fact that Koenig didn't consider Enid Rambler a mentally sick girl—thought she was shamming in order to stay on."

"And I also can't get away from the fact that Dr. Harlow believes she *is* sick," Dundee cut in. "My personal conviction is that she is using Mayfield as a hide out, that she has done something which has given her a very real claustrophobia—in other words, that she's afraid of being hauled off to jail. Strawn's trying to get a line on her before she came to Mayfield."

"Poor Bonnie!" Sanderson mocked, not unkindly. "One of his three beauties is married, one is a prospective jail bird, and the bespectacled one tells him a lie that he promptly catches her in!"

"Not only that, but *two* of my beauties have some of the identical roses that the murderer thoughtfully placed at the dead doctor's nose," Dundee admitted gloomily.

"Not—Claire Cantrell?" Sanderson demanded, startled.

"No. Justine Harlow and Enid Rambler. Each had a vase of those roses in her room this morning," Dundee told him. "I checked up with the Mayfield gardener, but he told me they're hothouse roses, a new variety, and very expensive. I'd hoped to find them growing on a hundred bushes about the grounds, but no such luck."

"What's eating on you, my boy, is that you're convinced it was Justine Harlow who paid that tearful visit to Dr. Koenig around nine o'clock last night—and you won't admit it. ... If she had pimples and greasy hair, you'd be a powerful lot quicker at putting two and two together, Bonnie. Face the thing! Koenig had suddenly made up his mind to discharge the little doctor. Why? *Because she was in love with him, and making a nuisance of herself!* He'd been so fond of her that he'd put her down in his will for half his estate, and undoubtedly she had some cause to think he cared for her in a marrying way "

"So now you're suggesting she killed him because he wouldn't marry her?" Dundee asked, in a dangerously calm voice.

"Keep your shirt on, boy!" Sanderson laughed. "I'm suggesting no such thing. All I'm trying to do is to explain why the girl drove only eleven miles in those two hours. You could hardly expect her to admit she'd had that kind of interview with a man who had just been murdered. But I don't believe for a minute she had anything to do with his death."

"That's a help anyway," Dundee admitted, more cheerfully. "Well, I'll be getting on. I intend to be a model 'patient' all afternoon—sit around on the lawn and gossip with all the biddies, male and female. Out of a ton of dirt I may winnow one small nugget of gold. ... By the way, Mr. Sanderson," the young detective added, so casually that it was obvious he had not really half forgotten what he was about to communicate, "I stopped off on my way here to check up on Norah Lacey's alibi. Strawn's man on the same job gave her a clean bill of health, but I wasn't quite satisfied. It seemed odd to me that she should give a fake alibi first, if she really had an airtight one that was true, and one so innocent as spending the evening with friends."

"Yes?" Sanderson prompted impatiently.

"The nurse was there, all right," Dundee said slowly. "She arrived at eight, as she said, and left exactly at ten. The Satterlees are nice people—a sixty year old grand mother, and a fifteen year old granddaughter, name of Mabel. It's a comfortable, but rather humble six room house "

"What are you getting at?"

"One of those six rooms is an extremely well equipped nursery—both beautiful and scientific," Dundee told him reluctantly. "Norah Lacey pays quite a stiff board bill for the three year old youngster that occupies that nursery."

"Whew!" Sanderson whistled thoughtfully. "No wonder she lied!"

"Yes. . . . And Norah Lacey was alone with the little boy, who is quite ill, from a few minutes after eight until ten minutes to ten. It seems that she persuaded the Satterlees to take the evening off and go to a movie. They've been very closely confined to the house on account of the child's illness. Therefore—" and he shrugged, his eyes unhappy.

"Therefore Norah Lacey has no more alibi than a rabbit," Sanderson supplied with some satisfaction.

"No—o. Except that I don't believe she'd leave that sick child alone. Remember she's a nurse, as well as—a mother, perhaps. . . . Funny thing, Mr. Sanderson, but that kid—and a cute brat he is—reminded me of someone. I've seen eyes like his somewhere recently–"

"*Koenig?*" Sanderson cut in sharply.

But Dundee shook his head. "Not Koenig, but–"

"But Koenig left Norah Lacey half of his estate," Sanderson reminded his subordinate grimly.

"I know," Dundee agreed dubiously. "Maybe I'm just a gullible, hero worshiping young fool, but without more positive evidence than we have so far, I'm not going to believe Carl Koenig seduced a nurse in his employ and then refused to 'do right by her.' "

"Got any idea whose baby it is, then?"

"Not the ghost of an idea," Dundee admitted hopelessly. "Another mystery. Just one of the half dozen that are sure to enter into the investigation of any murder. All of us have secrets in our lives, but fortunately most of us don't get mixed up in murders and have to see our secrets dragged into the limelight. . . . No use broadcasting this particular secret, is there, sir?"

"None that I can see so far," Sanderson replied. "No use slinging mud at a dead man, unless it becomes absolutely necessary in clearing up his murder. But bear this in mind, boy. Koenig had some good reason for leaving Norah Lacey—probably a good enough head nurse but easily replaced—one half of all he died possessed."

It was on that somber note that the conversation ended, and Special Investigator Dundee took his seat in his roadster, a well filled suitcase beside him. He began to drive rather slowly, but suddenly his scalp pricked in a way that always presaged disaster, and his foot bore down hard upon the accelerator. . . .

# CHAPTER 16

"I've been holding back your tray for you, Mr. Dundee," Nurse Lurline Doty told him archly, as he strode, suitcase in hand, into the reception room of Sunflower Court. "I've got a lovely lunch for you— breast of chicken, fresh asparagus, tomato aspic–"

"Thanks!" Dundee interrupted curtly. "Everything quiet?"

"Quiet!" the nurse echoed dramatically. "With all the patients knowing about poor Dr. Koenig, and having hysterics–"

"Has anything serious happened?"

"No one has committed suicide or confessed to the murder, if that's what you mean," she answered, a little sulkily.

In his suite at last, Dundee unpacked his suitcase, made sure that the precious trayful of case history scraps gathered from the floor of the dead doctor's office was still in the drawer where he had placed it, then gave hasty and rather unappreciative attention to his excellent luncheon tray. . . . Was he developing an appropriate neurasthenia, to fit his role of patient? And if not, why the devil should his scalp go on prickling in that way it had of warning him of approaching disaster?

Ready to go out and make the acquaintance of his fellow guests, Dundee suddenly felt a curious reluctance to play the role he had elected. Himself completely sound mentally, he felt a shrinking aversion to contacting those whose brains were warped and whose faces betrayed the disintegration of their minds. There was shame, too, in the fact that he was about to deceive unfortunates who had not the power to match wits with him. But duty was duty. . . .

He found that the largest number of patients out for air and exercise had chosen the wide expanse of lawn that lay between Sunflower Court and the main building. A man and two women were playing croquet, the silly, unprovoked laughter of one—the very fat girl he had seen that morning—shrilling out an almost constant accompaniment to the crack of mallet against ball. Her shots were wild, never making a wicket. . . .

"Play bridge, buddy?" a blithe voice hailed him, and Dundee turned gratefully to accept the invitation of the jolly attendant, Happy Day.

There were two tables of bridge. One foursome was made up of Samuel Rowan; a majestic, white haired woman with protruding eyes, who was introduced as Mrs. Asbury, and who immediately assured Dundee she was at Mayfield merely for a "rest cure"; a silent, homely girl whose name was Helen Rand; and Howard Salter, the writer, who seemed to be completely recovered from his attempted suicide.

"Needed a fourth pretty badly," Happy Day assured the detective, as Dundee took the vacant seat at a table where the attendant, his patient, Archie Webster, and a dignified, thin haired, erect old man were already sitting.

"And this is Mr. Hepple, Dundee," Happy Day concluded the introductions, indicating the elderly man. "Used to be a banker— responsible for the depression, ain't you, old sport?"

The ex banker bowed with grave and exquisite courtesy to acknowledge the introduction. "We are very glad to have you with us, sir. . . . Yes, Mr. Day, it was my sad destiny to bring about this world wide catastrophe, which is euphemistically referred to as the 'depression.' The gigantic scope of my unwise manipulations—"

"Tell him all about it some other time, grandpa," Happy Day interrupted, tossing a merry, significant wink Dundee wards. "Let's cut for deal. . . . Hi! Ace of Spades. And you and me's pardners, Dundee. How's that for a break? . . . Archie, I wish you luck with grandpa."

"My name is Hepple, sir," the gentle old man reminded him, still with beautiful courtesy.

"Excuse me for living!" Happy apologized gleefully. "The old boy doesn't play contract, Dundee, so auction it is, if you can bear it. ... Oh, Lord!"

"Got a pain in your tummy?" Archie Webster asked hopefully.

"Worse'n that," the attendant groaned. "Look who's coming."

Dundee looked, too. Across the driveway and toward them he saw a tall woman striding purposefully, and waving a raffia knitting basket from which trailed yards of purple wool. Her height was accentuated by the Grecian tunic of pale yellow silk which, sleeveless and girdled by a silver snake, hung in voluminous folds from shoulders to ankles. Long curls of gleaming black hair hung below her shoulders, escaping from a floppy leghorn hat weighted down with pink roses. At a distance she looked like a great beauty, but as she drew near Dundee saw before him what could only be called the caricature of a beautiful woman. The lines and coarseness of middle age were smeared over with heavy, theatrical makeup. The once glorious black eyes were thickly mascaraed and deeply shadowed with blue grease paint. Yellowish teeth, some of them false, spoiled the calculated effect of the scarlet Cupid's bow. But Dundee's eyes, after a fleeting summary of her appearance, riveted themselves upon a long stemmed rose that bobbed above the silver girdle. For it was an exact mate of the rare and expensive flower that had adorned the dead doctor's desk, as well as the rooms of both Enid Rambler and Justine Harlow. . . . Did he say *rare*? Why, the damned flower seemed to be an epidemic!

"*Don't* tell me you've already got a fourth!" she sang out, in a vital, throaty voice—the voice of a concert stage contralto. "Why, *hullo,* darling!"

And Dundee was amazed to find that the happily surprised and loving greeting was for him.

"Archie, my own true love, where did this gorgeous male thing come from?" she demanded of young Webster, as she bent to kiss him on the cheek.

"Quit smearing me up with your damned lipstick," Archie commanded ungallantly. "This is Marjorie Merrick, Mr. Dundee. ... At least that's her story and she sticks to it."

"A stage name, darling," Miss Merrick assured Dundee tenderly. "I am the world famous contralto. Of course you've heard of me. . . . What eyes! What a noble brow! What a chin! What a head of hair—" and she suddenly ran her thin fingers through Dundee's crisp black mane.

"In short, what a man!" Archie laughed. "Don't mind her, Dundee—"

"Jealous, my pet?" the odd creature crooned, encircling the young man's neck with a freckled arm. "He simply can't bear to have me pay the slightest attention to another man, darling—Oh! To think I nearly forgot!" and she fixed Archie Webster with glittering black eyes, a red nailed forefinger tapping warningly against her pursed lips. "Not a word, Archie! *For God's sake, not a word!*"

"I'm not saying anything!" the boy almost shouted. "But dry up yourself, Marjie. We want to play bridge."

"Take my place, Miss Merrick," Dundee insisted, rising.

"No, really," as his three table mates protested vigorously, "I'd rather look on."

"Sweet!" Marjorie Merrick breathed, as she slipped into his chair. "*He's head over heels* already, Happy!" she confided in a gusty whisper. "Sit right here by Mama, darling. . . . Well, can you bear it, children? . . . My sweet old Carl—*murdered!*" She turned swiftly to Dundee. "He always called me Marjorie and I called him Carl. . . . Madly, hopelessly in love with me, the poor dear. . . . And now—*now he's dead!* Oh, God, why should I be cursed with this terrible power—But not a word!" and again the forefinger tapped the scarlet mouth.

Again Dundee felt the hair rise pricklingly on his scalp, but this time he knew the cause. Weird and horrible to hear this scatter brained caricature babble on. ...

"I bid two spades—no, I mean I bid three hearts!" she announced triumphantly. "Not my bid? . . . Well, what difference does it make? I'm going to bid three hearts anyway when it gets around to me."

And although she played the hand to a running, rapid accompaniment of relevant and irrelevant chatter, the amazing woman made a little slam in hearts, with a dummy that seemed to promise not a single quick trick.

"That's bridge!" she applauded herself, with justice, her eyes beaming fondly upon Dundee. "Listen, darling! Be a lambkin and run and get Enid Rambler for me. There's something I simply have to tell her—"

"She has a sprained ankle," Dundee told her.

"Then bring her in a wheel chair, idiot!" she commanded imperiously. "Run!"

"I'll go," Happy Day offered. "You take my hand, Dundee."

"No. I'll go along with you," the detective offered, glad of the chance to ask a few urgent questions of one who knew his status. . . . "What a woman!" he breathed, with awe, as the two of them set off across the lawn. "What ails her?"

"She's a manic," Happy Day explained, proud of his knowledge. "Not a *maniac*—a manic. You know—up in the air all the time, happy as hell, and impulsive as a wild mare. Makes her nuts on men, poor girl! But I don't see why we should pity her. *She's* having a swell time—all the time!"

"A nymphomaniac?" Dundee asked interestedly.

"Sure! But not when she's herself. Awful decent sort, really," the attendant assured him, in a suddenly assumed English accent, at which he himself grinned. "She thinks every man that lays eyes on her is dippy about her. Has a tall story to tell about a man getting a job here as attendant in order to kidnap her. . . . That sort of thing."

"And Archie Webster is her present choice?" Dundee asked.

"Until *you* came along," Happy Day laughed. "Sure! She thinks Archie is insane about her, and only pays attention to Enid to make her jealous. Matter of fact, the kid's honestly dippy over Enid. . . . Swell girl, Enid Rambler. You were the lucky guy that found her last night and brought her back, weren't you?"

"Yes," Dundee assented curtly, for the attendant's blithe familiarity with himself and all the patients did not particularly please the detective.

"Yeah, Archie'd marry her in a minute if she'd have him. But she's not taking on any drunks, thank you kindly."

"Any truth at all in Miss Merrick's story that Koenig was in love with her?" Dundee asked, knowing the question to be a foolish one.

"Hunh! Are *you* crazy, too?" the attendant gibed. "She called him Carl, all right, and he humored her by standing for it. ... Greatest guy that ever lived—Doc Koenig! . . . Wonder what she wants Enid for?"

To Dundee's amazement, the crippled girl readily agreed to be taken out upon the lawn in a wheel chair. And as he lifted her slender body from the couch to place it in the chair he told himself, with a catch at his heart, that here was the real thing—beauty incarnate. She was wearing a sleeveless tennis dress of turquoise crepe de chine and a crocheted silk beret of the same color enchantingly set off the chestnut curls and vivid blue eyes.

"Hello, Precious! Did Muwer's baby hurt its poor little foot?" Majorie Merrick greeted the invalid, her voice rich with real tenderness.

"It did," Enid Rambler laughed. "And did Muvver want to see her baby?"

"God! I'll say I did!" the ex singer breathed fervently, dramatically. "Listen, Enid " and she briskly wheeled the chair to a safe distance, bending low and speaking in an urgent, rapid voice.

"Always cooking up something," Archie Webster laughed. "Enid's an angel to humor her as she does."

"Miss Rambler is indeed an angel of beauty and good ness," the elderly banker intoned solemnly. "But may I again remind you, gentlemen, that Miss Merrick was, in her day, a shining ornament of the concert stage? It was my good fortune to hear her sing, back in 1914—"

"Tell us some other time," Happy Day interrupted rudely, with another wink at Dundee. "Let's shuffle. They're coming back now."

And again Marjorie Merrick took her place at the bridge table, her forefinger tapping a warning of silence to Enid Rambler and Archie Webster alternately.

As the strange, hectic play progressed, Dundee watched the game, first at one table and then at another. Samuel Rowan was a clumsy but thoughtful player, his whole mind apparently upon the game. Mrs. Asbury played a shrewd, pitiless, aggressive game, brooking no conversation and rigidly enforcing the rule, "A touched card is a played card." She was not popular.

"Grand sweep!" Marjorie Merrick announced with loud triumph, as she showed down the last four cards in her hand. Then, with eyes narrowed and voice throatily significant, she asked of the table in general: "Has any one seen Justine? How's she taking it? ... The poor, poor darling! Of course I forgive her, but she never quit trying to keep Carl and me apart."

"Of course we've all seen Dr. Harlow," Archie Webster frowned at her. "She's been as busy as six doctors in a smallpox epidemic. And so has Cantrell. . . . And you'd better bite your tongue to keep it from saying any thing against the little doctor, Marjorie."

"Go roll your hoop!" the strange woman derided him. "As if it wasn't plain enough for a blind man to see that she was simply mad about Carl. To say nothing of Norah Lacey and Rose Caplan—"

"Are you crazy?" Webster cut in angrily.

"Sure! What do you think I'm here for?—ingrown toe nails?" and Marjorie Merrick laughed loudly. "And so are you, you sweet old alcoholic, you! . . . What's the matter with *your* attic, Big Boy?"

"Nothing, I hope," Dundee answered, flushing.

"That's what they all say at first," the woman laughed. "But you'll get so you think it's funny. . . . How's your stomach? Strong?"

"Fair to middlin'," he answered. "Why?"

"Because Jack Hubert's going to throw a fit," she told him calmly, and pointed toward the croquet field.

Dundee looked, then hastily averted his eyes.

"That's nothing," she assured him, almost gleefully. "You ought to have seen Clyde Powell when he was going good. Jack's a true epileptic—can't toss a fit when ever he wants to, but Clyde was a D. P. with epileptiform seizures. Just let him catch sight of anybody he was afraid of or hated, and—pfft! Perfect artist at fits, Clyde was, before he got too bad to come out on the lawn. . . . Have you seen Roy White? Our sleeping sickness exhibit," she explained, and distorted her face and crooked her fingers in a perfect imitation of the paralytic Dundee had seen that morning. "Staggers along as if he can hardly take a step, but one day I saw him run a race with Jack— and win!"

Dundee did not comment, and the ex singer began to shuffle the cards. Suddenly, however, she threw them down and beckoned Webster imperiously. Reluctantly the young man followed her, and another mysterious conversation ensued, Marjorie talking rapidly and earnestly, her finger frequently at her lips, and Webster nodding his head in impatient agreement with everything she said.

To conceal his interest in this by play Dundee strolled to the other table. Mrs. Asbury was announcing in a calm voice, as she reached for pencil and score pad:

"Down three tricks doubled. . . . Sorry, partner. But every cloud has its silver lining, Mr. Rowan. Just because you took that set like a gentleman, and didn't try to show me how a couple of finesses would have saved the game, I'm going to do you a big favor. . . . That stupid police captain thinks you murdered Dr. Koenig, doesn't he?"

Samuel Rowan flushed darkly, but did not answer.

"Well, the next time he has you on the grill, you just tell him that Josephine killed the doctor. She promised me she would kill him if he didn't let me go away with her yesterday."

Before Dundee could speak out of his amazement, Happy Day twisted about in his chair at the other table, clapping his hands. "So Josephine did it, eh, Mrs. Asbury? . . . Good old Josephine! What a load off the captain's mind *that* will be!"

Very calmly, and without a word, Mrs. Asbury rose, overturning her chair. With one sweep of her large right arm she scattered the cards and upset the bridge table. Then, very politely, she bowed to her bridge partner and opponents. "Thank you for a very pleasant game," she said, and strolled off across the lawn.

"Good Lord!" Dundee breathed. "Who *is* Josephine?"

"A lady who exists only in Mrs. Asbury's mind," Happy Day chuckled.

"A poor unfortunate—Mrs. Asbury," the aged Mr. Hepple intoned solemnly. "I should have liked the opportunity to assure her that her beloved and imaginary Josephine did not kill the doctor—but that, to my certain knowledge, he was struck down by the hand of God, as just retribution for keeping me here, when, in one day on the Stock Exchange, I could restore the country to an unparalleled era of prosperity. But he refused to release me, and the hand of God has struck!"

Dundee felt an icy sweat break out upon his brow and upper lip. "The hand of God"—"the voice of God." . . .

"Attaboy, Hepple!" Happy Day applauded. "But I hope *you've* got an alibi, or the bad old police may get you!"

"I?" There was gentle scorn in the old man's voice. "I sat next to Mrs. Asbury during the entire showing of both motion pictures last night."

Slightly sick, Dundee stared at the old man. If there was no one but that insane woman to support his alibi . . . Suddenly a feeling of desperate helplessness swept over the detective. How futile to try to apply sane, normal methods of investigating murder in a place like this! Why, anything—any ghastly thing that a De Quincy could dream of—could happen here! Had he not seen an apparently normal and highly intelligent woman suddenly go to pieces? Had he not heard a fine example of gentleman of the old school babbling matter of factly about the hand of God? In a place where victims of claustrophobia tried to run away, and nymphomaniacs deluded themselves that every man was in love with them

"Someone's calling you, Dundee!" Archie Webster, temporarily free of Marjorie Merrick, reported as he strolled back to the bridge table. "Guess they want to get your case history. Better think up some good complexes and psychoses, to make it interesting reading."

Dundee rose hastily, excused himself, and almost ran across the lawn to where Norah Lacey stood on the steps of the main building. And as he ran a concerted shout of laughter—blending the contralto notes of Marjorie Merrick with the sweet voice of Enid Rambler and the deeper rumbles of the men—followed him mockingly.

He clenched his hands. Had they discovered who he was and plotted this whole mad afternoon to tantalize and confuse him? What—whom—could he believe?

"What's happened?" he panted, as he reached the steps.

The nurse's face was drawn and ashen. "It's Dr. Mayfield. He's dead."

# CHAPTER 17

"WELL, thank God, it wasn't murder!" Captain Strawn ejaculated, mopping his heavy, flushed face. "We've got enough trouble on our hands as it is."

"I'll say we have," Dundee agreed gloomily. "No need of an inquest, I suppose?"

The two detectives were temporarily alone in the small sitting room of Dr. Mayfield's suite on the second floor of the main building. Beyond, in the bedroom, with the newly dead body, were Drs. Harlow and Cantrell and Miss Lacey.

"No doubt of its being a natural death, according to Cantrell and the little doctor," Strawn answered. "Just died in a fit–"

"Senile delirium," Dundee corrected. "Best get it right when you tell the reporters. . . . Wonder what's keeping Baldwin? . . . There he is! ... Come in!"

Roger Baldwin, the business manger, stepped into the room, followed by Dr. Mayfield's attendant, who had been sent in search of him.

"Another bad break for the sanitarium," Baldwin commented sourly. "I hope to God the traditional third blow falls quickly, so all three will make the same nine days' wonder."

"You were with Dr. Mayfield when the attack seized him, I believe?" Dundee asked abruptly.

"I was. Granger here asked me to see him, thinking perhaps I could pacify him," Baldwin explained. "He couldn't have made a poorer choice, as it happens. The old doctor hated the sight of me, and 'fired' me every time he saw me. He believed he was still head of Mayfield Sanitarium, and that I was only a salaried cashier."

"How did you happen to call Mr. Baldwin, Granger?" Dundee asked the attendant.

"Gosh! I didn't know what to do," the attendant protested plaintively. "The old doctor was in his right mind, and raising the roof because I wouldn't get Dr. Koenig. He told me flat I was lying when I said he was out of town, because he'd seen Dr. Koenig yesterday and knew he was just back from a trip."

"What did he want of Dr. Koenig?" Strawn cut in.

"I didn't pay much attention," the attendant evaded uncomfortably, "but he kept saying something about that man couldn't stay here another day, that he was a 'menace to Mayfield'–"

"Meaning Mr. Baldwin?" Dundee asked sharply.

"No, sir. It sounded like he meant—like he was referring to Dr. Koenig!" the attendant blurted miserably.

"I got the same impression," Baldwin said drily. "Not that it means a damned thing. The old doctor was always turning against one of us and ordering us off the place—"

"Just what happened when you came up?" Dundee interrupted.

"Granger stayed in this room and I went into the bedroom," Baldwin answered. "I knew it was unwise for me to go, but Granger was afraid to handle the situation alone, and everyone else—Dr. Harlow, Dr. Cantrell and Miss Lacey—was busy with patients. . . . The whole place is at sixes and sevens, now that the patients know about the murder—"

"And Mr. Baldwin is one of the bosses here," Granger justified himself.

"I found Dr. Mayfield in bed," Baldwin went on. "He recognized me and ordered me to get out. Said he wanted Koenig and no one else. I tried to soothe him—told him Koenig was away, but he told me I was lying. Said I was trying to shield Koenig, but that he was still head of this institution, and he'd see that 'that man' didn't stay here another day. But before he finished the sentence the attack came on. I called Granger and then hurried off to find Cantrell or Dr. Harlow. Both were with him when he died—about ten minutes after the attack started. . . . I've been getting off a cable to his daughter, Madame Arnaud, in Paris."

"Do you think she will come?"

"I doubt it. On her last visit she made all arrangements for his funeral, his death having been expected for more than a year."

"Why did Dr. Mayfield hate you, Baldwin?" Strawn asked abruptly.

The business manager shrugged, and grinned wryly. "He got an idea that I was extravagant, wasting the institution's funds. My colleagues accuse me of erring on the other side."

An hour later Dundee was concluding a detailed recital of his own day to Captain Strawn. The two men sat facing each other at the murdered psychiatrist's desk.

"By the way, Captain, when you questioned Hepple and Mrs. Asbury this morning, were you satisfied with their alibis?" Dundee asked, when he had finished his account of the mad bridge games on the lawn.

"The Asbury dame said a friend of hers, name of Josephine, sat in the seat where the old boy, Hepple, swears he was sitting," Strawn grinned.

"Just as I expected," Dundee groaned. "I'll be crazy myself before this case is finished. . . . Come in!"

It was Dr. Harlow. Spectacles could not hide the violet shadows beneath the gray green eyes. But the little doctor scorned to droop with fatigue or to abate one whit her professional briskness.

"Will you tell me if there is to be an inquest upon Dr. Koenig?"

Dundee sprang to his feet and offered his chair. "Captain Strawn and I have talked by telephone with both the district attorney and the police commissioner, and we have all agreed that, under the circumstances—many of the witnesses being psychopathic patients—it would be unwise to hold an inquest. Under the laws of the state, an inquest can be waived, you know."

"Oh!" A tremulous sigh of relief deflated the little doctor's chest and she slumped a bit in her chair. "Thank you—with all my heart."

"Then," Dundee suggested gently, "will you do us a favor in return? Will you tell us frankly and truthfully, Dr. Harlow, where you were last night between eight and ten o'clock? . . . You see, doctor, we know that you traveled only eleven miles in your car after five o'clock yesterday, so I am sure you will want to amend your story that you were driving the two hours between eight and ten."

The small hands clenched to still their trembling, but the tired eyes met Dundee's steadily. "Yes, I did not tell you the whole truth. I was making an unofficial call on a sick person."

"On a three year old little boy?" Dundee asked softly.

The proud shoulders fell then. "Yes."

"On Dr. Koenig's son, in other words?"

She did not flare out at him, as Dundee had half expected. But she shook her head wearily. "I don't know whose child he is."

"Did Miss Lacey ask you to have a look at the child?"

"Yes. She telephoned about eight o'clock that she was worried about Sonny, and not at all satisfied with the doctor the Satterlees had called to attend him. I could not refuse to go, but told her that my visit must be unofficial."

"Then you and Miss Lacey were with the child all evening?"

The girl doctor hesitated, then her eyes met his bravely. "I can't lie again. It would be no use. . . . Norah asked me to stay with Sonny while she went out on an errand."

"When did she leave and how long was she gone?"

"She left about eight thirty and returned at ten minutes to ten. Sonny was asleep, had been asleep for nearly an hour, and I was waiting outside the house in my car, anxious to be back here. The house is set almost flush with the sidewalk and the nursery is a front room, so I should have heard him if the child had cried out. As Norah drove up, I drove off, waiting only to assure her that Sonny was better. I drove home very fast, arriving at ten o'clock, as I said last night."

"Do you know where Miss Lacey was during all that time?"

"I do not," she answered with flat finality, then turned, with obvious relief, as Maizie Home appeared in the doorway from the reception room. "What is it, Maizie?"

"A telegram for you," the secretary said, and handed over the yellow envelope.

The little doctor tore it open and read, then she frowned. "They're in an awful hurry," she said, with the first note of querulous complaint Dundee had heard in her lovely voice. "It's from the State Hospital, asking me to rush them a resume of Clyde Powell's case history. . . . Will you get his history for me, Maizie? I suppose I'll have to attend to it this afternoon."

"Dr. Koenig had a special delivery letter from Dr. Wiggin the first thing yesterday morning, asking for Clyde's history," the secretary explained in a subdued voice as she tiptoed across the room to the file cabinet.

"Then Dr. Koenig must have attended to it, and his letter simply hasn't reached them yet," Dr. Harlow said.

"No, doctor. He had so many interruptions yesterday that he hadn't got to it by five o'clock," the secretary excused her dead employer. "He told me to get the history from the file for him, and I did. I clipped Dr. Wiggin's letter to the folder, so's Dr. Koenig could see just what Dr. Wiggin wanted—Why, it isn't here!" the girl broke off to exclaim.

"*Missing?*" Dundee sprang to his feet.

"It's not in the files," the girl quavered, "but I suppose Dr. Carl hadn't finished with it when he—when he was–"

"Have you sorted out those letters that were scattered over the floor?" Dundee slashed across the girl's hysteria sharply.

"Yes, sir. I smoothed them out and filed those that didn't require an answer–"

"Was Dr. Wiggin's letter among them?"

"No, sir."

"And did you find any letter from Dr. Koenig to Dr. Wiggin?"

"No, sir."

"It seems quite clear, Mr. Dundee," Dr. Harlow interrupted, "that whoever destroyed the other two case histories that are missing tore up Clyde Powell's too."

"Sounds reasonable," Strawn commented. "Convenient to the murderer's hand it must have been, right out here on the doctor's desk. Just more dust in our eyes."

"I've had a hunch all along that the one case history that was a menace to the murderer's safety was not torn up, but completely destroyed later," Dundee told them, his eyes burning with new hope. "What we've got to find out is—which history that was!"

"How?" Strawn demanded, but Dundee, without pausing to excuse himself, dashed out of the office and across the lawn to Sunflower Court.

Within five minutes he was back, carrying the glass tray into which he had piled the precious scraps gathered from the office floor.

"I need help," he announced briskly. "Everybody rally 'round! First, I want to verify my suspicion that only two case histories have been torn up. Begin by sorting the scraps—manila folder scraps in one pile, white paper scraps in another."

He dumped the tray of paper fragments upon the rug, and a moment later four pairs of hands were swiftly busy at the task. When the two piles were complete, Dundee rose from his knees and, his voice crisp with excitement, asked of Dr. Harlow:

"Have you a scales—very delicate and accurate?"

The girl doctor frowned thoughtfully, then nodded. "Gram scales, used in the diet kitchen. I'll get them."

She returned very quickly, carrying a pair of white enamel scales, whose pointer was set at zero.

"Good!" Dundee cried, and, after placing a light wicker letter tray upon the flat top of the scales, he transferred the small pile of cream colored manila scraps from the floor to the tray.

"Hocus pocus!" Strawn growled, as Dundee made a note of the weight of the scraps in grams.

"Yeah?" Dundee grinned. "Now, Miss Home, if you'll be good enough to bring me three manila folders— the exact kind you use for case histories–"

The girl obeyed, wonderingly. From the wicker tray Dundee removed the scraps, replacing them with the three new folders.

"See that?" he cried, pointing to the indicator on the face of the scales. "Three untorn folders weigh exactly *one third more* than these scraps!"

"Proving?" Strawn asked.

Dundee looked at his old chief in amazement. "Proving, Captain, that, while three case histories are" missing from this office, only two have been torn up. The third is completely missing—or at least its folder is, and if you can suggest a single plausible reason why the folder alone should have been removed by the murderer, and the case history torn up–"

"I getcha," Strawn conceded. "But looks like we're no forrader–"

"Down on our knees again!" Dundee cried happily. "What we're looking for now are scraps of paper bearing the typewritten names of Samuel Rowan, Archibald Webster, and Clyde Powell—the whole names or any recognizable part of those names."

It was Maizie Home who made the first discovery, as her nimble fingers picked up and rejected scraps from the sizable heap.

"Here's a scrap that has 'owa' on it!" she exulted. "And I can't think of any word in common use that has those three letters together— except Iowa."

"Neither can I," Dundee assured her approvingly. "Looks as if Sam Rowan's in the clear, doesn't it? But let's try to find more corroboration."

Dr. Harlow announced the next find. "Here's the top left hand comer of page two of Archie's history," she said quietly. "Look!" and she exhibited a scrap that read: # 2—Webs

"That's right!" Maizie Home dapped her hands. "We always put the last name of the patient after the number of each page of his history. I *knew* it wasn't Archie–"

"And here's additional proof that Rowan's history  was torn up," Dundee interrupted. "Look, Captain!" and he showed a fragment bearing the letters, "amu." "It's a safe bet that the complete word was Samuel. . . . Well?"

Captain Strawn sat back on his haunches, his heavy face sadly puzzled. "That leaves only the Powell boy's history, Bonnie," he deduced worriedly. "Looks like you've run into a blind alley, boy."

"Clyde Powell," Dundee repeated, frowning.

"*Clyde Powell?*" Dr. Harlow echoed incredulously. "Then the captain's right, Mr. Dundee. We've wasted our time. Clyde was transferred to the State Hospital on Monday, before Dr. Koenig returned. He left here with a guard and a nurse."

"Do you know that he actually arrived at the State Hospital, that he did not escape *en route?*" Dundee asked sharply.

"If anything had happened, I am sure we should have been notified," Dr. Harlow assured him.

The young detective whirled upon Maizie Home. "Did Dr. Wiggin's letter to Dr. Koenig, received yesterday morning, actually state that the patient had arrived?"

The girl's baby blue eyes narrowed in concentration. "I can just *see* the letter, as if I were looking at it now," she answered proudly. "It began, 'Relative to the patient, Clyde Powell, transferred to this institution on Monday from your private sanitarium—' That proves he really got there, doesn't it?"

"You say you can 'see' the letter," Dundee countered eagerly. "Anything distinctive about it—the paper, I mean?"

"Why, yes, there was," the secretary answered readily. "It was a bright canary yellow, and both the printing and the typing were in green ink!"

"That clinches it!" Dundee struck a fist into a palm. "You say no such letter was found among the crumpled correspondence found on the floor. Well, there's been no such letter torn up, along with the case histories! You can see for yourselves that there are no yellow scraps in the whole lot! Just to make sure, however, that the letter is actually missing, I want you, Miss Home, to search the correspondence files and your own desk, while I go through Dr. Koenig's desk from top to bottom."

Ten minutes later there was no blinking the fact that the canary colored letter from the State Hospital was nowhere in the suite of three offices. Waste baskets had not yet been emptied of their Wednesday accumulation, since the cleaning woman, who did her work here between six and seven in the morning, had been kept out by the plainclothes men on guard. Neither was the letter among the small heap of papers and personal belongings taken from the murdered doctor's pockets.

"So—Clyde Powell's case history is the crux of the whole matter," Dundee said slowly. "The missing letter clinches the thing. The murderer figured it out extremely well. He guessed that the file would be searched for missing case histories of only those patients who are still here. He was right. But it was necessary to *remove* the Wiggin letter, so that no one should be reminded of Clyde Powell's history. If you had not received that telegram from the State Asylum, Dr. Harlow, the fact of the missing history might never have been discovered!"

"But—*Clyde Powell!*" the little doctor protested, in puzzled distress. "He could not have been here last night. Not only is he in a locked ward at the State Hospital, but he is physically and mentally incapable of having committed the crime."

"You're undoubtedly right," Dundee told her, "but— *he has relatives!*"

"By God, boy, you've hit on something!" Strawn ejaculated. "Maizie here says the boy's father paid a visit to the doctor yesterday. It's a cinch the old man was feeling pretty low over his boy's being kicked out just because he couldn't pay Mayfield's big bills any longer–"

"That's absurdly wrong, Captain!" Dr. Harlow cut in angrily. "It was old Mr. Powell who asked that the boy be transferred, and I happen to know from Dr. Koenig himself that he was much upset over our letting Clyde go, and that he assured Mr. Powell yesterday of his eagerness to get the boy back, for as long as he lives—which won't be long—and at the minimum rate, with no charges for attendants. Carl was going to pay the attendants out of his own pocket. And *that's* the reason poor old Mr. Powell had tears in his eyes when he left here yesterday! He had refused the charity—too proud!—but he was touched by Dr. Carl's offer."

Dundee's mind had registered the unconscious slip— the one time she had referred to the dead man by his first name without a prefix, but there was no indication of the fact in his deferential manner as he asked her:

"Dr. Harlow, did Dr. Koenig ever say anything to you about Clyde Powell's reminding him of someone?"

"Why, of course not!"

"Perhaps I'd better put it this way: did Dr. Koenig ever wonder aloud to you 'where he'd seen those eyes before'?"

" 'Those eyes'?" the girl doctor repeated blankly. "Certainly not!"

"I getcha, boy!" Captain Strawn exulted, slapping his thigh. "I knew Mrs. Cantrell's story was the biggest step forward we've made yet. Clear as day, ain't it? The doctor's talking along to the little lady on the phone. His eyes light on Powell's case history, lying open on his desk. Suddenly something clicks in his brain. Funny how the good old memory works, ain't it? . . . Well, he remembers where he has seen Clyde Powell before—"

"He'd seen him here almost daily for five years," Dr. Harlow cut in acidly. "Clyde was here when Dr. Koenig took charge."

"That makes no never mind," Strawn assured her. "He'd been puzzled for five years as to where he'd seen Clyde Powell before, and suddenly he remembers. And he's horror stricken. That's the very word Mrs. Cantrell used to express the way his voice sounded, ain't it, Bonnie?"

"Correct," Dundee agreed.

"All right, then!" Strawn went on vigorously. "It's pretty easy to dope out what happened. The doctor remembers where he'd seen this Clyde Powell before— *and it was in a courtroom!* A boy criminal on trial for some pretty nasty offense—criminal assault or murder. Under some other name, of course. All right! The boy has either been acquitted or has escaped from prison. But Koenig knows that he's dangerous—ought to be in jail, or certainly in the asylum for the criminally insane—"

"And for seven years he was a docile, obedient, harm less patient in this institution," Dr. Harlow reminded him sternly.

"But the Big Doctor knows damned well there ain't no telling when he'll bust out, and there'll be hell to pay," Strawn retorted. "Well, then! He's got to act and act quick. He telephones his lawyer for advice. The lawyer ain't at home. Then the doctor thinks it only fair to warn the Powell family what he's on to and up to. So he telephones Powell to come down for an interview. Old Powell comes, realizes his son is doomed to spend the rest of his days in the asylum for the criminally insane, disgracing not only himself but his family, or that he'll be hauled back to the prison he escaped from. So–" and Strawn shrugged his massive shoulders.

"It fits, all right," Dundee assented, but without joy. A nasty job, this of his—"But before we get out a warrant for Powell senior's arrest, I think we'd better get him and his wife here for questioning."

"Oh, I'm sure you're wrong!" Dr. Harlow wailed, wringing her hands in the first abandonment to distress that she had shown.

"How can we reach Mr. Powell by telephone, doctor?" he asked gently. "I'm going to give him a chance to come without being brought in."

"The Powells own a grocery store on Hubbard Street," she told him, her voice shaking. "The family lives over the store. The initials are J. C."

"Telephone book? . . . Thanks, Miss Home!" and Dundee turned the pages quickly until he found the number.

Seating himself at the murdered doctor's desk, he lifted the combination transmitter and receiver from the French type telephone which still stood on the typewriter table at right angles to the desk. Laying the one piece instrument on the desk, he began to dial. The dialing completed, he reached for the instrument.

But to the watchers' amazement he did not complete the movement which would have settled the receiver against his ear and the transmitter before his mouth. . . .

"What are your eyes popping out at, boy?" Strawn demanded sharply.

Dundee continued to stare at the receiver for some seconds. Then, still without answering, he began to scrape with a finger nail, very carefully and delicately, against the inside surface of the receiver. Moistening another finger on his tongue, he wet the substance under his nail. And then he spoke:

*"One drop of blood!"*

# CHAPTER 18

CAPTAIN STRAWN, Dr. Harlow and Maizie Home stared at the young detective in stupefied amazement.

"And now I know," Dundee went on, with deep satisfaction, "how that blood came to be on the corner of the desk, why the murderer had to wipe it away, and—*how the doctor's chin was bruised after death!*"

Captain Strawn was the first to recover the power of speech. "Seems to me like one little drop of blood is doing a powerful sight of talking!" he commented sourly.

"You said it!" Dundee exulted. "Not only has it told me those three vitally important secrets, but—it will eventually send the murderer to the gallows! One drop of blood that he could not see at the time. Oh, he was careful, all right! Look at the inside of that receiver! Wiped clean, probably with the same gauze swab he used to wipe the blood off the corner of the desk. But one drop of blood was hidden from his sight, inside the receiver. The murderer could not see it. But when the receiver was again placed on the prongs, upside down, that betraying drop of blood seeped down until it clogged one of these six tiny holes—a silent witness, waiting to tell its story and, eventually, avenge the man who shed that blood."

"Yeah?" Strawn snorted. "How about a little explanation for them that can't hear blood talk quite so plain?"

"Sorry!" Dundee apologized with a broad grin. "I'm unpardonably melodramatic, but I can't help being excited. . . . Look, Captain! It's plain as day. Dr. Koenig was *not* typing when he was murdered. He was talking over the telephone. That's why he did not see and possibly did not hear the approach of his murderer. Which broadens the scope of our investigation, I admit, since it leaves room for doubt that the murderer was someone privileged to enter this office without knocking. While the doctor is still absorbed in his telephone conversation, the murderer secures the bronze statue and crashes it down upon his head. The doctor is facing the desk, although the base of the telephone is on the typewriter table to his right. As the doctor's head is crashed down, the combination receiver and transmitter is pinned between the head and the desk. As the coroner and Dr. Cantrell assured us, the blow caused a slight hemorrhage from the ear. The blood oozed into the receiver, which must have stayed in that position for several minutes, while the murderer was engaged in faking his stage setting and tearing up case histories—"

"Just a minute," Strawn interrupted. "Why didn't the person the doctor was talking to hear the sound of the blow, and make a fuss when the conversation was cut short?"

"I believe that the murderer pressed down on this bar," Dundee answered, pointing to the telephone base on the typewriter table, "before the blow was struck. It was the work of a second, and his action could not be observed by the doctor, whose back was turned. Dr. Koenig must have thought he was accidentally disconnected, if he heard the resulting buzz above the sound of his own voice, but before he could reach for the dial, he was struck down."

"O. K.!" Strawn grunted.

"Therefore," Dundee continued, "the murderer was safe in leaving the instrument pressed against the doctor's ear and mouth until he had time to remove it—or he thought he was safe to do so. He could not reckon with that one betraying drop of blood. At his leisure, he raised the head and removed the instrument, swabbing out the receiver, which, to his horror, dripped blood upon the blotter, and, as he was carrying it back to its base, upon the corner of the desk. It was natural for the murderer to invert the instrument, before he knew there was blood in the receiver. He did his best. He thought he wiped away all traces of the fact that the doctor had been killed while he was telephoning. Which brings us to the most significant deduction yet. It seems to me that it was vitally important to the murderer that no one ever know the truth—that the doctor was telephoning at the very moment he was killed. . . . Why?"

"Because the telephone conversation concerned the murderer, I presume," Dr. Harlow answered, in a dazed voice.

"Exactly!" Dundee cried eagerly.

"He was telephoning the Powells," Strawn cut in, "and spilling the beans about this Clyde—to the mother, probably. And in walks old man Powell. He's reconsidered his refusal to let Koenig get the boy back, and has come to tell the doctor so. But the first thing he hears when he steps into the office is what Koenig is saying to Mrs. Powell about having the boy turned over to the authorities. The old man goes berserk and kills the doctor."

"Please!" Dr. Harlow interrupted, her face pale and drawn with distress. "I'm sure Mr. Dundee is right about the telephone, but I'm absolutely positive you are wrong, Captain, about Clyde Powell."

"It is *his* case history that is missing, the letter concerning *him* that is also missing—not torn up," Dundee reminded her, to Strawn's obvious satisfaction. "Are you familiar with Clyde Powell's case history, doctor?"

"In a general way only," she admitted. "I've read it, and have made additions to it, but I have not gone over it carefully for years. The poor boy's condition was not interesting, psychiatrically. It changed in expected ways, growing steadily worse. He is a dementia praecox, with epileptiform seizures. That is, he is not a true epileptic, but is subject to attacks which resemble epilepsy. For more than a year he has been increasingly helpless. His mind is hopelessly gone."

"Any distinguishing or unusual aspects of his case?" Dundee asked.

"No," she answered. "Like many cases of dementia praecox, he had ideas of persecution, delusions of grandeur, and occasional hallucinations. States of depression and of excitement alternated, sometimes accompanied by epileptiform seizures."

"How long had he been ill?"

"About eleven years, I believe. He came to us from a private sanitarium near Los Angeles, seven years ago— two years before Dr. Koenig and I came to Mayfield."

"Do you remember anything in his case history that would account for its being destroyed by his father or anyone else?"

"Nothing whatever!" she answered emphatically.

"Do you remember whether there was a record of Clyde's having been involved in any serious trouble before he was committed to a sanitarium?"

"There was positively nothing of the sort! He was considered entirely harmless, both because of his past history and because of his behavior here."

"I see," Dundee said slowly.

"Well, *I* don't see, and I'm going to get the Powells here in short order," Strawn declared in no uncertain tones. "Give me that phone!"

"I think it would be wiser if no one else touched this instrument until Dr. Price has had a chance to make an analysis," Dundee suggested. "I'm positive it's blood, but I want official confirmation."

"O. K. Guess it's better to send one of the boys after the Powells, anyway," Strawn agreed, and strode out of the room.

"May I see Miss Lacey, please?" Dundee asked of Dr. Harlow, when the older detective was gone.

"Will you call her, please, Maizie?" Dr. Harlow asked wearily. "Then I'll join you in the reception room. There's work to be done."

When the white faced head nurse arrived, Dundee was grateful for the little doctor's tact which had made it possible for him to conduct the interview privately.

"Please sit down, Miss Lacey," he directed gently. "You've seen the morning paper? You know that Dr. Koenig's will, unless he has changed it without Dr. Cantrell's knowledge, leaves one half of his estate to you and one half to Dr. Harlow?"

"Yes," she quavered, and a thin, work worn hand strayed nervously to her silver threaded black hair. "I was dumfounded–"

"Then you know of no reason why Dr. Koenig should have been so generous to you?"

"No. I couldn't believe my eyes—" she faltered, but those eyes did not meet the detective's.

"Did it not occur to you, Miss Lacey, that Dr. Koenig wanted to help you provide for—Sonny?" Dundee asked, and again he hated his job.

"Sonny?" she repeated, in a voice that was scarcely more than a gasp for breath.

"He's a remarkably handsome little boy," Dundee assured her sincerely. "Whose child is he?" he added with startling abruptness.

Strength came back to her. "He's mine!" she cried passionately. "That's all you need know! He's mine!"

"Did you—give birth to him, Miss Lacey?"

She collapsed again, and Dundee was afraid she was going to faint. "I've said he's mine. That's enough. You can think what you like."

"Then I'm afraid I'll have to think you are his 'natural' mother," Dundee said gently. "Wouldn't it be much wiser and simpler for you to tell me the whole truth about the child?"

"I'd rather die!" she assured him with terrible intensity.

"Again you force me to draw my own conclusions," Dundee told her soberly. "My guess is not a pleasant one, but—here it is. Sonny's father is a man you love more than you love yourself—a man you would the to protect from scandal. Either that, or"—and he shrugged,—"to save yourself now you must protect *him!*"

"What on earth do you mean?" she cried starting up from her chair.

"What is Sonny's name, Miss Lacey?" he countered.

"His name is Lacey!" she cried. "I told you he's mine!"

"What is his first name, Miss Lacey?" he insisted.

Her knees were shaking as she sank back into her chair. "I suppose you'd dig it up somehow," she accused him bitterly, "so I may as well tell you. ... I named Sonny after—after Dr. Koenig. His name is Carl."

"I see. . . . Carl—Lacey. And you wanted him to have the right to be called—Carl Koenig, Jr.?"

She sprang to her feet again, her gray eyes blazing wide. "No, no! That's a lie—a terrible, vicious lie!"

"If it is not true that Dr. Koenig was little Carl's father," Dundee persisted quietly, "will you tell me who the father is?"

"Never! I've told you I'd rather die!"

"I'm sorry. . . . Miss Lacey, last night you were so worried over Sonny's illness that you called Dr. Harlow, begged her to come to see him "

"So *she* told you, did she?" the nurse interrupted bitterly. "I thought I could trust her—of all women!"

Her emphasis and bitterness surprised the detective.

"She told only after I'd learned the truth from a visit to the Satterlees," he assured her. "She obeyed your summons. She went to see Sonny. And almost as soon as she reached the Satterlee house *you* left—on an errand. What was that errand, Miss Lacey? What business was so pressing that it took you away from your desperately sick boy?"

"I refuse to answer!" she cried, shaking as with a chill.

"And I submit, Miss Lacey, that the errand was indeed an important one," Dundee went on inexorably, although his stomach revolted at his own tactics, "that it took you to the child's father!"

She gasped, and her pale lips parted, but she did not or could not find breath to deny the charge.

"Miss Lacey," he went on coldly, but with pity in his heart, "if you had known last night that Dr. Koenig's will left you one half of all he possessed, would you have —behaved differently while you were out on that vital errand?"

"Of course not! Dr. Koenig's will could not help— could not alter— oh, what am I saying? Stop digging at me! I've told you I'd rather die than tell you any more than you've already found out!"

But Dundee considered himself amply answered. He gladly let her go. But when he was alone again there was no triumph in his tired blue eyes. He had uncovered a woman's shame, and his own sense of degradation was the only result. For while he was now fairly sure whose voice had pleaded hysterically with the psychiatrist for a love he could no longer give her, he was equally sure that Norah Lacey had not murdered her betrayer. An ugly word. And a strange word to apply to the austere, almost saintlike Doctor. But human nature—Dundee shrugged. No, the nurse adored him too much to do anything more drastic than reproach him. Women were strange creatures, he reflected tritely. But men, he reminded himself, were no less unaccountable. The "Big Doctor"—so big in every other way—would leave the unwed mother of his child half of his estate, oblivious to the possibility of scandal, but would stubbornly refuse to give their child its rightful heritage of a proud and famous name. But wait! Had Koenig been so oblivious to scandal? Was not that the explanation of the divided estate? If two women were named in his will, to share equally—two respected and capable colleagues—would not the possibility of scandal be reduced to a minimum? But somehow the deduction did not cheer Dundee. He was young enough to be still something of a hero worshiper, and his ideal of Dr. Koenig, whose stature had increased hourly since his murder, was sadly tarnished. . . .

He was still sunk in gloom, still alone, when, ten minutes later, Captain Strawn burst into the room, his heavy face red with excitement.

"Looks like it's all over, boy! Here's a confession. After all this hullaballoo, it was a patient all the time!"

"A patient?" Dundee grinned. "Didn't Dr. Harlow warn us to expect a raft of confessions from upset patients?"

"But this one's no nut," Strawn protested. "The little doctor swears she's legally as sane as you or me—just flighty."

"All right! I bite! Who killed Carl Koenig?" Dundee laughed.

Strawn scowled at his levity, but he shouted the answer triumphantly:

"Marjorie Merrick!"

# CHAPTER 19

GRINNING skeptically, but with delighted anticipation of the lively scene that he was to witness, Dundee took his place behind the door of Dr. Cantrell's office, first making sure that the wall mirror was still so placed that it would reflect what took place at Dr. Koenig's desk.

As he waited for her to appear, the detective re read the "confession" note that Marjorie Merrick had written and sent to Captain Strawn:

*"Sir:* (it began haughtily, and Dundee chuckled) *Concealment is no longer possible. I can see, feel an invisible net closing—closing, tightening inevitably. Would God that— But remorse cannot interest you. Only THE TRUTH, terrible and shocking though it may be, matters to YOU—representative of the hard hearted police. . . . So, sir, to ease the burden upon my soul, I must tell you that I—I, Majorie Merrick, I ALONE, am responsible for Carl Koenig's death."*

There was no formal signature to the melodramatic note, and again Dundee chuckled. This was going to be fun! What the picture producers called "comedy relief." . . . Well, he could do with a bit of comedy–

A vibrant contralto voice cut across his amused reflections. The mirror was blank for a moment more, then gave him a full sized portrait of the ex singer. With heaven only knew what fantastic notions of propriety, the strange woman had changed from the yellow silk tunic to wide trousered black lace pajamas. Unfortunately, however, for any calculated effect of mourning, the undershirt and shorts she wore beneath the open patterned lace were of vivid scarlet satin. Dundee gasped, and was afraid he had betrayed his hidden presence, but the vital contralto was continuing unchecked:

"We meet again, Captain—Strawn is the name, I believe? ... Thank you! . . . No, no! Don't ask me to sit at *this desk,* where only last night—" and her bony shoulders heaved in terrific shudders.

"Stand then," Strawn told her sourly. "You wish to make a statement, Miss Merrick? . . . Ready, Brede?"

The police stenographer, who was blushing like a schoolboy, fumbled nervously with notebook and pencil.

"Captain!" the woman began, after taking a deep breath, and fixing the Chief of the Homicide Squad with her glittering black eyes, "do you believe that a person who is crazed with drink and mad with love is responsible for his actions?"

"What's that?" Strawn ejaculated. "I thought you said *you* killed Koenig!"

A thin hand went up in a melodramatic gesture, while the other hand settled more firmly the red rose tucked among the too black curls.

"No, Captain! Be accurate, I implore you! I wrote in my note that I and I alone am responsible for Carl Koenig's death!"

"Well, what the devil-?" Strawn sputtered.

"I meant exactly what I said," the vibrant voice pulsed on. "Crazed by drink which some unprincipled stranger gave to him, maddened by love for *me*, driven insane by jealousy which I—*I*, accursed enchantress that I am—"

"Can that stuff!" Strawn exploded angrily. "Listen, lady, I kid easy, but not *that* easy-"

Behind the door, Dundee nearly choked with laughter, but even if he too had exploded he doubted if Marjorie Merrick would have heard him.

"You're insulting, sir!" she stormed. "In good faith, and with a heart heavy laden with grief and remorse, I come to you-"

"All right, all right! Play out the comedy and get it over with!" Strawn interrupted helplessly. "But speed it up, lady! I'm a busy man."

"*Comedy!*" the woman cried bitterly, a black lace hand kerchief dabbing at her mascaraed eyes. "I come to you with the terrible truth of how Carl Koenig was murdered by poor, irresponsible Archie Webster–"

"*Webster?*" Strawn shouted. "Say, begin all over again and tell your story in plain American, without gestures— *if you please!*"

"I find that I must sit after all," the woman gasped weakly, and sank into the chair Strawn had first offered. "I shall try to be brief," she promised, with forlorn dignity.

"Archie Webster loves me madly. That is the secret of his frequent returns to Mayfield. Separated from me, he drinks himself nearly to death, but behind his debauches is the definite plan that they shall land him here again, where he can be with me!"

"Yeah?" Strawn grinned wryly. "I've heard it hinted around that it's the Rambler girl he's stuck on."

"Ah, you know so little of the subtleties of love!" she assured him tragically. "To make me jealous, Archie pretends to be interested in Enid—and a dear, sweet child she is, although God has not seen fit to curse her with the power over men which—"

"Sure! I getcha," Strawn interrupted rudely. "Get along with this yarn of yours."

"Yarn'!" she repeated, more in sorrow than anger; then she shrugged. "Very well! . . . Last night I dropped in on Enid and asked her to forget her fear of crowds and strangers—to go to the movies with me. She consented at last, and, in a burst of affection for me, presented me with a sheaf of lovely roses which, she said, some unknown admirer had sent her. . . . Ah, dear, dead flowers!" she broke off her narrative to croon in a tender voice, and Dundee saw her touch reverently the withered roses on the murdered doctor's desk. "You made *his* last moments sweeter, but you caused his death!"

"What in the name of God are you raving about?" Strawn demanded, mopping his sweat beaded brow.

"I am ahead of my story," she assured him calmly. "Enid and I went to the movies. Of course Archie joined us, but he came with a horrid, fat little man, too late to sit beside me. But they found seats on the same row, and the dear boy and I managed to carry on a conversation of sorts."

"I can imagine how your neighbors enjoyed *that!*"

She ignored his levity superbly. "He asked me where I got the roses," she went on, her voice somber now. "The devil that always lurks just below the surface of my mind whispered an evil plan to me then. I saw how I could repay the foolish boy in his own coin—make him as jealous as he had tried to make me. ... I sent him word that I was taking my roses to my own true love. Of course he asked the name, and I answered—'Carl!' "

"Carl? Pretty fresh with the doctor, weren't you?" Strawn asked, settled now to enjoyment of the comedy.

"Fresh!" she repeated scornfully. "I called him Carl almost from the first. It was as little as I could do, since the poor doctor was hopelessly, madly infatuated with me!"

"Being in love with you seems to be the regular mental disease around here," Strawn chuckled.

"Can I help it if I am cursed with this power over the hearts of men?" she countered with sad reproof. "I was not in love with Carl. The man interested me enormously, but—" and she shrugged. "No sex appeal, if you know what I mean. A great man and a good man, but, except for his passion for me, less man than doctor. . . . But my personal devil sent me to him last night. I went, knowing full well that Archie Webster would follow, would listen, would—Oh, God! No! I did not dream that he would *kill* for my sake—"

"What time did you come to this office last night?" Strawn cut in, thoroughly interested at last.

"Let me think! . . . Ah, my poor head!" She dosed the blue shadowed eyes and suffered visibly. "It was just after the comedy ended, and just before the feature picture, 'Manslaughter,' came on. About ten minutes to nine, I should say—"

"Ah!" Strawn grunted the syllable that was so often breathed by his witness, and behind the door Dundee echoed it with startled amazement. So it was *this* voice that Roland Morse had heard pleading hysterically with the doctor last night! Good bye to his own theory that it was Norah Lacey who, desperate with anxiety for her illegitimate child, had come to plead with Koenig. . . .

"What was Koenig doing? Was he alone?" Strawn asked.

"Alone, yes," the vibrant voice assured him somberly. "And working as always. I shall never forget how swiftly his thin, brown fingers flew over the typewriter keys–"

"Did you see what he was writing?"

"He was working on Sam Rowan's case history," she told him, more matter of factly. "I saw Rowan's name at the top of the paper in his machine. . . . Well, I gave him the roses, then found a vase and filled it with water. As I set the vase of roses before him I heard footsteps— someone entering the reception room. I knew it was Archie, come to spy upon us. Swift as a bird, I sprang to the door leading into the hall and closed it. Carl told me to open it, but I ignored him. For Archie's benefit I began to babble hysterically to Carl about my great love for him and his love for me. He, the poor dear"— and she broke off to laugh richly— "looked as if he thought I'd gone crazy!"

"I can just imagine!" Strawn assured her.

"Suddenly I forgot I was playing a role. It became real to me. The man's restraint was remarkable — simply incredible! Instead of taking the riches that were offered him, he forced himself to spurn my love. And no man had ever looked at me like that before. ... It did something strange to me, drove me to saying and doing terrible things that I would never have dreamed of doing if he had behaved differently—"

"You accused him of betraying you, of making him love you?" Strawn suggested.

"Ah!" she breathed. "So you knew all the time! I told you I felt the net closing in upon me — and poor Archie! ... As if I were indeed a woman scorned, a woman betrayed, I pleaded with him for his love, charged him, as you've said, with having made me love him, only to spurn me. He tried to soothe me. Once his love broke through, the love professional ethics could not let him show to a patient. He called me his 'darling girl." . . . Ah! I'll never forget that he died loving me!"

"Yeah?"

"But Archie, listening to my wild charges, could not know the truth," she went on mournfully, "that I was only playing an accursed role in a fiendish drama of my own writing! He listened, thought the woman he adored had been foully betrayed. ... Of course he killed him," she added simply.

"Sure!" Strawn agreed. "Guess you hung around and watched him do the deed?"

"Certainly not!" she denied indignantly. "Not then did I realize what a terrible thing I had done. I left Carl, and before I had reached the front porch I was laughing. . . . *I shall never laugh again!*"

"Did you see Webster?" Strawn asked heartlessly.

"No! How could I? He was—in here! I wandered out onto the lawn, waiting for him to join me and protest his undying love and his fierce jealousy. . . . He did not come. After some minutes I realized that I had been crying and that my makeup—I use only a bit of rice powder and the merest brushing of rouge, but—" and she shrugged her thin shoulders. "I did not want the effect of a moonlight reconciliation to be spoiled by a tear streaked face. I went to my room in Aster Cottage, renewed my makeup, changed my frock, wandered about the lawn again, and finally returned to the O. T. Shop, my heart heavy with forebodings. My worst fears were justified. *Archie was not there!*"

"What time did you go back to the shop?" Strawn prodded.

"About half past nine. I came in right in the middle of 'Manslaughter.' I left and returned by the back door of the shop."

"Was Miss Rambler still there when you got back?"

"No. The horrid little fat man, Archie and Enid were all gone. And there I sat, heavy hearted but still not *knowing*–"

"Have you talked with Webster today?" asked Strawn, remembering Dundee's account of Marjorie Merrick's mysterious behavior on the lawn that afternoon.

"Yes!" she cried. "And I don't believe the poor boy *remembers one thing that happened last night!* I warned him not to breathe a word, and he seemed not to know what I was talking about. How could he remember? He was drunk—had gulped down that whole pint of whisky the fat man gave him, to screw up his courage to avenge my betrayal— as he thought!"

"I see," Strawn commented drily.

"Tell me!" she pleaded, clasping her knuckly, thin hands. "Ease the pain in my heart! Tell me that you, too, believe he cannot be held responsible!"

"I don't think Archie will ever be hanged for this murder," Strawn assured her, with a grin he could not suppress.

Clyde Powell's parents, to receive whom Strawn summarily dismissed the ex singer and called in Dundee, were a striking contrast to Marjorie Merrick. They routed melodrama from the dead doctor's office and quietly brought real drama into it. One of those stark tragedies which love to happen to people like the Powells. . . .

Because of the possibility—now looming large—that this man was the murderer, Dundee gave his attention first to John C. Powell, grocer. A small boned, thin old man, who peered diffidently out of pale gray eyes through steel rimmed spectacles. A man whose cadaverous face seemed to Dundee to be the living graveyard of hope and ambition and interest in life. But there was something in it that was not dead—a sort of dogged tenacity, or perhaps it was that pride which had made him refuse charity for his mindless son. Like an ancient and docile child he looked frequently toward his wife—obviously the man of the family. A big, soft fleshed but iron nerved woman, whose brown eyes were stern and uncompromising toward long endured sorrow. . . .

Captain Strawn bridged over the strain of the meeting with two or three routine questions, then, with an almost imperceptible gesture, delivered the couple into Dundee's hands.

"You saw Dr. Koenig yesterday, I believe, Mr. Powell," he began gravely.

"Yes, sir. A great and good man—the doctor. His death is a personal sorrow to the wife and me," Powell answered, in his meek, apologetic voice.

"What was the nature of your interview with the doctor?"

"They had telephoned me to come for a suitcase full of odds and ends that Clyde had left behind when he was transferred Monday to the—the State Hospital," the old man explained, with difficulty. "I got the suitcase and thought I'd like to thank the doctor for all his kindness to our poor boy. The doctor seemed to feel pretty bad over Clyde's transfer—said if he'd been here he'd not have let them take him away. But I explained as how the wife and I couldn't afford the added cost of day and night attendants, and that since the poor boy wouldn't realize much now—" His voice broke and he coughed to hide the shame of his weakness. "Well, the doctor said that, with our permission, he'd try to get Clyde back, and take care of him for the rest of his life, at a nominal cost to the wife and me. I telephoned Susie from the doctor's office—"

"And I said no!" the woman who was incongruously named Susie interrupted emphatically. "Me and John ain't taking charity—not as long as I've got breath to say no. We pay our taxes regular, and we've got a right to take what the State can do for our boy, but charity—no!"

"I understand," Dundee assured her sympathetically. "How long has Clyde been ill, Mrs. Powell?"

"Eleven years come Christmas," she answered promptly. "He was terrible bright in school, was going to be valedictorian of his class when he graduated in June. Just eighteen he was then."

"How did the illness start?"

"Well," the woman hesitated, "he got all wrapped up in religion suddenly, and we all thought it was kinda nice —him wanting to be a preacher and all. Read his Bible all night long many's the night, but on Christmas Day he marched up to the pulpit in church and began to preach something awful—wildlike, and wanting to fight the regular preacher because he wouldn't come out flat footed against kissing and dancing. Couldn't bear the sight of a girl, hardly," she added, and sighed heavily.

"Did he create a very great disturbance then?" Dundee asked.

"It was terrible embarrassing, but the deacons—the deacons overpowered him, and nothing bad happened. Our pastor advised us to put him in the insane asylum then, but we was too proud. We was living in California then and was doing well with our own store out in Glendale. So we put our poor boy in a private sanitarium near Los Angeles—the Good Hope it was called."

"Before you put him in the sanitarium there did he get into any serious trouble?" Dundee persisted.

"Oh, no!" old Mr. Powell assured him earnestly. "We didn't let him out of our sight from Christmas Day till we put him in the sanitarium."

"And while he was at Good Hope?"

"A good biddable patient he was there, except when he got to arguing about religion. He always wanted to fight then, and he got what the doctors call a persecution complex, but of course they watched him too careful for him to hurt anybody," the old man confessed sadly. "Dr. Sandlin used to say the boy had a chance to get well—"

"Sandlin?" Dundee interrupted sharply.

"Yes, sir. A young doctor that worked there," Powell explained. "He was in charge of the mental cases. There wasn't many of 'em; it was a general hospital."

"Then in 1924 we moved to Hamilton," Mrs. Powell took up the story, oblivious to the fact that Dundee was only half listening. "My oldest daughter, Phronsie, married a Hamilton man and she begged us to come here. So we transferred Clyde to Mayfield and opened up a little store here."

Dundee forcibly pulled himself out of a riot of speculations, induced by the name of Sandlin. "Circumstances have arisen, Mr. Powell," he said courteously, "which makes it necessary for us to check up on the movements last evening of every person who came in contact with Dr. Koenig yesterday. A matter of routine, you understand."

"You want our alibis, don't you?" Mrs. Powell demanded, in her downright manner. "I'm glad to see the police are on the job. You don't know us from Adam. Far as you know, me or my husband might have had a grudge against the doctor. Of course we didn't, but you can't know that. . . . Well, Papa and me was in the store all day, except when he come here to see the doctor. I wait on trade, right alongside my husband. After supper my youngest daughter, Belle, was having a little bridge party in our rooms up over the store. I don't play bridge—I used to be quite a shark at 'Forty two' and 'Five Hundred,' but bridge— anyway, I was in and out of the parlor all evening, watching the game and scolding Belle for grouching over bad cards, and fixing a little snack for the party. Downstairs in the store, Papa was fixing up his books—we do a credit business—and writing up bills for our customers. Our youngest boy, Johnny—he's in third year high—was helping his Papa from seven o'clock till ten o'clock, when both of 'em come upstairs for the refreshments. Of course there was customers in and out of the store all evening," she added.

"Thank you, Mrs. Powell," Dundee said, with real admiration. "I wish all witnesses had your gift for telling a straightforward story without resentment."

"You've got your work to do, and I'm not blaming you for doing it, though it's a work I wouldn't choose myself," Mrs. Powell answered frankly.

"It has one advantage," Dundee smiled. "I do get to meet a lot of nice people," and he bowed. "Now, Mr. Powell, one other question: at just what time did Dr. Koenig telephone you last?"

"Telephone *me?*" Powell echoed. "There's a mistake somewhere. The doctor didn't telephone me or the wife last night at all, neither did we phone him."

When they had gone, Strawn turned toward Dundee and shrugged hopelessly. "So that's that! . . . Got it all down, Brede? ... A fat lot of good it'll do. Ain't a doubt in my mind that their alibis will check. . . . An other blind alley, Bonnie boy. I feel like I was lost in a Mirror Maze. . . . What did you think of that Merrick scream's yarn?"

"She was telling the truth, according to her lights," Dundee answered, with a reminiscent twinkle. "Naturally it's all the bunk about Dr. Koenig's being 'madly, hopelessly in love' with her and the same holds true of Archie Webster. I'll lay you a wager it was Archie who sent the roses to Enid Rambler and that she gave some of them to Dr. Harlow as well as to Marjorie Merrick."

"That Rambler baby again!" Strawn caught him up disgustedly. "Whichever way we turn we get back to her, sooner or later. If your hunch is right, Bonnie, and that girl knows who killed the doctor, I'm ready to put the screws on her—"

"Not while she's a patient in this sanitarium!" a lovely voice with a hard edge to it cried from the doorway into the reception room.

"Yeah, Dr. Harlow?" Strawn turned upon her almost savagely. "There's such a thing as conspiring to obstruct justice "

"Then book me on that charge now!" the little doctor challenged defiantly. "For I warn you that if you resort to third degree methods with Enid Rambler, whom I consider to be in a precarious state nervously, I'll put her in "Ten," and nothing short of a troop of militia will get her out of her locked room!"

"Be reasonable, Doctor!" Strawn pleaded, with sudden humility. "The girl's mixed up in this like a fly on fly paper. Not only does she know something about the murder she ain't telling, but she's hiding something pretty smelly in her own past–"

"Bosh!" the girl doctor interrupted inelegantly. "Enid Rambler is as clean and decent and sweet; as–as–"

"As you are," Dundee finished for her, under his breath.

"Well, there's such a thing as striking a bargain," Strawn told them, his eyes grim with purpose. "I'll find out what that young beauty is hiding, and then I'll make her a proposition—immunity in exchange for information about Koenig's murder."

"How are you going about it, Captain?" Dundee asked respectfully.

"First I'm going to find that fat man," Strawn answered. "In my opinion, him and the girl was working in cahoots "

"But according to Archie Webster, the fat man didn't know her name," Dundee objected.

"Ever hear of a hired assassin?" Strawn asked scornfully. "Suppose she'd got cold feet on the idea of murdering the doctor herself, and got in touch somehow with this fat man. She describes herself to him over the phone or in a note, but don't tell her name. . . . All right! He looks her up. She gives him the high sign during the movie to meet her outside. Both leave about the same time, the girl having fixed it with Webster to be waiting for her some where else—at a safe distance. . . . Check? . . . Sure! Then the deed is done. But the fat man ain't satisfied with the bargain he's made and tries to hold the girl up for five or ten times the amount she'd agreed to pay him— either that or the girl welches. Hasn't had a chance to get hold of the dough she'd promised him. He ain't having none of that—says he'll kill the girl too and make a good night's work of it. The girl runs away, you find her crippled on the highway, Dundee, and today she's holding on to the coat tails of a plainclothesman for dear life! . . . How's that?"

"Very diverting, Captain," Dundee smiled. "But if you honestly believe in that theory, how can you promise her immunity? In the eyes of the law, Enid Rambler would be more guilty than her pot bellied hireling!"

"Aw, go to hell!" Strawn sputtered feebly.

# CHAPTER 20

LURLINE DOTY posed, hand on hip, in the doorway, after depositing Dundee's well filled dinner tray upon a table drawn up to his sitting room couch.

"Ain't you the Miracle Man, though?" she kidded, hennaed head tilted, eyebrows arched provocatively.

"And I've just been telling myself that, as a detective, I'm a washout," Dundee retorted wearily, his interest in the food before him rather than in the nurse.

"But, oh boy, as a doctor!" she smiled archly. "Mrs. Morse is so well that Dr. Harlow says she can go home tomorrow—if *you* will let her! And Mr. Salter has borrowed a typewriter from Mr. Baldwin. He told me just now he'd already written five hundred words on the first chapter of a new novel. I asked him if I was going to be in it, and he said yes, and so I said I could tell him a story that would be a best seller, if he'd split fifty fifty–"

"Well—anyway"—the nurse evaded—"it's the most thrilling story you ever heard—all about a girl who goes wrong, and gets 'that way' and dies, and her sister says the baby is *hers*, so her poor little dead kid sister's name won't be disgraced–"

"Un hunh?" Dundee grunted, without interest, knife and fork busy upon the excellent *filet mignon* this silly creature had broiled for him.

"And he snatched at the offer like a starving dog at a bone, I suppose?" Dundee grinned.

"And the beauty of it is, it's a *true* story!" the nurse went on, her voice sinking to a thrilling whisper.

"True?" Dundee repeated, and lost interest in his steak. "Listen, Miss Doty, *does Miss Lacey know you're broadcasting this yarn?*"

"On, I wouldn't tell Mr. Salter the real names, and I'd change the name of the sanitarium, so nobody would recognize the story," the nurse assured him, falling without a thud into the trap the detective had set for her.

"That might be a help," Dundee said very casually, "but unless you've already told Salter, I don't think I'd say anything more about this story, if I were you."

"He wouldn't listen," the nurse admitted. "But I thought I'd write it up myself. I always did want to write, and I've read lots of stories that I know I could write better ones–"

"Not a doubt of it!" Dundee assured her, with a straight face. "You know all the facts personally, of course—not just by hearsay?"

"I'll say I do!" Lurline Doty was delighted with his interest. "Why, me and Colleen Lacey was chums from the time she first started taking Maizie Home's place when Maizie was on her summer vacations. . . . An awful sweet kid—Colleen—even if she did go wrong, and Norah simply worshiped the ground she walked on. Little and cute, with great big blue eyes, and silky black curls, and a dimple in her chin. She looked exactly like a movie actress–"

"And she died when the baby was born?" Dundee interrupted sympathetically.

"Yeah! *And with her lips sealed!*" the nurse whispered with dramatic intensity. "Not even to me would she tell who the man was, although I was with her not five hours before she died. I'd have been right there when the poor kid passed on if Norah hadn't chased me off–"

"Of course Miss Lacey made you promise not to tell the story on her sister?"

"Well, I'm not telling now!" the nurse justified herself aggrievedly. "You already *knew*, and I was going to make up new names when I told Mr. Salter–"

"Of course!" Dundee soothed her for the sake of further information. "And I'll bet you had a good idea who the man was, didn't you? Otherwise," he added craftily, "it wouldn't be much of a story."

"In my story I was going to have it that it was the famous doctor that had betrayed the poor, little innocent stenographer, because that would make it a good story, but I don't think it was *really* Dr. Koenig, although Norah named the baby Carl, and a blind man could see that Doctor thought Colleen was simply the cutest, prettiest, sweetest little thing that ever lived–"

"And why don't you think Dr. Koenig was the man?" Dundee cut in sternly.

"Why, he was too good!" the girl answered simply. "He'd have put out both his eyes rather than let them lust after a virgin–"

Dundee laughed. "I'm afraid you've been reading books that tell more than a young girl ought to know!"

"Oh, I'm old enough to know my way around," she assured him, immensely flattered.

"You're also old enough, Miss Doty," Dundee caught her up grimly, "to realize that the story you've just been telling me should be kept a sacred secret! . . . Don't worry about giving plots to Salter! Keep that story under your white linen cap!"

"You go to the devil!" the nurse cried, in a strangled voice, before fleeing the room in a starchy rustle.

Condemned to the nether regions for the second time that afternoon, Dundee cheerfully concentrated upon his excellent dinner.

Perhaps he'd been rather rough on the nurse, he reflected ruefully, as he drained his cup of its superb coffee. True, she was a malicious little scandal monger, but she'd given him valuable information. While he had made no progress toward solving the murder, the nurse had helped him eliminate Norah Lacey from his formidable list of suspects, and had thereby given him a moment of pure pleasure. Swell woman—this Norah Lacey! he told himself with supreme satisfaction. A genuine heroine, right out of the old school of romantic fiction. And a grand guy, this doctor whose murder he was so clumsily trying to avenge. For Dundee now felt sure that Carl Koenig's shining memory need never be tarnished by the breath of scandal. It seemed quite dear. The "Big Doctor" had been devoted to Norah Lacey's unfortunate little sister, in a purely fatherly way. And Norah Lacey, trusting to his love for the girl and his great understanding, had told him the whole story. With his permission, and without ulterior motive, Norah Lacey had given the child the name she loved best, because it was his. And Carl Koenig, regarding himself as a sort of foster father to the "love child," had left Norah Lacey half his estate, so that that child should have a chance in life. . . . Yes, a great guy, Dundee summed up, his impressionable heart swelling. . . .

"But what good can hero worship do the doctor now?" he demanded of himself truculently, and settled down to work. It was slow going without the typewriter to which he was accustomed, but he forced himself to be content with a pad of the sanitarium notepaper and a freshly filled fountain pen.

*Things I ought to know and don't*, he headed the first sheet of paper. Then, in his sprawling, untidy writ ing, he penned the following questions:

*1. To whom was Dr. Koenig talking when he was murdered? (Put paragraph in morning papers, asking such person to come forward.)*

*2. Whose eyes had puzzled Koenig? Man's or woman's?*

*3. What had Koenig's own eyes lighted upon, when he was talking with Claire Cantrell over the telephone, causing memory to click? Could that name have been Sandlin, which—as the name of Clyde Powell's doctor at Good Hope Sanitarium—undoubtedly appeared on the first page of Clyde's case history?*

*4. Why was Clyde Powell's case history completely missing, along with the Wiggin letter?*

*5. Who was the mysterious fat man? What was his connection with Enid Rambler?*

*6. What was Enid Rambler concealing? Was she really mentally ill, or shamming, as Koenig believed?*

*7. Who was the father of Carl Lacey?*

*8. Where was Maizie Home on Wednesday evening? (Probably unimportant, but should be checked up on.)*

*9. What had Koenig wanted of his lawyer, that could not wait until morning?*

*10. Why had Koenig suddenly determined to dismiss Dr. Harlow?*

*11. Why had Dr. Mayfield demanded, almost with his last breath— and while lucid, according to all evidence— to see Dr. Koenig?*

*12. Had Dr. Mayfield meant Koenig when he said that "that man" must leave Mayfield? If so, what had Koenig done to incur the old doctor's hatred?*

There came a knock on the door, and a woman's white sleeved arm appeared, a newspaper extended.

"Here's the afternoon paper," came a strangled voice from behind the slightly opened door.

"Just a minute, Miss Doty!" Dundee called. "I'll bring you my tray."

"Set it down outside," the choked voice answered.

"No! Please wait!" the contrite young man begged, and sprang toward the door. "I'm terribly sorry I hurt your feelings, Miss Doty. Won't you forgive me?"

The door opened slowly. A tear stained face reproached him "You— you act like I was a leper or something, just because I'm only an attendant, and not a baby doll beauty like Enid Rambler "

"No, no!" Dundee protested, genuinely shocked at the effect of his rudeness. "You've been awfully good to me–"

"I'd do simply *anything* for you, and—and to help you solve the murder," she sobbed. "My boy friend says he's already jealous of you, because I've raved so about you–"

Dundee was acutely embarrassed. "Who is your boy friend?" he asked hastily and without caring in the least what the answer might be.

"Happy—you know, Happy Day," she confided, snuffling miserably. "But we had a tight last night, because a woman had the nerve to call him up at my house, and he had the nerve to leave me flat. . . . And now today he's sore because I've been raving about you—and it wasn't just to make him jealous, either–"

Dundee's cheeks burned. Cooks and policemen—nurse maids and policemen, comic strip combinations. . . . "He's a fine chap! Jolly, and quite the sheik, for a fat

man–"

"He isn't fat!" the nurse flared angrily, and Dundee grinned happily as she snatched his tray and flounced out into the patio with it.

Picking up the paper she had dropped in the doorway, the detective, his work mood broken, scanned the murder story headlines.

*"PATIENTS QUIZZED IN SAN MURDER,"* he read. Smaller head type, pyramided above the two column front page story, announced:

*"SECOND DEATH IN 24 HOURS AT MAYFIELD SANITA RIUM CLAIMS FORMER HEAD; DR. MAYFIELD FOLLOWS COLLEAGUE TO MORGUE; MURDER THEORY SCOUTED."*

The last three words made Dundee smile. "Murder Theory Scouted," indeed! What a blow the coroner's certificate of "Death from natural causes," must have been to the city editors! Not since the double "Murders at Bridge" had Hamilton's newspapers missed so good a chance at front page sensationalism. His eyes swept down the ten point type of the story's opening spread, then on into the smaller single column type. . . .

"Thank God for Strawn's discretion!" he murmured fervently, as he read the story whose skillful padding concealed the paucity of its facts.

But the concluding paragraphs startled him into scowl ing attention:

"Leading physicians of the city, a symposium of whose eulogies of Dr. Carl Koenig appears on Page 2 of this edition, are speculating interestedly upon the question of who will succeed the murdered doctor as psychiatric head of Mayfield Sanitarium, an institution which has brought added lustre to the fair name of Hamilton," wrote the star reporter whose by line topped the story.

"Queried upon this important point, Dr. Bruce Cantrell, head of the medical department, told the writer today that efforts will be made to complete negotiations initiated before his death by Dr. Koenig to bring Dr. Horace Sandlin to Mayfield.

"While Dr. Sandlin is unknown to the local medical fraternity, the fact that Dr. Koenig approached him on his recent stopover in Chicago, in the hope of adding him to the Mayfield staff, is, in the opinion of Drs. Cantrell and Harlow, sufficient guarantee of the psychiatrist's ability.

"Dr. Sandlin, formerly on the staff of the Good Hope Sanitarium of Burbank, California, is at present connected with Howard Memorial Hospital, a private sanitarium for mental diseases located at Evanston, Ill.

"Dr. Justine Harlow, popular young woman psychiatrist and for five years assistant to Dr. Koenig, today handed her resignation to the surviving partners, Dr. Cantrell and Business Manager Roger Baldwin, effective upon the arrival of psychiatrists to take her own and Dr. Koenig's place. Dr. Harlow stated, however, that at this time she has no intention of selling her share of Dr. Koenig's financial interest in Mayfield Sanitarium, bequeathed jointly to herself and Head Nurse Norah Lacey in the famous doctor's last will and testament. No reasons for the resignation were vouchsafed the writer by the charming little doctor, but it is safe to surmise that she wishes the new psychiatric head, whoever he may be, to have a free hand, uninfluenced by the doctor's will, in choosing his assistants. The resignation has not yet been acted upon by Dr. Cantrell and Mr. Baldwin."

"Hell's bells!" Dundee ejaculated, in deep disgust. "That's carrying loyalty a bit too far! If Cantrell and that ass, Baldwin, accept her resignation, they deserve to have Mayfield go bankrupt in a year. . . . And why the devil didn't the little spitfire tell *me* she was going to take such a step?" he grumbled aggrievedly. "Lets me first learn a thing like that from the papers—"

That there was no earthly reason for Justine Harlow to take him into her confidence, in such a personal and heart wrenching matter, did not occur to the indignant young detective.

Those annoying paragraphs completely ruined his evening, which he had intended to devote to a painstaking resume of the Koenig case, from every angle.

"Damn me for a susceptible young fool!" he swore at himself more than once, but his profanity did not prevent his heart's aching for the girl who was undoubtedly tossing upon a sleepless bed, stricken by two grievous blows—the death of the man she had worshiped, and the knowledge that, if he had lived, he would have discharged her. How her pride must be suffering, too, Dundee told himself bitterly. Forced to be a beneficiary under a will which would have been changed if the doctor had lived long enough—

The thought brought to mind that major, unsolved question: To whom was Dr. Koenig telephoning when the murderer's blow struck him down?

Impossible, he mused, sprawling tiredly in a big easy chair, to trace local calls over a dial telephone. But there was an obvious way to ask that question, with some hope of having it answered. He reached for pencil and paper, scribbled a few lines, then lounged out into the reception room of Sunflower Court.

"Telephone?" Miss Hunter, the extremely fat night nurse beamed on him. "There's none closer than the main building. ... By the way, Mr. Dundee, Enid wants you to drop in on her, if you feel like it. She already has company, but she seems to think her little party won't be complete without you."

His fatigue forgotten, Dundee raced across the lawn to the main building, and brushed past Strawn's guard out side the dead doctor's door. A minute later he was talking to the Chief of the Homicide Squad.

"No, nothing new, Captain," he assured Strawn. "But I wish you'd give this paragraph to the newspaper boys when they make their rounds tonight," and he read the few carefully chosen sentences he had scribbled. "Right! We may draw a blank, but it would help a lot if the person Koenig was talking to when he was killed should see this notice and come forward. . . . Yeah, I saw that, and if Baldwin and Cantrell let that girl resign, they're worse nuts than any of their patients. ... By the way, Chief, have you heard from Price? . . . You have? And does he say that was blood in the telephone receiver? . . . Good! Same type as Koenig's, eh? . . . Well, I guess that clinches that! So long, Captain!"

And back Dundee raced to Sunflower Court, his susceptible heart faster than his feet. After all, a man had a right to some relaxation. . . .

He was greeted with a joyous smile from his hostess and an enchanting wave of her beautiful hand, but she did not speak. For, at a baby grand piano which Dundee had scarcely noticed on his earlier visit that day, Marjorie Merrick was playing and singing. Standing on either side of the singer were Archie Webster and Samuel Rowan, the latter an incongruously shabby figure in that luxurious room, the former listening with unconcealed admiration upon his handsome, reckless young face.

But Dundee scarcely saw the men, for, on half of the "love seat" to which Enid Rambler motioned him, a woman was sitting. Exquisitely graceful, Lora Morse sat very still, oblivious to the intrusion, in an attitude of pensive listening. Her beautiful, Madonna like face, framed in smooth dark hair, was sad but not blighted with grief. And in the great black eyes there was a quality of resignation, of hard won serenity, which touched the young detective's heart more profoundly than agonized tears could have done.

"She's well now!" Dundee exulted to himself, and took a mite of credit for her second cure. . . .

A glorious voice, with a rollicking gayety pervading its rich contralto beauty, was dignifying a song that had been popular a couple of years before.

" 'You're the cream in my coffee,' " Marjorie Merrick sang, her black eyes rolling a provocative confirmation to ward Archie Webster, who grinned engagingly, and most respectfully.

"What a voice!" Dundee murmured to Mrs. Morse.

"I'm praying that Marjorie will get well, too," Lora Morse whispered softly.

Enid Rambler lay on the couch, hands clasped behind her shining chestnut curls, her dark blue eyes softly luminous, her lips parted in a smile of happiness.

"Oh, you're so lovely!" Dundee's heart called out to her. "Can any creature as lovely and gentle as you have done any wrong?"

As if she had heard him, Enid Rambler turned her soft, shining gaze upon him, and smiled. . . .

"Well! There's life in the old girl yet, Archie, what the hell!" Marjorie Merrick cried, the instant she had finished her song, and the patness of the quotation from Don Marquis' *Archie and Mehitabel* surprised and delighted Dundee.

"One more, Miss Merrick, please!" Samuel Rowan begged, one of his rough brown hands making an awkward movement toward the singer.

"Gawd! Here's another victim of my accursed charms!" the singer laughed stridently, but her eyes were kind, and her thin fingers fell again upon the piano keys.

"Not till we've had tea, please," Enid Rambler called. "I'm afraid it will be as strong as lye if we don't drink it now. . . . Rally 'round, boys and girls! . . . Oh, Mr. Dundee, it's sweet of you to come! And will you call in my darling plainclothesman? I'm spoiling the man dread fully, but I want to make sure he likes it here and will stay."

"You wouldn't have to feed *me* cakes and tea to keep me around," Dundee assured her gallantly, but sincerely.

"Nor me!" Archie Webster joined in. "Send the dick about his business, Enid, and let me and my attendant watch you—you foul murderess, you!—to see that you don't escape."

Not even the presence of the awkward, blushing plainclothesman and of Webster's sissy looking night attendant—very different from the irrepressible Happy Day— could dampen the gayety of Enid's impromptu tea party. In addition to a pot of tea and a tall, Wedgewood pitcher of chocolate, there was a silver basket heaped with tiny sandwiches, a glass plate overflowing with Viennese *petit fours* of a dozen varieties, and a bonbon dish filled with expensive candies.

"Pretty swell having a Rockefeller Vanderbilt heiress in our midst, *ne c'est pas*, Laddie darling?" Majorie Merrick challenged Dundee, as she cuddled close against him at the tea table. "What a break for us poor nuts that you picked on Mayfield, Enid. For God's sake, don't be in any hurry to get well. We'll be sunk without you."

"I don't think I'll ever have to leave now," Enid answered happily, apparently oblivious to the sinister interpretation which could be put upon the words.

"I feel another song coming on!" Marjorie Merrick set down her cup and strolled toward the piano. "I'm going to warble *Always* this time. . . . Just an old fashioned girl—that's me! And listen, boy friend," she turned threateningly toward Archie Webster, "keep those Don Juan eyes on me while I'm singing, not on Enid, or I'll smash one of your curly locks clear down into your medulla oblongata."

But not even this threat could keep Archie Webster's eyes off Enid Rambler as the sentimental song soared richly from the singer's throat. And Dundee's own eyes were so occupied in watching lovely Enid Rambler that they almost missed the fact that Samuel Rowan was gazing in the same direction, doglike devotion shining in the brown eye that was not obscured by a cast.

But he did recall that fact later, with a cold chill of shock. In that room that evening were two men—one young, eligible, rich, accustomed to a reckless flouting of the law, the other oldish, life beaten, freshly unburdened of some dreadful secret—two men who, judging by the love that shone from their eyes, would have stopped at nothing to protect Enid Rambler from Dr. Koenig's determination to cast her out of Mayfield against her will.

But that realization came later. As Marjorie Merrick sang. "I'll be loving you always," Dundee's own infatuated eyes scarcely left the young girl. So it was that he saw the storm brewing, from the moment the first quiver passed over her delicate face and the first tear fell from her bronze eyelashes, until she covered her convulsed face with her hands and chokingly begged her guests to leave. . . .

Dazed, the detective stumbled out of the room, his offers of assistance and comfort rejected along with those of all the others.

"Strike me dead for an idiot!" Marjorie Merrick exploded. "I know damned well the poor kid's eating her heart out for some black hearted wretch that's done her dirt, and here I go and babble the sloppiest love song ever written! Kick me, somebody!"

And Archie Webster obeyed, with too much earnestness to suit the singer, who chased him vengefully across the lawn, then embraced him fiercely when she caught him.

Although it was nearly nine o'clock—bedtime for Mayfield Sanitarium—Dundee felt so restless in spite of his fatigue that his extremely comfortable suite in Sunflower Court seemed like a prison cell. There was nothing to read, no more work he could do before morning. . . .

Finally, in desperation, for he felt the need of some thing, anything to lift him out of the slough of despond into which Enid Rambler's tears had plunged him, he gathered up the scattered sheets of the afternoon newspaper. Might as well cast a stony eye over the comics, and dare them to make him laugh

Then he uttered a sharp exclamation as a brief, boxed item on page two leaped at his attention.

*MYSTERIOUS MIDNIGHT VISITOR AT MAYFIELD* was the two line, italic head over the blackface type of the boxed story. Swearing under his breath the detective began to read:

"Characteristically unable to see farther than the nose on his face, Captain John Strawn, Chief of the Homicide Squad, will first learn from this issue of *The Evening Sun* of a mysterious visitor who arrived shortly before midnight on Tuesday at the cottage shared by Dr. Carl Koenig and Roger Baldwin, Mayfield Sanitarium's business manager, and was closeted for two hours with the psychiatrist who was murdered in cold blood less than twenty four hours later.

"This information was divulged to a reporter for *The Evening Sun* by Mr. Baldwin himself. The business manager, when questioned concerning the murdered doctor's movements since his return from a business and lecture trip, which included New York, Boston, Washington and Chicago, stated that he was awakened by the sound of voices in low toned, earnest conversation. The voices, which undoubtedly came from the cottage living room, according to Mr. Baldwin, and one of which he identified as that of his partner, Dr. Koenig, continued for approximately two hours. Mr. Baldwin says he did not rise to investigate, that he did not see the mysterious visitor, whose voice was unknown to him, and that he did not recall the strange occurrence until the reporter questioned him as to Dr. Koenig's movements on Tuesday. Asked if the doctor and his unknown visitor seemed to be quarreling, Mr. Baldwin said that he got no such impression. On Wednesday morning Dr. Koenig made no mention of his visitor and Mr. Baldwin made no inquiries. Perhaps if he had, the murder of Dr. Carl Koenig might not now be the apparently baffling mystery that it is."

"Hell!" Dundee swore again, as he flung down the paper.

The district attorney's special investigator did not sleep much that night.

# CHAPTER 21

KNOWING the enterprise and efficiency of American city editors, Dundee was prepared to find a front page story with a Chicago date line in his Friday morning paper, but *The Star's* revelations were more important than he had guessed they would be. He read as he breakfasted off his tray:

"Chicago, June 4—Dr. Horace Sandlin, when interviewed late today at the Howard Memorial Hospital, where he is a member of the staff, confirmed Hamilton, —, newspapers reports that Dr. Carl Koenig, psychiatric head of Mayneld Sanitarium, who was murdered in his office at that institution Wednesday night, had opened negotiations to bring the Chicago doctor to Mayneld.

" 'I am indeed sorry,' Dr. Sandlin said to this reporter this evening, "that the news of my negotiations with Dr. Koenig had to come to the Howard Memorial Hospital board in this way, but the report is true. On his recent visit to Chicago, for the purpose of delivering a lecture at Northwestern University, Dr. Koenig did me the honor to extend me an invitation to join his staff at Mayfield Sanitarium near Hamilton. It was agreed at that time that I should call upon him at Mayfield, and go further into the question of salary, duties, etc.'

"At this point the psychiatrist laughed ruefully. 'I see by dispatches from Hamilton in the evening papers that 'a mysterious midnight visitor' is likely to be a favorite suspect in this baffling murder mystery. I am sorry to have to furnish so prosaic an explanation of that mysterious midnight visit, but I am glad to be able to clear up this minor point. *I* was the mysterious visitor! Unable to spare a day from my work at Howard, whose accommodations in my department are taxed to the utmost by patients afflicted mentally by the nation wide depression, I took a six o'clock train from Chicago, arriving in Hamilton at 11:30 P.M. I went immediately to the Sanitarium, or, rather, to Dr. Koenig's cottage on the grounds. There we conferred for about two hours, the interview terminating in time for me to catch a slow local at 2:45, getting me back to my work without loss to the institution I now serve. If the doctor and I had known that Mr. Baldwin was awakened by our voices, we should have taken advantage of the opportunity for me to meet Mayfield's very efficient business manager,' the psychiatrist added with a smile.

"When asked if he was still favorably inclined toward leaving Howard for Mayfield, the psychiatrist said: 'Naturally such a suggestion will now have to come from Dr. Koenig's surviving partners, and must be in line with the agreement already arrived at between Dr. Koenig and my self. For instance, Dr. Koenig was planning to devote most of his time to psychoanalysis, with an office in Hamilton, and to turn over the bulk of his sanitarium work to me, permitting me to choose my own assistant. Since Dr. Koenig is so tragically dead, however, any further negotiations must be instigated by Dr. Cantrell and Mr. Baldwin, his surviving partners."

Dundee lowered the paper, frowning intently. "Meaning," he muttered, "that Sandlin plans to be psychiatric head of Mayfield—or nothing! And that Justine Harlow must go! For who can say now whether Sandlin is lying or not? Koenig is dead and can neither confirm nor deny anything that Sandlin may say. Pretty clever of him to realize that the dead doctor's wishes will be sacred. A golden opportunity, and little Horace—damn his fat face!— seems to be making the most of it!"

He raised the paper and studied the rather indistinct photograph of Dr. Horace Sandlin, relayed to *The Hamil ton Star* by television. A smiling, fat cheeked face, with prominent, pale eyes, a broad nose, and thin hair, either blond or gray. Dundee conceived an instant, unreasoning dislike of the well fed doctor, felt a childish desire to stick his tongue out at those beaming, pale eyes. . . .

Eyes! Could these be the eyes which had puzzled Carl Koenig? Had Koenig suddenly remembered where he had seen Dr. Horace Sandlin before—a memory that called for instant action and brought horror in its wake? Certainly Sandlin's name had been mentioned, probably more than once, in Clyde Powell's case history. And Powell's history had been on the desk under the murdered doctor's eyes. *And*—Powell's history was completely missing. Not a scrap of it remained behind–

His head spinning in the vicious circle, Dundee shrugged and raised his paper again. . . . Yes, there was his own paragraph, prominently featured on the front page in a box to itself, asking all persons to whom Dr. Koenig had telephoned on the night of his murder to come forward for questioning by the police. But the request was worded so tactfully as not to alarm the prospective witness. "Merely to aid the police in fixing the exact time of the doctor's murder," the paragraph concluded.

Fat lot of good it would do, in all likelihood, Dundee prophesied gloomily. But at any rate he would have to await possible developments from that source. . . .

"Come in!" he called, as a knock interrupted his unhappy reflections.

It was Archie Webster, in a purple satin bathrobe and exuding health and vigor.

"Hydros are swell things! You look like you could do with one yourself, old man," the intermittent alcoholic suggested heartily. "So you've seen the bad news, too?" he added, indicating the morning paper. "If that fat slob is going to take charge here, I'm signing the pledge today."

The word "fat" crashed through Dundee's brain. "Have you seen this man before, Webster?" he demanded, his tired eyes suddenly keen with excitement.

"Does look sort of familiar, doesn't he?" Webster agreed. "Might be a composite picture of all the ward politicians—"

"Does he look anything like that fat man who gave you the whisky Wednesday night?" Dundee interrupted sharply.

Webster laughed. "Are you turning amateur detective, too? . . . But, you know, there is a sort of resemblance, at that—"

"Can you identify Sandlin as your uninvited guest?" Dundee persisted.

But Webster shook his head. "That's not a very clear picture, and I'm pretty sure that my fat man was a whole lot fatter—"

"This picture may be an old one," Dundee suggested, loath to relinquish his startling new theory.

"Better leave detecting to the police," Webster suggested with unconscious cruelty, "and come out for a game of peewee golf."

But Dundee excused himself so curtly that Webster quickly took his departure. After a hurried bath and shave the young detective sprinted across the lawn to the main building, cursing the fact that the telephone was so inaccessible.

Having let himself into the dead doctor's office, he dialed a number.

"Hello! Consolidated Ticket Offices? . . . Information, please! . . . Hello! Will you tell me, please, whether there is a train in from Chicago at about half past seven in the evening?" he asked, and waited for two or three minutes. Then: "At seven twenty, you say? . . . Leaving Chicago when?"

When the answer came he thanked the information clerk and slowly replaced the receiver. If it could be proved that Dr. Sandlin had not been on duty at Howard Memorial Hospital on Wednesday afternoon

The telephone rang. Captain Strawn's unmistakable voice came over the wire: "Lemme speak to Mr. Dundee!"

"This is Dundee, Captain," the younger detective answered. "Anything new?"

"Just got a funny telegram from Chicago," Strawn's voice replied. "Listen—and you might make a copy of it if you've got a pencil handy. . . . All right! Here goes:

*"PUZZLED BY SANDLIN STORY IN MORNING PAPERS STOP DR. KOENIG MY GUEST WHILE IN CHICAGO ON LECTURE TOUR STOP KOENIG WITH ME CONSTANTLY ENTIRE*

*TWENTY FOUR HOURS HIS VISIT HERE STOP AM POSITIVE
HE DID NOT CONFER THIS TRIP WITH SANDLIN RELATIVE
MAYFIELD STAFF POSITION STOP DOCTOR DID ASK MY
ADVICE REGARDING ASSISTANT PSYCHIATRIST STOP
SPOKE HIGHLY OF DR. HARLOW'S WORK WANTED TO FIND
YOUNG MALE PSYCHIATRIST WHO WOULD WORK
CONGENIALLY WITH HER STOP HAVE NO DESIRE TO
INTERFERE BUT AM OFFERING ABOVE IN INTERESTS OF
MAYFIELD
STOP PLEASE KEEP CONFIDENTIAL.*

"Got all that? . . . It's signed Edward Livingstone, Professor of
Abnormal Psychology, Northwestern University."

"Whew!" Dundee whistled. "Nigger in the woodpile somewhere,
Captain!"

"You said a mouthful," Captain Strawn's voice retorted gloomily.
"But what's all this got to do with the price of eggs?"

"Young Webster has halfway identified Sandlin's picture in the
paper as that of the fat man who presented him with a pint of whisky
Wednesday night," Dundee explained quietly, and it was Strawn's turn
to whistle.

When the younger detective again replaced the receiver, he had
secured Strawn's promise to check up discreetly on the Chicago doctor's
alibi for Wednesday afternoon and evening.

Still he was not satisfied. He sat there in the chair where Carl
Koenig had died, and stared gloomily at the telephone which had
yielded up the clue from which he, Dundee, had hoped so much. That
one drop of blood! How confidently he had banked on it! And yet,
according to Strawn, no reader of the morning papers had come for
ward so far with the admission that it was to him—or her —that the
psychiatrist had been talking when death had cut short the
conversation.

Useless to try to trace such a call, if the information was not
volunteered, Dundee told himself. Then, with a muttered oath at his
own mental laziness, he seized the telephone and dialed 1 1 0.

"Hello! Long distance? . . . Let me speak to the supervisor, please. .
. . Hello! District attorney's office speaking. I want to know if there was
a toll or long distance call put through over this number—Sheridan
0100—on Wednesday evening."

It was not quite so simple as that, for Dundee had to repeat his
request to three different officials before it was finally answered.

And the answer was "No!"

Feeling a little dashed, and that his hunch had betrayed him, the detective absently studied the copy of the telegram Strawn had read to him over the telephone.

"Telegram—telephone" . . . the words seemed to float lazily up from his subconscious mind.

"Lazy idiot!" he apostrophized himself, as he grabbed the instrument and dialed so hastily that the operation had to be repeated.

"Hello! Western Union? . . . Let me speak to the manager, please!"

Five minutes later, not even taking time to get his hat from Sunflower Court, Dundee hurled himself into his roadster, which was still parked in front of the main building. His hurry and excitement were due to no specific in formation which the Western Union manager had given him. He was merely playing a hunch, which, as he had talked with the telegraph manager, had grown to lusty proportions.

He made one brief stop on his way into the business section of Hamilton, a visit which the district attorney vainly tried to prolong. And within twenty minutes after he had hung up the receiver in the murdered doctor's office he was shaking hands with a brisk young man who made no effort to conceal the fact that he was almost as excited as the detective himself.

"I followed your suggestion, Mr. Barrow," Dundee told the Western Union manager. "Here is a note from the district attorney, asking you, as a personal favor to himself and to his office, to waive formalities."

"Well, I hope I shan't get into trouble," the manager smiled, as he accepted the note and read it. "But when it's a case of murder, I believe it is the duty of every citizen to extend whatever aid lies in his power–"

"Absolutely!" Dundee assured him heartily. "Now, you were saying over the telephone, Mr. Barrow, that a file is kept of uncompleted messages–"

"That's right. 'Bust' messages, we call them," the Western Union man explained, with a trace of superiority. "There are several such messages in the course of a day's business here, but not enough of them to file separately. We keep each day's 'bust' messages in a single folder, bearing the date. Naturally, these messages are all received over the telephone. Accidental disconnections are responsible for most of the 'busts,' of course. The client calls back, and is usually pretty sore because he has to repeat the message from the beginning. He does not realize that it would be a truly remarkable coincidence if he should" get the same operator who was taking down his telegram be fore the connection was broken. We have ten girls who do nothing but receive telegrams, night letters, etc., over the telephone."

"Yes, yes, I understand," Dundee fretted, for he had heard all this on the telephone twenty minutes before. "Now, if you could show me the file of 'bust' messages for Wednesday night "

But the manager hesitated. "I'm afraid I can't do that, not even with this request from the district attorney. But I can read off the names and addresses of those messages—"

"Have you looked through Wednesday's file since I called you?" Dundee interrupted. "I had hoped you might have found one with either the doctor's name or the Mayfield telephone number—"

"In that case, it would not have been a 'bust' message," the manager reminded him, with a smile of superiority. "Consider how a telegram is sent by telephone. You call or dial Western Union. One of our operators answers. You say: 'I want to send a night letter, please'— that is, if you are polite!" and the manager chuckled at his own wit. "The operator's first query is: 'To whom is the night letter going?'—Not, 'What is your telephone number or your name?' "

"Of course!" Dundee acknowledged, a trifle chagrined. "And it is not until the complete message has been taken down by the operator that she asks, 'What is your telephone number, please?' and then, 'In whose name is this telephone listed?' Naturally, if any of this information appeared on the message it would be complete, or so nearly complete that, if the line was disconnected, the operator herself could get the client back on the telephone."

"Correct!" the manager applauded. "And that's exactly why it will be no easy matter to point to a 'bust' message and say with any certainty, 'Dr. Koenig was telephoning this message to Western Union when the line was disconnected.' "

"When he was killed," Dundee corrected grimly. "But if my hunch is right, and Dr. Koenig was sending a telegram at the moment he was murdered, the name of the addressee or the nature of the beginning of the message should be quite sufficient."

"Perhaps you're right," the manager answered, very respectfully. "I'll read the names and addresses of Wednesday's bust messages—"

"Just a moment," Dundee begged. "Have these messages been checked against Wednesday's completed messages? My point, of course, is that *only those which were never completed need concern us.*"

"Completed messages are filed only under the names of the senders," the manager informed him, and he began to read off the names and addresses from a small sheaf of telegraph blanks.

And at each of the first three names Dundee shook his head. For one was the name of a girl whose address was a sorority house at the State University; another belonged to a firm of stockbrokers in New York, and the third "bust" message had been intended for the room reservations clerk of a Detroit hotel.

But the fourth name, even before the address was read off, brought a sharp exclamation of triumph from Bonnie Dundee.

" 'Buron Fitts, District Attorney of Los Angeles County, Los Angeles, California,' " the manager was in toning in his slightly sing song voice.

"That's the one!" Dundee cried. "Surely you will let me see that message? It fits a number of known facts–"

"Very well," and Barrow surrendered the half filled blank.

Dundee read the incomplete night letter avidly:

*PLEASE CONSULT YOUR RECORDS YEAR NINETEEN NINETEEN AND WIRE ME COMPLETE DESCRIPTION OF E D I*

And there, as if Fate chuckled at the detective's annoyance, the message ended.

## CHAPTER 22

BUT Dundee was more than grateful for Fate's small favors when he again reached the bedside of his pleurisy stricken chief.

"Progress, boss!" he exulted, as he flung down a copy of the "bust message."

The district attorney's enthusiasm was slower to kindle. "You're sure this message wasn't being sent by the Chief of Police, to check up on some crook they've picked up on suspicion?"

Dundee laughed. "Thought of that myself! . . . Bright lad—your special investigator! No one at headquarters knows a thing about this highly interesting night letter. And I'll wager my roadster it never reached District Attorney Buron Fitts—"

"I'm concerned with facts, not wagers," Hamilton's district attorney told him cruelly. "Can't the Western Union manager here tell you whether it was finally sent through another operator?"

"I suppose he could, but it would take hours to go through all the files from A to Z, in a blind search for the sender's name," Dundee acknowledged. "The simplest thing is to query Fitts himself. . . . I'll call him long distance—"

"Hold on!" Sanderson stopped him. "While it's half past ten o'clock here, it's only 7:30 A.M. in Los Angeles, and if Fitts and I have anything in common, my fellow district attorney is still in bed at that hour. Send a wire, then prepare to wait at least three hours before you can hope to get an answer. Even so—"

"Don't toss the wet blanket so blithely, Chief," Dundee pleaded. "I tell you I never had a stronger hunch! The way I dope it is this: While he was talking to Claire Cantrell, Dr. Koenig's gaze happened to light on *something*—a name, probably—that caused his memory to click. Now, that name *must* have appeared in Clyde Powell's case history, because, for no other reason that we can even remotely imagine, Clyde's history is completely missing—not torn up like the others, which were destroyed merely as a blind—"

"Yeah, I know all that," the sick man interrupted peevishly.

"Sorry, Chief," Dundee grinned. "Well, the good old memory suddenly functions, and Dr. Koenig remembers where he has seen those eyes before. *Before*—he said to Claire Cantrell! That means, in my opinion, that the owner of those mysterious eyes was either somewhere about or that the doctor had seen them very recently. Right?"

"Go on," the district attorney agreed obliquely.

"As we've said all along, the doctor's horror was such that he had to get busy without a minute's delay. Why?— Because the owner of those eyes was a possible menace either to himself or to Mayfield Sanitarium. Right?"

Again Sanderson commanded, but less irritably: "Go on!"

"Dr. Koenig calls his lawyer. Whatever it is, it's the sort of mess that the law must deal with. Attorney Forrest isn't at home, and Koenig says he'll have to handle the matter himself. What then? He telegraphs the district attorney of *Los Angeles*–"

"Yeah, I see—where Clyde Powell used to live," Sanderson supplied, as Dundee paused impressively.

"Not only where Clyde Powell lived, but where he was confined in a sanitarium of which *Dr. Horace Sandlin* was psychiatric head!"

"You're off the track there, my lad," Sanderson cut in drily. "In 1919 as well as in 1931 Dr. Sandlin was known as Horace Sandlin— neither part of his name beginning with E d i "

"I'm not saying Sandlin is 'E d i' and hence the murderer," Dundee retorted. "In fact, Strawn has checked up on Sandlin and has found that he has an iron clad alibi for all of Wednesday, day and night. Sandlin was in his office or at work among the patients of Howard Memorial Hospital near Chicago from noon Wednesday until midnight. But I'll wager that same roadster that Sandlin—accidentally, perhaps—is mixed up in this thing somehow."

And Dundee exhibited the copy of the telegram Strawn had received from Professor Livingstone of Northwestern University.

"Professors must be better paid these days," Sanderson chuckled, as he finished reading the long message, which scorned the economy of day letters.

But Dundee was not smiling. "There's something damned queer about Sandlin," he worried. "In my opinion, those last lines of the telegram are the most significant," and he repeated them: 'Am offering above in *interests of Mayfield*. Please keep confidential.' . . . Dr. Livingstone, bless his heart, spares no expense to warn us that Sandlin would be very bad medicine for Mayfield patients, and yet I suppose professional etiquette would seal his lips against any more specific charges. . . . Now why the devil, if there's anything smelly about Sandlin, did *Koenig* practically close negotiations to bring him to Mayfield?"

"Carl Koenig," Sanderson began slowly, "was a very great doctor, but not a particularly good business man. In sudden need of another assistant, Koenig probably listened to the advice of some colleague he met during his trip, and impulsively, without investigating very thoroughly, offered the job to Sandlin."

"But Livingstone wires that no such conference took place while Koenig was in Chicago," Dundee pointed out.

"Livingstone is probably mistaken," Sanderson decided reasonably. "It is unlikely that the good professor was actually with Koenig 'constantly,' as he says in this wire, and even so, the first negotiations might have been made over the telephone, and a personal appointment arranged for Tuesday night. That would explain Sandlin's coming along so soon after Koenig's return."

"Probably you're right," Dundee agreed, but with no conviction. "At any rate, it's pretty obvious that some thing clicked in Koenig's memory on Wednesday night that made him get busy in such a manner that his murder had to take place before that telegram could be finished and on its way to Los Angeles!"

"And what possible connection could there exist between 'E d i' and Sandlin?" the district attorney insisted.

"I don't know," Dundee confessed frankly. "There's this possibility: Koenig, in the role of alienist, served as an expert witness on some case in which Sandlin also testified, as an alienist. The defendant was this 'E d i.' In 1919, let us say, since Koenig himself gives us that year in his wire to the district attorney. 'E d i' has eyes that Koenig remembers, but the rest of his features fade from the doctor's memory. Before him, on Wednesday night, was Clyde Powell's case history, joining Los Angeles with the name of Sandlin. The juxtaposition of the town and the doctor's name brings about one of those freaks of memory. Koenig remembers where he has seen a pair of eyes that have puzzled him. For he and Sandlin, in Los Angeles, both looked upon the owner of those eyes. The whole case flashes back into Koenig's memory. 'E d i' is a dangerous person—and 'E d i' is where Koenig can lay hands on him, if the police still want him."

"Well, who *is* 'E d i'?" Sanderson demanded, irritable again

"I can't read a dead man's mind," Dundee admitted, shrugging. "My guess is that he was either the relative of a patient or a patient at Mayfield."

"Meaning that he may be our mysterious 'fat man,' or Rowan, or Roland Morse," Sanderson deduced. "Or—to change the pronoun, *she* may be—Enid Rambler!"

Dundee flushed, but his hot protest died out before it had made a good beginning.

"Keep your shirt on, boy!" Sanderson advised, paternally. "But you see where idle speculation can lead us. Suppose you put that wild imagination of yours on a leash and keep it there until we've at least had confirmation from Fitts in Los Angeles that that 'bust' message never reached him. If it didn't get through—and I admit that anyone starting a message like that would naturally finish it, in spite of disconnections, if it was humanly possible to do so—we can go on from here. Wire your query to Fitts, then possess your soul with patience until you get an answer."

Rather subdued, Dundee obeyed. But he had better use for the next two hours than to devote them to attaining a Buddha like calm.

# CHAPTER 23

ALTHOUGH he was sure that Enid Rambler had lied when she had said she had been staying at the Randolph Hotel before going to Mayfield, Dundee made inquiries there as the first step in his investigation into the girl's "past." The blank he drew there did not at all discourage him.

The city of Hamilton boasted two excellent hotels: the Randolph, the newer and more fashionable—swimming pool, roof garden, radio in every room; and the Hamiltonian, a dignified old house, whose noble spaciousness and graciousness extended beyond the lobby and public rooms into the guests' accommodations. A French chef, who made the only real *croissants* to be found in the city; hospitable and more than efficient service, and an air of leisured dignity seldom found in a Middle West hotel, made the Hamiltonian exactly the sort of temporary home which a girl of Enid's obvious breeding and apparent wealth would have chosen. But faced with the necessity of lying to protect herself, nothing could have been more natural than that she should have given the Randolph as her last address.

The manager of the Hamiltonian was Francis Drake Littleton, an Englishman, who had spent many hours talking London with the young detective, one time holder of a lowly job at Scotland Yard. He received Dundee cordially.

"An interesting case—the Koenig affair," Littleton began, with relish. "Scotland Yard would make short work of it. A great institution, sir—nothing like it in this country. You should have prolonged your training there."

"Oh—we blunder along and find the criminal occasionally," Dundee grinned. "By the way, sir, I need your help–"

"Anything I can do–" the hotel manager assured him, vastly pleased.

"Thanks!—It's just a side issue to the main case, I'm fairly sure, but we can't ignore it," Dundee told him, lighting one of the English cigarettes his host had offered. "There's a devilish pretty girl at Mayfield, who says that, before going to the sanitarium, she was stopping for a few days at the Randolph. My hunch was that she was exactly the sort of young woman who would demand only the best— hence that she was lying; that she really stayed at the Hamiltonian."

The Englishman bowed, and his very mustache registered pleasure in the compliment. "Her name?"

"Oh, she lied about that, too," Dundee laughed. "But I don't think she's at all expert about lying, or really an adept at choosing aliases on the spur of the moment. However, on the off chance that she was not lying, the name she goes under now is Enid Rambler."

The manager shook his white head slowly. "I'm sure no young person of that name has been a guest here, yet it has a vaguely familiar ring to it. ... On what day did she enter Mayfield?"

"The evening of Wednesday, April second," Dundee told him. "May I suggest that you look over the hotel register sheets for a week preceding that day, to see if a Miss E. R. was a guest here."

The manager reached for a telephone and was soon relaying the request to an assistant manager. Within five minutes the seven sheets from the hotel's loose leaf register were in front of the detective, and his quick eyes were racing down the topmost page of legible and illegible, neat and bold signatures.

Not until he reached the third sheet—the register entries for May 31—did he find what he was looking for.

"Here we are!" he cried jubilantly. " 'Miss Edith Ramsey, New York City ' "

"Edith Ramsey!" the manager ejaculated. "Good Lord, Dundee! Are you sure? Is *that girl* at Mayfield Sanitarium?"

"Careful of the good old blood pressure, sir!" Dundee warned. "What's up?"

The manager tried to control himself, but excitement still rode him as he exclaimed: "But this is astounding, sir! Simply amazing! Fearfully ironic, and all that sort of thing! While private detectives scour the country for her Well, well! A bit of a shock, I assure you!"

"Would you mind explaining, Mr. Littleton?" Dundee suggested, his impatience difficult to curb.

"Yes, yes, certainly! But it is *most* amazing, I assure you– Will you describe the young lady who you think may be Miss Ramsey?"

"Perfectly beautiful," Dundee began, with enthusiasm. "Curling chestnut hair, dark blue eyes; quite tall, very slender–"

The manager smiled. "I see that Miss Ramsey has had the same effect on you as she had upon my entire staff— myself included! . . . Yes, I am glad to say there seems to be no doubt that you have discovered the missing heiress."

"Then she ran away from the hotel?" Dundee asked. "Running away seems to be rather a habit of Miss Ramsey's."

But the manager shook his head. "Not exactly. But I'll be glad to tell you all I know. . . . One night—let me think! Yes, it must have been Wednesday evening, April second—Miss Ramsey and the young man of her party–"

"Young man?" Dundee repeated, with a premonitory twinge in his heart.

"Oh, yes!" the manager assured him. "A most estimable young man. One of America's aristocrats, I should say. Family—money—"

"His name?" Dundee interrupted the eulogy.

"Paul Van Twing—the Dutch Van Twings who were among the earliest settlers of New York," the manager answered, with relish. "The young man seems to be the worthy scion of a fine family— distinguished in appearance, with a grace of bearing that one so seldom sees in this—"

"There was a party, you say?"

"Only Mrs. Van Twing, a schoolgirl daughter who was ill, the son Paul, and Miss Ramsey," the hotel manager answered, with a faint air of reproach for these curt interruptions. "It was quite obvious that the young couple were in love. In fact, Mrs. Van Twing confided to me that they were to be married after the party reached California, their objective, toward which they were traveling by easy stages, due to the child's illness. . . . Tuberculosis, I'm afraid."

"And what happened Wednesday night?"

"The young couple went for a drive in one of the cars in which the party was making a luxurious cross country tour," Littleton went on wordily. "Mr. Van Twing dismissed the chauffeur and drove himself. Just before midnight the young man returned alone in quite a dreadful state. I happened to be in the lounge when he arrived. He asked immediately if Miss Ramsey had returned. I said I had not seen her, but made doubly sure by asking the night clerk and by ringing her room. The young man almost collapsed then, and I urged him into my office here and braced him with a spot of brandy. . ,. . Very decent brandy, too! Would you like a sip?"

"No, thanks," Dundee said, sitting on the edge of his chair. "What had happened? Did he tell you?"

"He did—and in the wildest possible way," the manager assured him, smiling. "Young Van Twing begged me to telephone for the police—"

"What?" Dundee shouted.

"For the police," Littleton repeated. "He said he had knocked down a man on the highway and killed him."

"Oh!"

"In a most distressing condition he was, the poor chap. Kept insisting that it was all his fault—and so vehement about it that I deduced"—and the manager smacked his lips over the word—"that it was really Miss Ramsey who was responsible for the accident."

"I see," Dundee said slowly. "I understand a lot of things now—"

"Oh, but it was all what you Americans call a false alarm," the manager assured him. "The poor blighter on the roadside had not been killed at all—was scarcely hurt, in fact. Merely stunned."

"Then why ?" Dundee began.

"Don't you see? Miss Ramsey fled the scene of the accident, believing the man had been killed. Poor Van Twing told her to 'beat it'—as you say over here; that he would assume the entire blame. He thought, naturally, that she would return to the hotel. He telephoned at a filling station for an ambulance and waited until he saw it arriving in the distance, then he 'beat it,' too. . . . Very bad policy, but the poor chap was frightfully upset. His whole thought seems to have been for Miss Ramsey, who, he told me, had become hysterical. He wanted to see her first, reassure her that her name would never be mentioned in the report of the accident, then go to the police and give himself up."

"I saw nothing in the papers about all this," Dundee frowned.

"There wasn't a line," Littleton assured him proudly. "That is, about the accident. I myself went with young Van Twing to the receiving hospital, and there we found that the man was able to leave. Had been stunned, but not seriously injured at all. At my suggestion the young man gave the accident victim a check for five hundred dollars, which made the unfortunate man glad that he'd been bowled over. Of course Van Twing reported the affair to the police, but a word from me kept it out of the papers."

"I see," Dundee repeated, dazedly.

"When we returned to the hotel, Miss Ramsey was still not in her room, and had not telephoned," the manager continued. "Young Van Twing was in a truly pitiable state. I suggested that he tell his mother—a fine, capable lady—and it was Mrs. Van Twing that took charge then and carried on. She telephoned every person with whom the party had become friendly during their brief stay here, but not one of them had seen or heard from Miss Ramsey. And three times during the remainder of the night she made telephone inquiry of every hospital in Hamilton."

"Did she ring up Mayfield Sanitarium?" Dundee asked.

"I rather think not," the manager told him. "Mayfield, you see, is quite remote—at least five miles from the city, I understand. And even if Mrs. Van Twing had inquired, she would have been told that no young person named Ramsey had been received there."

"And so the party shoved off?" Dundee asked.

"Not for several days," Littleton answered. "But the little girl— Alicia, her name is—became worse, and it was necessary finally for the party to move on toward the West, where the child was to be put in a sanitarium. Young Van Twing was in a dreadful state, but he had apparently done all he could, and his mother needed him badly. Mrs. Van Twing, however, did arrange with the society editors of both morning and evening newspapers to display prominently, with headlines, a social note to the effect that the Van Twings were to conclude their visit to Hamilton and go on to California, as soon as Miss Edith Ramsey, a member of their party, had returned from a visit with friends in a near by city. Her hope was that Miss Ramsey would see this item and realize that the coast was clear. But nothing developed. In case Miss Ramsey returned to the hotel, I was to give her a message, and also wire Van Twing in San Francisco."

"You mentioned private detectives, I believe."

"Right you are! A few days ago a person came here, making inquiries about Miss Ramsey. I asked him if he were a private detective—a rather neat deduction as it turned out, for that was exactly what the fellow was," Littleton commended himself. "A rum sort of codger —expert at pumping me, but quite the clam when it came to answering my questions–"

"What did he look like?" Dundee interrupted, but he was sure of the answer before it came.

"Disgustingly fat little bounder," Littleton told him. "Middle aged, fairish sort of hair and light eyes—most ord'n'ry, really."

"Has he been here more than once?"

"No. I particularly asked him to return and relieve my own anxiety, if he discovered Miss Ramsey's whereabouts, but I have not seen him since."

After ten minutes or so, during which the hotel manager plied the detective with questions concerning the Koenig case, which Dundee answered with apparent frankness, the young detective made his escape.

District Attorney Sanderson listened to the story with only an occasional exclamation by way of interruption, his brown flecked gray eyes fixed very intently upon the narrator.

"Hard lines, old man," he said surprisingly, when the narrative was concluded.

Dundee flushed, shrugged, but did not deny the insinuation behind the kindly words.

"I suppose you've wired the Van Twings?" Sanderson asked.

Dundee flushed more darkly. "No. And I asked Littleton not to. There's practically no doubt that Enid Rambler and Edith Ramsey are one and the same, but I can't have her snatched away before the mystery is cleared up. She may be a material witness against the murderer–"

"If your first theory about her is correct," Sanderson asked reasonably, "why don't you simply swap information with her? Tell her it's all a mistake, that she didn't kill any man in an automobile accident, and ten to one she'll be so grateful that she'll tell anything she's been hiding about Koenig's murder."

But Dundee shook his head. "No, Chief, if you don't mind, I'll work this thing out before I try to make use of the girl. Her testimony might be practically worthless if I had no case built up against the murderer. You know how much it takes to convince a jury that a man is a murderer. . . . Besides, the girl may be mistaken. Her story may be entirely worthless, the product of hysteria."

"Wonder why that fat private detective hasn't wired Van Twing?" Sanderson suggested thoughtfully.

"The way I dope it out is this: Fatty saw Enid all right, after she left the movie. Met him on the grounds probably. He made the mistake of spilling the beans first— that he was a detective, I mean. The girl thought he had come to arrest her for manslaughter—we understand now, of course, why the movie of that name scared the poor kid half to death!—and she played her part so well that the fat bloke was completely taken in—thought he had the wrong girl, in spite of the fact that the description tallied. Of course she didn't give him time to tell her what it was all about. . . . Lord! No wonder the blessed little idiot has claustrophobia, and an anxiety neurosis and God knows what else the matter with her poor nerves!"

"Yes, it seems rather obvious that she was running away from the fat man," Sanderson admitted. "And it's entirely possible she doesn't know anything about Koenig's murder."

"Then why is she so damned happy over having a cop to guard her?" Dundee worried.

"Ask me another," Sanderson shrugged. "But here's an answer to one of your questions," and he reached under his pillow for a telegram. "Fitts says no such telegram has been received in his office."

Dundee brightened. "Swell! Mind if I spend a wad of the taxpayers' money, Chief? I'd like to talk to Fitts long distance. If he has a normal amount of curiosity he's already been digging into the 1919 records, and can give me the information I want without delay."

"Hop to it!" Sanderson consented, with only a decent pretense of reluctance. "I'll undoubtedly be 'investigated,' but—I'm curious, too."

To Dundee's amazement—he had never before talked long distance with Los Angeles—it was less than five minutes before the operator's crisp voice informed him: "Ready with Los Angeles, Hamilton!"

There was a moment of disappointment, however, when a man's voice—as clear as if it were coming from a Hamilton telephone—told him: "I'm sorry, but Mr. Fitts is out of the city today." But Dundee's disappointment gave way to exultation when the dear, friendly voice continued, with scarcely a pause:

"This is Assistant District Attorney Boykin speaking. It was I who received and answered your telegram, and I confess it excited my curiosity. . . . May I ask if the matter has any connection with the Koenig murder?"

Dundee grinned and nodded vigorously toward Sanderson, to indicate that all was going well. "I'm pretty sure it has a whale of a lot to do with the Koenig case," he said into the receiver, "and I'm counting on you to help us, Mr. Boykin."

"Delighted, Dundee! We've heard about you, even 'way out here. Better come to the land of sunshine and flowers—"

"Maybe I'll get a vacation on pay if I can clean up this mess," Dundee answered. "Los Angeles is a great town for big time murders, too—"

"Hey!" Sanderson pleaded, in agony. "Cut it short!"

But there was no need for the admonition, since the man at the other end of the wire, the amenities attended to, was swinging whole heartedly into the business at hand.

"Told you I was curious over that wire, Dundee," he said. "I took the trouble to dig into the 1919 files, looking for both first and last names beginning with E d i— "

"Stout fella!" Dundee applauded. "Find anything hot?"

"Plenty!" the genial voice came back clear and strong. "Funny coincidence, too. Dr. Koenig's name figures in *two* separate and distinct cases—"

"What!" Dundee shouted in his excitement. "In *two* cases where the defendants' names begin with 'E d i '?"

"One case never got to the point of the person involved being a defendant," the Los Angeles attorney corrected him. "A flapper by the name of Edith Ramsey—"

"*Edith Ramsey?* . . . My God!" Dundee groaned, and Sanderson jerked upright in bed, regardless of pleurisy.

"Know her? She must be quite a gal by now. I remember seeing her in 1919, when she was only fifteen, but pretty enough then to launch at least a small fleet. . . . Say! She isn't mixed up in this, is she?"

"She's a patient at Mayfield Sanitarium," Dundee answered dully. "What have you got on her?"

"Well, I'll be " the man at the other end of the wire marveled. "Say, I'll sketch her story briefly. It sort of stuck in my mind, but I read up on it a bit, just to refresh my memory, in case I was on the right track about your wire. . . . Here's the dope: Edith Ramsey, daughter of a multi millionaire fruit grower in the Santa Clara valley, was given an automobile on her fifteenth birthday—"

"Another automobile!" Dundee groaned, but not aloud.

"The kid was too young for a license, of course, but her dad pulled wires and she got one—lied about her age, maybe. Anyway, the family had one of their half dozen homes here in Los Angeles, and one day the kid took her parents driving. There was a nasty accident. The kid ran the car smack into a P. E. train, and the mother and father were both killed instantly."

Again Dundee groaned "My God!" and this time the exclamation was wrung from the very depths of his heart.

"Yeah, pretty tough on a fifteen year old kid," Boykin agreed. "Well, Edith simply went nuts—tried to commit suicide two or three times, until they had to put her in the psychopathic ward for observation. Mrs. Ramsey's sister, a Mrs. Henderson, happened to be in Los Angeles at the time, and she was afraid the kid was going stark mad. She called in two or three neurologists, including Dr. William Huntington Edwards, one of our best alienists, and finally got hold of Koenig, who was here on the *other* case I'll tell you about later."

"Whew!" Dundee whistled, and dug into his pocket for a handkerchief with which to wipe the icy sweat from his brow.

"Koenig said it wasn't anything but a nervous break down, although the kid kept insisting she was a murderess, and ought to be hanged by the neck till she was dead. The Hendersons put the girl into a private sanitarium out here–"

"Not the Good Hope, by any chance?" Dundee asked.

"Right!" came the emphatic answer over the wire. "A couple of months out there fixed her up—they said she had what you call 'manic depression,' if you get me–"

"I get you!" Dundee assured him grimly. "I'll be a manic depressive myself if this keeps up. ... Well? How did the girl get into the court records?"

"Merely a guardianship matter," the clear, friendly voice assured him. "She wasn't old enough to come into her parents' money, of course, and this Mrs. Henderson, the girl's maternal aunt, was appointed guardian until the girl was twenty one. I understand the Hendersons took her abroad to finish her education, and that she has lived abroad nearly ever since. At any rate, she's never been back to Los Angeles."

"I see," Dundee said, and used one of the precious minutes that were being marked up against the call to brood hopelessly.

"Don't be so down in the mouth, old man," Boykin, two thousand miles away, advised sympathetically. "After all, what possible motive for murdering the doctor could that kid have?"

"Thanks, Boykin," Dundee answered tonelessly.

"What's the other case?—though I suppose it's useless to look further for the subject of Koenig's inquiry to Fitts."

"I'm not so sure of that," the Los Angeles man retorted over the wire. "I've been saving the hot stuff. . . . Listen to this, young fellow, and get an earful!"

# CHAPTER 24

"SHOOT the works, Boykin, but make it snappy," Dundee advised, a sympathetic eye upon District Attorney Sanderson's distress over the leaping toll bill.

"Right!" heartily agreed the voice of the Los Angeles assistant district attorney. "Sanderson's listening in, is he? —and chewing his nails? . . . Well, tell him there's a bare possibility he can bill Los Angeles County for half this toll call, for it looks to me like Koenig was ready to slip us the dope on one of our own pet fugitives from justice. Have you seen a bad boy by the name of Edinger out at Mayfield?"

"Edinger?" Dundee repeated blankly. "Never heard of him."

"Then I guess Koenig bumped into him on this trip the papers say he'd just returned from when he was murdered," the voice from Los Angeles surmised, with its first trace of gloom. "And Koenig's dead. . . . Too bad!"

"You say the name is 'E d i n g e r'?" Dundee asked.

"Correct!" Boykin assured him. "Wanted to answer to an indictment on charges of conspiracy and misappropriation. Skipped out before the grand jury met, and never been heard from since. In 1919 that was."

"What's the story?" Dundee asked. "Just the bare facts, of course," he added hastily, as Sanderson groaned.

But it was not Boykin's money that was being burned up by telephone wires, and he was not going to have his yarn spoiled. "In 1918, a youngster by the name of Marvin Cooley—only seventeen years old—lied about his age and got into a training camp. He was among the last of our boys to go to France, but he was unlucky enough to be shoved into the front line trenches. He was erroneously reported killed in action. But before the news came, his mother—a widow—had married this guy Edinger, Steven F. Edinger. At least, that's the name he was using out here. Mysterious sort of bird. We knew literally nothing about him before 1918, and mighty little after that. He was in the real estate 'game' when he married the rich widow–"

"But you have a description of him?" Dundee interrupted.

"Oh, yes," came the reassuring words over the wire. "He was then— in 1919, when the blow up came— about 38 years old, medium height, weight about 190 pounds–"

"Good Lord! Another fat man! . . . *Or is it the same one?*" Dundee asked himself, but he said nothing to interrupt the story which was costing the taxpayers a pretty penny per word.

"—eyes brown, hair thick and black—" the voice from Los Angeles went on.

"You're sure of the hair and eyes?" Dundee asked aloud, while he said to himself, "*Not* the same fat man!"

"I'm reading the description from the police circulars," Boykin assured him. "Ruddy complexion, black mustache, pug nose. No scars or disfigurations."

"Fingerprints?"

"Not a one. By the time the police wanted them, Edinger had cleared out, and too many other people had handled his things both in his hotel room and his real estate office," Boykin answered, but added helpfully, "Got a specimen of his handwriting, if that will help."

"It will—if I ever get the ghost of an idea who Edinger is. ... But what was he indicted for?"

"I told you he married a rich widow whose minor son was later reported killed in action," Boykin explained. "Edinger got his paws on the whole fortune by one of the lousiest schemes ever pulled in our fair city. He conspired with a woman who called herself a nurse, although she'd had no training, to get his wife adjudged mentally incompetent—"

"What!" Dundee shouted.

"Stop that, fellow! You'll bust my ear drum," Boykin pleaded. "Didn't I tell you I had a hot tip for you? . . . Well, once she was tucked away in a sanitarium—"

"Good Hope Sanitarium, of course?" Dundee interrupted again.

"How'd you guess it?" Boykin laughed. "As I was say ing, once he'd got her stowed away in Good Hope, he made ducks and drakes of her fortune, or—as everyone believes and no one can prove—he salted most of it away, in a good safe place where it would wait for him if things got too hot for him here—as they did. You see, the kid, Marvin Cooley, blew into town one day, all hot and bothered because his mother, whose name was no longer Cooley, of course, and who had moved from the old Cooley home, hadn't answered his letters. He got on her trail somehow, and found she was supposed to be crazy. He located her at Good Hope, without paying a call on his step papa, and then the fat was in the fire sure enough. The old lady was no more crazy than I am!"

"How did the son find that out?" Dundee asked, a little skeptically.

"Easy!" Boykin retorted over a wire two thousand miles long. "That's where the conspiracy comes in. You see, Edinger had ribbed up the nurse to work a ouija board with the old lady—"

"How old *was* she?"

"Fifty or so," Boykin answered impatiently. "Just the right age to be roped in by a fortune hunter. Well, when she went into a real nervous prostration over the news that her boy was killed in action, Edinger ribbed up the nurse to work the ouija board with her, getting messages for the old lady from the 'Beyond'—supposed to be from the kid, of course. The poor old lady got so she wanted to be at the ouija board all the time. Then Edinger played his trump ace–"

"Not a *voice* from the Beyond?" Dundee interrupted quickly.

"Say! Who's telling this yarn?" Boykin demanded, aggrievedly. "But you're right–"

"Ah!" Dundee breathed, and paid no more attention to Sanderson's agony over the telephone bill.

"Ain't it hot?" Boykin boasted. "The nurse—dame by the name of Whitson—swore it was Edinger that stood under the old lady's window late at night and pretended to be the ghost of the dead boy. She squealed, of course, to save her own hide. . . . But I'm getting ahead of the story. The old lady told everybody how her son not only came to her by way of the ouija board, but that she heard his voice. After that, it was pretty easy to get her adjudged incompetent and put away. 'Auditory hallucinations,' the alienists said, and you've got to remember the poor old lady was pretty well shot, nervously, anyway."

"My God!" Dundee breathed.

"Yeah! Pretty rotten!" Boykin, in Los Angeles, agreed. "Of course the jig was up when the boy returned, safe and sound, and madder'n hell at finding his mother in such a fix. The kid had grown into quite a lad, and he made short work of taking the matter of her 'incompetence' into court. There was a swell battery of alienists lined up on each side, Edinger calling in Dr. Sandlin from Good Hope, along with two or three other big shots, in a desperate effort to make the first ruling stick. But the kid got hold of Dr. Koenig as *his* big gun, along with Dr. Edwards, and finally the nurse squealed, and it was all over. But as I said, before the grand jury could indict or a temporary warrant could be clapped on Edinger, he'd skipped—and hasn't been heard of since."

Another precious minute was consumed by Dundee's thanks and his request that a copy of the grand jury proceedings in the Edinger case be rushed to him by air mail. Then he hung up the receiver and faced his chief.

"What a yarn!" he gloated, and himself spun the amazing tale for the district attorney's benefit.

"It ought to be," Sanderson grumbled. "It cost us at least ten cents a word. But as far as I can see, it doesn't butter any parsnips for us."

"You wouldn't kid me, mister, would you?" Dundee pleaded. Then, seriously, "Of course it may be, simply, one of those astounding coincidences that are always popping up in real life. But— Looky, Chief! Koenig was killed when he was telephoning that night letter to Los Angeles, before he could finish spelling a name that begins with 'E d i.' The reason he sent that telegram is that, while talking on the phone to Claire Cantrell, his eyes lit on something on his desk—and we can safely guess it was Clyde Powell's case history—that made him remember where he had seen a certain pair of eyes before. Now, in Powell's case history appeared two names that appear in the Edinger story—Dr. Sandlin's name and the name of Good Hope Sanitarium–"

"Wait a minute!" Sanderson interrupted. "If Koenig was figuring on hiring Sandlin as his assistant at Mayfield, he *knew* Sandlin was formerly connected with Good Hope Sanitarium. Nothing in the juxtaposition of those two names to make him have a brain wave. And no reason that I can see why this chap, Edinger, would have to destroy Powell's case history, just because Sandlin's name and the name of the Los Angeles sanitarium were in it."

"You're right!" Dundee assured him eagerly. "I admit there's a missing link—something else in Clyde Powell's case history that, *connected with those two names*, fired off a bomb in Koenig's brain. Can't you guess what that missing link was?"

"Edinger's name, I suppose," Sanderson obliged sourly. "But what in the name of heaven should it be doing in *Powell's* case history?"

Dundee considered for a long moment. "Both Powell and Mrs. Edinger were patients at Good Hope during 1919, but I admit I can see no reason why either Edinger's or Mrs. Edinger's name should get into Powell's history.

. . . Wait a minute!" he cried suddenly, and reached for the telephone.

"Another Los Angeles call?" Sanderson moaned.

But Dundee was dialing the number of Mayfield Sanitarium. Fortunately it was the staff's luncheon hour, and it was only a matter of seconds before Dr. Harlow's lovely treble came over the wire.

"Listen, Doctor!" Dundee urged. "Try hard to remember something for me, won't you? . . . Thanks! Did Clyde Powell have delusions of persecution against real or imaginary people?"

"Both," she answered promptly.

"Were the names of his 'persecutors' recorded in his case history?" Dundee continued eagerly.

"Clyde had a pet imaginary enemy whom he called 'Frank,' " she told him. " 'Frank' was responsible for nearly everything bad that happened to Clyde, and some times he shadow boxed with his imaginary foe, or held long, abusive conversations with him. But I can't remember any other names."

"Was the name of—*Edinger* among them?" Dundee asked tensely. "E d i n g e r?"

"Edinger?" came the slow, sweet voice very thought fully. "No, I'm positive it was not."

"That's tough," Dundee admitted, out of the depths of his disappointment. "Miss Home is familiar with the history, I believe. Will you ask her if the name of Edinger appeared in it, in any connection whatever?"

"Hold the line," Dr. Harlow directed.

As Dundee waited, Sanderson spoke, frowningly:

"Even if Powell got a persecution complex against this Edinger, through meeting him at Good Hope, when he was visiting his wife, I don't see why it was so damned necessary for Edinger—supposing he was the murderer— to destroy the case history. The history had been on hand at Mayfield for years, and it's hardly likely his name occurring in the early pages of it would have meant a thing to anyone but Koenig."

"You forget that the first three letters of that name were spelled out in Koenig's wire," Dundee reminded him, his hand cupping the transmitter of the telephone. "This murderer was the most cautious, cold blooded, farseeing bloke I ever heard of. He left absolutely nothing to chance—except that one hidden drop of blood! He foresaw that there was a bare possibility that the 'bust' message would be traced to Dr. Koenig. Any scrap of paper left in Koenig's possession, which would give the remaining letters of the name, Edinger, had to be destroyed. He couldn't simply file Powell's case history, in the hope that it would not be read again, for there was the letter attached, from the State Hospital, asking for excerpts from it. ... See? . . . Hello! Yes, Dr. Harlow?"

He listened for a moment, thanked the little doctor, and slowly replaced the receiver.

"No luck," he admitted gloomily. "Miss Home is as positive as Dr. Harlow that the name of Edinger was not in Clyde Powell's history. She says she skimmed through it when she got it out of the files for Dr. Koenig on Wednesday, and had handled it several times before, when additions were made to the record."

"Too bad," Sanderson sympathized. "Looks like an other blind alley."

"No. I'll swear we're on the right track," Dundee insisted stubbornly. "The key to the whole mystery lies in Clyde Powell's case history, which, undoubtedly, has been thoroughly destroyed by this time, and Steven Edinger is the murderer. The question is: who is Edinger?"

"The answer to that, to put it obliquely," Sanderson grinned, "is that Edinger isn't Edinger. A fugitive from justice doesn't parade a name under which he has been indicted."

"That's a foregone conclusion," Dundee agreed, a little curtly. Did his chief think he was that dumb? . . . "The question remains: who is Edinger—whatever name he may be using now? Have we had the pleasure of his acquaintance? In other words, is he Samuel Rowan, or the mysterious fat man, or—Roland Morse?"

"In the order of their probability, eh?" Sanderson suggested. "But why the mysterious fat man? I thought he was accounted for—as a private detective hired by Van Twing to find Enid Rambler, or, I should say, Edith Ramsey."

"I was willing to write him off, too, until I remembered that Littleton, the manager of the Hamiltonian, took it for granted that the fat man was a private detective, when he turned up at the hotel asking for Edith Ramsey. In fact, Littleton asked him if that was his job, and of course, whether it was true or not, the fat man said yes. But we can't blink the fact that somehow, innocently or not, Edith Ramsey is mixed up in this case. Otherwise, we've got a most amazing web of coincidence. Edith Ramsey was in Los Angeles in 1919. Koenig was called in on her case. Also, in 1919, she, as well as Mrs. Edinger and Clyde Powell, was a patient at Good Hope Sanitarium, where Dr. Horace Sandlin was employed as psychiatrist. We have the further coincidence that Koenig was called as an alienist by Marvin Cooley in the suit to restore his mother's status as a competent person. I tell you, sir, there's a solution to this case which will explain and include all these apparent coincidences, leaving only the coincidence that Edith Ramsey, under the name of Enid Rambler, was a patient at Mayfield at the time Edinger turned up to murder Dr. Koenig. An unlucky coincidence for her, poor girl, for it puts her in danger of her life."

"Then we'd better make sure that her guard isn't a victim of sleeping sickness," Sanderson said grimly.

"Right!" Dundee agreed heartily. "And I'll rest easier tonight if I know our friend, Roland Morse, is also under the watchful eye of an uninvited guest."

"How does he fit into Edinger's description?" Sanderson asked.

"Fairly well," the special investigator answered. "He's heavy, rather than fat, but diet and a medicine ball could have taken care of that. I'd say he's a couple of inches over the average in height, but police descriptions are not apt to be astonishingly accurate, especially when they concern the height of a very fat man. You've noticed that a wide girth apparently takes inches off a man's height. Morse's eyes are brown, all right, but I wouldn't call his nose pug. It's quite a nose, in fact, but the nostrils are rather noticeably wide. And it is an easy enough matter to change one's nose, plastic surgeons being what they are today. Morse's hair is pepper and salt, Edinger's was black in 1919. In fact, Morse fits the bill so well that I'd very much like to know exactly where he was during the latter half of 1918 and the first half of 1919."

"Odd, isn't it, how a criminal repeats himself," Sanderson mused with satisfaction. "The voice of a 'dead' son offering ghostly comfort to his mother in 1919, the voice of God wailing 'too late!' under a bereaved mother's window in 1931—with the same fiendish purpose: that of driving a rich wife crazy."

"Yes," Dundee agreed soberly. "And by a criminal's repetitions ye shall know him—and hang him!"

# CHAPTER 25

IT was a very thoughtful young detective who, after a lengthy conference with Captain Strawn of the Homicide Squad, drove slowly the five miles from Hamilton to Mayfield Sanitarium.

One question, which seemed rather irrelevant, persisted in annoying Special Investigator Dundee: Why had Dr. Koenig, so outstanding a man in his field, planned to bring Dr. Horace Sandlin to Mayfield, if, as Professor Livingstone of Northwestern University broadly hinted in his telegram, Sandlin had a none too flattering reputation among his colleagues? Certainly Koenig had had first hand opportunity for judging Sandlin, since the two psychiatrists had been opposing expert witnesses in the Edinger case.

The twin to that question also buzzed like a persistent gnat at his ear: Why had Koenig determined, quite suddenly, it seemed, to dismiss Justine Harlow, who had served him so faithfully and so well that he had willed her half of his estate?

Even if Morse should prove to be Edinger—and who else came anywhere near fitting that description, except possibly Samuel Rowan?—how should he ever learn the answer to those two questions? And Dundee wanted them answered. A solution with loose ends was no solution, to his type of mind. . . .

Mayfield's lawn looked like the pleasure grounds of a fashionable resort hotel, as Dundee drove in and parked near the main building. In the warm late afternoon sun, patients were playing croquet, miniature golf, and bridge. There was even a horseshoe pitching contest, Night watch man Whalen as champion challenging all comers. Archie Webster and his attendant, Happy Day, were proving to be unexpectedly formidable opponents as Dundee strolled by. He refused an invitation to join in the sport, and continued his apparently aimless stroll.

A bridge game was being held up while Marjorie Merrick checked a small heap of parcels which Business Manager Baldwin had evidently been delegated to purchase for her.

"My God, Roger!" the singer was exclaiming in a tragic voice. "You didn't get that perfume! I told you I simply couldn't live another day without it—"

"They didn't have it, Marjie," Roger Baldwin answered conciliatingly. "I tried the best drug stores and department stores—"

"Cheap hicks!" she dismissed all of Hamilton scornfully. "Wire Chicago to send me some, Roger—there's a lamb."

Dundee was about to stroll on when a sudden thought halted him.

"May I speak with you a moment when you're at leisure, Mr. Baldwin?"

"You can have him, darling!" Marjorie Merrick called out stridently. "As a personal shopping bureau, he's a bust, although he did bring me a box of candy—the pet!"

"The pet" flushed darkly as he backed hastily away from the bridge table and joined Dundee.

"Good business—that's all," Baldwin muttered, as if he were afraid Dundee might give him credit for a kindly impulse. "This shopping for the patients is the devil's own nuisance," he grumbled. "Just let the word get out that I'm going into town and I've got to bring back everything from face powder to pink silk step ins. ... If you wanted to see me about the rates on your suite, there isn't going to be any bill," he added gruffly.

"You're very kind," Dundee smiled, knowing that Baldwin would hate the soft impeachment. "But I wanted to speak to you about something else. . . . You handle all checks that are given in payment of bills here, don't you, Mr. Baldwin?"

"Not all; in fact, not many of them," Baldwin denied. "The cashier attends to that phase of the routine here. . . . No, I'll amend that statement somewhat," the business manager interrupted himself conscientiously. "Before the checks go to the bank, I see that their amounts tally with the deposit slip the cashier has written up. And I usually attend to the banking myself."

"Then I wonder if you have ever received a check here signed with the name 'Edith Ramsey'?" Dundee asked.

The business manager frowned, knit his brows. Then his face cleared. "Thought that name sounded familiar!" he exclaimed with mild triumph. "We haven't had a patient here by that name, but another patient, Enid Rambler—funny coincidence, the initials being the same, isn't it?—endorsed over to us a New York check made out to her and signed by the name of Edith Ramsey. That was the first week she was here, and the amount of the check was nearly a hundred dollars more than her bill."

"And you took a chance on the check's being good? Handed the change over to her?" Dundee marveled, knowing the business manager as he believed he did.

But Baldwin grinned wryly. "No. I issued a credit on her next week's bill, and by the time it was due, the check had cleared O. K."

"Did she pay by 'Edith Ramsey' checks after that?"

"No. After that first time, she gave us checks on a Hamilton bank."

"Signed 'Enid Rambler'?" Dundee asked.

"Certainly!"

"Did it occur to you, Mr. Baldwin, that Edith Ramsey and Enid Rambler were one and the same person?" Dundee asked.

"No! Why should it?"

"Was the handwriting similar?"

"Not similar enough to attract my attention, certainly!" Baldwin retorted. "Let me think. I'm pretty good at remembering details of that sort. . . . I've got it now! The Edith Ramsey check was written in a bold, large hand, that slanted sharply toward the right. Miss Rambler's signature is always written in a very round back hand."

"Exactly what I should have expected," Dundee murmured.

"Look here, Dundee!" Baldwin commanded sharply. "I don't know what you're driving at, but if you've got any wild notion that that girl is mixed up in Carl's murder, you're crazier than any patient we've got here. She's as fine and straight a girl as I ever met—and I'm not speaking now as Mayfield's business manager, out to protect a rich patient from scandal. If, for some reason of her own, Miss Rambler is here under an assumed name, I'd stake my life that it's an innocent reason."

"I'm sure you're right, Mr. Baldwin," Dundee assured him, and again set off across the lawn toward Sunflower Court.

It was obvious, he reflected, that Enid Rambler—as he still called her to himself—had managed to open a bank account in Hamilton, by mail. Easy enough to send in a large check, made out to Enid Rambler, signed by the name of Edith Ramsey, and endorsed by Enid Rambler, with a request that the money be deposited, when collected, to the account of Enid Rambler. Even if a handwriting expert had detected that payor and payee were the same person, it was no legal offense to open a bank account in an assumed name. But that first check, given to Baldwin, had wiped out the last vestige of doubt that Enid Rambler was Edith Ramsey. In this business, Dundee congratulated himself, it paid to be *sure*—not "practically certain."

"Yes, Enid's in her rooms," Miss Doty assured him, when he entered the reception room of Sunflower Court. "Now, don't blush! I just knew that was what you were going to ask!"

Having given up hope for herself, the day nurse had apparently decided magnanimously to sponsor a romance between this handsome young detective and the girl she had previously acknowledged as a formidable rival. Though what all the men saw in her, beyond the fact that she was pretty "in a way," Lurline Doty for the life of her could not say. . . .

Barney Flynn, the plainclothesman on duty outside the door that led from Enid Rambler's suite into the patio, showed a grateful inclination to talk when Dundee paused to greet him.

"Yep! Everything's swell!" Flynn told him enthusiastically. "Say, Dundee, I don't care if you never solve this here murder. It's the softest job I've struck in a coon's age."

"No trouble at all, I take it?" Dundee asked, smiling.

"You mean, does she try to make a get away?" Flynn asked. "Not that baby! She peeps out a dozen times a day just to make sure I *am* here—cautions me not to budge an inch. Pretty as paint, ain't she? . . . And sweet? Umm!" and the plainclothesman smacked his lips. "But at that, I'm kinda sorry for the poor little thing. Acts gay and chipper all the time, but she's scared, Dundee —scared stiff. Why, today she made Miss Lacey, the head nurse, have a set of heavy, barred screens put before all her windows. Seems like they keep sets of 'em on hand, to stick 'em in the windows of patients that suddenly go off their nuts."

"Is anyone with her now?"

"Sure! They's always somebody running in and out," Flynn assured him. "That baby could win a beauty and popularity prize in a Ziegfeld chorus. Rowan it is now. Been there about fifteen minutes. And I'll bet she's making that moth eaten old bozo feel like he's the Prince of Wales."

"Yes, that's a gift of hers," Dundee agreed, grinning, as he opened the door.

He was treated to a sample of Enid Rambler's gentle and exquisite courtesy as soon as he entered the girl's sitting room. She was lying on the couch, her injured foot resting on a pillow, and, in a chair drawn close, sat Samuel Rowan. The shabby charity patient was freshly and closely shaved; the coarse gray hairs had been plucked from his nostrils, and somewhere Rowan had found a not too dingy tie and a frayed but very clean white shirt.

The man's meek brown eyes—one clouded with a cataract—peered upward at Dundee with just a hint of disappointment at the interruption, but his greeting was respectful and friendly.

"So glad to see you, Mr. Dundee," Enid Rambler told him, and motioned toward a chair with one hand. In the other she held a small, limp leather book. "Mr. Rowan's trying to cheer me up," she continued, and there was gentle gravity in her eyes as they rested on the little book. "Isn't it dear of him to bring me this book—*The Casting Out of Fear?* ... If only there were no fear in the world, what a wonderful place it would be to live in!"

Rowan flushed, and turned his hat slowly in awkward hands. "It's a real good book," he said humbly. "It helped me a lot. In fact, that little book and Dr. Koenig have given me a new lease on life."

"I'm sure it's wonderful," the girl said warmly, but in the dark blue eyes which flicked a quick glance toward Dundee there was no hope.

"I'd like to read it myself," Dundee lied politely.

"There's nothing like it, if you've got something preying on your mind and haunting your dreams, night in and night out, like I had," Rowan told them, sincerity vibrating in his uncultured voice. "Mr. Baldwin gave me that little book, not dreaming what a miracle it would work in me–"

"But I'm sure he said it was 'good business' to give it to you!" Enid laughed, but Dundee's quick ear caught a note of hysteria in her voice. Probably old Rowan had been boring her intolerably. . . .

"Then I reckon he'd be right," Rowan told her, in nowise offended by her laughter. "Good business for the sanitarium to get rid of a charity patient, and good business in a larger sense to set a man on his feet and put him back into the world."

"You really want to go back into the world, don't you?" Enid asked softly. "I envy you, Mr. Rowan. But I'm afraid I–"

"Afraid! Afraid!" the old man repeated solemnly. "If *I* can get rid of that 'Old Man of the Sea'—that's what the little book calls Fear—a young girl like you, with every grace that God ever endowed a woman with "

"But you don't *know!*" Enid interrupted, and tears filled her eyes.

"If there's anything I do know, it's what fear can do to a body," Rowan corrected her gently. "That big police man has been pestering me to tell him my story, but I don't see no call to tell it to people it wouldn't help–"

He paused uncertainly, and Dundee cut in, gravely, without too much eagerness: "I think you're right, Mr. Rowan, but I'm sure both Miss Rambler and I would be greatly helped by your experience."

"Of course we should, Mr. Rowan," Enid agreed kindly, and Dundee saw that not even the prospect of being bored could dim the fine luster of her courtesy.

The older man settled himself a bit more easily in his chair, and Dundee waited, scarcely daring to breathe.

"Young people like you," Rowan began, "with the world before you and your hearts full of romance and hope, don't have no idea what life looks like to people who're getting old and never have had the good things you two take for granted. . . . Now, me and my wife," he began again, less sententiously, "was in love with each other, in a manner of speaking, when we got married in a little town down in Texas. She was a peart, high stepping girl, and I had my health and the sight of both eyes."

Unexpectedly, Dundee felt his heart contract with pity, not asked for by that quiet voice.

"We got hitched, and things went pretty well for a time," Rowan went on. "Then, somehow, I didn't seem to be turning out no great shakes as a money maker. My wife, Melcie, got pretty much disgusted

with me, and her tongue got to be sharp as a razor. Long about '28—
when our third child followed his two little sisters to the graveyard—
Melcie got it into her head that California was the Promised Land.
Nothing would do her but I should pull up stakes and light out for
California. I had a few acres of land that got so all it could raise was
boll weavils and mortgages, so when cotton picking was over that fall I
give in. Sold out for what I could get and bought a Ford. . . . Well, me
and Melcie had a pretty good time the first week, seeing new country
and spinning yarns with the neighborly sort of folks we met in the auto
camps. Her brother, Curtis, was along, and it was him buttin' in that
turned a little spat between me and Melcie into what you might call a
first class row. At one of them auto camps it was, and I needn't bother
you folks with telling you what it was all about. Maybe I was a mite
jealous the way Melcie carried on with that barber fellow at the camp,
her being old enough to behave herself–"

He stopped abruptly to brood, and Dundee and the girl exchanged
pitying glances.

"Well, Curtis butted in and I told him he'd better hitch hike the
rest of the way, if he wanted to get to California," Rowan went on.
"Melcie was pretty sore, but Curtis stayed behind, and we hit the trail
alone the next morning. Come night, I didn't feel much like mingling
with the folks in an auto camp, so we struck camp by our selves in a
ravine among some of the biggest mountains in Colorado. I didn't sleep
so good that night. I'd et a big mess o' canned beans, and I reckon they
didn't set so well on my stummick. Anyways, I had a nightmare. I
dreamed the whole side of the mountain was tumbling down on me and
Melcie, sleeping there by our camp fire."

Again the slow, uncultured, flat voice dragged to a stop. In the
intensity of his interest, Dundee was gripping the arms of his chair.
Enid Rambler's blue eyes were wide and dark with premonition of
tragedy.

"Well, sir," Rowan went on, with no intention of excluding the girl.
"Till this day I can't say where the dream left off and the real thing
begun. All I know is, whether it was in the dream I saw it or whether I
was actually awake by then, I saw a big rock come sliding and crashing
down the mountain side–"

"A landslide?" Dundee interrupted.

"No, sir," Rowan denied. "Except for some trash that it brought
along with it, that big rock was the only thing that fell. Likely some
animal brushed against it and tipped it over. . . . Well, there it come
and there I laid, watching it, but no more power to move a hand or a
leg than if I'd been paralyzed. ... It hit my wife. It killed her."

The awful suddenness of the conclusion struck both his hearers dumb. While Dundee's hair was still prickling on his scalp, Enid Rambler found her voice, brought it out in little, quivering gasps:

"Oh! But you—*you* couldn't help it, Mr. Rowan!"

The old man drew a deep breath and brought his hand down heavily on the arm of his chair. "No! I couldn't help it, child! . . . But for more'n two years I've called myself a murderer, and lots of other people think I'm a murderer, too. That little book there, and Dr. Koenig "

"But I don't understand!" the girl protested hotly. "It was simply a terrible accident!"

"You see, little girl," Rowan told her gently, and with no hint of familiarity, "if I'd acted soon as I saw that rock coming down the mountain side, I could have saved Melcie. And the rock would have killed me."

"But you *couldn't*—one can't *think* as quickly as all that–" she cried brokenly, and Dundee knew that her defense of Rowan was also a defense of herself.

"Melcie's brother, Curtis, found us there next morning," the quiet voice went on. "I'd waited till dawn, not knowing what to do—half crazy–"

"Of course!" the girl agreed passionately.

"Well, Curtis told the folks he was with—a couple giving him a hitch—all about the quarrel between me and Melcie," Rowan continued very quietly. "The three of 'em got their heads together and Curtis didn't have much trouble making 'em believe I'd pitched the rock down on my wife. They took me in to the nearest town in the county, and turned me over to the sheriff."

"Oh! Oh!" the girl moaned.

"I didn't much care what happened to me," Rowan comforted her obliquely. "I stayed in jail till the grand jury met, but they refused to indict, for lack of evidence."

"I should think they would!" Enid cried.

"They might as well a hung me," Rowan said soberly. "I knowed I was the biggest coward that ever–"

"No! No!"

"They let me go, but I didn't seem to take no interest in living," Rowan went on. "Finally, by the grace of God, I got sent to Mayfield. Wednesday, after I'd read that little book about casting out fear, I felt like I owed it to Dr. Koenig, being as how he was so good to me, to put the thing up to him fair and square. He asked me if, deep down in my heart, I wanted my wife to be killed by that rock. And I said no, she's been a good wife to me, and I didn't bear no malice after that tiff we had at the auto camp. Then he asked me—and there he hit the nail on the head—whether I'd ruther it would a been her than me. And I told him, God being my witness, I'd ruther a thousand times that rock had cracked my own skull wide open than to a seen it hit Melcie."

"Of course you would!" Enid championed him almost hysterically.

"Then he asked me what was eatin' on me," Rowan went on. "I said I couldn't get over it that I'd been a coward—laying there like a lump o' mud and letting it hit her. Then he told me that the way I'd 'reacted,' as he called it, was exactly what a psychiatrist would have expected. 'Suspended between the dream world and the real world,' he said, my brain refused to 'differentiate' between them. He said I'd been locked in a paralysis of horror, just as real as if I'd been actually paralyzed. He said I couldn't a moved to a saved my own life. He said I wasn't to blame," Rowan summed up simply.

"Oh, he *was* good!" Enid Rambler sobbed, hiding her face behind convulsed hands.

"I just thought I might help you to get a new light on your own little troubles," Rowan said awkwardly, and bent to touch one of her clenched hands. "I don't want to see *you* old before your time, child. . . . How old would you take me to be?"

The girl dropped her hands and stared blankly at Rowan with drowned eyes. Then her beautiful courtesy asserted itself.

"Why—why, I wouldn't take you to be a day over fifty five," she quavered.

"I'll be forty three years old, come August," Samuel Rowan said simply, and again Enid Rambler's face hid itself behind her hands.

Rowan was gone before Dundee realized his intention.

It was not often that the young detective found himself at a complete loss. Now, every instinct of his susceptible heart prompted him to soothe and console this girl whose grief was certainly as much for herself as for the poor devil who had tried to help her. But, equally, every instinct of his professional nature urged him to press his advantage, until the girl's own unhappy story should come tumbling out.

Enid seemed to realize that they two were alone. A thin, exhausted voice came from behind her sheltering hands.

"Please! I'm sorry, but—would you mind—? I can't talk now–"

The gentleman rather than the detective rose to his feet, hastily. "Certainly!" Dundee ejaculated. But it was the detective who paused in the doorway to ask, in a carefully casual voice:

"By the way, Miss Rambler, do you know a chap named *Edinger?*'

# CHAPTER 26

As Dundee left Sunflower Court he told himself ruefully that he now knew how a navigator must feel when, steering confidently into port, he finds himself in a strange harbor hundreds of miles off his course.

It was simply no use telling himself that Enid Rambler had lied. Caught with her defenses down, called upon to answer a question which should have been the exact touch needed to bring on an attack of hysteria during which anything or everything might have been revealed, that question had, perversely, served to steady her nerves. Because it was obviously so irrelevant, so meaningless to her!

"Edinger?" she had repeated blankly, her eyes meeting Dundee's candidly but with a sort of hurt wonder that he should try, at a time like that, to strengthen the slight bond between them by discovering a mutual acquaintance. "I don't recall. . . . Edinger? ... I met a writer by that name in London. . . . No! *His* name was Edington. . . . *Edinger!* . . . The name does sound vaguely familiar, but I can't think—I'm really awfully tired," she had pleaded pitifully.

And he had left her, believing she had spoken the absolute truth. At first the acuteness of his disappointment made him feel lost, almost physically ill. For his whole case against Edinger began with and rested upon the hypothesis that Enid Rambler, or Edith Ramsey as he should call her, was not only innocently involved but actually possessed proof of his guilt, if she could be persuaded to furnish it. And now Dundee would stake his life on the conviction that the name, Edinger, meant nothing to the girl.

But a few minutes' reflection served to assuage the detective's disappointment. That Edith Ramsey had not recognized Edinger did not really affect the case against the unknown murderer in the least, except that it eliminated the possibility of an easy and quick solution. Edinger, whether a casual visitor to or an inmate of Mayfield Sanitarium, had seen and recognized Edith Ramsey in Enid Rambler. That had been almost inevitable. In 1919 Edinger's pathetically persecuted wife had been an inmate of the same sanitarium near Los Angeles which had sheltered Edith Ramsey after the tragic accident in which her parents had been killed. Undoubtedly the girl's pictures had been featured in the newspapers for many days, not only because of the shocking accident, but because of her great wealth and her efforts to commit suicide. Dreadfully conspicuous, even in Good Hope Sanitarium, she had been gazed upon by all visitors, among them the then unnoteworthy Edinger, calling to see the wife whom he had driven to the verge of insanity. Of course Edinger would remember her, and use his knowledge of her pitiful past to terrify her into silence now when she had inadvertently stumbled upon proof of his guilt. And that proof, Dundee believed, consisted in nothing more than that Edith Ramsey, hysterically seeking medical aid on the murder night, had seen Edinger—an unknown and meaningless figure in her eyes— leaving Dr. Koenig's office.

Dundee frowned mightily as he reconstructed that hypothetical scene. Edinger—whoever he was—had recognized the girl, had terrified her by calling her "Miss Ramsey." Entirely ignorant that a murder had been committed, but sure that, now she was recognized as the heiress who had not only killed her parents in an accident but had recently killed another man in a traffic accident, Mayfield Sanitarium could no longer serve her as a hiding place. And so she had fled, only to be brought back, crippled, by Dundee himself. And not until the next morning, when Strawn, in an effort to heckle her into a confession, had brutally broken the news of the murder, had she had the faintest inkling as to what had happened, nor that her flight, if it had been successful, would have been a God send to the unknown who had accosted her.

And why had she not told, when the truth burst upon her? For the very simple reason that she believed her own liberty was at stake. If— she must be reasoning in her overwrought, always slightly hysterical mind—she "told on" Edinger—whom she did not know by that name, and possibly did not know by name at all—he would "tell on" her—tell that she was Edith Ramsey, wanted for manslaughter. For Edith Ramsey undoubtedly believed, with every terrified cell in her brain, that she was a fugitive from such a charge. In her unbalanced condition, she must be telling herself that the 1919 accident would be brought into the new case against her, making conviction and imprisonment doubly sure.

Dundee's heart throbbed heavily with pity for the girl. His almost overwhelming impulse was to go to the girl and say to her:

"You are not guilty of manslaughter. I know who you are. You are Edith Ramsey. The man your car struck on the night of April second did not die. He was only stunned. Now—whom are you shielding?"

But the inevitable consequence of that revelation instantly presented itself. Edith Ramsey now feared not only arrest on a charge of manslaughter, but she feared death at the hands of the unknown, if she told what she knew. And not even Dundee's adroitness could conceal from her the fact that the murderer's identity, beyond a name and a description that was eleven years old, was unknown to him. *She* could furnish a description, of course—probably an inaccurate or hazy one, registered upon an hysterical mind—but, she would ask herself, did she dare take the chance of telling what she knew when the murderer was still at large? In her opinion, would even a squad of plainclothesmen serve to guard her against his rage, and his supreme need to remove from earth the one witness who could actually connect him with the scene of the crime?

If—Dundee prided himself—he had one gift, it was the ability to *be* another person mentally. And now for five minutes he had been Edith Ramsey, thinking her thoughts in her own hysterical fashion.

No, he decided. It was not through Edith Ramsey— *yet*—that Edinger, whoever he was, could be brought to justice. How, then? Just as Dundee felt himself slumping into baffled weariness one tiny bit of information, scarcely noted at the time, came crashing through his brain like a streak of lightning.

Regardless of the fact that it was almost time for his dinner tray and that he was very hungry, the young detective sprinted across the lawn to the main building.

He found Dr. Harlow in Dr. Koenig's office, which had finally been turned back to the sanitarium by the police. With her was the secretary, Maizie Home, taking dictation.

Without preliminary, Dundee began:

"Wednesday night, Dr. Harlow, you said something about old Dr. Mayfield's habit of interviewing patients, during his lucid intervals. Tell me: did he remember Clyde Powell, and occasionally send for him?"

The little doctor's look of dignified annoyance at the interruption gave place to vivid interest.

"Why, yes! He did—frequently!" she answered eagerly. "You see, Clyde was a patient of Dr. Mayfield's for two years before the old doctor became incompetent to carry on his work. He was fond of Clyde, as we all were, and whenever Dr. Mayfield asked for a patient who was either dead or no longer with us, we made a practice of sending for Clyde, so that the old doctor's love of continuing with his profession might have an outlet."

"Dr. Mayfield made notes of his interviews with the patients, to add to their case histories, I suppose?" Dundee asked, excitement making his blue eyes bright as diamonds.

"No," Dr. Harlow answered, and Dundee's heart sank. "When he was in active practice it was his theory that note taking embarrassed and impeded a patient. But"— and Dundee's hopes skyrocketed—"Dr. Mayfield had used a dictaphone for years. As soon as he had dismissed a patient, he dictated a record of the interview and his comments upon it, into the dictaphone. Naturally he continued the habit until his death."

If Dundee had been seven years old instead of twenty seven, he would have clapped his hands with joy.

"That's great!" he cried, instead. "May I see the transcriptions of all the records dealing with Clyde Powell's case?"

Dr. Harlow smiled pityingly. "Transcriptions? You forget, Mr. Dundee, that Dr. Mayfield was—not himself, that, while some of his comments on patients might have been very valuable "

"Then that hunch is a washout!" Dundee interrupted, so like a deflated, forlorn small boy that the little doctor took pity on him.

"I don't know exactly what your hunch is, Mr. Dundee," she said gently, "but there's a chance that it is not a 'washout.' "

"You mean there were actual records in the dictaphone?" Dundee pounced happily.

"Exactly! . . . Everything possible was done to make Dr. Mayfield happy, to foster his delusion that he was still head of the sanitarium. Not only were there actual records in the machine, but they were all kept—every record he dictated during the five years since his retirement," Dr. Harlow assured him. "Such a precaution was necessary, since Dr. Mayfield's memory was very erratic. A year after he had dictated his comments on an interview with a patient he might demand a transcription of the record, sure that the interview had taken place only the day before."

Maizie Home spoke up. "Sometimes I'd have a simply terrible time finding the one he wanted," she said indulgently. "But I always humored him—no matter how busy I was. Then maybe after all my trouble he'd have forgot all about it by the time I handed him the typed copy."

"Did you keep these occasional transcriptions that Dr. Mayfield asked for?" Dundee asked the secretary.

"Oh, yes. In a folder all by themselves," Maizie Home told him.

Two minutes later Dundee was in possession of the small collection. It was a pitiful exhibit. Crisply phrased, masterly commentaries on all sorts of psychopathic cases either ended abruptly, on an unfinished note, or trailed off into incoherencies that were, in themselves, indisputable evidence of the writer's own mental condition. Not only was Dundee disappointed to find nothing referring to Clyde Powell, but he was inexpressibly saddened.

That feeling of rebellious sadness continued with him after the young and mentally proud detective was admitted to the old doctor's private apartment on the second floor —primly neat now that its puttering old occupant was dead—and left alone with the dictaphone and the huge box of wax cylinders.

Dr. Mayfield had kept his dictaphone on a table beside his bed. Resting there after the fatigue of interviewing his "patients," he had recorded those facts and opinions so important in his own eyes and so worthless in the eyes of all others.

Now Dundee sat beside that table, listening to the record which contained the last words Dr. Cyrus Mayfield had ever dictated. The wax of that cylinder had not been called upon to immortalize a great many of Dr. Mayfield's last utterances, but as Dundee listened to that reedy, quavering, but dignified old voice, the hair stirred on his scalp. During the last hours of his life the old doctor had tried valiantly to get an audience with a man he did not know was dead, and now Dundee was to know what Dr. Mayfield had died trying to tell.

"Memorandum for Dr. Carl Koenig," announced the thin voice in his ear. "It has just come to my memory, which I am afraid is not so good as it once was, Carl, that I am by accident in possession of certain facts which require immediate attention."

Dundee held his breath as the record, blank for a few revolutions, spun in silence. Then:

"A few nights ago when my attendant, 'Happy' Day— and let me here register another protest against the useless expense to my establishment of having attendants idling about me—I repeat, when my attendant, Day, believed me to be asleep he was visited in the sitting room of my apartment by a young woman whom he called—ah— ah— Mavourneen. . . . No, another Irish word—Ah! Colleen! That's it! Colleen! The old man's memory is pretty good after all, eh, Carl?"

And while the ghostly chuckle spun the wax cylinder, Dundee whistled softly in awe and astonishment. "A few nights ago!" Good Lord! Colleen Lacey had been dead three years!

"Without eavesdropping intentionally I learned that the young woman, whose voice I recognized as belonging to the stenographer who takes Miss Home's place occasionally, is about to become a mother. She demanded of Day that he keep his promise to her to marry her, but he told her that he was already married to a Catholic who would not divorce him.

"It was my intention to inform you of this state of affairs the next morning, and have you attend to dismissing the man immediately, but it temporarily slipped my mind. All day today I have tried to see you and have failed. Please see that Day goes immediately. He is a disgrace to Mayfield. And do what you can for the poor child he deceived. Cyrus Mayfield."

That was all. But Dundee, as he slowly removed the last record Dr. Mayfield had ever dictated, felt that, doubly futile though that memorandum had been, it constituted a rather fine monument to the founder of Mayfield Sanitarium. And it was not wholly useless after all, for it removed the one possible shadow from Carl Koenig's name. Not, Dundee assured himself, that he had ever seriously suspected that Norah Lacey's adopted child was Koenig's. . . .

But—and Dundee braced himself to an arduous task— he had not found what he was looking for. Shrugging at the hopelessness of trying to apply any system to his task, the detective selected a cylinder at random, fitted it into the machine, and began to listen.

Although he ran the machine at its maximum speed he was discouraged and very tired when at the end of an hour he was no wiser, so far as his quest was concerned. His knowledge of abnormal psychology and of the treatment of mental diseases was enormously enlarged, and, specifically, he learned a great deal about the advance stages of *dementia pracox*, as exemplified in Clyde Powell. But in all the many dictated additions to Clyde Powell's case history to which Dundee listened over the dictaphone, he could discover no single conceivable reason why Edinger or anyone else should have destroyed it.

And yet that reason had to exist! Otherwise the murder of Dr. Carl Koenig was as stupid and insane as its perpetrator had tried to make it appear. Regardless of hunger and weariness, Dundee kept on at his task.

When the clew did come the detective was so weary, so nearly asleep, lulled by the dignified cadences of that reedy old voice, that he almost missed it.

"—identifying him with his delusional persecutor, "Frank,' and being subject to epileptiform seizures whenever he encounters him," was the conclusion of the sentence which finally aroused Dundee, and made him, with frantic haste, turn the machine back so that he could again hear and this time take in the opening words.

When the voice of the dead doctor had obediently repeated the words which, to Dundee, seemed the most brilliant ever uttered by a doctor, the detective sat in stunned silence for a long minute. And as he sat, effort less, every fact, like a well trained soldier, marched forward and took its place, forming a perfect "British square" before which Dr. Carl Koenig's murderer would have not the slightest defense when the battle was joined.

But it was not in military terms that Dundee sounded the battle cry when, having plunged downstairs to the murdered man's office, he got Captain Strawn on the telephone. The office was temporarily deserted, the staff being at dinner. But Dundee had taken the precaution to close the door into the hall, and his voice, while jubilant, was little more than a whisper.

"How soon can you get here, Captain?" he demanded urgently. Then he added the words which had announced the end of the chase in every murder mystery upon which he had worked in Hamilton:

"Got a pot on to boil, Captain!"

# CHAPTER 27

TWENTY minutes later, Captain Strawn, Chief of the Homicide Squad; Brede, the police stenographer, and James F. Dundee, Special Investigator attached to the district attorney's office, entered the reception room of Sunflower Court.

Fat Miss Hunter, the night nurse, looked up from her work at the chart table with her usual beaming smile, which became rather strained as she realized who her visitors were.

"Is Miss Rambler in her room, Miss Hunter?" Dundee asked, unsmiling and without greeting.

"I—I think she's in the patio, down near the back gate," the nurse stammered, her florid face turning very pale.

"Thanks, Miss Hunter. . . . No, don't call her!" and Dundee turned to whisper instructions to the older detective.

In silence the three men crossed the room, passed through the little hall and stepped out upon the stone porch that bounded three sides of the patio.

Luck was with them. The girl who was known to Mayfield Sanitarium as Enid Rambler was seated at a table near the iron fence which stretched across the rear end of the patio. She was alone, and her head was bowed upon her crossed arms, which rested on the table. A pair of crutches propped beside her told how she had achieved this solitary outing. Nearby, stationed outside the door of her suite, the plainclothesman who had been detailed to guard her at night watched her stolidly. In the twilight he looked something like a faithful mastiff, watching the suffering of an adored mistress with dumb sympathy.

Dundee remained where he was until Strawn and Brede, as noiselessly as Indians, had reached the guarded door of Enid Rambler's suite. He saw them pass in, the greased hinges of the door making no sound. Then, walking normally, the young detective crossed the patio.

"Is there anything I can do, Miss Rambler?" he asked softly, when he had reached her side.

The girl raised her head, then strained away from him, cowering as if she expected him to strike her.

"Go away!" she panted. "I can't talk to you—I mean " Her hoarse whisper tripped over a terrible fear that blighted her beauty. "I mean," she repeated, "I don't feel well. I don't feel like talking to anyone."

"You mean," Dundee corrected her gently, "that some one has just told you who I am—why I am here."

"You—want me?" she said, and the words scarcely moved her white lips.

For a dreadful moment Dundee thought she was going to faint, and that his carefully planned climax would have to be delayed. But after that moment she opened her dark blue eyes and looked at him with a hopeless sort of courage that tore at his heart.

"I want to talk with you—yes," Dundee again corrected her, very gently. "Shall we go into your sitting room? . . . Let me help you!"

"No, thank you!" she refused his offer, struggling with her crutches.

And Dundee, although his heart was nearly bursting with pity for her, noted with keen satisfaction that, as she swung herself painfully ahead of him, awkwardly manipulating the crutches, her eyes darted terrified glances in every direction, as if her supreme fear now was that she be seen in his company.

Still preceding him, and avoiding even an accidental contact with him as if he were a leper, the girl passed through the little hall of her suite and on into the sitting room. Dundee, following her, glanced quickly toward the bedroom door. It was slightly ajar, but no carelessly planted boot or protruding elbow hinted at the presence of Strawn and Brede, who, he knew, were stationed in the bedroom, impatiently awaiting developments.

In spite of the girl's repugnance Dundee drew up a chair and relieved her of her crutches.

"I don't want to sit down!" she told him, bracing her self against the arm of the chair. "There's no need to talk. . . . Shall we—go now?"

"Go where?" Dundee asked, as if great surprise.

"To jail, of course!" she cried passionately, scornfully. "There's no use pretending any longer—"

"Really, Miss Rambler, there's no reason in the world why I should take you to jail," Dundee assured her, in a reasonable, soothing voice. "Of course, *material witnesses*"—he stressed the words, and paused to let them sink in,—"are frequently held in technical custody, but in this case–"

"Wait!" she cried, and sank weakly into her chair.

And Dundee knew that, as he waited obediently, she was trying to adjust herself to an incredible hope.

When she began, it was with a smile, a ghastly but gallant smile. "I—I thought you were going to arrest me for —for Dr. Koenig's murder, which would have been ridiculous, of course," she babbled. "But detectives do make the most absurd mistakes–" Her voice broke on a sob of relief, and again Dundee waited patiently for her to go on. "I see now that you merely think I know something about the murder that I've been concealing. *I don't know anything!*" She concluded in a suddenly loud and ringing voice.

"Is that so?" Dundee asked mildly, his face and voice giving no sign that he understood for whose benefit that loud declaration had been made. Not that he was in the least afraid that person had heard her and been reassured. . . . "Then it looks as if I've been wasting my time, Miss Ramsey."

At that casual use of her real name the girl's face be came like a death mask. Not even the eyes which stared at him in fixed horror looked as if they had any life left in them.

"I'm very sorry you had to learn from someone else that I am a detective, Miss Ramsey," Dundee remarked, in an easy, conversational tone, to give her time to recover from the shock. His very attitude, as he lounged in the chair he had drawn close to hers, was one calculated to reassure. "Please believe that my purpose in calling on you this evening was to tell you the truth, and to bring you a bit of good news."

"Good news?" she repeated blankly, with stiff lips.

"Yes—good news, but of course there, too, I may be wrong— blundering simpleton of a detective that I am," and he grinned at her companionably. "You see, I've had the impression all along that you were burdened with a very real terror, a fear that once you left this sanctuary you would—lose your liberty."

"Yes," the girl whispered.

"So, being a detective, and disliking all unsolved mysteries, I did some work on your behalf," he went on easily.

"On—my *behalf?*" she repeated, incredulously, but life was coming back into her frozen face.

"And, you know, Miss Ramsey—strange as it may seem —I believe you still don't know what actually happened on the night of Wednesday, April second!"

"Oh, don't I?" she shuddered, and covered her face with shaking hands, as if to shut forever from sight a picture she could not bear to look upon. But hands could not shut it out, and from behind them she moaned, "I'll never forget it! Never! If I could only die! . . . One minute he was walking, his whole body swinging as if he were so glad to be alive, and the next—Oh, my God!"

"You thought you had killed him, didn't you?" Dundee asked.

"Why are you torturing me like this?" she dropped her hands to demand wildly. "I admit it! I killed him! It was all my fault! I was simply paralyzed when he stepped in front of the car. I didn't know what to do—I didn't realize what I was doing when I let Paul persuade me to run away. And I don't *really* blame him for telling the truth–" But her crucified love rose up to choke her, even as she lied for it.

"Miss Ramsey, how do you know your sweetheart betrayed you?" Dundee asked softly.

"Why should he stand trial, when it was *I* that killed the poor man?" the girl defended her man passionately. "But I know he wouldn't have told the police if he hadn't thought I was safe—somewhere!"

"Paul Van Twing is a lucky devil," Dundee remarked, with just a hint of ruefulness. Then, because all his unspoken questions had already been answered, he could deny her relief no longer. "Miss Ramsey, I'm terribly glad to be the one to tell you that—you are not guilty of manslaughter!"

"Not—guilty?" she gasped. "You mean—oh, please!"

"I mean that the man your car struck was only stunned, not seriously injured; that his injuries were so slight that Paul Van Twing was able to adjust the matter without a charge being entered against him."

"But—But—" she gasped, and struggled to her feet, the sprained ankle forgotten.

"Miss Ramsey, who told you that you were guilty of manslaughter?"

"Who told me?" she repeated, and suddenly her body was electrified with the most terrible anger Dundee had ever seen.

He did not try to restrain her as she snatched up her crutches, let her swing herself strongly, head high and eyes blazing, from the room. For she was carrying out the part he had devised for her as exactly as if she had read the lines.

"No! Don't come in yet!" Dundee called in a low voice to Strawn, who was edging into the room. "But have your gun out—and ready!"

He himself waited in the sitting room until he heard the tapping of crutches in the little hall. Then, noiselessly, he joined Strawn and Brede in the sitting room.

"There's one difficulty," Dundee whispered to the older detective. "She may be terrified to face him alone, when he gets here."

"You're pretty sure she telephoned him, ain't you?" Strawn asked skeptically. "But don't worry about her being afraid! She's so damned sore she'd face him if he was a man eating tiger."

And he was right. The girl was still in such a towering rage that she did not seem even to notice that Dundee was no longer there. She did not sit down, but stood, swung between her crutches, her blazing eyes fixed upon the door which Dundee confidently expected the murderer of Dr. Koenig to open. For if the murderer did not come of his own accord, after receiving that telephone message, Dundee had made sure that he would be brought forcibly. . . .

The sounds of an arrival came, however, before Dundee expected them. How had he got here so soon?

With their eyes at the door crack Dundee and Strawn heard the knock upon that other door, heard the girl's ringing "Come in!" saw the door flung wide and a man's figure framed for an instant before it leaped forward.

"Who's that?" Strawn hissed into Dundee's ear.

And Dundee muttered, blankly, "I don't know!"

But he knew in the next instant, for the newcomer, far from assaulting the girl who, her crutches dropped, was swaying toward him, was sweeping her off the floor into his arms.

"Oh, Paul!" Edith Ramsey gasped. "Paul, Paul! I thought you didn't love me any more—"

The blond, six foot two young giant laughed exultingly, and Dundee gave him time to kiss the girl once before he stepped into the room.

There was scant time for explanations, and the young detective ruthlessly brushed aside the astounded new comer's protests.

"Come with me, Van Twing! Explanations later!" he ordered curtly. "Miss Ramsey is expecting another—guest. Quick, I say! . . . Don't be afraid, Miss Ramsey! Captain Strawn is in the bedroom, too—"

"Afraid!" she laughed, and anger returned, in nowise diminished by her joy at Van Twing's arrival. "Do as he says, Paul! Quick!"

The bewildered young man obeyed, even chuckled. "I say! What sport!" he gloated. "The hounds and the fox, eh?"

"Fox is right!" Dundee assured him grimly, but he felt that he was going to like this wholesome, handsome young giant, when he had time to think about him. "Stand back, Van Twing! . . . Ready, Captain?"

"Look! Is Edith in danger?" the young man protested, at sight of Strawn's leveled gun, and started for the door.

"Stand back, I tell you, Van Twing!" Dundee commanded savagely. "We are all delighted to see you, but I'll be damned if you spoil everything now! . . . Shut up!"

And Van Twing subsided just in time, for again the door from the hall was opening, and this time it framed no unfamiliar figure.

Roger Baldwin stepped into the room.

# CHAPTER 28

"WHAT do you want?"

From his place of concealment behind Edith Ramsey's bedroom door Dundee's very flesh felt the blight of the quiet, deadly coldness of Roger Baldwin's voice.

But apparently it had no power to chill the girl's terrific anger. She was magnificent as she faced him, head high, blue eyes blazing, her crutches forgotten.

"I want the joy of seeing your face when I tell you that I am going to have you arrested for the murder of Dr. Koenig!" she told him, her voice vibrating with a terrible exultation.

Roger Baldwin smiled, but no light gleamed in the strangely cold opaqueness of his brown eyes. Weird eyes they were! No wonder Dr. Koenig had been haunted by the certainty that he had seen them somewhere before. . .

Braced upon Dundee's shoulder, its muzzle thrust into the crack of the partly opened door, was Captain Strawn's revolver, and behind it was Captain Strawn's steady trigger finger and steadier eye. Otherwise the young detective would have been in a sweat of fear as the business manager of Mayfield Sanitarium walked slowly, but with deadly purposefulness to where the girl stood.

"You are insane, Miss Rambler," Baldwin said unemotionally. "You are suffering from a suicidal mania—"

"Suicidal?" she laughed scornfully. "You *know* I saw you come out of Dr. Koenig's office! You *know* I heard you tearing up papers—"

"—from a suicidal mania," Baldwin repeated, in his flat, unemphatic voice. "It will always be a great grief to me that I arrived too late to prevent you from shooting yourself with your own automatic. I struggled with you, but—"

But the shot that shattered the moment of silence which followed Baldwin's calm words did not come from the small automatic which he had lifted to press against the girl's right temple. . . .

"Won't be much of a job for you, will it, Doc?" Captain Strawn asked regretfully two or three minutes later. "I'd have liked to plug the devil through the heart—"

"I'm afraid this right hand will never be much use to him again," Dr. Cantrell answered. "But since he seems to be ambidextrous, the inconvenience won't be very great."

"That baby's not going to need either hand very long," Strawn gloated, but not even then did Roger Baldwin's opaque eyes, fixed on Strawn in an unwinking stare, register any emotion.

The murderer lay on Edith Ramsey's couch, where unsympathetic hands had placed him after his one spasm of fury had been subdued. Bending over him, silent and white faced, administering to his wound as carefully as if he had been any other patient, was little Dr. Harlow. Dr. Cantrell's rubber gloved hands were selecting instruments silently handed to him by Norah Lacey. For Dundee's preparations for the boiling over of his pot, as he called it, had been prophetically complete. Close upon Baldwin's unsuspecting heels had walked the little procession of the business manager's associates, half informed of what they might expect.

When all that they could do for the not seriously wounded man had been done by the doctors and nurse, Dundee took Dr. Harlow's place in front of the couch.

Solemnly but very quietly, in the deep hush, he spoke the dread words:

"Steven Francis Edinger, sometimes known as Frank Edinger, alias Roger Baldwin, I arrest you for the murder of Dr. Carl Koenig, and it is my duty to warn you that anything you say may be used against you."

The silence was profound for a long minute. Baldwin closed his eyes in token that Dundee's warning was superfluous.

"Won't you please take him away now, out of my rooms?" Edith Ramsey broke the silence, her voice sounding very small and pitiful, but there was no hysteria in it. Paul Van Twing's arms were around her. . .

"I'm sorry, Miss Ramsey," Dundee answered sincerely, "but I want to submit you to one more ordeal. I want you to tell your story in this man's presence."

Brede, the police stenographer, automatically opened his notebook.

"I shall be glad to!" the girl cried, righteous anger returning to give her strength. "I've been sure for two days —ever since Captain Strawn talked to me Thursday morn ing—that I was shielding Dr. Koenig's murderer, but I didn't dare—Oh, I can never forgive him for making me hate myself so!"

"Will you begin by telling how you happened to come to this sanitarium, Miss Ramsey?" Dundee suggested soothingly.

"Paul and I were driving on a lonely road. A man stepped from the bushes right into the path of the car," she answered obediently. "I was driving. The suddenness of it paralyzed me. I—it's happened to me before. ... I couldn't think, I couldn't act. I—hit him. Paul and I both thought he was dead. I seemed to go crazy. I *must* have been crazy, or I shouldn't have run away when Paul, who understood me, told me to. He said he would take all the blame, that no one need ever know I'd been in the car. I was a coward. I ran away. But I took my own automatic that I've always carried on motor tours. It was in the pocket of the car. Paul didn't know I took it. I meant to commit suicide before I'd let them take me to jail. The thought of a cell–"

Dundee's sympathy cut across her shuddering sobs. "We understand, Miss Ramsey. You have not really been your self since you were fifteen years old. . . . But bow did you happen to come to Mayfield?"

"I didn't know what to do. I had quite a lot of money with me, and Paul had told me to walk for a mile or so, then telephone for a taxi from a filling station, and go on back to the hotel But I—couldn't. I remembered meeting Mr. Baldwin on Main Street in Hamilton. He came up to me and said, 'How do you do, Miss Ramsey? . . . Don't you remember me?' I said I didn't, and he said he had known my father in California. Then he told me he was business manager of Mayfield Sanitarium now. He said again, "You're sure you don't remember seeing me before?' and I thought it was odd, but Daddy had so many friends mat I only met casually–"

"Baldwin was glad of the chance to test the completeness of his changed appearance," Dundee interrupted to explain. "You *had* met Baldwin, or had seen him but he was no friend of your father's. He was the husband of Mrs. Edinger, a patient at Good Hope Sanitarium at the time you were there."

"Oh!" Edith Ramsey breamed. "So that's why the name seemed vaguely familiar. . . . She was awfully sweet, so gentle, so good to everyone. I remember how devoted one poor boy was to her. . . . And that's an odd coincidence!" she discovered. "The boy was Clyde Powell, who was a patient here until Monday, I believe. I recognized him, but he didn't remember me at all. I was afraid at first that he might–"

"You distinctly remember, however, that Clyde Powell and Mrs. Edinger were friends?" Dundee interrupted eagerly.

"Oh, yes!" the girl cried. "Clyde simply adored Mrs. Edinger. And because she blamed 'Frank,' as she called her husband, for putting her in the sanitarium, Clyde adopted 'Frank' as his own persecutor—hating and fearing him exactly as Mrs. Edinger did."

"Thank you, Miss Ramsey," Dundee said triumphantly, though her statement only confirmed his own deductions. "So—in your extremity—you thought of this friend of your father's, business manager of a sanitarium?"

"Yes. Ever since 1919 I've thought of a sanitarium like this as a haven of refuge," she confessed. "And I believed no one would think of looking for me here. If they did find me, my record as a 'psychopathic patient' would keep me from being sent to jail. ... So I telephoned Mr. Baldwin from a filling station. He came for me in his own car. I told him the dreadful thing I'd done, and he said he'd hide me—*for ten thousand dollars!*"

"Good God!" Paul Van Twing ejaculated, and started up from the "love seat" he was occupying with Edith Ramsey.

"Sit down, Van Twing!" Dundee ordered curtly, but not unkindly. "I sympathize with your reactions, but Baldwin, or Edinger, is going to be amply punished for his crimes. . . . Go on, Miss Ramsey!"

"I gave him a check on my New York bank, and he explained to me how I could open a bank account here, in the name of Enid Rambler. He chose the name for me himself, because it fit the monogram on my handbag and the gun, and everything."

"He took the gun away from you?" Dundee asked.

"Yes. He said I must not think of committing suicide, that he'd protect me. . . . And all the time," she added, "he was planning to kill me with it if I told on him. These last two days, after I knew he had killed Dr. Koenig, I knew what he could do to me. Being the business manager here, he could walk into my suite any time he chose, and the plainclothesman on guard would not dream of trying to prevent him. And I couldn't tell a soul—I couldn't even say that Mr. Baldwin was to be kept out of my rooms—"

"My poor darling!" Van Twing said huskily, and tightened his arms about her. "I don't see how you kept from going crazy!"

"That's what he planned!" she cried, with passionate anger. "All the time I was here he knew I hadn't killed that man. But not only did he remind me somehow, almost every day, that I was a murderess and a coward, he made me believe you had turned against me, Paul, that from information you had given there was a warrant for my arrest—"

"But didn't you see the papers?" Paul Van Twing interrupted.

It was Dr. Harlow who explained, bleakly: "That is our fault, I am afraid. New patients, in Miss Ramsey's condition, are not permitted to see newspapers, for fear the stories of suicide will influence them."

"But Mr. Baldwin saw the papers!" the girl cried. "He knew! ... Of course, after he had got all the money he could out of me, his plan was to drive me crazy, so that nothing I said against him could be believed—and so that I'd never get out of here and learn the truth! ... I gave him thirty five thousand dollars altogether," she added, "but if he'd only told me the truth—that I was innocent of manslaughter and that Paul had not betrayed me, I'd have gladly given him every cent I had in the world, out of sheer gratitude!"

"Now, as to Wednesday night, Miss Ramsey?" Dundee hurried her gently.

The girl sank back into the shelter of her sweetheart's arms.

"I'd never gone to any of the entertainments in the O.T. Shop," she said quietly. "I was always terrified of strangers—afraid someone would recognize me and inform the police. But Wednesday evening, just before seven, Mr. Baldwin came to my suite and told me to go to the movie. He said I'd enjoy it particularly. He didn't tell me the name of the picture, said it would be a 'pleasant surprise.' I knew it was a command I did not dare disobey, so I went, along with Marjorie Merrick. It was—'Manslaughter,' " she added, in a horrified whisper. "He'd got it because he knew what effect it would have on me. It's about a girl who kills a traffic policeman, and is put in prison. I couldn't bear it. I thought I was really going crazy. It was horrible. . . . But I meant to tell you some thing else he said to me when he ordered me to go to the movie," she interrupted herself. "He said Dr. Koenig was 'suspicious,' that the doctor didn't believe there was any real reason why I should be here. Of course I was terrified at the thought of leaving my 'sanctuary.' I didn't know that Mr. Baldwin had got the picture with the express purpose of making me so hysterical that Dr. Koenig would let me stay on."

Her voice shuddered to a pause, and Dundee took advantage of the opportunity to glance at the girl's audience. Little Dr. Harlow sat very still and very straight, her eyes disks of horror set in the chalky whiteness of her face. Dr. Cantrell was listening with head bowed and shoulders slumped, the image of despondency. Norah Lacey was weeping silently and apparently unconscious of the tears that trickled down her thin, freckled cheeks. Only Roger Baldwin seemed unmoved by the girl's story of an incredible inquisition.

"So you left the movie, Miss Ramsey?" Dundee prodded gently.

"Yes. About half past nine. As I told you, I was in a terrible state. I tried to find someone to give me a bromide. Finally I went to Dr. Koenig's door off the main hall, but it was closed. So I decided to wait until he was not busy. I sat down in the reception room. I heard some strange noises, but they were not loud at all. Then I heard someone—I thought it was Dr. Koenig—tearing up paper. That sound went on and on. I was about to knock, because I couldn't hear him talking to anyone, but the door opened and Mr. Baldwin came out."

Dundee drew a deep breath of triumph. Strawn slapped a thigh in mighty exultation.

"He looked terribly queer when he saw me there," the girl went on tonelessly. "Then he bent over me and whispered, as if he was afraid Dr. Koenig would hear him. He said the doctor had just telephoned the police to come and get me, that he'd found out somehow who I was. And then Mr. Baldwin told me to run away. I started to run, and he stopped me. He gripped my shoulders and whispered: 'Run along the highway, my girl, and if you happen to get hit by a car, remember it's a quick, easy way to die. You ought to know. *You've killed three people that way yourself!*"

"I'll be damned if I sit here and—"

But Dundee sprang toward Van Twing and forced him back into his seat.

"He's right, Paul," the girl soothed her sweetheart. "I'm really safe now, and we're going to be happy. I'm well now—I'm *well!*"

But Dr. Harlow must have thought otherwise, for during the interruption she had slipped from the room. Now she was back, and silently offering a sedative to the girl.

"I don't think Miss Ramsey need talk any more now," Dundee said soberly. "We know the rest of her story. We know that she tried to carry out Baldwin's diabolic suggestion, but that she sprang out of the path of a car in time, suffering no more than a sprained ankle as she stumbled into the ditch."

The girl nodded mutely, and Dundee went on:

"As the district attorney's representative, Miss Ramsey, I thank you with all my heart for the aid you will render to the state in this man's trial for murder."

"But I'm still in a fog, boy," Strawn protested. "I know all about Edinger, and the mess he got into back in 1919, but why the devil is he here, and why in the name of God did he want to murder Koenig?"

"I'd like to know the answer to those questions myself," Dr. Cantrell said heavily.

"I know nothing of Edinger's story between 1919 and 1926, when he ingratiated himself with Dr. Mayfield's party on board ship," Dundee acknowledged. "From the looks of the man—and I judge he has not changed much during the last five years, I should say Edinger, who had adopted the name of Baldwin, had gone through some devastating illness. At any rate, he had lost so much weight and aged so drastically that scarcely any other disguise was needed to make him unrecognizable to those who had known him as Edinger."

"Amebic dysentery. Picked it up in China," the murderer astounded them by explaining in his emotionless voice.

"Thanks, Edinger," Dundee said drily. "As for the nose, a plastic surgeon would make nothing of the job of converting a short, stubby nose into a Roman beak. . . . At any rate, Baldwin felt safe when his enemy of the Los Angeles courtroom, Dr. Carl Koenig, met him and failed to recognize him. Baldwin did not know that his eyes haunted Koenig, nagging at his memory. The partnership was formed— *suggested by Baldwin*, who had had good opportunity to gauge the chances of fraud in a private institution for the treatment of mental diseases.

"Koenig was, of course, a severe check to Baldwin's schemes. But he found Mayfield to be a profitable field, in a perfectly legitimate way. If he had not been a born crook, he would have been satisfied with the profits which Dr. Koenig's skill and reputation made possible. It is possible that he was almost satisfied, until he chanced to meet Edith Ramsey, and later found the girl flinging herself at him for protection. The temptation was too great. Possibly there have been other patients here whose recovery Baldwin has cunningly retarded. Certainly we know of one other. . . . But let that rest for the moment.

"Tonight, after I was sure that Edinger was Baldwin, I asked Dr. Harlow if Baldwin had been away on a business trip recently. She told me that he had been to Chicago, to confer with architects, during the month of May. I knew, then, that the Sandlin mystery was solved."

"Sandlin?" Cantrell echoed incredulously, and Dr. Harlow lifted her eyes, which seemed suddenly to come alive again.

"Of course it was Baldwin who negotiated with Dr. Sandlin," Dundee assured them impatiently. "I feel sure that Baldwin ran into Sandlin by accident, when looking over the Howard Memorial buildings with an architect. Sandlin recognized Baldwin. And Sandlin, being as big a crook if not so clever a one as Baldwin, threatened exposure, if a suitable price for his silence was not forthcoming. Baldwin could not face trial on the Edinger indictment in Los Angeles, and he was much averse to turning over hard cash to the man who had helped him in his scheme against his wife. But he could—and would—pay another price."

"Get Sandlin into Mayfield and split the crooked profits with him," Strawn deduced happily.

"Right!" Dundee smiled. "But Koenig, when Baldwin broached the subject to him, was not having any Sandlin, thank you. That doctor wasn't good enough for Mayfield! Baldwin, who had had a long conference in his own cottage with Sandlin on Tuesday night—for of course it was Baldwin and not Koenig whom Sandlin came to Hamilton to visit—could see no way out. He insisted, as a partner, on Koenig's considering Sandlin as an assistant psychiatrist. Koenig made a note of the name on his desk calendar, intending, no doubt, to investigate Sandlin thoroughly enough to convince the business manager. I think it was probably true that Dr. Koenig intended to devote most of his time in the future to psychoanalysis. The two crooks would have had practically a clear field here—except for the annoying fact that Dr. Harlow, as straight and incorruptible as Koenig himself—would still be here!"

"Oh!" the little doctor breathed, and light began to shine through the horror in her eyes.

"On Wednesday afternoon," Dundee went on, "Dr. Koenig told the business manager that Mrs. Morse would be leaving in a day or two—

cured. That was a severe blow to Baldwin's cupidity. Mrs. Morse's monthly bill here was well over a thousand dollars, a sum Baldwin could not bear to lose, if human—or inhuman—ingenuity could prevent it. But first he protested to Dr. Koenig, or so I firmly believe. Koenig was astounded at Baldwin's suggestion that the woman be kept on indefinitely, on the chance that she was not really cured. Something of Baldwin's true nature must have betrayed itself to the psychiatrist at that moment. Not only did Baldwin want Mrs. Morse to be detained, but he argued against 'Enid Rambler's' being sent away, although Dr. Koenig was convinced she was not a definite psychopathic case, and that such an atmosphere was harmful to her."

He paused, and the silence which awaited his further revelations was electric with suspense.

"Picture to yourself, as I have tried to picture it, Koenig's state of mind in regard to Baldwin. The business manager, he suddenly realized, was becoming a definite menace to Mayfield. Not only was he opposed to patients being cured, but he wanted to add to the staff a doctor against whom Koenig had heard vague but sinister insinuations, and Koenig must have remembered his impression of Sandlin's insincerity at Mrs. Edinger's sanity hearing.

"Koenig was troubled, but there was nothing definite— yet. He worked all evening, unconscious of the fact that Baldwin had slipped out of his own office just before nine o'clock, and had staged that dreadful 'Voice of God' farce beneath Mrs. Morse's windows.

"Shortly before half past nine Dr. Koenig remembered that Mrs. Cantrell was not well. He interrupted his work of typing the excerpts from Clyde Powell's case history, wanted by the State Hospital doctors, and telephoned Mrs. Cantrell. As he talked, his eyes roamed idly. Then they were arrested by a line in Clyde Powell's history that had seemed unimportant before. That line was to the effect that, *at the sight of Roger Baldwin, the patient showed fear, and suffered epileptiform seizures.*"

"Has the case history been found?" Dr. Harlow asked.

"No, it must have been completely destroyed," Dundee assured her. "But Baldwin did not know that a senile, feeble old man had recorded the same interesting fact."

"Did that doddering old fool–?" Baldwin began, then his lips snapped to.

"Exactly," Dundee assured him. "It would have been 'good business' to clean out Dr. Mayfield's rooms thoroughly, wouldn't it, Baldwin? . . . But possibly you were saving those useless old dictaphone records of his, planning to have them shaved for future use?"

Baldwin did not reply.

"But how did that sentence in Powell's case history tip the doctor off?" Strawn demanded, sorely puzzled. "It wouldn't have meant anything to us if we'd seen it!"

"Right you are!" Dundee agreed triumphantly. "Baldwin's guilty conscience made him a little too far sighted. Without the fact of that completely destroyed case history But to answer your question. The sentence concerning Baldwin would have meant little to Koenig, even troubled as he was about Baldwin's attitude toward the sanitarium, if it had not occurred on the same page with two other names—Good Hope Sanitarium and Dr. Horace Sandlin. Those three names leaping into his vision almost simultaneously caused something to click in Koenig's memory. Suddenly he knew where he had seen Baldwin before! I am sure the whole picture of that Los Angeles courtroom flashed into Koenig's mind. Baldwin was 'placed' at last. And Baldwin was Steven Francis Edinger, 'wanted' in Los Angeles!"

"So Koenig tried to put the matter in his lawyer's hands," Strawn supplied with satisfaction.

"Yes," Dundee agreed. "After all, Baldwin, or Edinger, was connected with Mayfield, and the doctor must have planned to avoid publicity as much as possible. But when he could not reach Forrest, he acted. He was killed in the very act of dictating a night letter to the district attorney in Los Angeles."

For the benefit of Dr. Harlow and Dr. Cantrell, and partly, it is just possible, to let Baldwin know how his undoing had come about, Dundee told briefly the story of the "bust message," which had ended with the three letters, "E d i ."

Then he turned to the quiet, apparently uninterested man on the couch.

"You congratulated yourself on your luck in having entered Dr. Koenig's office just in time to prevent that message being completed, didn't you, Edinger?"

The murderer scorned to answer.

"And as you busily 'dressed the set' to make it look like murder committed by a homicidal maniac, you boasted to yourself of your coolness and far sightedness, didn't you, Edinger?"

There was still no answer, but Dundee expected none.

"Yes, you were clever, Edinger," the young detective went on relentlessly. "Damned clever! But—just a little too clever! You made three very bad errors, which—"

That drew fire. "Three!" the murderer snorted. "I didn't overlook anything—except that single damned drop of blood."

Dundee smiled. Brede was taking down everything in shorthand.

"I admit, Edinger, that that one drop of blood was in dispensable to us—that it led directly to your undoing. But you made two other serious errors. Not being a psychiatrist, Edinger, and having had only one really original idea in your life, you chose to repeat. *But Mrs. Morse does not hear voices.* She is not, and never was, that type of psychopathic case."

"The third error, Bonnie," Strawn reminded him. "What was that?"

"He told a lie," Dundee answered simply.

"Guess he's done a lot of lying these last three days," Strawn retorted, puzzled.

"Not much," Dundee corrected, in all fairness. "But he told one lie that has stood out like a signpost from the first hour of this investigation. He said that Dr. Koenig told *him* he was going to dismiss Dr. Harlow. . . . Very bad, Edinger! . . . Now, it was just conceivable that Dr. Koenig might have come to the conclusion that the little doctor was too credulous, too soft hearted for her job, even though he thought enough of her to put her down in his will for one half of his estate. But—Koenig would never in this world have told Roger Baldwin, whom he did not like particularly, of his intention to dismiss a woman who had served him faithfully and devotedly. With the utmost tact and gentleness he might have broken the news to the little doctor herself, but he would never have told anyone else *first*. And of all people, he would not have told you, Edinger! . . . And the more fool I, that I didn't follow that signpost more quickly!"

"I'm glad you made a detour," Edith Ramsey said softly.

"By the way, Van Twing," and Dundee turned to the young man who had arrived so opportunely, "I presume your fat private detective, who, incidentally, almost succeeded in getting himself suspected of murder, notified you of Miss Ramsey's presence here, incognito."

"Fat, is he?" Van Twing grinned, but without amusement. "He's fat mentally, too, it seems, for in his regular night letter report to me of his activities I was informed on Thursday morning that he—Fuller is his name—had located a girl strongly resembling Miss Ramsey, at Mayfield Sanitarium, but that the business manager had convinced him of his mistake. Naturally, when the newspapers blazoned forth the news of Dr. Koenig's murder, I was intensely interested. Late Thursday editions carried a paragraph describing 'Enid Rambler,' as one of the patients who had been 'quizzed,' and I was so positive it was Edith that I took a plane as soon as I could charter one. . . . There is some excuse for Fuller, however. The photograph he has of Edith shows her with bobbed hair, and considerably plumper than she is now. She has let her hair grow since I saw her last."

"I see," Dundee commented, and was silent for a long minute. Then, very soberly, he turned toward Dr. Harlow.

"For those who are grieving for Dr. Koenig," he said, almost apologetically, "I am presumptuous enough to offer this bit of consolation: Dr. Koenig did not die in vain. His tragic death saved Edith Ramsey. For this girl was doomed. Edinger would never have permitted her to leave this place until she was dead or hopelessly insane. Dr. Koenig would have given his life to save her. . . . And he did!"

**THE END**

# MURDER UNLEASHED
## BY DOROTHY BENNETT

Murder Unleashed

*by* Dorothy Bennett

A Resurrected Press Mystery

**ORIGINALLY PUBLISHED IN 1935**

EDITOR'S NOTES:
# MURDER UNLEASHED
## BY DOROTHY BENNETT

The 1935 mystery novel *Murder Unleashed* is interesting for a number of reasons. First it is interesting for what it is not as much as what it is. It doesn't follow the then prevailing pattern of the English mystery with a clever crime presented as a puzzle and an even cleverer detective to unravel it. Nor does it fit the mold of those light hearted American mysteries full of witty dialog and snappy one-liners and a hint of romance that were so popular in the films of the period.

Stylistically, it owes most to the hard-boiled school of detective fiction pioneered by Dashiell Hammett and Carroll John Daly. The settings and the crimes are gritty and realistic, not glamorous, the motivations of many of the characters petty and shallow. And as with many of those stories, the hero finds himself caught up in events he doesn't understand against a backdrop of the corruption that money and power bring. Yet the hero is not a hardened private detective, not a Sam Spade or Phillip Marlowe, or even a jaded newspaper man, but instead is a singer on a late night radio program, a former college boy and football player who has had his life turned upside down by an incident in his past.

The setting of the novel is San Francisco and central California in the early 1930's, in many ways the same San Francisco as that of Hammett's *The Maltese Falcon* and the same California as his Continental Op stories. But it is also the California of Steinbeck, not the Steinbeck of *The Grapes of Wrath*, but the Steinbeck of *Tortilla Flats* and *Cannery Row*, for the roots of this mystery lie in the small towns of the agricultural country south of San Francisco.

The crime, itself is brutal enough, a young woman lured to a hotel room only to be stabbed with a kitchen knife and left for a stranger to discover. Yet the novel is not so much about the solution of the crime, but about the hero coming to terms with himself and the incident in his past that had caused him to cut himself off from his past life. It is this emphasis on the psychological aspect that separates Murder Unleashed from the hard-boiled school. Detectives such as Sam Spade have already made their choices in life, while Dennis Devore still has his in front of him.

The author, Dorothy Bennett, is something of a mystery, herself. Her only two works are *Murder Unleashed* and *How Strange a Thing*, a mystery in the form of a poem that came out in the same year, 1935. After that, despite the promise of Murder Unleashed for all intents she disappears.

Whatever the facts of her life may be, for a first (and possibly only) novel, Murder Unleashed is a remarkable work, well written, well plotted, and well thought out. Resurrected Press is pleased to offer this new edition of a long forgotten work.

**About the Author**

Little information is available about Dorothy Bennett. It would appear that she grew up in Berkeley, California and probably went to the university there. Her mother was Mary Richardson Bennett, to whom she dedicated a murder mystery in the form of a poem entitled *How Strange a Thing* which was published in 1935, the same year as *Murder Unleashed.*

# MURDER UNLEASED

## I. BEGINNING OF WISDOM

IT BEGAN that foggy November night in San Francisco when Dennis Devore stuck his key in his hotel-room door, shoved it open onto blackness, and lit the light.

He stood on the threshold of the little snug, neat room. It might have been anyone's room, or no one's, so neat, so impersonal it was, with its bed neatly made, sheet turned down, reading light over the headboard, graceful walnut furniture, windows looking out onto the dark and the scattering lights below the hill, where Market Street and the downtown theater district still crawled along like great gold snakes through the night. Only a pocket-size radio standing on the table, a few packages of cigarettes thrown around on cloisonne ashtrays, and a pile of untidy books spilling over on the bureau made it his.

He preferred it that way. Light travel, long journey. He always felt nowadays as if he had to be free to get up and go in a second, if he wanted to. He carried his personal life in his dark and ruffled head.

So now he looked with satisfaction around at his snug and tidy den where he'd holed up for the winter. And as he looked, he saw something dark and untidy—like a solid sort of shadow—on the floor beyond the central table. He stepped around to see better, and then he stood staring down at the floor, eyes widening—widening . . .

He put his hand out automatically and clutched the edge of the table. His eyes still stared downward. They were wide with horror, as a moonless night is wide open to darkness.

There was a woman on the floor—a woman he'd never seen in his life before. She had red hair, loosened, coming down to her shoulders—a very white face—dark blue eyes that looked at him—and she was dead.

He knew that. He couldn't mistake it. She was dead, and those dark sapphire eyes stared at him incuriously. Her skin had the whiteness of milk, and her hair was like flame playing over her head. She was beautiful, and she was dead.

He didn't quite know what he did in the next few minutes. When he caught himself up again, he was still looking down at her, and his hand had clamped the table edge as if it had grown onto it. He couldn't have moved, then. But he'd gone through a very dark way in that short time.

But now he had hold of himself again. What had to be done would be done. He gave himself orders to move, to break that intolerable vise of stillness and horror that held him. And very slowly he went on over to the telephone on the wall, took up the receiver, and said, "Get me the Hall of Justice, will you?"

He listened a second, then, "Police department, please. Hello—will you . . . you'd better send someone over. There's a woman dead here."

It sounded for another second like a hoarse deep crackle of machine-gun barrage at the other end of the line. Dennis shrugged his shoulders wearily. He gave the name of the hotel.

"How do I know?" he said. "I found her."

He hung up. Then he passed one hand over his head, in a puzzled gesture. He couldn't think. He only knew that he had to keep that still figure within the edge of his sight. It couldn't hurt him, of course, but— he couldn't quite turn his back on it. He discovered that he was shivering, uncontrollable deep shivers like waves that tried to wrench his sanity from its moorings.

He had to hold onto himself. He did.

There was something he'd forgotten to do. Notify the hotel people. That was it. They'd have the police busting down doors in a minute if he didn't.

He went to the phone again. Suddenly, desperately, he needed communication with some outside help, the sound of a human voice. He felt like a diver abandoned on the ocean floor.

He raised the reassuring voice of the desk clerk downstairs.

"Listen," he said, "send the manager up here right away, will you?"

"He's just gone up in the elevator," the clerk said. "Told me he was going up to your room. The telephone girl gave him some message. Anything wrong?"

Dennis said, "Thanks. I'll let you know later."

The still figure on the floor was always within range of his vision. He mustn't lose sight of it. He'd go crazy with a primitive, superstitious fear if he did. The powers of darkness . . .

You had to face them boldly. Then they couldn't get you.

He knew that. He'd faced them.

There was a knock on the door. Life thundering out its command to open and face things. A quiet, sharp knock that meant to be obeyed.

Just as Dennis said, "Come," hoarsely, the door opened anyway and the hotel manager came in. He stopped inside the room and looked at Dennis, before he let his glance go around. His face was rigid, pitiless, hard with distaste that anything had happened in his hotel. His eyes were keen as lights shining in darkness.

"What's happened Ah!" he interrupted himself, as those keen hard eyes came to the woman.

"Someone—killed." Dennis found his voice dry. He forced it out of his throat and found that it dried up on him like one of the little California rivers sinking into a sandy bed in summertime.

"Killed?" The manager took him up sharply. "You said over the phone just now . . . dead."

"Look," Dennis croaked.

His hand pointed. There wasn't any need to say anything else. They both saw it—a little dark river drying on the taupe plush carpet. A little river of blood, whose source had been the back of that silent, black-clad figure. It had crawled a few inches and then sunk into the carpet. Or else—she had been killed at its farther end and had moved, before she died, in a convulsive gesture of escape. Not a pleasant little stream.

Dennis thought wildly for a brief moment of escape, of cottonwoods waving along a wide, sunny river, of water so shallow you could wade across, seeing the sun on the sandy bottom—of the wind in his face, the same wind that waved the trees.

That was far away—months and sunny afternoons away. It was a foggy November night, and he was in a close little hotel room, and that beautiful, white-skinned figure in the filmy black evening gown was lying at their feet. The grave blue eyes questioned them, swept them aside as unimportant. She looked as if she mustn't be disturbed—as if she were listening to, were looking at, something really important. Her whole attention elsewhere, beyond them.

And slowly, beyond the horror and the superstitious dread of death, Dennis began to feel stirring in his heart an ache of resentment that something so beautiful should die—should die before its time. The waste of beauty—the pity, the pity!

What had she done? Did it matter? She didn't deserve to die. No one so beautiful did. Not, his heart said fiercely, even if she'd done things terrible or treacherous. She'd given the world something in return, anyway. She'd been—her own excuse for being.

"Who is she?" asked the hotel manager, still staring at her.

Dennis's dark head came up on that with a jerk.

"How do I know?" he retorted. "I never saw her before in my life!"

"H'm," said the manager.

On that exchange they ended, until the police arrived about a minute later. The room seemed suddenly full of very substantial men in overcoats and felt hats, of deep voices questioning, commanding—of wide shoulders, hard eyes, straight glances.

The passage with the hotel manager had been just a preliminary. This was the main event.

There were two of them—Inspectors Sullivan and Cassidy. Dennis didn't have a chance.

The hardly veiled doubt of the hotel manager was nothing to the unbelief expressed by Inspectors Sullivan and Cassidy. Cassidy was a sharp-voiced man with a driving manner. He asked questions and expected answers. But Sullivan was like a smothering mountain in bulk and in manner. He sort of loomed. His comparative quietness was all the more impressive. Dennis felt smothered by that watchful silence and that ominous reticence.

They asked questions.

"Who is she?" Cassidy demanded, jerking his head first at the woman and then at Dennis.

Dennis said wearily and a bit automatically, "I never saw her before—in my life."

"Huh," said Cassidy, dropping this for the minute.

They crossed over to her, after warning the two men watching them not to move or touch anything in the room. They dropped to their knees and touched the corpse gently. Dennis and the hotel manager, who looked like a sharp black-and-white glossy raven in his dinner clothes, looked on silently.

Cassidy's head went up like an alarm signal. His hard blue eyes sought them.

"She's still warm!" he rasped. His sandy face flushed a bit with excitement. "She's still warm, I tell you. And the blood hasn't dried yet. This was done recently."

Sullivan nodded. The massive head went up and down once.

Cassidy jumped to his feet, turned on the other two.

"Who did it?" he demanded. "Who did it?"

He was like a fierce little hunting terrier now, sharp in excitement, merciless. He turned to both of them in turn.

"I don't know," Dennis said. That brought the gaze of those pitiless blue eyes on him then. He braced himself to meet them, and Sullivan's appraising deeper ones in the background.

"Who are you, anyway?" Cassidy snapped.

"I phoned you," Dennis said dully. "I—I'm in this room. When I came home tonight—just now—I found —that. I found her there."

"Yeah?" Sullivan came into it now. "What's your name?"

"Devore," he told them. "Dennis Devore."

It sounded like a silly sort of name now. He wished he'd picked a better one while he'd been at it. At the time, it had sounded good enough for what he wanted to do.

"What time'd you come here?" Cassidy asked.

"I don't know exactly," Dennis said. "I was on at the studio—broadcasting studio, you know—at eleven forty-five, for fifteen minutes "

"Broadcasting studio?" Cassidy picked him up.

"I'm a radio tenor," Dennis said. "I sing over it every night, at the same time."

"Eleven forty-five to twelve, eh?" Sullivan said, expressionless. "That brings you to twelve o'clock. Go on."

"I guess I left the studio just after twelve," Dennis thought back. "The next number was on when I left. It was a one-o'clock program tonight. It took me, say, fifteen minutes to walk home—I climbed the hill—and came right in here."

"Clerk might remember," Cassidy said briefly.

"It was about twelve fifteen, I guess." Dennis set his guess at that. "Then I came in " He set his teeth on that.

"Lights on?" Cassidy said, glancing around the room.

"No, out," Dennis went on, grateful for the shove over that hard place. "It was all dark in here. I had to open the door with my key and then turn on the lights at the door."

"The door was locked, eh?" Sullivan boomed in.

"Locked," Dennis nodded. "But anyone could have opened it—with a passkey. *He* did, just now." He jerked his head at the hotel manager, that unfriendly black-and-white raven in smart glossiness.

"Did, eh? What for?" Cassidy asked.

The gentleman he indicated shrugged.

"The telephone girl passed on Mr. Devore's message to the police to me," he said. "The policy of the hotel —well, there are some things we like to handle ourselves. Unfortunate publicity, you know "

"Some things you like to handle for yourselves!" Cassidy took him up, snarling. "To *keep* to yourselves, you mean! But not murder!"

The manager shrugged again and lapsed into silence.

"Go on. What about this passkey business?" Cassidy was on Dennis's trail again, yapping at his heels, as it were. "Why was it necessary?"

"It wasn't," Dennis retorted. "He knocked on the door, and before I could open it he'd shoved right in on his key."

"Before you could open it?" Sullivan said. "What were you doing that took up your time, anyway?"

At that Dennis looked at him with the first faint shine of a smile in his dark eyes, like a rather rueful sunrise coming in on a cold and wintry day. A smile at his own expense.

"Just—looking," he said softly and huskily.

"I was afraid that Mr. Devore might have stepped out, after—er— doing his duty by the police," the hotel manager struck in smoothly and nastily.

An unfriendly bird, Dennis decided dispassionately.

"Stepped out a second? Did you?" That was Cassidy.

"No, I tell you! I was in the room when he came in. I told you—I was—just looking."

Dennis had too much to do to hold his own with these two men to think about the hotel manager just now.

"Touch anything?" Sullivan asked now.

"Only the phone—and the table, I guess. And the door, of course."

"Fingerprints?" the hotel manager said.

"We'll see," grunted Sullivan, turning from them. "Coroner's men'll be here in a minute. Get the doctor's opinion. Not much doubt, though. Someone stuck a knife in her—and it's still there. Accounts for not much blood shed."

He turned softly, prowling lightly for all his bulk, to the windows, staring down at the sills a minute, at the latches still on the catch, at the dark fire escape beyond going down into the night. He didn't touch anything there, though.

Cassidy turned briskly to the hotel manager.

"Have to get list of people on this floor," he said to him. "Who're in these rooms along this hall, anyway? Did they see anyone or hear anything? What were they doing when she was killed here?"

The manager shrugged again, as one who gives up riddles.

"If it comes to that," he said, slowly, "I should be glad to have an explanation of some things myself. Why, for instance, should anyone select Mr. Devore's room in which to do such a terrible deed—a murder?"

The implication wasn't pleasant. No one pretended that it was. You couldn't gloss such a thing over. They all stared at Dennis for a second like, he decided swiftly and irrelevantly, hungry tigers picking out their special steaks.

There was now a confused noise beginning in the usually noiseless, plush-padded corridor outside.

"Doctor—coroner's men—likewise police reporters," diagnosed Cassidy quickly. "Let's get going."

Sullivan moved into action, slow, massive, somehow like the fabled irresistible force joined to the immovable body.

"We'll have to take your fingerprints," he said to Dennis, "if that's agreeable."

"Why not?" Dennis said. "Of course."

Cassidy was letting in something that resembled a pack of hunting hounds, eyes bright with excitement of the chase, giving tongue impartially to any trail that looked good. A blue-coat was helping him sort out visitors at the door. Cassidy had underestimated the population waiting outside. There were elevator boys in trim blue uniform, plainclothes clerk, and a few negligee guests from the same floor joining in the chorus.

The officially approved ones came in. Sullivan nodded to one unobtrusive little man with a case.

"Prints," he said briefly. The little man nodded and set out things on the walnut center table. There was something black and smudgy, like the sort of thing you press an election rubber cross against to ink it. Dennis reached out one hand. The little man seized it suddenly, firmly pressed down his fingers one by one in a quick rolling motion over the black stuff, transferring each print to paper before he took another finger. Then he dropped that hand, took the other one, and went through the same procedure. Dennis was left with two black-fingered hands. He was a bit ashamed and angry with himself because his hand shook a little. There'd been something so impersonal and ruthless in the procedure of taking his fingerprints that there was a sort of degradation about it—about him, he felt.

It was sort of frightening. Was this the way they treated prisoners—real prisoners? It was like being a wild animal in a cage. No regard for your personal will or spirit.

Someone came up to Sullivan, leaving the group gathered at the woman's body in a buzzing circle. A little man, with eyes like birds', bright and inquisitive and not unfriendly, in a thin brown face. A black overcoat almost too big for him draped him grandly. A black felt hat tilted jauntily over the lean little face.

"Kennedy—from the *Star*," he introduced himself in a hoarse chirp. "Took me off a losing poker game Can we smoke, chief?" he interrupted himself and lit a cigarette without waiting for Sullivan's approval or disapproval. That huge detective glared at him, but the undaunted intruder was conveniently blind and deaf to certain rumbles from the big throat.

"Murder, eh?" he went on.

"And what else would it be, with a knife sticking in her back?" broke in Cassidy with a certain bitter sarcasm.

"Trace the knife?" Kennedy thrust at him.

"Sure—if you want to trace every breadknife the chain stores have ever sold here," Cassidy thrust back. "You saw it—you can buy one like it for fifty cents. We could indict anyone in San Francisco who ever cut a loaf of bread, nearly, for having one in their possession."

"Yeah—and you could find out where it was last sharpened," the police reporter cut in. "I've got one of those things myself—I'm baching it—and I'm here to tell you they couldn't cut putty unless they'd been darn near a grindstone, a good grindstone, for an hour or two."

Sullivan turned to Dennis.

"You can go in the bathroom and wash your hands of that ink," he said.

Dennis went through the crowd. He caught Kennedy's half-whisper to Sullivan as he went. He tried not to see what was on the floor or what they were doing.

"Who's that guy?"

Sullivan rumbled an answer. Dennis knew what it was.

When he came back, Sullivan was waiting to meet him.

"We're going over to the Hall of Justice to report," he said. "You'll have to come with us, Devore, and explain why someone used your room for a murder party. I'm curious myself."

Dennis caught Kennedy's bright eye as Sullivan tried to hustle a way for the two of them out of the crowded room, without answering any of the questions that blocked his way.

"Listen," said that bright, keen little man intently, not unfriendly, "you're in a bad way, kid. Anyone you want me to call up?"

Then Dennis remembered someone.

"There's a man I know," he said, "a bird named Peter Byrne. If you'd call him up—I'd be glad. Thanks."

"Don't thank me. It's a swell story," Kennedy retorted. "A bird named Peter Byrne, eh? Right! What is he—a friend?"

"He's a lawyer," Dennis said hurriedly, as Sullivan grasped his arm and made a way for them impatiently.

Kennedy whistled, keeping pace with them.

"They find a beautiful dame dead in your room, and they haul you off to the coop," he remarked appreciatively. "You sure are in a tight place, kid. My boy, you don't want a lawyer—you need a can opener, to get you out of this."

"Will you shut up?" growled Sullivan and swept Dennis with him past the half-opened mouths and wide-open eyes of elevator boys, half-dressed guests, and other onlookers, down to the elevator, and so out to the street.

# II.  A BIRD NAMED PETER

Peter Byrne, awakened by a wild ringing sometime well after midnight, wondered why there were such things as telephones in this very imperfect world. He was a wide-awake young man when he was awake, and he went in for sleeping just as whole-heartedly.

After a few seconds he decided to answer the call.

He collided first with the bureau, whose location he knew as well as he knew that of the nose on his face, and then with the telephone chair. After that he was ready for anything, sleep shaken out of him.

"Huh?" he said to the crisp voice over the line. "What's that? Dennis Devore?"

"He's a tenor over the radio—one of these midnight canaries," chirped the shrewd, not-to-be-denied voice. "Come clean, Byrne—he says you're his lawyer—a lawyer, anyway. And he's in a jam, all right."

Peter forgot the midnight cold waves coming through his pajamas, attacking his bare feet. He clamored for details.

The voice then identified itself more explicitly. "I'm Kennedy, doing police for the *Star*," it said. "Devore asked me to call you. He's on the carpet at the Hall of Justice now."

"Not," thought Peter grimly and a bit wistfully, "such a bad place to be, at that."

He couldn't think of any Dennis Devore he knew who was a tenor over the radio. However, he was willing to learn more, as long as he didn't have to turn on the radio and listen to this Devore canary at this time of night.

"What's he in for?" he asked.

"Not what you think," the shrewd voice sort of grinned at him over the phone. "There ought to be a law, I admit—but we haven't got around to it yet. We will, we will. Just give us time—"

"Say," said an indignant and now thoroughly roused Peter Byrne, "what is this, anyway? A debate? Go--"

"Whoa!" said Kennedy calmly. "I'm coming to it. There's no law against tenors, as I said—but there certainly is against murder. Your friend Dennis is up for entertaining a lady corpse unbeknownst to him in his room tonight. He claims it was there when he got home from the studio. The police just said 'Yeah?' and hauled him off to the Hall of Justice—about 1:30 a. m. Pacific Standard Time. Are you standing by? The gong will indicate the police patrol, this time."

"Wh-what?" said Peter, inadequately.

"And so, friends of radioland, we come to the end of another swell pogrom—I mean program—and the beginning of the next. It's probably going on at the Hall of Justice now, where they're socking the truth out of your client."

About to say, stunned, "He's not my client!" Peter Byrne paused, on the very words.

The picture this shrewd chirper indicated wasn't a pretty one. Murder? Maybe so. A woman killed in this Dennis Devore's room. And no one to stand up for Dennis, whoever he was—and what a rotten name he wore! thought a fastidious Peter—except a casual pick-up acquaintance of a police reporter. And this Devore had given him Peter Byrne's name. Sort of last resort, maybe, because Peter couldn't place him at that. Not even with all the details he'd just listened to, that surely should excite any faint memory of this Dennis whatsoever. It was, when you came to think of it, sort of like an S O S coming out of the night to him.

And, as though accurately guessing the state of Peter Byrne's mind about that time, Kennedy's cool bird chirp changed to something colder and harsher, more like a challenge.

"Well?" it said, slowly, deliberately, a bit contemptuously, into the continued silence.

"Well what?" Byrne growled back at him.

"Are you in this or aren't you?" the police reporter wanted to know, still in that deliberate, rather deadly voice. "That is the layout. Either pick up your cards and play 'em or pass. I've told you all I know, Byrne. Just that Devore handed me out your name. I told him I'd get the situation before you. Are you in or not?"

A muffled roar answered him. To anyone who had ever spent an afternoon at the zoo it would be reminiscent of an aroused bear, shaking a shaggy head from side to side, coming out to battle. Peter was getting mad. His friends simply didn't go around bumping people off and then getting insolent, cold-voiced police reporters to call him up at an ungodly hour at night to bait him like this.

"Okay," said Kennedy, perversely mistranslating this roar. "I'll slip word to the boys his lawyer is coming around. You probably won't be able to get your client out of hock before morning, though. Might use a habeas-corpus grip on 'em to make them give him up if they're holding him too hard."

Peter had quieted down to deadliness himself. "I'll get him out," he promised simply and grimly. "I want to talk to him myself."

He hung up with a bang.

The light went on in the hall then and revealed Peter sitting there in blue-and-white pajamas, shaggy brown head at one end of his attire, large brown bare feet at the other. He blinked a startled pair of deep blue eyes from under strongly accented eyebrow ledges. He was impressive, built on the battering-ram principle.

His sister Blake was coming down the stairway. She wore a striped flannel dressing gown of blue and orange and brown, and a pair of blue bedroom slippers with orange pompons. She had a bright head of boy's golden brown hair weirdly ruffled up now, and a sleepy red mouth. Even when she was walking half asleep she carried her head with a sort of pride that straightened her slim body into a rushing grace.

"Blake," Peter said, puzzled, "do you know a guy named Dennis— Dennis Devore?"

"Heavens, no," Blake said. "Who is he, and why?"

She dropped into the big chair by the hall table and managed to wind herself up in its seat like a cat.

"I *thought* I'd brought you up better'n that," Peter grunted in great satisfaction. "I bet he's someone I knew at Stanford. There's always a lot of fellows you never remembered seeing in your life before, calling you up and saying they were at Stanford with you, when they want something."

"What does *he* want?" Blake asked, to be agreeable, seeing that her adored Peter was ready for a bit of midnight conversation.

Peter gave her the conversation, briefly.

"Guy's in jail. On a murder charge. Lady friend of his killed. He says he never saw her before, stranger to him. He gave a reporter my name to call up. Oh, yes—and he's a radio tenor—sings over the radio."

"Pete!" said Blake. She sat up. Her eyes were shining. Her bright boy's head lifted swiftly. "Go in and get him!"

"With what?" said Peter. "My bare hands?"

"He gave your name," Blake said softly.

Her brother grunted again.

"What are you doing down here in those clothes?" he demanded. He rose slowly, impressive in his scantier ones. "You'd better go to bed again."

"Where are you going?" his sister asked, preparing to go.

"I'm going to dress," he said briefly. "They don't allow pajamas down at the Hall of Justice when you're calling there just for a short visit—not a week-end stay."

"You lamb!" said Blake very softly and surely, pausing on the turn of the stairway to smile down at him before she disappeared.

That was about three o'clock in the morning. Peter was patient, he was forceful, he pulled wires. But it was around eight o'clock in the morning when the police decided to release his involuntary client from further questioning—for the moment.

They met in a small gray anteroom. Peter surveyed the wilted figure with frank interest. Dennis gazed up at Peter's more respectable and imposing heights.

"Hullo!" Peter said. "You Devore?"

Dennis nodded. "You're Byrne, aren't you?" He hesitated a second. He gave the impression, to Peter, as if he'd just held out his hand and then decided to snatch it back swiftly. A gesture of the mind rather than of the body.

He grinned faintly, instead.

"'Dr. Livingstone, I presume,'" he murmured.

Peter couldn't help grinning back before he thought about the seemliness of it.

"How'd you know me—of me?" he asked. He dropped onto the strongest-looking chair and motioned his client toward another. They settled down more at ease. Peter produced smokes, with a guilty glance of defiance toward the door. The dark head opposite him bent down swiftly over a match held out, inhaled luxuriously, exhaled a long wreath before it straightened up again.

"Missed those," he said simply. "You? Oh, I'd seen you at the studio—you came in with a party one night, remember?—and last night, when I couldn't raise any other name to save my life, you for some unknown reason stuck out in my mind. Favorably," he added hurriedly and respectfully, looking at Peter's two hundred pounds. "Perhaps it was because I'd remembered what a devil of a good guard you were and I knew I'd need a good fighter with me in this mess."

Peter grinned again. Then he made his face sober.

"Well, what happened in there?" he nodded toward the closed door.

"Plenty," said Dennis.

His eyes were dull and impenetrable all of a sudden.

"You didn't get fresh with them, did you?" Peter asked.

The wilted figure faced him indignantly.

"Fresh!" he echoed. "Do I look as if I was fresh?"

"You look as if you needed a shower and a shave," Peter commented frankly on his appearance. "And breakfast."

"Breakfast?" said Dennis wistfully. "What's that?"

"An old American custom," Peter explained. "We have it at our house every morning."

"I'd sort of lost track of it," Dennis apologized.

He got to his feet rather quickly, as if something had just got into his mind.

"Well," he said, "thanks very much—for all you've done. Sorry to have bothered you, but—thanks."

"What for?" Peter asked.

"Thanks for the lift," Dennis said. "I—I suppose this is where I get off. Good-bye." He did hold out his hand this time.

He couldn't very well make a graceful exit with two hundred pounds of solid Peter at the other end of his hand. He wanted to make a swell exit, too. He thought he had just about that much left in him.

"I said we had breakfast at our house—every morning," Peter repeated. "An old American custom."

"Oh!" Dennis said. "As I said, I'd sort of lost track of it."

☐

# III. TRICKS

After Peter had taken care of the necessary formalities they left the Hall of Justice and returned to Peter's house, where Dennis was now being introduced to that good old American custom, breakfast, at the Byrnes'.

"Tell us about it," Blake said, leaning brown elbows on the white cloth.

So Dennis told them about it.

At the end Blake's eyes were wide and almost as dark as Dennis's own, and Peter's eyes had narrowed like an armed force behind strong walls, ready, watchful, wary.

Dennis watched Peter like a man at the end of a long dangerous journey, beneath the walls of a strong and safe refuge, wondering if those walls would take him in.

Peter came out of his fortress then, having surveyed the countryside.

"What a beautiful jam!" he said with professional joy.

Dennis grinned, a bit crookedly this time.

"That's what Kennedy said," he reported. "'My boy, you don't need a lawyer—you need a can opener!'"

"Well, Devore—where did you get that name, anyway?" Peter paused to inquire en route.

"Pulled it out of a hat," said Dennis.

"Never do," grunted Peter.

"Oh, well—most people never get past the Dennis part." Their guest was still engrossed in pancakes and coffee, but willing to do his part in polite conversation at that.

"Well, Dennis," Peter gave in, "what happened down at the Hall, after that?"

"It was a great deal like being X-rayed," he replied. "Any little secret I'd ever had couldn't have stood a chance with those birds."

"But they do think you are holding something out on them?"

"Well, I must be cleverer than I give myself credit for being, then," Dennis said cheerfully. "They even shared my baby days with me."

"Well,"—Peter was being ponderous, but walking softly—"they did find the body in your hotel room, you know. And people don't—"

"Don't they?" Dennis asked grimly and surveyed the abashed faces about him. "I'm here to tell you they did!"

Something old and cold and wise had entered that bright and gay little sun room in that minute. They felt it.

Things did happen that way. People were murdered. Innocent men were accused. Innocent men had been hung.

"We've got to get Dennis out," Blake announced firmly. "First, who was she? We must find out everything—everything the police find out, and more. The whole truth. Then, was she killed outside somewhere and then brought into the room, or was she killed in your room?" Blake went on keenly.

"The police think so," said Dennis. "In the room. They hardly suspect me of lugging her along under my arm from the broadcasting studio."

"Yes, but we have this advantage," Blake pointed out. "We aren't narrow, like they are. We are free to suspect anyone, and we aren't trying to pin it onto Dennis, especially."

"Thank you," said Dennis, with that faint grin flashing out. "Only I plop for the room, too. Because why? First place, it's too darn risky doing it outside and bringing her in. Second, I saw her. And I don't think she'd moved—much."

Peter asked the same question the hotel manager asked. But he asked it in a very different sort of way.

"But why," he wanted to know, "your room?"

Dennis looked at him steadily with dark eyes staring through him and far away beyond him.

"'An enemy hath done this,'" he said, under his breath. "That's one answer. To put me in bad, maybe. Whoever had a grudge against her may have known me.

"There's a link there," Peter pointed out cautiously.

Dennis nodded, as though the interruption had been hardly registered on his mind.

"And then—why *not* my room?" he went on. "No one who's actually committed a murder can afford to have a body around. Put it on someone else. Say it was someone staying in the hotel—must have been—and they knew I was singing every night except Sunday from eleven forty-five to twelve at the studio. Room would be absolutely free then. Smallest risk of any in the hotel, probably. They arrange then for a murder party between those fifteen minutes. Easy, if it's been planned out. Wrong room. Lady enters it—it's in darkness, you know. Killed before she realizes it's a trap. Murderer goes out. Back to own room. Waits for alarm."

"Clever!" said Blake, shuddering a bit.

Dennis cocked an appreciative eyebrow at her.

"Oh, yes—if you like cleverness," he agreed. "Personally, I think it's a very overrated quality. I prefer depth."

"Quit sparring," ordered Peter. "This brings up a new line. Do you realize that it needn't have been anyone you know, any enemy of yours? It might be an absolute stranger!"

"Ye-es," said Blake. "But—let's combine both theories. Keep the best qualities of each. She was killed by someone who knew and hated Dennis, too, and she was killed in Dennis's room because he was away singing over the radio at the time. That clear?"

"Perfectly," said Peter. "Only—who did it?"

Dennis withdrew his gaze from the tablecloth that he'd been staring at.

"Look here," he began, "you're taking an awful lot on faith. Me, I mean. Isn't there—isn't there anything you'd like to ask—about me?"

"Well, but—I've seen you before," said Peter. "Were you at Stanford?"

He waited suspiciously for those familiar words of a claim on him to come.

Dennis laughed.

"No, I went to your dearest enemy and rival," he retorted. "At Cal we look upon Stanford as a training place for a good practice team for us."

"Got it!" said Peter suddenly in great satisfaction. "Last time I saw you, you were pushing your hand in my face. It was two years ago, at the Big Game. I was playing in the line, and you were a back trying to come through with the ball. You straight-armed me, and when I got up you'd wriggled past the second defense and were about thirty-three yards to the good. I remember that play, all right."

"I never did like guards," said Dennis airily. "They are apt to get in your way when you're in a hurry. You did, even when you weren't supposed to."

"Only I don't remember anyone on that team named Devore." Peter's relentless memory was still tracking.

"There wasn't any," Dennis said softly.

"Oh?" said Peter as softly.

"No. But it would be easy, of course, to look up the names of the team and find out who played in the backfield," Dennis said.

"Got no time," said Peter. "I'm a busy man. Don't play kid games any more and get my face shoved in."

"Well—" said Dennis softly but more huskily.

They heard a faint ring at the front door. Blake opened one of the casement windows and leaned out in the morning sunshine, peering down, trying to see who stood below.

"It's your police-reporter friend Kennedy, Peter," she reported. "He's on our doorstep."

She called down, and a minute later Kennedy came in and nodded to them.

"How's tricks?" he asked. "Mind if I smoke?"

"Do," said Blake. "Tricks are rather slow, at first," she told him. "You see, we don't know what's trumps. Would you say—clubs?"

"I'd say spades," Kennedy said. "For day after tomorrow, anyway. Coroner's inquest. If the verdict is death by someone unknown, you've still got a chance on the outside, kid. But if it's death by the hands of one Dennis Devore, the police'll take charge of your case for you and your client."

"A labor-saving device," said Dennis, "the police force."

He tried to smile.

"Go in with us," said Blake suddenly to Kennedy.

That hard-bitten gentleman eyed her suspiciously. "Oh, yeah? How?"

"We want to keep Dennis out of jail and get the right person who did the murder."

"I'll accept the invitation," Kennedy decided, after a second, grinning. "And it's not for your *beaux yeux* either, guy," he informed Dennis. "It's simply because I believe that a radio tenor is a subject for murder, a murderee, not a murderer."

"First, who was she?" Blake cut in ahead of Peter, to his indignation. "We've got to know!"

Kennedy's lean brown face hardened. He leaned forward.

"Listen," he said, "I'll tell you who she was. She was Bianca Fior! That mean anything to you? She played in big-league company, and she could hold her own beside a battery of beauties like Helen of Troy or Cleopatra as a siren."

"Bianca Fior," Dennis only said slowly. "That means white flower, doesn't it? I told you I felt that way when I saw her. As if I'd stumbled by mistake into some kind of bloody fairy tale."

"This isn't being in a fairy story," Blake said softly and sharply.

"It's better than being in a nightmare," Dennis answered.

# IV. DE MORTUIS

"Bianca was a home-grown goddess," Kennedy said. "Statue of Liberty of North Beach. There's a lot of mystery about her beginnings, and a lot about her end. You see her like that big dame in New York Harbor, big, beautiful—God, she sure was!—and with a past and present like a sort of foggy mist around her. Who was keeping her? The police'd like to know. They might run up against something dangerous. Some big politician, maybe. An ex-rum-runner's gal, maybe. They're moving cautious. Too many prominent men in her background. Too much politics, maybe. They'd be a lot easier in their minds if Bianca hadn't been bumped off."

Blake nodded wisely.

"She was beautiful—and bad," she emphasized. "And we're going to find out about her. Peter, you'll take headquarters, won't you? And tackle Dennis's inspector?"

"Okay by me," said Peter. "What's his name? Sullivan? I'll find out about the inquest, too. I've got to get to the office first, and I'll go on from there."

"That reminds me, brother," Kennedy said to Dennis, "you've got to come clean with me. We need pictures—lots of 'em. Papers are hollering for them. And that's a funny thing. I looked around your room a bit after you'd gone last night, and I couldn't see a single picture, or letter, or anything of yours there. Just some cigarettes and books. No wonder the lady mistook that room for hers, or for an empty one. No one'd know you'd ever lived there. Nothing personal around."

"I don't like a lot of truck," Dennis said.

"I'll say you don't," Kennedy said dryly. "Your room would make the Sahara desert look all cluttered up with Victorian keepsakes. But don't let me trouble you."

"You don't," Dennis retorted, grinning. "Was that all you had on your mind?"

Kennedy, under cover of lighting another of his eternal fags, gave him a long, cool appraising look from bright cold eyes.

"All," he said briefly, puffing out blue smoke. "Just to find the lady's stabber, and to cover police at the Hall, and to get some pictures of one Dennis Devore, radio singer, released by the police after an all-night questioning."

The bright little green-and-gold sun room had begun to be filled with blue tobacco smoke since Kennedy had come. He'd turned it into an office.

"Is that necessary?" Blake asked.

Kennedy nodded. "Play in with me, and I'll play in with you," he said. "That's fair, and I've got to hold down my job. Do I get them?"

"Yes," Dennis said. "You'll have to take them yourself, though. I mean—the broadcasting studio hasn't any of me."

"So I discovered," Kennedy said. "We'll take 'em on our way to our good deeds today. Stop by at the office with me, and it's done. Where'll we four meet next?"

"What are you going to do, Blake?" Peter asked.

She raised innocent eyes to his. "I'm a lady novelist looking for local color," she said simply. "I'm going to interview the hotel staff, on Dennis's corridor. To find out about those other guests who *didn't* find a body in their respectable rooms."

Peter got up then, preparing to go.

"We part here," he said, "then. Dennis, what are you going to do? We've ruled you out of the Hall of Justice and the hotel part of it."

"I'll have to go to the studio and settle up accounts," Dennis said. "I'll bet you a nickel, even, they'll cancel my contract."

"Or else raise your salary," Kennedy grunted. "You'll be a great drawing card now, kid."

"Oh, yeah?" asked Dennis coldly. "Because I might be a murderer? If they offer to do that, I'll fire myself!"

He'd gone white around his nostrils. His eyes blazed darkly, and he breathed a bit quickly. Kennedy watched him, that inquisitive bird's head of his on one side.

"I'd sure like to play poker with you," he said.

Dennis cocked an arrogant eyebrow at him.

"Do you think I look like a professional card player?" he asked, rather coldly still.

Kennedy grinned.

"No, you wouldn't be as dangerous if you did. You're scared, and yet you're cool and dangerous," —he emphasized his points with his lighted cigarette stabbed into the smoky air, leaning forward—" and you're picking your way through this with the brains of a quarter-back. The way you're using all of us— you remind me of a great back I once saw picking his way through a broken field at full speed."

Dennis looked at Kennedy and finally smiled it off.

"I've often wondered what happens to great football players," he said, airy again. "Beyond becoming wrestlers or candidates for the Old People's Home."

His eye lit on Peter in passing for an infinitesimal instant, without expression. Peter blushed.

Kennedy said, "This one I'm telling you about got in a jam, after he graduated. He ran down a man on a dark night on the highway down near Salinas way, and he didn't stop. Didn't even turn up till next morning to leave his name. Man died. He was some Italian wholesale dealer up here, I think. Pretty important. And this guy'd been speeding, evidently. They tried him for manslaughter, and he got off pretty well—on probation for a year, I think. Then he disappeared."

Blake said, in a soft rush, "Oh-h-h!" and stopped.

"He didn't stop, or come back until next morning?" Peter inquired, expressionless. His big brown face was like a rock.

"There was a girl in the car with him," Kennedy said. "Her name never came out. I think this football bird I'm telling you about got her home okay."

"Really?" said Dennis.

Kennedy stared at him. There was a short, intense second of silence, almost unbearable to Blake and Peter. Dennis went on smoking.

"I *said* I'd like to play poker with you," Kennedy remarked. His voice was that of the most lively admiration.

He hoisted himself to his feet.

"Well, come on," he said. "You're coming with me to the office, you said, for pictures."

Dennis got up, too, in a swift motion that reminded Peter of Blake's way of moving.

"After today," he said, "there probably won't be any Dennis Devore, radio tenor. I—I hope you'll think kindly of him."

That irrepressible grin of his just faintly touched dark eyes and sober mouth.

"He wasn't a bad guy," he gave him his requiem. "*De mortuis*, you know."

He turned to go, after Kennedy.

"Dennis," Blake said suddenly, "where are you going?"

"I don't quite know." Dennis wrinkled his brow mildly. "I can't live at the hotel—I suppose I'll get a room somewhere."

"I told you I was baching it," Kennedy broke in grudgingly. "I've got two rooms over on the north side of the city. Lots of room there for two. Thought I told you."

"You didn't," Dennis said. "But thanks. I'll accept." His voice was brief and bitter.

"You needn't thank me," Kennedy growled as ungraciously. "I like to have my exclusive story under my eyes all the time."

Clearly it wasn't one of those hospitable impulsive invitations. It looked regrettably like an invitation by *force majeure*. Dennis had an ominous semblance to a prisoner being led off to a dark dungeon that he hadn't inspected and chosen himself.

"Be here for breakfast tomorrow," Blake said hastily and impulsively, as this aspect of it struck her.

Dennis nodded and smiled at her reassuringly and followed Kennedy down the stairs.

Peter said, a bit heavily, in the silence, "I feel as if I were riding a surf board. Things seem to happen fast, when that Dennis guy is around. But—I don't know. It may be dangerous, but it's exhilarating." He grinned sheepishly.

"Yes," Blake said. "I feel that way, too. Rather— short of breath."

"What are we in for, anyway?" Peter said, sobering.

"I don't know," Blake said. "But we sort of had to do it, Peter. There didn't seem to be anything else to do."

"Not at the time, no," Peter agreed. "We just held onto our surf board and let it ride. But now—you heard what Kennedy said. About that ex-football hero who ran a man down and let him die in the road? If I thought Dennis was the one he meant who did it, it would be something else again. What do you think, Blake?"

He was suddenly impressive again, with a stern weight of integrity in him that bulked sheer as his big self.

"I think," Blake said slowly, "the only thing the matter with Dennis is that he's too chivalrous."

"What?" said Peter.

"Look how he acted about that Bianca woman, and she's the one that's got him into all this trouble," said Blake sturdily. "I shouldn't wonder—if he hadn't been too chivalrous at some other time in his career."

"Well," Peter said, "you'll cure him of that if anyone can, I'm sure."

"*De mortuis*," said Blake softly, "*nil nisi bonum*—indeed! I wonder just what he was thinking of—besides Bianca."

Peter began to laugh.

"I've just thought," he explained to her questioning eyes. "I've got two old codgers coming in to make a change in their wills today. I'll have to put 'em off. They're in no danger. They've lived to their placid eighties already—they can wait. Nothing's ever happened to them much. It's Dennis who needs to worry about reaching the ripe age of thirty alive!"

## V. CHURCH OF SAINTS PETER AND PAUL

Another conversation was going on between Dennis and Kennedy, on the front smoker of a Kearny Street car going down into Market Street.

"What's the idea," Dennis asked stiffly, "of the third-degree stuff?"

"Meaning what?" Kennedy said, raising an eyebrow and impassively puffing away.

"Well, I'm coming to stay with you, and it's not for your *beaux yeux* either, guy," said Dennis bitterly. "You practically blackmailed me into coming," he reminded his host.

"Better than being blackballed at your hotel," Kennedy grinned. "Listen, Devore—you want to keep out of jail right now. That's your aim in life—or it ought to be. Undercover stuff. And I'm not keen on having a good story wandering around under other people's noses—and eyes. I want to keep it to myself—for a while, anyway. You stay under cover at my place, where no cop'll think to look for you, and we'll both be covered."

"Why don't you spill your story right now?" Dennis asked. "Afraid? Or looking for fingerprints? There aren't any—I can tell you that. Nothing for the cops to compare, either."

"Or anything else," said Kennedy. "I noticed that. You sure made a clean break. I don't doubt someone swiped the records and the prints and all that. They would."

He looked sidewise at his rather sullen companion.

"Her folks had quite a lot of influence down there, didn't they?" he asked, grinning.

"Will you shut up?" said Dennis in a restrained but ferocious voice. "And go to—"

"The office," interrupted Kennedy brightly. "Here we are."

They climbed off at Market Street, where the traffic swirled around Lotta's slim fountain. They crossed the street and went up into an elevator, then left that and changed to another, rickety one.

"About that story," Kennedy finally said. "I might aim to keep it, and then produce it for what our British cousins would label 'Sensation in Court.' And then again I might not. It all depends."

"On what?" asked Dennis.

Kennedy grinned at him again.

"On people," he said. "I've seen a lot of 'em. Especially at the Hall of Justice. And they nearly all wilt, innocent or guilty, when they get in there. Something in it gets them. You didn't, and yet you had a lot to be scared about—things like this coming out, for instance. But you didn't lose your nerve. I don't think you've ever lost your nerve. And yet this bird back in Salinas did, according to the story. But it never did seem reasonable to me that a great back, used to thinking quickly, would have lost his nerve so completely, the way that bird did. He'd have thought things out quicker. People are funny. But I know them. That's one thing being on police does for you, anyway. You get so you can't be fooled about people much."

"Oh," said Dennis, thinking this out.

They got out and banged on a rickety wooden door that reminded Dennis of a model speakeasy. A center hole in it opened. A face appeared. Kennedy nodded at Dennis, and the face withdrew. The door opened.

"Scotch," murmured Dennis hopefully.

"No, Danish," Kennedy said following him in. "He doesn't like to be disturbed, that's all. Danes are funny that way."

"I know," Dennis nodded. "I had a Great Dane once. He didn't like to be disturbed, either—especially when he had a bone to pick." He fingered a scar on his right wrist reminiscently.

He sat on a hard chair and looked around a very bare room. It had great windows to the north and west, and an unpainted kitchen table and a couple of hard kitchen chairs in it. Otherwise it looked as if the carpenters and plasterers had just gone away and nobody else had moved in yet. Their host appeared in silence, a round rosy face, and a wet and chemically-smelling black rubber apron. He set up black apparatus, a little way in front of Dennis.

Dennis stared at it calmly and curiously. Only his eyes went black and impenetrably dull again, and the white lines came around the base of his nostrils.

He thought in a vivid flash of Sullivan standing by while a little unobtrusive man seized his hands, and, finger by finger, rolled them in inked stuff. There was a sort of degradation in having these things happening to one, instead of making things happen as you pleased. Like being an animal, and having to stand for whatever people did to you!

The flashlight went off then in a great sound, lots of smoke and a bright light. The little man nodded to them and disappeared into his warren. Kennedy got up.

"We won't wait for the prints," he said. "Thanks. I guess they'll turn out okay."

"They'd better," Dennis said. He got up, a bit stiffly.

"Smoke?" Kennedy said and fished out a packet of cigarettes. Dennis took one out carefully and lit it from Kennedy's light. His hands didn't shake. He could control his poised body more coolly than he could his hot and impatient mind.

"We'll go all the way down in this crazy thing," the police reporter said when they were in the rickety elevator again, descending slowly and cautiously. "No use letting people know where you are, if anyone's watching the front entrance."

They got out in a basement of gray concrete and walked through a sort of gray tunnel, landing outside in the dirty sunshine of an alleyway. Kennedy looked away carefully and quickly.

"Okay," he said softly. "No one'll pick you up here, anyway."

He signaled to a lurking plain dark taxi just on the corner where the alley joined a main street.

"Our special brand," he murmured to Dennis. "Warranted not to talk out of turn."

They got in the taxi without another word. Kennedy leaned forward and spoke to the driver.

"We can stop by at your studio, kid," he explained, sinking back again. "You can fix things up there, and then we'll go on to my place. I wouldn't go back to the hotel if I were you."

Dennis involuntarily shuddered and then held himself rigid again, commanding his betraying body. He saw a lighted hotel room, the graceful walnut furniture, the bed with the sheet turned back—and, beyond the table, that dark and untidy sort of shadow . . .

"I haven't the least desire to go back there, I assure you," he said through stiff, dry lips.

Kennedy looked at him again, that sidewise, quick, stab of a look from bright birds' eyes.

"Don't let it get you, kid," he said more gently.

Dennis looked at him coldly with his dark head haughty again.

"Nothing's ever 'got' me," he said coldly. "Not even getting my picture taken like a San Quentin boarder!"

Kennedy shrugged. They stopped before the entrance to the studio building.

"I'll wait here," the police reporter said. "You won't be long, I guess."

"Not if I can help it," Dennis grunted, getting out.

He wasn't. It was about five minutes later when he came down the stairs to the street again, the hatless dark head moving swiftly and surely through less sure traffic of people.

"I told you," he said only, getting in. "There goes Dennis Devore, poor fellow! Canned."

"By request?" Kerinedy asked.

"Does it matter?" Dennis retorted. "Sure it was by request—my own request. I asked for my time."

"And you got the air," Kennedy punned pitilessly. "Well, there's one less radio canary singing. That's all to the good."

Dennis laughed. He was oddly released and happy.

"You never heard me!" he said. "That remark proves it."

"And I hope I never will!" Kennedy said grimly.

They were in the sunny north section of the city now. Brown-faced, beautiful children with dark hair and great soft dark eyes like deer played about the narrow streets. The taxi went up, and stopped in that position, still going up. They climbed out precariously.

"My joint," said Kennedy. It was a new, clean-looking apartment house—two stories, four apartments, Dennis estimated swiftly. Better than he'd thought it would be. And there'd be a swell view of the Gate, glittering in noon sunshine.

There was. There was something else, too, that he hadn't reckoned on. A grand piano in the small living room. His eyes widened, seeing this. A swell grand piano! He knew the sort of tone it would have— dark and lovely, like itself.

"*Cantabile*," he muttered reverently, like a sort of Italian oath.

Kennedy's place was a surprise. He'd thought of something bohemian, which meant dusty and rather bare, like the camping place of a hardened old campaigner. Or else cluttered up so you couldn't move. This was—different. A grand piano. And the shelves of the room covered with books of phonograph records, music scores.

Kennedy was in the small bedroom. Dennis stepped over and looked at some of the books of records. His eyes stayed wide and dark with astonishment. He whistled softly. Into those astonished eyes came the faint flickering of mischief beginning again.

Kennedy came back again, slipping an overcoat on quickly.

"I'm due at the Hall now," he explained in a hurry. "I'll be back around six, I guess. You'll stay holed up right here till I get back. Get me? There's some stuff in the icebox when you get hungry."

"Aye, aye," said Dennis a bit absently. His eyes were veiled, but eager.

He surveyed the records gleefully when his host had gone.

"Blackmail, eh?" he said thoughtfully. "So I'm to stay in all day? We'll see."

He then proceeded to get drunk. He had a cocktail of Gershwin's, consisting of the Concerto, and the Rhapsody in Blue, then a full-bodied draft of Wagner's Ring taken straight, and blissful ecstasies from Beethoven. He began tapering off with Mozart. When Kennedy came back around six o'clock, he was sitting bright-eyed and white-faced at the piano playing and singing, lustily.

His host muttered softly. Dennis turned around, letting one finger pick up and trail the tune in the meanwhile.

"I saw Sullivan," Kennedy announced, discarding coats. " He got after me for letting you go this morning. He's just about made up his mind to take you in again. The inquest is coming, and he needs a goat to sacrifice. Threatened me with lese majeste and a few assorted crimes, but I told him there wasn't any warrant out for you yet and he'd better wait till the inquest is over. You're not to go out till then, either. You stay right here, holed up."

Dennis nodded, trailing a cigarette from the corner of his mouth and turning loose on the piano.

Above the syncopated din his voice rose, melting, tender. He was in the throes of sentiment.

Kennedy writhed, bearing up nobly. Finally:

"Do you *have* to do that?" he yelped.

Dennis looked at him.

"I have to do *something*," he said gently. "I'm bored."

Kennedy sat down in the armchair and groaned aloud.

"He's bored," he said bitterly and blankly. "Sullivan's after him, and that big stiff usually grabs what he's after; there's a murder inquest up, and he's bored. Did anyone ever tell you there was wirehaired fox terrier in you?"

"No," said Dennis truthfully.

"Well, there is," Kennedy grunted. "If you wait till I can get my things on again will you promise not to sing? There's a roof-garden ex-bootlegger across the street, on top of that apartment house. No one'll be likely to look for us there."

Dennis grinned and gave up the desecrated piano reluctantly.

"It's blackmail," Kennedy said as they went on down the stairs cautiously. "And you know it. You looked at my music stuff there."

"Blackmail?" said Dennis. He raised an elegant eyebrow. "Where have I heard that word before?"

The roof garden was cool. It had a view of part of the city to the south and sloping down to the north, where the dark Gate ran swiftly in the darkening evening. There were nondescript potted green things around, palms or rubber plants or what Dennis called hotel foliage.

Kennedy talked to the proprietor, a dark-faced but pleasant person with a picturesque version of a dinner suit. Dinner began to come— chicken, taglierini, red wine. They had a table at the edge of the roof, where the wall came up to their shoulders as they sat there.

"What's that big building—the gray one?" Dennis asked.

"Church," Kennedy said. "All the Italians go to it. It's St. Peter and St. Paul's."

Their host bent over them in an aroma of garlic, dark mustachios highly perfumed, and greasy vestments.

"All," he said, gutturally mysterious about it. "Yes. But not one—no more. She will be there for Mass, and she will never hear it. No more. Ah, *bella—fior d'Italia!*"

All of a sudden he wasn't a greasy, intrusive speak- easy host trying to be mysterious. He was a poet, a lover, a representative of a lover's race, mourning a lost beauty.

"Who d'you mean?" asked Dennis, with quickening breath.

"I mean her—the one they killed." He turned to Dennis as to a confidant. "You heard? They called her Bianca—Bianca Fior."

"You know her—about her?" Kennedy thrust in, keen as a bright thin dagger's blade.

The man shrugged. His dark eyes looked at them from beneath a dark fringe of hair. Honest, mournful eyes.

"No one knew her," he sighed. "Just—the house she lived in, the restaurants she danced in. No one knew her, signor, as she really was. Only I—a little. Two nights ago, just before sundown, I saw her. She was coming from the church, and she was weeping. I saw that. She had been to speak to her friend, the priest. Old Father Malletti. She came there sometimes."

Kennedy looked at Dennis. His eyes were bright as steel.

"Confession?" he barely breathed.

Their host shrugged again and mopped the table absently.

"No, not Confession, I think. She went to the parish house. Not to the church. I think old Father Malletti knew all her sorrows. As a friend, not a priest, perhaps. He would come to the door and stand on the stairs watching her go away. He did so the last time. He raised his hand. She did not dare to go too directly to God, I think—that beautiful one!—but old Father Malletti would dare to go for her. He is—a saint."

He made the swift, almost invisible passage of one brown, unwashed hand across his greasy white shirt-front, and went back to his noisy kitchen region. Dennis and Kennedy stared out at the thickened darkness. In the closing night the tall gray church of the Saints, Peter and Paul, stood impassively fronting them.

Dennis cleared his throat finally.

"Well," he said, "I'm not such a dumb dick after all, am I?"

Kennedy stared at him pityingly.

"Kid," he said, "for dumb luck, no. You ought to be down on your knees."

## VI. "HE IS GONE ON A JOURNEY"

Dennis yawned with immense exertion, through the thick soft feathers of sleep smothering him. His head drooped forward.

"Wake up!" said Kennedy hastily. "We're going places."

"Now?" said Dennis wonderingly.

He sighed deeply and shook sleep away from him, and obediently followed Kennedy down the stairs and across the street. He stood swaying a little, wand-in-the-wind fashion, waiting for Kennedy to take the lead into the apartment house.

That bothersome, small, hard-bitten gentleman sized him up wearily.

"Look here," he decided, "can you stay awake long enough for me to ask a question at the corner church?"

Dennis just nodded, or rather let his head drop down once. It was too much trouble to open his mouth and say yes.

He followed Kennedy, still half in his dream, to the still-lighted doorway of the priests' residence of St. Peter and St. Paul's. Kennedy rang the bell. After a minute the door opened. The housekeeper stood there, light falling on her old-fashioned big white apron and on her sturdy, lined face.

"Father Malletti?" asked Kennedy.

"Oh, you're wanting to speak to *him*?" the woman asked shrewdly. "In particular? Well, I'll have to call someone, sir. I don't just know . . ."

Dennis heard the voices, saw the lighted faces, from far away. Like people on a lighted stage.

The housekeeper turned. A tall young priest stood there behind her. A beautiful masculine voice, like a struck bell, thought Dennis, enchanted, spoke out effortlessly.

"You wanted Father Malletti?" said the beautiful voice. It came from the tall young priest. "Ah, he's away. He's not here."

"Where is he?" Kennedy took him up quickly.

"He is gone on a journey," said the young priest, "to the country. He went Saturday night. A former parishioner of his was dying, and they sent a big, dark car for him to come."

"Where is this place?" Kennedy asked.

"It's near Delroy." The beautiful voice seemed to hang in the air, sighing, over each word. Dennis listened to the sound, not the sense. He was too sleepy. But a word caught his ear.

"That's funny," he said, after they'd thanked the priest and had gone down the sidewalk again. "Delroy! That's where— "

He yawned and forgot again.

"Aren't we ever going to sleep?" he said plaintively. "Or will we keep this up all night? The Chinese torture. You're as bad as Sullivan."

"That's where—what?" his active small tormenter said.

"Oh—that's where I've got a small ranch," Dennis answered. "I'll invite you down some time. We've got the best beds—"

"If Father Malletti doesn't get back tomorrow morning," Kennedy said, halting at their door, "I'll take you up on that right away."

Something seemed to strike him then with a curious kind of worry, as though something were—out of tune, and he couldn't locate the note.

"Some people," he said slowly, "are a long time dying, aren't they? A big, dark car coming . . ."

He shook his head. He was blaming himself for the wrong notes. They were in his head, not in the things he'd heard.

There was a wall bed let down in the living room for Dennis. He was in it almost as soon as it was down. A pair of Kennedy's pajamas draped him sketchily. He tucked his head down into the pillow. The light began to grow dim.

"Delroy!" he said very drowsily. "There's a river . . . and cottonwoods . . . cottonwoods . . ."

They were waving in the little wind. He saw the shallow ripples of the broad stream, and the glint of gold under them as the sun struck through to the ledges of smooth sand underwater. A smile curved his mouth. .. .

"Say," Kennedy said, "I'm going to the Hall of Justice to take the night shift. I may be back late, but I'll try not to wake you up. Can I trust you to stay here while I'm gone?"

There wasn't any answer. The bright light fell full on the face of one who was far away.

"I guess so," Kennedy grunted, turning off the light.

# VII. THE LONG LEASH

"Fellow-members of the Dennis Defense Society," said Blake impressively, "we are met here to—to—"

"To do honor to a man who," rattled off Dennis glibly, "I should say needs no introduction—a man who has the welfare of this great country at heart—a man who, under a cast-iron exterior, has a heart as soft as a properly boiled egg—a man who—"

"Charter members of this society will please come to order!" said Blake. "Silly nuts—"

"Decline the nomination," said Dennis. "I was only calling attention to your cook. Under that Mongolian exterior rests an artist. His pancakes are a poem. I," he said pensively, "should know."

Blake succumbed. "Louie is an old-timer," she said carelessly, puffed with pride. She helped herself to a cup of clear topaz coffee, sniffing delicately with pleasure as she did so. "He says he used to wash gold in the Sierra creeks, just after the forty-niners were there."

"There's gold in them thar eggs," said Peter, opening one as if he expected to find a nugget in it.

Dennis grinned. He'd been absurdly blithe at an absurd—to his reporter host—hour in the morning. Ever since he'd gotten up around half-past seven, rustled around the small apartment shaving, bathing, and borrowing things from a Kennedy sound asleep, and had finally shaken his indignant host awake to tell him he had a breakfast date, he'd been, if not obnoxious about it, at least fearfully glad-handed. He belonged, said Kennedy bitterly, with one of those early-bird exercises on the radio. The cheerful kind. And now would Dennis let go his shoulder and let him get some sleep? He didn't give a hoot if he was going out to run into the entire homicide squad, out for his blood. Dennis, said Kennedy, growing eloquent, could go to several places whose location Kennedy seemed to know well. Or he could get taken up by the police if he wanted to. Let the police, if so, do the worrying. He didn't owe them anything.

"I'll be back after breakfast, maybe," Dennis said reassuringly, giving that indignant limp shoulder a final shake, this time meant in all friendliness of good-bye.

"Not," said Kennedy, "if I see you first!"

"Your ties are rotten, anyway," Dennis retorted. "I had to wear my own."

That final sally woke Kennedy up completely. He spent some uneasy moments wondering just what Dennis had decided to borrow from him before he decided to call sleep a lost cause and get up and see the worst.

By that time Dennis was knocking at the door of the dark old Byrne house on Russian Hill, being let in by Louie, the Mongolian image graven with nearly inch-deep lines on his mahogany old face.

And the Dennis Defense Society had greeted one another and were assembled for breakfast again by Blake, in the little green-and-gold sun room. The day was beginning with a little mist, a slight fog of San Francisco, so they had a fire in the very small fireplace by the north wall. Blake wore a creamy sort of silk dress, with blue heavy beads around her neck. Peter had blossomed out in a dark blue tie with minute red dots in it, worn with his usual blue suit. This would have signified, in a lesser man, an outbreak of vivid whorls, lightning blazes, and patterned arrows—something, as the salesmen say, pretty dashing, sir. Dennis gave the impression that he was actually wearing something of that sort anyway—red and gold, or blue and orange in heavy bars. He wasn't. His tie was immaterial, though. It was his vivid face, his eyes lit up in excitement, his dark head poised, that gave that impression. His spirit was wearing that sort of tie. All uncontrolled color and dash.

Just about this time Kennedy said to himself, with immense conviction, surveying the somehow crowded room that Dennis had so blithely left behind him, "Talk about serpents! I'd trade a wirehaired terrier in the house for a serpent, a nice quiet serpent in my bosom, any day!"

But Blake, curiously enough, at this time was looking at Dennis across the table, seeing the altogether blithe and somehow untouched spirit in him, and she felt a sort of sadness coming on her. She couldn't explain it. She only knew that suddenly she felt as though she were growing old—and Dennis wasn't. A sort of cold feeling, as though she were lonely. She couldn't understand it. The merest touch of a loneliness of spirit. She thought:

"Doesn't he *feel* anything?"

It was like a curious sort of balance. As Dennis's mind and heart and spirit went up, hers went down.

As though she'd lost him, a little. She didn't want him sad—but she wanted him with her.

Not so young and—untouched by sadness or mortal pang.

Dennis himself didn't know what was the matter—he simply felt that all was right with the world, like a lark charging skyward, as it were. At the very back of his mind, beyond his own hearing, a sound like a bell swung, clapping, "Delroy! Delroy!" at measured intervals. Perhaps its vibrations came to him, making him merry.

"Who reports first?" he asked, looking up. "We must get to business."

"I like that!" said Blake. "When I've been trying to get you two to pay attention!"

Peter strolled into action, like a large rock detaching itself from the landscape.

"Ladies first," he said.

"I was going to." Blake leaped to the invitation before anyone could get in ahead. She planted her elbows on the table and stared at them with very blue eyes. "You can't *guess* what I've found out!"

"My dear child!" Peter protested beyond endurance. "This isn't charades. If we'd guessed, you wouldn't have had to go and find out anyway."

"Well, then," Blake sorted her thoughts, "I spent the afternoon associating with the hotel servants. If the hotel manager knew he'd have had me thrown out. But the servants weren't a bit averse to making some extra money and to telling all they knew to a writer lady. They were thrilled. I started in with the cloakroom attendant—ladies' maid, you know—and gave her a big tip. Then she smuggled the others in for questioning. She wanted to know,"—she turned to Dennis gravely—"if her picture would come out in the paper."

"I'll take it up with Kennedy," Dennis said. "If she's pretty, that bird would commit grand larceny to get her picture."

Peter looked from the rock ledges of his eyes at Dennis, and then decided not to speak of pictures being in the paper this morning. It didn't seem tactful. He remembered that Dennis had been practically sand-bagged into having his taken yesterday.

"Bianca," Blake was saying, "came up in the elevator to the fourth floor—your floor—alone, about eleven fifty-five or a few minutes to twelve, that night. She didn't stop to ask the desk clerk for the number of any room, or anything—she just crossed the lobby to the elevator. She was wearing a black chiffon evening dress, and a bright Spanish shawl over it. And she was alone."

"That means," Dennis said intently, "that she was going to meet someone—a man—upstairs. We must look for a man alone, then, in the corridor I was in. He probably wouldn't have associates."

"Not in this kind of a deal," Peter rumbled. "Remember, we've decided he had it all planned out—going into the wrong room with her, and all that. He knew what was coming. It wasn't a sudden impulse."

"That makes it terrible!" Blake said, in a softly agonized rush of words. Her eyes darkened. That bright figure, going to death—to a planned death . . .

Dennis nodded. Something of her shadow seemed to have fallen on him. Or his spirit had come down to meet hers, from its first wild swoop upwards this morning.

"Who were my pleasant neighbors?" he asked grimly.

"Your immediate neighbors were"—Blake consulted a scribbled piece of paper—"(1) a honeymoon couple, on your right-hand side. She had dolls with long sprawled legs stuck around the room, the chambermaid told me. Just an ordinary good-looking young couple in looks—she could hardly remember anything extraordinary about them. They're on their way to Detroit now, anyway—to Papa's mills or something.

"Then, (2) a shoe salesman was on your left side—a traveling salesman. He had an exhibit of shoes down in one of the smaller ballrooms. He's there now, for the week, taking orders from the shoe men."

"A man alone?" said Peter, keen-eyed.

"He's a hearty-looking fellow," Dennis said. "I've met him in the lobby. Borrowed a light. Talked. About himself and his business. Brown hair, rather full face. I'm sure you can rule him out. He wouldn't have stuck a knife in Bianca—he might have playfully pushed her out of the fourth-story window at the height of a wild party, but he'd have been awfully sorry afterwards. No, this was cold-blooded and cruel. It was all arranged. That's what makes it so horrible. She came up in the elevator to meet someone, in her bright shawl and black dress, and they were laying for her."

"By the way, that shawl—" Peter said.

"It wasn't found?" Dennis asked. "Why, it wasn't in my room. I'd have seen it—"

"No," said Blake. "Nor an evening bag. Any woman would have had a dinky little bag with her, dressed as Bianca was. The chambermaid says they didn't find a thing like that. They looked in the lobby, and the corridors, too. The detectives asked them questions about these things."

"Make a note of it," Peter said briefly to Dennis. "Someone's got them."

That gentleman, bright-eyed, nodded. "Go on," he said softly.

"The entire corner next to the shoe salesman is a suite of several rooms. It's taken by an old lady who's had it for ages. She's a sort of cornerstone of the hotel. She has a maid, too. But if she's turned from respectability, I'd expect an outraged earthquake to topple the hotel walls down in retribution."

"Always suspect old ladies," Dennis said darkly and helpfully. "I do. All the unlikely people, you know."

"The hotel manager?" suggested Blake, wrinkling her nose.

"If you'd seen his face that night!" Dennis sighed in negation. "I'm afraid that's no good. He'd have thought out a better way than doing it in a guest's room. A man doesn't deny his own character, even at the moment of murdering. No, he'd have lured the guest on to a ferryboat ride and then dropped him overboard neatly. Without a trace, you know."

"How about the elevator man who brought Bianca up?" Peter asked. "He was alone with her up there for a second or two—or more."

"He's a nice young lad," Blake said, reminiscently smiling and shaking her head. "Fresh as daybreak—face, smile, manners, everything. He—if you're going to reconstruct this thing from people's characters, Dennis—would have gone for the point of anyone's jaw with a straight right—anyone that he'd a quarrel with. He wouldn't have stabbed anyone in the back. Least of all a woman. Besides, he's got an alibi. Or else he's the author of the quickest murder in history. He went right down again, after he'd left Bianca on your floor, to take some other people up to the seventh. The clerk noticed that. The people who went up will swear to the exact time, too. One of the women in the party glanced at her wrist watch, while they were wait-

ing for the elevator to come."

"No-o," said Dennis, half to himself. He leaned one elbow on the table and draped himself thoughtfully on it. His eyes were half closed in concentration.

"The man who did this," he said, "wasn't like any of the people we've discussed. He was like this: He had hell's own nerve, to do it this way. Do you realize that? It took all of it to do it—waiting for her, not knowing whether she'd be late or not—or if other people would get out at that floor with her. He bet on his luck. He'd choose a room near as he could get it to mine—across the hallway, say. I can see him," said Dennis, in a queer low voice that made them see pictures, too, in the bright daylight, "with his door open just a crack, listening for the elevator—making sure she was alone on that floor—coming out of his room quickly— 'Bianca!' coming to meet her with his arms out. He was a friend, a lover. She didn't have the least idea she was going to meet an enemy. She wasn't on guard. A woman like her would have been, otherwise. She was a wise baby. He even," said Dennis, in that monotonous thread of a voice with scarlet and black in its even tone — "he even took off her shawl and laid it across his arm, very gallantly— helping her off with it, in my room—and then she turned around, to see the room— his room—"

"*Dennis!*" Blake broke it off', in a sharp gasp. "Don't!"

"The seance," said Peter, "is ended."

He shook himself like a great dog when it comes up out of deep water. He eyed Dennis a bit askance.

"I think we know now," he said, "what the man was like, Dennis. Your demonstration was very effective. All I can say is that I hope for your sake he picked on you just because you sing over the radio at stated intervals. I wouldn't care to have anyone like that in my intimate circle of enemies."

"*Was* he?" Blake asked keenly.

"Known—as the police say—to me?" Dennis shook his head. "He wasn't—favorably or unfavorably. I haven't got anyone like that in my past, thank heaven."

"Well, is that all the bag?" Peter asked Blake.

"No," she said. "It isn't. I was going to say, across the hall from Dennis was, (1) a stage couple, those musical-comedy people who're playing at the Columbia in *Honeyblossom* this week."

"Ah, they'd do it with their tongues," breathed Dennis.

Blake looked at him. He sunk back abashed, making dumb-show promises of penitence and silence.

"And (2)," said Blake severely, "the Anstruthers, and we've gone to dinner parties and met them there, Peter, which I *hope* lets them out."

Dennis showed signs of life again. Peter caught his eye in sympathy. Dennis subsided, satisfied. Blake glanced up from her notes, suspiciously, but seeing no sign of communication attempted, went on.

"Then there's— Dennis, what were you going to say just now?" she pounced suddenly.

"I was only going to say," Dennis murmured, "you can bore people to death, too—at dinner parties. That's one way of doing it."

Blake snorted. A ladylike little snort. Peter grinned.

"Then there's," said Blake with immense dignity, "a Mr. Morgan, a very nice man, at the end room across from your side. And he was down in the Etruscan ballroom all evening dancing."

"What a pity," Dennis broke his silence drowsily, like little bubbles of speech ascending from a recumbent floating swimmer in a calm pool, "what a pity," he repeated, "that it wasn't the Attic ballroom. Morgan— Attic."

"*Den*-nis!" said Blake. He opened his eyes to a frozen atmosphere.

He broke the ice and got out of his perilous position. "What," he inquired intently, "does Mr. Morgan do, besides being so nice?"

"And besides dancing all night in the—uh, Etruscan Room?" Peter wanted to know.

"Why," said Blake doubtfully, "I don't think he does anything, much." She frowned down at her notes. "The help all like him. And he's got money. He just hasn't any business. Maybe he buys stocks sometimes, to keep him busy. But I suppose he plays around, mostly. He knows a lot of people. Plays golf a bit. Likes sailoring—has a nice little launch, or motorboat, or some kind of an amateur ship, at the Yacht Club anchorage. Gives parties. Goes to 'em."

"A clubman," said Peter in a tone of complete discovery. "There must be such beings. You always read about them in the papers."

"Noted," said Dennis, nodding. "Or well known."

"Ah," said Peter, "but do we?"

"Of course you do," said Blake briskly. "I told you all there was to tell about him. He was dancing all evening, anyway."

"We'll file Mr. Morgan for reference, anyway," said Dennis soothingly, " though I agree with you that he's probably harmless. How would a clubman dispose of his enemies anyway, Byrne? I'm a bit at sea there, I confess."

"He'd just drop them," Peter considered and gave a verdict. "Not know them at all—socially, you know."

"I don't think Bianca was the sort of person you could drop," Dennis pointed out. "Not if she didn't want you to."

Peter wagged a dubious head. "It's supposed to cut people to the heart," he said. "Being dropped, you know. They stagger out of their clubs—you've seen them, in the movies—"

"If you two have quite finished your humor," said Blake, gently, "we'll have some more business. That's all my report. The other rooms were vacant. Those were all your immediate neighbors, Dennis."

Dennis smiled at her. "Thanks a lot," he said.

"That's all right," said Blake a bit gruffly.

Darn Dennis! You couldn't get really mad at him, Blake thought, balked. He disarmed you. He was doing it now.

"The committee of the whole has read and approved of Miss Byrne's report," he said, "and orders it filed for reference. And the chairman wishes to say that it's a very nice report indeed."

He turned briskly to Peter.

"Byrne?" He cocked an interrogative eyebrow at that immovable but somehow forceful large person.

Peter smiled slowly. His blue eyes were very clear and untroubled in the depths of their rock ledges.

"Do I hear the whip crack?" he asked. "All right, here come the elephants into the arena."

"You were to meet Sullivan," Dennis reminded him affably.

"What's Inspector Sullivan like?" asked Blake with a proper awe of the constabulary.

"He's like Peter, a little." Dennis turned to her. "That's why I wanted to send Peter against him. He—looms. They remind one a great deal of two tall cliffs standing face to face, and I feel a bit crushed and very vulnerably puny between them. Man facing Nature, and all that, you know. Peter, if not actually getting anything out of Sullivan, could at least outface him. I can't."

"The inspector doesn't like you, Dennis?"

"I wouldn't say that," Dennis considered. "Not me personally, that is. He just wouldn't care much for any criminal. Particularly one he thinks may be a murderer. He just isn't made that way."

"But then—why didn't he arrest you straight off?"

Dennis took another of his long looks into a darkened future.

"The long leash has strangled many fool dogs," he said slowly. "I think that's the inspector's idea, in this case. He's giving me all the rope there is—to get tied up in."

"Oh!" said Blake.

"Not entirely," said Peter. "He's after Dennis, sure. But he told me he wouldn't want to help hang an innocent man. He's puzzled because some of the pieces don't fit in. He said, 'You can tell Devore it was lucky for him the windows weren't open.' Don't you remember—"

"But they *were* closed," said Dennis, bewildered. "I told you—the room was locked, and all the windows were locked, too. Sullivan saw them."

"Sure he did—and he saw the fire escape just outside them. And he said to himself, if you'd just staged a murder there and wanted an out for yourself, wouldn't you have opened the windows and left the way to the fire escape open, and then called the police? And when the police came, you'd have said, 'A thief's been in here—and he's killed this woman!' and you'd have pointed dramatically to the open window, Dennis. And that's what you didn't do. You let the police come into a closed, locked room and told them you'd found it that way, and expected them to believe someone else had done it. You blundered into the murderer's trap. And, luckily for you, Sullivan had sense enough to see it. Then he wondered if you were outsmarting him, at that.

"He took your fingerprints. He searched the room for strange prints, and he didn't find any. He didn't expect to find any. Anyone that smart wouldn't have left prints there. There weren't any prints at all on the knife. But on the window latch, where he found your fingerprints, he did find a set over yours. It was the chambermaid's. She was the last one to shut those windows. So you hadn't outsmarted him and closed the window and put yourself into a trap so obvious that he couldn't help seeing it. It was the murderer who'd put you there. And, luckily for you, Sullivan saw that and you didn't. Otherwise you'd have gone clever and tried to get yourself out of it."

There was a short but very full silence.

"Well," said Dennis, summing it up at last, "I *told* you cleverness was a very overrated quality!"

# VIII. DELROY! DELROY!

"Well," said Peter, "we seem to be agreed that everyone we've discussed in this case couldn't be a murderer. That helps a lot."

The phone rang. Blake took the call on the French extension phone by her chair and then handed the instrument over to Dennis.

"For you," she said.

It was Kennedy. That noble soul had risen above his injured feeling about the rape of his socks and shirts, to answer the higher call of his profession.

"Dennis," he said without preamble, "Father Malletti hasn't come back."

Dennis said, "Then that means—Delroy."

"Uh-huh," agreed Kennedy. "I've been to the church, and they're worried. Young Father O'Bannon —that's the one we saw last night— sort of blames himself. But—well, he can't give us any more help on the details. That's all we've got to go on—a big dark car coming, and a dying parishioner somewhere in the country near Delroy. You say you know the place."

"It's my inning," said Dennis instantly. "I'll go, Kennedy, and if I find him I call you up. Okay?"

"There must be some white man's blood in you," Kennedy said gratefully. "Sew it up tight, Dennis, whatever the dope is, and I'll remember this. I can't get away from the Hall just now."

Dennis put the phone down, softly, thoughtfully, and turned to his frankly interested host and hostess.

"There *is* news," he said. "Listen."

And he told them of the Italian ex-bootlegger's roof garden just across the street from the gray bulk of the Church of Saints Peter and Paul, and of old Father Malletti standing on the steps and watching Bianca, weeping, hurrying across the square—and later that same night, a big, dark car coming and taking him away. . . .

His voice faltered to silence. His eyes were dark and somber, unlit by any light within. He saw pictures. He sat with his hand propping up his chin—he saw the old man going into darkness—Bianca's friend. . . .

"Father Malletti was a saint!" he protested. He turned to Peter and Blake. "The Italian said so! No one would hurt him!"

"Oh, Dennis," said Peter reluctantly and slowly, but with his terrible strong honesty, "sometimes saints get in the way—of devils. And your murderer—you told us so yourself—was a devil."

"I think," said Blake, on a queer high note of breathlessness, "we'd better get the car out, Peter. Can you come with us?"

That stout-hearted gentleman shook his massive head, still more reluctantly.

"I've got a case coming up in court," he said. "But —I'll get a postponement! You can go on without me, and I'll follow later. That okay?"

"Swell!" said Dennis. "I'll see you at Hasta la Vista."

"Wherever that is," said Blake, once again cheerful at the prospect of action, and persuading herself that all would go well, since Dennis's face was brightening.

He told them, briefly. "I've got a ranch there. By the Little San Ramon River. Hasta la Vista—it means, 'Until I see you again,' or something like that. Sort of a good-bye."

"Ah, a landed gentleman!" said Peter lazily but keenly.

"Not yet," said Dennis. "A bachelor. Always have been."

He flashed that somehow grave, faint grin of his at Blake.

"Come on," Blake said, getting up.

He was light-hearted again. She felt her own spirits going up recklessly. She put on her brown tweed coat with the big badger fur collar sticking up all around her face, and a snug brown turban on her bright hair. Her eyes looked bluer and bigger, and her cheeks were fresh and cool and pink, in the brisk breeze outside the house. The fog was driving inland, in little puffs of white across the city, in the fresh wind, and the sun was out in a blue November day that was almost a copy of spring.

They got out the old red roadster and waved goodbye to Peter, standing there at the casement window with his pipe in his teeth and his mouth drawn back in a smile. Blake waved and smiled at him, but Dennis's white flash of a smile was almost like a knife cutting them away from him. He was glad to be out, and free, and away.

" Dennis," Blake said curiously, watching him drive, "you love this place of yours, don't you?"

"'Where the heart is . . .'" said Dennis, and fell silent.

But she could almost hear the little merry whistle in his heart, not quite coming up to his lips. He drove with the sound of it in his ears.

Through the warm dust of the Santa Clara Valley, set out with small fruit trees on the brown fields in even rows like rooted chessmen; through the little towns, whose names rang like sweet-toned bells in the sleepy noon sunshine, Palo Alto, San Jose, Gilroy, San Juan, Salinas; through the dark and wooded Santa Cruz mountain pass, to the salt marshes of the open seaside county of Monterey, where the wind blew and lonely cattle grazed; and so at last, about three o'clock in the afternoon, to sunshine again, and the Little San Ramon River winding across yellow fields in a flat country, singing to itself, very sleepily, very softly.

Dennis's country.

There was a little whitewashed ranchhouse set up among a few tall guardians of trees on a little knoll; there were empty corrals a little to one side; there were white chickens scratching in the dirt in a run set conveniently near the kitchen door; there was a wide veranda across the front of the house, and a few bright flowers, dahlias and chrysanthemums, lifting their heads in the brief garden around the front steps.

"Darling!" said Blake approvingly, getting out of the car a bit stiffly.

Dennis said nothing. He only looked. He stood and looked at it all as if he were—hungry, Blake decided. Dennis said, "I haven't seen this place for—nearly a year. I wasn't quite sure—it would be here."

The kitchen door opened. Blake caught her breath. An almost perfect copy of Louie, the old, graven image of a Mongolian, was out on the back stoop with a pan of chicken feed in one thin brown claw. His white apron was spotless. His head was brown and nearly bald. His black eyes glittered from wrinkles numerous as those in a thoroughly dried prune.

"It's Wong," said Dennis briefly.

The graven image saw them. The black eyes glittered. The thin brown hand clutched the tin pan. Wong drew himself up.

"Moah *bettah* you come back!" Wong addressed the errant young master in a thin, indignant high cackle that suggested an extremely nervous hen. "Wotsa mallah you! You think Wong he laise this chicken, laise these egg, laise these applicots, bettah fo' nothing! Wotsa mattla you, Dennis, fo' not coming back heah?"

The thin high cackle of a hen disturbed in her maternal duties beat on them relentlessly. Blake grinned. Dennis was getting nicely done to a lobster red.

"Come on, Odysseus," she said. "The speech of welcome seems to be drawing to a close. Wong's getting out of breath."

"Whew!" said Dennis.

The torrent died down to a mere muttered trickle. The black eyes glittered balefully. The wrinkled old face gasped for breath.

"You darned old heathen!" said Dennis.

Odysseus was home from whatever wars he'd been engaged in, Blake thought.

Pretty soon Dennis came out of the kitchen and grinned at his guest rather sheepishly.

"We stay here for chicken dinner," he said. "And Peter, when he comes. In the meanwhile messengers go forth among the heathen, from house to house and ranch to ranch, assembling the multitude and requiring them to come out and say if any strangers have been around

Delroy, or if any big black car has been here—if anyone's dying, and wanting to be prayed for—if Father Malletti's been here, and if he's gone. You see, Delroy is more of a district than it is a town. There's only a main street with a few stores on it, and hitching posts and parking space for us rustics and cowboys when we come in to order our sombreros and neckerchiefs. We'll inquire there, of course. But Father Malletti wasn't called there. He was called to some outlying ranchhouse or shack around here."

"We'll find out!" Blake sounded her battle cry.

"Sure we will," Dennis echoed her blithely. "And there goes the one who'll do it for us."

A thin brown figure was scrambling aboard an antiquated Ford roadster. The Ford roadster went bucking down the dirt road, hitting each deep rut as it passed.

"Dennis," said Blake admiringly, taking off the hat from her hot forehead, "you have, a genius for using people."

"Really?" said Dennis politely.

"Go on being like that," said Blake, undaunted. "I feel a distinct coolness in the air. Delightful."

Dennis grinned and got down from his high horse.

"Sometimes I've been sorry I never had a sister," he said reflectively. "It would have been nice at times to tie her to a post and play Indian-at-the-stake with her. I'm sure."

"Didn't you have?" said Blake.

"No, never. Neither sisters nor cousins nor any aunts," said Dennis briefly. "I'm an orphan."

He got up quickly.

"Do you want a drink of water and to rest in the shade here," he asked, "or do you want to come down and see the river?"

His tone was so hopeful that Blake got up, the obedient guest.

"Let's go see the river," she said responsively.

Dennis and Blake walked side by side through the hot gold sunshine, feeling the warmth of the sandy earth up through their shoes as they went, down to the green-shaded water. The Little San Ramon rippled in the sun brightly, like a shield held up, and the cottonwoods stirred gently, and the world was warm and golden and very peaceful. They had come, Blake thought, from the autumn fogs of the morning through spring to summer again, and it was rather unbearably peaceful and lovely, as though this were a lost summer —last summer's golden day, for instance, forgotten by time. She told this to Dennis, and he nodded gravely and stood looking a moment at the shifting river, from where they were halted up from the bank.

"'Tinkers to Evers to Chance,'" he murmured. "I see what you mean, Blake. Reverse play—going back to last summer instead of forward. Maybe you're right, and I'm making up for the summer I missed here. Time's justice doing me right."

He smiled at her.

"I always see what you mean, Blake," he repeated. He caught her hand suddenly and swung it as they went on again to the river.

Then his eyes went far away, absently, again.

"I'm thinking of Father Malletti," he said softly. "I didn't expect to find him in my house, all ready for us, exactly, but—well, Delroy's such a wide county. He might be anywhere around here, and what chance have we of picking up his trail? Just—chance, that's all."

Dennis dropped her hand.

They walked on in silence. They came to the bank of the Little San Ramon, and Blake sat down on the soft sand, while Dennis propped himself along the trunk of a cottonwood tree and stared at the stream going by, dazzling his somber eyes.

After a while, Blake said softly, urgently, "Dennis?"

He didn't turn around. "Yes?" he said.

"There's something else," Blake said. "You're putting me off, Dennis. You've something else in the back of your mind, always. What is it? We're friends, Dennis. Peter and you and I. You can trust us."

He turned around then in a roughly impatient, single movement that yet held appeal.

"What are friends, Blake?" he asked. "I haven't got a thing to give you—you and Peter. Nothing that'll satisfy you. You know—you must have guessed—I'm the hit-and-run hero Kennedy was talking about. The man who ran into someone down near Salinas here a year ago last July, and didn't give himself up till next day, and all that. I was lucky—I got off with probation. Lucky! How'd you like to report every doing of yours twice a week to a hard-boiled probation officer? It makes you feel like a beast in a cage. You want—space. Freedom. Loneliness. Well, after a year I got 'em."

"And what are you going to do with them, Dennis?"

"Oh, I'm not a woman hater," he said more calmly. "You needn't be sorry for me, Blake. I'm not soured on life, or anything like that, and I don't think all women are crooks because one of them took me for all I had. She was in a tough place, and she used me to get out of it—that's all. She was engaged to a fine guy, and she was a flighty little piece who wanted some fun. He was away right then, so we went around together a lot. And one night we were coming home, along about two in the morning, and she was driving—"

Blake gave a sharp gasp.

Dennis eyed her wearily.

"I thought you knew," he said, uninterested. "Something you said—well, anyway, Kennedy guessed —she was driving lickety-split, and all of a sudden she bumped something, and she began to cry out about hitting someone. But she didn't stop—she stepped on the gas. And by the time I could get her stopped, we were on a side road. So I made her come back, and we saw another car stop and pick him up, taking him to a hospital, I guessed. She was just about crazy then, thinking she'd have to tell all this to her fiance—he was a nice guy, but very strict—so I drove her home and then came around to the town to report it. And they took me up, for hitting him. He was dead.

"That's all, I guess," Dennis reviewed past history dispassionately. "I'd probably have done the same thing if I'd been in her case. I don't blame her. No, it's just that I feel like the name of that ship the Canadian captain had—the one the Coast Guards sunk. *I'm Alone.* I prefer to be. I feel safer that way."

"You pig!" said Blake.

Dennis bowed.

"'At your command!'" he said.

"I wish I had a mustache to twirl," he added plaintively. "I always feel not having one at such moments as these."

Blake laughed—she couldn't help it—above an immense gulf of loneliness.

# IX. THE HONEST PLOWMAN

☐ They had no news of Father Malletti—no news of him anywhere. Neither of his coming, nor of his staying, nor of his going from there. Not from the dusty, sun-parched, incurious little town, or from any of the neighboring ranches. Peter, who'd come down by train and been gathered into the red roadster at the station at five o'clock that afternoon, thoroughly scouted the idea of there being any news.

"This is the last place they'd take him to," he asserted, driving them off the main paved highway into the dirt road to Dennis's ranch. "If he was 'taken' anywhere at that, instead of being legitimately sent for. They'd never give the real name of a place in such a case.

Dennis disagreed. He shook his head wearily, stubbornly, unconvincedly.

"I've got an idea they did," he said simply. "They made a slip there. Someone was thinking of this part of the country, and the name came out. It's so pat, somehow. Why Delroy, anyway? It's miles from San Francisco. It's not so—well, convincing, if you want. Why not just say there was someone sick in San Mateo, or Palo Alto, or any of the near-by peninsula towns? No, they were thinking of this country, and they had to say it—it came out almost against their will. It was in their thoughts so deeply."

They left it at that.

"Maybe you're right, Dennis," Peter finally was forced to say. "Maybe even your devil can make a mistake."

"Don't call him mine," Dennis said.

The quiet words were a horror of loathing.

"Sorry!" said Peter. He drove along a little way, big hands loose on the wheel, obviously deep in thought. Then it had to come out.

"And yet, you know," he said slowly, "perhaps there's a connection. Have you thought of any, Dennis?"

Dennis looked at him with wide dark eyes of astonishment.

"Why, what could there be?" he asked.

"Well, this," said Peter, jerking his head at the surrounding sun-soaked and monotonous country through which their dirt rut of a road led. "Delroy! Doesn't it occur to you that both you and he seem to have this country in common? It's your own home stamping grounds—and yet he chooses it for a bait for Father Malletti—if he *is* playing that game. Anyway, someone summons Father Malletti to this place. Is that the someone who killed Bianca, Father Malletti's protegee, and so involved you in the case, Dennis, because he did it in your room?"

Peter turned those deep blue eyes, small-looking in their depth of eye-socket bone, on Dennis intently.

"'An enemy hath done this,'" he quoted, keen-eyed. "Do you remember saying that, Dennis, yesterday morning? What more is your enemy going to do to you? He involves you, it seems to me, whenever he can. He has plans for you. And they aren't at all nice plans. He wants you to get out of his way."

"A—a sort of sideswipe of revenge at Dennis, when he's doing his dirty work," Blake contributed breathlessly. "Oh, he is a devil! Dennis, don't you really know him?"

"I wish I did," said Dennis simply. "You make me feel as if I were standing in a lighted room with all the shades up and someone watching me from the darkness outside."

He raised his head from the comfortable leather back of the car seat, at a sudden thought.

"And if there is someone like that watching me," he said reflectively, "he knows more than you do about what's ever happened to me—down here. You'd better know, too. I've already told Blake."

Then he told Peter what he'd told Blake about the hit-and-run episode of a year ago.

Peter was silent, at the end, but not unfriendly—just thinking it over. Then he nodded.

"That was all there was to it?" he asked.

"All," said Dennis straightly. "Exactly as it happened. And it couldn't have any bearing on this thing that's happening now. It's ended for good. I just thought—you'd better know about it, Byrne."

"I see," Peter accepted it then." I'm glad you told us."

"I wanted to," said Dennis. "Before Kennedy or the police told you. Sullivan'll get onto it sometime."

They were at Hasta la Vista now. The sun was setting. It was all red and dark gray in the flat west country behind the tall elm trees around the house. The little white house had a flicker of red color on it, changing momentarily.

Wong met them. Dinner, he informed his straying master sternly, was on the table. He kept a beady eye on Dennis like a nervous hen ready to pounce on an errant and rather senseless chick. Dennis ushered his guests about.

"We," Blake said pointedly to Peter, who wanted to linger and look at things, "are starving. Dennis and I had only a couple of hot dogs, coming through San Jose."

"Wong!" yelled Dennis, at the head of the table in the small room lit by two bright oil lamps. "We're here!"

"He's not so swell at pancakes," he said modestly to Blake, of the old retainer, "but he's a shoutin' bearcat on hot biscuits and chicken."

Ten minutes later Blake looked up and caught Dennis's eye blissfully.

"Yes," she said. "He is, isn't he?"

The shoutin' bearcat cackled in delight.

"You're adopted," Dennis said to her. "That's our war cry."

"Smoke?" said Peter. He passed cigarettes around, and they lit up.

Wong fired a high-pitched and weirdly accented string of syllables at Dennis. That gentleman cocked an unaccustomed ear and finally got it.

"Man coming to see me," he announced briefly. "After dinner."

"What kind of a man?" asked Blake.

"Well, if we had any hills around here, he'd be a hillbilly," said Dennis, rather puzzled. "You know the type. Long and lean and lanky-looking, never washes, does a bit of plowing sometimes, helps out in fruit season or cattle driving. Got too much sun in him—all ambition and get-up been baked, out of him long ago Name's Bowden, I think. Lives in a sort of shack and on an acre of ground."

"Wonder what he wants to say," Peter said.

Dennis shrugged.

"I think I'll phone Kennedy," he said, getting up. "Promised to report to him. No news yet, anyway."

"Maybe," said a Peter soothed and a bit facetious from the extraordinarily good combination of hot biscuits, chicken, and cigarettes—"maybe your honest plowman can tell you a tale."

And that was the way Kennedy first got the "Honest Plowman " phrase of the later, terrible headline streamers. Dennis repeated it to Kennedy for a jest, and Kennedy remembered it—afterward.

Peter and Blake strolled out to the small front yard to finish their cigarettes in the fresh, nearly frosty air, while Dennis was inside phoning.

"What do you think of this guy, anyway?" Peter demanded.

"I don't know," said Blake, a bit troubled. "I feel as if I'd known him for a long time."

"That's the trouble," Peter grunted. "You can't get far enough away to see him good. To see what he's really like, I mean," he grumbled.

"No," said Blake. "You can't take him or leave him —he's already there."

Dennis came up to them. In the gloom of the evening his face looked white.

"I talked with Kennedy," he said. "He says—he says the police know Bianca's real name. She was Mrs. Victor Farnese!"

"What of it?" asked Peter.

Dennis's emotion seemed a bit unaccounted for.

"I forgot you didn't know," he said dully. "Victor Farnese was the man we ran over on the Salinas highway a year ago. The man they thought I killed."

He looked at them, puzzled, tortured, through the dusk.

"Things don't come to an end, do they?" he asked huskily. "They don't—ever—end."

He swayed a little. Peter put an arm around his shoulders.

"Well," Blake said, looking quizzically at the lately doubting Peter, "thunder clears the air, anyway!"

Dennis shook himself.

"It gave me a jolt," he said more practically. "What in hell is Victor Farnese's name doing here? He's been dead for the past year. What is his widow doing, getting murdered in my hotel room? I'd like an answer, please."

"Hi, Dennis," drawled a soft voice out of the dusk. A man had slouched up to them, unnoticed. An over-ailed, lanky, loosely hanging, soft-stepping man. They couldn't see his face.

"Name's Bowden—John Bowden," said the visitor. "You remember me? Ranchin' right next to you, across the south gully. Been away, haven't you?"

"Come back," said Dennis. "Hi, Bowden. Friends of mine. You wanted to see me?"

The other man nodded. "Yeah. Been wantin' to—a long time. Only you lit out of here so quick. And I had to be sorta careful around those days—was runnin' a still on my place for some fellows and didn't want too much company—po-lice, an' such. Fust thing, your trial was over, an' you'd gone. Always meant to get over here, before it was too late."

"Thanks for the kind thought," said Dennis. "But why?"

"Heard you say Farnese's name just now," said Bowden, without a direct answer. "Long's he isn't restin' right easy in his grave, or in your mind, might's well tell you now. No harm in it. You got probation, anyway—and they wouldn't never have been able to do anything about it, prob-ly, if I *had* told 'em "

"Told 'em what?" asked Dennis.

"What I saw that night," said their visitor very simply. "I was goin' along the highway on foot—on some business I wouldn't tell to the district attorney or the sheriff of this here county—and along just about that time you come along, drivin' like all get out. Couldn't see who was in the car—saw your headlights comin'. And just for a minute—just for a bare minute—saw somethin' in the road, in your headlights. It looked like a man on the highway. He was layin' down."

"You mean—you saw us hit Farnese?" Dennis said quietly, from a dry throat.

"No," Bowden drawled. "I mean when your head-lights was on ahead. Say thutty feet ahead of you. Looked like somethin' was laying there—like a big shadow—before you ever got on to it. Then you came by, hell-for-leather, and passed me, an'—whatever it was, and I heard your girl screamin' out."

Dennis couldn't speak. He was thinking of shadows— of another dark shadow he'd seen in a hotel room—on a floor. . . .

Peter cleared his throat. "Dark night?" he asked.

"Dark as hell," said Bowden. "No moon, ner fog. If you didn't want to be seen . . . Dark as tonight's goin' to be."

"Listen," said Dennis desperately. "Listen. Do you mean—we ran into a *dead* man on that highway?"

His visitor shrugged, faintly seen.

"I ain't sayin'," he said. "Only—it looked like a man might, layin' down."

"Did you touch it—afterwards?" asked Peter. "Was it—Farnese?"

Bowden shrugged again, less clearly seen than ever.

"No use," he said. "Figured whatever it was, you'd hit it square. People'd be comin', right away, and I didn't want to be there. Less *I* knew— "

"But you came and told us," said Blake. "Why?"

"Always meant to," said Bowden lazily, "sometime. Never got over here till now. Heard you was back. Last year Hell, nobody'd care now. You wouldn't spill it. Thought you'd like to know, though. Might be — sort of restless in your mind."

"Well," said Peter dryly, "we've got news for you, too. Mrs. Victor Farnese was murdered night before last in Dennis's hotel room in San Francisco!"

For a minute their self-invited guest stood motionless, soundless. As if Peter's words had cracked a hard-baked crust of indifference, were slowly entering his mind, becoming sensible, believable. . . .

He cried out once, a hoarse cry, astonishment, denial, belief— They heard him; then he was gone, swifter than shadows.

# X. THE REST IS SILENCE

They hadn't expected to get such action on that single remark of Peter's; Peter last of all. For a minute they stood there, the two men lost in the darkness, only Blake in her cream-colored dress a dimly seen ghost.

Bowden's curious cry still rang in their ears. Now that he was gone, it took on another quality—the quality of fear. The man had been terribly afraid. They knew it. They'd loosed something on him—fear. The hounds of fear.

Then Dennis broke the charm of stillness. He moved into swift and startled action.

"He knows something!" he cried furiously. "What does he know?"

He started to run, and Peter caught him by the arm.

"Hey, Dennis!" he said. "Gently—"

Dennis was beyond all that. He wrenched himself from the cumbering big hands.

"Gently?" said Dennis. "The hell with that! I asked a question and I want an answer! And I'm going to get one! You'd better stay here—this isn't your mix-up."

"Blake," said Peter, quickly, as his host disappeared down the path to the open fields, "you stay here."

He ran after Dennis, as well as he could see to follow him.

"Blake," said Blake to herself, breathlessly, "you stay here."

Then Blake started to run, too. She and Peter and Dennis ran smoothly, recklessly, over sandy ground, stumbled over heavy plowed ground broken beneath their feet, ran breakneck down a little rounded hill to halt, half-sobbing for breath, at the shelter of its valley. The keen night air had turned warm and heavy to their bodies, the breaths they labored to draw into their aching lungs were unbelievably heavy and smothering.

Dennis grasped each one by the arm to get their attention, and then pointed up to the opposite slope.

"House," he gasped huskily. "His. This is—south gully. We go—up."

Peter groaned. "We would," he said bitterly, drawing great drafts of air into his big chest. "My legs weigh a ton."

Miraculously, all of a sudden they had their second wind. They made it to the top of the opposite hill, slowed to a more sober pace, but not suffering so much. Dennis didn't seem to mind that they'd come on against orders—even Blake, he didn't so much not notice as take for granted there. He was too keen on something else. On getting his answer. He'd sort of broken loose on his own hook at last.

The shack was set on the top of the round foothill between two humps of it, protected by some chaparral bush from the winds. It was dark. Dennis didn't even knock on the door. He pushed it, and it swung open.

"Matches?" he asked Peter. "Or a flashlight, any of you?"

Peter struck a match. Dennis looked around quickly, before it should go out, and located the oil lamp on the table. He bent over it, and it slowly flared into bloom, and Dennis's intent, stern face showed above it, the eyes veiled under level brows, the mouth grave and calm.

He looked at the one room slowly, fully—iron stove, bunk-cot, table, cooking things hung up, shelves, dirty rough clothes hung up on nails in a corner.

"He hasn't got back yet," he said. "Perhaps he's scared to yet. Meanwhile "

He went over to the clothes and began going through them methodically, gravely intent, searching with a curious abstract young sternness, as if he were a rather scornful but just young judge searching out truth from an unsavory case. He put his hands into the blue denim overall pockets, lifted out bits of twine, crumpled cigarette papers, once a pocketknife, other uninteresting odds and ends. He didn't find anything worth looking at twice. Then he looked under the soiled pillow of the bunk-like bed, under the thin mattress, ruffled the blankets—Bowden evidently had no use for sheets—and put it in order again deftly, quickly.

Peter and Blake found seats, he on the kitchen table, she on the one kitchen chair, and watched Dennis without saying anything. There really wasn't anything to say. This, as he'd told them, was his business. Tracing a year-old lie, a year-old injustice, to its hiding place. They didn't blame Dennis for making free with his neighbor's shack in his absence. Bowden, if he'd been telling the truth, had been making pretty free with a good year of Dennis's life by holding out his information. Peter privately thought he'd like Dennis and Bowden to meet again. It would be a swell fight. He'd second Dennis.

Meanwhile he waited. And Blake with him.

Dennis finished with the bed and stood in the center of the room, looking around. He ran one hand through his already ruffled head and surveyed the ground with a certain puzzlement. Then he turned to the interested witnesses watching him.

"It must be here," he said. "Don't you see?" appealing to them as a judge would instruct a jury, patiently. "He didn't come over to tell me about Farnese's death out of kindness. He wasn't that kind of a guy. He had something to get out of it. What? I've got to find something—or make him tell "

He turned suddenly to the kitchen table where Peter was throned, and ordered him off peremptorily.

"Beat it," he said, and was hauling out the one battered drawer, shallow but filled with odds and ends of untidy things, with the industry of a terrier after a promising rat, before Peter was halfway off his perch. The drawer was the record of a rather messy sort of life—a futile, unpathetic sort of life. It had kitchen knives and forks and spoons of tin and of thin cheap silver plate worn through, mixed up with a couple of *Love Nest* magazines on cheap rough yellowed paper that had been handled a great deal by unwashed hands, and there were a few letters on cheap blue-lined stationery written by women who had evidently joined the Love Nest Letter Writers' Club and could find nothing better in life for a romance than a correspondence with such men as Bowden, and he with them. Dennis's very hands expressed a disdainful distaste, looking over the scrawled things, but he didn't neglect them. He read them and then put them by silently, and then rummaged around among the string and paper and magazines, to come up with a crumpled bit of blue paper. He held this out, curiously, with a different look dawning on his intent face.

"Hullo!" he said. "Recognize this?"

"Money-order receipts," confirmed Peter.

"Look at the dates," ordered Dennis. He passed two or three of the crumpled things over. Peter looked at the dates and place of buying them, stamped in a round circle on the scraps of paper. He looked at the amounts. They were, as far as he looked from the collection in his hand, all for ten dollars, even. They were all sent from the post office at San Francisco. He whistled. . . .

Dennis was tearing things apart in the drawer and bringing up more of them for inspection.

"Why, we've stumbled onto a little fortune," said Blake, eagerly. "Or does your plowman send these home to his old mother, Dennis?"

Peter and Dennis began spreading the receipts out on the table. They sorted them out. They counted them. There were eight. They were all for ten dollars. They were all from San Francisco. It didn't make much sense. Bowden wouldn't have gone up to the city to send these. Where'd he ever get the money, anyway? And he didn't have anyone to send them to, at that. Dennis only laughed a bit scornfully and harshly at the idea of that sun-scorched, wind-beaten person sending ten of his precious dollars out every month to a dear old white-haired mother. He just couldn't see it somehow, he told Blake.

Then they began looking at dates again. There was something funny about those dates. They weren't recent.

"Why'd he keep these?" Blake asked them, her eyes going wide and bluer in the flare of the oil-lamp light. Her hair caught the light like a short-haired halo around her young face. Her gold-touched hair got in Dennis's eyes like a light. He couldn't ask her to move away from the lamp, though. That would be silly. He said:

"Bowden was the kind of person who didn't throw anything away, Blake. For one thing, he was too lazy —just stuffed things in drawers and kept 'em. Too stingy, another thing. I guess he always had a sneaking idea any little bit of string or paper or anything was worth something. He was the kind of person that can't make a clean sweep of things anyway—sort of clutters up his life with truck all the time, until he dies."

None of them noticed that they were speaking of the absent owner of the shack as though he were himself in the past tense. They had such a disdain of the man that they simply didn't accept him among them there. They knew he wouldn't come in while they were there, anyway. They were sure of it. He was too mean-spirited. They'd seen him, He was afraid.

"Got it!" said Peter triumphantly.

The big head bent over the tidy rows of blue slips. He put out one big finger and pointed as he explained along the rows.

"Got the dates—see?" he said. The finger moved along the rows as he spoke. "They're a month apart, except for a gap of one here and here, and over here and here. The first one is for August, of a year ago. It's not too improbable to assume that the gaps represent missing receipts that are lost, I think. He must have lost some, in this rather careless system of book-keeping. In other words, there were twelve receipts for ten dollars each, covering a period of exactly a year. They began, you see, about a year ago, and ended this July."

He looked up then at the funny sound that came from Dennis.

"That mean anything to you?" he asked. "Think, Dennis."

"Think?" cried Dennis furiously, hopelessly. "I don't have to think! I know damn' well what it means—do you think I'd forget those dates so easily? They were last year, the year I was convicted of manslaughter and put on probation for Farnese's killing!"

Silence quivered about them. Peter broke through it.

"Well, what does it mean, Dennis?" he asked hoarsely.

Dennis stared at them, his face white and bitter as the bitter and unbelieving hurt in his voice when he spoke, slowly:

"Don't you see? Don't you see? Someone—must have known he was there on the highway when I ran over Farnese that night. They knew Bowden was there—and they didn't know how much he'd seen, maybe. And they approached him—and he sold me out for ten dollars a month—someone sent him the blackmail price of his silence all the time my sentence was due to run. Then I was free—this July—and they quit sending any more money—and he thought he'd get even on them, and waited—he waited for four months to tell me, when I finally came back here."

The slow, hurt voice stopped. They stared in silence at the silent blue slips of paper.

## XI. THE HOUNDS OF FEAR

"Then what?" said Peter. "Then what?"

He wanted to be doing something, to be in action. The muscles of his big body tensed, relaxed, like a man stretching himself after sleep. It was hard to be sitting there when something was going on—outside. He wanted to be in on it.

He went to the door and opened it, and Dennis and Blake came to stand at his elbow. In the dark night they heard the rising wind charging up the hillside, rustling the bushes near the shack, dying down again—and getting up again.

Somewhere out there was Bowden, in the dark and windy night, a man afraid—running, perhaps, or hiding —Dennis couldn't forget the way he'd cried out, the way he'd run.

They couldn't hope to find him now. They didn't know where he'd gone. They could only wait, hoping he'd come back at last.

The wind tore around the corner of the hill, and the night came alive again with its rush.

"The hounds of fear!" said Dennis softly. "The hounds of fear out night-running. You sicked them on him, Peter. He won't come here. He's—running."

Peter let the door slam shut, and they turned back to the table and the oil lamp again.

"No, he didn't expect to hear that Farnese's wife was dead," Dennis went on in that same soft voice, as though he trod down a dangerous trail warily. He seated himself at the table and put his elbows on it, resting his head on his two fists. He lifted his head and put his chin on his hands at rest instead, and grinned a crooked, unamused grin at the other two.

"Professor Dennis in his famous seance performance," he remarked. "Shall I give it to you now?"

"All you've got," grunted Peter, dropping down onto the side of the bunk. He drew Blake down beside him, and they sat facing Dennis like an attentive audience.

"Here it is, then, as far as we've gone," Dennis said. "We think we're almost as much in the dark as before. Maybe so. But do you realize that every time we find out something—even a trail that goes blind on us—we find out something more about the man who put it there? Our devil who killed Bianca.

"This is the plot. And you were right, Peter, this evening when you said it did involve me. It's getting clearer now all the time. It begins 'way back a year ago last July. Farnese was killed. I think our devil killed him. Why? We don't know that. Maybe it's not important. A local quarrel. Anyway, it happened here, and I was the fall guy. Only Bowden saw him lying on the highway, before I hit him. Bowden was paid blackmail to keep quiet, and I went on trial for the killing. Okay so far?"

He cocked an eyebrow at his audience. Blake nodded, quickly, beyond speech. Peter nodded a massive head slowly.

"Neat," he said. "I give him that, anyway."

"Is that all?" asked Dennis. "Wait till you hear what I give him. That guy's good—in his way.

"Now we come to recent events. Bianca was killed by our devil. Very coolly, very systematically. I told you what I thought about him then. She was killed because she was Farnese's widow, and she'd heard at last that he didn't die-—of an accident. The same man who killed him found out he had to kill her, to keep the first murder quiet. Otherwise, why the long wait? It doesn't make sense. If he was just finishing off the family, why didn't he do it all at once, a year ago? He was a friend of hers—a lover—and she was about to find out he killed her husband. So she was killed. In my room. If it ever came out that Farnese was dead before I hit him, people would think, maybe, that I'd killed him on purpose a year ago, then run over him to disguise it as a manslaughter accident, and that I'd killed his widow to keep her quiet about it afterwards. See? Our murderer saw that. He was a neat guy, at that, Peter. He didn't want to leave any loose ends if he could help it. And he thought he could help it along by adding me to the cast once more. The police would suspect too much of a coincidence like that, maybe, he'd think. I give him a swell mark on that. At first I thought he was a loose performer, letting me in for that without any seeming motive to back me up.

"Then,"—Dennis dropped that dark head down to his hands again, and that determinedly light voice went dark on him, too—"then Father Malletti came into it. Have you forgotten him? I haven't, for a second, all this night—not even when we were running after Bowden, across the fields in the dark and the wind. He's been at the back of my mind. I can't help it—I think I'm going to meet him sometime. I'm going to meet him," he repeated, and stayed for a second lost in some dark dream. "It's a funny thing—I even seem to know what he looks like. And I've never seen him, either. Maybe I've just made up a picture of him out of my mind. An old man, going into darkness—I can't get him out of my mind."

Dennis shivered, once, sharply, then stayed still.

"*What* does he look like, Dennis?" Peter said quietly.

"He's got dark eyes that go right through you," Dennis said. "They're very stern eyes. I'd be afraid, only—there's his mouth, and his smile. It lights up his face, when he smiles. He's got a thin face, and a great beak of a thin nose, beautifully arched, and a thin mouth. I think he had a quick temper, when he was a young man, but he's gotten over that now. He's worn down past the flesh and the passions to the light of the spirit. It burns in him like this oil lamp burning here in the dark. He's got thin white hair, too.

"For the rest," said Dennis thoughtfully, face propped in both his hands, staring ahead of him, "he's a rather tall, thin old man in a long black robe. That's all, I think. All I see of him."

Peter whistled, softly, like a long-held breath coming out at last.

"All!" he said, respectfully.

"I told you," pointed out Dennis, "that I couldn't tell whether that's just my idea of Father Malletti, or whether I really do see him, and he does look like that. Only—I think I'd be able to know him, if I met him, and without knowing his name."

"Dennis," Blake put in, hushed of voice, "will they— What do they want of Father Malletti?"

She'd put into actual solid words the thing they'd kept thinking around, not daring to approach too closely.

Dennis went forward to it.

"They want silence," he said straightly. "The way Father Malletti comes into this is because he knew Bianca Farnese. He was her confidant. She found out something that would have put her on the track of her husband's murderer—and Bianca, whatever she was, wasn't an accomplice to such a thing. I bet she had a kind of loyalty as splendid as she was—nothing small about her build or make-up. A home-grown goddess, Kennedy said. Well, she probably told Father Malletti what she knew, or suspected, and what she was going to do to find out more. That was the time she saw him last, when she went away crying. Someone knew she'd been to see him. They had to have his silence."

"What d'you mean—silence?" Peter said hoarsely, in a cold and drafty sort of voice. "You mean—he's dead?"

Dennis shook his head.

"I don't see anyone killing Father Malletti," he said simply. "It wouldn't do any good to them. He'd be with them all the rest of their life. It would be too much like killing themselves. And they can't buy or beg his silence. He'd speak out anything he thought should be spoken out, if he were free. No, I bet they're sort of puzzled what to do about it themselves—whoever 'they' are. I bet they're—just waiting."

He spoke with an assurance that, strangely enough, Peter and Blake didn't contest. He was like someone who knew the path, in a strange country, and led the way unhesitatingly. In a bit of a hurry, in fact, anxious to arrive at some unknown destination.

"That's it so far," he explained to them again. "I told you we know a lot more about our unknown than we did!"

"What, for instance?" Peter suggested.

"Well," Dennis considered, "I told you before that he had hell's own nerve, and that he was a cool, canny customer; I'm not taking any of that back. Only he's canny this way—he wants to let someone else take the credit for him. Me, for one. He's got nerve, but he's not taking any risks he can avoid. Then—you're right about this, Pete—he's got Delroy as a well-known country to work in. Farnese was killed in Delroy; Father Malletti was lured to Delroy; Bowden lives in Delroy; he knows something about me, and I come from Delroy. But he sent his money orders from San Francisco; he's not a native here. He lives up in San Francisco, where Bianca lived. And—he's someone who's got free access to my hotel floor, and can get to my room easily from where he lives— in my hotel. That narrow it down a bit? Think of a guy like that we know."

"I will," said Peter grimly.

"He *is* a devil," said Blake softly, passionately.

"I don't know," said Dennis thoughtfully. "He's pretty bad, sure; but I don't think he's so inhuman any more, the more I know about him. I think he's very humanly puzzled, say, about what to do about Father Malletti; if he's of the faith of Father Malletti, as he may be—Bianca was—he's probably thinking he's got a lot more than he can handle now with a priest on his hands. I think there's things he'd stick at, and this is one of them. You know, the more I see of life,"—Dennis regarded them very thoughtfully indeed—"the more I'm inclined to think there aren't any stage 'villains' in that sense of being what I'd call 'rapiers of wickedness,' that have a delight in evil and in their skill in it —like keen blades made only for fighting, and for being wicked. I think perhaps there're only two really wicked classes of people in the world, though—and those are the cruelly stupid, and the stupidly cruel. They aren't rapiers, they're bludgeons. They smash things in the first place because they're clumsily wicked, not really meaning to act like the rapiers of wickedness."

"Is this a bludgeon's work or a rapier's, Dennis?" asked Blake with fascinated attention. "This case?"

"Rapier's." That was Peter's judicial opinion, briefly.

"I vote bludgeon," Dennis said.; "Look at the case already! We've spotted holes in it as big as our heads! There's Father Malletti, for one. He can't be held silenced forever. The other way—well, our human devil doesn't want to take it. Then there's Bowden—he's a big gap in the defense. When we get Bowden, we'll make a hole in it you can see through! Those are two gaps that ought to be plugged, and aren't. And, if he'd been a rapier, he'd have done for Farnese more skillfully. All these later events, my sentence and Bianca's murder, have been the outcome of him smashing around regardless, trying to cover up his own traces through the general wreckage of lives he's made. He's cruelly stupid. And he's failed."

"What about Bowden?" Peter asked. "Where does he belong?"

"Bowden belongs to the stupidly cruel, I think," Dennis answered. "He's the kind that would set dogs onto a stray cat for the fun of it. That's the way he felt about setting us onto the trail of a man who'd been paying him money for silence, and who thought his safety was bought a year ago for good. Bowden wanted to have some fun with him, harrying him out of safety."

"Well," said Peter grimly, heavily, "he sure started something."

Dennis nodded his dark head gravely.

"Yes," he replied. "More than he wanted, or meant to. He's the one who's being hunted now. He's afraid."

And on the silent chill of that last word, they heard the, wind rising around the top of their hill, and, in the night, the hounds of fear baying in the windy dark outside.

☐

# XII. THE PLUGGED GAP

"So you see—" Dennis made a gesture with one hand that spread the whole case before them on the worn kitchen table like a pack of cards, or like the blue money-order receipts that lay spread out there already.

"And here's another gap he left, our devil," he said as afterthought. "How'd these receipts get here? They should have been left with the sender. But the murderer didn't want to have anything to do with them—even to tear 'em off and then throw them away, or burn them. He was afraid he'd get careless about one of them one day, and maybe the orders would be traced and one receipt found in his possession. He was, you see, always afraid, even though he reasoned to himself that he'd made everything safe. So he left 'em on the original orders, and they were preserved through Bowden's shiftlessness, or craftiness, and came to us. He couldn't, really, make anything safe, no matter how hard he tried. It's all coming up again. Like earth on a restless grave. Poor devil!"

Blake shuddered—she couldn't help it. Peter considered Dennis thoughtfully, deeply.

"You talk as if you were getting to know him—to be sorry for him," he said at last. "Even for Bowden, too, with his hounds of fear pursuing him. You make them too—humanly frail, Dennis, for us to have much anger left for them. Only pity. Is there anyone on God's earth you couldn't make friends with, Dennis?"

Dennis grinned. "I don't care much for the police," he said. "Or for Sullivan, if it comes to that. Or for that hotel manager."

He got up and went to the door again and stood listening to the wind outside.

"It's getting cold here," he said. "No reason why you should have to stay here all night. You and Blake go back to my house; you can stay there all night, if you want, or drive back to San Francisco if you have to be there in the morning. Bowden won't come back here as long as there's a light in this place. I'll go back across the gully with you to the house—if he's watching, he'll know we're all gone. Then I'll leave you there and come back here quietly and maybe catch him. And if I do, he'll tell what he knows."

He opened the door a little, and the keen, damp night air came like earthy darkness into the lighted room.

"You'll get cold, Blake," he said. "You'd better have something over your dress."

"She can have my coat," Peter growled and began getting out of one sleeve.

"I *am* cold," Blake admitted. "Talking of graves—" and promptly shivered again.

"Here, take my coat," Dennis said. "It'll fit you better—it's not a circus tent like Peter's."

He had it off and slung it around her, draping it over her shoulders, while Peter was still getting his off. He did it up carefully, putting the lifted collar up to Blake's cool round chin.

"Dennis," Blake said impulsively, "I think you're wonderful, the way you don't fuss about my being here. You don't treat me like a girl in that way. You let me in for things like you do Peter. I love it. Most girls miss these sort of things. But you don't treat me like that—like a *mere* girl."

"How else would I treat you?" asked Dennis, surprised.

Something faintly demure come over Blake's vivid face.

"I've been told," she said softly, "there're—other ways."

"Not by me," boomed Peter. "I need a kid sister as long as I can keep one—they're handy things to have in a house."

"You old Victorian!" scoffed Blake.

They stepped out into the night and waited while Dennis turned the lamp down and it flickered into darkness. For a second, it was totally dark around them. Then the shapes of things came out a little, darker bushes and the hill against a paler sky. Bright points of stars appeared overhead. They got their bearings and began to walk away, down the hill. Blake put her hands through Peter's and Dennis's arms, and they walked in step, stumbling once in a while over shadows that turned out to be solid clumps.

As they went down into the gully the sweet, frosty air of November came around them; the earthy smell, the smell of wet winter coming on, and the smell of dead dry grass rotting on the fields, and of leaves turning to mold, was in their nostrils. It was like a sort of nostalgia; it was a season smell they all loved, for the same reason. Peter said it wistfully, lovingly, the stolid giant made articulate.

"Football weather," Peter said, drawing the keen and fragrant air deep into his capacious chest like a loved draft. The other two sighed wordlessly.

Then Dennis began to sing absently, not caring how much noise they made to let Bowden know they were gone. . . .

*"Sweet—and lovely . . ."*

Dennis heard himself singing softly, in the starry night beside Blake wrapped in his coat.

After a few seconds—"Radio singer!" said Blake bitingly, under her breath.

Dennis stopped. Then:

"How do you like this?" he said expressionlessly. He began again. The cold night flowered into beauty. Something sharp of point as a needle went through Blake's heart.

*"Drink to me only with thine eyes"*

sang Dennis,

*"And I will pledge with mine . . ."*

It was like being kissed. Only Dennis had done it to hurt her.
*"I sent thee late a rosy wreath"*

—the old song was like a record that couldn't die, so beautiful it was, all these hundred years—

*"Not so much honoring thee,*
*As giving it a hope that there,*
*It could not withered be."*

You couldn't withstand beauty like that. It was a knife at your heart. It was someone you loved singing to you. It was something that wouldn't ever die. How could Dennis be so unmoved by it, making it so beautiful? He sang as if his love were on his lips, as if all the tenderness of the song were on his warm, young mouth, and his arm through hers didn't even tremble. He was happy, making such sorrow of love, such a havoc in the hearts of others listening to him. Was that what it was to be an artist? Blake was learning.

*"But thou thereon didst only breathe,"*

sang Dennis,

*"And sent'st it back to me-e-e;*
*Since when it grows and smells, I swear,"*

the deathless love song rose triumphantly,

*"Not of itself but thee!"*

And suddenly, it was all right again. She was Blake Byrne, walking across a frosty dark field, and Dennis was Dennis and not the disembodied spirit of deathless love seeking utterance. For Dennis had pressed her arm against his, once, closely, comfortingly, roughly, a friendly gesture, a careless gesture.

*"Not of itself but thee!"*

he sang over again, very softly, letting the song shatter itself against the silence.

He wasn't an artist any more, punishing others but not being punished himself by his song. He hadn't been angry. He was just Dennis again. Blake was silent. She was learning.

"Swell!" said Peter approvingly. "That's pretty."

"You think so?" said Dennis. "Pretty, nothing—hell, that was perfect! That reminds me, Peter, I have a bone to pick with you. Or I would have if I didn't have this unfortunate idea of picking opponents that could give Dempsey weight and height. You damn' near called me an Abou Ben Adhem back there in the shack —you said I was a little friend of all the world. Take back those words—or else."

"What's the matter with 'em?" asked Peter warily.

"It isn't like that at all with me," protested Dennis hotly. "It isn't that I love my fellow man ... go around with a smirk on my face loving 'em! It's just that—I don't know what it's all about. What anything's about. Half the time I think my fellow man is the lowest form of worm," said Dennis pensively, "only—then I'll remember what even worms come to in time. Dust. And then I can't help thinking how brave men must be, so casually brave, to go on living and to love life so much, knowing that at the end of it there's—nothing. Dust again. Some people have consolation. They think there's something more. Maybe there is. I don't know. I do know, though, that we have to die in this life, and that's a terrible thing to have to happen when it's a life like this. And they're so brave. They accept it so casually. How can I think they're so rotten, even the worst of them, when I see them going on to that? I don't know," said Dennis carefully, "what *it's* all about, but I think *they're*—splendid, anyway.

"Oh, Peter," Dennis went on with a quiet passion, "think how you'd feel knowing things are going to end for you. No more days like today, no more nights like tonight, for you ever! No more the sun shining in your face and the wind in your hair, and you driving along the dusty warm roads of Delroy. No more running down the fields in the cool autumn night, and the smell of the earth in your face, and the black frost rising to touch your cheeks as you run!"

Peter gave a deep murmur of sound and drew a deep, deep breath, earthy of frost and autumn, into his lungs.

"When I think of that," said Dennis, "I doubt if I could kill a fly. I'd want to give everything a chance. Even a murderer, who doesn't give anyone a chance. It's just that—I don't know what it's all about," he repeated.

At that suddenly forlorn note in his voice, it was Blake's turn to press her arm against his, hard, once.

"Only," said Dennis more cheerfully, "it's splendid, all of it. I wouldn't want to miss any of it. And when I think of that, and that our murderer made Bianca miss a lot of it, and Farnese, too, whatever kind of a guy he was, why then I feel like asking Sullivan for an invitation to see the hanging at San Quentin—the private showing. Bianca—she wasn't meant to miss any of it. She loved all this, too—every day, every hour. I don't care what she was, or what she did—she didn't deserve — death. I don't think anyone really does. Peter, you don't want to die?"

Peter murmured, like a cello string plucked hard, as if Dennis had picked out a chord on his heart.

"Well, that's the way I feel about this," said Dennis. "There may be other worlds, other faiths—I think there must be. You can see some of 'em up there now, all these bright stars. And maybe there are other lives, too, but all I know and love is this one. Maybe there are others, though. Perhaps," said Dennis lazily, the wind in his face bringing the smell of smoldering dead-leaf smoke—"perhaps God lets us out on a long leash, after all, and this life is it."

They went on a little silently; then, after a while, they began to talk softly together, in comfortable pauses. But they could feel that they were friends now truly, because they had talked of immortality together.

Blake and Dennis began to bicker, idly, as two players will toss a tennis ball back and forth across a net, purely for practice and enjoyment.

"You scrap so beautifully, Blake," sighed Dennis. "I almost wish we'd never get home."

"Good God, are we only going to your place, Dennis?" Peter boomed. "I thought we were halfway to San Jose by now!"

He brought up short in the dark and stood drawing great deep breaths, half puffing them out and in again. The others stood waiting for him.

"It only looks farther than it did," said Dennis helpfully, peering at the dark earth around them. "Coming back always does. Besides, you didn't notice landmarks before—you didn't have time, anyway. You were just about flying. The house is right around the dark clump of things to the left, and you can see the tops of the elm trees around it mixing in with the stars up there. And there's the light from the kitchen window. We're here."

"Well, if Bowden doesn't know we're out of his place and back here again, he must be deaf," said Peter contentedly, as they came through the yard and around by the lighted kitchen doorway.

"He knows, all right," Dennis said grimly. "And I'll know some more too, when I get back there. I'm going to get an overcoat—that shack's darned chilly, and it'll get colder later on in the night."

Blake slipped out of his coat and handed it over.

"Thanks a lot, Dennis," she said casually. "What was that bumpy thing in your side pocket—a gun?"

"Cigarette case." Dennis showed it to her, grinning. "Think I want to shoot myself accidentally some day? I can get someone else to do it for nothing!"

"D-Dennis," Blake said, wide-eyed, "don't you think I mean, hadn't you better let us come back with you? If there's sh-shooting—"

"The perfect host," said Dennis. "I'd invite you all for it, only—there's not going to be any. You must come down when the duck season's on, or when Wong and I are out for the jack rabbits and ground squirrels. Don't let me forget." He grinned again and opened the door to the dark hallway.

"Wong sleeps in his own place, that lean-to beyond the kitchen," he said. "There's room here, if you're staying. I'd like to have you. Wait'll I get my other coat—it's in the hall closet—" He broke off suddenly, with an almost ludicrous expression of astonishment on his face.

"Why, no, it isn't!" he said, bewilderedly. "It's in the hotel with all the rest of my things, waiting to be packed off by me, I suppose. I bet that hotel bird's hopping! You know, I keep forgetting—that it's a year since I've been here. I suppose—I suppose things do change. Even here. I would have thought—if I'd thought about it at all—that I could have gone in the dark to any place on this ground and picked up my stuff where I used to leave it. My coat in the hall closet, my car in the garage, the bumpy place where it leaves the garage floor for the dirt road, the squirrel gun standing in its place in the tool shack outside—it all comes back so clearly, as if nothing had happened in between to push it back into dimness. Only—a lot's happened. Well, I don't get my coat, but maybe there's chicken and stuff in the icebox like there used to be."

"Philosopher!" said Blake warmly, approaching the icebox cordially. "Maybe there is."

There was.

"Help yourself," said Dennis, waving his hand largely. "Wong won't mind, and if he does, why, who's the boss here, anyway?"

"Wong," said Peter.

Dennis laughed. "Right the first time. I'm only the young master. I forgot you had a Louie in your lives. He'd die for me if he thought I needed it, but he wouldn't let me put on any airs in my own house."

"He probably knows what's good for you," Peter observed.

"And you," said Dennis, "with your mouth full of my chicken!"

He looked at his watch and got up.

"Make wassail," he said hospitably. "It's five to eleven now, and I'm going back to get Bowden. He's had lots of time to come in by now."

"Want us?" Peter rumbled. Dennis shook his head, smiling.

"I think we'll take you up on spending the night here then, and make an early start back to the city in the morning. There's an inquest due there tomorrow—it may have slipped your mind—and if the chief witness doesn't show up there'll be ructions, especially in the detective bureau. As your lawyer, Dennis," Peter sighed, "I feel as if I were just hanging onto the tail of a kite!"

"This is our only chance," Dennis reminded him, "to do anything on our own hook. It's the long leash, and I'm going to take advantage of it. Otherwise—I may be watching you hopefully through a nice thickness of wire mesh up at the jail while you say that while there's life there's hope, and you'll carry it up to the State Supreme Court, and other polite things "like that to cheer me up! No, thank you. We'll do what we can on our own first."

"Sure you don't want company?" Peter tried again.

"Quite sure," Dennis said. "Thanks. It may scare him off if he sees or hears a crowd of us coming. I've got a better chance of getting him, going alone this way. So long—"

He stopped at the doorway and turned halfway back.

"—rather, *hasta la vista,*" he said, smiling at them. A curious gracious courtesy fell on him all at once, like the mantle of the old dons who had lived in his sunny county, who had listened to the gentle stately courtesy of the Little San Ramon River rippling through the long sunny afternoons. As though the sight of guests reminded him, for a brief second, of other, more gracious days.

"My house is yours," said Dennis gravely in the old formula and was gone, armed only with the cigarette case bumpy against his side pocket.

"Dennis—" Blake began, a bit lost.

Peter shook his big head at her and laid a big brown hand reprovingly for a second on her arm.

"His play," he said. "Don't spoil it."

So Blake—she didn't forgive herself for that—stayed back for once, and Dennis went on alone.

He went down the yard, through the dark fields, across the south gully—and as he looked up he saw a dim red glow in the sky, beginning at the top of the hill. So he began to run, and he reached Bowden's shack as the flames took hold of the wooden walls and began to roar in the wind. He went in and saw the broken oil lamp on the floor and Bowden sprawling in an attitude of surprise, arms thrown out. He knelt beside Bowden, and saw, in that second before the flames drove him out again, that the top was blown off from Bowden's head and the greater part of his face with it. That gap had been effectively plugged.

# XIII. AMONG THOSE PRESENT

About one o'clock that morning Dennis got Kennedy on the phone in the press room of the Hall of Justice.

"Shoot," invited that debonair gentleman cheerfully, when his caller announced himself.

"Don't be funny," said Dennis. "I've got a lot to tell you."

"Well, my ears are still in working order," said that slightly exhilarated person still more airily. "I guess they must work automatically. The rest of me has signed off for the night—eyes see red and black spots in front of 'em, complicated by red, white, and blue round things that look to me like poker chips. Hands can't handle a pencil any more—they make funny motions like shuffling—"

"Kennedy," said Dennis hoarsely, "do you *have* to be drunk just now, when I need you sober?"

It was just a last shot, but it seemed to work. There was a slight but electric pause at the other end of the line. Then Kennedy's voice again, crisper.

"Not," said that cool voice, "if you need me that bad. I'm as sober as a judge, Dennis. Spill it."

Reassured, Dennis went on talking. He told about Bowden's visit to Dennis's garden, of the visit to the shack, and the finding of the blue money-order receipts —and the conclusions drawn therefrom.

"Blackmail, eh?" Kennedy commented. "You're shattering my illusions, Dennis. I thought all rustics who had anything to do with the soil were one hundred per cent pure at heart before they came to the big city."

"You wouldn't think that," said Dennis grimly, "if you'd ever lived around in the country, as I have. Your 'simple' sons of the soil can be mean as dirt, some of 'em. They get a lot of time to think up things to do, I guess. Well, anyway, Bowden was blackmailing this bird—we found that out."

"Go on—he didn't come in?" Kennedy murmured, as though he were writing it all down at the other end of the line.

"Not till I went out with the others," Dennis said. He kept his voice steady, along a monotonous tone, for fear it would shatter itself to pieces. He didn't let himself think, he just went on talking to Kennedy, as though oral contact with him even at that distance kept him from seeing the fearful cliffs of danger plunging down on either side of his path. "Then I came back— alone. It was about eleven o'clock. He was there. He was there, Kennedy—lying on the floor. Someone'd shot him—so close it blew off most of his head. And the oil lamp had broken, and fired the place. It all went up."

"Whew!" said an appreciative Kennedy. "It's lucky I'm talking from a private booth! I took the call here instead of on my press-room phone as soon as I heard it was a long-distance call. I had a hunch, all right. Besides, it was too noisy there—the press room's a merry hell tonight, a dozen extra reporters sent in to cover the Hall, and the Hall is humming from top to bottom like a wasp's nest that someone's kicked open. Dennis, the Farnese and Malletti cases look like the biggest thing since the Trojan War! If these rats around here thought I was holding anything like this out on them, they'd mob me. About this Honest Plowman accepting money for silence,"—Kennedy was talking now as though he were writing it down straight for the hot metal of the print.

"He was a dirty blackmailer!" said Dennis hotly. "What's the idea?"

"Under your hat, Dennis. Sure he was. Only he's dead now, and this case is very, very alive. And we're not going to impeach our only good witness, since he's dead, by implying that he was a pretty worthless sort of skunk. We're going to play him up for a martyr. His testimony may come in handy one of these days, and by that time he'll be almost canonized by the *Star*. Another thing—keep off the subject of those money orders and receipts to the sheriff and any police officers, yet. Let the federal post office at San Francisco keep the original applications in the murderer's handwriting safe there, until we get more of a line on this case. I don't want these press-room rats climbing aboard our ship—they might swamp it. And the police would grab them without a thank-you from you. They're worth something."

"Sullivan'll be here soon," said Dennis, reminded. "The sheriff's gone to head him off at Monterey, near here. He's down following some clue or other, and Henry's letting me talk to you—he's the deputy, and I told him it was important, and he knows me."

"Sullivan? Yeh, I know," Kennedy's voice grinned. "Someone saw an old man with a black gown on coming down the street, and they phoned the San Francisco police and it turns out to be Mrs. McGuire, aged eighty, widow woman who's lived there all her life. They're getting hundreds of calls like that that always come in on a 'missing' case like Father Malletti's disappearance. Well, good luck, Dennis, and I'll be seeing you, maybe at the inquest tomorrow. Thanks a lot for this stuff."

"Inquest?" said Dennis. "Which one—Bianca's? I'm afraid I'm unavoidably detained, Kennedy, from going to anyone's inquest unless it's for Bowden's."

"This is a previous engagement," said Kennedy. "What would keep you, anyway? Where's your friends, the Byrnes?"

"How do I know?" said Dennis wearily. "I haven't seen 'em since the sheriff and his deputy detained me in Delroy. One thing that's keeping me here is an adobe jail they've got here. That's where I'm phoning from. And the sheriff has gone in to get Sullivan to explain to him that I can't attend any inquest. I'm wanted here."

"Hey, they can't do that!" protested Kennedy. "You tell them—"

"Can't they?" said Dennis. "You tell 'em. They want a lot of telling, anyway. They want to know how come my own squirrel gun was found all dirty, and with the barrel still warm from being used, stuck up in a clump of bushes near Bowden's shack! The last time it was seen by anyone it was in my tool shed, and I knew where it was kept, too. You think up an answer to that—*I* haven't been able to satisfy them!"

And he hung up with a bang and turned round to the desk of the sheriff's office in the Delroy jail.

"Thanks, Henry," he said. "I'll go back to the cell now and catch up on some sleep, if you're through for the night."

Only he didn't sleep. That was bravado. He kept seeing it all again—a red glare of fire, and a faceless thing. . . .

Peter and Blake weren't doing much sleeping, either. They sat up around the wood stove in the kitchen, with blankets wrapped Indian fashion around them and their sleepless heads sticking out at the top, their eyes tired and heavy and their voices hoarse as a crow's croak from weary talking. And yet they couldn't stop. They had to keep on.

Their host had left them, in the custody of the lanky and rather embarrassed undersheriff, who'd known Dennis when they were kids together, it seemed, and the sheriff who'd hastily come up at his undersheriff's phone call. The undersheriff and a deputy had driven up in a flivver around twelve o'clock in response to Dennis's call from his place, backed by a horrified and silent Blake and Peter, listening. Dennis after that hadn't been able to talk much about what had happened on the knoll of Bowden's shack. They'd got the main line of it from his phone call. It was too late to do much about it. The shack was nothing but hot wood ashes in a few minutes, and the main fire had already died down when Dennis had come back to them. The undersheriff and his deputy had come and looked over the place where the shack had stood, and raked over the pyre of hot wood ashes, and the two of them had searched the surrounding ground pretty thoroughly by lamp and torchlight, without saying much, but, like good hunting dogs, as it were, with a subtle current of silent communication between them. And then they'd found the squirrel gun, where someone'd thrown it in the bushes, roughly hidden, and they'd shown it to Dennis, still without saying much, their eyes reserved, judgment withheld.

Dennis had identified it as his. They wanted to know where he kept it. It was usually kept in the tool shed, eh? Well, it wasn't there now. They poked around a bit to make sure.

With this observation, and still more silence, they'd phoned and got the sheriff out of his bed, and received orders. They informed Dennis that they had to hold him. Dennis went a bit wild-eyed at that and said something about its getting to be a habit with the police, and then quieted down suddenly. The lanky under-sheriff was looking at him with grieved blue eyes from a thin tanned face. He expected his acquaintances to keep their composure better when being carted off to the jail. It made for uncomfortableness otherwise. Dennis couldn't go back on him.

Only, "Have you got them?" he whispered to Peter fiercely, as the flivver engine started and all other noise was undercovered by it.

"What?" said Peter.

"Those money orders," Dennis said. "You took them."

"I put 'em in my pocket," Peter said.

"Don't give them up," Dennis said. "We may need them."

"I won't," said Peter simply as a rock.

Then Dennis looked at Blake. He hadn't before. Blake was holding onto Peter's big arm hard with both hands and not saying anything. She smiled at Dennis—a small white smile, beyond tears, beyond words, beyond anything but a sort of still white bravery. As if there weren't anything left of her but that smile.

And the undersheriff and his deputy drove off in their flivver and took Dennis away with them, leaving a rather wild-eyed Peter and Blake behind . . . talking . . . talking . . . till their voices husked on them.

They didn't get anywhere, at that. They went over and over it again, past the ground that Dennis had already led them over before. They accepted that as tried territory now—that Bianca knew her husband had been killed, and she'd had suspicions—or near proof —or something—and all the rest, even Bowden's murder, followed from that.

Then Blake thought of something, from utter weariness, just as, sometimes, the tide going back on a muddy beach will uncover treasure—abalone shells shining, or an oyster with a pearl in it.

"You know, it may not be like that at all!" she said huskily, her eyes shining dark and wide. "Have you thought, Peter, we may be all wrong about these last two killings? The recent ones, Bianca's and— and this man's? The first man was killed by someone—and so we think the last two were killed by the same man. It may not be that at all!" She leaned forward in her chair, and her voice dropped still lower. "Where's Wong?" she asked, in a curious dark voice.

"Wong? I don't get you," Peter said. "Where is he? In his lean-to, I suppose. Sound asleep. Lots of these old Chinese take a breath of the pipe before they turn in. You know that, Blake. They're used to it. He's sound asleep. We didn't make much disturbance around, you know."

"Is he?" asked Blake. "That's good."

"Why'd you think of Wong, Blake?"

"Because I don't think we've thought of him enough, Peter. Everyone will be sure that Dennis is a murderer now. They'll think it's very suspicious that as soon as he comes back, murder happens. To people he goes to see. Well, maybe it is. I grant you this—it was probably his presence here that did make that murder come about. Not, of course, that he did it. But—don't you see?—someone knew he was here, and seeing that Bowden person, and that caused Bowden's murder."

"Yes, I see that," Peter said.

"Well, I think we're wrong about that someone. We think he's a San Francisco man who killed Bianca, too. And who killed her husband, Victor Farnese. Suppose he isn't? Suppose he was here in Delroy all the time? Suppose he is someone who knew Dennis's movements, who'd do anything for Dennis, who knew Farnese was murdered, and that Dennis might be accused of murder instead of just plain manslaughter about that? So—he killed Bianca to protect Dennis from the charge of murdering her husband. He killed Bowden for the same reason. Suppose Bianca was going to put it on Dennis? And suppose Bowden was in on it, too?—perhaps she'd paid him for saying it was Dennis killed him. He'd have turned traitor or liar for money. We know that. Maybe he thought it up himself, and put Bianca onto Dennis, thinking he could blackmail Dennis over it later!"

"The honest plowman!" murmured Peter in admiration. "Well, grant that—for the sake of argument. It was going to be a put-up job on Bowden's part to get money from Dennis, scare him on threats of this faked evidence to buy his silence. Who was the obliging friend who put out Dennis's enemy, Bowden, and his danger, Bianca?"

Blake was white and blazing now. She didn't need a blanket about her. She was on fire, whitely.

"Who," she retorted, "knew as much about Dennis's affairs as he did himself? Who loved Dennis so much he'd take anything on himself to get him out of a thing like that? Who lived in Delroy? Who knew where Dennis kept a squirrel gun here? Who knew that he'd come back again today? Wong."

"Prove it," said Peter quietly. "How'd he know anything about Dennis, up in San Francisco, away from here for a year?"

"Of course he did," Blake said. "You know yourself what a grapevine system these old Chinese have, all up and down the state. I bet he didn't miss a thing about Dennis. Why, when Dennis wanted to find out if Father Malletti'd been around here, this afternoon, he sent Wong out to gather the news from the other old heathen here. They know everything that goes on. You know that."

Peter nodded.

"And he knew Bianca was going to meet Dennis—maybe he'd been approached by Bowden and had arranged a meeting. I can see him double-crossing Bowden blandly, and then going up and doing for Bianca—swiftly—silently—that night—"

"In Dennis's room!"

Blake shrugged. "He had to. He couldn't pick his spot very much. Bianca may have known it was Dennis's room, thought she was going to see Dennis there and get the truth about Farnese's killing—sent off at that tangent by Bowden, you see—and met Wong instead. He may have reasoned that the short time between Dennis going up to his room, and giving the alarm, would clear Dennis. It practically has."

"Yes—until *this* came up," Peter said. "You can't blame Sullivan and those birds for giving him the cold eye on this."

"If he'd had witnesses—Dennis, I mean—tonight when he went back there, or if he hadn't gone back, he'd have been safe, with Bowden dead," Blake said swiftly. "It was chance, just chance, that we didn't all go back with Dennis."

"Chance," said Peter heavily, "and his own insistence."

"Don't blame yourself for that, Peter."

"I'm a fine lawyer! I let him walk right into it!"

He raised his massive head and tried to smile at her.

"All right, go on. Why did Bowden get his tonight, after we'd gone there to see him? Explain that, Sherlock, if it wasn't our First Murderer."

"Because," said Blake, "Wong was afraid—of what would happen when Dennis and Bowden did meet. He'd heard Dennis say tonight he was going to get an answer from Bowden. He knew that Bowden was a lot more dangerous than Dennis imagined. He had a picture of the two of them meeting, and Dennis flaring up, and Bowden cool as a rattlesnake, and as nasty-tempered— he thought Bowden was a danger to Dennis, and so he put him out of Dennis's way. That's one way of showing your love for a man—killing his enemies off."

"With Dennis's squirrel gun?"

"With Wong's squirrel gun," corrected Blake. "He'd been using it for a year by himself. He probably didn't even think of it as Dennis's any more. He took it because it was handy, and he was used to it. That's all."

"And now he's sleeping it off while young master's in jail?" asked Peter. "A—a sort of communistic crime, you might say. Wong commits it, and Dennis goes to jail for it. You might call that an involuntary act of brotherly love on Dennis's part, too, Blake."

Blake smiled, a curious little smile.

"I don't think you'll find him asleep," she said. "I don't think you'll find him there. I think he's going to hide himself in the nearest big Chinese city quarter. He thinks they'll be after him, not Dennis."

"So you think there's a First and a Second Murderer, do you?" asked Peter grimly. "The First Murderer killed Farnese, and the Second Murderer killed Bianca and Bowden, and skipped. Well, we'll see about that skipping part right now, anyway."

He went out, and Blake sat by the stove and shivered in spite of the fire until he returned, a few minutes later.

"Gone," he said, nodding his head in a heavy sort of gloomy satisfaction. "You're right about that, Blake. Hadn't slept in his bed, either." He shivered. "Gosh, it's bitter outside—that damp frost."

He took up a bit of rolled newspaper from the wood box and opened the lid of the stove to begin stoking again.

"Local paper," he said, talking idly to take Blake's mind off things. "News of all the county. Want to read? It's yesterday's. Here's a shipping column, from the Monterey Bay harbor. 'Among those in today from San Francisco—' let's see whom we know who has a boat in— Blake! Blake, do you remember Morgan? The guy on Dennis's hotel floor? His yacht *Margarita* came in yesterday. William Morgan, of the Hotel Ancaster. Must be him."

Peter gave a harsh croak of laughter. His hair was wild on his head; his eyes were deep storm blue.

"Among those present," he said grimly. "Do you get it, Blake? This man was in San Francisco when Bianca was killed—he was at Delroy when Bowden got his, in this county. He had access to those places. He's at home in Delroy. You've got competition for the post of Second Murderer. He might even be the First one, too, if our original theory holds. He was here tonight. You see, Blake, among those present tonight was also—the murderer!"

# XIV: BUT NOT FOR LOVE

Dennis was writing to Blake. He sat on the edge of his cot in his little cell in the Delroy jail, and put a blunt-pointed pencil to lined paper, industriously. The light

came in shyly from among piled-up gray clouds rapidly getting darker and grayer outside, in the early morning.

"Darling," wrote Dennis, dark head bowed closely over his inadequate tools, "do you wish me to be serious? At six o'clock on a cloudy November morning? I belong to a generation that would cheerfully die for you, but won't be serious for you. We aren't Hemingway's ' Lost Generation' of the war and post-war period, which was so deadly serious about everything, including the road to ruin. We're the generation after that, and we don't think they left anything that's worth taking so seriously. There's the third post-war generation coming up now, of course; my young brother and sister would belong to it, if I had them, it's about nineteen years old now and it's going back to the old ways. They believe in girls with long skirts and little shining topknots of hair done up on the backs of their necks, with a few silky straggles at the ears and the nape. They believe in love at first sight, and in lots of things that we thought died with the war, and the years afterward, and that perhaps didn't. Perhaps all those things are coming up again, like flowers out of fire-blackened ruins. Perhaps that young third generation's right, and things like that don't die . . . and radio tenors sing true things, about everlasting and extremely sentimental love. Wouldn't that be funny, if true? I'd have to revise my life, Blake. Or all that's left of it. It may be shorter than I think, at that. I had a talk with Sullivan this morning, earlier. Yes, Inspector Sullivan, of the homicide bureau. He was down here chasing a line on Father Malletti's disappearance, and naturally was interested in the recent events on my place. He seems to connect them.

"He came charging in with fire in his eyes and a shotgun in one large beefy hand, and I thought for a minute he was carrying out his own private economy program and was going to save the city the expense of a trial for me. Then he asked me if I recognized the gun, so I said, 'Sure, I recognize it. It's the one Wong uses to shoot jack rabbits and ground squirrels with. It's twelve-gauge, with a hand-carved walnut stock I made myself. It used to be mine.'

"'Sure you didn't borrow it?' he says, very quiet and sarcastic. 'And that it wasn't yours again—for an hour last night? I'm going to warn you anything you say can be used against you, Devore.'

"'Do you mean I'm under arrest?' I said.

"'I mean you'd better be careful what you say.'

"That was a fine incentive to open my heart to him! Peter would have been proud of the way his client clammed up on this occasion—I think he thinks I'm too talkative, anyway. I can see your large and laconic brother eyeing me with approval for once, Blake. My communication with Sullivan after that consisted chiefly of 'Yea, yea' and 'Nay, nay,' and not so much of them, either. I did unbend enough to inquire if this was to be my rather permanent address, so you'd know where to send mail to me, and it seems we are going up to San Francisco this morning (business as usual) for the inquest on Bianca, may she rest in peace, with Sullivan for my guard, and I'm not to be charged here until that's over. So we've got a few minutes of time, tell Peter. And tell him how funny it seems that time stretches out to hours and years sometimes, and then contracts to a few minutes, like an elastic band. It always seems to be doing that, lately. Most confusing. Since last night— (Last night? No, it must have been about a million years ago, Blake. And now I'm the last man on earth, remembering it, and you coming across the fields, and 'Drink to me only.' Surely you've forgotten?). Anyway, ask Peter if he remembers such a very long time ago. He'll be a famous judge yet. (That's in the future, and the future seems very close to me. Time has contracted again, and I can reach out and touch tomorrow with my fingers.) But he's getting some swell practice on my case! Everything seems to happen while I'm around, doesn't it?

"(Yes, that's what Sullivan commented on very freely this morning, around three o'clock. It seems he's been riding up and down this coast line on wild clues since yesterday, in a police car from San Francisco, and it hasn't improved his temper any. He knows I've got a manslaughter record here too, now—they can always identify me by a scar on my right wrist, and they did.)

"You know, I've been thinking about Father Malletti—and other things—all night. Do you remember I said that about 'an old man, going into darkness'? I nearly had the horrors last night, thinking of that and other things, and then I thought how that was wrong. It wasn't darkness, where he was. Father Malletti carries his own light with him, where he goes. So don't worry about that too much, Blake. I'm sure it's all right! I wish I could be as sure, about myself. Only I'm not exactly a saint.

"Sullivan'll come back soon, and then we'll go back to San Francisco in the police car. I'm writing this to keep from thinking of anything more after last night. Henry—the undersheriff here—has promised to smuggle this out to you. I told him he could read it first—he ought to, you know, being an officer. He doesn't say much, but he's a good guy. We used to play baseball and go swimming and hunting, before I went to college. We were in the same grades in grammar school and at Delroy High School.

"So now we're going to say good-bye to Bianca. She was beautiful, she reminded me of a gorgeous Venetian sunset painted by Turner in the '8o's. She was like a foreign country. But you, Blake, are like a picture by our own William Keith, of a California hillside by the sea, all tawny gold sand and orange poppies and deep blue lupin. You're home, to me.

"Dennis.

"P.S. Thanks for your note. Henry brought it to me. You're all wrong about Wong, you know. 'Men have died, from time to time, and worms have eaten them—but not for love.' I ought to know. Tell Peter—'Why don't you try this guy Morgan?' Adios.

"Dennis."

He looked up then at the swift first patter of rain outside the barred window and saw the darkened day.

# XV. THE BEAUTIFUL AND BLONDE

Blake and Peter sat at breakfast under the electric lights of the depressing Delroy hotel dining room at seven o'clock that same rainy morning. Blake was reading a letter, and Peter sat watching the landscape of her face where sun and windy clouds chased by changingly.

"Love letter?" he asked.

"Not nowadays," said Blake. "It's from Dennis, and he says I remind him of a William Keith painting of a field, and he calls me 'darling' once."

Peter shook his head.

"Nothing to that," he admitted. "You haven't got a case. What else does he say?"

"Dennis has discovered the Einsteinian theory of the relativity of time," Blake reported. "He says it's like a rubber elastic band."

"Does he, by any chance," Peter asked, "come down to current events?"

He looked up from his coffee to see Blake's blue eyes brimming deeply.

"He's going up to San Francisco with Inspector Sullivan," she said, trying to be casual about it. She helped herself to coffee. "They've started by now." Her voice went suddenly gruff on her. She took a too hot sip hastily. "He says you're mistaken about Wong, and to get onto Morgan as soon as you can."

"We will," said Peter, very satisfyingly solid about it. He sat back, thinking it over. "Blake," he said, "what about Dennis, anyway? Does he mean so much?"

Blake's eyes were two blue meadows, abloom with lupin.

"I used to have a picture of Dennis in his football uniform," she said simply. "I cut it out of the rotogravure part of the Sunday paper, and stuck it up in my mirror when I was in high school. I'd forgotten his name, but not him when I saw him."

"No!" said Peter, surprised. "I didn't know girls really did things like that."

"You'd be surprised," Blake said, grinning. "I'll bet there was many a damsel about my age or even in their later teens who had your picture, Peter, up in their mirrors. You looked keen with your football uniform on and your hair all mussed up, and your eyes frowning."

"No!" breathed Peter again, uneasily. "You don't say so!"

"I do say so," Blake retorted. "Don't be so bashful about your snapshots going into so many boudoirs, Peter. You and Dennis seem to have missed all this bleacher stuff—you must have played football for the fun of it. And what a lad Dennis is for getting his picture in the paper, isn't he? I don't wonder he didn't want to give Kennedy another shot at it. I suppose the papers simply spilled it all over their pages when he was on trial here for killing Farnese. Poor Dennis!"

"Sullivan knows," Peter said glumly. He set down his cup and eyed it with disfavor. " I don't mind drinking brown boots," he said mildly, "but I do draw the line at burnt rubber in my coffee. I loathe the taste of burnt rubber!"

He got up. His broad shoulders made the depressing little small-town dining room look littler and grayer than ever.

"Sullivan knows," he repeated, "that Dennis has a record here. That he's been going under a partly assumed name—Devore—instead of his own, whatever it is. That he's made the San Francisco police look more or less foolish by not yielding up all his information about his past to their first hurried vacuum-cleaning method. I don't blame him much for that—he thought he could get away with it, and maybe he would have, if *this* hadn't occurred just now. But with Bowden's killing, and the burning of the shack, the police have just that much more reason to suspect Dennis's holding out on them at first. Oh, I don't envy Dennis when Sullivan and the rest of them ask him frankly and fully for any stray bits of information they think he's still got up his sleeve!"

"What can *we* do?" Blake asked, pushing away her almost untouched cup of coffee. It may have been made partly of burnt rubber and brown boots, but it was tasteless to her.

Peter shrugged. He got into his overcoat and helped her into her brown tweed coat with the tall spiky fur Dennis had liked about her face. Only her cheeks weren't so fresh and pink now, nor her eyes so freshly blue. She was pale under her brownness, and her eyes were more deeply purple—blue, but older and tireder and bigger.

"What can we do?" Peter said. "Nothing much. I went to the jail before breakfast, Blake, and they wouldn't let me see him. Sullivan must have been in there then. Wait till the inquest's over—I can do more then, as his lawyer. He's in Sullivan's hands now."

Blake shivered and drew the fur up around her chin. "'Large beefy hands,'" she quoted distastefully. "Oh, Peter—you don't suppose—"

Peter laughed mirthlessly.

"Listen," he said. "I may not know much about Dennis, not even his last name, but I'm learning. Think of this, Blake—we've known him, man and boy, for just about forty-eight hours, or two days and nearly three nights, and already we've pretty well torn up our routine by the roots for him. We've chased down here to Delroy with him, we've gone man-hunting with him, and we've spent a nearly sleepless night over him. Kennedy's a police reporter, as tough-hearted as they make them, and he's bunked Dennis and kept his record from the police as long as he could. And, from the indications, his friend Henry at the jail here is running a free-delivery mail service for him, and I'll bet the sheriff's wife has probably cooked him a better

breakfast this morning than we got here at the hotel. No, I don't know what's going to happen to Dennis, but I wouldn't worry over him. I'd do all my worrying over his guardian angel, trying to keep up with him nowadays."

Blake smiled mistily.

"Peter, you *are* a dear," she said with conviction. She laid one brown-gloved hand on Peter's overcoat arm. "Where do we go from here?"

"To see Morgan and his yacht," said Peter staunchly, "before that guy can pull up his anchor and beat it back to the city. Let's go!"

They went.

By the time their car came into Monterey the sun was shining, and the marvelous blue bay, deeply blue as the sort of stuff in bluing bottles, and edged by a snowy line of white surf breaking on a white sand beach, lay incredibly lovely before them. Big white clouds sailed by in a blue sky. Smaller white yachts, slim and graceful, danced on the deep blue bay. A little gay wind ruffled the waters. It was the sort of day when nothing dark and terrible could happen. It made them, as a final magic, believe in it ... in spite of everything they knew.

They walked down past the old customhouse, and the old and mellow adobe houses left over from the Spanish California days, a hundred years and more ago. Time was gracious in this little sunlit city by the bay. A hundred years ago, *senor*, was only yesterday here. One slept in the sun, and when one awakened, the sun was as warm, the air as clear, the bay as blue, as— yesterday, under another flag and another people. *Vaya con Dios*, said Monterey softly, watching other cities rise to the skies, and foreign wars being fought, and airplanes landing on pontoons in its bay—and then turned over and slept again. It didn't really change. Blake felt it, too. Her eyes cleared, her face lightened, she gave a little joyful skip or two as they walked on down to the fishing pier and the white yachts.

"The *Margarita*?" Peter asked, of a brown-skinned fisherman.

The other pointed. "End o' the wharf, there. She come in yesterday morning."

Nets, brown like dried seaweed, were drying along the beach and the wharf. The pungent, salty scent of them with its reminiscent sardine smell clinging on, too, reminded them of seaweed brought home from its native element after a day's picnic, and hung proudly at first, then forlorn and forgotten, in their rooms when they were children, to be thrown out ignominiously at last. These scents had memory's dear and devastating power. They were by the sea again, and they were children again. . . . No, they weren't. They were Blake and Peter grown up, and their friend was in jail, and they were going to see a man they suspected of being a murderer. How did things happen that way, anyway? The bright blue-and-gold day clouded like sunshine threatened by dark storm clouds. Things turned out so differently from what you expected they'd be, when you grew up. Blake sighed.

Peter had halted before one of the slim white launches, tied up close to the wharf.

"Hello on board!" he boomed. "The Margar—"

A man's sunburnt blond head had popped up out of the companionway. Peter's voice died, then it picked up again to a roar.

"—Billy Morgan!" he shouted world-shakingly. "How in—"

The *Margarita's* owner showed more of himself. He was simply dressed in white duck pants and a white sweatshirt and a fine coat of brown skin. He stared at Peter from ingenuously frank blue eyes. The eyes wrinkled into a grin, that spread over his pleasant young sunburnt face.

"Hey, it's Pete Byrne!" he yelled back. He leaped out of the companionway to the deck, and thence clambered up to the wharf. He thumped Peter recklessly. "Hey, Pete! I haven't seen you since we left Stanford, you old sourdough! And you never looked me up afterward—I told you to. What's the idea?"

"Always meant to," mumbled Peter. He looked around a bit sheepishly, to find Morgan staring at Blake like a friendly pup waiting to be spoken to. "My sister, Blake," he muttered. Blake smiled. She'd been standing back, hands in her pockets, head on one side, gauging this affecting reunion of two old college pals. It seemed to be genuine. She was horribly disappointed, but she smiled generously, and young Morgan responded beautifully, like a friendly pup who's had the kind word thrown to him at last. He liked pretty girls. It was written on his admiring and extremely frank face.

"Your boat?" inquired Peter, going ahead grimly with his duty anyway. He eyed it stolidly, deep eyes steady. "Nice," he said. "Any objections—"

"Sure she's mine," said Billy Morgan. "She's a beauty, too. Came down from Frisco yesterday—just getting ready to pull out again this morning."

"I'd love to see it," said Blake softly.

She was surprised at the reaction she got. A red tide of hot crimson, red as a rose, swept over young Billy Morgan's face. His eyes went hotly bluer than ever with discomfort.

"I'd like to show you over," he said hurriedly. "Love to, Miss Byrne, but—you see, the old tub isn't quite in showing shape just now." His miserable eyes pleaded with her surprised cool ones. "I've just come down from the city in her, and—er—I'd love to show you over some other time. Will you? When I get back?"

"Of course," said Blake, holding him there. At the corner of her eye, beyond him, she saw Peter going into action. He dropped down lightly, for all his bulk, to the white holystoned hardwood deck, and from there addressed his involuntary host nonchalantly.

"You don't mind if *I* go over it?" he asked offhandedly and disappeared down the companionway to the cabin.

Billy Morgan, to Blake's secret surprise, seemed rather relieved at that. If she'd been he, and if he were hiding anything pertaining to Bianca's or Bowden's murders that he'd rather they didn't see, she wouldn't have taken a chance on Peter's passing it up. This man Morgan had been with Peter at Stanford, on the football squad with him—he should have known that Peter on attack was dangerously quick, even with his apparent rocklike stolidity. His mind worked quicker than most people thought it did. That was partly why he was dangerous to go up against, apart from the way he handled his bulk.

Meanwhile she chatted agreeably with the unsuspecting suspect, until Peter, a bit more flushed of face, came running up again to the deck and, jumping off again, made it to the wharf. Here he wrung his host's hand in his own large brown paw enthusiastically, accepted invitations for a visit and a yacht trip in the near future, swept Blake under his wing again, and beat it in an atmosphere of all-around good-fellowship.

"Well?" said a tense Blake, at the end of the wharf.

Peter leaned against a barrel and began to laugh.

"She is blonde and beautiful," he said, grinning. "What else did you expect her to be?"

"Was *that* why he wouldn't let me—"

Peter nodded. "She came down with Billy from San Francisco, and naturally it embarrassed the poor fellow—he's been raised right, Blake—when another fellow's sister was going to find her there."

Blake sighed. "Anyway, he didn't look like Dennis's 'devil.' What happened?"

"She's beautiful and blonde," reported Peter obediently, "and when I saw her I was struck dumb. She was in a blue satin wrapper sort of thing, and they'd been having breakfast there. Her hair was down over her shoulders, and her mouth was very red. She smiled at me. So I hissed at her, 'What's your name?' and she hissed back, 'June Oliver! I'm with the Honeyblossoms at the Columbia'—and she put out one delectable finger, all pink and pointed and shiny at the top, and put it to a ravishing red mouth and disappeared through a doorway, as we heard poor Billy's voice making valiant conversation above. She's bored with him already, I bet."

"So that's how it's done," mused Blake. "These girls have a great advantage over us. If any nice-looking male hissed at me, instead of hissing back my name and address I'd be obliged by a long line of scandalized Byrne ancestors to smack him down; or else you'd do it for me, I suppose. I've half a mind to join the chorus and see life."

"Yes, you will!" growled Peter.

Blake dropped the subject—for the time being.

"Well, what's Morgan like, really?" she demanded. "Apart from being a nice young man with a taste for chorus girls. Is he—could he be—our murderer?"

Peter shook his head positively.

"No chance," he said briefly. "I knew him when—and all that. He may have blondes in his past, but nothing else dangerous, I'll swear. You saw him, Blake. You can guess what he is. Father's head of a big stock company, Billy plays at the business, sort of ten-o'clock-to-three-o'clock hours with three hours off for lunch and the afternoon for golf stuff. He doesn't need to work, so he plays."

"You ought to know him," said Blake with a sigh. "You were a dear old college pal of his, if what I heard was true—or the half of it."

"Sure I was," said Peter, grinning again. "Sure he's a good guy."

"What do you think of him compared to Dennis? He's an old friend of yours, served a four-year stretch with you, and Dennis is a dear old pal of exactly two days' existence, as far as we are concerned with him. How does Dennis stack up with him? Would you back either of them as a murderer?"

Blake was a bit tense, but determined to see this through. She had to know.

"Morgan?" said Peter slowly, thinking this over. "He's a good guy. I told you that. How do I know if he'd be a murderer? I don't think it would ever occur to a guy like that that you could ever solve a problem, or have an out from a hard situation, by murder. He isn't conditioned to such violent responses to situations. Let me tell you, half of their living, with birds like Morgan, is being conditioned to things in a certain way —the conventional way. Dennis, on the other hand,"— Peter gave his slow, deep-eyed grin again—"Dennis, you might say, is a streak of lightning. I don't think anyone's ever thought of lightning as being conditioned to anything except lightning rods. Dennis's particular genius is that no one will ever quite know what Dennis will do in a particular situation. Not even Dennis. But I do think he's got a lightning rod somewhere around in his spirit that would keep him from murder."

"Peter, darling," said Blake softly, "sometimes you frighten me. You say things that are so extraordinarily true. The sort of thing that Dennis might say, just like that. Only you're not Dennis. You're not clever—but you're deep. You're what Dennis means when he says cleverness is such an overrated quality. He's talking about simplicity and depth—like a clear pool."

"Someone's been kidding you," said Peter, with that untroubled smile of his.

"So," said Blake, "we cross one more suspect off our list. Bowden, Bianca, Morgan, and Dennis says to cross off Wong. He says men don't die for love any more. Don't they? Maybe he's right, after all."

"I don't know about Wong, but we're right about Morgan, I'll tell you that," said Peter. "For one thing, he wouldn't have knifed a woman in the back."

"He might have," said Blake stubbornly. Peter shrugged.

"The *Margarita's* moving!" he said. "He's got the engine warmed up. I guess he's going to make the run back now."

They gazed at the slim white launch slipping off its moorings, edging slowly out from the pier, barely adrift in the crowded harbor.

Blake laughed suddenly. "Do you remember those rotten puns Dennis made?" she asked, a bit wistfully but with her eyes shining. "They were so terrible I liked them! I was thinking how true one of them was— the Morgan-Attic one. It did turn out to be that sort of a menage."

"He ought to be hung for them," Peter agreed, with a fatal absent-minded facility of phrase.

Then Blake broke down. For a terrible moment, tears reached as high as her heart. She couldn't help it.

She heard Peter's voice from a long way away, while she stood there drowning in that dreadful slow tide.

She stood there looking—not seeing anything—until her eyes caught the white *Margarita* as that shining thing put to sea, lightly as a feather floating on the blue water.

The tide receded. It might come again—would, she knew—like a sort of terrible awareness of what was happening, was going to happen, to Dennis, to herself, to life. But for the moment she was King Canute, and the wave *had* obeyed her.

She looked out to sea and grabbed Peter by the arm. The *Margarita* was curtsying to the harbor, putting about in a graceful arc of a gesture, her wake white-trained behind her. A woman was on the deck now, looking about her. Her gilt head was bright above a slimly wrapped heavy Spanish shawl, fringed and covered with embroidered red roses.

"Peter," said Blake, "look! She's wearing a shawl—a Spanish shawl!"

"What of it?" asked Peter, following that gay slim figure in the heavy silk with his leveled blue gaze.

"This!" said Blake huskily. "Don't you remember? Bianca had a shawl, too—and it was a white one, with red roses on it! He couldn't get rid of it—so he gave it to her to wear, thinking no one would connect him to it!"

"Lots of girls wear those kind of shawls," said Peter.

"White—with red roses?" asked Blake swiftly. "How come it's the same colors?"

"Listen," Peter said, "you may be right—they never found the shawl. But Morgan never gave it to this girl. You may be right about his being a murderer—Billy Morgan—and I may be wrong about that. He may have knifed Bianca. I don't know what devils a man may have in him; I don't think anyone really knows. But I am sure—I'm dead sure—that Morgan, even if he was a murderer, would never on this earth give another girl a shawl that he'd swiped from dead Bianca. I'll lay anything on that."

When Peter spoke like that, it was so. It had reached a far integrity inside him incorruptible as gold, unshakable and earthquake-proof as the center of the earth.

"But," said Peter grimly, "I practically made a date with her, and I'll get the truth out of her. I've got her name and theatrical company, and I'll look her up."

"Peter," Blake said suddenly, in a curious husky gasp, "of course! Don't you see it—her theatrical address? She's a member of the *Honeyblossom* company— and don't you remember, we found that among the people on Dennis's hotel corridor, right across the hall from his door, were a musical-comedy couple from the *Honeyblossom* company? These people were all—Dennis's neighbors that night."

# XVI. GOOD-BYE TO BIANCA

Morgan might or might not be a murderer; but Wong wasn't. Dennis knew that as unshakenly as ever Peter reached rock-bottom truth in himself.

Then where was Wong?

To Blake, in his note, Dennis made light of Wong's going; but he couldn't make light of it to himself. He sat in the back seat of the big police touring car, going up the peninsula highway to San Francisco at a sixty-mile clip, and he went over and over that in his mind. Sullivan sat beside him, twice as large as life in a big rough overcoat. Could he tell him about Wong? He didn't know. He might think—what Peter and Blake had already figured out. That Wong was a killer. Or that Dennis himself had put Wong up to killing Bowden, if not Bianca.

So Dennis sat a bit huddled, and silent, in his corner of the car and thought, "Where's Wong?"

Father Malletti had disappeared; now Wong had gone. Was there any connection? Had Wong gone willingly? Or had he gone—as Father Malletti had gone? He didn't know; but he'd have given five years of his life, or his good right arm, to know that Wong was all right. Dennis had stayed away from him for one forgetful-seeming year; he'd come back as casually as if it hadn't had much meaning for him, to be greeted by Wong again; but Blake had known, what Dennis now knew, that every Odysseus wants to find home unchanged when he comes back to it after one or many years. Dennis loved his place and all that was in it, though, like Odysseus, he'd been loving it at a distance, and he knew that Wong was his family. He didn't want him to be mixed up in murder. He wanted him in his proper place, wherever young master roamed and whatever he got mixed up in. And he wasn't in that place now. It was disturbing.

He could take care of himself and take what was coming to him, Dennis thought—but he couldn't take care of Wong. Darn families! They were the dickens of a responsibility. They took the half of your curse upon them, whether you wanted them to or not.

Only he couldn't quite still that queer ache in his heart.

So they came up the straight white road through the rain-clouded peninsula towns, past the Stanford fields, brown turning to a spring green in the November rains, past the tall avenue of eucalyptus trees at the deserted track of Tanforan, past the fields of the flower growers, the round hills of South San Francisco and the green graveyards there, into the wet gray streets and the gray hills of San Francisco, and the rain-washed purple violets and the dull burning of chrysanthemums on the corners under the big umbrellas, and the hurrying crowds, like the waves of the sea coming up from the foot of the shining gray streets.

Their siren cut through noise and traffic like the bow of a big liner through a choppy sea; they raced across the city in a shriek of sound that assaulted the populace as physically as ever the weight of their big dark touring car could.

Dennis saw blurred things he knew flash by—the clock on the corner as they crossed Third and Market, at Kennedy's place of business, the *Star* Building; slim copper-brown flash of Lotta's fountain, as they crossed the busiest corner in San Francisco, and the traffic held back for them on both sides; faces looking up, all along the sidewalk, startled, pale, seen and passed in a second; Kearny Street, the Hall of Justice tall and gray on their right-hand side; the Italian quarter beyond, as the hills began to climb to the north; the narrow gray hill streets, the gay-awninged restaurants, the children, brown-faced and beautiful, playing shrilly all along the streets, the fruit stores spilling over with bright oranges and red apples and bananas, lavish Florentine style—this was Bianca's country. Even the furtive little places with close-shut doors and blank windows, the soft-drink places, the pool parlors—these were Bianca's sort of things. She was a home-grown goddess, and the patroness of such places; the petty bootleggers as well as the gay restaurants flourished under the protection of her heavy-fringed shawl. Ceres for grain, the goddess of the harvest; but Bianca Farnese for red wine, the goddess of the grapes, Dennis thought, in California.

Her people were out to do her honor; it was more like the winter festival of the death of a goddess than a real funeral, Dennis thought. Perhaps it was incredible that Bianca could die, or that she wouldn't come again, in the spring, out of the hillside vineyards of Napa, out of the warm brown dust of the Santa Clara Valley, when the fruit trees were white in April like great sheets spread out over the brown earth. This was solemnity, but it wasn't really a funeral; it was a form.

Yet she'd been killed. Didn't any of these beautiful brown-faced children with the dark hair and the great dark eyes, didn't any of the bovine-eyed beautiful madonnas, the sleek fat men, the thin, keen men—didn't any of 'em know how Bianca died, by whose hand? Wasn't there a whisper of the murderer's name running through the quarter? It seemed incredible, incredible as Bianca's being dead, that they had no suspicion of her murderer. In a case like this, there were always whispers of names—among one's own people.

But none of them knew. If they had, they'd have told the police, in this one case. For Father Malletti was missing, and he was concerned in it, too. Dennis saw how quiet they were, standing in the streets, filling the street before the place where Bianca lay dead. He saw the storm-hush over them, and he knew then why it was that they weren't mourning Bianca more. For Father Malletti was missing. They were attending Bianca's funeral and her inquest, but they were thinking of Father Malletti. There would be women as beautiful as Bianca with every spring, and like pagan goddesses they might die with every winter, but Father Malletti and his faith didn't change with the seasons.

Dennis went up the steps between Sullivan and his partner Cassidy, and the crowd parted to let them go by. They walked into the overpowering sweetness of flowers, the sort of flowers that go with funerals—roses and carnations and lilies, too sweet and close. He had to breathe them in, like heavy perfume. There wasn't any other air in the place.

Dennis didn't like to see dead people. Yet he'd already seen two or three of them dead by violence, disordered, with the marks of their deaths on them. It wasn't as bad as now deliberately going to see the dead laid out in order. He found that he was shaking—little shivers of cold nervousness that ran over him like wind in the leaves of a slim aspen tree, never quite dying down to calm. This was worse than the first finding of her dead—because he knew what was coming. He was going to look at her again. The other time, he hadn't known—he'd just stepped in and found her lying there, the eyes open—now he had to do it all over again, deliberately. That terrible half-superstitious dread of the dead came over him again. It was like looking at creatures from another world. They were dead. Let them go in peace, without looking at them!

He stood with his head bowed a little, swayed, felt Sullivan's hand hard on his arm.

"Confession of guilt," he thought, dazed. "Murderer overcome by view of victim. I mustn't."

There'd be reporters here, police detectives, too—all watching him to see how he took it. Brace up, Dennis! Only—he'd had no sleep the night before, he'd kept seeing terrible things, and he was tired, and the heavy drenched air dazed him, sickened him with its sweetness. He was deeply afraid of death, of the dead, a primitive fear far inside of him.

But fear saved him. He was drugged by it. He moved forward dully, automatically, to the heap of flowers in the center of the expensively decorous, carpeted room. Guided by Sullivan's hand on his arm, he came to the side of the flowers, spilled in a rug of red and white over the casket, and raised his eyes and looked at dead Bianca's face.

There wasn't any shock. There was only, after a second, a sort of blessed relief. She was dead, but she wasn't—different. Her eyes were closed. But the beautiful lines of brow and cheek and chin remained, the lips were folded in marble calmness, her hair was as red as red gold. Was this what he'd feared? All the panoply of death, yes; all the paraphernalia and the majesty of death; he'd feared these. But the paraphernalia and the majesty of death led only to this—to sleep.

The utter peace of untroubled sleep was on that calm face. She wouldn't ever wake. She was done with them all.

Dennis looked at her fully, took leave of her, unhurried, at peace himself again. You couldn't be afraid —of her. He didn't know whether she was in a far country, or whether she had gone out for good like a light blown, out, but he knew that there was nothing to fear in what she had left behind her. She had no more use for it.

She had cast off beauty, the beauty of red hair and sea-blue eyes and a goddess's mouth, the beauty of a long white neck, of a walk that men remembered, a body like a goddess's braced against the wind—it was all here, like a shawl she'd never use again. She'd left it behind her. That was all.

Dennis sighed. It was all right. She'd gone. She had her peace.

Sullivan touched him. "Recognize her?"

"Oh, yes," Dennis said.

"That's all right then. We're through here."

He went away from that room in peace, wrapped in calm.

The coroner was holding his inquest in another sort of a room entirely—no thick gray carpets here, and rugs of red roses and white lilies, and suave attendants. The room was bare-floored, businesslike: long center table, chairs around it, other chairs lined up in rows for the jury and the spectators, a table for the press, windows dingy with the grime of officialdom's drabness.

They came in late. The inquest had begun. They had to push their way through the crowd before the door, and the room inside was crowded. The coroner's jury was in the row of chairs up front, the press table was jammed with men like the press box at a Big Game, Dennis thought fleetingly, and the witnesses sat around the center table with some lawyers. They couldn't be anything else. Lawyers! The word gave him a shock. Peter was more than twenty miles away—he was nearer two hundred, if he was still at Delroy or at Monterey Bay.

And the inquest might decide whether the police would hold his client or not.

Sullivan and Dennis emerged from the spectators like divers coming through the breakers. They came out at the center table. Sullivan began whispering to the coroner, after he'd put Dennis at a chair a bit apart from the other witnesses. The jury, a group of respectable-looking citizens, gazed at him with intense curiosity. The press table began whispering and writing furiously. Dennis felt fearfully and terribly conspicuous. Peter would have made a darned good windbreak then.

Sullivan came back and dropped heavily into the vacant chair between him and the rest of the witnesses and lawyers. The coroner, a small round man, partly bald, with a clever, round face, turned to the witness he'd been questioning in the stand. This was a fresh-faced young man, with very blue eyes and very sooty brows and lashes, and a very rugged sort of chin and tenderly humorous, cynical mouth. His cheap suit was all right, quiet and brown, and his tie was something terrible. Dennis liked him. He thought he knew him.

"Who's that?" he whispered hoarsely to Sullivan. "What're they doing?" Sullivan, he thought, might as well make himself useful as a guide as well as the guard for Dennis that he evidently was.

"Filling up time until we came," Sullivan informed him behind one huge hand. "He's taking all the hotel people now. That's the elevator chauffeur, Malloy."

In the jury row a motherly looking large matron gazed at Dennis with mingled emotions on her usually placid face. She felt that this dark-eyed and desperate, white-faced young man appealed to her natural kindliness—and yet she'd heard that he might be a criminal, and it was perplexing. You couldn't feel motherly toward a murderer, she thought.

"Er—Mr. Malloy," said the coroner dryly, "you've heard the testimony given by the clerk at your hotel. He says that Bianca Farnese—the deceased—came directly through the lobby to the elevator."

"Yes, sir."

"You were on duty at the elevator then?"

"Yes, sir."

"Did you notice the time then?"

"No, sir, but it must have been jist before twelve o'clock, I'd say."

"You can't fix a more definite time when you took the deceased up in your elevator?" the dry, precise voice persisted.

Dennis began to feel sweaty hot and then too cold. He knew that a lot hung on this question of time, not to make a pun of it, either. He didn't know how long it took to do a murder, but he knew the jury'd think it took several minutes at least to work up to an unpremeditated killing, a quarrel first, probably, and a bit of argument to heat the blood. Cold-blooded killing was different. That took a question of seconds. He knew, and Peter and Blake knew, that that was what had actually happened that night in his hotel room. It had been a cold-blooded killing. But the jury, and everybody else who thought Dennis might have done it, would think it had been preceded by enough argument to make it unpremeditated. A man didn't come home from a radio station and stab the woman he found in his room just like that. There had to be preliminaries.

Had there, in this case then, been time for those preliminaries between the coming of Dennis and the alarm he'd turned in? He fervently hoped not.

They were getting to it now, though.

Malloy couldn't fix the arrival of Bianca definitely, more than "jist before twelve, sir. The theayter and dancing crowds hadn't gone up from the ristaurants and hotel ballrooms yet, and they came around anywheres from twelve o'clock on. It was the quiet sort of time, sir, for the elevators, though the lobby was full."

"All right. You saw Bianca Farnese at the funeral parlors earlier this morning?"

"Y-yes, sir." Malloy moved his tough big hands in his lap. His eyes were dark.

Dennis thought, "He feels the same way about her as I do."

"Do you identify her—the deceased—as the same woman you took up in the elevator that night—three evenings ago—at about eleven forty-five?"

"Yes, sir!"

"You couldn't make a mistake from among a million women, with her," thought Dennis.

"What directions did she give you? Did she ask for any room number, or floor?"

"She jist said 'Fourth, please,'" Malloy remembered in a low voice.

"There was no further conversation between you?"

"No, sir. There was not."

"How was she dressed?"

"She had on one of them white shawl things, with her hair coming down to her shoulders," Malloy said.

"Did she wear any jewels?"

"Sure, she might have, sir. I wouldn't know," Malloy said in a troubled voice.

"Her hair was shining right in your eyes," thought Dennis. "You wouldn't have seen them if she had been wearing diamonds."

He rested his arm on the rather dusty oak table and regarded Malloy intently with his chin resting in the palm of his hand.

"Well, what happened then? Did you take her up to the fourth floor?"

"Of course," said Malloy a bit blankly, looking at the coroner with frank surprise. "Why wouldn't I?"

The shadow of a grin went around the room.

"I didn't think you'd take a guest to the basement if she asked for the fourth floor," explained the coroner a bit testily. His baldness turned a bit pink, too. "I'm asking you this merely for the purpose of the records. We must have a definite statement of events. Suppose you tell us just what happened when you took the deceased up to the fourth floor."

"I stopped the car, opened the door, and the lady got out," Malloy said. The big hands moved again, uneasily, in his lap. "That was all, sir."

"How long did you stay with the car up there after she got out?"

"Not a second, sir. I shut the door and went downstairs again—the light was on from the lobby."

"Did you notice anyone—anything unusual at all—in the hotel corridor as you opened the door for her, and in the time she took stepping from the car?"

"No, sir. There wasn't anything."

"Where was she when you went down again? Had she stopped in the hall, or had she kept on walking down the corridor, do you know?"

"She walked right off, sir. To the right. I could see that. She didn't have to stop at all to look around."

"You didn't notice any room doors open, or ajar? Were the lights in the hall on as usual?"

Malloy paused briefly, to answer both questions. He raised his dark blue eyes, sooty-lashed, in a level look at the waiting room.

"The doors were all shut, sir, as far as I could notice. The lights were on jist like they always were—are. The last I saw of her, she was going down the corridor, and I saw the back of her red hair and her white shawl going away down the hall."

Dennis caught his breath. It made a harsh sound like a rasp in his throat, and he hoped Sullivan and the others hadn't noticed. He couldn't help it. He thought somberly, "Down the hall—into darkness. Into—my room . . ."

That was the last anyone had seen of her—except the murderer. The red hair shining, and the slim white-shawled back, walking like a goddess—into darkness, in that soft-lit corridor.

The others hadn't noticed the sound he made. Only Malloy with his grave dark blue eyes looked at Dennis briefly, and the two of them held that look level for a second.

The coroner was asking, "Did you see what time it was when you got down to the lobby again?"

"No, sir. I did not. There was a party—a lady—could tell you—"

"We'll call her later. Let's get on with your testimony. You took the deceased up to the fourth floor, had no communication with her except the words 'Fourth floor, please,' and left her there walking away to the right-hand side corridor. Then you immediately brought the car down to the main floor level again, as you saw the light signal on your board. That right?"

"Yes, sir."

"No communication!" thought Dennis scornfully, of the little dry-voiced coroner. "You fool! She didn't have to say things to you. She stepped into that guy's elevator and out again, and he'll never forget her as long as he lives. There'll be a sort of brightness dazzling him all the rest of his life."

However, you couldn't say things like that to a coroner. Dennis sighed, and shifted his elbow more comfortably, and dug his chin in, and followed events closely.

They were coming to him now.

"You took these people up to the seventh floor," the coroner was repeating. "You passed the fourth floor twice, once coming up and once going down. Did you stop on the return trip going down?"

"No, sir, I did not."

"At any floor?"

"No, sir," Malloy said patiently.

"Did you hear or see anything on the fourth floor on either occasion you passed it?"

"No, sir."

"Or on any further trip you made?"

"No, sir."

It was like a patient litany, in a gray Celtic voice.

The coroner gave up.

"Well, we come to the arrival of the hotel guest in whose room the deceased was found," he commented. "At what time, Mr. Malloy, was it, should you say, that Mr. Devore entered the hotel lobby?"

"It was afther twelve o'clock a bit—more than a bit," Malloy answered, consideringly. "I'd say—around twelve-fifteen, sir."

"You've heard the testimony of the manager of Station KDO, the broadcasting station," the coroner reminded the jury and the interested room, "that Mr. Devore's program ended at twelve o'clock, and that he left promptly."

"Oh, my cat's whiskers," commented the equally interested Dennis gleefully to himself. "They had to drag that guy in. I bet he was about ripe for murder himself, being hauled away from the studio like that on a busy morning."

"Leaving the broadcasting studio, which is situated in the Market Street district," the coroner went on precisely, "and arriving at the Hotel Ancaster, on the hill district to the north of Market Street, would be a trip of about five minutes on a street car, or about fifteen minutes' uphill walk, that is, if the walker were a young man and brisk."

He shuffled papers for a second.

"That is, the times twelve o'clock at the broadcasting station and twelve-fifteen arrival at the hotel would agree, if Mr. Devore had walked from the studio. We have the hotel clerk's testimony, you'll remember, that it was actually 'some time' after twelve—that is, not directly after twelve—that Mr. Devore came in, although he didn't know the exact time. He did not stop at the desk for his key—he apparently had it with him. Mr. Malloy, will you tell us anything you remember about his arrival? Anything—you can think of?"

"You mean," Dennis thought grimly, "did I come in all wild-eyed and ready to kill any visitor I had."

Malloy didn't look at him.

"He come in—well, prompt," he replied, echoing the. manager of the studio unconsciously. "Like he always does—as if he was going places, and in a hurry."

"Indeed?" said the coroner. "What was his appearance? His clothes?"

"He didn't have a hat," Malloy said. The room leaned forward at that. It sounded promising—coming in in a hurry and without a hat on a foggy midnight. Malloy disappointed them, and so, to a degree, did Dennis.

"He hardly ever wears a hat," that honest young man informed them. "At least, I've never seen him with one, all the times I've took him up and down in the car."

"Was he wearing an overcoat?" the coroner asked.

"No, sir," Malloy said. "Sometimes he wears one and sometimes he don't, but he wasn't that night. That's why I thought he'd been walking, let alone the time he come in. He wasn't cold-looking, he was briskcolored like he'd been walking up the hills in the fog."

"That's why I walked," said Dennis to himself. "It was a swell way to get warm that night."

"All right. Then what happened?" The coroner made his favorite move again. "Tell us just what happened, what was said, everything."

"Well, Mr. Devore, he come—came—charging in like he does, and walked across the lobby, and into the car. There were two others, a couple, came in then, and I took them all up together. They got off at the third, and he went on to his floor, and just said 'Thanks' when I opened the door for him to get out there. He walked off down the right-hand side of the corridor, to his room, I guess."

"Oh, yes," thought Dennis. "It was—to my room, all right."

He wanted to bury his head in his hands at that memory. He'd been feeling swell, a sitting-on-top-of-the-world sort of feeling that comes to brisk young men who've been walking up San Francisco hills at midnight in the fog and lights and sounds of a city in their eyes and ears, and then he'd opened the door of his room—onto darkness and murder and nightmare happenings. He wanted to bury his head in his hands and shut it all out. He couldn't. He sat there with his eyes dark, no reflections at all in them.

There was the slight stir of concluding testimony through the crowded room—a shuffle of movement, a murmur of whispers.

"Er—one moment, Mr. Malloy," said the coroner, looking up dryly as the witness moved tentatively, too. "One more question: Do you recognize Mr. Devore from among those in the room now?"

Malloy's deep Irish eyes rested on Dennis for a second.

"Sure I do," he said. "That's Mr. Devore there," and he half pointed at him. The room made that stir again, as everyone turned to look in Dennis's direction.

He stood up, automatically. The coroner seemed to expect it of him. He felt like Exhibit A being shown off.

"Is Mr. Devore wearing the same suit he was wearing three nights ago, when he came into the hotel just after twelve o'clock, can you tell me?" the coroner asked hopefully.

"I think so, sir," Malloy answered conservatively.

He looked at it intently. Dennis looked down at it fondly. He liked that suit. He'd paid a lot more for it than he should have, and it didn't look aggressively expensive, and it stood up under hard wear like a thoroughbred. It was dark, almost black stuff, but with a little pattern of white running through it like light on a black night. It had been his constant companion these past three days and nights, too—he'd gone to two jails in it, gone man-hunting in it, he hadn't had it off him now since he'd dressed at Kennedy's and borrowed shorts and socks and things from that elephant-memoried gentleman yesterday morning, and it was still good enough to stand the gaze of the coroner's jury and the spectators. He loved it. He always felt for it as a man does who has paid more than he should have paid for a good dog or any thoroughbred who is worth the money—that he'd got a lot more than his money out of it.

So Dennis looked down at it fondly, and the coroner's jury and the crowd and the press table looked at it with more varied emotions, among them fascinated horror. This might be . . .

"Looking for bloodstains," Dennis thought. "I suppose they'll call it the 'death suit.'"

"Thank you, Mr. Malloy," said the coroner now. "That will do."

There was the slight stir, more decisive now, of a concluding witness. Malloy stepped down and came to the long oak table and dropped down heavily at his chair up near the front. The hotel clerk, a dapper gentleman who, Dennis had always felt, should have been a radio announcer, got up when his name was called again, went up and was sworn in again and briefly asked the same questions that had preceded Malloy's dismissal.

"Do you recognize the man who came into the lobby at a few minutes after twelve that night?" He did, and pointed Dennis out, by name.

"Is he, do you know, wearing the same suit he was wearing when you saw him come in that night at that time?" The hotel clerk thought he was. He hadn't noticed him especially. Thank you, that was all. He stepped down, dapperly.

## XVII. DANGER NEARER TO DENNIS

They called the lady who'd looked at her little diamond-set wrist watch as the elevator with Malloy and Bianca in it had reached the fourth floor that night. She was slim and cool and blonde and very well dressed, with nice make-up, a small blue hat, a tailored dark blue suit, and a brown fur that even Dennis thought might be a couple of sables around her shoulders.

"And what time was it, Mrs. Armstrong, when you looked at your watch that night?"

"It was—just—three minutes of twelve."

Her voice was cool and low and somehow amusedly detached in spite of its levelness. She didn't look at Dennis all the while she was on the witness stand. She carried her good manners and her breeding into even the distasteful duty of an inquest on murder, and she extended her manners even to a person suspected of that murder. Dennis wanted to thank her for that.

The coroner did, but not for that. He thanked her for adding another link to the evidence which might form a chain to snap around Dennis or around some "person unknown."

"Thank you, Mrs. Armstrong."

"Not at all."

She stepped down and sat quietly at her place again, gloved hand against her chin, listening.

"Madam Chairman," thought Dennis. "Or Madam President. She'd listened to meetings a lot."

They called the hotel manager next.

Dennis didn't know much about him, except that his name was Fersen, he was a Swiss of some sort, and he didn't have any use for Dennis at all.

Dennis didn't blame him much for that last. No hotel manager wants to see his hotel in the papers with an "X Marks the Spot" caption on it.

He was a rather pleasant-looking sort of man, brown done in tones of autumn coloring—face a bit full, but nice easy smile, brown well-brushed hair with a mere hint of red in it, brown shining eyes with a bit more red in them, figure square and very well dressed, square hands that he occasionally used to gesture with. A man who wanted to be pleasant, ordinarily—to get along with people. Yet a man accustomed to getting his own way, to being a bit of a disciplinarian, as a good hotel manager had to be. He could be, as Dennis had found out, brusque.

"You know this man—Devore?" the coroner asked as a form of beginning, indicating Dennis.

"I know him—yes," Fersen said guardedly.

"As a guest of your hotel?"

"He was." The answer was brief but somehow pretty comprehensive.

It sounded, thought Dennis uneasily, as if he hadn't quite realized what he was implying. It sounded as if he'd fired Dennis out of the hotel, wouldn't have him on any terms—as if he'd found out something about him—murder, maybe.

"He isn't there now?" the coroner followed that up quickly.

"I haven't seen Mr. Devore," the hotel manager stated distinctly, "since the night—the body of Mrs. Farnese was found in his room. He apparently hasn't returned to claim his luggage or any personal belongings awaiting him."

That was that. It did sound bad.

"He thinks I was scared to come back to a place where I'd killed a woman," thought Dennis resentfully. "He knows better than that! I didn't kill her! Only—he's making everyone else think that, on purpose. Why?"

It wasn't tangible. Nothing definite. The man was answering questions—yes, and truthfully. It was only in the way he was answering them—giving Dennis the worst kind of breaks, the worst implications.

It wasn't only unfriendliness: he was being deliberately nasty about it, in his pleasant way. The very way he said "Mr. Devore" in quotes was a sort of sneer. He didn't believe in the name, and he made everyone else see that Dennis had a last name that sounded like a chorus boy's dream.

He told of the hotel's brief but too lasting relations with Dennis. Mr. Devore had come in about three months ago—he didn't say from where, or if anyone had recommended the hotel to him. He'd registered from Los Angeles. That wasn't a crime in itself, of course, but unidentified lone gentlemen with pasts might very well come from Los Angeles. Every San Franciscan in the coroner's room knew that the best murders of past years had, in fact, taken place in Los Angeles. Even New York columnists had commented on it. A round half a dozen could come to mind—the Phillips hammer murder, the terrible Hickman crime, the chicken-farm murders, Mrs. Patty's killing, whose murderer is still being hunted—oh, there was quite a list to choose from. And Los Angeles was a swell place to come from if you had to come from somewhere, so to speak. In that big, sprawling, tourist center of a city, trails and the beginnings of trails might be conveniently lost and never traced back.

Mr.—er—Devore, in fact, had conveniently come from Los Angeles out of nowhere, with no friends, and had established himself at the Ancaster with no further recommendations. They all got that.

They were meant to get it, Dennis discovered in a helpless anger. It was put that way deliberately. Good Lord, did this man, this respectable man, hate him, the unrespectable, so much? It was like a class war. He knew why I.W.W.'s went blind with rage and surged to burn and destroy. It was a helpless feeling, seeing society, respectable society, down on you like that. It was the anger of the cornered.

They were told further about Mr. Devore. In strict answer to the questions put by the coroner, the hotel manager told them that he had no friends visiting him, that he paid his bills promptly, gave extremely little trouble—"sitting quiet because he didn't want to be noticed" was the version Dennis gave this, with the courtroom following suit—and that he hadn't been seen with any woman. This was given reluctantly, though honestly, and everyone got the reservation in Fersen's mind, that just because he hadn't been seen with any woman at his hotel didn't mean he didn't know any. He probably wanted to keep his woman friends out of the hotel to avoid talk about him there. He sure kept to himself in his room there, eh? Not exactly hiding—just "giving no trouble" to the hotel staff. Unobtrusive.

They went into the events of the night of the murder. The hotel manager acknowledged that he'd heard that Dennis sang over the radio. He hadn't heard him himself, he believed. He'd just heard that was what Mr. Devore did. He hadn't seen him come in that night, either. The office, where he was working late that evening, was on the ground floor of the hotel, but on a back corridor, away from the lobby and public dining and ball rooms. It was accessible to the kitchens and the chefs offices and the hotel garage, which were in the basement, and connected of course with all departments of the hotel by telephone through the switchboard in the lobby. It also had a back stairs near it, and a service elevator.

"You didn't see either Mr. Devore or the deceased—Bianca Farnese—enter or leave the hotel then, Mr. Fersen?"

"No."

"Could you tell us about when you were in your office that evening—the approximate times?"

"I was working there from about eleven o'clock on— until I was interrupted by news of what had happened on the fourth floor."

"Did you leave the office for any extended time during that time— between eleven o'clock and, let us say, the interruption?" the coroner asked briskly.

A slow red began to creep up the well-fleshed cheeks of the hotel manager. His hands fiddled a second with each other, then one of them began to turn a solid signet ring around his third left finger. The coroner hastened to turn away any coming signs of a storm.

"I'm asking this," he explained precisely, "in order to get everyone's action quite clearly set out during that evening—everyone of whom we have any definite knowledge, or whose actions might interest or influence the murderer. If, for instance, you had left your office open during quite a period of time, might not someone have passed unseen by your hallway, taken the service elevator or even the stairs, to the fourth floor, and there committed the killing?"

The hotel manager quieted down at this.

"He's a hot-tempered bird," diagnosed Dennis. "Not used to having to explain himself or what he does."

"I see," he was saying more graciously. He smiled, that easy and, in other circumstances to Dennis, rather charming smile. He was making himself pleasant. He unbent to explain:

"I didn't, at any time during that evening, leave the office for a long period of time. Twice I stepped into the lobby, once in response to a telephone call from the desk clerk to meet a friend and greet him, once to listen to the music from the dining room. Anyone who used the corridor to my office would have had to pass me then. No one did."

"Thank you, Mr. Fersen. How about someone coming up from the basement offices to use the back elevator or the stairs?"

"It's impossible for a guest of the hotel"—those brown eyes with the red shining in them lit on Dennis briefly for a second—"to wander into the basement unnoticed. Any stranger would have been seen at once."

"There are only two ways to get to these stairs and the elevators, I understand from the chart of the hotel —by the corridor running past your offices on the ground floor, and by entering them at the basement level?"

"That is so. And one other way. You could enter them from the higher floors."

"You suggest?"

"I don't suggest anything." The hotel manager spread those hands of his briefly in depreciation. "But it has occurred to me that one might get off from the front elevator at some floor—say the second, the seventh, any of them—and walk the length of the hotel to use, not the service elevator which is run by an employee, but the service stairs, in order to go up—or down—as he chooses, unnoticed. It would be less conspicuous than using the front stairs, which are for guests and are more likely to be noticed."

The coroner digested this for a moment. Then:

"You said 'down,'" he pointed out. "Do you think anyone, on the night of the murder, used those stairs to go—down, from Mr. Devore's room on the fourth floor? He would have had to go, assuming he was a guest and not an employee of the hotel, past your office to reach the lobby. You have pointed out that the basement descent would have been too perilous for a stranger or one obviously out of place there."

The hotel manager shrugged—a pleasant shrug.

"I don't know," he pointed out in his turn. "It's too mysterious for me to say that."

"He's got something up his sleeve," Dennis thought to himself, watching that well-tailored part of his clothing instinctively. "Wonder what it is."

The coroner went back to events instead of surmises.

But for a second Dennis didn't hear what he was asking. He was sick and cold with a wave of sudden fear that had swept over him. He knew what the hotel manager had been doing, what he'd had up his sleeve. The whole room had known. He had cut anyone—anyone not a recognized employee of his hotel—off from using the back elevator and the service stairs. The murderer had gone up—must have gone up—by way of the lobby and the front elevators, in full view of anyone there.

Dennis had gone up like that.

There wasn't, it seemed, any "unknown" in this case who could have slipped in conveniently.

A hotel, even a crowded popular one, was like a safe. It was pretty well guarded at its strategic points, under a casual exterior of smooth service.

That put it up to Dennis. He'd gone up to his room and then said he'd found a murdered woman in it. Had he had time to do the killing? He hadn't done it *before* he left for the radio station—Bianca, according to most competent witnesses, had come in at about five minutes to twelve. Dennis had been in the radio station then. That ran like clockwork. No question of false time there. Bianca had been walking along the corridor to Dennis's room then. Malloy had been bringing the elevator down to the lobby. Well. . .

That left the problem of time and Dennis to the period *after* he'd left the station. Bianca'd been in his room all that time. Waiting for him? He knew she'd been killed then. But no one else—no one except the murderer—knew that. She might have been waiting for him. He came back, and it was about fifteen minutes past twelve, and she was dead. Somewhere in that time it had been done—it had taken only a minute or two. But no one knew that, except Dennis and the murderer. Even his friends didn't know that. They just took it on faith. . . .

Dennis's eyes darkened there, thinking a second of Peter and Blake—and of Kennedy. He wished Peter could have been here with him. It wasn't any use wishing that, though. And at that, it was a pretty selfish wish. Peter might not want to be standing by with a suspected murderer in the full light of an inquest. It was asking a lot.

Well, then (his thoughts scurried briefly like mice surprised in the dark by a light flashing on them), Bianca had been dead at twelve-fifteen, even if only he and the murderer knew that. What time had Dennis come up to his room, and what time was it that he'd phoned for the police? It sort of hung on that, he thought.

He wasn't counting on anyone's malignity to corner him there especially. He'd underrated the contemptuous hatred felt by one sort of man for another, a different type—the hatred of the respectable for the patently unrespectable artist, the substantial for the unsubstantial, the man of property for the man to whom property was something binding, who didn't, deliberately, want any ties like that.

He'd underrated the hotel manager.

The coroner asked the hotel manager:

"Mr. Fersen, you were, you say, in your office when the telephone girl from the public switchboard rang for you. Will you tell us just what was said in that call, and what time you received it?"

"I don't know," Fersen said deliberately, "that I can put an exact time to it. Doubtless, as it went to the police station, the police noted the time, I should say. however, it was about twenty-five minutes past twelve that the telephone girl notified me that Mr. Devore had put in a call for the Central Police Station, and that he seemed to be having some trouble in making his meaning clear to the officer answering."

The room sort of rose in a whisper of sound, like a wind getting up among trees.

"Er—we'll go into that message more exactly," said the coroner. "Twenty-five minutes past twelve, you said? Thank you!"

"Satisfied," thought Dennis a bit dully. "They all are. Was it that late when I phoned? Must have been. I must have just stood there, looking at her . . ."

He remembered, from a long, long way off, how it had been that night. He'd held onto the edge of the table and gone 'way under for a while. Then he'd thought of telling someone—the police. Then he'd got onto himself and made himself walk across the room, away from Bianca's body, conscious of it—at his back. It must have been around that time that he finally phoned, and got through to that deep-voiced, question-asking officer. Then he'd stammered it out—there was someone dead here, in his room—at the Ancaster—how'd he know what it was about? She was dead— maybe he'd said "murdered," but, funny, he didn't remember that, quite.

Anyway, the hotel manager was saying that. The phone girl had told him that Mr. Devore was ringing up the police and claiming that battle, murder, and sudden death were prevalent in his room. She'd immediately rung up the manager and told him. The manager's instinctive reaction had been to safeguard the good name of his hotel. He'd wondered about calling the hotel physician, decided against it until he knew more about just what had happened, he'd gone up by the service elevator run by a hotel employee, and left that interested man at Dennis's door while he knocked on it, wondered at the silence behind it, and in a sudden spurt of unease had thrust his passkey into the lock and had opened the door—on Dennis and Bianca's corpse, there on the floor.

"What did Mr. Devore have to say about this discovery?" asked the coroner keenly.

"Why—he didn't say much, as I remember it now," Fersen hesitated. "He seemed—dazed."

"Dazed, eh?" Everyone looked at Dennis, dark head bent a little, gaze on his hands locked idly together, lips set tight.

"Why wouldn't I be?" thought Dennis furiously. "D'you think I see murder's work every day? It's your callous guy you ought to suspect, not the man who's bowled over by a glimpse of the body."

"Then what happened?"

"Mr. Devore began to tell me—to protest—that he'd never seen the woman—the deceased—in his life before," Fersen said smoothly. Too smoothly. The coroner's jury and the crowd caught it. There was a little whispering sound like a laugh going over the room. It was—funny, at that, maybe. My Most Embarrassing Moment! He'd found a strange woman in his room, murdered. It didn't sound true, somehow. A protest seemed faintly farcical. Sure, he must have known her.

The hotel manager obviously hadn't believed Dennis, and he'd made the room see the impossible side of the crime—that Dennis hadn't known Bianca, even as a casual acquaintance. It didn't sound true, told like that. It sounded as if Dennis had just lost his head then and had protested too much. If he'd come out and said it was an accident—or that they'd both been drinking—or that they'd had a scuffle . . .

Only he hadn't. He'd tried to get out of it, to hush it up. Dennis saw the coroner and his jury and the whole room going away from him, its belief or sympathy or even will to comprehension withdrawing like a tide that left him stranded there. He felt defenseless and very lonely, rather like a mussel left exposed at low tide.

He bent his head and stared studiously at the lower knuckle of the third finger of his left hand. He knew without looking about him what was going on. Sullivan was shifting his heavy bulk in the chair next to him, preparatory to taking the witness stand soon. The motherly-looking lady juror with the placid face and the comfortable width had decided that he was a murderer—that white-faced, desperate young man, poor thing!—and was staring at him with interest and repulsion mingled in her kindly, rather faded blue eyes. The hotel manager Fersen, having done his duty nobly by the city and by his hotel, was stepping down jauntily, sure that everyone knew that the Ancaster had cast out Dennis even before the police had decided to take him in among themselves.

The coroner decided to go catch minnows for bait for a while, and the bigger fellows could lie unmolested on the bottom of the stream with their tails waving gently, facing upstream in position. He called the service elevator man who'd accompanied Fersen upstairs to Dennis's door. That obviously thrilled person, exhilarated by his brief contact with the live wires of a murder case, gave negative information. He'd taken no one up or down that evening except a few employees, all of whom had accounted for every minute of their time and their errands to the manager. He'd seen no one around the corridor on Dennis's floor while he waited outside until the police came. The telephone girl came, red-lipped, blonde-haired, furred, a good deal like a hotel guest— a good imitation, Dennis thought.

No, she hadn't had a call from Dennis's room all evening except— the murder call. Her voice dropped. The room swayed forward.

"Murder?" emphasized the little round coroner. His eyes were very keen behind his spectacles. He wasn't a fool, Dennis realized. He was a clever man.

"Cleverness," thought Dennis forlornly, "may be awfully overrated and a surface quality, but it sure does count, Peter. He may be able to get your client hanged on it, regardless of any deeper superiority you and I may possess."

That would be a joke on—Peter, he decided.

"Well," said the telephone girl, "he asked for the police, and when I got the police and plugged him in through the outside board he began saying there was a dead woman in his room, and would they come around right away."

"And?" prompted the coroner, head poised like a bird—a rather choosy bird selecting his worm.

"And they said they would," said the telephone girl simply.

There was a subdued snort through the room. The coroner's bald spot got pinkish again.

"I mean—what further conversation did Mr. Devore have with the police about this dead woman—did he say, actually, that she'd been killed, or murdered, or did he make any reference as to who she was?" the coroner said brittlely.

The telephone girl got brisk, too. It was the sort of manner she assumed with too impatient customers, Dennis thought.

"No, he didn't," she said a bit snippily. "He said— she was dead. She'd been killed in his room, and he'd found her there. And for them to come at once. So they did."

"Very well," said the coroner. He couldn't ask too leading questions of the witness, of course. He couldn't say suggestively, "Did he actually say she'd been killed with a knife wound in her back, done with a kitchen knife at exactly seventeen and a half minutes past twelve, by one Dennis Devore?"

He'd already tried to lead her to suggest that Dennis knew the woman was murdered as soon as he saw her. That he had accidentally shown too much knowledge of it over the phone. The hotel manager had sort of backed him up in that. But the telephone girl had on the whole thrown him down on it. And she'd had the first-hand knowledge of the call.

She'd plugged in for the hotel manager, gasped out a story that had sent him upstairs, and—that was all she knew until the police came. She hadn't taken the time of the call.

"I bet the rest of the Ancaster got rotten phone service during those minutes," Dennis decided.

A uniformed policeman took the stand, his blue and silver spick-and-span in that rather grimy room. He had a broad face rather rarely done in pink, and a deep voice that Dennis found reminiscent. It was the sort of official voice he'd often found in policemen, especially ones with rarely done reddish broad faces.

They'd met before—over the telephone. At exactly—lemme see— twelve twenty-three p. m. on the night of the murder.

The coroner encouraged him gently. The policeman fixed his hard-boiled small blue eyes on a distant target at the other end of the room and fired words at it.

"I was on duty at the switchboard, sir, and took the call from the Hotel Ancaster. I made a note of the time when I had done so. The call was from a Mr. Dennis Devore, and asked the police to come to the hotel at once as there was a dead woman in his room. There was nothing said of killing or murder at the time by Mr. Devore." The cop took a breath and went on: "I then asked Mr. Devore what had happened. He said he didn't know. He had found the deceased there when he came home."

"Er—thank you, officer."

"I then notified the detective bureau, and Inspectors Sullivan and Cassidy, homicide squad, answered the call."

"Thank you, that'll do."

Inspector Sullivan was called next. He got up, leaving the seat next to Dennis empty, and a few more people got a good look at Dennis. Inspector Sullivan's testimony, given in a quiet voice, was depressingly familiar to Dennis. It was becoming as familiar, that story, as the well-known linked chain of his leash is to a dog. And it was closing around his neck. There'd been no one up there, around his floor and in his corridor, who hadn't had a right to be there, it seemed. There'd been nothing suspicious. Only Bianca going into his room, and Dennis calling the police. That left it up to him. Circumstantial evidence? Of course, but what else was there in this case? There was Father Malletti's disappearance, and the murder of Bowden, the "honest plowman." Murdered near Dennis's ranch, at the time when Dennis was alone near there, with a grudge against him, and with his own gun handy. There was Dennis's former record, concealed from the police.

"A bad habit—finding bodies," thought Dennis, shielding one side of his face with his hand. "They'll hold me, sure. All that about Bowden and the rest'll come out at this inquest. The police don't care if they do tip their hand all at once. They've got me, haven't they? They should worry about the surprise element. It'll all come out, and then the jury'll turn in a verdict mentioning me as recommended for further investigation, and they'll hold me. And the murderer's going loose and laughing somewhere. While Bianca's being buried. At that, I can't blame the jury. That's three killings I've already been mixed up in—Farnese's, Bianca's, and Bowden's. Three strikes and you're out, in any man's league."

He sat up suddenly, dropping his hand away from his face, at hearing the last question from the little coroner:

"Have the police, Inspector Sullivan, found out anything bearing—or that might bear—on the murder of Bianca Farnese in any events or acquaintances of her life?"

"She was a home-grown goddess," Kennedy had said. "Statue of Liberty of North Beach."

She was Bianca Farnese, from a rather bloody and gorgeous sort of fairy tale.

She had been the patroness of gay restaurants and little furtive bootlegging parlors.

Many men must have loved her.

There wasn't one of them that had come forward to say anything that might give up her murderer; there wasn't a restaurant where she'd danced and given her patronage that could tell of her true loves and hates. She'd been seen with this man and that man; she had lived in an apartment near Powell Street, on Nob Hill; she had had a pretty good bank account in the savings department of a big national bank; she might have been a light-o'-love, but to most people she had been more like a lighthouse that flashed its beams in their face, blinding them to anything behind that blazing light of her beauty, her vitality, her generousness.

Now that she was dead, that blinding, powerful light flashed off, a lot of people had scurried for cover like beetles seeking the friendly dark of an under-stone, before the fiercer light of publicity and the police would be flashed on them. Already some of their letters had been recovered, and frankly indignant and terribly respectable gentlemen had had to explain pettishly that she had been only a "friend." The letters may have mentioned money. Well, they had "loaned" Mrs. Farnese some money once when she was ill, and she had asked for it. The letters may have mentioned appointments. Yes, these suddenly frank gentlemen had replied, wiping their foreheads, Mrs. Farnese had wished to consult them about buying bonds, and had written to make an appointment at so-and-so's restaurant so they wouldn't be interrupted in their business talk. Or they had gone home with her after dinner for a cup of coffee and a quiet business talk. The city chuckled, and the police, after a long hard stare at the victims, had reluctantly given up most of the clues of the letters. None of these scared and reluctant gentlemen, dragged so painfully to light as "friends" of Mrs. Farnese, had had anything to do with her murder, they decided. Some of them had alibis, and some of them had acquired wives since their acquaintanceship with Bianca, and some of them, just plainly, weren't murderers. They were gay young men who could have afforded Bianca a lot more than they relished the publicity attending her murder.

"There wasn't," as Sullivan explained to the rather mirthful room hearing these primly official disclosures, "a murderer among them. We made sure of that."

There was a deep disgust in his voice.

"You suggest, then," said the coroner, "that although there were undoubtedly many men in Mrs. Farnese's life, there was no one affair serious enough to cause her killing?"

"I do that," said Sullivan stoutly. "She may have played some of her men friends for easy marks, but the ones she played around with could afford it. And there was no suggestion of blackmailing any of them, in any of the letters they wrote her. It was, on both sides, I should say, a casual sort of affair, a companionship more than usual in such cases."

"Friends with her victims," thought Dennis, eyes shining. "Oh, clever Bianca! She rooked 'em, and they loved it. She was civilized, and she picked civilized men for her sort. All except one. One was a wild beast in her civilized kingdom. One of them killed her. He pretended to love her—maybe he did love her. Only she found out about Farnese, and so he killed her. He didn't play the same game or the same rules as the rest. He was wild, under all his pretense of being civilized."

"Then, Inspector," the little coroner said, "can't you give us any information from Mrs. Farnese's life that might lead to a suggestion of who her murderer was?"

"The police are still investigating Mrs. Farnese's life,"—Sullivan on the witness stand crossed his knees comfortably and went on blandly— "but we have no information as yet to make public—except this: that the man who killed her probably wasn't in the limelight at any time while she lived, as a friend of hers. Otherwise he wouldn't have dared to kill her and think he could get away with it like that. He must have known that every acquaintance and incident of her life would be dragged up by the police after her death, and anyone unquestionably linked with her would be subject to a thorough questioning, if not being put actually under suspicion of the murder. For that reason, then," Sullivan took a deep breath and continued his speech, "we are inclined to think he was someone who has, so far, kept his connection with her a secret. None of the men we've questioned as friends of hers, according to the letters they wrote her, fill the bill in points of time, place, and other circumstances of the killing. Also they've been questioned by the police as to their relations with Mrs. Farnese, which questioning usually brings complete results," said Sullivan dryly. "It's only occasionally the police don't find out the whole truth of a man's story in their questioning."

His eye lit on Dennis for a moment, in passing. Was there—could there be—a sort of flicker of light deep in their small dark depths, like a passing signal? It had never occurred to Dennis before that Sullivan might be a kind of sportsman, feeling a sort of unprejudiced admiration for anyone who could beat him at his own game. But then, reflected Dennis philosophically, Sullivan could afford to feel that kind of admiration—he had, after all, finally hooked Dennis. It was easy to be a sportsman if you were on the winning side. You felt large and generous toward your opponent then.

It would be, anyway, in a split second now, Sullivan's inning. Because Sullivan's statement had put it entirely onto some "unknown," and the whole room knew that Dennis had strenuously denied any acquaintanceship whatever with Bianca Farnese. There couldn't be a more dark unknown in anyone's life than a man who protested he'd never seen the woman in his life before until the time she was found dead in his room. The more Dennis made that statement stick, the more, paradoxically, would he be under suspicion of her murder. He would fulfill Sullivan's sketch of the "unknown" then, to perfection.

Sullivan stepped down from the stand. Dennis was going to testify next.

The coroner was calling out his name.

Dennis felt the way he'd felt only once before in his comparatively carefree life—once when he was in an airplane and the darned thing had suddenly gone wonky, off balance, and begun to stagger and flounder wildly around in the blue air, about five thousand feet up; and the pilot, a friend of his, had pointed with a grin to Dennis's strapped-on parachute and then to the terrible emptiness below, which was coming up rapidly to meet them. He'd known fear then, the dreadful cold fear of utter cowardice, forced to walk off" like that onto nothing. His friend was waiting for him to jump, before he'd leave the plane himself; and he had to do it, by himself. It wasn't so bad, once he'd jumped. It was the decision over himself first that took strength. He'd thought then that if he won over the feat that weakened his physical self to the stuff of water he'd never know such fear again in all his life. It didn't come twice, that sort of thing. He'd be over it, having conquered it once. Once he'd jumped, it was all right. He'd won. He felt good, and as if nothing could ever touch him in that way again. He thought he'd won a sort of inoculation of sheer mental bravery over physical fear, forever.

But now he knew that a man could feel that same sort of fear twice. Even if he'd won the first time. Maybe he would go on feeling it, like this, whenever something extra frightening had to be done and he had to force himself to go ahead and do it. He was cold and weak again, with that fear that was almost unashamed, so strong, so crying out in him.

Things didn't ever end. You never won completely, once, for all the rest of your life. You always had to go on fighting as if every previous fight had never happened before. He knew that now.

He was standing up, one hand resting on the back of the chair, before he went up to the stand to tell away his life, his liberty—his precious liberty that meant his life. He knew now that the long leash had come to its end, that it was tightening, tangling around him. He knew the unbelievable story he was going to tell them all, and how they'd take it. It was the end of his liberty, and so of his life, because when he was in jail no one would bother to investigate any other trail but his. No one except—Peter, maybe, and Blake. What could they do? They could only follow him, and he'd come here, at last.

He didn't blame any of them. He saw now, for the first time, that his story of what had happened was unbelievable, except on the grounds of his guilt or guilty knowledge.

Things didn't happen that way, unless you made 'em happen. Men didn't get murdered all around you, and you not involved . . . unless . . . someone was involving you. No one would believe that, though. Only he and one other knew that was true.

Dennis swept weary eyes briefly over the crowded room, the jury with the shocked and kindly faces in it, the miscellaneous group of witnesses gathered around the shabby oak table. He gave up with a heavy motion of one hand and started up to the witness stand. The coroner was calling him, impatiently, repeating his name: "Devore! Devore!" Then Peter grabbed him.

## XVIII. THE MARINES

"Quick," said Peter, "before the gendarmes mass. Where are we?"

"H-how'd you get here?" asked Dennis huskily, instead.

"Flew, you fool. Don't waste time. Where are we?"

"Returns coming in from all counties. Landslide against me, I guess. No final count."

"You testified yet?"

"Just going to."

"What's the coroner like?"

That gentleman was getting ready to go into action and separate the huddle into its component parts. He objected to having unannounced meetings going on in the middle of an inquest, particularly with suspected persons taking part in them.

"He's an er—er," explained Dennis quickly but satisfactorily, with a side glance at that worthy. "Not an error, though. He knows his stuff", but he's awfully slow at a getaway."

"Good enough," said Peter, taking his hands off Dennis and straightening up.

The room, which had been seething a bit like a windy sea, began to subside.

"Mr. Coroner," Peter rumbled above it, standing staunch as a rock in the midst of the excitement, "I represent Mr. Devore here, and I'd like to talk with my client and with you and Inspector Sullivan before we go on further in this inquest. We haven't had a chance to confer yet."

"Sure you can," said Sullivan. "You can begin with us, Byrne. We'd like to hear it."

"Good enough," said Peter again and went on up front. A policeman, uniformed, moved unobtrusively to a place a bit behind Dennis's chair, as if he'd just happened to drift there in the shift of the crowd. The three men bent their heads close together over the coroner's part of the big table, where his papers were massed. You couldn't hear what they were saying, but you could hear the tone of the voices. Peter spoke first, quite a while, deep voice urgent. Then Sullivan spoke, a little shorter.

The coroner snapped them up on something, dry and businesslike, as if he'd stamped an okay with his signature on a signed paper, like a formality that ended the conference. They broke it up then.

Peter came back to Dennis, with Sullivan dropping into his chair on the other side. The coroner arranged his papers, regardless of the stares and whisperings that roved around him.

"Er—," he said, raising his partly bald head again, "we'll have Mr. Devore as a witness now."

Peter laid a hand on Dennis's arm as he started to get up.

"You can claim immunity from testifying," he said in a whisper, "if you want. Or you can waive immunity, as you please. Because you're the one witness they're liable to try to pin it onto."

"Immunity?" said Dennis, widening his eyes innocently. "What's that? Do you want 'em all, to think I did it?"

He grinned at Peter, and before Peter could stop him he was up and going forward. Peter gave a subdued grunt, whether of satisfaction or of disturbance no one could tell, and leaned back to watch his client. Dennis, he thought, wasn't afraid to take it, anyway. For anyone whose previous private life bore investigation as little as Dennis's did, he wasn't backward, Peter realized, about it.

Dennis, on the other hand, walking up to the witness chair, simply felt as if the marines had come. Perhaps not in the very nick of time, but enough in time to avenge his dead body, which was satisfactory to him. A man doesn't like to go down in a crowd of enemies and be totally forgotten, and no one even know of the fight he's put up. It's even more satisfactory to have a monument of dead enemies erected over him, and he felt that Peter would attend to any details like that in an elegant manner.

He put up his right hand and was sworn in. He seated himself and waited for the opening shot. It sort of ricocheted and hit him from an unexpected angle. Yet it was only a mere routine question, after all. No one in the room, with the exception of Peter and Inspector Sullivan, and maybe Kennedy if he was there among the reporters, could have known of its unexpected effect. Even the little bald coroner couldn't know.

All he'd said was, "What is your name?"

"Er—er!" stumbled Dennis helplessly for an agonizing second. He turned red, and the room began to titter. He'd forgotten how many names he was supposed to have, and which one he went under here, anyway. They all knew him as Devore, of course. What in the devil was the proper name to give now? Spring a totally new one on them? He thought that might have a bad effect. But after all, he was under oath.

He caught Peter's eye and stopped fumbling. His mouth closed more firmly. Peter was rising from his seat.

"Mr. Coroner," said Peter massively and very respectfully, "my client's professional name is the name that he is known by on legal contracts and in business, and with your permission, the police have agreed to accept that name as his proper one in this case—that of Dennis Devore."

The coroner caught Sullivan's small but wise elephant eye. Sullivan nodded an equally massive head. Peter sat down. For a man who had no idea of what Dennis's real name might be, he'd done pretty well on the spur of the moment, he felt. Of course a broadcasting artist could have a professional name, without any rude questions arising from that fact. It wasn't, then, an alias.

Dennis gave his name. Dennis Devore. His—er—former address, the Ancaster. The coroner asked him if he was returning to that address. Dennis said yes, all his things were there. He'd had every intention of returning to it. The hotel manager stared stonily in front of him at that.

Dennis didn't care. He was still a bit stunned from one amazing fact that had just penetrated his brain: Devore! He was Dennis Devore here! The coroner kept calling him that. Sullivan didn't rise and expose him. There were no questions about his manslaughter record down at Delroy.

Dennis realized in one dizzy second that the police weren't telling all they knew. Neither was Kennedy. He must have kept it quiet, as he'd said he might unless something broke to make it worth his while to spill the whole thing. That encouraged him. It sounded as if they wanted to keep things under cover, after all. For the benefit and surprise of—some other person.

The coroner asked questions that brought Dennis step by step over the route of that night when Bianca died in his room. That journey of his had been pretty well mapped out—by the manager of the radio broadcasting station KDO, by the hotel clerk, the elevator man Malloy, the telephone girl, the hotel manager, the police. Now in Dennis's low dark voice it gained a new interest. He answered questions quietly and briefly, but the room leaned forward and saw pictures as he spoke.

He'd gone up—he'd tried his door—it was locked— he'd had his key with him—he'd put it in the lock and turned the knob, and the door opened—the room was dark—it was a bit stuffy, the windows were all closed— he'd turned on the lights.

"What did you do then, Mr. Devore?"

"I thought of opening the windows," Dennis said.

"Did you open the windows?"

"No." Sullivan slouched in his seat. Dennis went on: "I—I meant to, and then—I crossed the room, and saw —her. The body. Lying on the floor."

"Just a minute," the coroner said. "You heard nothing when you came in?"

"Nothing," Dennis said tiredly. His dark eyes looked at the breathless room without interest, as if he didn't see them all there. As if he saw things, pictures, in his mind instead.

"How was the body lying?"

"On its back. Her—the face was upward."

"Did you touch it?"

"No." It sounded like a dark wing drooping, that low word.

"Did you see any cause of death, or know she was dead?"

"I knew she was dead," Dennis said simply. "I didn't see anything—I didn't know how she died."

"You didn't know it was—murder?"

"No."

It was a dark whisper of a word again, lower.

"What did you do then, Mr. Devore?"

"I called the police."

"By telephone?"

"Yes, through the hotel board."

"There was an interval of time before you called the police, after you'd come into your room and discovered the body?"

"I didn't know it," said Dennis simply. "I—at first, you see, I didn't even know she was there. I suppose it was a minute or two before I saw—the body. Afterwards—I thought I phoned almost as soon as I saw it. Maybe I didn't."

"I see. Er—what happened before the police arrived?"

"I called the hotel clerk," Dennis said. "Then I asked for the manager. He told me the manager had already gone up. The phone girl had given him my message to the police. A few minutes later I heard a knock at my door, and Fersen came in."

"What happened then?"

"We just waited for the police to come." Dennis recalled that brief passage at arms, and decided to say nothing about it. "Inspectors Sullivan and Cassidy came, and after that some reporters and fingerprint men, and—I told them about it."

"I see. Mr. Devore, have you ever seen the deceased before, to your knowledge?"

Dennis shook his head. "No. Never."

Somehow the room didn't laugh at that statement now. It was given too gravely. There wasn't anything funny about it after all.

"You didn't know who she was?"

"No. I didn't know that until—the morning after she'd been killed."

"How did you learn it? From the police?"

"No." Dennis grinned that brief glimmer of a grin over mouth and eyes, as he looked at the press table. "I learned it from a reporter."

There was a subdued but appreciative deep chuckle from the press table. Sullivan turned the nicely done color of rare beef under his brownness of face.

"Er," said the little coroner a bit hastily. There was a polite silence, all waiting for him to speak.

"You can tell us nothing, then, of the circumstances under which the deceased was found in your room that night?"

"The circumstances," said Dennis grimly, "were that someone took her in there and killed her. That's all I know. I'd like to know more about it myself!"

"Quite so," said the coroner. "We—er—appreciate your feeling on this subject. We should all like to know more. Er—can you tell us under what circumstances you came to San Francisco, Mr. Devore?"

Dennis leaned forward in the confidential attitude of one about to tell a longer tale. The room subtly became relaxed, as those about to listen to a life story. He put his elbow on his knee and rested his chin against his fist.

"It was about three months ago," he said engagingly, taking them all into his confidence. "A friend of mine who's a radio engineer suggested that maybe I could sing over the radio. So I did." He grinned, as though it were as much of a surprise to him now as it had been then. "They offered me a contract. So I went first to Los Angeles, and then came up here, and got a try-out at KDO, and I've been here ever since."

"Until this happened," he thought.

He was a Native Son, eh? They knew all about him now. The whole room felt sort of friendly to Dennis, as though they'd known him quite a while. There wasn't anything fishy in his story. His life history was as clear as crystal. He'd explained everything, in those few simple sentences.

Only Peter, and Inspector Sullivan, and maybe the wise little coroner perceived that Dennis had offered the courtroom his whole life all wrapped up in three months, with a fine frank gesture of confidence. His history hadn't gone back beyond that.

But then, most people in the room, if they'd stopped to think about this point, wouldn't have believed that Dennis could have much of a history by now. There didn't seem time for it. The motherly-looking juroress was beaming on him. She knew that her feminine instinct had been vindicated. That nice young man a murderer! It wasn't likely, and she'd known it all along.

Dennis, however, cocked a cynical dark eye at all this sudden relaxation toward him. He didn't dare take it too much to heart.

"Fine!" he thought. "If I could break it off now— What's the use? Now comes the grand exposure. Recent events are going to trip me up so hard I'll discover a new universe. I could have made it, too, if—all those other things hadn't happened."

The little coroner was rustling papers again, with a sound as precise and dry as his own voice, in the stillness.

He looked up.

Dennis took a deep breath.

"Er—thank you, Mr. Devore," said the little coroner dryly.

Dennis stared at him.

The room rustled again, with the sound of many people suddenly alert.

The coroner looked again, a bit testily, as the witness didn't take the hint.

"That'll be all," he said briefly.

Dennis came to. "Oh—er!" he remarked a bit vaguely, but finally he got up and came down to Peter in a state of beginning excitement, eyes shining.

He dropped into his chair beside Peter.

"They didn't ask me a thing!" he protested in an excited whisper. Peter seemed asleep, almost, lying back comfortably, eyes lost in the shadows of his rock-ledge eyebrows. Dennis went on: "Not about anything that counts, Peter—such as, had I ever been in jail before or up for manslaughter, or what Bowden had to do with it, or Farnese, or Father Malletti—or those money orders we found ..."

Peter grunted a warning. The coroner was looking at them even more testily. Dennis subsided. He didn't want to take any more chances on the inquisition chair.

"Ladies and gentlemen of the jury," the coroner was saying, "you've heard these witnesses testify that the deceased, a woman known as Bianca Farnese, met her death in a hotel room on the night of the 3rd of November in this city. The circumstances leading to her arrival in that room and of her death are unfortunately, at this time, er—obscured. The manner of her death, however, was made plain to you by the physician of the police department who examined her immediately after the discovery of her body, and, as he has testified, not more than an hour after her death. The cause of death was the wound made by a knife blade entering her back in such a position, stripped of technical verbiage, as to cause almost immediate death. The knife remained in the wound and was exhibited to you. Efforts to trace it have not been, so far, successful. There seems to be no doubt, ladies and gentlemen of the jury, that this adequately describes the cause of death. The immediate cause, or agency, that is. What further cause there may be—er—you've a pretty good idea, as I've said, of how the deceased came to her death.

"Er—it's been represented to me, by officials of the police department who are working on the case, that this death of the woman Bianca Farnese which we're engaged in investigating may be—undoubtedly, I should say, was—involved with—other recent occurrences. I suggest, therefore, ladies and gentlemen, that you bear this in mind when fixing not only the immediate agency of death, but also if you wish to fix any definite responsibility for the manner of her death on any person or persons. That definite responsibility will in due time, we trust, be legally placed by—er—the courts, with the aid of the police department. I can only suggest this—you are quite free to return your own verdict under the circumstances—but at this time—er . . ."

The jury nodded gravely. That last "er" meant more to them than the whole speech together. It meant all that the coroner meant it to mean. The police had clues, and didn't want to be burdened by a ready-made defendant handed over to them. The jury, in fact, "got" the coroner neatly. He and the police wanted a free hand. All right, they'd get it.

"The long leash," whispered Dennis irrepressibly to Peter. "He wants it, too."

He got it. The coroner's jury consulted briefly, came back, announced when questioned that Bianca Farnese had come to her death through violence, specifically by a knife wound made by the hands of a person or persons unknown.

The courtroom broke up in a great rush of sound. Dennis turned to Peter.

"How'd you do it?"

"This is an inquest, not a trial," Peter reminded him. "That's all they had to do, really. Just say how she died, not who did it."

"Yes, I know," said Dennis impatiently, "but how'd you get them to fall in with that? You know Sullivan wants a definite charge on me so he can hold me."

"Ugh," grunted Peter absent-mindedly, gathering papers.

"Listen, Indian," said Dennis threateningly, "that reticent ugh-ugh stuff you've been pulling doesn't go with me. Explain in words of more than one syllable."

"I made a dicker with the police and the coroner," Peter said. "I offered to hand over the facts about the money orders and Bowden's last words. Kennedy's held all that back until he had something to follow and spring on 'em all at once. In fact, with a great price, I'm afraid, obtained I this freedom for you."

"What price?"

"We're going to have Sullivan come to lunch with us, and then we're going to Tell All."

"Well," Dennis sighed, "I don't care if I do!"

# XIX. THE RESTLESS GRAVE

"In fact," said Dennis, "the more I think about it, the more I feel like a rather antiquated safe with the family jewels locked up inside of it and the fake butler, alias Sure-shot Mike, picking away at the lock, and no Rin-Tin-Tin to dash through the French windows at the last minute and rescue the diamonds. In other words, to tell the truth, Peter, we've been carrying pretty valuable information around with us, and if that 'person unknown' the jury was talking about knew that, he'd be apt to take us apart to get at it. He's already," Dennis reminded Peter, grave-eyed, as they put on their overcoats to go, "put Bianca and Bowden out of the way for that very thing—knowing too much about him."

Peter nodded. "He does know now, Dennis," he confessed. "It can't be helped. He knows we know something important. It's like this"—the logical Peter began to make his brief as exactly as if he were going to argue it out with the court listening—"he must have been here today, to see what would happen. It was too important for him to know that, let alone his unholy curiosity. He was here, then, and he knew you were going to be up for a target by the police. Then I come in and say something to Sullivan and the coroner, and the situation changes. I've brought information that lets you out. If it lets you out, it must implicate him in some way, if it's anywhere near the truth. He can't afford to have any glimmering of the truth come out. Not even the beginning of a trail to him. He's been so careful about that! The coroner and the police both let you off easily—too lightly, in view of the information they must have on your recent doings. Follows, then, that my information supersedes theirs. Therefore he knows they've got it now. Q.E.D. The family jewels are in the old safe, and the fake butler knows it now."

"Don't be so darned logical, Peter," Dennis protested. "You take away any appetite I might have had for lunch, if that's a satisfaction to you!"

The room was pretty well cleared by now. Sullivan remained by them, heavily putting on his overcoat. Dennis grinned fleetingly.

The three of them turned to go, and Dennis put a hand on Peter's arm, dragging him back.

"Where's Blake?" he asked hurriedly.

"She's bringing the car back from Monterey," Peter said. "I came up by plane from the Hotel Del Monte grounds there."

Dennis dropped his hand, freeing Peter. "Oh," he said.

"By the way," said that sisterless gentleman, following Sullivan's broad shoulders out of the room, "Morgan's a washout, Dennis."

"I thought so," Dennis said, "when you didn't say anything about him. Oh, well!"

He shrugged and went on behind the two of them, thinking what a battle-cruiser line he had in front of him now—Sullivan and Byrne, both broad-shouldered, tall, heavily built, alike in their rough-coated overcoats swinging along, in their soft felt hats jauntily pulled down over their right eye. Dennis thought the two of them were enough for any battle line.

It was sort of nice, and a relief, after all, to have Sullivan with them. It had been pretty hard on Peter, scouting alone for Dennis.

"Where'll we eat?" demanded Peter, as they stood on the outside steps beside Sullivan.

"Somewhere where it's quiet," Sullivan said. "These places around here are all crowded now. We don't want the world listening in on us."

"I know a place," Dennis remembered. That faint glimmering grin began in his eyes, but his face was grave. "It's a swell place, near here. On a roof."

They found themselves following his lead, along the narrow and crowded hill streets. Dennis climbed the stairs, nodded affably to the dark-faced proprietor in a way which chased some of the anxiety out of his large, dark, mournful eyes at seeing Sullivan there, and chose the same table among the potted plants that he'd had with Kennedy. They not only had a quiet table to themselves—they had a space around it entirely left to them, too. Peter looked all right—respectable, solid, but not official; Dennis was obviously a bosom friend of Alexandro, the boss; but no plainclothes suit could disguise Sullivan as anything but an officer of the police.

The other patrons, under the striped umbrellas and among the stranded sort of palms and things scattered about, gave them a respectful assurance of privacy and a sudden lowered tone of voices.

Dennis dropped into a chair with an air of homecoming and looked around for landmarks outside, under the blue and windy sky of a rainless November day. The warm wind ruffled his hair pleasantly, the sun was warm on his face. It was a swell day.

"What'll it be?" asked Peter.

"Some of the same," said Dennis, taking no chances with the rather illegibly written bill on the table. "And coffee," he added. The proprietor flashed him a smile, and departed, heavily, to his kitchens.

"That's the guy who saw Bianca coming out of the church there, down the street, the night Father Malletti disappeared," Dennis told them in a hushed voice.

"He told Kennedy and me about it night before last—remember? It was in the paper next day."

"All *I* know," said Sullivan bitterly, "is what I read in the papers. And at that, the little rat of a Kennedy has been holding out on us, it looks."

"Well," Dennis murmured, "there's a lot in them just now."

"Suppose," Sullivan suggested, "you tell us what isn't in them yet, Devore."

"All right," Dennis surrendered with a sigh of relief. "Here's the layout, as far as we've gone. Shall I tell 'em, Pete, or you?"

"You," said Peter briefly, beginning to eat.

So Dennis put his clenched hands on each side of his face, sunk his chin in them comfortably, and began to talk, ignoring the slowly congealing food in front of him. He told of their visit to Delroy, of Bowden's coming into their garden at dusk, and of Bowden's strange and last words about Farnese. "He said Farnese was lying on the highway, Sullivan, for a target for any car to hit. He was dead before we—I—hit him!"

"We'd know a lot more if we could get a line on Farnese," Sullivan commented. "He's been dead more than a year, though."

"But his widow," Dennis pointed out, "was killed—only the day before yesterday, Sullivan! That case is still alive, still recent. It must be. Farnese isn't resting easy in his grave, after all. Bowden was right. It's—the restless grave, betraying his murderer after all this time."

"Yeah," Sullivan said only, "but who?"

Dennis shook his head. He went on, but he couldn't get any answer to that question. He went on to the visit they'd paid Bowden—"I told you all about that, except finding the money orders and why we actually went there that night, when you saw me in the Delroy jail," Dennis commented virtuously at this point.

Peter grinned. Sullivan was turning that dull red again, under his tan. He laid down his knife and fork and looked at Dennis.

"All," he repeated. "Sure you did—all except anything that counted. We'd get somewhere, maybe, if you thought to inform the police about this case once in a while. We're in on it too, you know. It isn't your private case. We want to find out what's happened. That's our business. If I find out that you or that little squirt Kennedy have been holding out anything more on me after this, I'll shake it out of both of you at the Hall of Justice. Well, go on. Those money-order receipts— where are they?"

He picked up his knife and fork again.

"Peter's got the money-order receipts," said a more subdued Dennis. "Hand 'em over, Pete, will you?"

This ceremony was accomplished with no other formality than a grunt of acknowledgment by Sullivan. That large, solid gentleman had been shaken to his foundations by a gust of official wrath, and it took his bulk a little while to acquire calm again. He stowed the compact small packet away in his inside breast pocket carefully.

Then Dennis went on, picking his way carefully among the many pitfalls that seemed ready to trip up the unwary who went in threat of official displeasure. He told about the second trip, alone, back to Bowden's dark shack in hopes of catching him there—and its result. Its lack of result, all clues ended in that swift murder and blaze.

"Damned amateurs," observed Sullivan, still simmering, "to let Bowden go like that! Our only direct line on the case! *We* wouldn't have done that. We'd have had a squad of men spread around the shack to pick him up—and we'd have got the killer, too, at the same time."

"No," protested Dennis, "it wouldn't have done any good to wait for the police, and anyway, how could we have done that? We didn't know when we went down there we'd run into this. You had the alarm about Father Malletti being missing as soon as we did. That's what sent us down there. You had the same information on  that. Then I only got onto Bowden when I was actually there. I called Kennedy up and told him—it was too late to send anyone down there then from San Francisco and have 'em get there in time."

"You or Kennedy could have called me—or the bureau."

"It wouldn't have done any good. Kennedy didn't know where you were—anywhere between here and Santa Cruz on the coast line. He knew there were cranks' tips coming in all the time along the coast. We had to go ahead and handle it ourselves."

Sullivan was slowly getting convinced. He grunted, more pleasantly this time, a softer, more lenient grunt of almost assent.

"So that was that," ended Dennis, encouraged by that grunt. "Only—it wasn't, Sullivan. I wish it had been."

Dennis's eyes looked darkly out at the bright day, from between his clenched fists. "I wish it had been," he repeated.

"What happened then?" Sullivan asked.

"Wong disappeared," said Dennis simply but rather desolately. "I told.you who Wong is, didn't I? He's a great friend of mine, anyway. He's—I've known Wong for as many years as I can remember back." Dennis's voice had suddenly thickened. He cleared it huskily and said, "You go on, Peter, and tell him. I wasn't there at the time, anyway. I was with the sheriff and Henry back at the jail then."

"There's nothing to tell," said Peter, devastatingly. "That's all that happened. I went out to look for him where he was supposed to sleep and he wasn't there. Bed hadn't been slept in. We waited—Blake and I— until morning and then got the car and went in to Delroy, to the hotel there. He hadn't come back by then."

"Why'd you go to look for him just then?" asked Sullivan keenly.

"Blake thought he wasn't there," Peter said. "So I went to look. And he wasn't. We'd been talking things over, and Blake said that Bowden was shot with a squirrel gun that Wong had been using for the past year; it wasn't Dennis's gun any more; and that Bowden was Dennis's potential enemy, and he'd been killed before he could blackmail Dennis. She—we—thought that the same person might have killed both Bianca and Bowden, because they were both dangers to Dennis— they might both have raked up that old scandal of Farnese's killing, and have blackmailed Dennis about its being a first-degree murder charge, if they knew that Farnese was dead before he was hit by an automobile. And we thought that the person who put them both out of the way was—Wong."

"Listen," said Dennis hotly, "you tell me anything about Wong that we can use against him in this case, and I'll pay you a million dollars— cash. That's what I think of Wong!"

"Then why did he skip?" demanded Peter.

"Probably so he wouldn't have to listen any longer to you two theorizing," said Dennis ungratefully.

Sullivan lifted a heavy hand, checking argument.

"This is a sweet case," he said, in heavy sarcasm. "You say the only reason you can figure out, Devore, why they ever picked on you as the fall guy is that you ran over this dead man Farnese a year ago. Hell, that's no real reason for anyone to hate you so they'd try to pin another killing, a woman's murder, and then another, Bowden's, on you. And get this—there are no direct clues to the killer, if there is only one killer, except these bits of paper in my pocket. The absence of direct clues suggests a homicidal maniac's lack of logically reached conclusions, to my mind. You see, a maniac's mind leaps ahead in gaps that a normal man's mind has to have bridged. A normal man has to have pretty good solid reasons for his acts. Or," said Sullivan meditatively, "maybe we're the crazy ones, not to bridge the gaps with significant clues, probably staring us in the face."

"This is sweet," said Dennis with interest. "Either the killer's crazy or else we are, with betting odds on us. Sullivan thinks we're cuckoo, Peter."

"I wouldn't doubt it," said Peter.

"Or else," said Dennis, "I'm a killer."

"He doesn't think that," protested Peter, as the silence from the other third of the party became a bit uncomfortable.

"What does he think, then?"

"Well," Peter said, hesitating delicately, as he seemed to be the intermediary in this affair, Sullivan smoking on easily, "this may be a little hard to take, Dennis. He doesn't think you're a murderer, I believe, but he does think you're a little cuckoo."

"Hard to take!" Dennis echoed in astonishment. "If I never had anything harder than that to take, I'd be doing swell. That's what everybody thinks, probably including you, Peter."

"Well, you see," Peter grinned, "as your lawyer, Dennis, he does include me."

Dennis turned to Sullivan. "You don't think I'm a killer, do you?" he asked a bit apprehensively.

"No, I'm beginning to get a line on the kind of birds you are," that large and lethargic gentleman answered. "You like to go ahead and do things on your own, have your fun with the bombing squad, so to speak, and let the police department do the mopping-up operations for you afterward. You do all the damage, we clean up the case. That's dangerous work. It's apt to land you in jail as—accessories to murder, perhaps, unless the police know about it in advance. You do too many things on your own."

"You don't think I know anything about Father Malletti's going away, do you?" Dennis went on. "I swear I don't—"

"Listen, Devore,"—Sullivan pointed his pipe at Dennis, all lethargy gone from him now—"if I'd thought there was any chance of you knowing where His Reverence was, you wouldn't be sitting here offering to let me know things—you'd be begging me to take the information as a free gift, down at the Hall of Justice."

"Don't you really know where he went?" Peter asked gravely.

"No," said Sullivan. "Nor who took him there. But whoever it was,"—the big man knocked his pipe out, preparing to get up—"the curse of Cromwell on him."

"It will be," said Dennis. "I'm quite sure of that. Or an even worse one on him now. The curse of—himself. Because we know one more thing about our killer now."

"What's that?" Peter asked, as they went on down the stairs again.

"We've one more thing to add to the killer's description," Dennis said, "if Sullivan's right about the gaps he's left in his crimes. The very absence of clues. We must look for a man with the light of unreason in his eyes at times. The light—"

Dennis stopped there, groping for words, on the very edge of some great discovery, he felt. There was something—he almost knew . . .

They were in the street now, and they saw the tall gray Church of Saints Peter and Paul, with a crowd in front of it, and people coming down its stairs, and automobiles driving away. Bianca's funeral— Bianca's last Mass! Glimpse of flowers piled high—a black hearse, followed by automobiles—going to the green graveyard in the hills of South San Francisco, where Dennis had come past only that morning, very early. The crowd was going away, slowly, people coming past them, jostling—swarthy faces, bright black eyes, curious glances, bursts of excited talk, sudden lowering of voices—Peter and Sullivan standing like large, steady rocks in the midst of this oncoming sea.

Dennis leaned against the wall of the house, waiting for the crowd to go by. His eyes were half closed, concentrated, intent on something in the darkness of his mind. He couldn't quite get it. He frowned a little.

"The light—of madness," he repeated.

He looked up and saw Peter's eyes, those clear and deep blue pools set in the overshadowing rock ledges of his brows, and as he looked he saw the sudden change come into Peter's clear eyes. It was like a sudden flash of sun into them, a light—of warning, danger.

Peter roared out something.

And Dennis, responding instinctively, hearing again the old signals of combat through the years, flung himself forward, in front of Sullivan, arms outstretched.

There were red rockets whirling madly in a black world of pain. Then they disappeared, and Dennis fell forward into the thick, the stifling darkness of a restless grave.

# XX. DEAD MEN RISE UP

Dennis sat up and hastily held his head with both hands. He opened his eyes, and the light pierced them like a sharp bright sword. He closed his eyes. He was sitting, he'd discovered, on the edge of the curbing in a practically deserted street. Peter was the only human object looming around anywhere.

"How's your head?" Peter asked.

"It's a rotten head," Dennis said, sick and dizzy with pain. "What happened to it?"

"A bullet tried to make connections with it," Peter said, "but just missed the train. It just grazed you. You're lucky, Dennis."

"I was born to be hung, I guess," Dennis agreed.

He winced as a frightful noise began at the other end of the street and mounted to shatter his head to pieces. Sirens screamed in death agonies, and their echo beat in his brain relentlessly, against his too thin head. It made him feel sick.

"Sullivan's called out the gendarmes," Peter said. "That bullet was meant for him, Dennis, and you took it. He's very peeved."

"Well," Dennis groaned, "don't let him roar at me, Pete. I can't stand it."

He got to his feet in one swift act of will, saw the street swerving and whirling around him, and felt Peter's arm holding him up as he drooped. Funny, it was his head that was hurt, but his legs felt stiff and the world was rocketing around him. A police rifle squad in a touring car roared past them, siren sobbing and then screaming again, and Dennis shuddered.

"Do they have to do that?" he inquired piteously.

"Yes, but we don't have to listen to it," Peter said more practically. "Let's go somewhere."

Dennis became aware of a soft, insistent hissing somewhere. He opened both eyes in a heavy gaze and saw the dark-faced proprietor of the roof garden hovering around, apron anxiously clasped in both not too clean hands.

"Signor," said this person, weepingly, "this is very bad. They shoot you, yes?"

"Yes," said Dennis.

"Ah-h-h," said that somehow comforting dirty and dark person, conveying everything in one simple word: sympathy, execration, promise of brighter things to come, and dolefulness for what had happened to a patron of his. Dennis felt encouraged. He felt still more encouraged when the proprietor bolted and came back with a bottle and a glass, into which he poured some of the contents of the bottle.

Dennis drank it, and the world got more stable, his head became subdued, and he was able to take a faint interest in light and sound again.

"Thanks," he said, more firmly.

"I need some, too," said Peter grimly. "You only got shot at. I saw it being done."

"All right," said Dennis. "Only don't let go. I don't want to hit the pavement again. Where is everybody, anyway?"

"They left," said Peter, chuckling, "in a great hurry. Like spilled mercury. And our killer was among them, I'm afraid. The next thing I knew the sirens were screeching their heads off, and the streets were blockaded by cops and flying squads, and nobody dared show up till now. Here they come back again—we'll be mobbed."

"Let's get out," said Dennis. "That's Kennedy's place, that apartment house down the street. That's where I spent the night before last, remember?"

"So that's where you were hiding out!" observed Sullivan on his other hand. "If I'd known that then, you would have been down at our place instead, day before yesterday."

"Day before yesterday?" said Dennis, reviewing the events of the past hurriedly, as he went across the street partly under Peter's power and partly under his own.

He began to laugh helplessly.

"And I told Blake it was about a million years ago since last night! Things sure do move fast, don't they?" he unconsciously echoed a plaint of Peter's after he'd first met Dennis.

"They move fast when a killer's around," Sullivan said, leading the way up the stairs in the grim manner of a shotgun squad. "It's like having a mad dog loose."

Madness! Dennis stopped abruptly, racking his already aching head for something—something that eluded him. He sighed.

"How's the head?" Sullivan asked.

"I have got," said Dennis very carefully, "the father and mother of all headaches."

He sank onto Kennedy's davenport when he had the door unlocked and they came in.

"Do I look interesting?" he inquired.

"You look like a ghost," Peter said bluntly, standing over him. "The guy who shot you ought to see you now. He'd think you'd come after him to get him, and he'd probably babble it all out."

"Get some iodine and gauze," said Sullivan briefly. "We don't want to go to the Central Emergency unless we can help it. No use letting too much information out. If it's all right with you, Devore, we'll treat it right here. It's a scratch."

"It's all right with me," said Dennis. "What happened, anyway?"

"What didn't?" said Peter, sticking a cigarette in the invalid's mouth and striking a match to it. He sat down on the nearest chair arm, and his blue eyes shone joyously, reviewing battle. "One second we were ahead of you, in the crowd, and then—there was a big, dark car coming by, slowly, from the funeral, I guess— looked that way— and I just happened to look up at it and see—I don't quite know what I saw." Peter's brow was puzzled, but his eyes were very candid. "You know how it is when something—dangerous happens and you get just a bare glimpse of its action before you go to meet it? I saw something," repeated Peter, "something that was bright, like steel, and I knew it was a gun sticking out where it hadn't any business to be—and I couldn't jump for it, because I was too wedged in by people, and I couldn't knock them away to get to Sullivan—the damn' thing was aiming at him—so I yelled, and you jumped at Sullivan, Dennis. And the gun went off, and you got it on the side of your head and dropped down there—Sullivan left you there for me while he went forward to get the enemy—and in a split second all that mob had disappeared like silver balls of mercury rolling away—you've seen it, Dennis— and our big, dark car with them, a couple of taxis filled with mourners almost collided going over the hill, and the police sirens were raising hell along an empty street. And you began moaning, so I sat you up on the curbing, and the next thing I heard, to my great relief, was that you were swearing heartily away under your breath at all the noise around. So I knew you were okay."

"Okay!" said Dennis bitterly. "My head's filled with lead."

"It should have been," said Peter. "Or Sullivan's. I can't make out how that guy could have missed both of you."

"What I can't make out," said Sullivan, dabbing iodine on Dennis's aching head, "is why he went for me at all. I've been on the squad for a good many years, and those birds don't usually go out gunning for an officer like that. They'll shoot when you get 'em cornered, but they won't go out and look for it like that."

"I told you our killer wasn't—usual," said Dennis.

He sat up suddenly, regardless of a racking pain that tried to put him off his balance. He swayed and regained control. His eyes brightened. He had an idea.

"Listen," he said. "Sullivan doesn't know why that guy shot at him and missed. But I do!"

"One reason," said Sullivan,—"why he missed, I mean—was because you shoved in and took it for me, Devore."

Dennis tried to shake his head impatiently and gave it up with a faint groan. He had to be content to sit back again and let his tongue do all the talking without any help from his eager but pain-bound self.

"I mean why you were shot at all!" he said. "You're right—people don't go around potting officers. It's against the law, or something. Inhibition, maybe. Anyway, I know I'd a sight rather take a shot at an unofficial guy than at a cop. Retribution comes too fast, I guess, when the gendarmes get used as targets. Therefore, get this—our killer wasn't shooting at you, Sullivan. This may be a blow to you, but he wasn't."

"Well," said Sullivan, with a suspicion of a grin, "he made a darn' good imitation of it. It had me going."

"No, he wasn't shooting at you," Dennis insisted, slowly, " although he probably thought he was, at that. He was right, if he only knew it."

"Listen yourself," said Peter, getting worried. "Do you want me to get a doctor, Dennis?"

"Don't you see?" Dennis urged. "I saw it myself for a second, when you were both walking out of the coroner's room ahead of me this morning. You're both alike!—you're built alike, you walk alike, you wear practically the same sort of clothes, wear 'em the same way, too— that you-be-damned way, as if someone you didn't much care for were blocking your way and you were going to knock them over. And our killer didn't know that. He saw a big man in an overcoat and a felt hat standing there, looking like the guy he wanted, and he let go at him. And the guy he wanted, Peter—was you."

Dennis sank back again, eyes brilliant in his white face. He was picturesquely decorated, with a white bandage set high up around the right side of his head, curving lower on the left. Peter stared at him, his brown rock of a face getting darker and darker and grimmer and grimmer, until his mouth was only a tight line in it. His blue and candid eyes were dark with shadows, too. He looked at Dennis as if that picturesque young man were the ghost that he'd called him. The ghost of unpleasant memories.

"Why did he want me?" Peter asked, very quietly. Only his big hands clenched and unclenched very steadily, very quietly, unconsciously.

"He wanted to get you," Dennis said jauntily, as a man demonstrating a problem in perfectly plain geometry to a rather dumb class, "because of what he thought you had either in your head or in your pocket, Peter. In *this* pocket."

He reached out a languid hand and nicked with one finger the upper left side of Peter's suit.

"The receipts!" said Sullivan, in a voice like dynamite going off.

"I told you," said Dennis, a bit wearily, "I felt like a safe when the fake butler is picking away at the lock and the family diamonds were inside. Only—I wasn't the safe this time, Peter. You were. And you nearly got burgled, at that. He was aiming, you see, at your—or

Sullivan's—heart, so he'd get what you had in your valuables-carrying pocket just over it, and at the same time get what you had in your head. A thrifty guy. He darn' near made it, too."

"How'd he know?" asked Peter softly but thunderously.

"He guessed," said Dennis. "Same as I'm guessing. Only you've got to admit it's a swell guess at that. He may have been one of the customers up on the roof with us, and seen Sullivan stick the things in that pocket, but I doubt it. I just think he was at Bianca's funeral and saw us, going by, and guessed—and took a chance on it. But he mistook Sullivan for you, and not only that—he missed."

"Then that shot was meant for me, and you took it." Peter took this into the fastness of his mind, revolved it around thoroughly, and then looked at Dennis again. "I won't forget that."

"Don't be dumb," said Dennis. "What could I do?"

"All the same," said Peter, "it was fine of you—"

"No, it wasn't," Dennis interrupted firmly, in his element of argument now. "I want you to be clear on that point. It was a darn' fool thing to do, if you look at it from my point of view. Here was Sullivan, with his large, capable mind set on finding someone to hang all these murders onto, and he might very well set himself to proving my guiltiness in spite of all his reassuring words this morning. That might have been a bluff on his part, to lull my fears to rest. I should have welcomed the opportunity to remove him from among my opponents. But I didn't. And I didn't say to myself, either, in a drowning-man flash, 'If I save his life he'll be properly grateful to me and maybe think I'm innocent after all and lay off' of me.' I simply saw someone was going to go for our side, and I went for them first, that was all."

"I told you I was beginning to get you," said Sullivan.

"Well," said Peter, "after all this dissection of your motives I should say Sullivan ought to be thoroughly dead. You've got the Irish genius, Dennis, for proving that black is white if you happen to believe it at the time.

"Thank you," said Dennis, gracefully inclining his head.

Peter retired behind his cigarette, balked. Then he came out again with another remark.

"And," he said, grinning, "you've got a stiff-necked Armada pride from some black Spanish ancestor, Dennis, that's going to earn you a good working sock in the eye one of these days. If a man wants to thank you decently, why don't you let him?"

"All right, he can," Dennis said. "And if he wants to do it up properly, how about a little more of that nice red wine across the way to do it with? I could do with some of it right now."

"Got it," said Peter. "Brought it over in my coat pocket. Not the inside pocket, either."

He went to Kennedy's midget kitchen to get some glasses, leaving a Dennis considerably brighter. Dennis after a second broke into a whistle, found his head could stand it, and the thin sweet whistle broke into fuller song, as a thin brown twig breaks to flower.

*"Or leave a kiss but in the cup."*

Dennis sang, very thoughtfully eyes far off,

*"And I'll not look for wine!"*

"You bet you won't," agreed Sullivan. "Not while you're with me. You'll take it straight. Have some respect for the police."

"Do you know," said Dennis, sitting up and taking a glass from Peter's hand, "I'm beginning to!"

His tone was that of such honest astonishment that even Sullivan couldn't take offense. Peter laughed, and Dennis after a second began to laugh, too.

At last he said firmly, "I've got to get my things out of that hotel manager's clutches. But," a bit dizzily, "not just this minute. Give me a couple of hours to tear off some sleep, and I'll tackle anything. Even that fish-faced guy."

# XXI. DENNIS ENTERS A CAGE

He woke up to the soft bloom of lights, stretched himself in a long, beautiful ache of sleepiness, all pain gone, and yawned with his mouth very wide, open and his eyes very tightly closed.

There was something very nice going on; it was strangely like something he knew and loved; it was just outside the edge of his mind now. It was like the Little San Ramon River singing sweetly to itself through the sunny days, down by the river banks. It came closer to his consciousness and resolved itself into Kennedy's dark-toned piano, playing "Home to Our Mountains."

Dennis decided it was the loveliest song he'd ever known, except perhaps one. He lay there listening and presently decided that he wasn't sleepy any more. He turned over to the light and lay there on Kennedy's comfortable davenport, idly drinking the music in, and watching Kennedy's lean brown fingers going over the ivory-and-black keyboard in a pool of light.

*"There in our younger days"*

played Kennedy,

*"Peace had its reign."*

The swirl of music stopped, like a pool dammed up for speckled trout to lie in, and Kennedy fingered the last phrase slowly, more pointedly, with one intent
finger.

*"Peace had its reign"*

sang that dark and lovely piano in a final intent word.

Then Kennedy turned around on the bench to look at his guest, lighting his eternal cigarette and letting the song trickle away into silence.

He cocked an eyebrow casually at sight of the ruffled bandaged head and the general wild state of affairs in the visitor's still-white face, where even sleep hadn't smoothed out all the recent damage done there.

"Wirehaired pup," he said, "where'd you get the scratch?"

"Oh, that," said Dennis, sitting up and dismissing the subject with a casual hand to his bandage, "a guy shot at me. Where did Peter Byrne and that bird Sullivan go, Kennedy?"

Kennedy shrugged.

"They didn't tell me," he said. "All I know is that I came home for a few hours of peaceful rest, as I'm accustomed to before I go on what is now a practically twenty-four-hour shift at the Hall, and I find a big flatfoot of a cop standing guard outside my place on the stairs, and you with a souvenir of war on your brow sleeping it off inside. Where've you been, and what doing, Dennis?"

"I've been to the wars," said Dennis.

"I'll say," said Kennedy. "I hope you got the first shot in, that's all."

"Sullivan doesn't think so," said Dennis a bit grimly. "You see, it was really meant for him, only the guy thought he was Peter. So he took a shot at him when he was standing across the street, after we came out from lunch on that roof place. But he missed—he only got me."

Kennedy sat up straighter and whistled softly.

"I might have known it," he said, eyes bright. "That was what all the row was about a couple of hours ago in this district, and nobody down at the Hall would give out any dope to the press-room gang on it. We were all het up about it—thought Father Malletti's kidnaper had been found, not to mention Bianca's killer and Bowden's little shotgun pal. None of the cops would talk—they'd been told off not to. I've been chasing around on that for the afternoon. And I come home and find the story all neatly wrapped up and asleep on my couch, with a cop guarding my front door for me!"

He laughed soundlessly.

"I might have known it!" he jeered at himself. Then he eyed his visitor very pointedly indeed. "Peace," said Kennedy, "has had its reign here as far as I'm concerned. I think I'll order in a machine gun and a pair of sandbags to prop up against the windows."

"What d'you mean?" asked Dennis.

Kennedy pointed the end of his cigarette at Dennis.

"You go down to Delroy," he said, "and people get bumped off, burnt up in shacks with their faces blown off; you come up to San Francisco and someone starts shooting in the street—the Hall of Justice just about gets the lid blown off it in the excitement of having all the flying squads out with their guns cocked, and there's general hell to pay. Do you suppose," Kennedy asked himself an academic question, "he's sort of a natural force of disturbance, attracting these things? He reminds me a lot of the calm spot inside the center of a typhoon. You can't deny, Dennis, that things do happen in your vicinity, whether you want them to or not."

"It must be my head," said Dennis. "It just doesn't make sense. Oh, and by the way, Kennedy, if you want a good line on our devil—our killer—we've just about decided that he's a homicidal maniac. He leaves too many gaps in his reasoning. He doesn't make sense to any ordinary man who wants to link up his reasoning. Too much space between his bridge spans. What do you say, Kennedy?"

"If I knew just what you are talking about," that much-tried gentleman replied, "maybe I could do better. Begin at the beginning, Dennis, and—er, shoot."

"Gimme a smoke," Dennis said. He bent his damaged dark head over the flicker of light for a second and looked up, eyes lit by a deep reflected gleam from the match before he blew it out and settled back again. "Let's see—what d'you know?"

"All about Bowden and your squirrel gun," said Kennedy crisply. "A lot about the inquest—I wasn't there, our page-one guy covered it, and I got it from his story—and why you weren't served up on toast to the coroner there. In fact your lawyer Byrne asked me about it before he went in there, and I told him to play those money-order receipts. He did, eh?"

"He did," Dennis said. "He's a swell guy, Byrne is. He played 'em like a professional card sharp. That's why I'm here."

"Instead," said Kennedy, "of being *safely* in the city jail."

"Oh, I don't know," said Dennis thoughtfully. "Being shot at's no fun—at the time. But all the same, it's the breaks of the game. The breaks," he repeated, very thoughtfully indeed, dark eyes looking into some dimly lit future.

"Things are beginning to break, eh?" said Kennedy.

Dennis nodded. "I think so," he replied. "I think our killer gave a lot more away than he took. Listen!" Dennis gave his favorite exclamation and prepared to indulge in his favorite indoor sport of talking. "How's this look to you? We've made an alliance with Sullivan —treaty of peace, dancing around the council fire, and all that—up at Alexandre's roof place at lunch. We told him everything as far as we've gone about this case—"

"That must have been a treat to him," Kennedy interrupted.

"He wasn't pleased at first," said Dennis pensively. "But I persuaded him it was all for the best that we'd kept some things dark before. Anyway, we told him everything then, kept absolutely nothing back—Pete even handed over the money-order receipts—by request — and then we went downstairs, stood looking at the end of Bianca's funeral Mass going away from the church, and somebody going past slowly in a big, dark closed car takes a shot at Sullivan. Peter sees it in time, yells, and I jostled Sullivan. But that shot wasn't really meant for him, anyway."

"Well," Kennedy said judiciously, eyeing his smoke circles, "I can only say it looks a lot to me, Dennis, as though you and maybe Sullivan and Byrne had included a lot of Alexandre's good red wine in your peace pow-wow. People are getting more thrifty nowadays. They don't let off shots unless they've got a pretty good bead on someone at the other end of the line."

"You wrong us," said Dennis. "All of us."

"All right," said Kennedy. "Go ahead."

Dennis elaborated on his theory of Sullivan being shot at in mistake for Peter. He had a good listener. Kennedy sat in a deceptive quietness, brown head bent, body tense.

"Yeah," said Kennedy at last, "I see."

He lit another cigarette off the end of his lighted butt. Kennedy was working again.

"I see," he said again, slowly, "and it's possible. It's darned clever, too. Dennis, just how much of all this stuff do you believe, anyway?"

"Believe?" said Dennis. "All of it. Why shouldn't I? It's my theory, isn't it?"

"Well," Kennedy said, "I just wanted to make sure. You talk a lot, you know."

"And so do you," said Dennis indignantly. "And so, for that matter, has Peter Byrne been talking—recently."

"I make my living by talking," Kennedy said briefly. "Over the phone at the press room. Phoning stuff in to men who can handle a typewriter more flossily than I can. As for Bryne—sure he talks a lot at times, but it's always a bit surprising to hear him—like the stunt Moses did with the rock, making water gush out of it. He talks, but you'll notice he always says something. Your talk reminds me of a fountain playing, purely for decorative purposes—beautiful, but not so strictly utilitarian and necessary as the water from the living rock in the desert. At that, Byrne's been putting on a few accessory jets and frills, probably influenced by you, Dennis. What I meant to say, though, was if you do believe all this stuff of yours about the killer leaping ahead so quickly in his reasoning, and if you have traced him almost as quickly as he does things, like the way you got onto this shooting, the real purpose behind it, like a flash—why don't you put on a big spurt, Dennis, and instead of being one step behind him leap ahead of him and think out his next step before he takes it, for once. You've got the brains—no one else has even kept up with him as you have, up to this time. All it takes is a little extra pace, to reason out his next move."

"You think I lack logical reasoning power, too?" said Dennis. "That's why I'll be able to do it, I suppose —because I skip a lot, too. That makes it unanimous, I must be cuckoo."

"It might work," said that cynical person, his host. "On the theory— set a nut to crack a nut."

"I'll do it!" said an aroused Dennis. "You wait and see! But first," he amended, "I've got to go over to the hotel and get my things. Coming?"

"I'd like to," said Kennedy with conviction. "Although I don't see what could possibly happen on such a peaceful errand as that. But I've got to get some sleep before I take on the night shift, if I'm not going dead on my feet. When the fire engines go by I'll know what's happening, time enough. How're you going to get past that cop on the stairs, anyway? I'll bet he's got his orders to stop you from going out, as much as to stop anyone from going in here and getting you."

"I'll walk by him," said Dennis. "He doesn't know me from Adam. With a pleasant greeting."

And he did.

The officer, brave in blue and silver, responded handsomely to a cheerful "Hullo, Sergeant," especially as Dennis sauntered down the stairs waving a nonchalant cane, wearing a raglan coat hanging loose from his shoulders, and with a felt hat sitting pretty on his head, concealing any betraying bandage there. All the accessories came from Kennedy. The officer, who'd had Dennis described to him, hadn't heard any of these things mentioned. He stood aside and let this blithe young man pursue his pleasant and apparently very casual way down the steps to the outside door.

Dennis found the disguise had been so useful in one case that he didn't discard it in another. He hailed a taxi at the corner and was driven downhill and up dale to the heights of Nob Hill and the Hotel Ancaster.

He entered the pleasant little lobby, more like a private living room than a hotel public place, at tea time, and no one noticed him especially. The clerk over at the desk was murmuring soothingly to some people there, the music from the hotel orchestra came faintly from behind the closed doors, where people were having tea in the many-windowed, lamplit, flower-decorated Etruscan Room, the soft lights of the lobby glowed enticingly. Tea time. It was a pleasant hour.

Dennis had his own key still in his pocket, and he didn't want to talk to the clerk. He crossed the lobby to the elevator, and as he felt the soft thick plushiness of the taupe carpet underfoot he thought of Bianca walking across that same carpet, under these soft lights, going up to his room, three nights ago. And he thought of the last time he had entered this hotel himself, that same night, later. And of how he'd felt then, careless, unknowing of what was to come, in a hurry.

The elevator door clicked open, and Dennis stepped in, to meet Malloy's astonished eyes.

"Whisht!" said that shaken young man.

"Whisht yourself," said Dennis, leaning against the wall of the cage in a reassuring way. "Take me up like a good fellow, and don't talk so much about it. Unless"—he looked straight into those dark and Irish blue eyes, sooty-lashed, in their rugged setting of face—"unless you think I did it."

"You mean about killing the lady?"

"Yes."

There was a short but electric silence. Then Malloy clanged the door of the elevator shut on them.

"I don't think nothing of the kind," he said with a curious kind of violence in his voice. "What floor is it—fourth?"

"Yes," said Dennis absently. Then, "Who does think so?" he inquired gently.

The elevator cage rocked a bit. Dennis put his hand on the wall and steadied himself. The cage resumed service. Dennis felt that it had been a mistake, perhaps, to spring such a question on Malloy then, but he couldn't pick his time and place.

"Why do you say that, sir?" said Malloy thickly. His nice and rough-hewn face was paler, under the electric light.

"Someone thinks so," said Dennis, "evidently. And you've been arguing with 'em—in your mind. Good egg."

"Well, it was like this, sir," said Malloy, stopping the lift at Dennis's floor but not making a move to open the door, "I never did think so—about your doing that, the way you come in all bright and gay that night —it wasn't reasonable you'd be changed so quickly into a murderer, was it?—but at the inquest, Mr. Fersen did seem to think so, sir. The way he said no one could get up here without me and him seeing them."

"You mean no one did come except me," said Dennis softly. "That was right, wasn't it?"

"Yes," said Malloy sullenly. The stubborn blue eyes stared defiantly from narrowed black lashes into Dennis's dark ones.

"He's quite right," said Dennis. "No one did, besides me. Except the murderer. What do you think?" He looked at Malloy, broad and big in his dark blue uniform, there alone in the elevator with him.

"Malloy," he said, "suppose one of us two is a murderer. What do you think then?"

The silence seemed icy cold, in that little closed cage lit by the glaring electric globe above them. They stared at each other.

"What do I think?" said the boy bleakly. "Would I risk my mortal soul to do such a thing? And would I be afther kidnaping a priest?"

"No," said Dennis. "I shouldn't think so. But—did you kill her, Malloy?"

The tired dark voice persisted. There was a feeling like an icy cold wind coming up around them, in the elevator cage, a cold from the far, inhuman spaces of the ends of the earth, from the naked North itself.

Malloy stood up to the last truth.

"No," he said. "Whatever you want me to swear by, I'll swear. I didn't kill her. I— No, I didn't."

Dennis's hand dropped away from the wall. He sighed.

"I didn't think you did," he remarked. "Then that leaves—me, doesn't it? Me and—the murderer."

"Have you got any clues on him, Misther Devore?" Malloy said humbly, still a bit shaken.

"Clues?" said Dennis. "What are clues? The kind of things any street sweeper can pick up in the streets? Bits of string, and paper, and a cigarette butt? Sure, you can have all of those you want, out of the wastepaper baskets they empty and burn down in your basement!"

He leaned against the wall again and looked in front of him darkly.

"Or are clues the things you don't do? The only reason I wasn't arrested at the first go of this was because I *didn't* open and close a window here, and a dick was bright enough to see that. Is that a clue?"

"I wouldn't call it that," offered Malloy, frankly puzzled.

Dennis grinned at him suddenly, gravity gone again. "Neither would I. The kind of things I call clues is going along a dangerous place and seeing where someone's been—someone who hasn't any business to be there, and who was there—a killer. Seeing, not from what kind of cigarettes they smoked, or stuff like that, but from what they did, what kind of people they were, what kind of things they could do—what they were capable of—and coming at last, slowly perhaps, but inevitably, to—them. A man can't help leaving a vital imprint on a thing that's as close to him as—murder. It's too much his own work, his forces have been engaged in it so."

"Is it fingerprints you'll be meaning, sir?" asked Malloy.

"It is not," said Dennis, grinning again at him. "And will you let me out of this jail and keep your mouth closed about my being here? I'm just going to clear away my stuff and then see Fersen and pay my bill here, and I don't want the whole force charging up to restrain me as a dangerous character."

"I'll do that," said Malloy, his face lighting up in relief at hearing something from Dennis that was put in straight words meaning action.

Dennis stepped out into the softly lit corridor and stood there, seeing the dark shape of his door dimmer down the hallway. This was the hallway down which Bianca had come to meet her murderer.

He opened his door and went in.

# XXII. DENNIS IS TRAPPED

Dennis didn't waste any time in there; the police had evidently gone through his things pretty thoroughly, and the maid had then laid them out in order ready for his packing. He got his suitcase from the corner, stuffed in neatly arranged rows of socks, handkerchiefs, shirts, ties, threw his other suit and his dressing things into odd corners, strapped up the suitcase and turned to go.

The room seemed exactly the same as it had always been. The lights were the same, the furniture waited there, graceful and impersonal, chosen to suit almost any cultivated taste well enough. The bedclothes weren't turned back, though, with the white sheet partly covering the white counterpane as it had been —that other night. And as he crossed the room to get to the door, he saw—he couldn't help seeing, his eyes going there with a dreadful fascination-that there wasn't any stain at all, not even a slight trickle of darkness or a betraying lighter color there where it had been cleansed off, on the taupe carpet near the table. This must be an entirely new floor covering, from the Ancaster's supply department. You couldn't know that anything—anything unhappy—had ever happened there in that pleasant room. It was just the same as it always had been. Hotels were wonderful, Dennis thought a bit wryly. The minds of the people who ran them must be as impersonal, as uniform, as pleasant as—a hotel room.

He came out and closed the door behind him, hearing the lock click into place. He stooped to take his suitcase, set there beside him, and straightened up again, listening. Someone was saying, "Oh, Mr. Devore!" in that restrained but urgent voice of a well-bred person in a rather public place. He turned round.

One of the doors was open, down the hall. A woman was there, partly behind it. Dennis took his suitcase and went on toward the door, and as he came it opened a bit more and he saw an elderly woman standing there. She was imperious and tall and thin, with gray hair almost white piled up in a rather old-fashioned way over her thin hawk face. She was dressed in a fussy silk dress, with the color that Dennis thought of as lavender in it and a lot of pink, too, and an amethyst necklace around her once fine neck.

"Come in," she said more graciously, having had her way in attracting his attention so far.

Dennis hesitated.

"You're Mr. Devore, aren't you?" his hostess said a bit more sharply.

"Yes," said Dennis, "but—"

He wanted to explain that he didn't have any idea of coming in for a chat with this rather grasping person who stood at her doorway and summoned guests like that. He'd got onto who she was, as soon as he saw her clearly. She was the old lady who had the corner suite at this floor—the cornerstone of respectability of the hotel, as Blake had described her. And she wanted to chat.

"Always suspect old ladies," Dennis groaned to him- self.

She was waiting for him.

"I can't come in," said Dennis nicely. "I've got to catch a train."

That inspiration didn't work, in spite of the suitcase evidence in his hand.

"Nonsense," said the dragon sharply. "Just tell your taximan you'll give him five dollars to go faster. It always turns out that you've a few minutes to spare. Come in and have some tea."

Dennis came in.

His hostess sat down on the davenport by the wide windows that gave a view of the city and, beyond gray buildings, the bay. Dennis sat down in a comfortable armchair across from her, with a small table between them.

"Lucy will bring your tea," said the dragon kindly. Dennis always did have a particular charm for old ladies. He made them feel, somehow, young again. "I've been wanting to talk to you, Mr. Devore, and as Lucy saw you going to your room just now—"

"Lucy must do a sentry go at the door," thought Dennis, taking his cup of tea obediently from the rather gaunt hands of Lucy, a ten-year-younger edition of her mistress, but in severe black and white. "I wonder if she keeps a midnight shift there? It might come in handy."

He decided he'd ask. As soon as he got a chance.

"You sing over the radio, don't you?" his hostess asked. "I think that's wonderful, Mr. Devore. Lucy and I—we have a radio here—have often heard you."

"Yes," said Dennis. "I mean I used to."

"Aren't you singing over KDO now?"

"No," said Dennis. "Not any more."

He accepted very thin and tiny sandwiches from a plate offered him by Lucy and wondered how soon he could get in his question.

"Lucy," said that gaunt person's equally gaunt mistress, breaking into Dennis's thoughts, "you've cut the sandwiches too thick again. I've told you before how I like them. Or did these come from the hotel kitchen?"

"No'm," said Lucy. "They sent the things up here for me to make, Mrs. Appleby. I can't get 'em any thinner. They won't cut."

"Nonsense," said the formidable old lady. "Give the bread to me, I'll show you."

Lucy apparently wasn't at all surprised by anything her mistress chose to do, even to giving a sandwich-making demonstration in the midst of a tea.

"Yes'm," she said only and disappeared.

Dennis went on eating the rejected sandwiches placidly. He drank his tea. It was pretty good tea. He'd had coffee and red wine and now tea since he came to San Francisco only this morning, and he didn't despise any of them. They each had a place, he felt, and at that moment the place for tea was in him. He was hungry again. Five o'clock in the afternoon was a swell time to eat.

"Why aren't you singing over the radio now?" Mrs. Appleby came back to her guest briskly. She sat with her hands folded in her pale lavender-pink silk lap, and reminded Dennis a lot of the little coroner he'd met in the morning in her way of asking things.

"I'm going away," he explained.

"Because of that thing that happened here?" his hostess surmised even more briskly. "That woman being killed here? But I thought that was practically cleared up by now."

"It is," Dennis assured her. "Only for a few odds and ends. No, it isn't really that. I have to go on business."

"Lucy," said Mrs. Appleby as that patient servitor entered with a tray bearing bread, a bread knife, soft butter in a dish, and other paraphernalia of sandwich-making, "set those here and watch me. Stand here."

"Yes'm," said Lucy, taking her stand to the right.

"I'm sorry to hear that," said his hostess, jumping back to their conversation efficiently. "We enjoyed your singing so, Mr. Devore. Lucy and I always liked to tune in on it. You sing with such feeling."

"Yes'm," murmured Dennis. "I mean, thank you very much."

"That other night—the last night you sang," old Mrs. Appleby said, casting an aside of "Like this, Lucy" to her faithful subject as she cut slices of bread of about the same thickness as the first Lucy-made standard, "we listened to your entire program. We particularly enjoyed your singing 'Sweet and Lovely.' Didn't we, Lucy?"

"That was the last song on my program," said Dennis, remembering back. "If I ever come back here again, I've got a new program ready. Did you—did you happen to look out of your door at any time while I was singing? Or about that time, you know?"

"No," said Mrs. Appleby very decisively, "we didn't. There wasn't any occasion to go out of our rooms. Did we, Lucy?"

"No'm," said Lucy. "We were listening to the radio all through the program, Mr. Devore."

"Oh," said Dennis. "Thanks. I just wanted to know."

"The police," said Mrs. Appleby, "asked us that question, too. Didn't they, Lucy? I soon put them right. They didn't find out anything about that killing from us."

"No," sighed Dennis. "I'm afraid not. I just asked."

"There," said the old lady triumphantly. "Now you see how I mean to do it, Lucy. These are much better. I'll show you—where are the old sandwiches?"

"I've eaten them," said Dennis simply. "They were awfully good. And I don't feel hungry a bit now, I'm afraid. I really must be going."

He rose and stood waiting.

"Well," said the old lady, rising reluctantly, "if you must. I wanted to have a nice talk with you, young man. Some other day—it's been very nice to have had you."

Dennis smiled at her.

"I liked it," he said. "Some day—I may come back. I'd like very much to sing 'Sweet and Lovely' for you and Lucy if I do. May I?"

He shook hands and went away, leaving a sort of young light on two old faces, like a reflected bit of his smile.

He went on down the corridor to the front stairs, and, not being up to facing Malloy again, carried the suitcase quickly down the four flights winding around the elevator until he landed in the lobby again, by the corridor leading back to the manager's office. He set the suitcase down quietly there and turned to go down that corridor with the subdued lighting. Then he paused.

"They didn't see anything," he said softly, thinking it over to himself for a second there in the half-dusk and privacy of the hallway, a little apart from the lobby. "They were listening to their radio, and they didn't look out or go out of their rooms. That's all right. And the police didn't find or see anything that helped them to solve a murder, in their rooms. But I've been up there, and I've talked to them and gone into their rooms."

Dennis turned white at the thought.

"They're all right," he argued palely with himself. "No one has hurt them, or tried to, since that killing. Only—people I've talked to have died. You can't get away from that. If someone knew I'd been up there— and they will know—they know all about me—"

Dennis leaned up against the wall a bit faintly.

"I'll write a note to Sullivan and ask him to put a guard on their door," he said at last, decidedly. "He'll do it. He can take the cop he put on Kennedy's door to guard me, and just transfer him to this suite. Although you can get past a cop at the door—it's been done before."

He grinned and, feeling more cheerful, went on to Fersen's office. There was a snug little anteroom with a pretty, capable-looking tailored girl typing away behind a big desk in one corner of it. She had violets in a fragrant bunch in a jade-green bowl on the brown desk. She looked up and smiled as Dennis came in. The inner door to Fersen's private office was open, and the light lit in it. So Dennis just grinned back at the girl before she really knew who he was, and went on in.

Fersen was filing away some papers in a medium-sized but grim-looking safe along the opposite side of the office. His well-creased trousers were bent slightly at the knees; the light shone on his smooth and well-brushed brown hair. It was a peaceful scene—until he looked around, at some sensation of sound, and saw Dennis standing at the door watching him.

He came up to his full height with a slight hissing noise reminiscent of a startled cobra shooting up its hood. The papers actually dropped untidily from his hand and lay at his feet, mocking the neatness of the rather good-looking office.

Dennis smiled at him and remembered to take off the unfamiliar hat on his head. Fersen's eyes followed the gesture automatically, and widened still more as he saw the neat white wound stripe of a gauze bandage uncovered by Kennedy's concealing hat. Then those eyes began to narrow in a determined way. Fersen was over any flurry he may have felt at suddenly seeing his unannounced and troublesome visitor.

Dennis recognized that ominous narrowing of his eyes—he'd met it in other people before the storm broke —and he forestalled it.

"I've just been up to my room," he said pleasantly, "and it really looks very well now. I congratulate you on your nice, efficient organization here. Too bad you couldn't have removed any body before the police came and disturbed the place so."

"The floor covering," said the hotel manager coldly, recovering himself and sinking into his chair with no gesture of invitation to Dennis to do the same, "was handed over to the police department by their request, if that's what you're referring to. The Ancaster management has no wish to hide any clues to such a serious thing as murder, as you're evidently hinting."

"That's fine," said Dennis heartily, choosing a big chair himself. The office, he thought, was pretty well done—it looked just the club sort of place where two comfortable business men might get together over their cigars. A few posters with bright colors conveying news of conventions, black-and-white posters announcing symphony concerts and other musical events, and a few gayer resort pictures, one showing a man golfing on a green turf, supplied the only hotel-profession atmosphere around.

"I'm glad you think that," said Fersen pointedly. His square and very well-kept hands held the arms of his office chair rather hard on each side of him, though he was leaning back at his ease otherwise. His hands and his voice were the only things that gave away his distaste for his visitor. "I should have thought that under the circumstances the fewer clues left for the police the better, if I had been you perhaps."

"What circumstances?" said Dennis.

Fersen showed his nice white teeth in a surprisingly animal gesture of drawn-back thinned lips for a fleeting second. Dennis, evidently, as he'd done to other and not so well-polished persons, was getting under the top layer of civilization and culture to the more primitive person underneath the hotel manager's exterior.

"I think you know them," said Fersen, recovering himself again, but with an effort, perhaps, this time, "as well as I do. Better, should I say?"

There was a nice and calculated deadliness in his smooth voice. Dennis responded beautifully.

"If you're going around saying things like that," he said hotly, "it's about time I came back here!"

Fersen's eyes lit on the suitcase by Dennis's side.

"You don't think you're coming back here to stay, do you?" he asked coldly.

"I know I'm not!" retorted Dennis, the light of battle vivid in his eyes. "You don't think I'd stay in this dump, do you—after the way you tried to shove that killing onto me, though you were damned sure in your own mind I couldn't have done it in the time? How do I know that? Because of the way you talked when you first came up to my room that night! You weren't scared—you knew pretty well I wasn't a murderer— and you weren't alone up there with a killer— but you wanted someone to hand the killing to so the police wouldn't bother your darned old hotel any more and disturb the other guests! You didn't care about me —you only wanted a goat for the sacrifice. You'd have let the killer go without a murmur of help to the police, if you'd thought you could hush it up that way! I knew you weren't scared to be up there alone with me —you were just plain peevish at things happening! Any other guy who really thought I'd done it would have looked at me with horror in his eyes. You were just annoyed with her, and me, and the cops coming!"

He stopped to get his breath and go on.

"You don't give me credit for—overcoming any natural fears I may have had?" Fersen asked smoothly.

"Don't make me laugh!" said Dennis inelegantly. "I've seen brave men scared, and overcoming it, too —recently. Don't put yourself with them. You're just plain careful of your own skin."

He rose with an odd effect of violence in the suave room.

"Give me my bill, and I'll pay it here," he said. "I don't want any more of this hotel any more than you want me. Where's my statement?"

"Right here," said Fersen crisply. He reached among the drawers of his desk and drew out a paper. "I've made it up already. I told the clerk to let me know when you were coming, so that I could see you personally about it."

He tossed the statement carelessly and contemptuously across the broad desk in Dennis's direction. That hot-headed young man took it up and smiled, narrow-eyed, with a contempt that made the hotel manager's look like Grade C, slightly rancid.

"Don't worry," he said. "You weren't going to miss me. I was going to ask to see you personally and tell you to go to hell, anyway."

Fersen made a sound slightly like a strangled snarl in his throat.

"That covers it," said Dennis, putting a bill on the paper and shoving them both back across the smooth wood desk. "Do you mind signing for it?"

His voice was bland and innocent again. Fersen took out his fountain pen, shook it slightly, scribbled his signature across the paid bill. The second of action had given him back his poise again. He was the man of business, the older and much more suave man of the world regarding unpolished youth again. He looked at Dennis with veiled and slightly shining brown eyes in a pleasantly blank and fleshy face. His lips even smiled, slightly, showing a white edge of teeth behind them.

Dennis had regained some of his own poise again. He felt that perhaps he'd been a bit uncouth.

His eye fell on one of the brighter posters along the wall, the poster with the blue-sky background and the man in white knickers swinging at a golf ball on the green turf, with the ocean in the distance behind him.

"I see you've got the golf-tournament poster there," he said chattily. "That was for last week-end, wasn't it? Saturday and Sunday—let's see"—he leaned forward, making bright conversation with his unwilling host, "November 1st and 2nd, it says. At Del Monte. Do you like golf?"

"Do you mind getting out of here?" asked Fersen, restrainedly. "I might remind you that you're no longer a guest of this hotel. I'll have to ask you to leave at once."

"Or you'll call the police," said Dennis, but with an absent air of near-hostility that didn't do him justice. He was thinking to himself behind the light words. Something had caught like a jagged bit of torn silk at the corner of his mind. Some word had awakened a memory—a wonder—a puzzled effort at remembrance. He had it. Del Monte, of course. He'd heard the name before today. From Peter. Peter had flown up from Del Monte grounds, he'd said, in time for the inquest. Peter must know Del Monte pretty well. He wondered if Peter played golf much. If he was there often—for week-ends, as lots of sportsmen were. It was a swell hotel for a week-end.

He rose reluctantly and took up his receipted bill and looked at the signature across the bottom of it. In spite of all the hotel manager's wrath at the time of writing, the letters were small and distinct and beautifully written. "A. Fersen" said the neat and lovely signature there. "Paid. November 6th."

But Dennis saw it through a darkness and a coldness that made him feel physically sick. It was November 6th, and a Thursday. Bianca had been killed on a Monday. This last Monday, November 3rd. The golf tournament at Del Monte—Peter's Del Monte—had begun on a Saturday, November 1st. Two days before Bianca'd been killed here. It was on the evening of the 1st of November, a Saturday, that someone had taken Father Malletti away, in a big, dark car. Down to Delroy, they'd said. Delroy was in the same county as Del Monte. Anyone who knew Del Monte pretty well would have known the county about there well, too, on drives and trips. Dennis stood there staring at the comfortable, well-furnished, dark-shining brown walnut office, with the big, overstuffed armchairs and the taupe carpet and the brown-shining head of the hotel manager across the desk from him. But his dark eyes didn't see any of it. He was cold. This was the ultimate fear. He'd reached it at last. His eyes were dark with emptiness beyond any shadows. Something'd burnt out in him. He was cold, and sick, and shaken, and weary to death of the wickedness he'd caught a glimpse of, had been trailing all this time.

Nothing mattered. Nothing really mattered. He wanted to turn his head to the wall and die quietly. His spirit was already dead. Only it was so damned cold. As long as he could feel that awful cold, he supposed he was alive, and ought to be grateful to it.

He had to go on, anyway. He knew that, dimly, 'way down in him. You had to go on even when you were knocked out, and beaten by this glimpse of the terrific, implacable casualness of life—that had led them to this conclusion, through such deviating ways.

He felt the need of a clear space about him, a clear second of time to recover his bearings, as a man staggers up in the ring.

He wished he had Peter now with him, helping him. Peter would have helped him, cleared his head, given him a second of grace. No, he wouldn't, either. He wouldn't have had Peter ever, backing him up. Peter and he were opposing forces. They'd always been enemies, friendly enemies, and now it was real. He'd forgotten that. He couldn't have Peter now.

He fought for time himself, in a harmless ruse. He looked at the statement in his hand, and asked idly:

"What does the 'A' stand for?"

"Adam," snapped the hotel manager.

Dennis took a deep breath. He didn't feel quite so dumb and dazed now. His head was getting clearer, and the objects in the room were coming out of the almost total darkness that had enveloped them. He could go into action again.

"Good-bye," he said amiably, going toward the door. "I always seem to be saying good-bye to people lately. There was Bianca—Bianca Farnese. I said good-bye to her this morning. Just before her funeral."

"That woman!" said the hotel manager, and the words were somehow spitting with his unconcealed contempt.

"Her name," said Dennis, "was Bianca Farnese, and she was a human being, and she's dead now. You're the second person I've met today who's called her 'that woman.' Her name was Bianca."

Fersen's nerves, under the strain of the past few minutes of sparring, suddenly snapped.

"Don't call her name in here!" he ordered brusquely.

"Bianca—Bianca—Bianca," said Dennis very distinctly, and vanished suddenly—indeed, to the somewhat distraught hotel manager, like a light blown out. That sorely tried gentleman wiped a wet and well-fleshed face with an immaculate white handkerchief wielded by a square, well-kept but slightly trembling hand, and gave a hearty Swiss curse.

Out in the corridor again, Dennis leaned against the wall and grinned a fleeting grin. He felt a lot better. That last rally had done him good.

"That was a low brawl!" he rebuked himself. "It reminded me a lot of two cats spitting at each other. Here, of all places. Peter wouldn't have approved of it. All the same . . ."

The glow of brief battle began to fade again. Dennis felt as though his teeth were going to chatter. He felt entirely defenseless and extremely cold again—that sick cold that made him craven. He wanted to hide from what he knew was coming.

"All the same," he said steadily, to himself, "you'll have to face it. Peter or no Peter. He could have done it. He knows Del Monte. His car is red and a roadster —he would have taken one just the opposite from his, dark and big and closed. He c-could have done it. He went down to Delroy, to meet us. He knew what Bowden told us. He knew where my squirrel gun was—I told him. He and Blake weren't together in the house all the time I left them there—he said he went upstairs. It fits in. Oh, damn it, it fits in! He d-defended me when he didn't have to "

Dennis broke off. "I feel like a cur trying to bite a man who's given him a good dinner," he told himself soberly. "But I've got to go on. I've got to."

He went on, there in the dim corridor.

"He may have known Bianca," he reasoned. "Peter's been around town for a year since he left college, and he knows plenty of people in this town. He may have met her—the most beautiful and rather notorious woman here. And if she did treat him a bit lightly, he wouldn't take it like the others did. He's got more to him. He won't take too rough treatment. Pete's— dangerous."

Dennis sighed and changed his place against the wall.

"He knows the Ancaster," he went on, very monotonously now, as though dulled by emotion. "He's gone to dinner with people who live on my floor—the Anstruthers. They're—very respectable people. I count them out. They haven't the feeling for murder, or for much else. He knows the Ancaster, and he saw me singing one evening in the studio, and knew I was there on a scheduled time every evening. He happened to think of that—when he wanted to. Only—Farnese? How does he come into it?"

Dennis was frightfully tired. He hardly felt that he wanted to go back a whole year, yet he had to. He moved his head restlessly against the sustaining wall.

"He comes," he said to himself meticulously, "because Peter loved Bianca, maybe. 'Way back. It was such a strong passion it lasted. He may have hit Farnese rather hard—and Farnese died of it. He may not have meant to kill Farnese at all. Just to hit him. A man could die of Peter's blow, if Peter was very angry."

That faint grin flickered up through unimaginable deeps again to Dennis's haggard face and dark eyes. It lingered a second, and then went out, for good.

"He would be," said Dennis simply, "if he knew I was standing here and trying to trace back his life so I could swear it away. I could hardly blame him for that."

He let his breath out again in a long shallow sigh, as though his life were slipping easily away there with it.

"Farnese's skull was fractured," he went back relentlessly like a tired ghost driven back and back again to a scene. "They said the automobile had done it. I thought he'd been hit by a club, or something. But a man hit by Peter, hard, and falling on a cement highway, could have his skull fractured, very easily. Far- nese might have been down at Del Monte when Peter was there, a year ago, and Bianca too probably, and he may have tried to blackmail Peter. Or threatened him. Anyway, he got his skull fractured. Then it would have been very easy to dump him into an automobile and go along the highway with him out from Del Monte until the road was lonely enough to let him out and leave him there on the highway. Then I came along."

His mind cut ahead again. The field opened up, all of it, so damnably easy. He almost hated that clear mind of his now. It saw too much.

"Morgan was a friend of Peter's, and Peter clears him," he thought, dragging the thought out almost against his will. "I'm nearly charged with murder, and Peter defends me. He doesn't want anyone else charged with it. I'll say that for him. He doesn't want to put murder onto anyone else. Manslaughter's—different, of course. And there was Blake. He didn't want Blake to be in on a murder case a year ago, with her brother involved. No, that all fits in, too."

But at the thought of Blake, such an agony seized him that he couldn't go on. Not to any conclusion. He just stood and suffered in a dumb stricture of agony like an animal's, with no means of expression or of relief for himself. It was hardly endurable. You just held on as best you could. It was like something dying, very slowly, very painfully, inside of you. You couldn't do anything. You just endured—and after a while it became better. You'd lived through that, at least.

Dennis gasped. His face was wet. He became aware that he'd passed through something like a mortal sickness and was on the other side of it for the present. He was better. He felt a bit more alive again. He lifted his head.

He hadn't moved. He was standing in the corridor of the Hotel Ancaster, in the dimly lit dusk apart from the lobby, and he'd gone through all that without any movement of his body except that of his drooping head against the wall. Funny, how you could travel in spirit such strange and terrible ways, while your own material self didn't even budge a step. He felt—convalescent, now. Terribly weak, but not so bad. He felt more alive. Even—hopeful, with the irresistible if unstable hopefulness of a man who'd just passed through a serious illness and was getting better. His head was clear and bright, if he did feel a bit weak.

He'd go on.

Maybe something would happen—

That irrepressible hopefulness urged him on, like life springing up again from a recently frozen, hard winter ground.

But he had only the blind, unreasoning conviction that it couldn't be like that. Peter Byrne couldn't be a murderer. All the same, his clear mind pulled him that way; something blind and dark and stubborn tried to pull him the other way. He couldn't give in to it. He wanted to too much.

He came into the lobby again, and a young man in a dinner suit, with a fair sunburnt head, turned away from the desk and saw him at the same minute. Dennis knew him, but slightly. He was Morgan, on the same floor with him. The man Peter'd traced to Monterey Bay, near

Del Monte, this morning, and the man Peter'd let go clear of the case with the explanation that he was a friend of his and out of it.

Morgan nodded to Dennis, saw his suitcase, and crossed over to intercept him.

"Hello," he said, being sociable in his nice way that made Dennis feel about a million years older than this fair-haired boy who always seemed just out of college. "Leaving us?"

He took out his cigarette case and offered Dennis a smoke.

"Thanks," said Dennis. "Yes. I'm on my way. I think maybe I'll rest up a bit—at Del Monte, maybe."

"A swell place," said young Morgan. "I was down there this morning—near there, anyway. Ran into Pete Byrne and his sister Blake down there. She's a pretty kid."

"Yes," said Dennis carefully. "Very."

"Which is lucky," Morgan said, "because Peter likes to have pretty girls around him." He grinned, frankly.

"Oh," said Dennis, "does he?"

"Well, he's in there now with a very golden-haired girl," Morgan indicated the doors of the Etruscan Room with his head. "She's in the chorus of a musical play here. At the Columbia. Pete's squiring her."

"There's a very pretty girl in Fersen's office." Dennis made conversation automatically, while his mind digested this information about Peter liking pretty women. "I saw her just now."

"And that's all," said Morgan disgustedly. "She goes home promptly at six every day. Never stays in the evenings."

"Why don't you offer to take her home?" Dennis retorted.

"I have," said young Morgan simply. "I offer to nearly every night. I even offer to talk business—hotel business—with her while we're going home. It doesn't work."

Dennis cocked an impolite and incredulous eyebrow at that black and white and gold butterfly with the nice grin talking hotel business. "Business?" he said.

"My dad's buying in," Morgan said. "Syndicate, you know. Fersen's managed this place for years for some old birds who never bother their heads about it much. He's a darn' good manager. We'll keep him on. The Ancaster'll just join a chain of hotels under the syndicate, that's all. And I'm sort of keen to start in here. Funny, isn't it? I think I'd be pretty good at it, though. I like playing host, you know. Of course, to start with I'd be in a 'way-down-under job and work up. I wouldn't mind that."

"No, I think it'd be okay for you," Dennis agreed. "If you like this kind of work, you'd be swell at it. Playing host."

"Oh, as a host," said Morgan, "or nearly so—I'd like to tell you we liked your singing here the other night, Devore. Monday night, it was."

Dennis stared at him in a sort of whiteness.

"I wasn't here," he said stiffly. "I was at the studio most of Monday night."

"Sure you were," Morgan said. "We tuned in on you in the Etruscan Room—by request. Our party wanted to hear your program. That was about just before twelve."

That was the night that Bianca had been killed here, Dennis thought dizzily. Monday night. November the third. Bianca had been here.

"I'm glad you liked it," he said, carefully. "Fersen wouldn't have liked it, if he'd known. He doesn't care much for me as a guest or any other way. I've just come from his office now."

"Oh-h-h," said young Morgan, with an understanding, long-drawn-out drawl, "you mean because of that killing up there, in your room? You can't blame him —much—for not liking that. That guy's goofy about his hotel, of course. No reason why he should put the blame for all this publicity on you, though. Listen—if he acted up—I mean there's no reason—" Young Morgan floundered in a stiff, choppy sea of embarrassment. "I mean," he brought it out, red-faced and looking at the end of his cigarette instead of at Dennis, "my dad's buying in here—and I've got a say—if you

want to stay here—"

"That's white of you," Dennis said softly. "But all the same, I'd rather go—down to Del Monte. No, Fersen's not driving me out. We just don't jibe, that's all. Lucky for him he couldn't hear me when I was singing here the other night. He doesn't like radio singers, especially me."

"Oh, he heard you!" said Morgan, puzzled, but polite. "He must have heard you. I asked the orchestra leader to stop playing for a few minutes while we got KDO on the loud speaker, and they did. The orchestra leader's got a phone there, connects with the hotel switchboard—people sometimes phone him for programs and to arrange parties, you know—and I used it to call Fersen in his office and see if he minded my cutting the orchestra off. I knew he wouldn't, of course —it was just a formality. But he didn't answer—so he must have been in the lobby at that time, and I guess he didn't object to it— he didn't say anything about it, anyway, to me."

"He probably didn't know who was on," Dennis said.

"Sure he did. He didn't mind," young Morgan said reassuringly. "The doors to the Etruscan Room were open to the lobby then. And they announced you between every song, by name. He must have heard you, but he didn't mind. You're seeing things."

"Yes," said Dennis. "I guess I am. I thought he'd be ready to bite me, even hearing me over a radio like that. Of course, that was before—before things really happened, that night."

"That's right!" said Morgan, getting interested. "That was the night of the murder here, wasn't it? We all missed that—didn't know a thing about it until the police came in. None of us, in my party at least, left the Etruscan Room until the cops came. We were all listening in on you."

"It seems to be a habit around here," said Dennis a bit dryly. "That night, anyway."

"Oh, you're famous," Morgan grinned. "The Ancaster claims you— or did. Say, Peter Byrne's your lawyer, isn't he? He's one grand guy, isn't he?"

"Yes," said Dennis in a muffled voice. "You know him well?"

"Stanford together—met him around town a bit afterward," Morgan said.

"He used to play football a lot, didn't he?" said Dennis, hating himself a lot. "What does he play now —any golf?"

"I think so," Morgan said. "I've seen him down at Del Monte sometimes, going round."

"Did you get to the tournament last week-end?" asked Dennis very casually. "Or did Pete?"

"No," said young Morgan regretfully. "I stayed here, like a good boy. School's beginning already for me, though I'm not officially here in any position yet, you know. But there was some sort of a convention here that winded up at Del Monte, and Fersen was pretty busy shuttling around just then between here and there, so I stayed here as sort of assistant manager. No, I don't know if Pete was down there or not last weekend. He probably was, if he could get off."

"You had a pretty girl to help you," Dennis consoled him. "I suppose the assistant manager inherited the office and all its fixings."

"A lot of good that did me with her," said young Morgan frankly. "She still went home promptly at 6 p. m. every evening, very businesslike."

"I hope she didn't get into this mess the other night," Dennis said. "It was sort of ghastly for anyone, let alone a girl."

"No, she didn't," Morgan said. "She went home as usual that night, too. Say, Devore—it's a funny case, isn't it? Is it—would it be too frightfully indiscreet to ask you if you or Peter have a line on it? Clues, you know, and all that? Or do you know now who did it? I know you and Byrne have been working on it."

Dennis looked down at his cigarette.

"We're—beginning to know," Dennis said slowly and very softly, almost as though he were speaking to himself. "We're dealing with two

people—persons. One of them is out in the pleasant light of day during
the entire time. We know him. He may be a friend. He may be a casual
acquaintance. Anyway, we know him. Perhaps we like him. He may
be—a friend of ours. The other's —a bit mad. If you c-call it mad—to
kill and hide behind—the first person."

He raised desolate eyes to young Morgan's friendly, sunburnt fair
face and attentive blue eyes.

"You see, they're—the same person," Dennis said. "That makes it—
d-difficult."

He rose and threw away his cigarette into the nearest ashtray.

"It must," said young Morgan sympathetically and quite
uncomprehendingly.

"It does," said Dennis briefly. He was himself again. "Difficult as
hell. I've got to get on. I'll be seeing you."

"Driving down?" asked Morgan.

Dennis shook his head. "Train. Got no car."

"I could arrange for one," his near-host informed him eagerly,
professional hotel instinct aroused at seeing a guest go forth into the
night carless. "I've got a big old hack here, keep it in the hotel garage
as sort of common property. I use my roadster a lot of the time myself,
but I keep this thing here in case I've got a big party to take around
places. It's old, but comfortable—got a powerful engine, too. Wait a
second, I'll see. Phone the garage."

His fair head crossed the lobby quickly, leaned over the black
phone on the room clerk's desk. He talked into the mouthpiece for a few
minutes, put the phone down, and came back again to where Dennis
waited, with a more rueful expression on his extremely candid young
countenance.

"Washout," he said. "Sorry. After all I said about it, too. It's out of
the garage now. It's sort of common property, you know. Anyone in the
hotel who's responsible, like you if I vouched for you, or me, or the
manager, or the chef, could use it, on hotel business. I'm frightfully
sorry, you'll have to take the train."

He spoke as if it were a misfortune that couldn't be equaled. As if
he'd said, "Sorry, here's a parachute, you'll have to go overboard."
Dennis smiled.

"I was going to, anyway," he pointed out. "I'm not out anything.
Thanks for thinking about it, anyway. I suppose you've let Pete Byrne
have it sometimes?"

"Any time he wanted it, he could have it," said Morgan. "I've been
down there in the garage with him, and they know he's a friend of
mine. I think he has had it out, once or twice."

"Well, I thank you for him, too," said Dennis, "as he's my lawyer.
I'll be going. Got to phone first, though."

He crossed over to the telephone room, just off the room clerk's desk space, shut himself into a booth, dropped a nickel in the slot, and said, when he had his number, "Sullivan there?"

"No, he isn't," the deep voice at the other end of the line answered. "Who's calling him?"

"Devore speaking," Dennis said. "Know where I can get him in a hurry?"

"Well, he left word," the cop at the other end in the Hall of Justice said. "He's at the post office—he was, anyway, when he phoned here. He's tracing them receipts, he said to tell you if you called up, and he wants samples of your handwriting. He's getting them from everybody. He also left some kind of a message about an officer at a door—he wants to know why in heck there was or wasn't one, at some door when he called there on his way to the post office this afternoon."

"Oh, yes," Dennis murmured, while his mind worked busily. "There was one, officer. Only it was at the wrong door. That's what he meant. He wanted you to send one good stout officer over pronto to the Hotel Ancaster and station him outside the door of old Mrs. Appleby's suite, fourth floor—got that?—and take notice of every- one going in or out of that door. It's very important. And I'm in a frightful hurry."

"Yeah," said the cop, evidently writing this down in earnest heaviness. "I got that. What else?"

"Tell Sullivan," said Dennis more sweetly, "that I've been at the Hotel Ancaster, and I've found out practically all about it. All he has to do is arrest the man I tell him to. Got that?"

He hung up the phone, stood ruffling his hair impatiently for a second with the flat of his hand, came out of the booth and considered.

"A frightful hurry," he repeated absently. His eyes were darkly worried, crowded with thoughts. "Only I can't move—until I've made them safe. To go away like that—and leave them here unguarded—it just can't be done. Not anyhow. Not though—I know all about it."

And all of a sudden his eyes cleared of thought, became once more dark and untroubled and luminous, as though he smiled deep within them. A clear pool, in the dark of a calm evening, when even the night wind was hushed, Dennis's eyes reminded one of, then. Peter's eyes were clear pools in the daylight, reflecting calm blue sky, but Dennis's dark eyes reflected stars at night when they were calm and at peace.

Dennis thought to himself, standing there, hands in his overcoat pockets, hat on as a disguise for his bandaged head, waiting for promised relief from the Hall of Justice:

"Peter's in there with a gold-headed chorus girl. Peter likes pretty girls. Peter had access to a big, dark closed car. Peter knew Delroy country pretty well. Peter this and Peter that. Morgan let me drag it all out of him. Sure, Peter did this and that and had ac- cess to this hotel and to Delroy. And if I saw Pete Byrne with the bloody knife in his large brown hand coming out of my room two seconds after Bianca'd died there, I'd know he hadn't done it! And thank God," said Dennis very sincerely, "that I had sense enough not to really believe that—and the hell with split infinitives—in spite of Morgan and my own eyes and my very clever mind figuring it all out! I was—just being clever, that's all. Peter was right. I'm too apt to be."

Dennis laughed, soundlessly but very keenly, eyes very bright, face eager again. He felt like a too eager pup on the trail who thought for a while he'd scared up a mountain lion instead of a rabbit, and who knows now to his great and inexpressible pleasure that it was just a rabbit after all. He bounded forward again.

"Now," he said, "from what I know of him, what would he do with Father Malletti? Where would he take him? And—what did he want with Wong?"

He thought acutely for a second. His mind leaped forward in great bounds, like an eager dog clearing obstacles that ordinarily are too much for him. He was, so to speak, playing 'way over his head for a moment, caught up by the fire of chase and of battle. His mind caught up with—something. Began to worry it. Like a too eager dog, wouldn't let go. . . .

"Oh, no," said Dennis, in a very small voice, without any feeling at all in it. As if horror had dulled it. As if he were looking at something he wished he hadn't had to look at. He'd caught up with it. "No," he said, in a futile defiance again. "It couldn't—he couldn't do that. Not with Wong. That's why he wanted—"

He made a gesture, a forward movement to fling this thought away from him. It wouldn't go. Dennis's face was white again, as white as the bandage over his dark head. He had to move—to move quickly—his face was ablaze with a sort of white impatience and fear.

Only he couldn't go—yet. He had to stay. He didn't know where Sullivan was, either. He had to wait in this dim corridor away from the too lighted lobby, away from Peter, from young Bill Morgan, from any too curious eyes, until the promised policeman came, to station himself at that door he'd promised protection.

Only he couldn't wait. There wasn't any time. This was Thursday, and Father Malletti had been gone since Saturday. An old man—he couldn't hold out. Not any longer. And Wong was there, too.

Dennis at this moment saw with rather abstracted eyes something that said "For Fire Only" on the wall beside him. It seemed to be the sort of thing you pulled down, like a hook. It reminded him of something.

"Kennedy said this would be a nice friendly visit here," he thought. "He didn't see what could possibly happen here. I didn't, either. At the time. But now—if he's listening, he'll be able to hear the fire engines going by, all right."

He then knocked out a small pane of glass, pulled some sort of a small lever down, and released it again. Then he waited, leaning stilly up against the alarm box. He fished around for pencil and paper and began writing.

Pretty soon he heard the fire engines outside. They seemed to be making quite a bit of noise as they stopped outside the hotel. There'd be a great deal of noise and confusion within and without, firemen rushing around in odd places where they usually weren't, and perhaps a little water spilled around. There'd be protection. No one would go stealthily around—he couldn't—when there were firemen rushing around each corridor rescuing people. There'd be guests' heads popping out of doors with inquiring expressions. It wouldn't be any time for a killer who liked the shade and quietness to pick for another killing. Dennis thought he'd arranged it quite neatly, after all.

The first of the firemen rushed into the lobby. They had oilskin coats and long drooping-looking hats on, and one of them had an axe. Dennis stepped out to meet them.

"I'm expecting Inspector Sullivan around here in a minute," he said. "Would you mind giving him this note?"

He walked on quietly out of the lobby, leaving behind him a folded note which, when opened five minutes later by a white-faced Sullivan, turned out to be a hotel statement, marked "Paid. November 6th" and signed in a small and lovely handwriting by A. Fersen. Under that Dennis had written hastily in pencil, "This is a sample of my handwriting. Dennis Devore," in a much more sprawling hand, as requested.

Dennis was nothing if not obliging.

# XXIII. SO THEY CAME OUT—

Dennis came out to the sidewalk and said to himself:

"He may be dead! And if they find him there—I can't take any chances. I've discovered too many bodies already. Oh, it's damned clever! Even Peter would say so. If they found Father Malletti—dead— or dying—in my house at Delroy, I'd lose my last friend on that. And someone meant me to. And break my neck over it, too, into the bargain."

He was walking down the steep hill street now, going like a river unconsciously with the descent down into Market Street, at a pretty stiff pace. All the street lamps were lit, soft gold globes in the dark and misty night, and the Path of Gold flared softly and brilliantly and beautifully high overhead all down Market Street to the Ferry Building and the bay. Dennis felt as though he were an invisible ghost walking among all these people going by, hearing bursts of laughter, sounds of brief conversation, noise of cars and traffic whistles and street cars rushing by. He thought: "I can't go to Sullivan or Kennedy or anyone— for if they find Father Malletti dead in my house, I'm done for. Someone has seen to that. And I haven't much money—I paid out my hotel bill, and I'm pretty short, and the banks aren't open now. What'll I do?"

He halted at a particularly busy corner, staring about him as one awakened, and saw the slim copper shaft of Lotta's fountain in the middle of the intersection where three streets met, and across the street the clock, and Kennedy's tall gray *Star* building with lights in every window shining through the evening.

"There!" thought Dennis with a wild relief. He plunged into the traffic with an abandon which whitened several more hairs in the head of an already iron-gray traffic officer there, made it to the opposite side unscathed, coming up to the sidewalk again like a dog who has breasted a strong current, and disappeared around the corner of the building before any official action could be taken.

Here he stopped and caught his breath in a great sigh, almost a sob, of relief. It was the alleyway where he'd come out with Kennedy the other day—days ago—and there was the discreet taxi hovering, or rather sleeping near, its entrance, the driver huddled over the wheel reading a newspaper.

Dennis wrenched the door open and said:

"Quick! Get her going, will you? I've got to get down country to Delroy tonight!"

The driver raised a dispassionate thin face and surveyed his uninvited passenger.

"Can't be done," he said. "This cab belongs to the *Star*."

"But this is on *Star* business!" said Dennis crisply. "Step on it, guy."

"Got a press badge? Or an order from the desk?" the man inquired more alertly but still suspiciously, not stirring.

"Listen," said Dennis calmly but desperately, "you know me. I came here with Kennedy, the man on police, the other morning. You took me to Kennedy's house. I haven't got time to get any orders—this is urgent."

"Yeh, but—'way down to Delroy!" the driver demurred.

"I'm with Kennedy, I tell you!" Dennis insisted.

"Yeh, but how do I know if Kennedy is good for a long ride like this?"

"You'll know!" said Dennis ominously. He reached forward and picked the man out of his seat with one hand clamped on his shoulder, and as he'd heave a javelin on a long throw he sent him sprawling through the opposite door. The driver spoke, once.

"Things," said Dennis to him, "are just beginning to happen. That was nothing at all."

He drove away with the startled driver's expressions of astonishment half heard above the roaring shift into high. That was at San Francisco, at the beginning of night. Say six o'clock. Afterwards Dennis couldn't remember much about that ride except the way the engine droned so monotonously, so reassuringly, and the way his right foot got still and numb on the accelerator. Sometimes he was conscious of the towns going through, the little wayside towns with the lights in the streets and the houses, and sometimes he knew there were wide fields on either side of him, and the wind blowing past the windshield to his hair and face. But mostly he just drove in a suspension of thought. There wasn't anything to think about, any more. That was all over. All he had to do was to get down to Delroy, and there wasn't any use sending his mind ahead of him down there. He was so damned tired of thinking. He was so damned tired.

He lay back and drove on, without any thought or feeling. Occasional stray thoughts went by in the wide spaces of his mind, and out again, like birds flying through a dark night. . . .

Night was the best time to drive. Not so much traffic on the road then—and what there was, was making time. What was he doing, anyway, driving on and on like this? He didn't know—didn't want to know. He'd had a good reason at the beginning, anyway, and he couldn't be bothered to look it up and sort it all out again. Just keep on going. *"What country, love, is this?" "This is Illyria, stranger."* That was wrong, he knew, but he couldn't be bothered to straighten it out now. The sense was the same. The words sang themselves to him over and over—*"What country, love . . .""Illyria, stranger."* That was a very far-away country, too. Things happened in it.

He half checked the big car involuntarily at a remembered landmark—a white stone bridge showing up out of the black night. He swung it forward again, full speed ahead, through country that even in the dark was familiar to him now. Here a slight grade, going up — around the corner of a mountain—there straightening out, a curve on level ground again—he followed the white road in the dark, headlights shining on ahead. Here Farnese had died—Victor Farnese—killed by his car once. No, Farnese had been dead before the car hit him. He'd lain there on that stretch of road for Dennis to come along and hit again. Oh, you couldn't let ghosts reach out and grab your hands from the wheel now! Get going, guy. Dennis was miles past the place where Farnese had lain in the road a year ago. He'd laid that ghost.

He was on the dirt road to his place, off the highway. He had to slow up. It was nearing midnight, from the looks of the stars. It was deep midnight, and the stars were very bright. There were no lights in his house at all. There wouldn't be. He had matches.

He left the car before the house and went on up to the front steps. There was no sound from the silent and dark house. He tried the front door. It was locked. He listened. Whatever else there was was listening, too.

There wasn't any sound at all.

*"What country, love, is this?"*

It went through his head like sign and countersign.

*"This is Illyria, stranger."*

Illyria—the place where strange, where terrible things could happen. He was on its threshold. Should he go in?

It had already drawn him in. He was an inhabitant of that strange country. Whether he wanted to be or not. He was unlocking the front door with his key, and the noise grated in the quiet night. The door swung open. The house waited for him.

Dennis went up the inside stairs in the dark, the house creaking and protesting about him. He tried doors. They opened. He went into one room and held a lighted match up, and found nothing—only the usual furniture, bulky and dark in the dim room—bed and bureau and chairs.

The frost mist of November over the fields outside made the old house desperately chilly. Dennis was glad he had Kennedy's coat on. He couldn't help shivering a lot, at that. His teeth wouldn't clamp together tightly. —they insisted on trying to chatter. It was horribly cold here.

He left that room and tried the next, and another match flared up into his eyes for a second of confusing light. And he looked on the narrow bed and saw Father Malletti laid out there, a thin, long line of black against the white cover. Dennis's hand shook uncontrollably. The match flickered and went out. He lit another, set it to the oil lamp on the bureau there. Then he turned around and looked at the bed again. His eyes were blinded with darkness before them and in them. He couldn't see for a second.

The light caught, slowly, slowly, and grew in the room. Dennis watched things coming clearer. He looked at Father Malletti again.

Someone had closed his eyes. The thin face, white as the white bedcover, sunken and calm as a death mask, had his sweet life written on it in deep lines of nostrils and straight-set thin mouth.

Dennis found himself on his knees, beside the bed.

"O God," he said to himself intensely, "if he's dead—let him into his heaven."

He laid a tentative hand on Father Malletti's, lying there so frail. It was warm. Faintly warm. Like the merest flicker of life hanging on. Father Malletti had come to the end of the long leash of life, with very little farther left for him to go. Dennis recognized that.

The sunken eyelids opened, heavily, slowly. Father Malletti's deep eyes looked out at him, from great distances. They were dark eyes, like Dennis's, but deep-set in the arched caverns of their sockets.

"Alive!" thought Dennis. "Alive. Alive."

He hardly dared breathe for fear of blowing out that flickering bit of life before him, deep in the depths of Father Malletti's dark eyes. He feared that the pounding of his heart would be too gusty for the frail craft of Father Malletti's life, when he touched him with hammering pulses beating through his fingers.

He got up, a bit unsteadily, and went out through the door quickly. He left the lamp in Father Malletti's room, and lit matches, groping his way to the stairs again. He lit the lamp in the cold kitchen and started putting wood in the stove. He couldn't think very clearly. Father Malletti was here, and alive, and that was wonderful—but where was Wong? He was afraid for Wong.

He worked quickly, methodically, making some beef broth from cubes, sticking more wood in the fire, taking the cup up to Father Malletti when it was steaming in his hand. He couldn't wonder about Wong now. Later—later . . .

Father Malletti took the beef broth very slowly, fed by Dennis from a spoon. The room was getting warmer. The light glowed from the lovely lamp of the old-fashioned oil burner set on the bureau. Father

Malletti opened his deep eyes again and saw Dennis bending over him, intent frown between his brows, lips apart a little in his intensity. Father Malletti's face was warming to life again—the waxen whiteness displaced by a slightly softer color and contour. The soft gold light was kind to his face. Dennis breathed heavily and unconsciously through his parted lips, and looked at Father Malletti with his intent little frown stabbing his forehead.

"Are you all right, sir?" said Dennis, forgetting with the arrogance of superbly supple youth that Father Malletti was an old man and had a lot longer to go back from danger than he or Peter would have had. Father Malletti moved his lips faintly. Dennis frankly grinned. He took that for a good sign. Then he leaned forward to listen to that faint murmur of breath coming from the thin lips.

"Another," said Father Malletti in a thin thread of a voice.

"Another?" said Dennis. "Is there?" He considered this to himself. "Here?" he demanded.

Father Malletti said something that Dennis took for a "Yes." Only a very hopeful person could have translated that faint sign so.

"We'll get him," he said confidently. "Drink this, sir."

They finished the cup of broth. Dennis took Father Malletti's thin cold hands in his vital warm brown ones and rubbed them gently. He took off Father Malletti's shoes and rubbed the cold feet evenly and gently till he felt the warmth creeping into them. He put a white woolen blanket over the thin blackness on the bed, and Father Malletti lay there drowned in whiteness like snow, only his dark eyes alive, watching Dennis.

Then Dennis turned to go. He wasn't sure that Father Malletti understood what he was saying, but he felt that he owed it to him to explain anyway.

"I'm going to hunt for the other," he told him. "I'll be back, soon, sir—before you can get cold again. I've got to go."

He turned back again, slipped the overcoat from his shoulders, laid it over the white blanket carefully, and, satisfied with his work, departed.

He'd searched the two bedrooms upstairs. He'd been in the kitchen. He went, kitchen lamp in hand, through the rest of the house. There wasn't anything there except the dim furniture. Was it Wong that Father Malletti had meant? He wasn't there. Or was it—another? The other—the killer. Dennis frankly didn't feel like meeting him yet. Things were too darned uncertain. Father Malletti was just on the edge yet, and he might slip backwards into the cold again. Wong was somewhere, and he might need help. And Dennis was only one person—not really a fighting outfit, just a rescue squad. He needed reinforcements.

He wondered a bit dizzily why he hadn't thought of that before. He'd just gone ahead. Something inside of him had driven him on, regardless. Had taken charge of him for a while, all down the road to Delroy. He hadn't, in fact, been quite—responsible. He'd been like those monomaniacs, people with just one idea in their heads at a time. His idea had driven him down here, alone, without leaving any definite word to anybody. Dennis wondered vaguely why he'd been impelled to do it so at the time.

He came out of the kitchen door and surveyed the landscape, holding the lamp up. The whitewashed tool shed and the outhouses were dim bulks against the dark. The black frost caught his breath in a terrible damp chill, as though he were breathing ice. He left the kitchen steps and went on across to the sheds and lean-tos, and there was no one there. So then he thought that Wong was dead, after all, and the terrible cold chill fell on him silently, freezing all feeling, all tears.

He came back to the kitchen, went up to Father Malletti again, stoked wood downstairs, all in a silence that wouldn't let him go. Then he went to the phone, called San Francisco, got Kennedy on the line again.

"It's Dennis," he said.

"Wait a second," said Kennedy at that. "I'll take it in a closed booth."

He waited till that crisp and indomitably cheerful voice came over the line again: "Well, Dennis? What's the good news this time? I suppose you know Sullivan's searching San Francisco for you, looking behind every cushion and shaking out the curtains?"

"Yes, well," said Dennis dully, "he can find me down here, Kennedy. In Delroy. I've found Father Malletti."

Kennedy was stricken dumb. For a definite space of time there was silence on the line. Then he asked, only, quietly:

"Alive?"

"Yes," Dennis said, "but—"

"That's all, Dennis," Kennedy said in a new and very quiet tone of authority that Dennis unconsciously responded to. "Don't say any more—over the phone. You've said plenty! Only—wait a second. Are you at —the same place you were last time?"

"Yes," said Dennis.

"All right—stick there. We'll be right down. Are you—okay?"

"Yes," said Dennis. He heard the phone click as Kennedy hung up the receiver at his end of the line. He stuck his on the hook again and went up to Father Malletti.

Upstairs again he looked at his watch. How long would Kennedy take? He saw with a faint shock of surprise that it wasn't midnight, after all. It was only ten o'clock. He'd thought that hours and hours had gone by, in that ride down to here. The night was the longest he'd ever known. Longer than hospital nights, when he'd broken a leg once. It was the longest and darkest night.

He sat down by Father Malletti and sometimes he felt his face and hands and feet to see if they were cold, and sometimes he stirred to give him water or a bit of broth. A long time later Father Malletti looked at him more clearly and spoke in the lingering remnants of a tone of lifelong authority.

"What are you doing here, then?"

It was like a ghost summoning one to judgment. Dennis answered it straightly:

"This is my house, sir. Someone brought you here, and I found you. Someone wanted to know what Bianca Farnese told you, last Saturday night when she saw you."

Father Malletti considered this, eyes closed. Then he spoke.

"She asked me," said Father Malletti, "whether a dead man can live again. What do you make of that, now? I thought myself"—the thin breath labored to bring out each word—"it was a riddle."

"Either a riddle or a miracle, maybe," said Dennis. But his eyes were bright in thought. "What did you tell her?"

The deep old eyes shone darkly alive as Dennis's own eyes, in that sunken mask of an indomitable old face.

"I told her," said Father Malletti, "the best way for a dead man to live again in this world was in his works, and for her to be on her knees and pray for him in the next world."

Father Malletti was throwing aside the handicap of his frail and ill-used old body as a man much used to conquering it. His mind was bright and clear now.

"Dead men do rise up," mused Dennis. "Look at you, Father Malletti. Look at me. I'm supposed to be dead, too. And we're both here."

He smiled at his companion. "Are you warm, sir? It's a cold night, and very dark. It's like—death, I think."

He gave a little shudder.

"Be putting something around you," commanded Father Malletti, rising in spirit to the occasion from his bed of frailness. "And surely don't be telling me you're afraid of death. A fine boy like you!"

"That's just it," said Dennis frankly. "When I go, I'm—nothing. A body that can run a hundred in ten, sometimes, that can kick and block and tackle as well as you'd choose, that can feel the sun and the wind on it—all this means nothing. I can't take it with me. And it's all I've got. I have a great joy in it, Father Malletti. Can you understand that?"

Dennis could talk to Father Malletti the way he'd never talked to anyone before.

"Now you're different," he said earnestly. "You've got practically nothing to do with your body any more —you're a guest in it, you don't do things with it like running and kicking for the sheer joy in doing them, sir. You're different—you don't have to worry about going to heaven, or if*there is any heaven, sir."

"Haven't you any faith?" said Father Malletti sternly.

"I don't know," said Dennis. "I prayed for you when I thought you were dead here, sir. I prayed that you'd gone to heaven. I think that's a pretty good act of faith, to pray for another person's entrance to a place you hardly believe in yourself."

Something almost like a laugh came into Father Malletti's piercing eyes.

"That'll hardly be counted against you," he assured his host a bit dryly. He fell silent again.

After a while:

"When I was a young man," said Father Malletti, as though to himself, "I was a great swimmer. I loved to swim in the ocean, when it was a fine day or a rough one. Many a time . . ."

He lay there smiling a bit. Then he roused himself again.

"You're not of our faith?" he said again.

"I've never thought much about it, sir."

"You will," said the old man surely. "You will."

He didn't speak again after that, but fell into sleep again. Dennis thought that saints were very single-minded people.

After a while he heard false dawn being heralded from just outside by a sleepy cock, and he roused himself to go down to the stove again and stoke. He unwrapped himself from his blanket, thrust it sleepily away from him, stumbling in its folds, and went nearly in total darkness, eyes closed sleepily, down the stairs he knew so well.

He came into the kitchen, bent over the oil lamp again, struck a match—heard a slight sound, and remained, head bent, hand poised, above the globe as he looked up.

The kitchen door was opening. Dennis waited. The man who Dennis knew would come was there, pale face looking at him for a second.

"You!" said Dennis softly.

He wasn't surprised.

The match flared and went out. He dropped its blackened stem from his fingers. The door had closed. He knew that by the cessation of cold draft along the floor, by the slight thud of its jamming.

He was alone in there with a killer. The pale face still looked at him, the eyes burned brightly, in a sort of inhuman, unswerving, even dispassionate hatred. It was no use arguing with that sort of look—no use pleading, or playing for time, or doing anything but fighting now. Those eyes didn't see—reason. They hated, and watched their chance ... in the dark.

Dennis in the dark poised himself on his toes, ready for attack, hands held up to his chest, ready to launch himself. This was the last great line smash, maybe, and he wanted to make it good. He wasn't afraid. Not any more. He was in the game now, and he wanted to play it. He wanted to fight, and play a good game. He was impatient for the signal.

He heard the sound he'd been waiting for, body poised like a back's ready to plunge forward, and he located it —scrape of foot against the floor, there—and plunged. He hit something solid that grunted in a startled way as though the breath were out of its body. Then he was met by attack as fierce as his own, after that first  irresistible giving away as his body struck the other's.

Their arms around each other, they rolled to the floor, struck the table, wrestled up again. Dennis tore his right arm free from those powerful smothering ones and began hitting, with a monotonous regularity. He heard, above their hoarse breathing, the smacking thud of his fist going in each time. The other grunted in a distressed way and got an arm across Dennis's throat, pulling it back in a way that almost cut off breathing. Dennis knew he couldn't stand much of that. He couldn't see to hit, either. He put his fist straight forward, hit the other's face, and felt the arm strangling him slip from his neck. Encouraged, he hit again, missed, shook his dazed head and plunged in again, felt something solid in front of his blows again and stood there and socked like a boxer gone blood-wild, all science cast aside for the moment.

They used each other for punching bags for a minute, then Dennis felt his opponent soften, fade away from before his blows, slipping. He heard a heavy crash that shook the floor. He was down. There was only a curious rasping sort of snore from the ground. Dennis stood there a second, raised shaking hands and wiped the sweat from his wet face with the palms of both hands, gasping for breath. He was shaking, and his heart was hammering like a loud clanging bell in his body. He wanted air and plenty of it. He went to the door, opened it, stood there dizzily, heard someone say:

"Reach for heaven, guy!"

He sidestepped automatically, lunged forward, hand stretched out stiffly, in a last effort of command over his sagging body. His hand struck someone's hard chin  and shoved it out of the way.

There was a bright light there now. He looked with nearly darkened weary sight down at the man he'd spilled, and, in the bright glare of the automobile headlights trained on them, saw too late that he'd stuck his fist again too hastily into the face of his friend Peter.

He felt himself falling forward helplessly. He felt a heavy hand on his shoulder, yanking him to his feet. It spun him around, and as his dark head fell forward on his chest he saw Sullivan, and slid down to his feet.

A little while later he was talking to Peter.

"He looked at me," said Dennis, "at the inquest, and afterwards in the hotel, and his eyes were red as a cornered rat's. He was a very pleasant man," said Dennis dizzily, "only his eyes were red like a rat's."

"Dennis, come to," said Peter, shaking him. Dennis opened a pair of dazed dark eyes and found himself in some sort of semidarkness that shifted and moved a little, with his head on Peter's broad shoulder.

"You're so beautifully sane, Peter," he said drowsily. "I do like blue eyes. There aren't any shadows or red lights in them. Except once in a while clouds, like the sky."

"Dennis," said Peter, "how did you know?"

Dennis obligingly opened weary eyes again in slight surprise.

"He did everything short of shoving the knife in my hand and giving me a push," he said. "I sort of wondered. It was so perfect."

That was that. He heard Sullivan's deep voice say something about "concussed" and slid without any further interruptions into that sunlit ocean of sleep.

# XXIV. —AND SAW THE STARS AGAIN

It was afternoon in San Francisco.

"Dennis," said Kennedy, "doesn't it strike you as somewhat of a miracle that Father Malletti was kept alive, on a wild sea coast, from Saturday to Thursday— when he was placed in your house, in his condition?"

"Why—no," said Dennis wonderingly. "I didn't at the time."

"How is Father Malletti?" asked Blake of Sullivan softly.

That massive gentleman smiled on them affably.

"Getting along fine," he said. "He's got Father O'Bannon with him now. That was a smart trick of yours, Dennis, to get Father O'Bannon to identify that hotel-manager rat Fersen as their visitor that Saturday night, by listening to his voice in the next room."

"He didn't see Fersen's face that night," said Dennis, "but I knew a man with a voice like Father O'Bannon's had a good ear."

He smiled in great satisfaction at Sullivan. "As long as you give me credit for suggesting that, I'll take it," he said. "But to tell you the whole truth, I don't remember that part of it at all. When was that?"

Peter grinned. "That was in the police car coming back from Delroy," he said. "You sat and babbled to me, Dennis. You were talking at first about a man with rat's eyes looking at you. At first we thought you were punch-drunk. You and Fersen gave each other a swell cleaning up. He was very messy when we went in and found him. He's got a scalp wound where his head got laid open on the edge of the stove, too. It was lucky for you I'm a pretty slow shot, when you didn't stop, coming out of the house. I nearly got you, then I saw in time who it was. But you weren't punch-drunk."

"No," said Sullivan heartily. "It was just a little concussion."

"Just a little concussion," said Kennedy softly. "Nothing at all. In fact, a lot of people think that's the normal state of brain of a wirehaired pup anyway."

Dennis grinned at him. " Do you want me to go on?"

"By all means," Kennedy told him. "You might explain the main point of this, anyway, Dennis. Fersen sits there—he sat there last night—while we tried to reason with him about spilling the story, and he sort of snarls at us, showing his teeth slightly, and reminds me as you say of a nice plump rat that knows he's caught."

"Yes," nodded Peter to Dennis's inquiring look, "you weren't there in spirit with us, Dennis. We dumped you down on the leather couch in Kennedy's editor's office when we came back last night from Delroy, and you slept there peacefully while the *Star* Building was barricaded, telephone switchboard guarded, the chief of police and a number of detectives and reporters and such gathered around Fersen, trying to get him to talk—it was the biggest night the *Star* has ever seen. They didn't even issue any early editions until the other morning papers had all come out, so there wouldn't be any leaks. A couple of huskies from another paper tried to break in by the alley, and there was a swell fight. No one could get in or out after we came home with the bacon. And you were sleeping away on the couch in the same room with all of this rumpus about Fersen!"

"He didn't talk?" asked Dennis.

"Not unless you call that snarl of his articulate," said Peter. "I don't care much for it myself."

"Well," said Dennis, "this is it. There were two brothers—must have been brothers, or else why the change in name of one? One was Victor Farnese, a wholesale produce dealer of San Francisco. The other was trained in Switzerland, near Italy, for a hotel career. He came out here after a while, probably in accordance with his brother's suggestion. He got a hotel. He was a pretty good man at his job. But there was a flaw in him, a big one. It found him out. He and his brother Victor agreed to cook the hotel's accounts; they fixed it up on Victor Farnese's bills. I'll bet Farnese was the moving spirit in this, for two reasons—he was first on the ground here, knew the lay of the land, and also he was the one who either suggested that his brother change his name or actually picked it out for him. In fact, I know he did. Fersen never picked out that name for himself. So," said Dennis, "they fiddled with a lot of accounts, and took big profits for a while. For a lad who can't add three and four without getting something he shouldn't, I'm doing well in this rarefied atmosphere of high finance," added Dennis modestly, pausing to admire himself.

"You have us all gasping for breath," agreed Peter. "Go on."

"The inevitable happened," said Dennis, going literary under the stimulus of an audience. "He and Farnese had a fight. They didn't trust each other. I don't blame 'em. I wouldn't have either. He—Fersen— killed his brother down at Del Monte last year. Blamed it onto me. He was safe for a year. Then his brother rose up and slew him—or is going to hang him, anyway. The first intimation he had of it was what Bianca said to him."

Blake and Kennedy made it a dead heat.

"What did Bianca say?" demanded Blake.

"How did Farnese kill her?" demanded Kennedy.

"Don't you know?" asked Dennis. Peter growled warningly. "Well," hastened Dennis, "Fersen was in love with Bianca. I guess that was partly why he killed his brother, too. Envied him. But Bianca didn't know he was Farnese's brother. After Farnese was dead, Fersen made love to his brother's widow. Then the hotel was going to be sold and an accounting demanded. Fersen had made a lot of money. Some he'd spent on Bianca, and some on the stock market, I'll bet a nickel. Anyway, it went. He didn't have any to show the accountants, and he knew it. He was planning for a getaway with what he had. He wasn't cleaning up hotel affairs, he was cleaning up his own late at night. Then for once he got reckless. He knew he was going to be forced to leave soon anyway, and he wanted desperately to take Bianca with him. He sent her a letter. A passionate, signed letter. Probably begging her to come with him and giving her some directions for tickets—things like that—if she agreed to run away with him. And in his emotional stress he signed his real name—Farnese—to his reckless, desperate letter."

"Dennis," said Sullivan heavily, "have you been holding out on me again?"

Dennis shook his head decidedly.

"Then it's just a guess?"

"Oh, spring it on Fersen!" Dennis said impatiently. "He'll tell you it's true. It must be."

"Go on."

"And Bianca looked at the note and wondered. And she called Fersen around to her and asked him a question."

"What question?" Sullivan asked.

"She asked him why his name was Farnese," Dennis said.

The others sighed sharply.

"He couldn't answer. He was dumfounded, confused. He'd thought that was too well hidden from anyone. Bianca got suspicious. He couldn't bluff it out then—too late. She told him she was going to ask Father Malletti for advice. She went to Father Malletti. That night Father Malletti was—called away to a parishioner. Bianca didn't connect the two events then. Fersen called her and asked her to come see him privately at the hotel and he'd explain everything. Bianca came—and he killed her. He knew she would be merciless now that her suspicions were roused. She was his brother's widow. She'd already talked."

"But you said that all she had asked Father Malletti was if a dead man could live again?" Kennedy asked keenly.

Dennis nodded. "Yes. She meant Farnese. Why was Fersen taking the name of Farnese? She didn't know. She talked in riddles around the subject. She was puzzled. And Farnese did live again. He came out of his grave and slew his brother."

"Dennis!" said Blake in a soft little wail.

"D-darling," said Dennis to her alone, "you'll see it. Farnese had a sense of humor—rough, but serviceable. When he made up his brother's fake name, he made it up out of the letters of his own name.

No one saw it then. Bianca's been playing anagrams since then with some of her gentlemen friends. She saw it all, when she saw that signature—A. Fersen. It was Farnese and had always been Farnese. I saw it when he put it on the hotel bill. That's why I gave the bill to Sullivan. I was scared to tell him anything, in that hotel. I left him the bill as a hint. Fersen wasn't a humorous or a playful man. He'd never played anagrams in his life. Many people do nowadays. It amused Farnese to have his brother labeled with his own name all the time."

"It'll help hang him," said Sullivan. "I hope that'll amuse Victor Farnese."

"Probably," agreed Dennis. "Now you tell tales for a while. Just how'd you find Wong?"

"That was Blake," said Peter proudly.

"I sent for Louie," said Blake clearly, "when I came up from Monterey yesterday afternoon—I'd had lots of time to think on the road up—and I just said, 'Louie, where's Wong?' And he was hiding out in Louie's place in Chinatown. They belong to the same tong, and are very brotherly about it."

"The old heathen!" said Dennis proudly. A sharp high cackle answered him. Wong had been listening to his Dennis talking, hearing the sound of the loved voice, though he couldn't understand just what Dennis was driving at. "Why'd you skip out, Wong? Tell the company so they can understand it."

"He say, 'Dennis, he one mudderer,'" he shrilled. Peter stirred protestingly and got red.

"That was when Blake and I were discussing things around the stove at your place, Dennis," he protested. "After the sheriff took you up for the Bowden affair. We were saying what other people would say about you now."

"I know," said Dennis soothingly. "Go on, Wong."

"Wong say, 'Oh-h-h no,'" the brown heathen image shrilled out defiantly. "He say, yes-s-s, he one time kill man, one time kill woman, plenty bad fo' Dennis. What fo' Bowden dies when Dennis comes back heah again? He say, suppose one time Wong does that fo' Dennis. Wong think suppose he one time disappeah, no mo' Wong, they think Wong do it. Wong he makes bed, take his clo', go with tluck dlivah all up load, Sanfacisco. Goo'bye, till Dennis no mudderer again. Tha's all."

"Well," said Dennis, looking at them with eyes darkly bright, suspiciously bright, "I was wrong, that's all. Men have died for love, from time to time, though worms have eaten them for it. You know," said Dennis humbly, "I think at times I've been a damned fool," said Dennis very humbly indeed. "It's so difficult not to be, isn't it, Inspector?"

Sullivan got red under his broad tan. Peter snorted joyfully.

"But," said Dennis gravely, "if you hadn't skipped out for me, Wong, it would have been just too bad for you. Because Wednesday night, after Bowden was killed, after Blake and Peter had left my house, Father Malletti was planted there, still alive but very weak, from some hiding place where he'd been lying since Saturday night, to die. And if Wong had been there when the killer came to do that—there wouldn't have been any Wong.

"Here is the series of events: Saturday night, Father Malletti taken. Monday night, Bianca killed at the hotel, Dennis held for questioning by police. Tuesday, investigation in San Francisco. Wednesday, we went down to Delroy, didn't find Father Malletti, saw Bowden. Bowden was killed that night, afterwards. Wong went away. Fersen brought Father Malletti from where he'd hidden him since Saturday night in some little cove along the coast, up to my house, to be discovered—dead—in due time. Thursday, yesterday, up at the hotel here, Fersen was getting worried. Things were crowding him. He went down to Delroy to kill Father Malletti—in my house—for good. He was getting a bit cracked about me. He didn't like it because the police had let me go after Bianca's killing. He rang me in there because I was just out of a mansalughter sentence for Farnese's killing, and he thought it would be a swell coincidence for the police. Sure, he knew me, all right. He'd seen me at the trial. He was doing so well, after the Bowden killing, that he began to think he could wipe out anyone he didn't want on this case. He tried it on Sullivan, there, thinking he was Peter with some mysterious clue that might lead to him. As he was, of course."

"But the money-order receipts were found to be for printed applications," Sullivan objected. "It's hard to tell a man's handwriting from his printed writing."

"You didn't really expect to get a nice sample of the killer's writing especially written out for you on those very incriminating applications, did you?" asked Dennis, with lifted eyebrow. "I could have told you he'd print 'em, and saved you the disappointment. Only if I'd told you in advance, you'd have thought I was the one who'd printed 'em. Anyway, they served their purpose. They had Fersen getting panicky. What did we know that he didn't? He was a coward—and a most cautious guy, for a killer. Only bold when he was top dog. He chose his own hotel for the murder because it was safest. No one would think of a hotel manager capable of raising all this fuss in his hotel."

Peter bent a mild but accusing blue eye on Dennis.

"You knew I was in that hotel last night," he said. "Don't deny it. Billy Morgan told me he met you and talked about me. Why didn't you let me in on this midnight trip to Delroy?"

Dennis grinned. "You were having dinner with a chorus girl. Who was I to interfere? I withdrew."

"Withdrew!" snorted Peter. "You should have known I was following a clue—the clue of the white Spanish shawl. She was the girl we told you about, the one on Morgan's yacht."

"How'd I know you were following a clue?" said Dennis unrepentantly. "You didn't look an awful lot like it. You looked to me like Pete Byrne having dinner with a beautiful girl. Did you ever get around to the question of the Spanish shawl?"

"We did. We were talking about it when the fire engines came along," Peter said, brooding. "She said you could buy swell ones in Chinatown for practically nothing at all. She mentioned the store she'd bought it at. Then the fire engines came. That was a swell idea of yours, Dennis. I only hope you won't want to break up any more tete-a-tetes. Next time you might use tear-gas bombs, or something. We all tore out to the lobby, milled around a bit, quieted down, and I saw Sullivan looking at a piece of paper in his hand. It was your bill. We began putting the pieces of evidence together, Dennis, and found a dim sort of logic among them. Sullivan, for instance, thought this might possibly be your way of summoning him in a hurry."

"It was," said Dennis. "Kennedy gave me the idea."

"I? Me?" said the debonair gentleman, sitting up straighter. "I didn't tell you to go around ringing false alarms any time you wanted to see a friend, Dennis."

"Don't be so modest," said Dennis. "It was a swell idea. I wanted Sullivan there in a hurry, and he came."

"We all did," said Kennedy.

"Well, you see," said Dennis irrefutably.

"Dennis," said Peter again, "how did you know it was Fersen?"

"How'd you begin to suspect Fersen?" Sullivan asked. "There wasn't anything—"

"Enough," said Dennis, "when you came to add it all up. Bits of this and that. What he did. What he said. What he—was."

"He looked all right to me," said Sullivan.

Dennis dropped his cigarette carefully into the tray, put his clenched hands up to his face in the gesture that was as familiar to Blake and Peter as though they'd known him all their lives.

"Bits," said Dennis. "I don't dignify them by the name of clues. I leave that to the detective bureau. They want clues. Clues?" said Dennis with a certain scorn. "Clues are swell. But suppose a man doesn't smoke, drink, swear, or use profanity. How are you going to trace him then? If it's cigarette stubs you want, or empty glasses for fingerprints on them for him to be traced by, it ought to have been me. No, the clues I mean are the ones he leaves of his living self. First clue—he had a passkey, and he used it. Came busting into my room, when he really didn't have to. He was too eager. He wanted to make sure I wouldn't skip out. He was going to make sure I was held for and by the police, as a victim. Having one victim, they naturally wouldn't look around for more. He had a passkey.

"He knew I wasn't really a killer. That careful, rather soft-living guy wouldn't have stayed there alone with a killer, or someone he thought was a killer. No, he wasn't afraid of me. That was curious.

"Then he was too eager again to get me, when he didn't open a window in my room. He left it all locked and closed, so the police would be sure to suspect me of the murder. Sullivan outsmarted him on that one, and I got off—temporarily.

"At the inquest he laid himself out to get me, giving me the worst of every break he could. Nothing dishonest, you know, but it was a dishonesty of the mind, all right. And I saw him get mad there, too, once, when he was too closely questioned. He had a red light in his eyes. And when Sullivan said that about the killer being crazy at times, I saw, just for a second, the red light of madness flickering in someone's otherwise pleasant eyes. I couldn't quite place it then. It wasn't until afterwards—I placed it. He was a bit cuckoo, you know. He kept Bianca's evening bag and shawl.

"Then Fersen's alibi for that night was smashed. You wouldn't remember it like I did, maybe," said Dennis frankly, "because I've got some artistic vanity, I guess. At the inquest Fersen said he'd never heard me singing over the radio. Well, I was singing that night over the radio—in the Hotel Ancaster—in the Etruscan Room and through the lobby—and announced by name between each song, too. And Morgan called him up and found him out of his office then, when I was singing. He evidently wasn't in the lobby, though he'd said at the inquest the only times he left his office that hour were to go to the lobby. He didn't hear me singing. Where was he? Up in my room, reached from the service stairs in his corridor. He was up there with Bianca. He'd made this date with her because he was desperate; he went to it with a knife in one nicely kept hand. It's easy," said Dennis reminiscently, "to get knives in the Hotel Ancaster. I saw one sent up from the kitchens when I was in Mrs. Appleby's suite. It was the same sort of common breadknife Bianca was stabbed with. It put the idea into my head that if that one was from the hotel kitchens, probably Bianca's knife was, too. Easy to get, you see, for a hotel manager on a kitchen tour of inspection, earlier. That's why 1 was scared about old Mrs. Appleby and Lucy. It was a little thing, really. The police of course didn't get it—they didn't have tea there, in her suite. But I knew we were dealing with a man who made almost a mania of caution—a careful guy—and he might think I'd picked up something handy in that visit. As I had. So I was scared for them. But you put the policeman at their door, didn't you, Sullivan?"

"Sure I did," said Sullivan. "And Fersen, after the excitement of the fire, came up and touched off some fireworks about that, too. You were sure getting under his skin, Dennis."

"Yes, I meant to," Dennis said. "He was worried. He'd taken a shot at Sullivan and got me. Then you remember Peter said that about my being like a ghost. That I'd scare the murderer if he saw me. He probably thought he'd gotten me. The police veiled my end in mystery, as you'd say, Kennedy. They didn't give out any information about this particular shooting. So when I came into Fersen's office, and he saw me, and at first didn't see the bandage around my head—I had your hat on, Kennedy—he went up in the air. He looked at me as if he'd seen a ghost. I remembered what Peter'd said. I was a ghost, and he saw me there. For a second. But all this," said Dennis carefully, "isn't much good without a motive, is it? Why should Fersen, that nice soft-living pleasant man, want to kill Victor Farnese a year ago, and then his widow Bianca, and then stop Bowden's too loose mouth? Farnese was a wholesale produce dealer. Fersen was the manager of a hotel which he ran to suit himself. He didn't have to show his accounts to prying eyes. Not till lately. The hotel's going to be bought by Morgan's father and some of his friends. That meant an accounting. Morgan told me that, quite innocently. Then I remembered Fersen had been working late, alone, in his office the night Bianca was killed. Why should he? I wondered. So what?

"Then," said Dennis cheerfully, "I proceeded to get under his skin, for a couple of reasons—I wanted to see what he was like under all his fine walnut veneer, and I wanted to get his handwriting plausibly. And he was cheap wood under his fine grain, and he gave me his signature on the hotel bill, and I gave it to Sullivan. Then I played hob with him a bit more—fire alarms, cops, and so forth—and he scurried like a rat down to Delroy to kill Father Malletti and plant that on me. And he found—"

"A wirehaired terrier pup at his rat hole," said Kennedy.

Dennis grinned. "Being a detective's rather fun," he said. "I'm pretty good at it, I think. I think maybe I'll keep on."

"I never thought I'd be begging you to stick to radio, Dennis," said Kennedy. "But I am. Your detectiving is too rough on us—it's wearing. We're not all as young as we were. Stick to radio, Dennis."

"Oh, but I am," said Dennis. "I'm singing again tonight."

Kennedy said appreciatively, "There'll be a big mob to hear you, boy!"

Dennis said, "I don't mind that—as long as there's—one person."

His dark glance flickered on Blake's fair young face.

"I'll sing a song for you, Blake."

"Which one?" asked Blake.

"Ah, you'll know," said Dennis. "If you're listening."

He whistled, very softly, the first bar of "Drink to me only" as they all strolled out to the grass-covered terrace on the highest level of the hill-built house.

*"What country, love, is this?"* said Dennis to himself, as though he were trying to remember something he'd forgotten. It ran through his head. *"This is Illyria, stranger.* Stranger? No, not any more."

Peter and Blake stayed in the doorway, watching him.

"Are you really in love with him, Blake?" Peter said.

"Well," said Blake, thrusting her hands deep in her pockets, regarding Dennis, "he'll have to have someone to save him from being too chivalrous again. And then think of yourself, Peter. Life would be very dull for you without Dennis. You ought to be grateful to me for keeping him in the family permanently."

"I've felt like a three-ring circus since I saw him," agreed Peter.

"Besides," said Blake deeply, "I simply can't bear the thought of his marrying anyone but me. It must be love."

"I'm always waiting to see what he'll do next, or what'll turn up next," observed Peter with anticipation. "We'd better find out his proper name, by the way, if he's going to be our relative."

"Does it matter?" asked Blake.

"No," said Peter, consulting himself with surprise. "I suppose it doesn't."

Dennis looked at them from the goldfish pond and smiled and began to come over the grass to them. "I wonder what he'll do next," said Peter.

They stared in fascination at his ingenuous face.

**THE END**

# THE MURDER OF CECILY THANE
## BY H. ASHBROOK

Murder
of Cecily Thane
by    H. Ashbrook

A Spike Tracy Mystery

R. P.

A Resurrected Press Mystery

## ORIGINALLY PUBLISHED IN 1937

# THE MURDER OF CECILY THANE
## BY H. ASHBROOK

*The Murder of Cecily Thane* is the first in a series of seven mystery novels by Harriette Ashbrook featuring the amateur sleuth Phillip (Spike) Tracy. Ashbrook was a member of that school of mystery writers who looked upon murder as an entertainment in contrast to the "hard-boiled" writers of detective fiction such as Dashiell Hammett, John Carroll Daly, and Raymond Chandler. The style had been popularized in America by the writers S.S. Van Dine, Ellery Queen and Rex Stout, and in Britain by writers such as Anthony Berkeley. These mysteries are more concerned with antics and wit of their detectives than they are with the sordid details of crime, in particular, the ability of their amateur sleuths to twit the official police who are often portrayed as bumbling dim-wits. Murder, when it occurs, mostly happens off-stage and with a minimum of blood and gore.

The detective of the series, Phillip Tracy, though he prefers to be called Spike, is the younger brother of the district attorney of New York, a relationship that provides him with ready access to crime. Spike is something of a feckless playboy with a tendency for being arrested for being "drunk and disorderly," a source of endless embarrassment for his more responsible elder brother. Of course, this character flaw doesn't prevent him from solving crimes that leave the more established police completely baffled.

Despite, or perhaps because of, his irresponsible personality, Spike Tracy is an engaging character. Unlike S.S. Van Dine's Philo Vance, he doesn't come off as an arrogant know-it-all of as oddly eccentric as Rex Stout's Nero Wolfe. Instead, beneath Spike's jaunty exterior, there is a caring and compassionate character, one who is truly interested in seeing justice done.

Spike's long suffering brother Richard and Detective Inspector Herschman of the Homicide Squad serve as convenient foils to Spike's humor and repartee. His brother, the D.A. is serious and sober, sorely lacking a sense of humor, and more interested in his political future than solving crimes, while Herschman is a quintessential New York policeman, honest and competent in an ordinary sort of way, but not overly endowed with either culture or intelligence. Yet, despite the fact that they serve as targets of Spike's wit, neither is portrayed as either fools or bumbling.

The mystery in *The Murder of Cecily Thane* is the murder of a well-off woman approaching middle-age. She is found murdered in her bedroom after a night in which she has gone out dancing with a paid escort. She is the apparent victim of a robbery, as she has been shot and several hundred thousand dollars worth of jewelry is missing. Her dancing partner of the evening is the immediate suspect, but motives and opportunities soon surface for a number of other suspects.

Of interest is the way Ashbrook deals with the subject of gigolos, the young men employed by older women of means to escort them to night clubs and social functions in place of their husbands. This seems to have been a institution peculiar to during the Depression when work of any sort was hard and a man would do anything to survive. While the treatment isn't completely sympathetic, it is at least understanding. Ashbrook's willingness to address social and moral issues is one of the things that set her apart from other mystery writers of the period.

Reading the Spike Tracy mysteries, it's hard to understand how they have become so neglected. The writing is crisp and the pace is quick. The elements of the mystery, while not necessarily innovative, are handled in a manner competent and fair enough to leave any reader satisfied. The character of Spike is likeable and his foils—his brother and Inspector Herschman—handled at least as well as their counterparts in the Philo Vance or Nero Wolfe books. More importantly, despite their levity, there is some real substance to the novels. Yet despite all this, unfortunately the works of Ashbrook have languished in obscurity.

It is therefore with great pleasure that Resurrected Press offers this new edition of *The Murder of Cecily Thane* and the other books in the Spike Tracy series.

## About the Author

Harriette Cora Ashbrook (1898-1946) was the American author of thirteen mystery novels. Seven of these were published under her own name and feature Phillip (Spike) Tracy, a playboy turned amateur sleuth whose brother just happens to be the District Attorney of New York. She also published six more mysteries under the pen-name Susannah Shane featuring Christopher Saxe as the detective.

Greg Fowlkes
Editor-In-Chief
Resurrected Press
www.ResurrectedPress.com.

## Resurrected Press books by H, Ashbrook

*The Murder of Cicely Thane (1930)*

*The Murder of Stephen Kester (1931)*

*The Murder of Sigurd Sharon (1933)*

*A Most Immoral Murder (1935)*

*Murder Makes Murder (1937)*

*Murder Comes Back (1940)*

*Murder on Friday (1941)*

**Like us on Facebook to stay up-to-date on all of our latest releases: http://www.facebook.com/ResurrectedPress**

# The Murder of Cecily Thane

## I. X Marks the Spot!

"THERE are times, my dear brother, when I wonder why God lets you live."

As the district attorney paced in angry strides up and down the length of his office, his hands jammed into his pockets, he presented a severe contrast to the young man before him.

Slouched comfortably in a huge leather chair, one leg swinging nonchalantly over an upholstered arm, the young man blew long, lazy clouds of cigarette smoke into the air. A smile played about his lips, and the spring sunshine coming in through the open window bathed him with a pleasant, easy warmth, that seemed to match his disposition. He was gay and debonair despite the crumpled state of his Tuxedo and his obvious need of a shave.

"I repeat—there are times when I wonder why God lets you live and breathe and get into trouble."

"And this, I suppose, is one of them?" The young man spoke with the lazy indolence of great bodily ease and infinite amusement.

"Exactly!"

"Well, thank God, God isn't consulting you about the way He runs the universe."

"If you *must* get arrested, why not do it in some place beside New York? Paris—London—*anywhere* but here?"

"I have. Four times in Paris and three in London. Or, perhaps, it was the other way round. By the way, what was the name of the place where I bided the night?"

"Forty-seventh Precinct Station House."

"Not very interesting, is it? Still—" He drew a small black notebook and a pencil from his inner pocket and made an entry. "I'm keeping a list of the jails I've been in," he explained. "Perhaps some day I'll write a book—'Jails I Have Known.' It'll be frightfully amusing. In Munich they serve champagne and put it on your bill. Once in Paris—"

"Stop that nonsense and try to take this thing seriously."

"But why?"

"Why? Because every damned paper in the town will be carrying the story on the front page."

"Really?" The young man grinned. "A member of the front page elite at last. Do you suppose they'd like my picture? Or maybe both of us together. I know—a passionate one for the tabs like this." He sprang from the chair and prostrated himself before the glare of his brother, his face hidden in his hands, his shoulders drooping with synthetic shame.

### "'District Attorney Plays Erring Kin'"

"Look here, Philip," the older man's voice softened helplessly and he stopped his angry pacing. His tone was almost pleading. "If you can't take this thing seriously for yourself, look at it from my point of view. I'm supposed to be the public prosecutor here, to stand for law and order and decency, and my brother, my own brother gets run in on a charge of being drunk and disorderly."

"Well, what would you prefer—spitting in the subway or murder?"

At the last word the district attorney winced. "Don't talk about murder. I've got enough of it on my hands just now without a young ass like you adding to it in a jolly spirit of fun."

"Yeah?" The young man rose slowly from his ridiculous posture and dusted off his knees. "You mean you've got a murder on the pan right now?"

The district attorney nodded. "I was on my way up to the scene of the crime when I had to go chasing off after you and get you out of jail. Of all the times to get into trouble, you couldn't have picked a worse one, you couldn't have—"

"Really, old thing, there's nothing to be gained by going over all that again. And anyway, I think it would be much more interesting to talk about your murder."

"'My murder' is quite right. It probably will be." The district attorney became slightly calmer and much more gloomy. Then he burst out once more in sudden irritation. "Why did this have to come just now when I'm working on the state banking laws? The newspapers make such a fuss about murders. This sort of thing," and he indicated a copy of the morning paper on his desk, folded at the editorial page.

The young man picked it up and read the paragraph indicated by his brother's vehement finger.

> "The present police and legal administration may seek to camouflage successive failures with grandiloquent talk of 'civic progress' and 'worthy reforms,' but the man in the street is not deceived by such high-sounding phrases. The fact remains that since District Attorney Tracy has been in office there have been three unsolved murders to his discredit. As an officer of the

people, pledged to the punishment of those who transgress the law, it seems to us that he has been flagrantly unsuccessful in the discharge of his duty. A little bit more effective criminal investigation and fewer, 'worthy reforms' would do much to redeem his administration. 'Reform' like charity should begin at home."

The young man laid down the paper.

"It strikes me," he said, "that that fellow doesn't like you."

"'Doesn't like me?' They're just waiting for an opportunity to get me. Damn the newspapers! If there isn't something new to tell them each day, they make up something that is usually worse than the truth and they—"

"There, there," the young man broke in soothingly. "Tell me all and get it off your chest and then you'll feel better. Who killed whom and where and what and why?"

"Cecily Thane."

*"Cecily Thane?"* He opened his eyes with sudden interest.

"You know her?"

"No, I can't say that I know her. I've seen her around in night clubs a good deal and of course every one knows about her jewels."

"Well, she's dead—murdered last night—and $200,000 worth of jewels are missing from her private wall safe." The district attorney turned and with sudden belligerence shot a question at his brother. "What do *you* know about it, anyway?"

"Now, now, Richard, my pet, I didn't do it, I swear I didn't and if you don't believe it ask the excellent sergeant and the two patrolmen down at the police station who played poker with me all night."

"I mean what do you know about *her*?"

"Just gossip. She's always seen about with some young fellow, usually sporting about three pecks of diamonds. They say they don't all belong to her, but that she takes 'em out of her husband's store. They call her the walking showcase."

"Well, she's dead and I can't fool any more time talking about it. I've got to find out who killed her. Just my luck."

"Mine too." The young man reached for his hat and stick lying on the desk.

"What do you mean, 'yours' too?"

"I mean that I was going up to British Columbia and hunt elk, but now I think I'll stay here in New York and hunt murderers instead. Much better sport."

He put on his hat and motioned toward the door. "Come!"

"Come where?"

"To the X which always marks the spot where the body's found."

It was difficult to believe that R. Montgomery Tracy, known officially to the bar as the district attorney of New York County, was the brother of Philip Tracy, that insouciant young man who, under the more familiar name of Spike enlivened existence on both sides of the Atlantic.

The marital difficulties of the late R. Montgomery Tracy, Sr., and his wife, may to a degree have accounted for the divergence in the two sons. It was soon after Philip was born that Mrs. Tracy, always of a flighty disposition, refused point-blank to languish longer under the stern Puritan rule of her husband. Forthwith, she picked up her youngest child and went to Europe, becoming soon a part of that irresponsible, delightful European population that rotates from St. Moritz to the Riviera, to Paris, with an occasional visit to London or Berlin.

Philip had grown up a charming hybrid, half American, half continental, a pleasing combination of Piccadilly and Broadway, Oxford and Yale, dividing his time between school in France and England, and visits to his father and older brother in America.

He had not confused the issues of his existence with anything so dismal as a profession. College was a pleasant interlude between boyhood and manhood—an interlude of failures in the classroom and triumphs on the athletic field and the prom floor. Inability to graduate brought only a joyous feeling of release into a world that was waiting for a playboy—Paris, New York, Vienna. His twenty-five years had been lived with a gay intensity made possible by the unceasing flow of dollars from the paternal estate. His life was utterly useless and infinitely amusing.

Yet this could not be considered an entirely accurate estimate of him. When the occasion demanded he could display a shrewdness that seemed at complete variance with his more apparent character. There lay underneath his facetious  exterior, a quickness of perception that sometimes puzzled those who surprised him in the occasional exercise of it.

But his brother was not among them.

At forty R. Montgomery Tracy had a wife and four children, political ambitions, and a sense of humor so rudimentary as to be practically nonexistent. Many years of contact with the majesty of the law had imparted to him a certain depressing heaviness that at times clouded the sharpness of his vision when dealing with less abstract human factors. Life, he felt, was not to be taken lightly.

As district attorney of New York County he displayed a dogged efficiency that was at once the pride and the despair of his supporters. He served with the fearless honesty commanded only by a man whose inheritance puts him above financial temptation. There were many solid achievements to his regime of which his followers could boast.

But on the more spectacular side he was lacking. Already there were rumblings of disapproval at his failure to provide a good show for the masses. Of bread he gave them plenty but he was a poor ringmaster for their circuses.

For murders particularly he had an intense distaste. They interfered so with the solid constructive program which he in his unimaginative way believed would lead him on to higher and nobler political heights. They precipitated mobs of reporters into his office and brought a thrill-thirsty public howling about his ears.

And now here was another one on his hands—a gaudy, spectacular one. Elton Thane's sudden rise to fame as a jewel merchant had been broadcast throughout the success journals of the country. Ten years ago a salesman—now a millionaire. Importer of rare and precious gems which once had adorned the now defunct crowns of Europe. Owner of a costly shop on the Avenue and of a smaller branch uptown in the eighties on Broadway.

The district attorney shuddered to think of the afternoon papers. As he rode north on Lafayette with his younger brother toward a certain house in West Eighty-second Street, the argument which had begun at Police Headquarters was still in progress.

"But, my dear boy," he protested, "I refuse to permit you to make a Roman holiday out of the most serious crime in the penal code."

"But I'm not. I'm going to apply myself to the serious study of a serious crime and I shouldn't be surprised if I found it not too boring."

"In other words, you're fancying yourself in the role of a detective?"

"Well, something of the sort."

For the first time that morning the district attorney laughed.

"Herschman will enjoy that."

"Who's Herschman?"

"In charge of the Homicide Squad."

"And when will I have the pleasure of his acquaintance?"

"In about fifteen minutes. He's up there now."

"Oh, so you *are* going to take me with you?" Tripped up in the unsuspecting web of his own making the district attorney considered.

"Well, just this morning. You may come with me to the house but please don't bother with nonsensical questions. Make yourself as unobtrusive as possible."

"A sort of unofficial observer."

"Exactly. And try to look slightly serious. Remember a woman has been killed."

"Oh, absolutely!" and Spike grinned.

## II. Spike Makes an Utter Damn Fool of Himself

THE home of Elton Thane at 8 West Eighty-second Street was one of a row of brownstone fronts, dreary of exterior, but with a certain smartness in the shine of brass knockers and the glisten of well-washed windows that bespoke servants and money. Standing on the south side of the street just three doors to the west of Central Park West, it was a victim of the terrific din which accompanied the building of the Eighth Avenue subway which at that time was in process of construction.

The pavement of Central Park West was torn up, and what traffic was forced through it, bumped and jolted perilously over the rutted roadbed. Timbered shafts had been sunk at intervals, and men could be glimpsed working twenty or thirty feet below the surface. At Eighty-second Street, the site of a prospective station, the street was laid open as if by a great gouging fist and in the excavation men worked with electric drills, boring away at a stubborn rock formation.

Emerging from the transverse concourse of the Park at Seventy-second Street, the automobile carrying the district attorney and his brother picked its way carefully northward, threading in and out among supply trucks and cement mixers. At Eighty-second Street its occupants were forced to get out and walk the short distance from the corner to Number 8, for the station excavation was at its widest directly in front of the Thane house, closing the street to traffic from the east.

"Ideal spot for a murder, isn't it?" Spike spoke above the din of the drills.

The district attorney frowned in disapproval and started up the steps, but a restraining hand was laid on his arm.

"Really, old thing," Spike protested, "do you think you're approaching the problem just the right way? Isn't it always customary to stop and observe?"

"Observe?"

"You know—footprints on the doormat and automobile tracks and all that."

"There is no doormat and automobiles don't make tracks on asphalt."

"Well then, shouldn't something be done about those men?" and Spike indicated the workmen in the station excavation. "We at least ought to stop and note the color of their eyes and whether they have been vaccinated and how long since—"

"Philip!" the district attorney thundered, but it was a hushed thunder out of respect to the dead within. "Philip, I refuse to permit such levity. Either you drop your facetious manner or you leave me on the threshold."

"Why, Richard, I was merely trying to be helpful."

"Well, don't. The legal and police departments can handle this case without any assistance from a man who has just spent the night in jail."

Spike acquiesced meekly, but out of the corner of his eye he cast a furtive glance at the workmen—three sweating little Italians and a huge foreman with fierce black whiskers. He looked like pictures of a Russian Nihilist but his voice as he ordered the three little men about was unmistakably tinged with an Irish brogue.

At the top of the steps a policeman standing guard saluted respectfully and opened the door for the district attorney and his companion.

The door gave on to a small vestibule, and this in turn on to a long hall along the right of which rose a flight of stairs to the second floor. The interior of the Thane house was in marked contrast to its conventional façade. As the two men stepped over the threshold, they were assaulted by a flaring mass of color from green and mauve walls and vermilion hangings. Chairs of uneven architecture, tables at varying levels, bookcases holding futuristic statuettes instead of books, lighting fixtures concealed behind strangely angled pieces of glass. Bizarre, unrestful. Obviously the late Mrs. Thane had gone in for the newer things in decoration.

To the left was a wide arched opening into the drawing room, from which came a low hum of voices. Inspector Herschman and one of his men were seated rather incongruously on a triangular divan with three legs of perilous thinness.

Any reader of detective fiction would at once have recognized Herschman for what he was—a Headquarters dick. In face and form and haberdashery he conformed exactly to the popular idea of what a Headquarters dick should be. A massive fellow with that certain rough capability that comes of a long apprenticeship at pavement pounding in a city whose population is crowded into a space only half large enough for comfort. One could easily imagine him cowing a bunch of gangsters. But it was more difficult to picture him pitted against a Raffles or a Steinlin.

He looked a trifle ruefuly at the district attorney as if to remind him of his long delay in arriving at the scene of the crime. But Tracy made no explanation of the fraternal difficulties which had entangled him, and introduced Spike as briefly as possible.

"My brother. He just happened to be with me this morning so I brought him along."

Then nervously he got down to business. "Let me have a brief summary of the whole situation. I know only the bare outline of the case as you told it to me this morning on the telephone." And Herschman went ahead with his explanation.

Shortly before four o'clock that morning, Elton Thane had returned home and started up to his room on the third floor. Noticing a light in the sitting room of his wife's apartment on the second floor, he had knocked. Receiving no answer he walked in and discovered her body. She had been shot through the heart. Her jewels had been torn from her throat and her private wall safe had been emptied of $200,000 worth of diamonds, emeralds and pearls.

"The body hasn't been removed yet from the room upstairs," Herschman said, "and everything is just as we found it. I thought you'd probably want a look before anything was disturbed."

Tracy nodded approval and the inspector continued.

Elton Thane had immediately summoned a Dr. Partridge, a friend and physician, who lived next door, who had in turn called the police at the Eighty-sixth Street Station. After a preliminary survey of the situation, Groaty and McCarthy, the detectives who had answered the call, reported to Headquarters, and Herschman had himself personally taken charge of the case. Firearms and fingerprint men had already been there and Sayler, the medical examiner, was upstairs making his examination before the body was removed.

"Any leads?" Tracy inquired nervously.

"Well, I've got Groaty and McCarthy out looking for the man Mrs. Thane went out with last night. A chap named Spencer, Tommy Spencer. The two of them—Spencer and Mrs. Thane left the house last night about eight o'clock, bound for some dancing place. At eleven-thirty they came home and went up to Mrs. Thane's apartment on the second floor. About a half hour later he left."

Tracy was thoughtful for a moment. Then his gaze met that of Herschman and each nodded as if confirming the other's thought.

"It has a number of points of similarity with the Schlockenhass case," the district attorney said.

"Yeah. So many that I told Groaty and McCarthy to take a look at the photographs and fingerprints in that case before they started their hunt."

"Have you a description of the jewels missing?"

"Not yet. The husband, the only one that knows anything about them, is so busted up that he hasn't been able to talk yet."

"Well, suppose we go upstairs."

As the three men mounted the stairs—the district attorney and Herschman leading and Spike trailing in their wake, the very picture of meekness and unofficial observation—the Inspector outlined the general plan of the house. In common with most brownstone fronts it had four stories and a basement with three rooms on each floor. The kitchen and furnace room took up the entire length of the basement with the exception of a small room in front made into a sitting room for the servants. A small door and two iron-barred windows opened from the sitting room directly on to the street. At the back was a door from the kitchen opening on to a small grass plot surrounded completely by a high brick wall.

On the first floor was the dining room, drawing room and at the back a small bedroom and bath. The second floor was Mrs. Thane's apartment, consisting of a bedroom and bath and sitting room. And on the floor above, Mr. Thane had similar quarters. The three bedrooms on the fourth floor were occupied by the maid, and the cook and the butler.

"I suppose you have questioned them all?" Tracy asked.

"Only the maid. She was the only one who was home last night. It was the cook's night off and she was visiting friends in Jersey, and the butler left yesterday."

"That's unfortunate," the district attorney said. "When you have more than one story to go by it is easier to piece together the real one."

The second floor of the Thane house bore further evidence of the variety in interior decorating taste of its late occupant. The sitting room was done more or less in the style of Louis XIV with small gold-legged chairs, a Fragonard carpet, paneled walls and 'taffeta drapery in billowing loops of shirring. A doll dressed as a college flapper struck an ungainly note as it sprawled among the pillows of a chaise longue copied after the famous Récamier portrait.

To the right as the three men entered the sitting room from the hall was a wide archway leading to the bedroom whence came incongruously enough whistled snatches of a gay, lilting popular song. Dr. Sayler, official medical examiner of the New York police force, was seated in apparent contentment on a gold lacquered chair, in the bedroom, whiling away the time whistling and smoking, unmoved apparently by the lugubriousness of his surroundings.

"The inspector told me you were coming," he called cheerily to the district attorney, "so I stayed around a bit. Thought you might like to see exactly how things lie before I removed the body."

With an airy gesture he indicated the corner of the room directly to the right of the archway, leading from the sitting room to the bedroom.

Cecily Thane lay on her back, one arm thrown upward over her head, her mouth slightly open. She was a woman at that tragic, indeterminate age, somewhere between thirty-five and forty-five. At one time she must have been beautiful but with an ephemeral blond beauty that had begun to fade early. The hair, geometrically waved was just a shade too blond, and the thin angularity of her face was heightened by triangular spots of rouge under prominent cheek bones. The lips were thin, drawn tightly into a scarlet penciled line. The whole face bore a look of chronic strain, of nervous tension that could not be attributed entirely to whatever strange and terrifying events had immediately preceded the tragedy.

She was wearing an evening gown of opaline satin heavily encrusted with sequins. Over the left breast an ugly spot of red spread out through the glittering cloth.

On the wall about five feet from the baseboard, a wall safe stood open; and scattered about the floor were several small jewel boxes and one larger one with trays. Boxes and safe were empty. The body lay directly in front of the safe, about three feet from the wall.

The district attorney looked inquiringly at the medical examiner.

"It must have occurred some time about twelve or shortly after," he said. "Certainly not after one o'clock. A clean shot directly through the heart."

He stepped over to the body and with the unconcern of a laboratory lecturer, demonstrated. "You can see there are no powder burns. Probably fired at a distance of three or four feet. The bullet entered the body here just to the left of the breastbone."

"Have you the bullet?"

The doctor shook his head. "No, it came out just to the left of the backbone. I suppose one of your men picked it up, Inspector?"

"I have it here," Herschman replied. "It's from a .38 caliber Colt. About the commonest type of gun there is."

Walking to a point on the south side of the bedroom he indicated a spot in the paneling of the wall, just below one of the large windows that gave on to the rear of the house. "You can see the spot here where it hit."

Dr. Sayler, the district attorney and Spike crowded around the inspector to examine the small dent about one-fourth of an inch deep which the bullet had made in the soft painted wood of the paneling

"Well, suppose we have the maid up," Tracy said "I'd like to go over her story with her."

Herschman gave an order to one of the officers whom he had stationed just outside the door of the sitting room and presently a buxom, slightly pretty young woman of perhaps twenty-five appeared from below stairs. Her name, Emma Bloomstead, should have indicated a Scandinavian stolidity, an harassing inarticulateness, but she belied it. She was of the second generation of immigrants and she talked freely. Obviously shaken by the events of the previous night, she was also obviously impressed with her own role in the official limelight

"How long have you been employed in this household?" Tracy began his questioning

"About five years."

"And you were the only one of the servants in the house last night?"

"Yes, sir."

"Now, Emma," Tracy went on, using an entirely unnecessary propitiatory tone. "I want you to tell us just exactly what happened last night as well as you can remember it."

"Well, Mrs. Thane went out about eight with Mr. Spencer like she does quite often and—"

"You mean Mr. Spencer is a good friend, comes here often?"

"Twice a week, on Monday and Thursdays, and they always go out together. He must have lots of money because she always dresses up swell in evening gowns like she was going to swell places Well, last night about eight she goes out with him and she tells me they'll be back about eleven-thirty, which is sort of early because usually it's one and two and three and sometimes four when they get home.

"Well, then I came upstairs and sort of straightened things up up here, hung up dresses, and emptied the ash trays, and put away shoes and things, and then I went downstairs and pretty soon Mr. Thane rings for me and sends me down to the corner to mail a letter. And a little while later when I got back he went out, about nine o'clock.

"And then about eleven-thirty, Mrs. Thane and Mr. Spencer got back, and they rang for me to bring up some ice and vichy and I did."

"You mean up here in the sitting room?" the district attorney interrupted.

"Yes, sir, right in this room. I came up with the stuff on a tray and there was Mrs. Thane sitting over there on that chaise longue and Mr. Spencer sort of ranging around the room waiting till he could get his hands on a cocktail shaker. And so I left the tray there and went downstairs again."

"Downstairs? You mean to the first floor?"

"No, to the servants' sitting room in the basement. Then a little while later, after I had taken the tray up to the sitting room, the bell in the first floor front hall rings and there is Mr. Spencer wanting his hat and stick and I gave them to him and he left."

"How did he seem—nervous or hurried?"

"Not a bit of it. As calm as a cucumber. And took his time about things. Tried to joke a little bit with me but I didn't let him get away with it. No good ever comes of mixing with the mistress' boy friends."

"Does Mr. Thane know—know of this Mr. Spencer?" Tracy inquired with a significant inflection.

"Knows him and talks right friendly with him too. Why only last night when Mr. Spencer comes to call for Mrs. Thane, he meets him downstairs in the front parlor and they have me bring up the seltzer bottle and the Scotch, and there they were drinking a highball together just as chummy as you please."

"You don't by any chance recall any of the conversation which you overheard between them?"

The maid pondered for a moment, reaching into the recesses of her memory for any stray bits of talk.

"Well, they weren't talking about anything much. Just talking like men do, you know. Mr. Thane had a new golf club he was showing off and he was near busting up everything in the place, swinging it around. And then by-and-by Mrs. Thane came down and the three of them just stood there and talked for a minute or so; and then I heard Mr. Thane tell 'em to be home early just like she was his daughter instead of his wife, and Mr. Spencer said yes, they'd be home about eleven-thirty."

The maid sniffed. It was plain that she did not approve of the complacent attitude of her employer. He was not acting up to her standards of an outraged husband.

"To continue with your story—Mr. Spencer rang for his hat and stick and you gave them to him. And then what?"

"He left and I went on back downstairs."

"Do you remember what time it was?"

"Yes, sir. It was just about a minute after twelve. I looked at the clock especially because Mr. Thane had always told me to sit up until twelve-thirty in case he came in and wanted anything. I remember thinking that I'd only have about twenty-five minutes more and I was sleepy. And then pretty soon at twelve-thirty I went to bed."

"As you passed Mrs. Thane's door on your way upstairs did you notice anything peculiar?"

"No, sir." Even Emma Bloomstead's garrulity was stemmed as the thought that she had passed a room containing a murdered woman at twelve-thirty at night.

"Was the door open?"

"I didn't notice."

"You went right to bed and to sleep? You didn't hear any noise or sound in the house?"

"No, sir."

"No sound of a shot?"

"No, sir."

"When you were in your sitting room in the basement you heard nothing?"

"Oh no, you couldn't hear yourself shout with that racket going on down there where they're building the subway."

"In other words, neither before or after you went to bed did you hear the sound of a shot."

"That's right."

"And what was the next thing you knew after you had gone to sleep?"

"Well, the next thing I knew, the bell in my room was ringing and I came down here, and Mr. Thane was here and—" Emma looked apprehensively in the direction of the bedroom.

"And what did you find?"

"Mr. Thane was over there—" and she nodded toward the archway, "bending over Mrs. Thane sort of shaking her like he was trying to make her talk. He was sort of wild-like, and trembling, and talking fast. And he told me to call Dr. Partridge next door. So I tried to get the doctor, but the telephone wouldn't work, so then I went over there myself and Dr. Partridge came right over with me."

"You say the telephone wouldn't work?" the inspector broke in.

"Yes, sir."

"What telephone?"

"That one there," and she pointed to the instrument carefully masked behind a Dresden shepherdess with widespreading bouffant panniers. Beside it was a small indexed booklet containing addresses and telephone numbers.

Herschman crossed the room quickly and took down the receiver, but no answer came. Several times he clicked the hook but the instrument was dead.

"The one downstairs and the one up in Mr. Thane's room work, but not that one," the maid explained and Herschman's eyebrows went up. Suddenly he stooped over and examined the gilded cord that ran along the wall for a little way before disappearing into the box at the foot of the baseboard. The cord held tight against the plaster and woodwork by small staples appeared intact to the casual observer surveying it from a standing height. But as the inspector bent down he gave a low whistle.

"Cut!" and he indicated a point near the box where a closer scrutiny revealed the severed strands.

The four of them peered down at the baseboard and the district attorney looked inquiringly at the inspector. But Herschman, if he had any theory to offer, said nothing.

"The other phones in the house are they working?" Tracy inquired and the maid, nodded.

"Yes, we've been using them this morning. And last night I called the police on the one downstairs."

"That was after you came back here with Dr. Partridge?"

"Yes, sir. He came right up here and looked at Mrs. Thane and said she was dead and then Mr. Thane told me to call the police."

"Is Dr. Partridge available now?"

"Do you mean can you get him?"

The district attorney nodded.

"Yes, sir. He went home just a little while ago, and I guess maybe he's still there, because he don't go out much."

The district attorney made a motion of dismissal and Emma quit the room reluctantly. At the doorway she paused, hoping obviously that the keenly enjoyable situation might be prolonged by a suddenly remembered question. But none was forthcoming.

"Suppose you have one of the men outside bring the doctor over," Tracy said to the inspector. "I'd like to have a—what in the devil are *you* doing?"

Left to his own devices during the course of the questioning, Spike had been wandering about the room in an aimless contemplation of knickknacks, fiddling with the pillows of the chaise longue, gravely contemplating the ornaments of the writing desk, staring meditatively into ash trays. Now he was at the dressing table and from its litter of crystal and silver toilet articles he had chosen a lip stick and was carefully painting a simpering Cupid's bow on his own firm lips. At the sound of his brother's voice he turned a ludicrous smile upon the room.

"*What* in the devil are you doing?" The district attorney as was his habit when upset, repeated himself with growing emphasis.

"Charming, isn't it?" and Spike lighted a cigarette, just as if it were quite the thing for gentlemen at murder investigations to spend their time smearing pale orange rouge on their lips.

It was with difficulty that the district attorney controlled himself. For a moment he seemed on the verge of sputtering like an irate teakettle. Then he spoke with reproving hauteur.

"This, my dear brother, let me remind you, for you seem to have forgotten yourself, is not a vaudeville performance."

It was only the presence of the doctor and the inspector that kept him from elaborating the theme into another brother-to-brother lecture. His impulse was to repeat all the accusations of the morning with a few extra thrown in to fit the occasion. He was grateful for the arrival of Dr. Partridge, turning the attention of Herschman and the medical examiner from the humiliating sight of his own brother making a blasted fool of himself.

Peregrine. Partridge's name was his most adequate description. In christening him thus, his parents in the remote Victorian past had divined with remarkable foresight that some day their offspring would grow up to resemble nothing so much in the world as—Peregrine

Partridge. A little, fussy, meticulous man with bright bird eyes and a bustling air that did not match at all the sad droop of his walrus mustache.

It was apparent from his attitude as he greeted the district attorney that he was fully aware of his own importance in the case, and like Emma was quite a little setup by it. His chest beneath his old-fashioned, double-breasted vest puffed out with a slight pompousness—but not too far out. It was more than ten years since he had been in active practice of his profession, but he had not forgotten the correct bearing in the presence of death—particularly death under, strange and mysterious circumstances.

"If you would be so kind, Dr. Partridge," said Tracy, "I wish you would repeat for me the things which you told Inspector Herschman here earlier in the morning"

The little doctor was on the verge of saying, "Delighted!" but recalled himself in time. For a moment he considered Tracy's request in grave silence. Then he began his story in a careful, precise voice.

"Mr. Thane, as you doubtless know, spent the evening with me. Or rather I should say part of the morning. We are both troubled with insomnia and frequently we keep each other company over the chessboard. Last night we played until about a quarter of four. He hadn't been gone more than five minutes when Emma, the maid, came over to my house in great agitation and asked me to come over here. I came and found Mrs. Thane—dead."

He paused to let the full drama of his recital sink in.

"Would you tell us the position in which you found the body?"

"It was lying in precisely the position it is in now. I see your man has not disturbed it in the slightest detail."

"And did you make any examination?"

"Yes, a brief, but somewhat thorough one under the circumstances."

"What in your opinion was the time at which Mrs. Thane was killed?"

"Probably around twelve o'clock. Possibly a little before, possibly a little after. But certainly not after one."

Both Herschman and Tracy looked toward the medical examiner, struck by the similarity of the two doctors' findings. Then Tracy turned back to Dr. Partridge and posed his next question with tactful caution.

"Did you by any chance, Doctor, know this Spencer who took Mrs. Thane out last night?"

"Only by hearsay. Mr. Thane sometimes spoke of him."

"He was friendly with him?"

"Well, not exactly that. Mr. Thane and the young chap were not quite of the same mental caliber, the same tastes. But Mr. Thane was tolerant toward him. He understood Mrs. Thane's desire for dancing and theaters, and as he did not care to go himself, he raised no objections. I understand—" He hesitated as if uncertain of the propriety of the statement. "I understand she paid him well."

"Oh, a professional gigolo?"

"Something of the sort."

"The Schlockenhass case again," Herschman put in and the district attorney nodded.

"The what?" the little doctor asked.

"The Schlockenhass murder about six months ago."

"Oh, yes, I recall. There was a great deal in the papers at the time."

"Tell me, Doctor," Tracy went on, "after you made your examination of Mrs. Thane and ascertained that she was dead, what did you do?"

"I turned my attention to Mr. Thane. I could see that the living had more need of my services than the dead. Mr. Thane has for several years been a victim of chronic heart disease. He was suffering from shock, natural enough under the circumstances, but with increased severity in his particular case. After the police arrived, I persuaded him to leave things in their hands and to: come over to my house with me."

"And he is there now?"

"Yes, I suppose you would like to question him?"

"Of course, but if you think he is unable just at present, we could put it off for a few hours."

"No, I think perhaps it would be best if you saw him now. I gave him a sedative but the effects are beginning to wear off. It might do him good to talk"

"Very well, then, Doctor," Tracy indicated the doorway and the four of them—the district attorney, the inspector, Dr. Partridge and Spike went down the stairs to the first floor in follow-the-leader formation. But at the foot of the stairs just as they were prepared to leave the house, Emma appeared.

"Mr. Thane's come home," she announced, "and he says that if the policemen would like to see him he's up in his rooms."

The apartment of Elton Thane was on the same plan as that of his wife and directly above it But there the similarity ended. These were a man's rooms—dull greens and browns; soft, worn leather chairs; heavy walnut furniture bearing the marks of long wear; the carpet a little threadbare; smoking stands at comfortable intervals—a room that bore the stamp of living rather than the impress of an interior decorator's latest whim.

When the four men entered the room Elton Thane was standing looking out of the front windows, his back to the door. He was a tall man with bushy, iron-gray hair, and shoulders that drooped as if suddenly he had been dealt a staggering blow in the back. At the sound of their entrance, he turned slowly.

In his youth he had undoubtedly been a handsome man. Now at fifty he was still strikingly good looking, but time had bracketed his mouth with two heavy lines, and dulled the deep-set brown eyes. He was haggard, and his clothes were crumpled by the restless sleep from which he had just awakened. His face as he stood before them was curiously devoid of expression as if the tragedy of the night had left him stunned and but partly conscious of what was going on around him.

For a moment he only stood there, slowly taking in the presence of the four men. Then he motioned them to chairs and seated himself.

"Well?" A single syllable, but it was as if his voice had stuck in a parched throat.

"Mr. Thane," the district attorney began, "this is a very painful procedure for you, and I regret sincerely that it is necessary. However, you understand—"

Thane nodded silently, and Tracy continued. "Will you please tell us in as much detail as possible everything you know of the movement of Mrs. Thane last night."

There was a slight pause. Then in a low, controlled voice Elton Thane spoke. His story was substantially that of the maid and Dr. Partridge. After his wife had left at eight o'clock, he had written a letter, sent the maid out to post it, and had then gone off to his club, the Chatham, on West Seventy-sixth Street.

At some time about twelve he had returned to Eighty-second Street to Dr. Partridge's and played chess until about four in the morning, and had then gone home. Passing his wife's door and noticing the light, he had knocked. When there was no answer he had gone in and found her dead body lying in front of the rifled safe.

He paused, but his face, still as expressionless as ever, remained set.

"Tell me, Mr. Thane," said the district attorney, tactfully switching the conversation from this painful situation, "what do you know about this young fellow, Spencer?"

For a moment Elton Thane hesitated. "Well," he said finally, "I really know very little about him. He was—ah—"

"I think I understand. He was your wife's paid companion on dining and dancing excurions which you yourself did not care to attend." Thane nodded.

"Anything more than that?"

"No!" For the first time he raised his voice and his eyes flashed. Then as if this effort had suddenly weakened him he slumped into his chair and his hands hung limp over the upholstered arms. When he spoke again he had regained his control. "No, I am quite sure that there was nothing more between them than that. My wife was a good deal younger than I and—our tastes were different."

"Was he here frequently?"

"Twice each week. He was always engaged for Monday and Thursday evenings."

"And you were friendly with him?"

Thane nodded. "He was—he—I liked him. He seemed a good sort. As a matter of fact I took him golfing with me several times. I can't believe that—that—"

"That he is the murderer of your wife."

As his unspoken thoughts were put into words by the district attorney, Elton Thane gripped the arms of his chair until his knuckles showed white. But he only repeated himself.

"I can't believe it."

"Were there any other people in the house last night between eight and twelve?"

"No one, except the maid and myself and Spencer."

"Who beside Mrs. Thane knew the combination to the safe in her bedroom?"

"I was the only other person."

"Do you, by any chance, know where Spencer lives?"

"He used to have an apartment somewhere on West One Hundred and Fourth Street, between Columbus Avenue and the Park. I don't know the exact number, but I was there two or three times after we had played golf together. He has moved recently though. I think it's some place not far from here but I can't say just where."

"Perhaps," said the district attorney turning to Herschman, "you might find the telephone number on the pad in Mrs. Thane's room"

"As if I hadn't already thought of that," the inspector replied "The S page is missing. The only page in the alphabet that isn't there"

## III. THE LITTLE ROUND HOLE IN THE CHAISE LONGUE

AS Tracy, Herschman and Spike drove back to Police Headquarters, the two older men reviewed briefly the famous Schlockenhass case which had stirred the city six months before.

Greta Schlockenhass, middle-aged wife of a rich brewer, owner of many gaudy but expensive jewels had been found dead in her hotel apartment, a bullet through her heart and $150,000 worth of jewels missing. Investigation showed that she had been seen frequently in the company of several sleek young men in the night clubs. For their service as escorts she had paid them generously. Four of them were taken into custody by the police, but there had never been sufficient evidence to charge them with the crime, although two of them already had records for larceny. They had been released. The murderer had never been found nor, the jewels recovered.

The story had been a newspaper sensation for four weeks, with flaunting eight-column streamer heads, pictures of the murdered woman, her bereaved but complacent husband and the four young gigolos who had had the misfortune to be in her employ.

"Suppose we have a look at the Schlockenhass records when we get back to the office," the district attorney suggested.

"I was thinking the same thing myself," Herschman replied "Milliken should be ready with the fingerprints by then."

"In the meantime," Spike suggested, entering the conversation for the first time since his rebuff over the rouge incident, "let's read all about it in the newspapers."

The taxi held up by traffic was stopped immediately in front of a newsstand which had just received its pile of first editions of the afternoon papers. Spike beckoned to the boy in charge.

"A *Sun* and an *Evening Post* for these two," he said, "and a nice, juicy *Graphic* for me"

The taxi moved on and the three of them leaned back in contemplation of their papers—the district attorney with a certain distasteful apprehension—the inspector with an air of abstraction as if he were thinking of other things.

But Spike rustled his with gusto. "As usual," he said after a glance at the front page, "my trusty tab's about six hours ahead of yours. Here's the whole story."

And there indeed it was. Ninety-six-point headlines. "Diamond Queen Slain." Photographs of Cecily Thane and her husband resurrected from the office morgue. The Thane house decorated with an ominous X. "Police Seek Night-Club Sheik." Emma Bloomstead showing rather too much leg.

The district attorney gave one brief, pained glance at the gaudy page and heaved a sigh of resignation.

"It's begun," he said.

And when he reached the anteroom of his office at Headquarters, the full tide of it swept over him. The room was full of newspaper men, and rather irate newspaper men at that. Each one of them had received a thorough reprimand from the city desk for the manner in which the *Graphic* had beat them on the first-edition story. It was the only paper in town that carried the news.

It was twenty minutes before the inspector and the district attorney could escape the mob and their questions, but finally they emerged into the district attorney's private office where Spike had already made himself comfortable.

Milliken, fingerprint expert, had been even quicker in his work than the inspector had anticipated, and had already a group of photographs to lay before his chief.

Both Tracy and Herschman were struck with the same thought as they looked at them—the records in the Schlockenhass case—and Lovelace, Tracy's secretary, was accordingly sent after them.

"A nice variety," Milliken explained as he laid the still damp prints on the desk. "At least four different persons."

Tracy and Herschman examined the pictures with interest. Each one was neatly labeled with the exact spot in the room from which it was taken . . . from the edge of the mantelpiece . . . a corner of the dressing table . . . the arm of a chair.

"Anything on the wall safe?" the inspector inquired.

"Couldn't get a trace. It had apparently been wiped clean."

"Hm." The inspector appeared to consider this piece of information, but the arrival of Lovelace with the Schlockenhass records interrupted whatever train of thought it might have aroused.

There were a number of legal papers and two photographs, one front and one profile view of each of the four men who had been arrested in the famous jewel-murder of the year before. And underneath each photograph were five neat fingerprints.

It was with these prints that Milliken at the inspector's direction quickly compared the prints which had been taken from the room of Cecily Thane that morning. He had been at work with his small pocket glass no more than three minutes when he looked up with an expression of satisfaction, and pushed two of the pictures toward the two men eagerly waiting on the other side of the table.

"There's your man," he said quietly. And then with a tiny steel rod he proceeded to point out the similarity in markings. The thumb and forefinger print which had been taken from the edge of a small smoking table in Cecily Thane's bedroom was identical with the corresponding prints of one of the Schlockenhass arrests.

Herschman read from the back of the record card: "William Preston . . . 23 years old . . . 5 ft. 8 . . . weight 140 pounds . . . brown eyes . . . occupation professional dancer. No criminal record. . . . Was seen at the Lido Venice with Greta Schlockenhass three hours before her murdered body was discovered."

"Well," said the inspector, "it looks like the man we're after is the right one. Must have changed his name to Spencer."

A wave of obvious relief seemed to sweep over the district attorney at this satisfactory turn of the case. For the first time that morning he leaned back in his chair and relaxed, and the worried frown faded from between his brows.

The striking coincidence of the murder of Greta Schlockenhass and Cecily Thane under the same circumstances and with, obviously enough, at least one person involved in both cases, seemed to clear the way for a solution of the puzzle.

When Herschman and Milliken had left, Tracy helped himself to a cigar, lighted it in a leisurely fashion and looked in the direction of his brother. Spike, as was his habit, had immediately upon entering the room selected the most comfortable chair and slouched into it. While his brother, the inspector and the fingerprint expert had made their comparison of the fingerprints, he had been gazing out of the window at the gloomy, barred windows of the Tombs just across the street.

"Well," said Tracy complacently, "you see how it's done."

"How what's done?" Spike asked, pulling his mind back apparently from a long distance.

"You wanted to see how criminals are found out," he explained patiently, "and now you see it. Not so thrilling after all, is it?"

"In other words, you mean that this chap Spencer popped off Mrs. Thane?"

"Exactly."

Spike reached forth a hand and picked up the four sets of pictures from the Schlockenhass case and examined them one by one. Three of them were sleek-looking young fellows with carefully brilliantined hair, the type that can be seen by the dozens on any dance floor. But the fourth one, marked Preston, was different. The hair was an unruly dark mop. And the eyes were not the knowing eyes of a professional dancing man, but of a boy who seemed to have stumbled somehow into trouble. The chin both in profile and full face was weak, but the general effect of the face as a whole was somewhat appealing.

Spike looked at the picture carefully for a few moments. "Aren't you jumping at conclusions?" he said.

Tracy laughed indulgently. "The amateur detective has a theory?"

"Not a theory. Just a couple of questions."

"Let me have them and perhaps I can clear it up for you." Tracy was patronizing.

"Well, number one is, why, if this Spencer lad did do the trick, why did he take the trouble to lug the body from the chaise longue to the spot in front of the safe? Why not just leave the lady where she lay?"

"What do you mean?"

"I mean that she wasn't killed in front of the safe. Number two—why—"

"My dear fellow, I never heard anything so ridiculous."

"Quit 'my dear fellowing' me and hear me the to end. We are alone. No outsiders are present to witness the humiliating depth of my foolishness in thinking I can put my feeble brain against the mighty minds of the legal and police departments, so let me babble on.

"As I said before—number two—who was the woman, beside Emma, of course, who was in Cecily Thane's sitting room between eight o'clock last night and four this morning?"

"Now you're talking like one of your infernal tabloids. I wish you would read the *Times* occasionally and then your mind would not run so constantly to women."

"Just the same," Spike persisted, "it would be interesting to know"

From his inside pocket he drew out his cigarette case and opened it. But he did not take out a cigarette, for there were no fresh ones in it—only five half-smoked butts.

"You were justified, my dear brother," he said, "in thinking I was an utter damn fool this morning, playing with the late Mrs. Thane's lip stick. But as a matter of fact it was one of my infrequent sensible moments."

For a few seconds he held the open cigarette case before him and contemplated the five butts. Then one by one he lifted them out and put them on the desk before him.

"These two Luckies I found in the ash tray immediately to the right of the big easy-chair by the fireplace. You'll note that they're ringed with dark carmine rouge, the kind usually affected by dashing brunettes. And these two Benson and Hedges I found in the ash tray beside the chaise longue. They are, please observe, ringed with a much lighter shade of roug—pale orange in fact. And this Camel I smoked myself after I had painted the engaging Cupid's bow. The color on it corresponds exactly with that on the Benson and Hedges. And the maid said that she emptied the ash trays at eight o'clock after Mrs. Thane had gone out."

He paused to let these carefully assorted facts sink in.

"Which means?" said the district attorney

"Which means that when Mrs. Thane came home last night she smoked two cigarettes. And that some other woman was also in the room some time after eight o'clock when the maid emptied the ash trays and she too smoked two cigarettes. Under the circumstances, I think it would be rather interesting to know just who she was."

For a moment the district attorney said nothing, but shifted uneasily. "But did it occur to you," he said finally, "that the dark red lip rouge might belong also to Mrs. Thane?"

"Nothing, my dear brother, escapes me. I made a special point of taking an inventory of all Mrs. Thane's lip sticks on the dresser and in the drawers and all were the same shade—pale orange."

"Probably the maid sat down and took a rest while she was clearing things up."

"Probably," Spike shrugged his shoulders as if to let the subject drop.

"Means nothing," Tracy went on. It was plain that he was trying to lull his reason to sleep and let these disquieting points brought up by his brother rest unnoticed. "Herschman will probably be able to find a perfectly logical explanation in five minutes."

"Probably," Spike admitted. Then he reached for a cigarette from a paper packet in the pocket of his Tuxedo: and lit it and exhaled deeply.

"I wonder," he said, "I wonder if her eyes are blue. All my life I've been searching for a blue-eyed brunette and the only one I ever saw was a Dublin barmaid who had a husband who was forty pounds heavier than I. A charming little thing but really not—"

"Look here, Philip, the district attorney broke in, "you are an utter damn fool, but—but—"

"But sometimes out of the mouths of babes, sucklings and damn fools there sprout words of wisdom."

Tracy nodded grudgingly. "This cigarette business does look slightly suspicious. But on what do you base your statement that the body was moved from the chaise longue to the position in which it was discovered in front of the safe."

"I'm not so sure about that," Spike admitted. "I just threw that in by way of rousing your appetite for more and bloodier details. Still, I think I'm right at that."

Suddenly he rose from his chair and reached for his hat. Then he paused and looked at his brother with a certain eagerness in his glance.

"Listen, old thing, would you mind tremendously if I temporarily stepped out of my role of unofficial observer?"

"Why?"

"I'd like awfully to have another chat with the charming and gabby Emma. Not that I have ever been partial to blondes, but—"

"Certainly not. You are not going to turn this case into one of your notorious escapades with women, and a servant girl at that."

"My dear Richard, you wrong me. My pursuit of Emma is purely in the interests of criminal investigation. I shall do and say nothing in her presence that you and dear old Great-grandmother Tracy couldn't witness and retain your innocency. What I mean to suggest is not a rendezvous tête-a-tête, but a serious little chat. Just you and me and Emma. Something clubby—and revealing."

For a moment the district attorney hesitated.

"Very well," he said. "It isn't at all regular, but—" and he too reached for his hat.

"Oh, by the way," Spike said as he paused at the door, "would you mind bringing the fatal bullet along with you?"

In a few moments they were in a taxi speeding north for the second time that morning to Eighty-second Street.

"Another thing that's funny," Spike pointed out, "is that cut telephone wire."

"A very common precaution," the district attorney assured him.

"But in this case why was it necessary. Granting that this fellow Spencer did do the dirty deed, certainly he gave the lady no time to summon help before he shot her. And she was hardly in any condition to do it afterward."

The district attorney, if he had an explanation, did not offer it, and Spike continued more in the manner of one thinking aloud than conversing.

"The fingerprint business on the safe is intriguing too. If Spencer is the guilty guy he probably waited until she went to the safe of her own accord to put something away or take something out. And then he plugged her. But why wipe off her fingerprints?" He broke off, bewildered by the maze of his speculations.

As they stopped before the Thane house, the police ambulance carrying its grisly burden was backing away from the door. Cecily Thane's bedroom was just as they had left it, except for the spot immediately in front of the safe. An ugly dark stain spread out through the carpet where the body had lain. Two policemen were standing guard, one inside the two-room apartment and one in the hall outside. Tracy requested one of them to summon the maid.

As Emma entered the room a few moments later both the district attorney and Spike were struck by the change in her attitude. Her self-assurance was gone and she seemed noticeably more subdued than she had been in the morning. It was plain that this second interview filled her with no elating sense of importance. She eyed the two men with a certain uneasy distrust and said nothing.

Spike glanced questioningly at his brother, and the district attorney nodded to him. "Go ahead —but—" He broke off with a warning, apprehensive, look as if to say, "Go ahead, but try not to make *too* much of a fool of yourself."

Spike courteously indicated a chair, and Emma, unused to such mannerly treatment by the strange invaders who had been swarming the house since four o'clock that morning, seated herself uneasily on the edge. He opened his cigarette case, now replenished and offered her one fraternally. The district attorney frowned.

"Smoke?"

She shook her head. "No, sir."

"Never?"

"No, sir."

He selected one for himself and lit it and settled back comfortably in his chair.

"You really should learn to smoke, my girl," he advised sagely. "Splendid for the nerves."

"Yes, sir. That's what Mrs. Thane always said."

"And Mrs. Thane was very nervous?"

"Well—yes—lately."

"You've known Mrs. Thane a long time, haven't you?"

"I've worked here five years."

"Then you're pretty well acquainted with all of her friends, aren't you?"

"Yes, sir."

A sudden change seemed to come over Spike. He sobered, left off his casual air, like one who has dallied long enough and has decided to come down to business. As he posed the next question there was nothing in his manner to indicate that he had but a few hours before placed elk-hunting and criminal investigation in the same category.

He was in deadly earnest, and Emma grew more uneasy under his direct gaze.

"Tell me," he said, "did any of Mrs. Thane's friends drop in to call last night after she left with Mr. Spencer?"

"Why—no."

"No—women friends, for instance?"

"No, sir."

"Did she have any visitors earlier in the evening before she left?"

"Well—about six o'clock her brother came to see her."

"Her brother?"

"Yes, Mr. George Griffis."

"He is a frequent caller, I suppose?"

"No, he doesn't come very often—not since he moved away."

"He used to live here?"

"Yes, sir, until about a year ago."

"And this is the first time he has been in the house in a year?"

"Yes, sir."

"Sort of a family reunion?"

"Well—not exactly."

"What do you mean—not exactly?"

"I mean that—that—" She broke off abruptly with a look almost of fright in her eyes. "You'd —you'd better ask Mr. Thane."

"I see." Spike paused a moment. Then he continued his questions.

"Did Mrs. Thane go out at any time during the day?"

"No, sir, she was in all day."

"Did she have any other visitors except Mr. Spencer and her brother?"

Emma hesitated and ran her tongue over dry lips before she answered. "No, sir."

"Did she write any letters?"

"I don't know."

"What I mean is did she send you out with any to post?"

"No, sir."

"Perhaps she had you call a messenger?"

"Yes, sir."

"Did she send many letters that way—by messenger?"

"Well—quite a few—lately."

"You don't know by any chance to whom the one she sent yesterday was directed?"

"No, sir."

"But you called the messenger for her?"

Emma nodded.

"Western Union?"

"No, sir. Service."

Spike took a long pull at his cigarette before he spoke again. Then: "You are quite sure—quite sure, mind you—that no one came to the house after Mrs. Thane left last night?"

"Why—no sir." The denial was emphatic, but even as she made it, her feet shifted nervously.

He considered this for a moment. Then abruptly he changed his tack.

"Have you any idea when the furniture in this room was bought?"

The girl looked at him in slight bewilderment, unable to grasp the connection between the furniture and the murder of her late mistress, but a look of relief came over her at the sudden turn in the questioning.

"Well, Mrs. Thane was always buying new things and throwing away the old ones."

"Did she buy anything new recently?"

"She had the rooms done over about two months ago and she got that writing table and the radio cabinet and that chaise longue and the new easy-chair here."

"You did the dusting in here"

She nodded.

"When is the last time you remember dusting thoroughly?"

"Yesterday morning"

"And I suppose that in the course of your work you dusted that piece over there?" He indicated the chaise longue, soft maple wood and fine wicker skillfully combined.

"Yes, sir."

"You took all the pillows off?"

"Yes, sir."

"And you noticed nothing strange about it?"

"No, sir."

Spike rose and crossed the room to the chaise longue and swept aside its burden of down pillows.

"You didn't by any chance notice this hole, did you?"

The eyes of both the district attorney and the maid widened as they followed the direction of his finger. Through the fine wickerwork of the back, about the spot which normally supports the shoulder blade, was a small, round hole, with still fresh edges of wicker showing.

"I think, Richard," said Spike on whom the old air of nonchalance had suddenly descended "I think you'll find that the bullet which your man picked up back there in the bedroom just fit this hole."

# IV. Blots on a Blotter

FOR a few moments after the maid had left the room, Tracy stood gaping at the hole in the chaise longue. Then slowly he drew a small bit of lead from his pocket and passed it through the opening. Even as Spike had predicted, it fitted exactly. Quickly he turned to his brother in agitation.

"I can hardly see how even that alters the case," he protested in feeble defense. "He might just as easily have killed her here as over there."

"Of course, but what would be his object in lugging the body across the room and depositing it melodramatically amid the empty jewel cases unless—"

Spike stopped abruptly as if he had suddenly chanced on an idea.

"Unless what?"

"Unless the person who did it was aiming for just that. A woman shot through the heart . . . safe empty . . . the jewels gone. Plain as day. Motive robbery."

"I don't follow you."

"Of course, old dear. Don't try, you'll strain your brain attempting to keep up with my light fling deductions. You really should read the tabs, though, and you would be able to dope these things out better."

"But the dent which the bullet made in the woodwork over there is as plain as day."

"Certainly. You or I or any one else could duplicate it in two minutes with a nail and a shoe to pound it in."

"And your theory about a third person—possibly a woman—having been here is totally erroneous."

"Oh, do you think so?"

"Didn't the maid deny that any one else had been in the house?"

"Certainly, but she was lying. Did you notice that she didn't say 'No' right out when I asked her. She said, 'Why—no'. I always suspect denial when it's prefaced by 'Why.' I'm rather struck, too, by the change in Emma. I'm afraid she's losing her grip."

"Yes," Tracy admitted, "she doesn't seem to be so—so self-assured as she was this morning."

"I rather imagine she's been talking to some one since we were here this morning, and she has been warned against too much gab."

"Thane, perhaps."

"I shouldn't be surprised. Let's have another talk with him."

Tracy nodded assent and rose to summon the officer just outside the door, but Spike stopped him.

"Just a moment. This messenger business intrigues me frightfully. Suppose we find out first just where Mrs. Thane's letter was sent yesterday afternoon."

In a few moments he had the Service Messenger Company on the telephone in the lower front hall. At first they were unwilling to give out the information, but the name of the district attorney of New York County soon brought a more satisfactory answer.

"Our messenger called at the Thane house about four yesterday afternoon and took a letter to Mrs. Mortimer Fennel at 204 West Eighty-sixth Street," the voice over the wire admitted.

"Was there any answer?"

Spike hung up the receiver and took the stairs to the second floor two at a time. As he entered the sitting room his eyes traveled with a speculative glint to the writing table on the opposite side of the room. From the dressing table in the bedroom he brought a hand glass.

"Blotters," he explained to his brother, "are always interesting. Especially the blotters of ladies who have just been murdered. Or, at least, that is the way it has been in all the detective stories I've ever read."

The writing pad of the desk was clear of any blots of ink, but the small hand blotter, mounted on a pale blue and green enameled pad, bore several marks. It was apparently a fresh one, for what impressions there were stood out clearly, and only in one or two places were there marks superimposed upon others.

Spike held the looking-glass at right angles and the two men examined the reflection.

"Frightfully disappointing, isn't it," Spike admitted "I was all prepared for blackmail, rape, arson and blood. Still, we'll keep it for future reference," and he extracted the blotter from its holder and handed it over to his brother. "And now let's get at Thane."

Elton Thane was still in his apartment on the third floor, but when he was informed by one of the ubiquitous officers that the district attorney wished to speak to him again, he came down to the reception room on the first floor and waited for him there. By tacit agreement it was Tracy who posed the questions this time. Although willing to trust his brother in conversation with inconsequential servant girls, he was not willing to grant him an equal privilege with the master of the house.

"I'm sorry to disturb you again, Mr. Thane," he explained, "but there are a few points which are not yet quite clear to me. My brother here is—ah—assisting in the investigation so you need not feel constrained by his presence," he added as he noted Thane eyeing Spike skeptically.

"We understand that your wife had some visitors yesterday."

For a moment Elton Thane said nothing, merely looked out of the window, his lower lip caught between his teeth. Then with his eyes still averted he spoke.

"Yes?" but the word was a question rather than a confirmation.

"Yes. The maid tells us that Mrs. Thane's brother was here yesterday afternoon."

"Yes, he was," he admitted quietly.

"And what was his mission?"

"I don't know. I wasn't here at the time."

"But surely your wife told you."

"No, I came in at six and she was resting. I did not disturb her. I did not see her until just before she left and Spencer was with her. All she said was, 'George was here this afternoon.'"

"This is his first visit for quite a while, isn't it?"

"Yes. In almost a year. He used to live here with us."

"And why did he leave?"

"He preferred living closer to his place of business. He has a small real estate business in Nassau Street, and he found it more convenient to live on Brooklyn Heights."

"You have his address?"

"Only his office. 154 Nassau Street."

"There were no—no hard feelings when he left?"

"None whatever. As a matter of fact he still keeps his room here, in a way."

"What do you mean, 'in a way'?"

"I mean he still kept his latchkey, and his bedroom on the first floor has remained the same since he left it. He was free at any time to come and go in the house as he pleased."

"And did he ever avail himself of that privilege?"

Thane paused to think. "As a matter of fact, I don't believe he ever did."

"So that yesterday, to the best of your knowledge, is the first time that he has been in this house for a year?"

"Yes."

There was a short pause while the district attorney considered these statements. Then he switched to a new tack.

"And did your wife have any other visitors that you know of yesterday?"

"No women visitors, for instance?"

"No."

"No one by any chance came to the house to see her after she had gone out with Spencer."

"Why—no."

Again a short pause. Spike's glance met his brother's in silent appeal. The district attorney hesitated uncertainly and then nodded almost imperceptibly.

"My dear Mr. Thane," said Spike in a leisurely tone which was in pleasing contrast to the hammer-like quality of his brother's questioning, "would you mind my offering a bit of advice?"

"Why no."

"I mean that if you really intend to be convincingly you should leave off the 'Why'."

Elton Thane stiffened, and a slow red crept up his pale ears.

"What do you mean?"

"I mean just this—we have a very strong suspicion that some one beside Spencer and Mrs. Thane's brother came to this house last night."

"Why, I never heard of anything so preposterous."

"Really, Mr. Thane, it will be much simpler if you just tell us right off the bat. Certain things make me feel that it was a woman."

"A woman?"

"Oh, so it wasn't a woman. Well then, a man."

For a moment Elton Thane remained stiff and erect in his chair. Then suddenly he seemed to give way to the inevitable. He slumped back with a gesture of surrender.

"All right," he said, "I'll admit it. But—but may I ask you, if you possibly can, not to drag this man into the case?" There was a note almost of anguish in his voice

"You may rest assured," the district attorney broke in, "that we shall do everything we can to avoid involving innocent persons. But under the circumstances, we cannot know who is innocent and who is suspect, unless you are perfectly frank with us."

Thane nodded in assent. "You're quite right. Forgive me for my efforts to conceal—"

"And who was this man?"

"He was a very old friend of both Mrs. Thane and myself. He and his wife and daughter used to live in the same apartment house with us before we moved here. We have known them for perhaps twelve or fifteen years. He came to the house last night after both of us had left. Emma tells me that he said that he would come in and wait a while, thinking I might possibly return from the club. He went up to Mrs. Thane's sitting room—that's where we usually met—and stayed for a little while and then left."

"And was he alone?"

"Yes."

"He had no—no woman friend with him?"

"He was quite alone. His wife is an invalid—has been for many years. And as a matter of fact she has recently taken a turn for the worse. That is the main reason why I hope that his name can be kept out of it, even in the most innocuous connection. She is a very highly strung woman, and if she should hear about it in any way, it might have an extremely bad effect on her at this particular time."

"I quite understand. And what is this man's name?"

"Mortimer Fennel."

# V. THE ROUGE-RINGED CIGARETTE

THE district attorney and his brother walked briskly along Eighty-sixth Street in the direction of Riverside Drive and exchanged arguments.

"But my dear fellow," Tracy protested, "surely Thane told a straight enough story—after we pressed him—"

"After 'we' pressed him?" Spike laughed. "Straight enough for you, but not for me."

"Well, what lurid idea have you got up your sleeve now?"

"It's so lurid that even I blush to confess it."

"What is it?"

"Well, when a lady writes a note to a gentleman's wife and that very same night the gentleman comes to the lady's house and subsequently the lady is found dead with a bullet through her heart—well, it all sounds rather intriguing, don't you think?"

"Possibly, if I could follow you."

"The thing that puzzles me though is where my blue-eyed brunette—at least I hope she's a blue-eyed brunette—with the heavy, carmine lipstick comes in. I hesitate to accuse Mr. Fennel, sight unseen, of using rouge."

"And I hope that I can trust you to refrain from even making any ridiculous suggestion in that direction."

"Oh, positively. I shall be as silent as the tomb—unless, of course, you get in a corner as you did with Thane, just now." He grinned out of the side of his eyes at his brother.

"You know," he went on, "I can't get over the change in Emma. She was positively clam-like in comparison with her garrulous state this morning."

"Probably a let-down after the initial excitement of the case. It frequently affects people that way."

"Richard, dear, your psychology is rotten—and frightfully unexciting. I prefer to think that some one has forcibly impressed upon her the golden quality of silence. As my feeble brain has it figured out, Thane had no opportunity to talk to her until after we left this morning. And when he did he found out that this George Griffis and Mortimer Fennel had visited the house the night before. And for some reason which as yet I can't quite fathom, he would much rather these two gentlemen were left out of the case. This Mortimer Fennel especially."

The district attorney only grunted and the two of them walked on in silence—Tracy in heavy gloom; Spike with a singularly exhilarated air about him.

Number 204 West Eighty-sixth Street was a six-story apartment house of the older type distinguished by an oversupply of baroque ornament and a lobby that had originally been marble and red plush. Now all that remained of former glories were yellowed stone and worn armchairs, and an iron-grilled elevator presided over by an ancient black man. Its proximity to Riverside Drive gave it a certain air of refinement, while its out-of-date design stamped it as a place for people of limited means.

The Fennel apartment was on the sixth floor. As the district attorney and his brother stood in the hall outside the door waiting for an answer to their ring, Spike pulled out his watch.

"Twelve o'clock. We're just in time for lunch."

"I hardly think you have the proper costume for a luncheon engagement," Tracy remind him with a disapproving glance. Spike was still wearing the crumpled Tuxedo which he had slept in at the Forty-seventh Precinct Station House.

"Oh, that's not what's bothering me," he assured his brother. "I was just wondering whether by any chance Mr. Fennel has read of the recent disturbance on Eighty-second Street. I don't imagine he reads the *Graphic* and the other papers wouldn't have it until their second edition. If not, we—"

His sentence was cut short by the opening of the door. It gave on to one of those long dark halls for which the older New York apartments are famous, so that it was difficult at first for them to make out the figure of the girl who answered their ring.

"Mr. Mortimer Fennel?" the district attorney inquired.

"You wished to see him?"

"Yes."

"Won't you come in," and she led the way down the dark hall to the living room in the front. It was a comfortable looking place, tasteful and pleasant with gay chintz hangings and the soft gleam of old walnut and polished brass andirons. The girl motioned them to sit down, but she did not immediately summon Mortimer Fennel.

She was a young woman of perhaps twenty-two or three but her somewhat Junoesque build made her seem older. Almost as tall as Spike, she was handsome rather than pretty. There was a certain firm line to her chin that gave one the feeling that in character as well as figure she was a person of exceptional strength.

"Mortimer Fennel is my father," she explained. "Is there anything that I could do?"

"I'm afraid not, Miss Fennel," the district attorney said.

"You see, my mother is very ill, and my father is with her. He doesn't like to leave her even for a moment, unless it is very important."

"I'm very sorry to trouble him, but it is important."

"Very well," and she left the room with that soft tread that a sick room in the house develops.

In a few moments she returned, followed by her father. Mortimer Fennel was a man of perhaps forty-five or fifty—a strikingly handsome man. His heavy black hair, only just beginning to show gray, swept off his forehead in a Byronic gesture, and his nose, thin and sensitive, was high-arched and patrician It was his mouth that betrayed him It was full and sensual, but with a weak, defeated droop to it.

The sick vigil at his wife's bedside had told heavily on him. His unshaved face was pallid and his eyes stared out from deep circles of weariness. He had on a dressing gown over his clothes, and his shirt was collarless. For a moment he stared in slight bewilderment at the two visitors. Then the district attorney explained.

"I am exceedingly sorry to trouble you, Mr. Fennel, at this particular time, but unfortunately circumstances force me to. I am the district attorney of New York County and this is my brother who is— ah—assisting me."

As the three men seated themselves, Tracy looked inquiringly in the direction of the girl who still remained in the room.

"I would suggest that Miss Fen—"

But he was interrupted by a swift and courtly gesture from his brother. Spike drew forward a chair from one corner of the room and in his best Continental drawing-room manner bowed the girl into it. For an instant there was a lightning-like exchange of glances between the two brothers. Then Tracy capitulated.

"It has been my painful duty this morning," he went on "to investigate the murder of Cecily Thane."

Even R. Montgomery Tracy, the most unimaginative man who ever held the post of district attorney, was conscious of the crucial drama of the occasion, and had the good sense to let this single sentence stand unqualified. For a moment there was a dead silence in the room. The weak, handsome face of Mortimer Fennel suddenly, almost invisibly stiffened, but not a muscle moved. When presently he spoke, his voice seemed consciously under control.

"You mean that Mrs. Thane has been—murdered?"

Tracy nodded. "She was found at four o'clock this morning shot through the heart in the bedroom of her home."

Fennel made no move, but sat staring ahead of him. Tracy continued.

"In view of the fact that you were a visitor at the Thane house last night, Mr. Fennel, I am forced to draw you into the investigation."

"Why—why yes, certainly."

"Would you mind telling me of your visit?"

"Well—" Fennel paused to pass a thick, nervous tongue over his dry lips. "Why, I went there some time in the evening—no one was in so— so I just stayed around a bit, and then I came home."

"I'm afraid I will have to insist on a little bit more detail than that. What time, for instance was it when you went there?"'

"I—I don't remember exactly. Some time the middle of the evening. Nine o'clock perhaps."

"And who admitted you at the door?"

"Emma."

"And she told you that Mr. and Mrs. Thane were out?"

"Yes."

"But you remained for a short time?"

"Yes."

"And what did you do while you were there?"

"I—I went up to Mrs. Thane's sitting room."

"And about how long were you there?"

"Twenty minutes—perhaps half an hour."

"And what was the purpose of your visit?"

Again Fennel paused and with the same quick, nervous gesture moistened his dry lips. "Why—I was just walking by and I—I thought I would drop in for a little chat."

"Just a friendly visit?"

"Yes."

"It did not, of course, have anything to do with a letter which Mrs. Thane wrote to your wife yesterday afternoon and sent around by special messenger?"

"Well—as a matter of fact," he admitted, "it did. You see, my wife has been ill for a long time—many years. Lately she has grown worse and—Mrs. Thane wrote just a friendly letter to cheer up a rather dismal sick room, and I thought it only courteous that I drop around and let them know of Mrs. Fennel's condition."

"You don't by any chance have the letter still?"

"I—I don't think so. I threw it in the waste basket."

"Perhaps it is still in the house?"

"No." It was the voice of Nina Fennel, sharp and decisive. "I emptied all the baskets myself this morning and it was carried away in the weekly trash removal."

Both Spike and his brother turned and looked quickly in her direction and both were struck by the contrast between the father and the daughter. He was weak, nervous, obviously uneasy. But she sat calmly in her, chair, her mouth set in a firm line and her eyes meeting those of the two men with an unwavering gaze

"Tell me, Mr. Fennel," the district attorney went on, "did you, while you were in the Thane house, see any one beside the maid?"

"No."

"As I understand it then, you went immediately to Mrs. Thane's sitting room on entering the house, remained for twenty minutes or half an hour, and then left?"

"Yes."

"And then what did you do?"

"Why—why, I came home, here"

The district attorney was silent for a moment, apparently digesting these facts and considering his next question. It was Fennel himself who broke the pause.

"Tell me—tell me more about the—murder. Who—"

"As yet there is very little to tell. We have only just begun our investigation. You don't happen to know a young chap named Spencer?"

"Spencer?"

"Tommy Spencer."

"Yes, Ce— Mrs. Thane, I believe, went about some with him."

"You knew him?"

"I've—met him."

"He is the last person whom we know to have been with Mrs. Thane."

"You mean he—killed her?"

"The investigation, as I have already pointed out, has only just begun. We have come to no conclusions as yet. You don't know where this Spencer fellow lives?"

In the questions which followed the district attorney obtained from Fennel much the same information as he had had from Thane earlier in the morning. It had been in that very apartment house that the Thanes had lived before their increased prosperity had made possible a change to a more affluent home five years before. For ten years previous to that, they had lived on the floor below, so that altogether the two families had known each other for fifteen years. But despite this long acquaintanceship, Mortimer Fennel could throw singularly little light on Cecily Thane.

"You see," he explained apologetically, "the difference in our financial status has rather come between us and the Thanes these last few years."

On the corner of Eighty-sixth Street and Riverside Drive the district attorney and his brother waited for a taxi.

"Well," said Spike, "what do you think of it all?"

"Frankly, I don't know."

"You know, old thing, you really should have paid more attention to the lady."

"Speaking of the lady, your action in keeping her in the room was quite inexcusable. Women, in so far as possible, should be kept out of police investigations."

"But my dear brother, she wasn't an ordinary woman. If you weren't quite such a doddering old bird, insensible to the charms of womankind, you would realize that Miss Nina Fennel in spite of her somewhat Amazonian proportions is an extremely likely looking gal. And—"

"That hardly qualifies her to participate in the investigation."

"—and she has black hair and the most beautiful blue eyes in the world. Furthermore, if you hadn't been wasting your glances on pa, you would have observed that when you rang in that question about the special messenger letter, the daughter attempted to quiet her jangled nerves with a cigarette."

The sarcastic reply which was on the district attorney's lips was cut short by a taxi which slid to the curb in front of them. He stepped in and waited for his brother to follow. But Spike closed the door and leaned through the window.

"If you don't mind, I think I'll take a walk along the Drive and clear the crime from my brain."

"An excellent idea," the district attorney agreed, secretly glad to be quit of his brother and his disquieting discoveries.

"But before I leave you," Spike went on, "there is one more little piece of evidence that I should surrender. Here—"

From an inside pocket he drew forth a cigarette which apparently had lived a short life. Not more than a quarter of an inch had been smoked away. And about the other end there was a circle, of deep carmine rouge.

"This," said Spike, "dropped unheeded upon the carpet from the nerveless fingers of Miss Nina Fennel when you mentioned the name of Tommy Spencer."

## VI. Spike Acts Like a Low, Sneaking Cad

AT eleven o'clock of the second morning after the murder of Cecily Thane, R. Montgomery Tracy and Inspector Herschman sat in Tracy's office and looked glum.

"I tell you, we didn't waste any time," the inspector protested. "Two hours after the body was found Groaty and McCarthy were out looking for him."

"And they let him slip through their fingers."

"Slip nothing. The time he slipped was when he left the Thane house night before last. You didn't expect him to stick around and sit on the front doorstep until the police came, did you? Oh, he's slipped all right. He's probably slipped right out of the city."

"You know what puzzles me," Tracy admitted, "is this—if he was going to escape, why didn't he do it immediately instead of delaying a day. Would you mind going over once more the findings of Groaty and McCarthy?"

Herschman suppressed a harassed sigh and patiently repeated his story. "They went around to West Hundred and Fourth Street, the place Thane told us about. The superintendent there said that Spencer had skipped out about three months ago without leaving any address, owing three months' rent and God knows how many bills around the neighborhood. He said they were just as anxious as we were to find out where he is.

"So then Groaty goes down to some of the night clubs where guys like that hang out and finally finds some one that knows him. He's living in an apartment at 15 West Ninety-third Street, just off Central Park West. A big swell place and he's got a butler, or valet, or whatever you want to call him.

"The butler says Spencer came in about four o'clock Tuesday morning and went to bed. Got up at about eleven and went out and he hasn't been back since."

"You may get a line on him when he tries to dispose of the jewels," Tracy suggested hopefully, but Herschman laughed.

"That's likely. People don't steal $200,000 worth of jewelry until they have a reliable fence."

"But you've broadcast the description?"

Herschman nodded "Good one, too. Thane gave it to me yesterday morning just before we left the house. Being a jeweler himself, he knew how to give just the information we wanted. There's one diamond and emerald necklace he says is worth about $50,000, and a string of pearls about $10,000 and a lot of smaller pieces."

They relapsed into gloom and silence again. Presently the district attorney spoke in a voice that was half a groan. "Have you seen the newspapers this morning?"

"Yeah. They're playing it hard. We're in a hole if we don't get our hands on Spencer. I told the reporters that an arrest was expected any moment."

"I suppose you've got men watching Spencer's apartment now?"

"Of course." Herschman could not keep the disgust from his voice.

"What sort of a fellow is the servant?"

"English. Very ruffined and tight-mouthed. We had to pry every word out of him."

"Found Griffis yet?"

"No. He hasn't been at his office since Monday afternoon. He lives at 70 Pierrepont Street on Brooklyn Heights, but be hasn't been there either; I've got men watching both places."

"Another one slipped through your fingers."

"Listen here, Mr. Tracy," said the inspector, now thoroughly aroused, "if you would let me handle this investigation, instead of turning it over to that half-wit—to your brother, there might not be so many slips. Never in all the time I've been a detective have I been up against the situation I'm in now."

The district attorney bridled. He might have his own opinion about his brother, but he allowed no one else the same freedom.

"I think you'll have to admit, Inspector," he said heatedly, "that my brother has proved most valuable. He has certainly opened up a great many more avenues of investigation than were apparent, at first glance. I hardly think you are justified in—"

"Now, now, children, no quarreling, no quarreling. Kiss and make up, and Richard, tell the inspector you're sorry for having such a half-witted brother."

Into the heated, gloomy atmosphere of the room, Spike breezed like a breath of the spring sunshine outside. A gay flower blossomed in his buttonhole, and he swung his walking stick with jaunty abandon. It was evident that he was on his usual good terms with the world. If anything, he seemed more exuberant than ever. With a deft toss he landed his hat on the rack on the opposite side of the room, hooked his stick beneath it, and sprawled into a chair.

"Well," he said looking brightly from one disgruntled face to the other, "what is it that has taken all the sunshine out of your lives today? A new murder?"

"No," the district attorney said shortly, "the old one is quite depressing enough."

"Depressing? To the contrary, I find it frightfully exhilarating. What's new?"

"Nothing. Herschman located Spencer's apartment, but he hasn't been there since yesterday morning, and Griffis hasn't been at his office nor his house since yesterday."

"And so you two are just sitting around being mean to each other."

"Have you anything better to suggest?" said Herschman sarcastically.

"Well," Spike replied with mock apology, "not that I think I'm any great shakes as a raconteur, but possibly since you haven't anything else on your mind, you might like to hear what I've been doing since last I saw your two dear faces."

Herschman merely grunted and Tracy emitted an ill-tempered "Well?"

"Well, first of all," said Spike settling himself more comfortably. "First of all, I lied to you, Richard. I lied. I admit it right out. When I left you yesterday afternoon,, I had no intention whatever of taking a walk. As a matter of fact walking was the furthest from my mind. I had something much more sinister in view.

"I have bad a feeling all along that this case wasn't being conducted properly!" He paused to grin out of the corner of his eyes at Herschman, but the inspector did not even take the trouble to protest the reflection.

"In the first place I may as well confess that I've been disappointed at the way you've gone about things. Not angry, you understand, just terribly, terribly disappointed. You two simply haven't lived up to my idea of what a couple of sleuths ought to be. Not once have either of you examined a footprint through a magnifying glass. You've made no attempt whatever to delve back into the history of the Thanes to discover the family curse which in turn has taken one of each generation ever since the day old Whoosis Thane vowed never—"

"Say lissen, lissen," the inspector interrupted. "What's the idea?"

"I'm coming to that, Inspector, presently. Just give me time. What I'm trying to say is that feeling that the case lacked color I thought I would inject a little into it. Unfortunately I did not have my false whiskers with me but I did the best I could without them. I'm under the impression that false whiskers are what the well-dressed detective wears when he is in the act of—"

"Philip," the district attorney broke in peremptorily, "neither Inspector Herschman nor I have the time or the inclination to listen to your attempts at alleged humor."

Spike sighed. "So I see. Ah, well—to put the matter briefly, I went back up to the Fennel apartment house after you left and chatted with the elevator man. Most interesting. He says that Mortimer Fennel and Miss Nina went out together Monday at about eight-thirty and they didn't come back until after one."

He paused. The district attorney who had been drumming impatiently on his desk looked up with a sudden flash of interest.

"But Fennel told us he left the Thane house about nine-thirty and came directly home."

"Exactly," said Spike. "It took him over three and a half hours to cover a distance of perhaps a half a mile. Maybe it took him longer than that. The elevator man goes off duty at one o'clock and he swears that neither Fennel nor Miss Nina came in before then. After one the elevator stops and there is no one in the lobby, you have to walk up."

"Rather—ah—interesting," the district attorney admitted in a guarded manner.

"Rather? You're damn well right it's 'rather' interesting. And it's also 'rather' interesting to realize that Mortimer Fennel could leave his sick wife's bedside more than four hours Monday night for, according to his own testimony, 'just a friendly visit,' and he damn well didn't want to leave her for so much as two minutes when we called on him the following morning."

Herschman said nothing but his manner slowly altered. He was listening now with an ill-concealed eagerness.

"All right. Go on. Then what?" he said impatiently as Spike paused to light a cigarette.

"And now," Spike continued, "I come to the real dirt. After my little chat with the doorman, I went back down to the corner of Eighty-sixth Street and the Drive. You may remember that at that point there is a little park with a lot of trees and shrubbery, just west of the Drive. It slopes down to an iron picket fence, and the New York Central Railroad tracks along the Hudson rim directly beneath.

"Well, I crossed over to the little park and waited, trying my best to look like an idle pedestrian. It got rather boring, especially after three hours' and three very suspicious-looking policemen had passed.

"But presently came four o'clock and I was rewarded. The girl I left behind me, came out of 204 and started down toward the Drive."

The district attorney heaved a sigh of exasperation and disgust, but Spike forestalled whatever words were on his lips.

"No, Richard, you misjudge me absolutely. My intentions were entirely dishonorable. I felt like a beast, backing into the shrubbery and spying on the poor girl as she came across the Drive instead of following my natural and gallant pulse and stepping forth boldly and trying to date her up for the evening."

He paused and blew a contemplative cloud smoke. "As a matter of fact, I wish you'd get this beastly murder business cleared up, so I could do just that thing . . . A blue-eyed brunette. . . ."

"Suppose you go on with your story instead indulging in ridiculous day-dreaming," the district attorney said irritably.

"Let me see, where did I leave myself. Oh, yes, backing into the shrubbery, like the low cad I am. Miss Fennel crossed the Drive and entered the little park. Her manner was designed doubtless to give the impression that she was in the contemplation of Nature and the Palisades but I thought I detected a certain strain about her, as if she were hoping there was no one around to witness what she was about to do.

"She crossed the park and walked down the slope to the iron pickets along the railroad track and waited. Presently a freight train of open cars filled with sand came along. She waited for a few cars to pass her while she looked around somewhat in the manner of a frightened rabbit.

"I had slunk across the park in her wake and stepped out of sight in another clump of bushes, quite near to her, so I could see plainly what she was doing."

He paused and smiled benignly on his two listeners. "And would you believe it, that beautiful girl pulled out of her handbag one of the most murderous-looking revolvers I ever saw in my life."

Both the inspector and the district attorney were sitting forward in their chairs now.

"And what did she do with it?" Herschman snapped.

"Why," said Spike calmly, "she threw it into one of the cars passing below and it was buried in the nice clean sand and carted off to God knows wherever the train was going."

Herschman sprang from his chair and glared at him.

"Young fellow, are you telling the truth or is this your idea of a joke?"

"Really, Inspector, you misjudge my sense of humor."

"Would you get up and swear to that in court?"

"Well, being, as I have already pointed out, a low cad, I would if I were forced to, but if you don't mind, I'd really rather not. Miss Fennel, you know, is an extraordinarily charming girl and I wouldn't like—"

"Shut up!" Herschman barked and reached for the telephone with an excited gesture.

"Now don't," Spike cautioned, "be impolite to me, Inspector, because I might get mad and not tell you the rest of my story and it's really rather intriguing."

But Herschman had his own office on the wire and he paid no heed to the warning "Mallory?"

"Yes."

"Get in touch with the New York Center freight yards along Riverside Drive immediately and check up on all shipments of sand that went north yesterday afternoon. Find out the destination of every car and tell them no matter where the sand is, it's to be held for inspection before unloading. Then get men out after it. Search every car for a gun. Now have you got it straight?"

"Yes, sir."

"Well, then, hurry. Don't lose a minute." He jammed the receiver down on the hook and started out the door. "I'm going up to question this Fennel woman, and I'd rather do it alone," he said curtly.

"But, Inspector—" Spike too had risen from his chair and laid a detaining hand on Herman's arm. "I really think it would be to your advantage to hear my babblings to the end."

"I'm going to see Nina Fennel and I'm going now."

"Oh, really?" Spike's hand tightened about the inspector's arm in a firm grip, and he slowly pulled him back into the room. "If you go now, you won't hear the end of my story. And anyway, Miss Fennel had a very fatiguing day yesterday and I have no doubt she is still asleep."

"Lissen here, young fellow," Herschman turned on Spike with an ominous look in his eyes. "Are you trying to keep anything from my—"

"To the contrary, I'm doing my best to tell all, to bare my soul, and you won't listen."

Herschman shook off the restraining hand, hesitated a moment and then seated himself once more.

"Well?" he snapped.

"Well," Spike continued, "after Miss Fennel parked her gun, she retraced her steps across the little park and hailed a taxi and drove downtown, with me in hot pursuit in another cab. She stopped at an obscure little restaurant over on Second Avenue, near Fourteenth Street, and went inside and took a table and began crumbling bread, and drawing figures on the tablecloth with her fork and looking at her watch and all in all acting like a very nervous woman.

"Apparently it was a prearranged rendezvous of some sort because presently a young fellow came in and sat down at her table, and they went into a huddle with their foreheads together looking mutually distressed. Unfortunately I am not a lip reader, but I fancy that she told him something that surprised him greatly and then he told her something that made her start and grip the edges of the table, and by-and-by after they had ordered about three dollars worth of food and hadn't eaten three cents worth, she got up and left."

Spike paused again, apparently for breath.

"And you followed her?" the inspector asked.

"No, I didn't."

"You didn't?"

"No. As a matter of fact, I was beginning to be a little tired of my false whisker role, and quite a bit ashamed of myself, spying on the poor girl, so I remained in the restaurant and kept my eye on the boy friend.

Herschman threw up his hands in outraged disgust.

"Oh, my God!"

"Really, Inspector, you shouldn't take things so hard. Bad for the blood pressure. And anyway the boy friend was fully as interesting a Miss Fennel.

"While he was waiting for the waiter to bring his check, I sauntered over to his table and just casually dropped into conversation with him. Very delightful fellow. We got on famously together. As a matter of fact we got on so well that I invited him up to my apartment for the night."

He paused and selected another cigarette from his case and lit it leisurely.

"Well," said Herschman impatiently, "who was this Fennel woman's boy friend, and what's his name."

"His name," said Spike, "is Tommy Spencer."

## VII. "NIGHT CLUB SHEIK HELD"

FOR a moment neither the district attorney nor the inspector said a word. Then they spoke simultaneously.

"Tommy Spencer?"

Spike nodded. "Tommy Spencer. Cecily Thane's boy friend of the night before last. We had quite a long talk together. Very interesting."

"Where's he now?" The words fairly shot from Herschman.

Spike nodded toward the anteroom. "Out there. No—" he protested as Herschman started toward the door. "He's quite safe. I tipped off two of your officers to watch him. As a matter of fact I think Tommy's keeping something from me, and it irks me. I wouldn't like him to get away before we found out what it is."

Suddenly Herschman came over and stood squarely in front of Spike and glowered down at him. "Look here, young fellow," he said, "you think you're pretty bright, don't you."

"Well," Spike grinned disarmingly, "don't you?"

"No. You've just got plain damn fools' luck."

"Suppose," said the district attorney in a placating voice from which the surprise had not entirely disappeared. "Suppose, Philip, you tell us a little bit more about your evening with Spencer."

"I'm afraid there's not much more to tell. I was perfectly frank with him after I scraped up the acquaintance. I told him I was the district attorney's brother and that I was—ah—interested in the Thane case and would he be so kind as to tell me all he knew about it."

"And he did?"

"Well, I have a feeling that up to a certain point he repaid my frankness with frankness."

"Just had him eating out of your hand, didn't you?" Herschman's voice was heavy with sarcasm.

"No," Spike admitted, "I would hardly go far as to say that. There were moments in our conversation when sheer physical force was all that kept Tommy by my side. Fortunately I'm about fifty pounds heavier than he."

"Well, go on with your story."

"One rather interesting point, he did clear up. He was not involved in the Schlockenhass case."

"Oh, he wasn't, wasn't he? And how do you know that?"

"Because he told me so."

"And you believe him?"

"His explanation was most logical. He said that his unfortunate arrest was due to a misapprehension on your part as to his true character."

"He told you that?"

"Not in precisely that way," Spike temporized. "His exact words were, if I remember correctly —'That goddam, lousy Herschman couldn't get it through his wooden head that just because the old girl paid me to let her step on my feet, I wasn't the one that bumped her off.'"

"What else did he have to say for himself?"

"He said that you had almost ruined his career. That's why he had to change his name. And he told me what he'd been doing since he left the Thane house Monday night. Quite open and frank about it. At least up to a certain point. From then on—Well, I don't know. Really I would like to get an expert opinion of the lad's story from the combined legal and police minds of New York County."

"What's the story he told you?"

"Let's have him in and let him tell it himself."

Herschman nodded in agreement and the district attorney called the outside office on the telephone. Almost immediately the door opened.

The cold details of the police record card were hardly an adequate description of William Preston alias Tommy Spencer. As the slight, dark young man stood in the doorway there was an air about him that was undeniably attractive—an attraction made up of good looks and an almost pathetic helplessness—a type that is extremely intriguing to women. But it was plain that he was striving now to put up a bold front. His eyes as he met those of the district attorney and the inspector were apprehensive but defiant; his movements were of the nervous, jerky type peculiar to young men who sleep in the daytime and spend their nights drinking and dancing.

"Well," he said with exaggerated coolness, "here I am"

"Back again," said Herschman The inspector motioned him to a chair and looked at him with narrowed eyes in the manner of a sidewalk cop eyeing a crook from the morning line-up. Then his jaw set and he jammed his hands into his pockets. "You know what you're here for," he snapped.

"Yes, I know." He answered with a surly bravado that was obviously assumed. "You think I bumped off Mrs. Thane just like you thought I bumped off Mrs. Schlockenhass."

"Suppose you cut out the fresh talk and tell me what you know. Where did you and the Thane woman go Monday night?"

"We went down to the Club Paradis and had dinner and danced and we came home about eleven-thirty and went up to her sitting room on the second floor."

"It isn't usual, is it, in your line of business to get in at such respectable hours. I thought women paid you to keep 'em out late."

"Yes, but Monday night some special friends of mine were giving a party, and I told her I could only give her half the evening. It had been a party that was arranged for another night and then they suddenly changed the date. And she was a good egg, so she said it was O.K."

"Well, then, what did you do when you brought her home and got her up in the sitting room?"

"We had a couple of cocktails and then I left."

"What time?"

But before Spencer could answer, the inspector's question Spike broke in with one of his own. "Mind telling again, Tommy, in just what position Mrs. Thane was the last time you saw her."

"She was on the chaise longue."

"And she was, I take it, still alive and well?"

"Say, how many times do I have to tell you that I'm not the one that did the shooting?"

"It's distressingly evident, Tommy, that you're not familiar with that famous line of Shakespeare's, 'Methinks he doth protest too much.' You really should read—"

But he was cut short by a glowering glance from Herschman.

"What time did you leave the Thane house Monday night?" the inspector put in.

"Oh, I don't know. About half an hour later, I guess."

"And then what did you do?"

"I went back down to the Paradis and stayed there till four o'clock; and then I went home and went to bed and slept till eleven—and if you don't believe it you can ask the man I've got work—" He broke off suddenly in confusion.

"We have already."

"Wha—what did he tell you?" There was a sudden tenseness in his voice

"Never mind what he told us. I'm asking the questions, not you. Then what did you do?"

Spencer hesitated. "I went for a walk."

"You went for a walk?" Herschman's voice was sarcastic. "Your morning constitutional, I suppose."

"No, just a walk. Can't a fellow take a walk?"

"That depends on where he walks. Where'd you go?"

"Oh, just around—just along the Drive."

"You didn't just happen to walk down to Eighty-sixth Street and see Miss Fennel?"

At the mention of Nina Fennel's name there was just the flash of an eyelid, an almost imperceptible tightening of the jaw, and when he spoke his voice was just a shade more defiant and surly.

"No I didn't see Miss Fennel until four o'clock yesterday afternoon."

"And what were you seeing her for?"

"I had a date with her?"

"What for?"

"What do you mean, 'what for?'"

"Under the circumstances, Mr. Spencer," the district attorney's voice broke smoothly into the swift staccato of questions and answers, "it would be best if you were to state frankly just what your business with Miss Fennel was."

"I didn't have any 'business' with her. It was just a date. My God, haven't you ever had a date?"

"Don't attempt to delve so far back into ancient history, old thing," Spike put in. Then turning to Herschman and the district attorney. "I think what he means to say is that his engagement was purely a social one for the purpose of tea and conversation."

"Yes, that's it."

"What did you talk about" Herschman went on.

"Oh, different things?"

"What, for instance?"

"Oh—I dunno—people we know—things like that?"

"You didn't happen to be talking about Mrs. Thane?"

"Yes, we did talk about her. We spent most of the time talking about her. Why shouldn't we? After all if it hadn't been for Mrs. Thane, I'd never met Ni—Miss Fennel."

"Oh, so Mrs. Thane introduced you to Miss Fennel. When?"

"One night about three months ago at a night club. Miss Fennel was with a party at another table and she came over and spoke to Mrs. Thane and we were introduced."

"Tommy," Spike broke in, "let me get this just straight. Miss Fennel came over and spoke to Mrs. Thane first and Mrs. Thane introduced you."

"Yes."

"And since then you've known her quite well?"

"Well, sort of."

"Would it be impertinent of me to inquire whether she is one of your—ah—customers?"

"No. Nina Fennel doesn't have to pay men to take her around." It was evident from Spencer's voice that he was slightly contemptuous of his clientele.

"How did she seem the first time she met you? What did her feelings seem to be toward you?"

Spencer lowered his eyes and fumbled with one of the buttons on his coat. "Why she seemed to—well, sort of like me right off. I got a man I know to take care of Mrs. Thane and I went over and danced with Ni—Miss Fennel and she—well—uh—"

"She made it plain that your attentions were acceptable?"

"Yes, that's it."

"I don't see what this has got to do with the case," Herschman broke in irritably.

"Probably hasn't, Inspector," Spike admitted. "Just a quaint idea of mine. I'm so interested in people, you know."

"How often have you been seeing Miss Fennel since then?" the inspector went on.

"Oh, about once or twice a week."

"Just 'dates'?"

"Just dates."

"And after she left you in the restaurant yesterday afternoon, you went with Mr. Tracy here to his apartment for the night?"

Spencer nodded.

"And you're sure you didn't do anything but just walk yesterday afternoon?"

"Yes."

"Up and down the Drive?"

"Yes, up and down the Drive."

"Are you in the habit of walking from eleven-thirty in the morning until four in the afternoon?"

"No, but I had a bad head on me from the party the night before and I wanted to walk it off."

"You didn't have lunch any place?"

"Guys in my business don't eat lunch."

"And when had you made this 'date' with Miss Fennel?"

"I stopped in at a drug store and called her up and told her to meet me?"

"About what time did you telephone Miss Fennel," Spike broke in.

"Oh, I don't know."

"Rack the old brains and let me have the exact hour."

"Oh, maybe—two—three o'clock."

"And from where?"

"United Cigar Store on Seventy-second Street and Broadway."

"And you told her to meet you down on Second Avenue at four o'clock."

"Yes."

"Your witness, Inspector."

"You bet he's my witness," said Herschman, "and I'm so fond of him that I'm going to hold him as a material witness—without bail."

He turned a triumphant smile on the district attorney.

"Didn't I tell you I'd make an arrest any moment?"

Spike grinned and said nothing.

# VIII. Bribery and Corruption!

AS Spike rode uptown in a taxi he scanned the fresh ink of the latest afternoon tab which heralded the arrest of Tommy Spencer.

### "Night Club Sheik Held"

And underneath the inevitable picture—"Tommy Spencer, boy-friend of Cecily Thane and the last person known to have seen her alive, being taken to the Tombs by Inspector Herschman. Story on page 2."

There followed a carefully abridged account of the morning's events at Police Headquarters. Just how and where the elusive Spencer had been apprehended was not quite plain, but the obvious inference was that Inspector Herschman, like the true servant of the people that he was, had not been idle.

"I see," Spike mused as his eye came to the bottom of the column, "that in his elation at making an arrest the inspector has forgotten about Nina. I'm afraid he doesn't realize that for publicity purposes the female of the species is more effective than the male. However, far be it from me to bandy a lady's name about with tabloid reporters—God bless their bloody hearts."

The taxi stopped at 15 West Ninety-third Street and he got out. The apartment house which he entered was one of the newer buildings that had recently sprung up near Central Park West—a rather gaudy edifice with a lobby inhabited by a mixture of modernistic divans, Renaissance refectory tables and an imposing looking door man.

The apartment of Tommy Spencer was on the fifteenth floor, a rather luxurious suite of four rooms with a magnificent view overlooking the Park. The door was opened by a servant.

"You, I take it," said Spike as he stood on the threshold, "are Murray."

"Yes, sir."

Nothing more correct in appearance or demeanor had ever come out of an English servants' hall than Murray. It was rather a shock to find one of his patent aristocracy serving a professional dancing man. Anything less than a duke seemed beneath him.

"I have an unfortunate message from your master," Spike explained. "Here," and he thrust the newspaper into the servant's hand as he brushed passed him through the small reception hall into the living room.

It was a disorderly place, and it was apparent that it had not been cleaned recently. Murray's impeccability did not, it was plain, extend to the actual performance of his duties. Spike surveyed it carefully as he waited for the man to finish his glance at the headlines.

"Mr. Spencer is in prison?"

"Unfortunate, isn't it?"

"Most unfortunate, sir, but I was expecting it. The gentlemen from the police department were here yesterday and were most curious."

Spike slumped into a chair and took out his cigarette case.

"By the way, what was the story you told them? You see, I'm one of the gentlemen from the police department myself. I am the brother of the district attorney and I am assisting in the investigation."

"I only answered their questions, sir."

"Well," said Spike as he flicked the ash from his cigarette into a near-by ash tray, "suppose you answer a few of mine."

"I am sorry, sir, but I fear there is nothing more that I can add. We went quite thoroughly into the matter."

"Yes?" Spike's voice rose in that curious inflection which turns an affirmative into a negative.

"Yes. sir."

"As I understand it, Mr. Spencer came home at about four o'clock Monday morning and went to bed and got up at eleven."

"Yes, sir."

"Do you know by any chance whether he possessed a gun?"

"I couldn't say as to that, sir."

"You are his valet, aren't you, and you look after his clothes and go through his dresser drawers, don't you?"

"Yes, sir."

"And have you ever seen a gun anywhere in the apartment?"

"I couldn't say as to that, sir."

"But you remember what you've seen and what you haven't."

"I don't recall, sir."

The good-humored air which was part of Spike's habitual expression slowly faded, and a calculating look came into his eyes, carefully veiled by a disarming casualness.

"Working long for Mr. Spencer?"

"Four months, sir."

"You're not by any chance the John Murray that used to valet the Duke of Westbury."

"No, sir. My name is Angus Isaac Murray, and in London I was with Sir Jordan Henley."

"Quite a bit of mixed ancestry?"

"Yes, sir. My mother was Scotch and, my father was English and one of my grandfathers was Hebrew."

Spike smiled. "Well, that makes things easier."

"Beg pardon, sir?"

"I mean I find your family history highly diverting. Tell me more. How come you're now in a position which is so obviously below your talents."

"Misfortunes overtake us all, sir. I was so foolish as to be lured to New York by an American gentleman who wished a valet. We disagreed at a most unfortunate time—soon after I had dropped a bit too much at the Pimlico races. In my extremity, I was forced to take the first thing that was offered until I could get back to England."

"But surely in four months you could save enough to pay your passage home."

"No, sir."

"Pardon me, Murray, if I seem to intrude upon a rather delicate matter—but are your wages paid up to date."

"No, sir."

"Mr. Spencer was not in the habit of paying his bills promptly?"

"No, sir. That has been one of the most distressing features of my work here."

"How much does he owe you?"

"Two hundred dollars, sir."

"Why do you remain?"

"I'm only staying until I can collect what is owed me. Mr. Spencer said last week that he would raise quite a large sum of money soon."

"And the rent on the apartment?"

"It is two months, overdue, sir."

A slow smile twisted up the corner of Spike's mouth. With a leisurely gesture he drew his bill fold from his inside pocket and selected a ten and two yellow-backed twenties. When he had replaced the wallet he tapped the folded bills meditatively on his palm with a significant gesture.

"You know, Murray," he said, "I don't believe that the chaps who were here yesterday were very thorough. I have a feeling that you and I, perhaps, will—ah—understand each other better."

For a moment the valet remained silent, his eyes on the tapping bills. Then he spoke without the shadow of a change in his expression or demeanor.

"Yes, sir. Quite."

Spike's eyes under half-opened lids slowly felt their way about the littered room.

"When did you clean here last?"

"Monday, sir. Monday afternoon."

"Did Mr. Spencer by any chance have any visitors on Monday night."

"Yes, sir."

"And who were they?"

"There was only one, sir—a lady."

"Her name?"

"I don't know it, sir."

"A young lady?"

"Yes, sir."

"Was this her first visit here?"

"No, she had been once before. She was here last Sunday afternoon for tea."

"And at what time did she come Monday night?"

"At about a quarter to one."

"A quarter to one." Spike sat forward in his chair. "Are you sure of that?"

"Yes, sir. I always make it a point to note the time of visitors so that I can make a proper report."

"Suppose you just go ahead and tell me about her without my questions."

"Well, sir, she asked for Mr. Spencer and I told her he would not return until probably early in the morning. She came in and said that she wished to write a note to him. I left her in here alone, and in a few moments she called me and gave me the note and asked me to give it to Mr. Spencer as soon as he got up in the morning. She was most insistent. And then she left."

"What was her manner?"

"She seemed—ah—somewhat upset. I would say very upset."

"And in the morning you delivered the note to Mr. Spencer?"

"Yes, sir."

"You don't by any chance know what was in it? You didn't—ah—just happen to read it?"

Murray hesitated and his glance went to the bills in Spike's hand. "No, sir," he said firmly.

Again there was a pause. And again Spike reached slowly for his wallet and drew out two more yellow twenties and a ten and placed them with the hundred.

"Rack your brains, Murray. Are you quite sure you can't recall?"

"Well," he temporized and went through the facial gestures which usually accompany a racking of the brains. "As a matter of fact, it was, I believe, something like this, although I could not swear to the exact wording, of course: 'Tommy, Something terrible has happened. I must see you right away. Telephone me in the morning.'"

"And the signature?"

"I couldn't make it out. It was just a single letter, quite illegible."

Spike appeared to digest these facts for a few moments in silence. Then again the slow gesture to the inside pocket, and again two more twenties and a ten.

"Concentrate on this gun business, Murray. Are you quite sure that you never saw a gun in Mr. Spencer's possession"

Again a short pause while Murray searched his memory.

"Well—yes, sir, I have"

"He keeps one here in the apartment"

"Yes, sir."

"You don't happen to know what kind of a gun?"

"A .38 caliber Colt, I believe."

"Did you by any chance notice whether he took it with him Monday night before he went to Mrs. Thane's."

"No, sir, I didn't."

"Quite sure?" Spike gave a decisive flick with the bills.

"Quite sure, sir, but—"

"But what?"

"It is not in its usual resting place now."

"And where is it?"

"I don't know, sir. Mr. Spencer took it out with him yesterday morning when he left the apartment."

"How did he act just before he went out? Was he—ah—just what was his manner?"

"Well, sir, at eleven o'clock he summoned me and asked for the afternoon paper and his breakfast."

"The *afternoon* paper?"

"Yes, sir. You see Mr. Spencer says that the morning news is stale by the time he is up—he seldom rises before eleven—so he has the early edition of the afternoon paper delivered here in the morning."

"What paper?"

"This one." With a fastidiously offended gesture, Murray picked up from the reading table the glaring tabloid which Spike had brought with him and held it between his thumb and forefinger.

"You, I take it," said Spike with a slight grin, "read the *Times*."

"Yes, sir."

"And after you had given Mr. Spencer the paper, he ate his breakfast and then went out."

"No, sir. He went out immediately. He didn't touch his breakfast."

"Is he in the habit of going without food in the morning?"

"No, sir. It's the first time I've ever known it to happen."

"You have no—ah—theory, have you, Murray, to account for his sudden distaste for food."

"I think it was something he read in the paper that upset him."

"No doubt. Or perhaps it was the young lady's note. Did he read it before or after he read the paper."

"I couldn't say, sir. I brought them both in at the same time and then left the room."

"Did he telephone before he went out?"

"No, sir."

"Or say where he was going?"

"No, sir. He appeared in a great hurry."

"Well, Murray, you've been most helpful."

Spike rose from his chair and laid the $150 in bills on the reading table and picked up his stick.

"And Mr. Spencer's message?" Murray reminded him.

"Well, as a matter of fact, he's in need of clean socks, shuts and B.V.D's I suggested that I drop by and get them for him, but he seemed positively appalled at the prospect of having me get chummy with you. He told me to get them at a haberdashery, so just to keep his mind at peace on that score at least, I'll do as he asked."

"Yes, sir." For a moment the shadow of a comprehending smile lighted up Murray's correct countenance.

At the door Spike paused suddenly as if he had just remembered something.

"By the way, did you happen to notice whether the young lady was a blue-eyed brunette?"

"No, sir. Her hair was tucked up under her hat, and I am not in the habit of noticing lady's eyes."

"You should make it a point to do so, Murray. You miss a lot."

"Yes, sir."

"Perhaps you remember some of her conversation, though—the Sunday afternoon she had tea here."

Murray hesitated. Slowly he reached for the pile of bills on the reading table and counted them through, folded them and put them in his pocket.

"I'm afraid not, sir," he replied firmly.

"But surely you can tell me what sort of a person she was. What I mean to say, was she like most of Mr. Spencer's friends?"

"No, sir. If I may say so, she was greatly superior. Most of Mr. Spencer's friends are of a class to which I am not accustomed."

"In other words she was a lady."

"Quite, sir"

"And I suppose you served the tea?"

"Yes, sir."

"And now and again you caught snatches of their, conversation?"

"Well, occasionally."

"Do you recall any of it?"

"Well, sir, I—" He left the sentence trailing in mid-air.

"Strain your brain just this once more, Murray," Spike persisted, and as he spoke he crossed the room and laid a fifty-dollar bill on the reading table. "Surely, you found something diverting in this particular visitor's conversation."

"Well, at the time, sir, I didn't think. so—but—"

"But subsequent events, have added interest to her remarks?"

"Yes, sir."

"Suppose you tell me about it."

"Well, Mr. Spencer summoned me to bring in the tea and I caught the name of Mrs. Thane. I got the impression that the young lady was somewhat bitter. If I remember exactly she said, 'I've known her for fifteen years and hated her for seven of them. Ever since—' At that point unfortunately I left the room." He paused.

"But you returned?" Spike prodded him gently on.

"Yes, sir. About a half hour later to take away the tea things. I would not swear, you understand, that they were still talking about Mrs. Thane. At least I didn't hear her name actually mentioned. But the young lady had hardly touched her tea and she was still saying something about hating. She said—" He hesitated, earnest in his efforts to be accurate.

"She said, 'I hate her so much, I'll kill her some day.'"

☐

# IX. Nina Fennel Is "Perfectly Frank"

AN hour later at Police Headquarters Spike faced an irate district attorney and a highly incensed inspector.

"But why should this Murray withhold information from the legally authorized authorities and give it to you?" Tracy sputtered. "Groaty and McCarthy questioned him for an hour. I've a mind to have him arrested for obstructing justice."

"I think you're a bit hard on him," Spike defended. "And probably he answered all their questions right enough. They evidently didn't ask the right ones—in the right way. He has the correct English servant's dislike of the police and sensational publicity. But fortunately for us, his Scotch mother and his Jewish grandfather made it difficult for him to resist the lure of a good bargain. Your men appealed to the Murray of him and I to the Angus Isaac."

"Why it's bribery," Tracy persisted. "Pure bribery."

"Not at all, I was simply paying him his back wages. Two hundred dollars was the exact amount. As a matter of fact, just before I left I gave him another fifty and intimated that God had still more good things in store for him if he stuck around and didn't beat it off to dear old London on the next boat. I thought perhaps you'd like to confirm what I've just been telling you, Inspector."

"Say lissen, young fellow, what right have you got going up there and questioning state's witnesses without authority from me?"

"Surely, Inspector, it isn't within your power to prevent two private citizens from having a clubby little chat with each other."

"Well, I'm telling you this right now, you—"

"Don't! It's just possible that I might get temperamental and refuse to finish my story. And really, you know, I picked up two little souvenirs which I think you might be interested in."

"Get this straight. I'm not interested—". With difficulty Herschman stemmed the flow of his wrath as he realized that he was most decidedly interested. When he spoke again it was with sullen capitulation. "Well, go ahead, what have you got?"

"But first of all, Inspector, let me register my hearty agreement with you on one point. I think you were quite right in being skeptical of Tommy's devotion to Nature and the joys of walking in the open air. I have a feeling that somewhere in the course of that walk he disposed of the gun which Murray assured me he took with him when he left his apartment yesterday morning, because he didn't have it last night when I took him home with me."

Herschman grew slightly mollified and Spike went on.

"Number one of my little souvenirs is this." He took from his pocket a tabloid newspaper and unfolded its gaudy face. "The good old *Evening Graphic*, the only paper which carried the news of Cecily Thane's murder in the first edition, the paper which Tommy Spencer has brought to his apartment every morning at eleven o'clock."

"Well, what of it?"

"Frankly it may be just a coincidence, just another proof of the world-beating qualities of my favorite sheet. And then again— Well, I'll confess, I don't know.

"Here's something more definite, though." From his cigarette case, he drew forth a half smoked cigarette, one end ringed with heavy carmine rouge. "As soon as I palmed this souvenir from the ash tray beside the most comfortable chair in Tommy's apartment, I had a feeling that Murray had not opened his heart and told all to my predecessors. Hence my rather generous expense account."

Herschman bent forward and examined the butt. "The Fennel girl!" He gasped in spite of himself.

"Miss Fennel, Inspector," Spike reproved him. "Would you mind, Richard, handing over the other six in this set?"

From a drawer in his desk Tracy brought forth a small pasteboard box and opened it and Spike put the cigarette which he had just brought beside the others.

"A perfect match."

"Well," said Herschman, "where does that get us?"

"Let me remind you that a young lady visited Spencer's apartment at one o'clock Tuesday morning and that Murray assured me that he had not cleaned the room or emptied the ash trays since. I think therefore that we may assume that she smoked this cigarette. The rouge on it corresponds exactly with that on the three that were found in the Thane sitting room and with the one which I myself saw Nina Fennel light.

"The conclusion is fairly obvious. Nina Fennel was in Cecily Thane's sitting room Monday night and she was at Tommy Spencer's apartment early Tuesday morning—writing a rather desperate-sounding note.

"Less than forty-eight hours before Cecily Thane was killed Nina Fennel threatened to kill some one and I have a strong suspicion that she referred to Cecily Thane. And less than twenty-four hours after Cecily Thane is killed Nina Fennel is seen throwing a gun into a passing freight car of sand.

"I think it's all frightfully intriguing and I rather imagine that Miss Fennel is our next move."

"*Our* next move?" Herschman rose with a determined glint in his eye and started for the door. But once again Spike forestalled him and laid a firm grip on his arm.

"Inspector, I don't like your ironic emphasis on the 'our.' Surely you won't deny me the pleasure of an interview with the only blue-eyed brunette I've ever known who wasn't married to a man heavier than I?"

As the district attorney, the inspector and Spike stood in the dark hall outside the Fennel apartment, Spike cast a beseeching glance at Herschman.

"Remember, Inspector," he threatened, even as he implored, "even on such slight acquaintance, I have grown tremendously fond of Miss Fennel, and it would upset me no end if you handled her roughly."

"I know my business," the inspector grumbled and pressed the buzzer.

This time it was a maid who answered the ring, a slatternly young person dragging a dirty dust mop in her wake. She ushered them into the front room in silence and not until they were seated did she speak.

"Miss Fennel and Mr. Fennel's both with Mrs. Fennel. She's awful sick and they said I wasn't to disturb them unless it was important."

"It is important—very important," and the inspector fixed such a stern eye on the girl that she turned and hurried down the hall making a loud slip-slopping with her loose bedroom slippers.

In a few moments, Nina Fennel came into the room. She was wearing the same dress that she had worn the previous day. It was crumpled and her hair was mussed as if, perhaps, she had not had her clothes off all night. There were deep circles under her eyes and her face seemed to droop with fatigue and anxiety. Yet strangely enough she seemed even more striking looking than she had the day before. It was as if impending tragedy had lent her a passionate sort of strength and beauty.

As she stood in the doorway and looked at the three men she seemed to stiffen in every muscle. Her expression was suddenly just a shade too determinedly matter-of-fact.

"My mother—" she began but the district attorney broke in.

"Yes, I know, Miss Fennel. I am most sorry, but it is absolutely essential that I talk to you—you and your father. This is Inspector Herschman of the police department and there are certain matters he would like to go over with you."

"Very well." She came and sat down and seemed to surrender herself to the three men.

"I would like to talk to your father too, Miss Fennel," Herschman reminded her.

"I'm sorry but that is quite impossible. My mother is very, very low and one of us must be at her bedside constantly. Won't I do just as well?"

'I'm afraid not. I want to see your father too."

Nina Fennel did not move an inch, or lift so much as an eyebrow, but somehow she seemed slowly to become as steel, unbending, inflexible.

"I'm sorry," she said in the same level voice, "but it is quite impossible."

"But if I insist?"

"But you—you can't." She seemed beset by a sudden panic and her voice grew pleading, imploring. "Please—don't you understand? It may be my mother's last minute on earth—even now. She asks for him constantly. You mustn't drag him away. You can't."

Herschman opened his mouth to speak but before the words could come out, Spike cut in in a quiet tone.

"May I suggest, Inspector, that we accede to Miss Fennel's suggestion and use her as a proxy for her father?"

Herschman glared in Spike's direction, but the young man went on, unperturbed. "There are a number of things about which I am sure she will be even more helpful than her father."

The inspector grunted and chewed the edge of his lip. It was plain that he was wishing that Spike were taking a walk in Central Park or perhaps even better, in Hyde Park. That would mean the whole Atlantic Ocean between them. But finally he conquered his feelings and with no particular good grace turned once more toward Nina Fennel.

"Suppose, Miss Fennel," he said, "you tell me just what you were doing last Monday night."

For a moment there was a dead silence in the room. Nina Fennel sat staring straight before her with her lips in a tense line. Then she turned suddenly and faced the inspector.

"I was at Mrs. Thane's." Herschman started slightly at the suddenness of her capitulation. The straightforward answer where he had expected evasion had the effect of a slap in the face on him. He blinked and Nina Fennel smiled slightly. "That is what you wanted to know wasn't it?"

"Yes—but—"

"Won't you please go ahead with your questions. I want to get back to my mother as quickly as possible."

"What were you doing there?"

Again she paused, considering her answer carefully. "Inspector," she said finally, "I am going to be perfectly frank with you. Yesterday when the district attorney and this gentleman were here," and she indicated Spike, "they talked to my father, but they did not take the trouble to question me. They questioned only my father and he answered them truthfully."

"But that's not answering my question What were you doing at Mrs. Thane's and what time were you there and how did you get in?"

"I went with my father—"

"You went into the house with your father?"

"No, I went to the house with my father. He went in and a little later he let me in."

"About what time was that?"

"Eight-thirty, perhaps nine."

"And what did you and your father do while you were at Mrs. Thane's?"

"We sat there for a while—perhaps fifteen or twenty minutes. And then he went home."

"And you?"

"I remained."

"For how long?"

"An hour—perhaps longer. I'm not just sure."

"And what were you doing while you were there?"

"Just sitting. Sitting and smoking."

Spike looked triumphantly in the direction of Herschman, but the inspector went on doggedly. "And after you left?"

"I took a walk. Quite a long walk."

"You just walked. Where did you walk to? Did you go to any one's house or apartment?"

"No, I just walked. It—it was a nice night and I felt the need of air, so I just took a walk."

"And what time did you get home?"

"I'm not sure, but it was sometime after one. The elevator in the hall stops at one, and I had to walk upstairs, so it must have been after one."

"What, Miss Fennel, was the—uh—purpose of your visit to the Thane house?"

"As my father told the district attorney, yesterday, just a social call. Mrs. Thane had been kind enough to write to my mother and inquire about her, so we just dropped in for a moment."

"But why was it that you did not enter the house at the same time as your father?"

"I had an errand to do at the drug store on the corner and I told him to go on. I was a little longer than I had expected to be."

"And who let you in?"

"My father. He didn't want to bring the maid up from downstairs again to answer the door, so when he saw me coming, he opened it before I had even a chance to ring."

"I see. And then you and your father went upstairs and sat there fifteen or twenty minutes and he left."

"Yes."

"But why didn't you leave with him?"

"He got tired of waiting. The maid told me that she wasn't sure just where Mr. Thane was, and that he might be in any minute, so I thought I'd wait a little while longer."

"Miss Fennel, how long have you and your father and your mother been friends with the Thanes?"

"Ever since I can remember. Ever since I was quite a little girl."

"Did Mrs. Thane come here often to see your mother, now that she is so ill?"

"No. She was a very busy woman and then sickness depresses her so. She often wrote notes and sent flowers."

"Your mother has been ill long?"

"My mother has been confined to a wheel chair for the last twenty-three years. But it is only recently that she has been so seriously ill. She had a bad spell early Tuesday morning."

Herschman settled himself back in his chair and looked steadily at Nina Fennel for a moment, the corners of his mouth, turned up in just the suggestion of a smile. It was the expression one often remarks on the face of a cat, surveying an unsuspecting mouse, just the moment before it reaches out with its clawed paw.

"Tell me, Miss Fennel," he said at length, "do you happen to know a you—"

"Wait!" It was Spike breaking in. "Listen !" He held up his hand for silence "They're calling you, Miss Fennel, down there," and he pointed in the direction of the hail leading into the sick room.

Nina Fennel sprang from her chair and rushed down the hall, her face suddenly overspread with dread and fright.

Once outside the apartment house, Herschman let go on Spike. "Say, what the hell did you have to go butting in with a phony remark about some one calling, just when I was about to show that dame up."

"Exactly, Inspector, exactly," said Spike smiling blithely. "I knew you were going to do just that little thing and that's why the hell."

Herschman surveyed him with a look that said plainly enough "It's only the fact that you're the district attorney's brother that keeps me from throwing you into the Hudson River with a five hundred-pound boulder tied to your feet."

But Spike went right ahead, disregarding the murder that was in Herschman's heart "You see, old thing," he explained, "when a woman says, 'I'm going to be perfectly frank with you' you can bet your sweet life she's preparing a whole bushel of whoppers. And Miss Nina Fennel, despite her many other superior charms, is all too like her sisters in this respect She lied like hell. She was 'quite frank' about all those things which she knew we could check her up on. Her arrival at the Fennel's—her return home—that sort of thing. But she didn't know that we had already had a little tête-a-tête with Tommy Spencer's butler so she went right ahead with her lies and thought she was putting it over on us."

"Then why not tell her so right to her face"

"And put her on her guard? No, no. She thinks she has fooled us completely. She won't be so careful about watching her step!"

For the second time that day Herschman retreated into the mumbled silence of defeat.

"And it strikes me very forcibly," said Spike, "that she had rehearsed everything she told us. It flowed off too glibly."

"Say, lissen," said Herschman, "I thought you were gone on this dame, and now you seem absolutely pleased that we've got the goods on her."

"Pleased? Inspector! And you think you are an accurate reader of the human countenance. I'm torn—simply torn within. For the second time in my life I am suffering bitter disappointment. The other blue-eyed brunette, as I have already pointed out, had a husband forty pounds heavier than I. And this one—well, it looks very much like she may be a murderer." Spike blew a disconsolate cloud of cigarette smoke into the air. Then he added with philosophic resignation: "Still, I suppose all women have their drawbacks. You just have to take them as they come."

"Yes, and another drawback she's going to have," Herschman put the last word to the argument, "is a cop watching that apartment house from now on, and trailing her wherever she goes."

## X. Mr. Shansky Defends His Reputation

ON Thursday morning, the third day after the murder of Cecily Thane, Herschman entered the office of the district attorney and slammed the door viciously behind him. Tracy at his desk, scanning the morning papers with an harassed air, looked up quickly.

"Well?" he said irritably.

"Just got a report from Mallory on the freight shipments of sand on the New York Central," Herschman snapped. "Only six cars went out Tuesday afternoon on the tracks along the river up to the new bridge they're building at 168th Street; and the whole damn load was poured into the cement mixers late Tuesday night. The gun that Fennel woman threw away is cemented tight into one of the piles. Not a chance of getting it."

With a gesture of frustration he bit off the end of a cigar and spat savagely.

"If this case ever got taken up by the detective story writers," a leisurely voice from the depths of an easy-chair in a far corner remarked, "I suppose it would be called 'All Guns Missing.'"

"Oh, shut up!"

"Have it your own way, inspector."

"Got hold of Griffis yet?" Tracy asked.

"No, but I got a line on him. He's running a real estate business and he's in pretty deep. I've got Marks working on that end. He says he doesn't know yet whether there's anything crooked about his business but it looks shady. He owes a lot of money and he's keeping away from his office and his apartment. I got a good line on his history. Used to be very prosperous but in the last two years he's gone downhill."

"Well, what is our next move?" The district attorney tapped nervously with his pencil and looked at the inspector for a suggestion. But none was forthcoming. Herschman slid down on the end of his spine and puffed silently at his cigar.

"It's about time," Spike remarked, "that God gave us a break. So far we've gone ahead on our own steam. I really think we deserve a piece of good fortune, dropping unasked from the sky."

And as if in response to the hint, came Mr. Morris Shansky, not more than fifteen minutes later. At first glance Mr. Shansky's appearance was deceitful. He did not in any sense appear Heaven-sent. He was a little man, smartly gotten up with only a trace of his ancestral Yiddish accent; and as he sat in the anteroom of the district attorney's office refusing to tell his business to the secretary and insisting on a "private" interview, he was plainly nervous.

At length when his protests were of no avail, he played his trump card. Drawing Lovelace's ear down to his own level and looking about fearfully to be sure that no one might hear him, he whispered a single sentence. Even the adamantine Lovelace's stiff brows raised slightly and he disappeared into the inner office.

"A man here, Mr. Tracy," he said, "who wants to see you. He says it's about the Thane case. He insists on seeing you."

Herschman pricked up his ears, and the district attorney looked distressed. There were far too many disconcerting aspects to the case as it was, without further muddling. But with a resigned gesture he motioned the secretary to admit the visitor.

As Shansky entered the inner office he looked suspiciously at the inspector and Spike, but the district attorney cut short his protests. "This is Inspector Herschman and my brother who are assisting in the investigation. Anything you have to tell me you can tell them."

Shansky seated himself warily in the chair across the desk, not at all reassured.

"First of all, Mr. Tracy, I'm telling you," he began, "that never before in all my years in business has such a thing happened to me. Always Morris Shansky has a reputation for honor. Never has there been the slightest suspicion against my business. Always—"

"I can quite believe that, Mr. Shansky," Tracy interrupted impatiently. "What was it you wanted to tell me?"

"I'm telling you now. Ask any one on Third Avenue about me and they'll tell you that Morris Shansky deals only with respectable people. Never does he—"

"Just what is your business?"

"Pawnbroking. Licensed I am, and never have I taken anything but honest goods from honest people. Ask the cops in my district and they can tell you. Always—"

"Say lissen," Herschman broke in, "what is it you've got on your mind about the Thane case?"

Under this direct frontal attack Shansky cut short his ego-professional eulogy. In silence, he drew from an inner pocket a small box and laying it on the table pointed to it with a single word.

"That."

"Yeah, what?"

"Its—it's one of the jewels you advertised, missing from the safe of this murdered woman, Cecily Thane."

With a quick gesture Herschman reached for the box and lifted the lid. Inside, reposing on a wad of cotton, lay a diamond and emerald necklace which even to the uninitiated eye was worth a large sum of money. For a moment both the inspector, and the district attorney gasped. Then the inspector turned on Shansky, his voice tense with excitement.

"Where'd you get it?"

"I'm telling you, Mr. Inspector, always have I done an honest business. Never—"

"Lissen, brother, I know you're not a fence, so cut it. What I want to know is who brought this into your store and when and how much did you give for it?"

"A man, a small man with dark hair with a funny white streak like it was put on with a paint brush, brought it in."

"When?"

"The morning after the Thane murder—early."

"What time?"

"Early. About half past eight."

"What was his name."

"John Morgan. See, here I got the ticket."

"And how much did he want on it?"

"Five thousand dollars."

"And you gave it to him?"

"Not right away. I don't carry that much with me so early before the bank opens."

"So what did you do? Go ahead, tell it. We're not going to eat you."

"So I tell him I have to wait till nine-thirty and he says no he must have the money right away. He says his wife is going away on the boat and he must raise the money quick as she hasn't no cash with her. And I tell him, no, I got only about a thousand in the safe, will that do. So he says no, he'll come back at nine-thirty. So at nine o'clock I go to the bank and get the money and when I come back to the shop he's there again and I give it to him"

"Was he one of your regular customers?"

"No, never did I see him before. And when I read the description of the jewels in the Thane case that you send around to the licensed pawnbrokers, I know that he is the man that killed her and took them. Never has such a thing happened in my business. Always I—"

But Herschman had reached for the telephone and motioned for silence. He called the number of the Thane house, and in a few moments he had Elton Thane on the other end of the wire.

"Herschman at Headquarters, Mr. Thane. Do you know any one named John Morgan . . . No, I didn't think you did. . . . Well, do you know any one—any man with heavy dark hair with a streak of white right down the middle? What? . . . Yes. . . . Would you mind coming down here to Headquarters right away? Something very important has turned up, and we need you. . . . Yes. . . . About twenty minutes? . . .

Good! . . . Say, wait a minute. Bring Emma with you. . . . Oh yes, we'll need her. All right."

Herschman hung up the receiver and turned with a triumphant smile to the district attorney. "Well, we've got—" Then he caught himself in time and nodded toward Shansky with a significant gesture.

"I'm sure, Mr. Shansky," the district attorney said, "we're greatly obliged to you for your help. It has been invaluable. Will—"

"It isn't you that needs the help, Mr. Tracy, it's me. I got my license to think of. And my five thousand dollars. How about that's?"

"My dear Mr. Shansky, if there are any difficulties about the renewal of your license, please communicate with me and I will give the matter my personal attention. And as for the five thousand dollars, you are fully protected by the insurance on the jewels which will cover your loss. In the meantime won't you step outside and let my secretary have your name and address and telephone number in case we want to get in touch with you?"

With a firm and final gesture Herschman himself personally escorted Shansky into the waiting room before he had an opportunity to enter any further defense of his impeccable reputation. He could hardly wait to close the door on the pawnbroker's back.

"Thane says," he explained, his voice shaking with excitement, "that the only man he knows with bushy black hair with a white streak down the middle is Mrs. Thane's brother, George Griffis."

In the half hour which it took Elton Thane to drive from Eighty-second Street to Police Headquarters, Herschman was busy investigating the pawnbroker. He found that Shansky's record was all that Shansky had claimed.

Thane arrived, breathless and puzzled and left Emma in the anteroom while he went into the district attorney's office. The two days which had elapsed since they had last seen him had wrought a decided change in his appearance. The weariness and pain had disappeared from his face and there was a quiet sense of calm about him.

Herschman could hardly wait for the preliminary greetings to be finished.

"There, Mr. Thane," and he pointed triumphantly to the little pasteboard box in which the glittering jewels lay.

Thane's eyes went wide as he gazed at it. "The necklace! But how—"

"A pawnbroker brought it in this morning," Herschman explained. "Not a fence. We looked him up. A licensed pawnbroker."

"But where did he get it? Did Spencer—"

"No, not Spencer. A man who gave the name of John Morgan, a man with bushy black hair with a streak of white down the center."

"George!"

Herschman nodded. For a moment Thane was stunned. Then he broke out. "It—it can't be. He's her own brother. He—he lived in the house with us."

"Exactly! And even when he moved out he kept his latchkey."

"Are you sure, Mr. Thane," the district attorney broke in, "that you have told us all you know about Griffis' visit to your wife the afternoon before she was—last Monday afternoon?"

"Yes, everything. I saw her for only a moment, you know, before she went out with Spencer and all she said was, 'George was here this afternoon.'"

"I think we had better have the maid in," Tracy suggested, and nodded to Herschman. In a few moments Emma Bloomstead entered the room. She hesitated at the threshold and looked uneasily, at the three men before her. Then her glance traveled to Thane as if in silent question. But he spoke with gentle reassurance.

"The gentlemen here, Emma, have a few questions they would like to ask you."

She said nothing as she took the chair which Spike pulled up for her.

"Emma," said the district attorney going straight to the point, "Mr. Thane tells us that on last Monday afternoon, Mrs. Thane's brother, George Griffis visited her."

"Yes, sir."

"At what time did he come?"

"Oh, some time in the afternoon. About four I guess. I don't know exactly."

"Didn't you let him in?"

"No, sir. He used his key he used to have when he was living there."

"Did you see him when he went out or at any time while he was in the house?"

"No, sir."

"Then how do you know that he came to the house?"

"I heard his voice."

"Suppose you tell us about it."

"I was going up to my room from the basement to get a clean apron and I had to pass right by the door of Mrs. Thane's sitting room."

"The door was open?"

"No, it was closed tight."

"But you could hear the voices?"

"Yes, they were talking loud."

"Did you stop and listen?"

"Well—yes." Emma admitted her eavesdropping with a proper lowering of the eyes. "I couldn't hear Mrs. Thane. She was talking low and natural, I guess, but Mr. Griffis was talking very loud."

"And could you hear what he was saying?"

"Well—some." It was plain that she was loath to make the admission.

"And what did you hear?"

Again her eyes sought Thane's.

"Go on, Emma, tell them whatever you heard." His voice was quiet but there was a certain tenseness about his jaw as he spoke

"I—I couldn't make out all of it very well, but he kept saying something about the bank and $5,000."

The district attorney and Herschman exchanged significant glances.

"All right, go on"

"And then he'd say, 'I've got to have it I tell you,' and Mrs. Thane would say something low so I couldn't hear and finally he said something about—" She stopped and this time as she looked at Elton Thane there was positive fright in her eyes. "Then he said something about Mr. Thane."

"What?"

"He said, 'By —by Jesus, if I told all I know about that lousy husband of yours, you wouldn't dare be so damn stingy.'"

She stopped again, toying nervously with the edge of her purse, and again the district attorney pushed her on with the story.

"And what else did he say?"

"I didn't hear any more. The telephone rang just then and I had to go back down into the front hall to answer it. It was a call for the cook and I had to go downstairs to get her, and I stopped in the kitchen for a few minutes while she was gone to tend some stuff she had on the stove. And a little while later when I went upstairs the door was open to Mrs. Thane's room, and she called me in to tell me something about dinner, and he was gone."

There was a stiff, tense silence as Emma brought her story to a close.

"And you are sure that is all you overheard?"

"Yes, sir."

Tracy motioned her to withdraw and when she had left the room, both the district attorney and Herschman with one accord fastened their eyes on Elton Thane.

"Tell me, Mr. Thane," Tracy said, "have you any idea to what Mr. Griffis referred by the remark which your maid has just repeated?"

"I'm sure I can't imagine what he was talking about."

"You know of no financial difficulties of your brother-in-law?"

"As a matter of fact, I understand he hasn't been doing well lately, but I have no direct knowledge of his affairs."

"Can you explain in any way his reference to you?"

"George and I have never—well, we have never been on particularly good terms with each other."

"And yet he lived in your house until a year ago?"

"Yes."

"What was the nature of your difficulty with him?"

"Oh, just a difference in temperament. In-laws, you know, are not notoriously good friends."

"And you are quite sure that you don't know what he meant when he said, 'If I told all I know about that lousy husband of yours you wouldn't dare—?'"

Tracy paused and looked directly at Thane. Slowly Thane's eyes dropped.

"Mr. Tracy, I think perhaps I had better be honest with you," he said in a voice that was barely audible.

"So you do know?"

"Yes Three years ago I—I was up against the wall. Things had been on the upgrade for me, and then I lost heavily in the market. I had to have $50,000 or I would have lost $500,000. So I—I—I—signed my brother-in-law's name to a check."

No one spoke and for a moment Elton Thane let this simple and damning confession stand unqualified. Then quickly he went on in a louder, surer tone. "But I paid him back, every cent—later when I made money. Every cent and eight per cent interest."

"In cash?"

"Yes, he wouldn't take a check."

"Did your wife know of this forgery?"

"Yes, she knew. She—she got the check afterward and kept it."

"You mean to say, Mr. Thane," Herschman put in in a slightly incredulous manner, "that your wife held a check which you had forged for $50,000?"

Thane nodded.

"How did she get it and where did she keep it?"

"She persuaded George to give it to her—and, and I never did know where she kept it."

"Then how did you know she had it, still?"

"She—she used to remind me of it."

"Remind you of it? In what way?"

"Good God, man," Thane suddenly gave way.

It was as if the muscles which had been holding him calm and erect had melted within him. His shoulder slumped helplessly and his voice came hoarse and broken.

"God! Can't you understand that for three years she's held that check over my head—me—her own husband—and after she persuaded me to do it. I didn't want to. I swear I didn't. She made me.

"We went to George and asked him for the money and he refused. And I had to have $50,000 or my whole business, everything I had would go. So she made me do it. She said she'd keep George from prosecuting. She did—she kept him from prosecuting. But she got the check herself and she's held it over my head ever since She's—Oh, my God!"

With a sudden movement of despair Elton Thane Hung his head forward in his hands and choked back the torrent of words that came from his tortured lips.

## XI. Elton Thane in a Tight Place

FOR a moment there was a tense silence in the room, broken only by a sudden intake of breath from the bowed figure opposite the district attorney.

"Are you quite sure," the district attorney said at last in a very quiet voice, "that you realize what you are saying?"

Thane lifted a haggard, drawn face to the prosecutor. He seemed to have aged at least ten years in the last ten minutes. He nodded his head dumbly.

"Yes, I know what I'm saying—and I know what you're thinking. But I didn't! I swear to God I didn't." His voice rose hoarse and shrill.

"No one is jumping at conclusions, Mr. Thane, but under the circumstances I shall have to ask you to give us a very careful outline of your actions last Monday night."

Thane made an effort to pull himself together and ran his tongue over his dry lips. But when he spoke his voice was once more under control.

"All right. Go ahead. Ask me whatever you want to."

"Suppose you go ahead."

"I left the house about eight or half past, I don't know just when, and went to my club, the Chatham on Seventy-second Street, and stayed there almost all evening."

"Do you remember the names of any of the people who saw you there? Did you talk to any one?"

"Yes. About ten o'clock I got in a bridge game with J. P. Crandall and Horace Pullman and another fellow. I forget his name. Some friend of Crandall's."

"And how long did you stay there?"

"Till almost twelve. And then I remembered that I'd promised Dr. Partridge next door—you met him that first morning—I'd promised him I'd drop into his place for some chess. So I left the club and went to his house."

"You walked?"

"Yes."

"And you went directly without stopping off any place?"

"Yes."

"And you—"

"No. Wait a minute. I did stop at a cigar store. The one at the corner of Columbus and Seventy-sixth Street and got a couple of packages of cigarettes and some cigars. I'd promised Partridge to come much earlier in the evening, and I'd gotten so engrossed in the bridge game that I'd partly forgotten about my promise. So I thought I'd take some of his favorite cigars as a sort of peace offering."

"And that was the only place you stopped?"

"You went right from the cigar store to Dr. Partridge's house?" The eyes of Herschman seemed boring into Elton Thane, but they failed of their effect. Thane seemed to divine what was in the inspector's mind.

"No," he said, "I didn't go into my own house. I went directly to Dr. Partridge's."

"At what time did you arrive at Dr. Partridge's?"

"Oh, somewhere around twelve."

"That's pretty indefinite."

"I know, but it's the best I can do."

"And you stayed at Dr. Partridge's until when?"

"About four."

"All the time?"

"All the time."

Herschman's brows came together in a calculating line and he looked quizzically at Thane.

"I tell you what, Mr. Thane, I'm going to ask you to stay here for a little while. In there," and the inspector indicated a door at the far end of the office. Thane acquiesced without protest and followed him through the door, and down a long hall to a small office, where two patrolmen were playing cards.

"Don't let this gentleman here disturb you, boys," he said as he motioned Thane to a chair. "He's just waiting here a little while for me."

One of the men looked up from his cards and nodded with an almost imperceptible lift of his eyebrows

Herschman hurried back to the district attorney's office and grabbed the telephone. "Get me the house of Dr. Partridge on West Eighty-second Street." While he was waiting for the number he explained to Tracy. "I'm going to get Partridge down here double-quick and check on that story. I've left Matt and Parker with Thane."

In a few moments the connection was through and the high-pitched but pompous voice of Dr. Partridge himself answered. He would be delighted to put himself at the service of the police department One gathered from his tone that be felt that he had been rather neglected of late, and was only too glad to step once more into the limelight.

In the brief time which elapsed between the call and Partridge's arrival at Headquarters, Herschman dispatched a detective to the cigar store at the corner of Columbus and Seventy-sixth Street in search of the clerk who had been on duty the previous Monday night.

Dr. Partridge smiled genially as he entered the office. Removed by three miles and the lapse of three days from the night of his neighbor's tragedy, he seemed more naturally himself, much less impressive and ridiculously pompous.

"I'm sorry to trouble you, Dr. Partridge," the district attorney explained, "but there are certain points in connection with the Thane case which are not, as yet, quite clear in our minds. So I'm going to ask you to go over a few of them with us."

Partridge nodded in compliance and seated himself in the chair which had so recently been vacated by Thane.

"How long have you known the Thanes?"

The meticulous little man thought for a moment and then gave his precise answer. "It will be four years next month that the Thanes moved into the house next to mine. About five months later Mr. Thane called me in a hurry one night about half past twelve. His wife had been taken ill suddenly, and although I have been retired from active practice for the last ten years, in an emergency I answer calls. The case was a simple one—indigestion and hysteria, but mostly hysteria. My acquaintance with Mr. Thane dates from that night."

"Was Mrs. Thane subject to such attacks frequently?"

"Well, yes, occasionally. She was rather a highly strung woman, and, if I may say so, given to violent fits of temper, which usually ended up in an attack."

"And so you treated her off and on for these attacks of hysteria?"

"Yes, though it would hardly be called treatment. I merely administered a sedative which is all those cases usually demand."

"What in your opinion brought on these attacks?"

"Temper! Pure temper!" Dr. Partridge's small, precise little mouth under its drooping walrus mustache pulled itself down into a decided disapproving line.

"Temper brought on by a quarrel with her husband?" Tracy suggested.

The doctor nodded reluctantly.

"What did they usually quarrel about?"

"I do not inquire into the private lives of my patients, unless they ask me to do so."

"But surely, Doctor, you came to know the Thanes very well, and you could not help but understand any difficulties that may have arisen between them."

"No, I knew only Mr. Thane. I never saw Mrs. Thane except when I was called in professionally. But early in my acquaintance with Mr. Thane we discovered a mutual fondness for chess, and as I have already told you, we often played quite far into the night."

"How often were you in the habit of playing chess with Mr. Thane?"

"At least once a week, but lately twice and sometimes three times."

"How late do you usually play?"

"Sometimes until half past one or two."

"But last Monday night you played until four?"

"Yes. That is the latest that we have ever kept at it."

"Didn't you get very sleepy?"

"Yes, but Thane was having a run of bad luck and he was trying to recoup his losses. We always play for a small stake, you understand. A purely nominal sum, just enough to add a slight zest to the game. Under the circumstances, I could hardly suggest quitting."

"In what part of your house were you playing, Doctor?"

"In the front parlor on the first floor."

"You and Mr. Thane were in that room all the time until four o'clock when he left—both of you?"

"Both of us—all the time," the doctor declared emphatically. Then quickly he corrected himself. "No. Wait. Once Thane left the room, but just out into the hall to the front door. It was a fairly warm night and we both of us laid off our coats and vests, but even then it was not comfortable, so he stepped out into the hall and opened the front door."

"And how long was he gone from the room?"

"Twenty seconds, perhaps half a minute."

"And that was the only time that either one of you was out of the room?"

"Well, now that I think back, I left the room a little bit later to go down to the basement to fetch a decanter of wine."

"And how long were you gone?"

"I couldn't have been more than a minute. The stairs are just outside the door of the parlor, and the bottle was in the cupboard directly at the foot of the stairs. I had only to run down and back again."

"Now tell me, Doctor," Herschman broke in, "at what time did Mr. Thane arrive at your house last Monday night?"

The doctor thought for a moment, in an earnest effort at accuracy. "It was exactly ten minutes of twelve."

"Why do you say exactly?"

"I say exactly because that is exactly what time it was. Ten minutes of twelve."

"Do you usually remember time so accurately?"

"No," he admitted frankly. "I don't. But in this particular case I do. When I had seen Mr. Thane earlier in the day and he had suggested a round of chess that night, he said he would be over at eleven-thirty. I am a person who keeps appointments promptly, and I expect the same promptness in others. When he did not arrive at eleven-thirty, I grew impatient. When he did come finally, I drew my watch out, to reproach him and I showed it to him. He was twenty minutes late. It was exactly ten minutes of twelve. Of that I am positive."

"Did he bring you anything as a sort of peace offering?"

The little doctor suddenly smiled. "Indeed he did. He brought me five boxes of my favorite cigars."

"Five boxes?"

"Five boxes!"

"And you're quite sure about the time of Thane's arrival at your house?"

"Quite sure. There can be no mistake about that."

Herschman's expression was one of disgruntled defeat. When the door had closed on the doctor, he slumped down into a chair and looked ruefully at the district attorney.

"Well, another good theory all shot to hell. That is, if that little bird is telling the truth and I think he is." For some quite inexplicable reason which even he himself could not have analyzed, the inspector looked not to the district attorney but to Spike for confirmation.

"Yes, Inspector, I think you're right. Too bad isn't it. I'm all cut up. It would have made such a nice story for the tabs—'Slayer Plays Chess, After Shooting Wife.'"

"I think I'll ask that maid just once more when Spencer left the house," Herschman said with sudden decision. "See if she tells the same story twice."

But when Emma was once more before the three men, she only reaffirmed her original emphasis on the precise time of Spencer's departure

"Yes, sir. I'm sure it was almost exactly twelve. Or maybe just a minute or so after. I looked at the clock especially."

☐

# XII. THE GIGOLO RACKET

THE report of the detective whom Herschman had sent to the cigar store on Seventy-second Street and Columbus Avenue only lent further credence to Thane's story. The clerk in question remembered distinctly his customer of the previous Monday night.

"Sure I remember him," he replied to the detective's question "He bought five boxes of the most expensive cigars we carry. He wanted six, but we only had five in stock, so he took all we had."

"And what time was he in the store?" the detective asked.

"A little before twelve, about ten or fifteen minutes before. I noticed particularly because I close up at twelve and along about the last half hour, I keep a pretty close watch on the clock. Yeah, just about fifteen, twenty minutes to twelve, I'd say."

When the detective brought this information bark to Headquarters, Herschman merely grunted and relayed it to the district attorney's office.

"What I want to know," Herschman said, "is where are we headed for next? This case is getting too damn complicated."

"I should think a nice quiet little talk with George Griffis would be interesting," Spike suggested.

"Yeah." The word was heavy with sarcasm.

"Well, if you two can possibly do without my company for a little while I think I'll go up and chin a bit with Tommy."

As neither the district attorney nor the inspector paid any attention to his suggestion, Spike took their indifference for consent, left Headquarters and crossed the street to the Tombs. On his way he stopped and bought a bag of fruit, a carton of cigarettes, two hot dogs and the latest edition of the *Graphic*.

The story which it carried of the Thane case bore obvious evidence of a city editor's insistent demands for new and exciting developments when nothing new was forthcoming from the official source of information. Tommy Spencer was the chief preoccupation of reportorial ingenuity. From the morgue there had been dug up old pictures when he went more accurately by the name of William Preston and was just starting out in business as the dancing partner of Mrs. Greta Schlockenhass.

From Murray there was an account of Spencer's movements on Monday night. Quickly Spike scanned the type for the name of Nina Fennel or, at least for some reference to a "mystery woman." Knowing the tabloid penchant for mystery women, he did not trust even the chivalrous discretion of Murray under the unscrupulous onslaughts of wiley reporters. But apparently he had misjudged the butler. There was no reference to Spencer's feminine visitor on the momentous night of the tragedy.

At the jail he was readily admitted, his relationship with the district attorney proving an open sesame to the most heavily barred door. He found Spencer slumped disconsolately on the hard iron cot which was the only furniture which the cell afforded.

"Really," said Spike reprovingly, "you offend me, Tommy. Positively offend me, you're that gloomy. Here, lighten your soul, if not your stomach with a hot dog," and he sat cross-legged on the floor and opened his purchases.

"You're a hell of a one to talk to me about being gloomy," Tommy grumbled, and bit savagely into a hot frankfurter.

"It is rather nervy of me, isn't it," Spike replied complacently. "Me with the freedom of the city, and you shut up in this bloody cell."

Tommy looked at his visitor uneasily. Yet at the same time it was plain that he welcomed company after the monotony of solitude. His obvious impulse to talk was warring with a certain wariness which was only half concealed.

"Anything new?" he asked.

"Just chatting with Mr. Thane."

"Yes, that's the best thing he does."

"Oh, really? He always impressed me as being frightfully reticent."

"Thane? Why, he's one of the gabbiest fellows I know. I never once went to call for Mrs. Thane but what he was sticking around entertaining me in the parlor before she came, just like he was her little brother and I was her boyfriend."

"Well, you were, weren't you?"

Tommy shook his head. "No, it was strictly business between Mrs. Thane and me. She paid prompt—or fairly prompt, and I gave good service, and that was that."

"Tommy, you're shockingly commercial."

"The more 'commercial' you are the better you get on in my line."

"What sort of a person was she, anyway? You know we have surprisingly little information about the woman herself."

"Oh, she was all right."

"Meaning nothing at all. Be a bit more specific."

"Oh, well, she was the sort most of my customers are. Tired of their husbands, wanting some one they can't get, and nothing to fill up their time. Some of them get nervous breakdowns and call in a doctor to send them to Bermuda. And some of them call in me to take them to a nightclub."

"Incidentally, how does one go about working up a—ah—a clientele such as yours?"

"Oh, different ways. Usually if you're seen around a lot at a night club some woman will spot you and get a line on you. Sometimes you get called in to take extra women around—you know, when Cousin Susie arrives unexpectedly from Dubuque and there isn't a man for her. Sometimes the woman's husband even hires you. That's the way I got roped in on that Schlockenhass case. The old boy liked to sit around in his stocking feet with his bucket of beer and a corn cob, and his wife wanted something a little bit livelier, so he got me to keep her busy so he could have time nights to read his *Police Gazette* in comfort."

"Tommy, let me ask you just once more about that Schlockenhass case. Are you quite sure you've been truthful about it?"

"Honest to God, I'm telling you the truth. I didn't have any more to do with killing Mrs. Schlockenhass than I did with killing Mrs. Thane. It was just my damn luck, though, to be with each woman before the fellow that did the job came along."

"What makes you so sure that it was a 'fellow?'" Spike posed the question casually through a leisurely cloud of cigarette smoke.

"Sure it was a man," Tommy shot back quickly. "Women haven't the nerve for that sort of thing. Anyway, what woman would have it in for Mrs. Thane?"

"Well, for that matter, what man?"

"How should I know? I'm not the dick in this case I'm just the goat."

"You know," Spike confessed with a smile of amusement, "this situation despite its tragic ending, intrigues me no end. I mean your calling at the house for the wife and the husband entertaining you until she got ready. Sounds like something out of a Lonsdale comedy drama. Just what sort of thing does one talk about under the circumstances?"

"Oh, I dunno. Almost anything. What you read in the newspapers, or the weather or golf—Thane's a golf bug—(Took me with him once or twice, but I never could get much interested in it)—where you're going that night. He was always particular where I took Mrs. Thane. If she'd been eighteen and he was her mother, he couldn't have been any fussier about knowing that we were going places that he considered respectable, and what time we were getting home and all that."

"I suppose you hear lots of interesting stories from your—ah—clients?"

"What do you mean, interesting stories?"

"I mean most of your clients confess that their husbands 'don't understand them.'"

"Yes, that's their line. But I will say this for Mrs. Thane. She never pulled that one on me. She never talked about her troubles."

"Oh, so she did have some—troubles?"

"No woman hires a man to take her around to night clubs unless she's got something bearing down on her chest."

"And Cecily Thane never got hers off her chest?"

"Not to me."

"Just a straight business proposition."

"Strictly business, that's me."

"Frightfully embarrassing, though, I should think."

"Embarrassing? Why?"

"I mean the financial end. Did you submit a monthly bill or was it a pay-as-you-enter proposition?"

"At the beginning of each evening she'd give me $100. That was expenses and my rake-off."

"You never had any—ah—arguments with Mrs. Thane about money?"

"No, not arguments. Once or twice she didn't have the cash and she asked me to stand her till the next time and she'd pay double. Thane, you know, is as stingy as hell."

"Really?"

"Yes. Once when we drove out to his golf club the bill was $5 and he gave the taxi driver a quarter. Can you tie that?"

"And yet," Spike persisted, "you're quite sure that there were never any money troubles between you and Mrs. Thane?"

"Sure. I'm telling you."

"I know, Tommy, old thing, but under the circumstances do you mind if I'm rather skeptical?"

But Tommy only grunted and spat out a seed.

"By the way," Spike went on, "how did you happen to acquire Mrs. Thane's patronage?"

"A girl I know introduced me to her. Dame named Audrey Keating. She's a show girl and every once in a while she steers me on to something good."

"I didn't know Mrs. Thane had many friends in the profession. How did Miss Keating happen to know her?"

"She never said. I just met her down at the Lido Club one night after the show and she said she had a job for me, and the next night she brought Mrs. Thane to the club and we've been doing business from then on."

"Tell me, did Mrs. Thane ever—was shea— Well, what I'm trying to say, is—was she in love with you?"

"Say, listen I'm telling you that I'm running a business. And I use business methods. All she wanted was some one to go out and dance with her."

"Something you said a moment ago, intrigued me," Spike went on. "You said that most of your customers were women who were tired of their husbands, 'wanting some one they couldn't get.' Just who was it that Mrs. Thane wanted that she couldn't get?"

"How should I know?" Tommy bit quickly into a pear and filled his mouth with an overlarge bite.

"Oh, I just thought you might have a hint of it," Spike said nonchalantly and let the matter rest. "Interesting profession, yours. How ever did you come to select it?"

"I didn't select it. I started doing it because I was broke and down on my luck, and I found out the only thing I could do to make money was to dance. I wasn't good enough for stage dancing, but I could get by on the gigolo racket."

"You're not a native New Yorker I take it from your accent."

"No, I came from a little town out in the Middle West. You'd never think it, but I clerked in a grocery store. And then I came to the great city to make good as a popular song writer." Tommy paused as an expression, half wistful, half cynical crept into his eyes. "Poor goof! I didn't know until after I got here that song writing was a closed corporation, and I had about as much chance of breaking into it as I would breaking into grand opera. I got flatter and flatter, and finally just when I was down to my last five, I met up with a guy that put me next to this business. I've been at it ever since, almost two years. And I wish to hell I'd never set eyes on a night club or a jazz band."

"There's somethmg about the way you say all this, Tommy that makes me feel that your heart is not in your work."

"You're damn right it isn't."

"But really it seems to me that $100 a night is shockingly good pay, and for dancing with beautiful women."

"Beautiful women! God, if you could see some of the freaks that I've taken out. But that's not the worst of it. There's something about the business of being a professional dancing man, that when you meet a real girl—I mean a girl that really matters—why she sort of looks down—she thinks you're nothing but a—" Tommy stumbled hopelessly and Spike tactfully came to the rescue.

"I quite understand" He rose and stretched himself after his cramped position on the floor, and gathered up his hat and stick from the end of the cot. In the doorway of the cell he paused.

"I might be going up to see Nina Fennel," he said and smiled. "Any message you'd like to give her?"

For a moment Spencer only stared at him. Then he too smiled a little ruefully. "That's right, kick a guy when he's down. I suppose you're going to cop off the only real dame I ever knew, while I'm shut up in this goddam jail."

"Oh, no, Tommy, you mistake me. Much as I would like to do so, I wouldn't be permitted to go alone. I would be amply chaperoned by my brother and Inspector Herschman."

Out of the corner of his eye as be turned and walked down the corridor, Spike could see Spencer's knuckles go white as he gripped the edge of his cot and stared straight before him with frightened eyes.

## XIII. George Griffis in a Tight Place

AT eleven o'clock on the fourth morning after the murder of Cecily Thane, Inspector Herschman and District Attorney Tracy retired from their morning round with the newspaper men, after hinting that a complete denouement might be expected at any moment.

But when they closed the door on the last of the reporters they relapsed into a state of pessimism which was sharply in contrast to their attitude before their recent questioners. Spike, who during the week had assumed almost the aspect of a permanent fixture in his brother's office, was as usual sprawled in an easy-chair, smoking and regarding his two companions with a slight smile of amusement. Neither Herschman nor Tracy was in a talkative mood and the room was steeped in a gloomy silence.

"Well," said Spike at length, "since there doesn't seem anything else which demands our immediate attention, let's talk about the murder of Cecily Thane."

Herschman gave him a dark look and Tracy's mouth set itself in the disapproving line which his brother's carefree attitude usually evoked.

"As things stand now," Spike went on disregarding the frosty reception which his suggestion had received, "we have a most interesting array of people who were in or about the Thane premises on the fatal night of May 15. There is, for instance, Tommy Spencer. Tommy has already been involved in a similar case, he's hard up for money, and he quite definitely told his valet that he expected to 'raise quite a large sum soon'.

"And then there's George Griffis, estranged brother, who hocked a necklace known to have been in the dead woman's possession. . .

"And then there's Elton Thane himself, whose best friend and severest critic has for the last three years been making him toe the mark by threatening him with a check which he forged.

"Not to mention Emma the maid. On the occasion of our first conversation with her, Emma talked like one whose life is an open book and who joys in the confessing. But ever since then she has acted like a scared bunny.

"In sharp contrast to Emma's two-timing tactics is Dr. Peregrine Partridge who, I have a feeling, is one of the few persons involved who is telling God's truth and nothing else but."

Spike paused a moment. "And then there is Nina Fennel," he pointed out quietly.

"Yeah, that's what I say," Herschman snapped. "If I had my way about this I'd go up there and strong arm that dame."

"But, my dear inspector, you must realize that Miss Fennel is definitely not the type that one strong arms. I have a feeling that it is best to let matters stand just as they are with her for the present. For no reason at all I don't believe the time is ripe to call her attention to the fact that she lied like a lady.

"I don't believe that the letter which Cecily Thane wrote Mrs. Fennel was merely a kindly inquiry about her health, any more than I believe that Miss Fennel and her father dropped in on the Thanes Monday night for 'just a friendly chat'. And it looks very much like Miss Fennel and Tommy have a little secret between themselves that they're not telling us. Furthermore, throwing guns into sand cars is not precisely the sort of thing one does when one's conscience is carefree and spotless."

"I'll say it isn't," Herschman said

"But the thing that puzzles me is the delay. It seems to me if I had just shot some one and was going to dispose of my gun, I'd pick the first garbage can I struck."

"Say, lissen, brother," Herschman gave some patronizing advice, "when you've been dealing with crooks as long as I have, you'll learn that even the smartest of them do the damndest fool things."

"I suppose it was only from the naiveté of my own ignorance, Inspector, that I brought forth the quaint idea."

Herschman eyed Spike uneasily. Words like "naiveté" and "quaint" were not in his vocabulary and they annoyed him.

"Well, now you've got 'em lined up," he grumbled, "what are you going to do with them? Spencer, Griffis, Thane and the Fennel girl. Thane's got an alibi. He arrived at Partridge's at ten of twelve and his wife wasn't killed until after twelve."

"Unless," Spike reminded him, "Tommy did it."

The inspector nodded in agreement. "But there's some one you're forgetting, aren't you?" the district attorney broke in.

"Who?"

"Mortimer Fennel."

"Well," said Spike, "the inspector may have forgotten him, but not I. As a matter of fact, I find him most intriguing."

"But we haven't got anything on him like we have on the daughter," Herschman countered.

"No," Spike admitted. "Nothing except the fact that he was seen entering the Thane house Monday night. But no one saw him leave. And, what is still more important, unless I'm very much mistaken, he seems to be the object of a good deal of concern on the part of his daughter. I have a feeling that she much prefers having us talk to her, than to her father."

"You mean—" But whatever the inspector was about to ask was interrupted by the ringing of the telephone. With the nervous eagerness of one under a tension he grabbed it, before the district attorney had an opportunity to reach for it.

It was a summons for him to come to his own office down the corridor. He left the room but in less than five minutes he was back, an excited light in his eyes and a triumphant smile turning up the corners of his mouth.

"They've got Griffis."

Both Spike and the district attorney sat forward in their chairs.

"Got him! McCauley's just telephoned that he's bringing him over here. Got him through his bank. Got a line on him from a real estate company he was trading with and found that he did business with the Corn Exchange branch at Fourth Avenue and Twenty-ninth Street. McCauley buttonholes the president and finds out that on Tuesday morning Griffis appeared at the bank and met a $5,000 note that they held on him. But he had another note for $2,000 that came, due today. McCauley stuck around and sure enough Griffis turns up and renews it. As he walks out McCauley grabs him."

Fifteen minutes later Detective McCauley walked in with his prisoner. George Griffis was a young man, perhaps thirty-four or five with a pale pasty face that seemed prematurely etched with lines, from which peered apprehensive blue eyes. Although of average height, he somehow gave the impression of being a small man. Perhaps it was his sloping shoulders, perhaps the uneasy way he carried his head ducked forward slightly.

As he stood now before the inspector and the district attorney, his eyes jumped nervously and his bony fingers played with the side flaps of his pockets. A thin, negative fellow that you would have passed a hundred times without seeing, had it not been for the strange marking of his hair.

Heavy and bushy and black. You wondered where such an anemic, ineffectual creature had gotten the strength to grow, much less support such a vigorous healthy mop. And straight through the center, as if it had been put on with a paint brush, ran a streak of pure white.

He seated himself nervously in the chair which the district attorney indicated. At a sign from the inspector, McCauley withdrew.

"You are aware Mr. Griffis," the district attorney began, "why you are here?"

"Y—yes." For the first time he spoke and his voice trembled and broke even on the one word.

"Then just why," Herschman broke in, "have you been hiding out on us?"

"I—I haven't been hiding."

"Where have you been the last three days?"

"I had to go out of town on business."

"What business?"

"I'm in the real estate business and I had to see a man down in Camden about some property I have my eye on."

"His name?"

"Pearsall. He's with Jones & Pearsall. They're a firm I do business with often."

"And that's the one and only reason you've not been in New York since Tuesday morning."

"Yes, sir."

"Ever see this before?"

Herschman tossed Cecily Thane's diamond and emerald necklace down on the desk before Griffis with a careless gesture as if it were so much glass. Griffis swallowed and his eyes bulged slightly.

"Yes. It—it belonged to my sister. She gave it to me." He seemed to rush the words out.

"She *gave* it to you?"

"Yes, Monday afternoon, just the day before she was murdered."

Herschman, who had been pacing the floor in front of his victim, slowly settled himself into a chair and carefully folded his arms and let his half-closed eyes rest on Griffis.

"Suppose you tell us about it." His voice was quiet but steel edged.

"Well—I went to see her Monday afternoon, and I was rather pressed for money, and I asked her for some. She said she didn't have any, and she'd been spending so much lately that she hated to ask her husband for any more. He's rather close, you know. And so she said she'd let me have that, and I could raise some money on it temporarily. I've got some more coming in next month, you understand, so I could easily redeem it and I was going to give it back to her then."

"I see," said Herschman and a slightly ironic smile twisted up the corner of his mouth "Did you go to see your sister often?"

"Well—fairly often—"

"I suppose, of course, you were pretty fond of your sister. Her death makes you feel pretty terrible."

"Well, yes, naturally"

"On Monday afternoon when you saw her did she seem—worried about anything or upset?"

"No more than usual"

"What do you mean, no more than usual?"

"Well, she was always a nervous, excitable sort of person."

"And was she nervous and excited when you saw her?"

"Oh, she was just about as usual."

"How long did you stay?"

"About twenty or thirty minutes."

"Just a nice little brother and sister visit. You told her about your money difficulties and she promised to help you out and gave you her necklace."

"Yes."

"Just kind and helpful and sisterly."

"Yes."

Herschman paused. Then he shot the next question so suddenly that Griffis started visibly in his chair.

"Did Thane ever pay you back the $50,000 for the check he forged on you?"

"—Uh—no."

"Never paid you a cent?"

"No."

"Why didn't you prosecute?"

"On account of my sister."

"Where's the check now?"

"I don't know. Cecily made me give it to her very soon after it happened and I've never seen it since."

"I suppose she took it from you to make sure that you would never use it?"

"Yes, she wanted to protect her husband."

"Why did you move away from the Thane house last year?"

"Why—uh—I had a fight with Ce—with Thane."

"What about?"

"I was trying to make him pay back the money he forged on me."

"And did he do it?"

"No. I told you before."

"You didn't have a fight with your sister"

"No. We were always—very good friends." Again Herschman paused, and in the interim Spike spoke from his corner in the easy-chair.

"By the way, Mr. Griffis, did you by any chance notice whether your sister was writing a letter when you came in?"

"No."

"And I don't suppose you know whether she happened to be acquainted with any one by the name of Fennel?"

The muscles around Griffis' thin mouth seemed to tighten.

"Well—yes—she did."

"Very well?"

"Oh, no," he said quickly. "Mor—Mr. Fennel—the Fennels—" He floundered. "The Fennels used to live next door to them when they were on Eighty-sixth Street."

"And have they kept up the friendship since then—since the Thanes moved away?"

"No, they've hardly seen anything of them." Again the quick negative.

"Your witness, Inspector," and Spike lapsed once more into the indolence of smoking.

A sardonic smile twisted Herschman's face. He surveyed Griffis in much the same manner as a cat looks at a mouse with which it is playing in its quiet, torturing fashion. Griffis pulled out his handkerchief and wiped the beaded moisture from his forehead.

"What," said Herschman with a misleading leisureliness, "what was the situation between your sister and her husband—friendly?"

For a moment Griffis' nervous hands stopped fiddling with the edge of his coat. For the flash of a second a sudden alert gleam seemed to light his eye. When he spoke again his voice was more controlled than at any time during the meeting.

"They were not," he said carefully as if choosing his words; "they were not very well fitted."

"How do you mean?"

"I mean my sister, like any woman, did not enjoy being neglected by her husband."

"He neglected her?"

"Yes. She was a very lonely woman." Griffis' voice became low, shot through with a certain note of suffering.

"I suppose there were other women?"

"I can't say whether there were 'women.' But there was a woman."

"Yes?"

"Elton Thane has been running around with a show girl for the past year, and my sister was almost beside herself."

"Did Thane ever speak to your sister about a divorce?"

"Many times He begged her to divorce him."

"And she wouldn't do it?"

"Certainly not. She—she loved him." The note of pain increased.

"You know who this woman is?"

"She was in some revue, but I understand she isn't working now." The last part of the sentence was uttered with a certain quietness that spoke far more than the actual words.

"Know where she lives?"

"No."

"Name?"

"I only know her first name. It's Audrey."

Herschman reached for the telephone and got his own office on the wire. "McCauley," he said when the connection had been put through, "get all the programs of Broadway revues for the last year and locate any girls in them named Audrey. And bring 'em around to my office."

## XIV: Miss Keating Forgets to be Dramatic

ONCE more the papers buzzed with the news of an arrest in the Thane murder case—George Griffis, brother of the murdered woman. His picture three columns wide and beneath it a photograph of the necklace which had been turned over to the police by the impeccably honest Shansky Even Shansky came in for his share of the publicity posed in front of his Third Avenue three-balled shop.

And once more Spike glanced over the headlines as he rode north in a taxicab to an address on East Ninety-third Street—an address which he had only five minutes before obtained from Tommy Spencer in his cell in the Tombs. The number, a few doors east of Madison Avenue, proved to be an apartment house of the obviously swanky sort, with a uniformed doorman, and a telephone operator in the hall who discreetly took your name and relayed it to the apartment before permitting you to be shot up in the elevator.

The door of Miss Audrey Keating's apartment was opened by a black and white starched French maid who looked as if she might have dropped out of a moving picture. Indeed, the entire interior was not unlike the more luxurious Hollywood sets of ladies of easy but shrewd virtue. It was obvious that Miss Keating was all that is popularly expected of a lady of the chorus who plays with millionaires in her off hours.

Nor did Miss Keating herself differ greatly from the popular conception. She appeared in a luxurious scarlet dressing gown whose sleek, clinging folds revealed those melting lines which were her fortune. A tall, striking, blonde with that particular brand of eyes which are never known as merely blue, but baby blue. Yet with it all, there was a firmness to her smooth white chin and a certain determined line to her, carefully etched mouth that somehow counteracted the general impression of voluptuous softness which she produced. She came toward Spike with that artificial undulating step so assiduously cultivated by ladies who are in the habit of appearing before vast audiences, hung with rhinestones, and topped by amazing creations of spiraling plumes.

"Mr. Tracy?" she inquired. The voice had originally been pure Chillecothe, but somewhere along the way it had been heavily overlaid with the accent so commonly heard on the English drawing-room stage. Spike bowed low in his most Continental manner and brushed her outstretched hand with his lips. Miss Keating smiled the smile she reserved for managers and millionaires. As a matter of fact, Miss Keating was sure that this handsome young man with the charming manner was doubtless one of the two, perhaps both, which was all the better.

"Won't you—sit down," she asked in her best manner.

"Sorry," Spike apologized, "but I really can't. As a matter of fact I'm in a frightful hurry. I just dropped in to pick you up and take you out for a drive with me, and I assure you there isn't a moment to lose."

"But really—" Miss Keating protested, but she was obviously pleased with the unaccountable behavior of this strange young man. "But really—Mr.—ah, Tracy," she refreshed her memory from his card which she still held in her hand "I don't quite understand."

"I can quite believe that my request is unusual and precipitate, but run along and get your coat on and I'll explain while we're riding."

But Miss Keating had apparently no intention of running along. Instead she sank gracefully into a chair, carefully disposing her various comely members to achieve the best possible display.

"You are a strange young man, aren't you?" and she smiled archly.

"Dearie, you don't know the half of it. But I'm not half as strange as the young men and old ones too that are going to be up here in about five or ten minutes."

"And just what do you mean?" Miss Keating stretched herself like a sinuous cat, and laid one white hand on Spike's cuff.

"I mean that the district attorney and the chief of the homicide squad are probably on their way up here right now to question you in connection with the Cecily Thane murder."

The effect of these words on Miss Audrey Keating were not unlike a shock of electricity. She sat bolt upright in her chair and her baby blue eyes grew suddenly frightened and staring. Worse still, when she spoke she had forgotten her English comedy-drama accent and had reverted to pure Chillecothe.

"Wha—what do you mean?"

"Exactly what I said. And if you're wise you'll come with me before they get here."

"But how do I know—but what—but what you—"

"Here!" Spike shoved a paper into her hand. "I neglected to present my letter of introduction."

She snatched the paper from him and read the few scribbled lines: "Audrey: I think this is a regular guy, but I'm not sure. Do what he says and he'll keep you out of trouble—maybe. Tommy Spencer."

For a moment she stood undecided, crunching the paper in her hands. Then suddenly she rushed out of the room. In not more than three minutes she was back again with her coat and a small close hat that came far down over her eyes. When her coat collar was turned up her face was almost hidden.

Not until they were in the taxicab which Spike had held in readiness at the door, and were driving slowly through the Park did she speak again. Then she turned abruptly to him.

"Who are you anyway?"

"My name is Tracy."

"The district attorney!" she gasped

"My dear young lady, why, I ask you, does the name of the district attorney strike such terror to your heart?"

"Why, what, do you mean? I'm not afraid. I've nothing to be afraid of." She spoke quickly, as if in a vain endeavor to convince herself of what she was saying.

"Then why look so scared?"

"Say, listen," she appealed "What's the idea? What do you want with me?"

"Well, first of all, perhaps I had better correct the mistaken impression you're under. I am not the district attorney."

The girl seemed visibly to melt with relief. "Then who are you?"

"I'm his brother. No, no—don't mistake me," he went on quickly as she once more grew wary. "We've really nothing much in common outside of our parents. Richard thinks life is a great legal problem and I think it's a rightfully amusing show. However, just at present we do have a mutual interest—the Thane murder case."

He paused and looked out of the corner of his eye at his companion. She was sitting very still, her hands folded in her lap, her fingers clasped in, A tight nervous grip.

"Would you mind awfully telling me what you know about it?"

She did not answer.

"Because if you don't," be went on quietly, "I'll take you back home and by that time my brother and his dear friend, Inspector Herschman, will probably be there with the cortege of newspaper reporters and photographers that have been following them around this week."

"Please—please, don't get me into this." Impulsively she grabbed his arm "I can't afford to get mixed up in the newspapers in a murder case."

"My dear girl, you simply confound all my preconceived notions about actresses. I always thought publicity was an asset."

"But not this kind. Not a murder case. Look what's happened to the actresses that have been mixed up in murder cases."

"Well then," he continued philosophically, "you'd best tell papa all. That's really your only way out."

Suddenly he turned on her that charming, beguiling smile which had melted the hearts of scores of females on both sides of the Atlantic. Gently he took one of her stiff hands in his. When he spoke again his voice carried that note described by our more impassioned novelists as low and vibrant.

"Can't you—trust me?"

The histrionics of the situation were too much for Miss Keating even in the midst of her fright.

"Can I?" Once more she was in command of her comedy-drama manner.

For reply Spike only gave her hand a long, understanding pressure as if his feelings could not be put into words. Then gently he released it and reached for his cigarette case as if to restore their relationship to a more casual basis.

Reluctantly Miss Keating accepted a cigarette and let her glance travel over her companion. Not even the realization that he was neither a millionaire, nor a manager, but was rather the brother of the district attorney could quite remove the satisfaction from her appraisal.

"What do you want to know?"

"Everything you know."

"But I don't know anything really."

"Tell me, for instance, how you happened to be acquainted with Mrs. Thane."

"Oh, I really wasn't acquainted with her. I met her on a party one night."

"Do you recall the exact circumstances?"

"No. I go to a good many parties, you know. And you know how you meet people."

"Well then, perhaps you can tell me this, did you introduce Tommy Spencer to Mrs. Thane before or after you started—ah—going about with Mr. Thane?"

The girl stopped suddenly in the middle of a long exhale of smoke and the hand which held her cigarette trembled. "What do you mean—going about with Mr. Thane?"

"It's quite useless to ask such unnecessary rhetorical questions, my girl," Spike assured her.

"I'm sure I don't know what you're talking about," she said defiantly.

"Of course you know what I'm talking about. You know as well as I do that I am referring to the fact that it's fairly common knowledge that you and Elton Thane have reached a certain stage of intimacy where—"

"That's a lie."

"What's a lie?"

"What you just said."

"But really I haven't said anything."

"You just said that Elton Thane and I—" She broke off uncertainly. Her Chillecothe training had not endowed her with words sufficiently euphemistic for such a delicate situation

"You know, my dear," Spike went on, "you'd much better come right out and tell me the truth or I shall think the worst. The very worst," he emphasized "Here I find you, a beautiful girl, who has not been working for six months and yet you are living in an apartment that doesn't cost a cent under $300 a month. There's really only one conclusion to draw."

"Is that so? Well, let me tell you something. You're all wet."

"Yes?"

"Yes, that's what I said. I'm not that kind of a girl."

"No?"

"No. A guy's not getting me until he gets me with a wedding ring around my finger. I've seen too many dames all set up in nice apartments and just settling down and enjoying themselves, and about the time they begin to get too fat to get back into a show or get another man, the guy up and leaves them—flat—cold."

"Really? How brutally heartless."

"I've seen it done too many times to get caught. Little Audrey's too smart for that."

"So I suppose you told Mr. Thane that until he could divorce his wife and marry you with full pomp and circumstance, you would allow him only the privilege of providing you with a luxurious living, for which he would get nothing in return but the charm of your companionship."

For a moment the girl said nothing. Then reluctantly she surrendered. "Yes, that's it. You're pretty smart, aren't you?"

Spike turned upon her a look of flashing admiration. "My dear, beside you, I am a low-grade moron. To get away with what you're getting away with requires no mere surface sophistication like mine. It requires genius. But tell me—did Mr. Thane accept this arrangement?"

"There wasn't anything else for him to do"

"And now I suppose that with Mrs. Thane's death, there will be nothing to prevent marriage?"

"Well, we'll wait a little while, anyway, just to make it look better."

"How did you two happen to meet?"

"Some business men I know gave a party and asked me, and three of the other girls in the show I was playing in, and he was there."

"And since then you have been—friends?"

"Yes."

"But I still don't quite understand how Tommy Spencer got dragged in."

"I dragged him in. Mr. Thane was always afraid his wife would find out about him going out with me and I said that was simple. Just keep her busy with some one else. Get her a boy friend; and I got Tommy."

Spike sighed. "It's all distressingly commercial. But weren't you afraid of meeting them when you were out with Thane?"

"No. I know pretty much what night clubs Tommy works—he gets a rake-off from the clubs, you know—and we stayed away from them. But then we didn't go to clubs much. Just dinner and a show afterward. Mr. Thane's sort of a quiet person."

"Yes, that was my impression of him. I should hardly have picked him as a person to your taste."

"What do you mean," she bridled. "Just because a girl's been on the stage every one thinks she's wild and doesn't care for a nice, refined life, with a man that's got plenty of—that—"

"A good provider," Spike supplied. "I think I understand." He smiled and Miss Keating looked hurt.

"Tell me, did Mr. Thane ever try to get a divorce?"

"No."

"And yet he professed himself eager to marry you?"

"Yes."

"Strange, isn't it?"

"Well, he always said that somehow he just never, could bring himself to it. I used to tell him he was a fool. He could have got one easy as not. We've had a lot of quarrels on that point. But then, I figured, well, if he's satisfied with present arrangements, I should worry."

"Quite sensible of you, I'm sure. But tell me, Miss Keating, what do you mean, 'he could have got one easy as not?'"

She turned on him a look of surprise. "Why, don't you know? This Fennel fellow. He and Mrs. Thane have been lovers for years."

"*. . . lovers for years. . . .*"

"Oh, quite!" Spike remarked, but his nonchalant manner belied the sudden excited click which his brain had given, at the three words . . . *"lovers for years". . . .*

Two hours later, Spike was waiting for the district attorney and the inspector when they came back to Headquarters, both of them mumbling reproaches to each other in a disgruntled manner.

"We went after this Audrey woman," the district attorney explained to Spike. "Her last name's Keating. But she wasn't home. Herschman's having the place watched."

"I hardly think that will do much good," Spike remarked. "I have a feeling that Miss Keating is not going to return for some time. She tells me that she hates newspaper photographers and policemen."

Herschman whirled on his heel and faced Spike. "What do you mean?"

"I mean I've just been out driving with Miss Keating and she asked me to drop her at the corner of Fifty-ninth and Eighth Avenue, and the last I saw of her she was disappearing into the downtown subway. I pointed out to her that her apartment would undoubtedly be favored by a visit from the police and she seemed appalled at the prospect."

"You mean you had hold of her and you let her go?"

"Just her hand."

"No funny business. Where is she now?"

"I have no idea."

"Say, lissen, brother," Herschman began savagely, "what are you trying to do, double-cross us. I'm getting damn tired of your meddling. What business have you got, I'd like to know, butting in and balling things—"

"Inspector," Spike broke in, "remember your blood pressure."

"Damn my blood pressure!"

"You know, old thing, I had an idea that Miss Keating was just what she turned out to be—a devastating combination of ignorance and shrewdness—something that not even the combined legal and police minds of New York could batter through. Sex appeal was what was needed, and if I do say so myself, I rather feel that in that respect I have a slight edge on you and Richard."

"Damn your sex appeal! How did you find out where she lived? It wasn't in the telephone book and it took us two hours to track her down."

"Oh, I got her address from a friend of mine. Really, you know, our little drive was most revealing. Acting again like the low cad that I am, I gained her confidence and then pried loose some very interesting information."

While Herschman sat in glowering silence, Spike began the story of his afternoon's adventures. But when he came to the revelation of the unique financial relations between Thane and Miss Keating, the inspector suddenly grew alert

"You see," Spike explained, "she's a very, very clever girl."

"Yeah, and I also see that Elton Thane's a very, very guilty man." He rose in sudden decision.

"Where are you going?" the district attorney inquired.

"I'm going up to arrest Elton Thane for the murder of his wife. There you are. Motive absolutely proved and clear. He wanted to marry this Keating girl and collect on the money he'd been spending on her, and he couldn't as long as his wife was holding that check on him. And he couldn't get the check from her, so—" He made a gesture with his hands to indicate that it was all as plain as day.

"But you forget," the district attorney reminded him, "that Thane couldn't possibly have done it. He was at Dr. Partridge's from ten minutes to twelve on. And Spencer was with Mrs. Thane until twelve."

Herschman stopped abruptly in the act of reaching for his hat. As he considered the district attorney's words the determined set to his jaw gave way.

"Yes, that's right," he admitted. Then he turned to Spike with a disgruntled snap. "Well, go on with your story. Is that all?"

"Not quite," and Spike continued. As he drew to the end of his account he asked for the blotter which, had been removed from Cecily Thane's writing table the morning after she was murdered. Holding it up to a small looking-glass the letters were plain.

Taking a pencil he sketched in lightly the missing letters and handed it over to Tracy and Herschman. Now the reflection read:

"And that my dears, is what Mrs. Thane said in the kind letter of sympathy she wrote to Mrs. Fennel last Monday afternoon. Under the circumstances I think we ought to have another go at the Fennels— Mortimer Fennel in particular."

## XV. NINA FENNEL FAILS TO EXPLAIN

ONCE more the three men stood outside the Fennel apartment and waited for an answer to their ring—the district attorney, Spike and the inspector. They had to ring twice before the slatternly maid at last opened the door to them and led them almost as a matter of course into the front room.

A few minutes later Nina Fennel appeared in the doorway. There were deep circles of weariness under her eyes and her heavy dark hair, sliding low on her neck, seemed to elongate the lines of her face.

"Well?" she said as she stood in the doorway.

"Miss Fennel, we've come to see you—and your father." The district attorney put particular emphasis on the last three words.

"I'm afraid it's just about as useless this time as the last," she said in a tired voice. "My mother's condition is unchanged."

"I'm very sorry to hear that, I'm sure, but I must insist that we see your father too, this time."

"No. It is impossible." She stood in the doorway, blocking the way. Herschman rose and came toward her.

"No, it's not impossible," he said. "Not if I have to go down to your mother's room and bring him out myself."

"No—no!" A terrified look leaped into her blazing eyes. But the inspector never wavered. He took her arm in a grip that seemed to the observer a gentle one, but it was like steel. His eyes bored into her. She faltered. Then suddenly the backbone went out of her.

"All right," she said, "I'll call him." And she turned in defeat and walked down the dark hall.

Mortimer Fennel, if he had looked weak and tired that first morning on which he had faced the district attorney, now seemed as if he had scarcely the strength to bring one dragging foot after the other.

"You—you wanted to see me again?"

"Yes, you—and your daughter," Tracy said.

"You realize—that my wife—"

"I understand, and I regret greatly that we have to intrude at this particular time; but there are some things that we must ask you to repeat, Mr. Fennel. Please tell us again, every movement you made on the night Cecily Thane was murdered."

And again Fennel related his story of the previous Monday night. It was the same as he had told them once before.

"And you are quite sure, are you, that your little call on the Thanes had nothing at all to do with a letter that Mrs. Thane wrote Monday afternoon to your wife?"

"Why—yes, I told you that before." His voice was hoarse.

"And you're quite sure that after leaving the Thane house at nine-thirty you did not return to it later on."

"Quite sure"

"And you came directly home"

"No," put in the girl quickly. "He walked around a while."

"I'm not asking you," Herschman snapped. "I'm asking your father. You came directly home?"

"No—I walked around a while."

"How long?"

"Oh, I don't know."

"Half an hour?"

"No. Longer than that."

"What time did you get back here?"

"It was—it must have been quite late. The elevator wasn't running."

"And you, Miss Fennel, you're also quite sure, I suppose, that you left there not later than ten o'clock?"

Fennel shot a sudden surprised glance at his daughter.

"But—but she wasn't there," he protested.

"Yes, Father," the girl said, "I told them I was."

"What was your idea, Mr. Fennel, in lying to us, telling us that you were alone in the Thane house?"

"I—I didn't want to get Nina mixed up in it."

"What do you mean, in it?"

"Oh, all the publicity and scandal and—" Mortimer Fennel made a hopeless, weary gesture.

Herschman turned back to the girl. "You're sure, are you, that you left there not later than ten o'clock?"

Her chin went up suddenly in a defiant gesture. "I am quite sure."

Again the corners of the inspector's mouth turned up slightly and the cat-and-mouse expression, indicative of extreme pleasure spread over his face. He paused. Then slowly he spoke, boring the words in as he faced Nina Fennel.

"Since you're so ready with your answers, Miss Fennel, maybe you can explain why you went to Mr. Tommy Spencer's apartment last Monday night shortly after one, about the hour you told us you were 'just walking' along Riverside Drive."

Nina Fennel said nothing. The gesture of defiance seemed suddenly to freeze on her face, and Herschman went, on relentlessly. "And maybe you can also tell why on Tuesday afternoon you threw a revolver into a northbound sand car along the New York Central tracks."

Slowly she lifted a trembling hand to her mouth and her eyes grew wide with terror.

Herschman's voice grew louder. "And you don't need to tell me what Mrs. Thane wrote to your mother last Monday afternoon, because I know. She told your mother that she and your father 'had been lovers for—'"

Suddenly there was a stifled shriek. Nina Fennel flung herself on the detective and clapped both her trembling hands over his mouth.

"For God's sake—no—don't—" and her terror-stricken eyes signaled down the dark hall. There was a deathly silence. Not a soul spoke. All eyes were on the girl. And then like an eerie, weird wail came the voice, weak, palsied with sickness.

"M—Mortimer!"

The girl and her father looked at each other, their eyes exchanging desperate messages.

"Father—go—" and she pointed down the dark hall. Mortimer Fennel stumbled out of the room toward the faint, piteous wail.

When he had gone, the girl shut the door behind him and stumbled to a chair and sank weakly into it, as if her legs would no longer support her. She leaned her head on her hand and did not face them as she spoke.

"Well—go on."

"But it's your turn to go on," the inspector reminded her. "You haven't yet answered my questions. Why did you go to

Tommy Spencer's apartment last Monday night and write him a note in which you said, 'Something terrible has happened.'"

"I—I thought—I mean I thought he could help me—about the letter that Mrs. Thane wrote to my mother."

"And how could he help you?"

"I—I—didn't know. He knew Mrs. Thane so well and I thought—why, I thought he might be able to do something to stop her."

"But that doesn't explain why you went to such pains to dispose of a revolver the following afternoon. Why did you do that?"

"I—I thought—" She broke off suddenly and pressed her trembling lips together.

"You thought what?"

"I—I don't know."

"You don't know why you threw the revolver away. Whose revolver was it?"

"It—it's just one that's been around the house for a long time."

"It wasn't by any chance a .38 caliber Colt?"

"I don't know. I—I didn't notice."

"But why did you throw it away?"

"Oh—I never did like guns—and I just thought—I'd—I'd get rid of it."

The inspector paused to consider the situation for a moment. Then quickly he made up his mind. "Your explanations, Miss Fennel, are not satisfactory. I'm holding you as a material witness in this case—without bail. You and your—"

"No—no, please. Let me go. I'll go. Don't take him away from her. She's dying. She may not live till morning She's—Oh, God—"

Suddenly she collapsed forward on to the arm if her chair, a piteous figure, weeping hysterically, pleading.

"Don't you think, Inspector," the district attorney broke in in a quiet voice, "that it will be sufficient to hold the girl?"

## XVI. A CONFESSION

"WOULD it be impertinent to inquire," said Spike as he slouched lazily in an easy-chair in his brother's office the following morning, "now that you've got the three of them in jail what are you going to do with them?"

"What are we going to do with them?" the inspector repeated brusquely. "Why, we're going to—ah—"

"Yes, I thought as much."

"Lissen, young fellow," he burst out.

"Call me Spike, old man, just Spike. Neat and to the point."

But Herschman apparently did not get the point, for he relapsed into moody silence.

"I sympathize with you," Spike admitted with feeling. "I really do. Spencer talks too much. Miss Fennel won't talk at all—beyond a certain point. And Griffis is too scared to be of much account. That being the case, I'll take a hand myself."

He settled himself more comfortably and lit a cigarette. "Where do we stand? Well, it seems pretty certain that on the night Cecily Thane was murdered, her house was simply teeming with people who had no particular fancy for her. Who, in fact, wouldn't be at all distressed with her out of the picture.

"No. 1—her husband who, while waiting to be legally free, is put to the impertinent expense of supporting his girl friend without getting anything out of it. When he asked his wife for a divorce, she probably reminded him of the forged check which she held and told him to try and get it.

"No. 2—Mortimer Fennel and his Amazonian daughter, Nina, naturally have a grudge against the murdered lady, seeing as how she tried to spill the beans to their ailing wife and mother that for the past fifteen years Mortimer has not been all that a devoted husband should be. They probably intercepted that letter before it ever got to Mrs. Fennel, but they were afraid that another time, Mrs. Thane might be more successful.

"No 3—George Griffis who is hard up and needs money and has an ancient but quite understandable grudge against Cecily for helping her husband nick him out of $50,000."

"You forget," the district attorney, put in, "that Thane repaid him that money."

"So Thane says. But George seems to have suffered a lapse of memory on this particular      point. George didn't seem at all upset his by sister's death. And that is that."

"You forget Tommy Spencer," the inspector reminded him.

"No, I didn't forget Tommy. I can't quite decide about him. The fact remains that despite the disparity in their social position and disposition, Miss Nina Fennel went out of her way to meet him and has since encouraged him. And despite Tommy's obvious charms, they are not the sort I think would appeal to a girl of Miss Fennel's type. To be very frank, I'm rather of the opinion—"

But Spike got no further. It was at this particular junction that they were interrupted by the district attorney's secretary. "A gentleman to see you," he announced. "Mr. Fennel."

"There's going to be no bail for that girl," Herschman declared. "If the old guy thinks that he's going to come around and get the girl out, he's all wet."

Tracy nodded to Lovelace to bring Fennel in.

As Mortimer Fennel stood in the doorway facing the district attorney, the inspector and the insouciant young man, even the most casual observer would have been struck by the change in him. His nervousness was gone, his trembling hands were still. His whole being seemed diffused with a great despair, but a despair which he no longer fought. It was as if he had been clinging desperately to something, but had at last surrendered, quietly as one who realizes the futility of struggle. His shoulders sagged with defeat.

The district attorney indicated a chair, and Fennel dragged his faltering feet across the floor and sank into it. For a moment no one said anything. Then Tracy spoke.

"Well, Mr. Fennel?"

Fennel raised his haggard, despairing eyes "I have come to get my daughter," he said simply, and his voice was like something from the dead

"That is impossible," Herschman broke in. "She's held without bail."

"Yes, I know. But you must let her go."

"Let her go?"

"Her mother is dying I have just come from her bedside. The doctor says that she can't last until noon."

"Look here, Fennel, you don't need to come pulling that—"

But Fennel held up his hand and cut him short. "My, daughter did not murder Mrs. Thane. She knows nothing about it." He spoke the words in a calm, even voice, but he closed his eyes as he said them. Then even more quietly, even more calmly, he went on,      "I did it."

For a moment there was a dead silence in the room. Spike, Tracy, and Herschman had suddenly leaned forward in their chairs, staring at the man in front of them, scarcely breathing.

"Yes, I did it." He opened his eyes and looked about him. "If you will bring a stenographer in here, I would like to dictate my confession.

That is—I think that is the usual way, isn't it?" There was something tragic and piteous in the utterly calm manner with which he sought to comply with precedent.

Without a word Herschman rose and walked quietly to the door, summoning Lovelace from the outer office.     When the secretary had seated himself at a small table, Fennel looked inquiringly once more at the district attorney.

"It is customary, is it not, to give a brief description of yourself in— in such cases?"

The district attorney nodded.

In the same colorless voice, Fennel proceeded; slowly so that Lovelace might have no difficulty in getting each word.

"I am Mortimer Fennel, forty-six years old, commercial artist, free lance. Twenty-four years ago I married Maybelle Comminger, and a year later our daughter, Nina, was born. My wife has been an invalid since then."

It was as if he were merely reciting something he had learned by heart, as if he had written it down beforehand and memorized it. With never a pause for a word, never a single fumbling for a phrase he went on.

"When my daughter was eight years old I met Cecily Thane and her husband. She was dissatisfied with life and so was I. We became— lovers. Seven years ago her husband discovered our relationship, but it made no difference to him.

"During the last three years, my feelings changed, so that I no longer cared to continue the relationship, but Mrs. Thane insisted that if I did not do so, she would tell my wife. In spite of my conduct during the last fifteen years, I have always felt for my wife a greater love than I have ever had for any woman, and she has never for a moment suspected my infidelity. My daughter, Nina, however, has known the truth for several years, and has aided me in keeping it from her mother.

"The relationship between me and Cecily Thane at length became so strained that in desperation I told her that I would never see her again. Last Monday afternoon she sent my wife a letter by special messenger, telling her the whole sordid story. Fortunately my daughter intercepted it.

"Together we went to Mrs. Thane's house Monday night, to plead with her to desist. I did not wish my daughter to be drawn into it unless I could help it. When I found that Mrs. Thane was not there I summoned my daughter to the house. I don't know why I did this except perhaps that I have always been a weak character, and I have always leaned heavily on her youth and strength.

"I was in such a wrought-up state that my daughter forced me to leave the house and said she would remain and deal with Mrs. Thane. A half hour later, feeling that it was useless for her to wait any longer that night, she left."

Fennel paused, closed his eyes as if to summon strength for what was to follow. Then he went on, still calm, dead:

"I returned to the house at eleven o'clock and let myself in with the latchkey which I still kept from the years when I was on more friendly terms with Mrs. Thane. I hid myself in her dressing room until after she had come in with Tommy Spencer and Spencer had left.

"And after he left, I—I shot her. I took the jewels from her jewel safe to make it appear like robbery. I left the house immediately and threw the jewels wrapped in a newspaper in a garbage can. Then I came back to my home at 204 West Eighty-sixth Street.

"That—that is all."

Fennel sat now, staring straight ahead of him. Slowly he reached forth a hand and took a pen from the desk and dipped it in the inkwell. In a firm untrembling hand he wrote his name at the bottom of the long sheet which the secretary pulled from his typewriter.

And now," he said as he handed the paper to the district attorney, "will you release my daughter—immediately? She must see her mother—before—she—dies."

And very quietly Mortimer Fennel sank to the floor unconscious.

## XVII. Spike Reads the *"Times"*

ON Sunday morning, the day following the confession of Mortimer Fennel, Spike stood outside Police Headquarters and hesitated. The gaudy magazine covers of a corner newsstand caught his eye, and he stopped for a paper. Strangely enough, though, it was not the screaming pink of his favorite evening tab that he selected from the array spread out on the counter, but the dignified pages of the *Times*.

Slowly he strolled down Centre Street until he came to Sherman Park. He dropped down on to one of the benches and unfolded his paper. Even the erudite *Times* had given the Thane murder confession a two-column head on the front page, for not even erudition and dignity could disregard the pitiful, moving story of Mortimer Fennel.

There it all was, the secret that both he and his daughter had so painfully guarded, spread out for the world to read and relish. And yet even amid the welter of tragedy there was one comforting thought. They had succeeded. Mrs. Mortimer Fennel had died the previous day in the arms of her daughter, even to the end unconscious of the black shadow that for fifteen years had hovered over her home.

Spike read the news columns slowly, his own knowledge of the persons involved piecing out the story that had been unearthed by the reporters. He read to the end and then put down the paper, and let his mind reconstruct the whole pitiful, tragic tale.

Mortimer Fennel, a young man in art school with dreams of the Paris salons driving his brushes, had found that a passionate but too early marriage made his plans for study abroad impossible But he had surrendered gracefully to necessity, for he had been very much in love with his young wife. Commercial art paid the rent and the grocery bills. And presently came joy and tragedy. Nina was born, and from that day on Maybelle Fennel remained an invalid, chained to a wheel chair—a sweet, gentle shadow whose physical weakness was matched only by the moral instability of her husband.

Endowed with all the intensity of an artistic temperament, his ambitions thwarted by lack of money, Mortimer Fennel soon found that he was not of the fiber of which martyrs are made. He still loved his wife with a strange, mystical tenderness. He adored his baby daughter. But the inherent weakness of his nature coupled with the desires of the flesh proved too much for him.

His acquaintance with Cecily Thane had started quite casually enough; The Thanes moved into the same apartment house in which the Fennels lived, and the common cause of tenants—lack of hot water, a broken elevator or a delinquent janitor—brought them into each other's lives

And Cecily Thane was ripe for change. Elton Thane, a salaried jewelry salesman, could not provide her with the luxuries to which her upbringing had never accustomed her, but which she desired avidly. And because her mind and her time and her life were empty, she welcomed the entrance of Mortimer Fennel. He was young, and quixotic, and good looking, and had that peculiar charm for women which weak men so frequently possess; and the hopeless state of his own family life, which offered no outlet for his passionate nature, soon resulted in a liaison.

He would have been content to let it be just that, but Cecily Thane for once in her life found herself touched by a real emotion. She wanted Mortimer Fennel and wanted him desperately—wanted him in all his poverty and weakness She had arrived at that love-is-all-and-the-world-well-lost emotional state where she would willingly have run off with him to any romantic, quixotic end of the earth which he selected.

But Mortimer Fennel was not even a strong enough character to do the cowardly thing. He longed desperately to rid his life of the trying complications of an invalid wife and an infant daughter, but he lacked even the courage to make the break. And so for fifteen years he and Cecily Thane were unmolested in their love making. By the time Elton Thane had discovered the true state of affairs, he was too engrossed in making money, in building up his own business to care—much.

At first it had piqued his pride. But gradually he found that it was after all a rather convenient arrangement. It left him more or less free to pursue his own desires. And since the time had long since passed when Cecily was any part of those desires, he let in drift. And so they drifted—drifted. And all the time Nina Fennel was growing up. At fifteen she had an instinctive dislike of the beautiful Mrs. Thane of whom her father occasionally spoke. At twenty she actively hated her, and at twenty-one she had divined the whole hateful story.

Just when she had come to know, she could not have told, no more than Mortimer Fennel could have told when he became conscious of the fact that he had gradually begun to lean on the daughter that had so recently been just a little girl, and was now a grown woman. The years of his entanglement with Cecily Thane had not dealt happily with Mortimer Fennel. It was only the strong pull of the flesh that kept him at her side, for his instinctive fastidious discernment, so ill-combined in his weak nature, showed him plainly the vacuity, of this woman. After the first year he ceased to love her, but he did not cease to desire her.

However, even desire at last becomes faint, and in Mortimer Fennel this diminishing process was premature. The swift passion of his nature had spent him, until at forty-five he found that he no longer even desired her. Upon her, the years had just the opposite effect. At thirty-eight her physical charms and her lover were slowly slipping from her. With a desperate fury she fought to recreate the old ardor; but Mortimer Fennel was weary. He wanted only the peace of his own home, and the gentle companionship of his shadowy, fading wife. He was like a runner who has run too swiftly and suddenly finds himself broken and winded with a wish for nothing but infinite rest.

She even tried the obvious device of what was apparently a new and younger lover, but in reality was only a hired dancing partner. And then with a swift rush the whole lingering tragedy of the last fifteen years had resolved itself into an imminent terror. Cecily Thane had told him that unless he returned to her she would tell his wife of the relationship which had existed between them. She had used the last and lowest weapon of a desperate woman, a woman beyond love or hate, carried away by an avenging despair—moral blackmail. She had made good her threat, but Fennel and his daughter had intercepted the letter before it reached Maybelle Fennel.

"In less than twenty-four hours after she wrote the letter to Mrs. Mortimer Fennel, Cecily Thane was found dead with a bullet through her heart."

It was a damning juxtaposition of two facts, and Spike frowned as his eyes rested on them at the end of a column. Presently he rose from the bench and slowly retraced his steps in the direction of Police Headquarters. But he did not go in. For a moment he stood uncertain, two thoughtful lines between his eyes. Then he hailed a taxi.

"Bellevue Hospital." A few moments later when the cab cut in toward the curb in front of the hospital he told the driver to wait while he went inside. In less then twenty minutes he was back. He was still puzzled and thoughtful, still hesitant as to his next move, but a certain excited eagerness had replaced his sober dejection.

"15 West Ninety-third," he directed, but a few moments later as they were driving up Second Avenue he leaned forward and gave another address. "8 West Eighty-second Street."

But when he arrived at the Thane house he did not get out. Instead, he merely sat and looked at its innocuous façade. It was as if he sought to find in some turn of masonry or woodwork, the answer to the puzzle that had brought two deep furrows between his eyes. Slowly his gaze traveled over the front of the house up and down the street . . . across . . . and at last in defeat they came to rest on the yawning maw of upturned asphalt, disjoined sewer pipe, and heavy beamed timbering that marked the site of the future subway station. The fierce, bewhiskered Irishman and the three little sweating Italians were still at work. Or at least the Italians were. The Irishman sat in magnificent detachment on an upturned keg and gave orders and stroked his Victorian whiskers.

At last with a shrug of defeat, Spike motioned the driver to go on, and the car backed out of Eighty-second Street and presently drew up in front of 15 West Ninety-third Street. As he shot up in the elevator he reflected on the last time that he had been there and the ill-fated fruit which his investigation had borne. He was met at the door of Tommy's apartment by Tommy himself. Despite the fact that he was clad only in rumpled pajamas, there was a haggard, drawn look to his face as if little sleep had come to him his first night out of jail.

"Where's your man," Spike inquired as he settled himself in a chair, and Tommy stretched out wearily on the davenport.

"I fired him. He wanted his wages and I didn't have a cent, so I gave him about $400 worth of clothes and junk and put him out. The nerve of him, and me out of jail only two hours."

"Absolutely no consideration for the feelings of a gentleman. You did quite right to fire him. But tell me, old thing, how are you feeling this morning after your week's rest cure?"

"Rotten!"

"That's extraordinary. You really should be in the pink. No late hours, and only the simple coarse fare which doctors are so frightfully keen on."

"That's not what I mean. I mean I'm feeling rotten."

"Exactly. You mean that being slightly struck with Nina Fennel, you're all cut up about her father."

Tommy nodded. "God!" he broke out suddenly. "I'd almost have rather they'd plastered it on me, than have it happen like it has."

"A very worthy and chivalrous sentiment, I'm sure. Far more than Nina Fennel deserves."

"What do you mean? 'Far, more than Nina Fennel deserves?'" Tommy bridled.

"I mean, my lad, that Nina Fennel just played up to you because she thought you might be able to help her crab Mrs. Thane's deal."

Tommy flushed hotly. "That's not true. She wouldn't do a thing like that."

"Yes, I think she would. My impression of Nina is that she's a very strong-minded and calculating girl. She simply thought you might be used as a handy tool. Just how, I don't imagine she had all worked out."

"Yes," Tommy admitted disconsolately. "I guess you're right. She's not my class. But anyway I'm sorry for her sake that her father killed Mrs. Thane."

"The sentiment does credit to your kindness of heart but not to your perspicacity."

"That's all right with me. Whatever it is you're talking about."

"I mean, my dear fellow, that Mortimer Fennel did not kill Mrs. Thane."

"What?"

"Really, Tommy, you are difficult. You seem to understand neither my best four-dollar words nor the simple forty-cent variety. I said, Mortimer Fennel did not kill Mrs. Thane."

"But he confessed."

"Of course. He partakes of your chivalrous nature."

"But if he didn't do it, what's the idea?"

Spike settled himself more comfortably and lit a cigarette before he spoke again. "It's too bad, Tommy, that you don't understand human psychology better. Then you'd realize that for the first time in his life, Mortimer Fennel is really being noble. And the usual thing has happened. He has overdone it.

"All his life he has been a weak soul, continually leaning on some one else. Before she fell ill, he probably leaned on his wife. And then he leaned on Cecily Thane. And when he grew too old and tired for the rather arduous attention which she demanded, he leaned on his daughter. Leaned heavily. That, perhaps, is why Nina is such a strong-minded person. She has had to be."

"Well, I don't see anything noble in all that."

"Of course not. That's just the point. Mortimer Fennel is suffering from an attack of accumulated decency. All his life he has been a weakling. And like many weaklings, he has experienced a delayed realization of just what an egg he has been. So he's making a noble gesture of expiation. He's doing it because he has at last realized that he's no good, and that the best thing he can do is to give up his worthless life to save his daughter."

"What do you mean, 'save his daughter'?" Tommy was suddenly alert, defiant.

"I mean save her from the electric chair."

"You don't mean to tell me that you think Nina did it?"

"Her father thinks so and I imagine he is rather better acquainted with her than we are."

"Do you think so?"

"My dear fellow, I never jump to conclusions—especially when there are so many alternatives. Just because I am convinced that Mortimer Fennel did not do it, is no sign that I think his daughter did. Especially in view of the fact that there were a number of other people in the house during the evening."

A sudden, wary silence seemed to descend upon Tommy. He tamped out his cigarette and sat immobile, only his eyes moving, shifting about the room.

"Well," he said finally in a dogged, voice. "Go ahead. Give me the works. I'm used to it by this time."

Spike laughed. "You sound as though you were a criminal and I was a member of the third degree squad of the police department."

"Well, you think I am, don't you?"

"I admit the possibility. But I admit other possibilities, too. After all there were other people in the house that night beside you."

Spike drew from his pocket a small memorandum book and a fountain pen. "Suppose we're very businesslike, and put things down neatly in black and white.

"There was first of all, the maid."

"No. 1—the maid," he wrote.

"And then there was the husband—the outraged husband. For years his wife has been unfaithful to him. But because he was a nice meal ticket she wouldn't divorce him. And in the meantime he had fallen for some one else. Excellent reason for murder.

"And then there is the boy friend—the hired boy friend. His record shows that he's traveling under an assumed name, and that once before he was involved in a similar case but was released for lack of evidence."

"But I'm telling you that I never had a thing to do with that Schlockenhass case. Not anything more than I had to do with this one."

"Tommy, my dear, do try to look at it more objectively. I'm merely putting things down as any right-minded, reasonably suspicious person would regard them.

"And then there is brother, who finds himself in serious financial difficulties. Unless he has five thousand dollars he'll go bust. And his sister refuses to give it to him.

"No. 4 is Nina Fennel. She—"

"But she didn't do it!" Tommy broke in vehemently. "I'm telling you, I—"

"Tommy, spare me, spare me," and Spike held up his hand in a pained gesture. "Don't, I beg of you, tell me that you did it. Things are altogether too complicated already with one gentleman confessing to the dastardly deed to save the beautiful Nina, without another one messing things up."

"Oh, well!" Tommy gave a helpless shrug to his shoulders and settled once more, into gloom.

"So you see, old thing," Spike went on, "there were at least five persons in the house that night that might reasonably have been interested in Cecily Thane's death. Take yourself, for instance."

"All right, take me if you insist on being stubborn. I've told you everything. I've come absolutely clean."

"I know, but there are still a few little puzzles in my mind. I wish you'd repeat, if you don't mind, just exactly what you did after the maid brought in the cocktail shaker and the ice."

"Well, I mixed up some drinks and we had a round apiece. I had this date I was telling you about and I had to hurry off and so I left."

"Just where was Mrs. Thane when you left the room?"

"She was lying back in the chaise longue."

"And you went directly downstairs and rang for the maid to bring your hat and coat and stick?"

"Yes. And then I went out the door and started down toward Central Park West to get a cab. And at the corner of Central Park West and Eighty-second Street I hailed—No, wait a minute. I came out of the house." Tommy went back over his story meticulously, trying earnestly not to omit any detail however slight. "I came out of the house and I stopped a few minutes looking at that subway excavation.

"They were working with a drill you know, one of those things that bores down into rock and makes such a God-awful noise A big fellow with whiskers, and two or three other fellows. And I stopped watching them for a few minutes and pretty soon they quit work and then I went on up to Central Park West and got a cab."

"Have you any idea how long you stood watching the subway workmen?"

"Oh, five—ten minutes. You know, how it is when you're looking into excavations."

"And while you were standing there did you notice any one going into the Thane house?"

"No. I wasn't looking at the house, I was watching the hunkies."

"Very well. Go on."

"Well, I got the cab and drove down to the Club Paradis and met my friends there. I don't remember just what time it was, but I had three or four drinks, and got a little tight, and danced a while, and then I went home and went to bed. And that's the honest-to-God's truth."

For a moment Spike said nothing but sat in silence digesting these facts. "Then why," he said presently in a quiet tone, "why immediately on reading of the murder of Cecily Thane in the *Graphic* the next morning did you dress hastily and go out and dispose of your gun?"

Tommy's hand in the act of lifting his cigarette to his ups paused in mid-air. Then slowly he lowered it.

"What do you mean" he said.

"Really," Spike protested. "It's difficult to speak any plainer. You'd best answer me right off. Why did you go out and dispose of your gun and where did you dispose of it?"

"Oh, all right—all right," Tommy at last gave in with a surly air. "A fellow that's been in a jam like I'd been in with the Schiockenhass woman doesn't like to get caught in another one. And the less guns you have around you at a time like that the healthier it is for you."

"Oh, quite."

"Especially when the one you've got happens to be the same caliber as the one that did the murder."

"I can quite understand your apprehension."

"So I wrapped it up in a piece of newspaper and tied it with a string and threw it in a garbage can."

"But surely you know that a pistol expert could tell whether the shot had been fired from your gun or from another."

"Oh, do you think so?" Tommy laughed derisively. "Sure, the one I'd hire for the defense would get up and swear that it wasn't, and the expert hired by the cops would get up and swear that it was; and who's going to tell which one is lying. No, no, dearie, I know my stuff. By this time I hope the damn thing's at the bottom of Jamaica Bay."

"Undoubtedly is," Spike said and rose to go. "Well, old dear, you've been willing, if not very helpful." But at the door, after he had gathered up his hat and stick and gloves, he paused. "By the way, your undue haste the morning you read of the murder of Mrs. Thane was not in any degree heightened by reading the note which Nina Fennel left for you the night before, was it?"

Tommy's hand paused halfway to his mouth. His eyes met Spike's and slowly, they were invaded by dread and apprehension, which he strove valiantly to conceal.

"Wha—what do you mean?" he said at length striving to be casual.

"Never mind," Spike said airily. "It really doesn't matter," and he walked out closing the door softly behind him on Tommy Spencer's face which had suddenly gone a pale, ghastly green.

# XVIII. Spike Takes an Eye-Opener

OUTSIDE the apartment building Spike paused once again in indecision. The heavy frown between his eyes was even deeper now. At length he summoned a taxi and gave the address of the Thane house. But neither his gestures nor his commands were at all sure. He was still groping. Still playing for an off chance.

At the corner of Eighty-second Street and Columbus Avenue he dismissed the taxi and walked the half block to the Thane house, hesitated once more with his foot upon the lower step, and then turned irresolutely toward the subway excavation. For a few moments he leaned against the board railing which kept chance pedestrians from falling into the hole, and watched the workmen.

For once the bewhiskered Irishman seemed to be taking part in the proceedings. A large and stubborn bowlder clung tenaciously to its rocky moorings, and the men were laboriously prying it loose with a crowbar. All four of them heaved and sweated at the iron rod, and at last with a great cracking sound the under strata gave way and the bowlder shivered loose.

The Irishman straightened up and wiped a dripping brow with a very red but none too clean handkerchief. Having done his share of the manual labor, he retreated once more to his upturned keg and proceeded to supply the mental direction of the enterprise. The steady persistence with which Spike gazed in his direction at last had its telepathic effect. He rose from his keg and picked his way over the rocky floor of the excavation until he was directly in front of the observer.

"Hot work," he said just by way of opening the conversation, and indicated the bowlder.

Spike nodded in sympathy and inquired politely when the new project would be in operation.

"Not for two or three years. Maybe four."

"Frightfully slow, don't you think?"

"Slow? Say, brother, we been working three shifts every twenty-four hours for the last six months. We're burning it up."

"You're always on the day shift?"

"We take turns. Up to a week ago I was on the 4 to 12 shift, but I changed two days ago to the 9 to 4."

Spike's eye lighted up with a sudden gleam of interest. "Then you must have been working here the night—" He nodded significantly in the direction of the Thane house.

"Yes, right here all the time, thinking how nothing exciting ever happens, and not twenty feet away from me a murder." The workman laughed heartily at the quaint humor of life. "Funny," he went on, relishing the idea of discussing the astonishing events of which he might be said to be a part. "Funny, but I always thought that that Spencer fellow did it, 'til I read in the papers this morning that Fennel fellow's confession."

"Really?" Spike opened his cigarette case and shared it with the man. "What made you think that? You know I'm frightfully interested in murders."

"Well," the workman went on puffing contentedly between words. "You know the night that Fennel did the job? Well, along about twelve, little before, I noticed some one hanging over the railing, just like you are now. But there's so many people that come along and gawp at us that I didn't pay much attention. And I wouldn't have noticed this fellow only one of the hunkies here lets fly his pick by mistake, and the head comes off and shoots up, in the direction of this fellow that's leaning over the rail.

"And then I looked up and got a good look at him right in the face. The pick head came just about two inches of hitting him. Of course at the time I didn't think much of it, but the next day when I see it in the paper, and see his picture I remembered.

"And then I thought, godamighty what a nervy bastard! Shooting a lady and then coming out and standing around ten minutes looking at a hunch of hunkies excavating. If I'd just committed a murder, I'd be running as fast as I could in the opposite direction."

"That does seem the natural thing to do," Spike admitted; but his reply was perfunctory as if he were thinking with one corner of his mind and paying little attention to what he was saying aloud. Then he looked sharply at the workman and posed a question.

"You say the night shift ends at twelve?" The workman nodded.

"Promptly? You don't ever linger on for a few minutes?"

The workman laughed. "Say, brother, when you been working eight hours you don't do not even one minute of overtime if you don't have to. You quit prompt the second that little bell rings." And he motioned in the direction of the timbering on the opposite side of the excavation where the small metal circle of an electric bell gleamed. "It goes off automatic all up and down the line, here. Got it hitched up to Western Union."

"Really? How extremely efficient. And so, on the night Mrs. Thane was murdered you went off duty promptly at twelve—after young Tommy Spencer had been standing here watching you for about ten minutes?"

"Yes, we—Say, young fellow," the workman broke off uneasily. "Are you a cop?"

"My dear fellow, I hardly know whether to be insulted in appearance or mentality."

"Eh?"

"I say, it's quite all right." And with a thoughtful pursing of his lips Spike suddenly stepped away from the excavation and bounded up the steps of the Thane house and rang the bell.

"Say, what the hell?" The workman stood open-mouthed, puzzled, as he watched the door close on Spike's back.

Inside Spike found a new and strange servant—a butler, who discreetly took his name, and his hat, and his stick, and informed him when he asked for Mr. Thane that Mr. Thane was at his uptown shop and would not be back until the evening Spike hesitated for a moment and was about to retrieve his hat and stick, when he thought better of it.

"Then may I speak to Emma for a moment?"

The butler nodded but it was plain that he did not approve of the master's visitors consorting with servant girls.

Spike went into the drawing-room and in a few moments Emma appeared. When she saw him her face lighted up with a smile that was slightly coquettish. It was as if the confession of Mortimer Fennel had in some mysterious fashion restored to Emma her old grip on life.

No longer was she wary, frightened.

"Oh, Mr. Tracy," she said, but the sudden business-like greeting of Spike soon made it plain that his errand had not the personal connotations which she had hoped.

"Tell me, Emma," he said; on the night that Mrs. Thane was murdered, did you—" He broke off and appeared to reconsider. When at length he spoke again it was with the disarming airiness which usually characterized his conversation.

"Tell me, Emma, are you acquainted with Miss Nina Fennel?"

"No, sir."

"Had she as far as you know ever been to see Mrs. Thane?"

"No, sir."

"Quite sure about that?"

"Yes, sir. If she ever was here, I never let her in."

"But do you always answer the door?"

"No, sir. Just when we haven't any butler."

"And you have a new butler now. Very charming chap, isn't he?"

Emma blushed slightly and merely nodded. It was plain that she too had felt the new butler's charm.

"When did the old butler leave?"

"Just a few days before Mrs. Thane was mur—About a week ago Thursday."

"Of his own accord?"

"No, sir. He and Mr. Thane had a quarrel and he got fired."

"You don't by any chance know what the quarrel was about"

"No, sir. Hickson, that was the old butler, didn't say. He just said he got a dirty deal."

"And it was Hickson previous to last Thursday who always opened the door and admitted visitors?"

"Yes, sir, except when he had his day off and then I did it."

"So it is quite possible that Miss Nina Fennel could have come to the house previous to last Thursday without your knowing it?"

"Yes, Sir."

Spike rose. "Thank you very much Emma, for your help. You don't mind if I look around a bit before I go?"

"Oh, no, sir," and she gave him a willing carte blanche to search the house.

"Just wait here a few moments for me," he said. "There may be one or two other things I've forgotten."

He bounded up the stairs two at a time until he was at the top of the landing on the second floor. Then quickly he started what was apparently a fruitless search. He went from room to room, sweeping each one with his glance—Thane's sitting room and bedroom, Cecily, Thane's apartment, and even the servants' rooms on the top floor. And when he returned to the first floor, he glanced in at the small bedroom-den at the back of the hall. In the drawing-room Emma was still waiting for him.

"If you don't mind," he said, "I'd like to take a look around downstairs too."

The basement floor laid out on the same plan as the other floors was divided into three rooms—the servants' sitting room in the front, a large butler's pantry that was a room in itself, and the kitchen in the back. Briefly his glance swept the three of them. And slowly a smile of dawning satisfaction seemed to light up his face. Then quickly he grew serious—very serious as he looked at the maid.

"And now, Emma," he said, "I want you to think very carefully. Very carefully, you understand."

Emma nodded and looked apprehensive.

"When Mr. Thane summoned you from your room last Monday night, you went directly down to Mrs. Thane's sitting room?"

"Yes, sir."

"And who was there?"

"Mr. Thane and—and—Mrs. Thane."

"And then what did you do?"

"Why Mr. Thane told me to run quick and get Dr. Partridge."

"And did you?"

"Yes, sir, you know that already."

"I suppose you didn't have time to dress?"

"No, sir, I just had on my kimono and slippers."

"And you went out the front door and next door to Dr Partridge's?"

"Yes, sir."

"Did you leave the door unlocked behind you?"

"Why, I don't know. I guess I must have."

"You didn't take a key with you?"

"No, I was too upset to think about a key."

"So, unless you had a key you couldn't have gotten back in—unless you left the door ajar behind you?"

"Yes, sir, that's right. We always keep the lock on."

"And you did get back in without any trouble?"

"Yes— No, wait a minute, let me see. No, I remember now. The door slammed to and I had to ring, and Mr. Thane came down and let us in."

Again the slow smile of dawning satisfaction lighted up Spike's face.

"Well, thanks very much again, Emma, for your help."

At the door she stopped him. "Mr. Tracy—" She hesitated.

"Yes, Emma?"

"Isn't it true—about Mr. Fennel? I mean, didn't he do it?"

But Spike only smiled and slowly closed the door behind him. Once outside the Thane house he did not hesitate but went directly next door to Dr. Partridge and rang the bell. The doctor fortunately was in, sitting complacently in his shirt sleeves, with his toes comfortably wriggling in his stocking feet. As soon as his housekeeper announced the visitor, he hastily slipped on his shoes and became once more the bustling, slightly pompous person which be usually was when any one was about to observe him.

"Ah, Mr.—ah—"

"Tracy," Spike supplemented.

"Yes, Tracy. Sit down. Sit down. I've just been reading here," and he indicated the morning paper lying on the table, "the splendid work the police department has been doing. Splendid! Splendid!"

Spike smiled indulgently. "The difficulty is, though, Doctor, that it is only half done."

"Only half done? Why I understand that Mr. Fennel has confessed."

"Quite true. But the fact still remains that—" Spike paused as if uncertain quite how to proceed "Listen, Doctor, I need your help."

"Why, I'm sure, Mr. Tracy, that I have been at all times willing to do what I could and I still am, but I hardly see now—"

"I know. But just let me ask a few more questions."

The doctor nodded in assent and Spike went on, picking his words carefully and glancing up, now and again, to see just what effect they had on the little man.

"Tell me, Doctor, are you acquainted with Miss Nina Fennel?"

"No, I am not."

"Well then, do you know her father?"

"No. You must remember that outside of Mr. Thane, I know very little about the Thane household."

"I quite understand that. But did Mr. Thane ever speak to you about Mr. Fennel or his daughter, or any of the people involved in this case?"

The doctor thought carefully. "Well, once or twice he referred to Mr. Fennel but in an entirely casual way—just as he might refer to any other acquaintance. There was, I may say, on these occasions no suggestion of venom or animus in his attitude."

"Ever anything about the daughter?"

"No."

"Quite sure?"

"Quite sure."

"Strange," Spike mused. For a moment he sat thinking. Then he looked at the little doctor with his most engaging manner. "Dr Partridge, I am going to make a very strange request and I wish you would grant it without asking me just why I am making it."

"Well," the doctor temporized, "that depends, of course, on what it is."

"It's quite simple. I'm going to ask you to let me take a look at every room in your house. You may go along with me to make quite sure that I don't make away with the family plate.    All I want is just to look."

"That seems easy enough," the doctor said indulgently. He rather liked this young man, and he was in a mood to humor him "Take as many looks as you like. Where shall we start?"

"Let's be systematic. How about beginning with the basement and going up?"

The doctor assented and led the way to the hall and down the flight of steps leading into the basement. The plan of the Partridge house was almost identical with that of the Thane house. For the second time that day Spike went from floor to floor, giving each room a minute but swift scrutiny—the kitchen and dining room in the basement, the doctor's sitting room and study on the first floor, the bedrooms on the second and third floors, and the servants' rooms on the top floor.

"Well," said the doctor when they had completed the search. "Did you find what you were looking for?"

"No," said Spike and grinned with great satisfaction.

But as they stood once more in the front hail of the first floor, he seemed loath to take his leave. It was as if something was still troubling him. Instead he went once more into the sitting room and sank into a chair with a somewhat weary sigh, and let his head rest on his hand.

"My dear fellow," the doctor, protested, "you're not ill, are you?"

Spike shook his head "No, I'm not ill. But this thing is rather getting on my nerves What I need just now is a good strong shot of liquor.'"

"Ah well, if that's all that's troubling you, just wait here a moment," and he disappeared into the hall and down the stairway to the basement.

As the sound of the doctor's slippers padding down the basement steps came to Spike, the weary droop seemed to melt from his shoulders and again the broad grin of satisfaction spread over his face. Quickly he reached for the doctor's coat and vest that lay over a near-by chair. But when the doctor returned not more than a minute later, he had resumed his crumpled, done-in attitude. With a grateful sigh, he sipped a glass of brandy and seemed visibly to brighten.

"Well, Doctor," he said at last, "thanks for your forbearance with the whims of youth. And thanks for the eye-opener. It certainly was."

And with a debonair twirl of his walking stick, Spike shut the door behind him and ran quickly down the steps of the house. There was no hesitation now in his movements. He hurried to the corner of Eighty-second Street and Columbus Avenue and hailed a taxi.

"Three Forty-six Hudson Street," he said. But on second thought he changed his mind. "No, just take me down around Times Square some place."

It was not until the early hours of Monday morning that he again hailed a cab and gave the Hudson Street address. The city room of the *New York Graphic* between the hours of twelve and four is a dreary place peopled only by grumbling charwomen struggling futilely with overflowing waste baskets, two or three tousled reporters pecking sleepily at typewriters, and a young man of serious mein sitting at the big horseshoe desk reading copy.

As Spike stood in the doorway surveying the room he had a sudden feeling of disappointment. For years when in New York he had been an assiduous reader of the highly colored tabloid, with its "thrill slayers," "torch murders," "gang wars," "love feuds" and assorted journalistic atrocities.

It hardly seemed possible that this highly seasoned fare could emanate from so commonplace a sanctum. *The Graphic* office he had always pictured as a ridiculous, mad, frenzied bedlam of rushing reporters; and instead he found it only a barn-like and very littered room, with the few sleepy inhabitants smoking and confiding to each other their secret dreams and longings.

Stifling his disappointment, he crossed to the serious young man at the copy desk and drew up a chair. The serious young man paused in the midst of the confessions of a bootlegger's mistress and looked up inquiringly.

"The name is Tracy," said Spike and tipped back his chair and settled his feet comfortably on the desk as he proffered a cigarette.

"Thanks," said the young man, "and what of it?"

"Oh, nothing. Nice name though, don't you think?"

"Yeah, but what the hell's that to me?"

"My dear fellow," Spike protested, "you should read the newspapers, really you should."

"Read the newspapers? Say, boy, I read the newspapers before they are newspapers," and he pointed impatiently to a pile of copy at his elbow that was waiting to be edited.

"Such is fame," and Spike sighed philosophically. "What I mean to say is, that it will be a terrible blow to my poor brother to realize how soon the world forgets."

"Say, lessen, what do you want, and spill it quick because I haven't got any time to fool."

"Very well." Spike immediately became businesslike and ceased his bantering. "I'm Spike Tracy, the brother of Richard Montgomery Tracy, the district attorney and I've been—ah—listening in on this Thane murder case."

The whole demeanor of the serious young man underwent a quick change. He pushed the pile of waiting copy aside and the impatient frown was supplanted by a look of keen curiosity, not unmixed with admiration.

"So you're the guy that's been throwing the monkey wrench into the works," he said.

"Well, of course, to the outsider it may seem that way. Personally, I've just been trying to be helpful."

"Just a regular little Pollyanna." The young man smiled for the first time "Of course," he explained quickly, "we don't dare tell the world that the Thane murder case was really brought to a successful conclusion by you. There are going to be other murders, and we wouldn't exactly like to get in bad with the Headquarters crowd by intimating that it took an amateur to show them up; but all the boys that are covering the case know."

"Stop—Stop—You'll have me chewing my thumb and looking flushed and coy."

"But really, the way you've solved this case is remarkable."

"But really, the case isn't solved."

"What do you mean?"

"I mean that it isn't solved."

"But Fennel's confessed—"

"My dear fellow," Spike looked at him indulgently, "you're almost as naïve as my brother and Inspector Herschman. You really should understand that in love and murder men always confess to scores of things that aren't true."

"But how do you know?"

"That's a long story. Too long to go into now."

"But if he didn't what's the idea of confessing?"

"Mr. Fennel has a very beautiful and hot-tempered daughter," Spike-said quietly.

"You mean—he's shielding her?"

"I don't mean anything just at present. I'm just groping around with a hazy idea in my mind about certain things. That's why I've come to you."

"Yeah?" There was a breathless note in his voice.

"Were you here in this office at four o'clock last Monday morning?"

"Yes."

"And, what happened just about that time?"

"Matthews called up and gave us the tip on the story. Charlie Matthews, the man that covers the Eighty-sixth Street Station."

"Just what did he say?"

"He was in an awful hurry. He just said to send some one up to 8 West Eighty-second Street immediately. A woman had been murdered."

"Anything else?"

"No. He hung up right away. He explained his hurry afterwards. He said that the cops weren't giving it out at the station and he just happened to overhear it. He knew that if he went himself they'd probably get sore and hold out stuff on him so he had me send up some one else."

"Matthews told you all this?"

"Yes."

"When?"

"The next night when I came on."

"Does Matthews ordinarily work in the daytime or the nighttime?"

"Daytime But he hangs around the station quite a bit at night too— just playing poker with some of the other fellows down there in the pressroom."

Spike frowned. It was apparent that this turn of events did not fit in with some slowly forming theory in his mind. He picked up a pencil from the desk and tapped it with an, irritated gesture against his teeth and finally brought his chair down with a bang.

"Are you sure it was Matthews you heard over the phone?"

"Of course it was. Why he got his $100 bonus the next day for it."

"What do you mean?"

"Well, every fellow that turns in a tip on what proves to be a big story gets a bonus if we beat the town on it."

"Oh, I see" Spike's frown melted into a smile. "Matthews doesn't happen by any chance to be around tonight does he?"

"His day off."

Spike rose slowly and stamped out his cigarette on the floor. "Thanks awfully. You've been very helpful."

"But say, lissen," the young man protested, "what's the new dope?"

"Nothing—yet. But if you see Mr. Matthews give him this card of mine and tell him if he wants to make another $100 to call around at my place at eight o'clock tomorrow morning."

## XIX. A TEA PARTY AT POLICE HEADQUARTERS

IT was Monday morning, almost a week after the murder of Cecily Thane. The district attorney of Kings County settled himself comfortably at his desk and rang for his secretary. He looked happier than he had for more than a week. The peculiar combination of depression and impatient irritability which had worn him down during the preceding week, seemed to have vanished completely.

In his buttonhole was a scarlet spring flower, and on his face an expression of happy anticipation like one who having been disagreeably interrupted in a pleasing task, is suddenly released to pursue once more his pleasant way.

"The folder with the bank examiner's reports, Lovelace," he said, and took a deep breath of satisfaction as it was laid before him on the desk. Soon he was mulling happily through columns of figures and hefty tomes on financial jurisprudence. So engrossed was he in fact that he paid no attention to the leisurely entrance of his younger brother.

Spike as usual dropped into the nearest easy-chair and lit a cigarette. For a few moments he said nothing, but let his eyes rest in amused silence on his brother. At last by a slight movement he betrayed his presence, and Tracy looked up.

"Oh, hello," he said absently and reached for the latest report on the Fidelity Finance and Trust Corporation.

"Oh, hello," Spike responded lazily. "Still working on the Thane case?"

"The Thane case?" It was as if he were trying to search through his memory for a bit of ancient history. "No, thank Fortune, that's settled. Lovelace, please bring me Britt's Abstract of Laws Governing Bank Examiners in Great Britain."

For a few moments more he worked in silence, a pleased, zestful smile hovering about his lips. Spike sat and smoked in a leisurely fashion, his face now thoughtful, now over with a smile of satisfaction, now drawn into a puzzled frown. At last as if he had come to some conclusion, he broke his silence.

"I say, Richard, do you feel in an awfully benign, indulgent mood?"

"Eh—huh?" Only the surface of the district attorney's absorption was scratched and he went serenely ahead with his, work almost as if no one had spoken.

"I say, do you feel like humoring the whims of an erring but well-meaning brother?"

Tracy put down his pencil and looked over his glasses. "If it's money you want you can't have it. You've way overspent your allowance and you'll have to suffer."

"Richard, you have an absolutely putrid mind. You're always thinking that I'm thinking of either money or women."

"And I'm usually right."

"Usually, but in this instance you're all wet. I'm thinking of neither. I'm thinking of murder."

"Still thinking, I see, that you know more about the Thane murder than we do."

"I'm not thinking I know more about it. I do."

"Do you know, Philip Tracy, your conceit is appalling?"

"I haven't a doubt of it, brother. It is equaled only by my charm and perspicacity."

"Well, I'm very sorry, but I haven't the time to argue the matter with you this morning. I'm busy."

"Not half as busy as you're going to be."

"Now listen here, Philip, please go away and don't bother me. I've a great many things to do to get this report in shape for the next meeting of the Bar Association and I can't—"

"Can it, dearie, can it." And Spike reached forth a lazy hand and pressed the buzzer at the corner of the desk.

"Lovelace," he said, when the secretary, appeared, "would you ask Inspector Herschman to be so kind as to step this way?"

When the secretary had left, the district attorney laid down his pencil with an exasperated frown. "Well, go ahead. What crazy idea have you thought up now?"

"Crazy is right. It's so utterly fantastic that I can hardly believe it myself."

In a few minutes Herschman strode into the room. Like the district attorney he too seemed to have just emerged triumphantly from a trying experience,, and to have been restored once more to the favor of the gods. He was smiling broadly —even when his glance encountered Spike.

"My brother here," said Tracy with the deprecating gesture which he used when referring to Spike, "insists that he has something to add to the Thane murder case."

Herschman grinned. "With Fennel's signed confession in our hands, I don't think there's much to add."

But Spike was not at all daunted by the unfriendly reception. He offered Herschman a cigarette, held a light for him and even smiled benignly while doing it.

"Well, seeing as how you two are all frothing at the mouth with impatience and enthusiasm. I'll come right down to the point. I'm going out for a bit and while I'm gone, I want you to get Nina Fennel, Elton Thane, Emma, Tommy Spencer, Dr. Partridge and George Griffis down here in this office.      Get them all here and hold 'em until I get back from where I'm going."

"Come now, Philip, you're being ridiculous."

"Perhaps," Spike admitted. "And then again I may be being tremendously clever.    Just at present I don't know myself."

"What's the idea?"

"The idea, Inspector, is so wild, crazy that I haven't the heart to tell even you until. I'm a bit more sure. All I want to know is will you or won't you?"

"Certainly not," Tracy said emphatically.

"Oh, very well, then." Spike shrugged his shoulders and reached for his stick and hat. "It will be frightfully embarrassing for you two, though, when I write my confessions as an amateur detective for the *Graphic* and call attention to the fact that you are about to send the wrong person to the electric chair."

"Wrong person? What do you mean?"

"I mean, old thing, that Mortimer Fennel did not kill Cecily Thane. Well, au revoir. I'll send you marked copies of the paper."

But he got no further than the door.

"Stop!" The district attorney's voice had an uneasy edge to it. "Where are you going?"

"I think I'll go up to Columbia and register for a course in journalism to prepare me for my career as a writer."

"Come back and sit down."

For a moment Spike hesitated. Then with a leisurely air he re-crossed the room and sank into the chair he had just vacated.

"Inspector Herschman," Tracy pointed out, "who was tracking criminals when you were still crying for your bottle, has gone very thoroughly into Mortimer Fennel's confession. and has assured me that we will not have the slightest difficulty getting a conviction for first degree murder on it."

"Oh, quite. I haven't a doubt of it. But I was under the impression—please correct me if I am wrong—that the highest standards of the legal profession demanded justice rather than convictions."

With an exasperated sigh of surrender the district attorney pushed aside the papers on which he had been working. "All right, go ahead. What have you been doing now?" His tone was very much that of a mother who strongly suspects that Willie has broken a window or made a forbidden raid on the pantry. "What makes you say that Mortimer Fennel did not kill Cecily Thane?"

"Well, Sunday morning I went over to the prison ward of the hospital and talked to him. No, perhaps that isn't entirely correct. He's too weak for sustained conversation. I asked him just one question. The answer he gave me convinced me that as far as murdering goes he's still a bum commercial artist."

"And what was the question?"

"I asked him where Cecily Thane was standing when he shot her and he said in front of the safe. If you're not too weary to rack your brains, you'll remember that a very revealing little bullet hole was found in the chaise longue."

"He was delirious," Herschman put in sharply.

"No, he wasn't delirious. His brain was perfectly clear and his temperature was normal. I asked the nurse."

The inspector and the district attorney eyed each other uneasily in silence and Spike watched a hurdy-gurdy man who was grinding away on the sidewalk below.

"Well, gentlemen," he said finally, "will you or won't you?"

"Will we or won't we what?"

"Ask Nina Fennel, Elton Thane, Emma, Tommy Spencer—write 'em down so you won't forget 'em—Dr. Partridge and George Griffis to drop in this afternoon and have a dish o' tea with you, and then hold 'em here until I get back? My own contribution to the gathering will be Mr. Charlie Matthews of the *Evening Graphic*, one of the greatest little opportunists I know."

Again the district attorney and the inspector exchanged glances. "Oh, all right, all right," Tracy finally gave in in an exasperated voice. With an irritated gesture he pressed the buzzer for his secretary and indicated the papers in front of him. "Lovelace," be snapped, "gather these up and put them back in my working file."

When Spike walked into the district attorney's office two hours later his brother and Inspector Herschman were making a valiant but unsuccessful attempt to conceal from their six guests the feeling that something was up. One glance at the satisfied air with which Spike stood in the doorway and surveyed the room convinced the uncomfortable hosts that whatever had been his errand, it had been successful.

Despite all elaborate efforts to be casual, there was a certain excitement in the air. George Griffis and Elton Thane, disregarding the differences which had come between them in the past, were sitting close together as if for mutual protection, and occasionally they exchanged a low-voiced remark.

Dr. Partridge was like a nervous, curious little bird, mystified but rather enjoying the situation. Charlie Matthews, a young fellow of engaging appearance and exceedingly rumpled clothes, in the best reportorial traditions, was alert and waiting for whatever might break. And Emma, the maid, sat in one corner obviously frightened.

Nina Fennel was by herself, a little apart from the others, scarcely ever looking at them, her hands listless in her lap. Only her eyes which rested with tragic intensity on the Tombs across the way, gave a hint of what was going on in her mind. And directly across the room from her was Tommy Spencer, looking at her with an expression in which apprehension was mingled with an almost touching wistfulness.

Of the ten people in the room, Spike alone seemed untouched by the general atmosphere of tense expectancy. With his usual airy greeting he addressed them collectively and proceeded in a leisurely manner to lay aside his hat and stick, and draw out his cigarette case. But for once he did not slouch down into the nearest easy-chair. Instead he stood before them slightly in the manner of a guest at a house party about to do card tricks.

"Frightfully good of you all to come down," he assured them in a tone which was designed to put them at their ease but which failed dismally of its purpose. "I hope I haven't inconvenienced you any."

But as no one either protested or affirmed he went ahead. "The fact is that we've discovered who murdered Cecily Thane, and as you all are more or less interested—or perhaps I should say involved, I thought you might be curious to hear about it."

Out of the corner of his eye, he cast a glance at the district attorney and the inspector sitting to the side of the group, and finding them both slightly pop-eyed, he smiled.

"My brother and Inspector Herschman here, have not been satisfied with the confession of Mr. Mortimer Fennel. They have felt all along that Mr. Fennel in assuming the guilt was acting from a motive which although noble was slightly misguided. It is only natural, of course, that a father should strive to protect a daughter."

He paused. Nina Fennel's eyes suddenly tore themselves away from the Tombs. It was difficult to tell whether the glance she shot at the young man before her was one of frantic question or pure terror. Quickly she pressed the back of her hand across her mouth as if to stifle a word—a cry. But Spike only smiled benignly in her direction much in the manner of a Sunday-school superintendent addressing the primary class, and went on.

"Mr. George Griffis' possession of at least one of the pieces of jewelry missing from the safe has seemed an incontrovertible bit of evidence in refutation of Mr. Fennel's confession."

Again he paused and the eyes of every one in the room focused on Griffis He sat stiff, immobile, his glance shifting nervously from the toes of his shoes to a far corner of the room, to the side, back to his shoes, but never once meeting the gaze of any of the other nine people.

"The case, you see," Spike went on, "has many mystifying aspects. Perhaps not the least of these is Mr. Tommy Spencer. Gentlemen—and ladies—" here he bowed to Nina Fennel and Emma, "I offer as exhibit A in this puzzling situation Tommy's frank and open face."

But at the moment Tommy's face failed dismally to fit the description. Like Griffis his glance was shifting from one side to the other and his fingers toyed nervously with the watch chain across the front of his vest.

"Not, I will admit, a very convincing performance," Spike remarked, "but nevertheless I offer him in evidence. Evidence of the amazing difficulties which gentlemen of his sort are likely to encounter in the peculiar type of business by which they earn their living.

"Gentlemen, and ladies, let me introduce—the goat. Tommy has been so unfortunate as to embrace a profession which seems to be characterized by a high and spectacular mortality rate among the clientele. You all remember the Schlockenhass case. Tommy, as you are doubtless aware, was the gentleman who was known to have been the last person to see Greta Schlockenbass alive. And he is also the last person who is known to have seen Cecily Thane alive. The coincidence is rather striking, don't you think?"

Spike looked around with a bright inquiring glance.

Then suddenly and for the first time that afternoon his demeanor underwent a quick change. No longer was he the parlor entertainer. His face became set into grave lines and his voice lost its note of levity. He stood now perfectly still, his arms folded in front of him.

"The person who killed Cecily Thane deliberately framed the crime on Tommy Spencer. Knowing Tommy's previous connection with the Schlockenhass case, knowing his ill-repute with the police, the guilty person laid careful plans to throw the blame upon him. The plan as executed was one of clock-like precision, timed to the minute.

"In less than five minutes after Tommy Spencer left the Thane house last Monday night, the guilty person shot Cecily Thane through the heart as she lay on the chaise longue, dragged her body across the floor, placed it in front of the safe, picked up the bullet which had gone through the back of the chaise longue and drove it into the wall of the bedroom, giving the impression that she was shot as she stood in front of the wall safe. To complete further the illusion of robbery the safe was rifled."

Spike paused and there was a deathly tense silence in the room. Not a soul moved—breathed.

"The murderer knew that Tommy Spencer would be suspected immediately. The murderer believed that as soon as Tommy learned of the murder of Cecily Thane he would realize his own peril and disappear.

"It was necessary, therefore, that Tommy should learn the news as soon as possible. So the guilty person took the one sure way to do it. The murderer telephoned the *New York Evening Graphic* the story. And then to make sure that Tommy would have plenty of time to get away in, the murderer removed from Cecily Thane's telephone directory the S page containing his number, so that, the police would have to spend at least five or six hours locating his apartment."

Spike paused again and his eyes swept his audience. Nina Fennel still sat with the back of her hand pressed convulsively against her trembling lips. George Griffis gnawed at his knuckles. Elton Thane nervously wiped his mouth with his handkerchief.

All of them were staring straight at Spike now as if hypnotized by his unfolding of the murder plot. Then slowly the eyes of one of the nine people before him wavered, glazed, grew wide and agonized and a gasping, tortured voice spoke.

"He's— He's right—I—I killed her—I did—just what he said—I—"

With a sudden rasping moan, Elton Thane pitched forward, face down on to the floor. His body jerked convulsively and then was still.

For a moment no one moved. They stood, transfixed by the sight before them. Dr. Partridge was the first to recover himself. He sprang forward, turned the prostrate man upon his back. Quickly his hand sought the pulse. He listened. Then he laid the hand down.

"Dead!?"

The ghastly quiet of the room was broken only by the hysterical weeping of Nina Fennel. "Tommy—my father—didn't—Tommy!"

# XX. Spike Borrows $5,000

SPIKE woke from a deep, dreamless, twelve-hour sleep. Slowly, lazily he stretched and then lay still, enjoying to the full that first delicious drowsiness that immediately follows sleep. Presently he reached out a hand to the bedside table and fumbled in a small leather box for a cigarette, lit it and lay back against the pillows, puffing contentedly.

"Your brother and another gentleman to see you sir." It was Meeks, the servant, who stood in the half-opened doorway leading to the sitting room. "They've been here twice before this morning, but I told them you left word you were not to be disturbed."

Spike smiled. "The Mountain comes to Mahomet. The combined legal and police minds of New York County sit patiently on my doorstep."

"Yes, sir."

"Well, show them in."

As Montgomery Tracy and Inspector Herschman entered the room there was in their attitude toward the man in the bed a suggestion almost of awe and respect. The district attorney attempted to smile, and the inspector fumbled with his hat. Spike apparently was the only one completely at his ease and he was very much so.

"Meeks, a couple of drinks for the gentlemen, and one for me. And have one yourself, Meeks. I feel particularly set up this morning."

Tracy and Herschman seated themselves.

"Well?" said the district attorney, but this time there was none of that peremptory irritation which usually characterized the word when he addressed it to his brother. It was rather as if he were discreetly suggesting that if it were not too much trouble, would Spike mind beginning.

"Yeah," supplemented Herschman, "go ahead. Spill it."

"But first, Inspector," said Spike, "tell me if I was right."

"Oh, you were right, all right. Everything checks exactly."

"And Thane?"

"Strychnine sulphate tablets. We found a box of them in his pocket. Partridge says be must have taken about three grains, it acted so quick."

"Any trace of the jewels?"

"Up in Thane's room, hid in some old books that he had taken the stuffing out of."

"I didn't imagine that a man of Thane's close nature could bear to chuck $150,000 worth of Jewelry into the river. He'd probably planned to cut up the larger and more distinctive stones later on and use them in his business. How about the gun?"

"Not a sign of it."

"All guns missing—Tommy's, Nina Fennel's, Elton Thane's. Really, you know, if I'm ever suspected of murder I shan't make the mistake of egging on the police by chucking mine away. And how is Miss Fennel?"

"Oh, she's all right. She's been over to the hospital most of the time with her father. They've moved him into a private ward and he's coming along O.K. But say, lissen, young fel— Mr. Tracy—"

"Inspector, spare me. After all we've been through together, just make it Spike."

"Well, what I mean is, we want to know all the dope. You—you pulled a pretty neat job—and—" Herschman fumbled He was not used to his new role and his lines were halting. "I got to hand it to you. And if I've said anything in the past that—well—"

"Quite," said Spike magnanimously. "I understand perfectly, Inspector. How were you to know that Richard's impression of me was false. A most natural error, which only adds to your human, lovable qualities."

The inspector looked slightly bewildered but relieved. He was not used to being called 'lovable" but he was glad to be spared putting his apology into words.

Meeks entered with three frost-clouded glasses. Spike lifted his toward his two guests. "Yours for bigger and better murders!"

He and the inspector each took a big gulp, but the district attorney only sipped his. The toast was apparently not to his liking.

"Now Philip," he said, "we are most curious to know how you arrived at your conclusion that it was Elton Thane who murdered Cecily Thane. I may say that I join with Inspector Herschman in a sincere—ah—regret that I have at times been not wholly confident of your abilities. You have, I may point rendered me a great service."

From his inside pocket he drew forth a newspaper clipping with a morning date line on it. It was from the same paper which less than a fortnight before had been calling the district attorney to task for his failure as a criminal investigator. The editorial read:

"It is apparent that District Attorney Tracy and his aides in the police department have turned over a new leaf. The dispatch with which they have handled the Thane murder case will do much toward re-establishing the confidence of the people of New York in their administration. Confronted with a difficult criminal tangle of many muddled and misleading aspects, the issue clouded by a false confession, they brought the guilty man to justice and saved an Innocent man from the electric chair. They are to be congratulated."

Spike handed the clipping back to his brother and smiled.

"And I may say," the district attorney began, "that I am grateful to you, that is—your modesty—ah—I feel most uncomfortable at receiving credit which by right—ah—"

"Quite!" Spike interrupted. "Credit for having made a few pertinent suggestions as to the murderer of Cecily Thane will be of no use whatever to me in my subsequent career of debauchery and light living. But you can use it quite neatly and you're welcome to it." He waved his hand in magnanimous dismissal of the subject.

"Well, go on," Herschman urged with impatient curiosity. "Shoot the works. What tipped you off to the fact that Thane, himself, was the guy."

"Well, Inspector, if you would be a more assiduous reader of detective stories you would realize that it is always the person with the iron-clad alibi who is the guilty one—the person who apparently couldn't possibly have been there to do the dirty work. And in this case that person was Thane."

"Tommy, Nina Fennel, Mortimer Fennel, George Griffis, all of them quite possibly could have been there. Tommy easily enough Nina Fennel and Mortimer Fennel just as easy. Emma you remember saw neither of them leave. They said they left at nine and nine-thirty, but did they? One or the other or both of them might easily have hidden in the house, waited until Cecily Thane returned and Tommy left."

"Well, I never thought of the girl and her father working together," Herschman said. "I thought there was something between her and Spencer."

"I rather imagine that there was something between them. Nina Fennel probably planned months in advance to use Tommy Spencer in some way to break Mrs. Thane's hold on her father. Just how, I don't believe she knew. Actual murder I'm sure she never contemplated. And then on that Monday afternoon when Cecily Thane finally made good her threat and sent a letter to Mrs. Fennel she and her father both went all blah.

"The father particularly. As he explained in his 'confession' he's been pretty much of a clinging vine to that Amazonian daughter of his. They went to the Thane house to appeal directly to Mrs. Thane. Then both of them lost their heads and wandered about aimlessly.

"Finally Nina went down to Spencer's apartment and wrote what turned out later to be a most incriminating note. But how was she to know that the police would interpret the 'terrible thing' that she mentioned to mean the murder of Mrs. Thane. At any rate, that was the way Tommy Spencer interpreted it. He has thought all along that she did it, and he's cringed every time her name was mentioned in connection with the case. What she really meant, of course, was the letter sent to her mother."

"But since she was innocent and knew she was, why in hell throw away that gun the next day?" Herschman persisted.

"Certainly she knew she was innocent, but all she knew about her father was that he did not come home the previous night until after one o'clock. And she probably jumped to the conclusion that in his desperation he did it."

"But why didn't he tell her he didn't?"

"Because, my dear fellow, he was thinking just the same thing about her. And when two people begin thinking things like that about each other, they usually end up by making damn fools of themselves.

"She threw the gun away because she was afraid the police would find it and suspect her father. And he confessed because he thought she had done it, and he was having a delayed attack of nobility. Each one was trying to shield the other."

"What about George Griffis. How did he get one of the missing pieces of jewelry?"

"He probably just lifted it when he went to see his sister Monday afternoon—"

"Then why did Thane include it in the list of things he gave me?"

"If you'll think back you'll realize that up to the time that he gave you that list he didn't have  much time to take stock. He probably stuffed the jewels into their hiding place immediately after he shot his wife. Then he hurried directly to Dr. Partridge's. He had no time to look the stuff over when he came back to the house to 'discover' his wife's dead body. Five minutes later Partridge arrived and was with him constantly until we saw him the next morning.

"In all that time he had really no opportunity that he dared risk to take an invoice. It was not until after he had given you the description that he was alone long enough to look over the swag and realize his mistake. As the piece which Griffis took was one of the most spectacular and distinctive, he simply jumped to the conclusion that of course it was in the lot that he had removed from the safe.

"Griffis, for his part, was scared, of course, of grand larceny. What probably happened was—when he found out that he wasn't going to get any money out of his sister, he simply waited for a moment when her back was turned, and then picked up the nearest bit of pawnable stuff that happened to be handy. And, by the way, did the forged check come to light anywhere?"

"Yes," Herschman answered, "we located the bank where she kept a private lock box under another name. That check was the only damn thing in it."

"Probably the most lucrative investment she had," Spike pointed out.

"But you're still not telling us," the inspector persisted "how Thane could have been in two places at once. The maid swore that it was just twelve o'clock when Spencer left and Partridge swore that it was ten minutes of twelve when he arrived at his house where he stayed until four. So how could he have been in his own house at twelve and shot his wife?"

"If you'll just lend me your pencil and fetch me a piece of paper from that writing desk I'll draw a picture of it."

But the picture which he drew was not a floor plan of the Thane and Partridge houses. It was merely a series of crossing lines filled in with figures, with a few notes written at the side. When he had finished it he handed it to the two men.

"I think from the very start I suspected Thane, but it was just one of those groundless sort of feelings which all the evidence seemed to refute. How could he have been in his own house at twelve o'clock or shortly after and shot his wife when all the time he was in another place?

"And it was just one of those little inconsequential things that we didn't pay much attention to at the time that kept aggravating my belief in the apparently impossible. You'll remember that the fingerprint pictures showed that the knob of the wall safe had been wiped clean.

"Thane was firm in his statement that only he and his wife knew the combination. If she opened the safe, as the circumstances seemed to indicate, why did the murderer take the trouble to wipe her fingerprints off the knob? Especially in view of the fact that the whole thing was staged to give the impression that she had opened the safe and had been shot the second afterward.

"The only other person who knew the combination was Thane. And if he opened it, naturally, he wouldn't want to be leaving his print around. The logical thing for him to do would be to wipe it off. Am I right?"

Herschman nodded in agreement. "Yeah, that's sense."

"After I talked to Miss Audrey Keating that certain feeling increased. Here was a perfectly sound motive for Thane. He wanted to marry another woman. And his wife wouldn't divorce him. And when he tried to force her into it, and God knows he had enough evidence with Mortimer Fennel at hand, she probably pulled that forged check on him and dared him to go ahead and start action. Her death was for him the only solution.

"But then I didn't have another thing to go on—just a hunch, and a theory, and one insignificant piece of evidence. Until—" Spike paused and turned a reproving gaze upon his brother.

"I think, Richard," he went on, "that my very first attempt to be helpful in this case was dismissed by you as facetious. When I suggested the very first morning as we mounted the steps of the Thane house, that we stop and have a little chat with the workmen in the excavation in front, you reminded me that there was a time and a place for levity.

"As a matter of fact it was one of those workmen that set me on the right track. You remember that Emma testified that she heard no sound of a shot after she let Tommy Spencer out of the door and added something of this sort—'but heaven knows that's not to be wondered at with all that racket going on outside.'

"However, my little chat with the foreman who was working there the eventful Monday night revealed the fact that the racket stopped that night promptly at twelve, when the automatic shift bell rang and the shifts changed.

"So it's reasonable to believe, isn't it, that if the shot had been fired after twelve when there was no noise outside to drown it out, Emma would have heard it."

He paused and looked inquiringly at his audience.

"Yeah, that's right," Herschman said. "Even if the shooting was done with the door to the sitting room closed, there's a pretty, clean sweep of sound from the second floor to the basement."

"Well then," Spike went on, "I decided that the shot must have been fired before twelve o'clock."

"While Spencer was still there?"

"No, after he left."

"But he didn't leave until twelve. You remember how hard the maid stuck to that point. She swore that it was almost exactly twelve by her clock in the basement when she let him out."

"And so it was—by her clock. But the right time was really ten minutes of twelve."

"I don't get you."

"It's really quite easy when you look at the diagram. But wait! Let me explain what I did after I talked to the workman. It was really he that gave me the idea that perhaps the time played a bigger part in this than we had suspected.

"You will recall that almost every one who came in contact with Elton Thane that night for some reason or other remembered the exact time. The clerk in the drug store on the corner of Columbus Avenue and Seventy-sixth Street. Naturally enough, to be sure. It was his last half hour and of course he was clock watching.

"But to make doubly sure that the clerk would remember him, Thane bought five boxes of very expensive cigars. Five boxes. He would have bought six if the store had had them. And both Tommy Spencer and Dr. Partridge hinted at the fact that Thane was notoriously tight with money. One box would have been sufficient as a gift. But five fixed him more clearly in the clerk's mind.

"And because Thane was late to his appointment with Partridge, the good doctor naturally drew out his watch and looked at the time and upbraided him—and remembered therefore that it was ten minutes to twelve, exactly, when Thane arrived."

"Yeah, and where does that leave you?" Herschman protested.

"It would leave us still high and dry, had I not lowered myself to lawful larceny." Spike paused and grinned.

"What do you mean?"

"Well, if I tell you, will you promise that nothing I say will be used against me?"

"Sure, go ahead."

"Well, to get back to my break with the workmen. When I left off talking to them, I went into the Thane house and had another chat with Emma. I was rather afraid she would suspect what I had on my mind, so I threw in a lot of misleading questions about Thane's quarrel with the butler and whether she had ever seen Nina Fennel and gave the impression that I was hot on the young lady's trail. My real object was to search the Thane house thoroughly for just one thing—clocks."

"Yeah, clocks. What's the idea?" Herschman was sitting on the edge of his chair now tense with excitement.

"The idea is that I found only one clock in the entire house. The alarm clock which the servants keep down in the servants' sitting room and carry up to the top floor with them at night. Not another clock in the whole place.

"At Dr. Partridge's I went through the same rigmarole and found several. One on the basement floor in the kitchen. One in the housekeeper's room on the third floor. None in the rooms in which he lives on the first and second floors.

"The doctor, I should point out, was, most fortunately for me, in his shirt sleeves when I arrived. He had laid his vest and coat across a chair in the sitting room—even as he did the night that Cecily Thane was murdered. So I summoned up all the dramatic talent I could, faked a great weariness and asked little Peregrine for a drink. He went down to the basement to get the decanter of wine—the very same decanter that he had fetched up the night Elton Thane played chess with him. And while he was gone I swiped his watch."

Spike paused and grinned "Remember," he reminded them, "that I have your word that you'll not send me up the river."

"But what was the idea" Herschman was still puzzled.

"The idea was that by this time I had a wild crazy notion in my head and I wanted to verify it. I'll admit I was slightly, dramatic—

melodramatic, if you will. I took a chance on being right. I went down to Headquarters and had you two assemble the gang. And while you were rounding them up I went up to Elton Thane's branch store on Broadway at Eighty-seventh Street and waited around a bit until I was sure that he wasn't in the place—that he was on his way down to meet you two.

"Then I went in and pulled out Partridge's watch, pretended that it was my own and raised hell because it hadn't been keeping good time. Just as I suspected, the Thane establishment like every well-run jewelry place keeps a careful record of each watch that is brought in for regulation or repair. A sort of case history. I had them look up my watch and found that the truth was even as I had suspected."

Spike paused, tantalizing

"Yeah?" Herschman could hardly contain his curiosity. "Go ahead. What did the jewelry shop records show?"

"They showed that on May 15, the day Cecily Thane was murdered, Dr. Partridge's watch was taken from the shop by Elton Thane himself, and delivered to Dr. Partridge."

"And on the way home, Thane set it back," Herschman broke in.

"Exactly."

"Well now, who would have thought of that?"

"Elton Thane, I imagine, had thought about every detail for quite a long time," Spike went on. "May 15 was probably the culmination of months of planning. And then suddenly everything resolved itself into his hands. Dr. Partridge turned his watch in to be fixed and it was an easy enough matter for Thane to hold it until a night when he knew his wife was to be out with Spencer. And then fortune played right into his hands, gave him an advantage he had scarcely hoped for. Spencer reported that he would be home early that night.

"From then on things were easy. You remember that Emma said that Thane sent her out about eight o'clock to post a letter. While she was gone he probably turned her clock downstairs forward ten minutes. Partridge's was already turned back ten minutes. That means that he had twenty minutes' leeway. The rest is easy if you just look at the diagram."

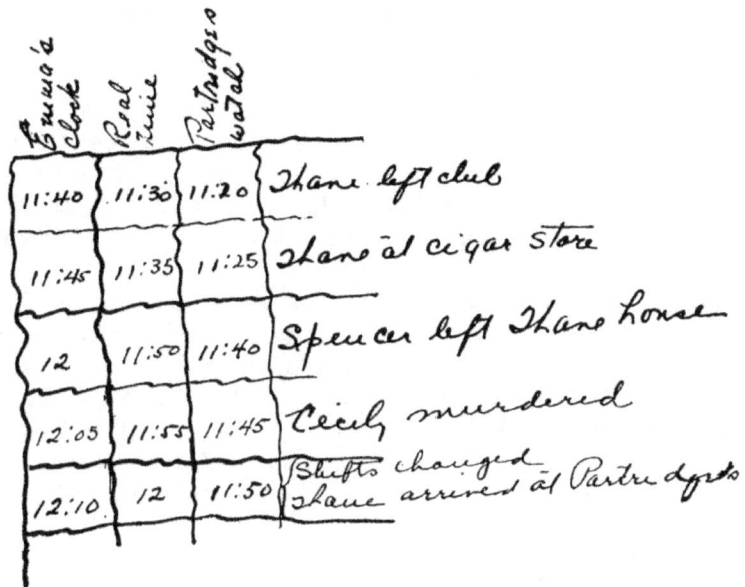

The three men bent their heads over the hasty pencil chart that Spike had just made and he explained as he went along.

"When Spencer left the house, Thane was probably watching from some vantage point near by. When the coast was clear he slipped into the house, went up to his wife's room and shot her while the drilling machines in the subway excavation were still making a terrific racket Then he went down immediately and went next door to Dr. Partridge's, arriving there, according to the doctor's watch, at ten minutes of twelve. Actually, of course, it was just twelve. Neat, eh?"

Spike laid down the pencil and leaned back against the pillows. The district attorney and the inspector were silent, but it was the silence of admiration, of tribute.

"Well, I got to hand it to him," Herschman said finally. "The kid's clever."

"Don't be so ambiguous, Inspector. Who are you referring to—Elton Thane or me?"

"Aw—you know I mean you."

"Well, it goes for Thane, too. He had every detail planned carefully ahead of time. Take the cutting of the telephone wire."

"Yeah, what the hell did he do that for? His wife couldn't put in a call after he'd shot her."

"Of course not. It was just his way of playing for a most necessary bit of time. It's quite plain that if his alibi was to be any good, the watch and the clock which he had tampered with would have to be set back or forward again to the right time."

The inspector nodded in agreement.

"Very well then, Thane just trusted to pure blind luck and the mildness of the night that Partridge would take off his vest with his watch in it. And luck was with him. Knowing where Partridge kept his decanter, he probably suggested a drink and Partridge went downstairs to get it. While he was gone Thane turned the watch forward to the correct time.

"Then his problem was to turn Emma's clock back ten minutes. And so when he returned to his own house and aroused her, he told her to summon Partridge, by telephone. When the telephone wouldn't work, it was quite the natural thing to assume that all the telephones in the house were out of order and he told her to foot it. That left him with time to do two very important things. Go up to her room and set her clock back, and put in a call to the *Graphic* from the telephone downstairs."

"Yeah, but why didn't the paper get hep? I should think that a tip like that with nothing to explain it would get them going."

"Of course. And there again Thane played into luck. I don't imagine he was personally acquainted with Mr. Charles Matthews. But fortunately for him Mr. Matthews is not above taking money which in the strictest sense of the term he has not earned. In view of the fact that the paper offers a $100 bonus to a reporter who turns in an exclusive tip, far be it from Charlie to inform the hand that signs the checks that he had nothing to do with the call which caused the *Graphic* to beat the town on Tuesday morning.

"You see, up to this point every one concerned played right into his hands. But he hadn't counted on the visit of Mortimer Fennel. You'll remember that not until after he talked with us on Tuesday morning did he have a chance to talk to Emma. And when he learned that Fennel had been there, he probably threw the fear of God into her and told her not to be so gabby with policemen. Naturally he didn't want Fennel drawn into the case. People might think he had killed his wife because she was unfaithful. He hadn't an idea, of course, that we'd ever even know of the existence of Miss Audrey Keating. She—"

Suddenly, for no reason at all, Spike grew pensive, slightly appealing as he looked at his brother.

"Richard, my boy," he began tentatively, "I don't suppose you could lend me some money?"

Tracy stiffened. The admiring mood vanished.

"How much and what for?"

"Quite a lot and if I were to tell you what for you'd look even more sour than you do already."

"A woman, as usual."

"Simply a mind reader you are, Richard. Simply a mind reader."

"Let me remind you, Philip, as I have many times before, that I will not lend myself to—"

"Before you go on, old thing, would you mind letting me read that editorial from this morning's paper over again—out loud?"

For a moment the two brothers looked at each other. Then slowly the eyes of the older fell. "About five thousand," said Spike and Tracy reached for his check book.

"Thanks awfully," he said when at last he held the still inky check.

Suddenly Herschman broke into a hearty, paternal laugh. "Go to it, boy! But tell the gal the next time she's mixed up in a murder case to hang on to her gun."

Spike turned a questioning glance on the inspector.

"Nina Fennel, ain't it?" "Herschman went on. "I could see you fell hard the first very day."

"Oh, my word no, Inspector. You know I've decided that there is no such thing as a perfect blue-eyed brunette. They either have husbands or else they, have strong, noble characters which is even worse. As a matter of fact I was wrong about Nina Fennel, or at least partly wrong."

"What do you mean?"

"Well, I think I was quite correct in thinking that she originally took up with Tommy because she intended to use him. And then after she got to know him—well—" Spike made a gesture to indicate the utter simplicity of the whole thing.

"She's a strong-minded sort of person who has to have some one around her who's leaning and depending. She's just the sort to fall for a weak but appealing chap like Tommy. He took her home from the bit of melodrama we staged yesterday at Headquarters, and from the ecstatic letter which I got from him this morning, I have a feeling that Nina has consented to lead him on to a higher and nobler life. He says he has definitely abandoned his precarious profession." Spike paused and threw off the covers and stepped out of bed.

"No, no, inspector! I'm sorry to destroy your little idyl of dreams and romance, but I've decided to go in for blondes from now on—Middle Western blondes who try to talk like Lady Oxford's drawing-room."

**THE END**

# RESURRECTED PRESS CLASSIC MYSTERY CATALOGUE

**E. C. Bentley**
*Trent's Last Case: The Woman in Black*

**Ernest Bramah**
*Max Carrados Resurrected:*
*The Detective Stories of Max Carrados*

**Agatha Christie**
*The Secret Adversary*
*The Mysterious Affair at Styles*

**Octavus Roy Cohen**
*Midnight*

**Freeman Wills Croft**
*The Ponson Case*
*The Pit Prop Syndicate*

**J. S. Fletcher**
*The Herapath Property*
*The Rayner-Slade Amalgamation*
*The Chestermarke Instinct*
*The Paradise Mystery*
*Dead Men's Money*
*The Middle of Things*
*Ravensdene Court*
*Scarhaven Keep*
*The Orange-Yellow Diamond*
*The Middle Temple Murder*
*The Tallyrand Maxim*
*The Borough Treasurer*
*In the Mayor's Parlour*
*The Saftey Pin*

## R. Austin Freeman
*The Mystery of 31 New Inn from the Dr. Thorndyke Series*
*John Thorndyke's Cases from the Dr. Thorndyke Series*
*The Red Thumb Mark from The Dr. Thorndyke Series*
*The Eye of Osiris from The Dr. Thorndyke Series*
*A Silent Witness from the Dr. John Thorndyke Series*
*The Cat's Eye from the Dr. John Thorndyke Series*
*Helen Vardon's Confession: A Dr. John Thorndyke Story*
*As a Thief in the Night: A Dr. John Thorndyke Story*
*Mr. Pottermack's Oversight: A Dr. John Thorndyke Story*
*Dr. Thorndyke Intervenes: A Dr. John Thorndyke Story*
*The Singing Bone: The Adventures of Dr. Thorndyke*
*The Stoneware Monkey: A Dr. John Thorndyke Story*
*The Great Portrait Mystery, and Other Stories: A Collection of*
*Dr. John Thorndyke and Other Stories*
*The Penrose Mystery: A Dr. John Thorndyke Story*
*The Uttermost Farthing: A Savant's Vendetta*

## Arthur Griffiths
*The Passenger From Calais*
*The Rome Express*

## Fergus Hume
*The Mystery of a Hansom Cab*
*The Green Mummy*
*The Silent House*
*The Secret Passage*

## Edgar Jepson
*The Loudwater Mystery*

## A. E. W. Mason
*At the Villa Rose*

## A. A. Milne
*The Red House Mystery*

## Baroness Emma Orczy
*The Old Man in the Corner*
## Edgar Allan Poe

*The Detective Stories of Edgar Allan Poe*

**Arthur J. Rees**
*The Hampstead Mystery*
*The Shrieking Pit*
*The Hand In The Dark*
*The Moon Rock*
*The Mystery of the Downs*

**Mary Roberts Rinehart**
*Sight Unseen and The Confession*

**Dorothy L. Sayers**
*Whose Body?*

**Sir William Magnay**
*The Hunt Ball Mystery*

**Mabel and Paul Thorne**
*The Sheridan Road Mystery*

**Louis Tracy**
*The Strange Case of Mortimer Fenley*
*The Albert Gate Mystery*
*The Bartlett Mystery*
*The Postmaster's Daughter*
*The House of Peril*
*The Sandling Case: What Would You Have Done?*

**John R. Watson**
*The Mystery of the Downs*
*The Hampstead Mystery*

**Edgar Wallace**
*The Daffodil Mystery*
*The Crimson Circle*

**Carolyn Wells**
*Vicky Van*
*The Man Who Fell Through the Earth*

## About Resurrected Press

A division of Intrepid Ink, LLC, Resurrected Press is dedicated to bringing high quality, vintage books back into publication. See our entire catalogue and find out more at www.ResurrectedPress.com.

## About Intrepid Ink, LLC

Intrepid Ink, LLC provides full publishing services to authors of fiction and non-fiction books, eBooks and websites. From editing to formatting, from publishing to marketing, Intrepid Ink gets your creative works into the hands of the people who want to read them. Find out more at www.IntrepidInk.com.

www.ingramcontent.com/pod-product-compliance
Lightning Source LLC
Chambersburg PA
CBHW051929020726
47501CB00001B/42